Scimitar

Scimitar

by
David Grainger

PERCHERON BOOKS

For Janice who has been the foundation stone for a most wonderful life.

PUBLISHED BY:
Percheron Books

An imprint of Why Knot Books
5443 8th Line
Erin, Ontario
Canada N0B 1T0
519-833-1242

ISBN 978-0-9810609-4-1

Scimitar

PROLOGUE

March 22.
Mexico-Arizona border.

Nate Cohn, a pharmacist by trade, swept the rugged brush-strewn hillsides with his cheap Russian nightscope. Nate and his two companions were members of a group of vigilantes called the Minutemen, an unofficial and unsanctioned private militia who had taken it upon themselves to help out the U.S. Border Patrol with the interception of illegal Mexican immigrants. They were not equipped quite as well as the government agency, but unlike the patrol's officers, they were able to drink beer and smoke the odd joint while they waited to intercept the wetbacks who'd managed to slip past the agents.

Nate's feet were killing him, his orthotic insoles a bad fit for the Vietnam-period military boots he affected as part of the tough-man vigilante image he was trying to foster. To further his discomfort, sweat streamed down his chest soaking his vintage Desert Storm combat jacket. The extra sixty-five pounds he'd gained in the thirty years since his high school graduation made these evening excursions to the border region a lot more arduous than he'd imagined they would be. He found few ways to avoid his shifts, however, as his barbershop rants about illegal Mexicans streaming across the border had left him without a credible way of refusing to help out when his friends asked him to join. The truth was he'd rather be at home dozing in front of his new flat screen television.

Nate flinched away from the nightscope, dazzled as headlights and a small searchlight sprang from a Border Patrol truck perched on top of a hill that overlooked the border's tall fencing. The truck began to move, a pool of jiggling light about a quarter mile south from the position that he and his companions had assumed.

"Something's going on up there, Ted. Take a look, will you," Nate said. "Damned night-vision scope just blinded me."

Ted Jefferson, tall and lightly built, resembling more the scarecrow from The Wizard of Oz than a vigilante, rose from the lawn chair parked next to the beer cooler on the tailgate of Nate's Lincoln Navigator. "Hold my beer for me for a sec, will you, Pepsi?"

He handed his beer to Jack Fergus, the myopic third of the self-proclaimed citizens border patrol unit. Fergus was a primary school teacher who wore glasses so thick that some of his friends still called him Pepsi, a high school nickname he'd earned decades before in reference to his spectacles.

Ted raised his 20 x 50 binoculars to his eyes and focused them on the headlight-lit tableau playing out a quarter of a mile away. He could see six men framed by the headlights of the Border Patrol truck and one of the officers walking up to them. The other patrolman, he guessed, remained in the truck, likely calling in on the radio. As Ted watched he could see the six figures gather around the Border Patrol officer, obscuring him from view.

"So what's going on?" Nate asked.

"Not much. Looks like they just bagged themselves a half-dozen," Ted replied. He kept the binoculars trained on the men above for a few more seconds and then exclaimed, "Oh shit!"

"What?" both Nate and Pepsi piped in unison.

Ted had just seen the Border Patrol officer stagger from the centre of the small group of men, stumble to the front of the truck and then lurched from view into the darkness outside of the headlights' glare. Ted turned for a moment and said, "Looks like those pricks just cold-cocked the Border Patrol."

In turning to address Nate and Pepsi, he'd missed two quick flashes of light that emanated from the knot of men above. Raising the binoculars again, Ted saw the six men moving toward the truck.

"Let me see," Nate asked. Ted passed him the binoculars. The darkness outside the blaze created by the truck's lights hid what was going on above. The truck's spotlight suddenly swung upwards, stabbing the sky briefly, and then winked out.

"What's going on?" Pepsi asked again.

"I don't know," Nate replied, passing the binoculars back to Ted, "but something's not right."

The truck started to move, bounced twice and then began winding its way down the rough track. Behind it, sprawled on the gravel and desert scree and invisible to Ted, lay the bodies of the two Border Patrol officers.

"They're coming this way," Ted said. "We'd better get ready just in case they need our help." He let the binoculars drop to his chest and plucked his old .30-30 Winchester from its resting place in the back of the Navigator. The rifle was old, a hand-me-down already worn by years of hard use when Ted was given it as a young teenager. Its familiarity comforted him in a way that Nate's high-tech Ruger and Pepsi's Glock 17 handgun did not. He considered his weapon a classic.

While none of the men dreamed of using their weapons, they were not averse to swaggering back and forth with them, terrifying any illegals they were detaining while they waited for the Border Patrol to show up.

"You guys ready?" asked Nate. In the distance the truck had reached the bottom of the hill and was snaking along the track towards the three men. Nate's disquiet grew. Something didn't seem right. He'd never seen the Border Patrol stuff six men into a small truck and then abandon their post. Usually they called in backup and a transport vehicle. His palms grew slick with perspiration as he picked up the Ruger and positioned himself on the far side of the rutted trail they'd parked beside. "Pepsi, you'd better get in the truck. If it looks like there's going to be trouble, get on the cell and call for some help. Ted, you stay on that side and flag them down. I'll cover you."

"Yeah, right. You cover me," snorted Ted.

"You don't think those Mexis have done anything to the Patrol boys, do you?" asked Pepsi.

"I doubt it," replied Nate. "But better safe than sorry. You never know these days. Used to be the damned wetbacks would cross the border, steal a little water from your livestock and take off their hats when they saw you. Hell, they even used to open and close the damned cattle gates behind them on their way through. Now the arrogant bastards are just as likely to flip you the bird or tell you to fuck off."

"Heard it before, Nate," grumbled Ted under his breath, and then he said, "I don't like it. You didn't see that officer stumble toward the truck like they'd just blindsided him."

"Could be he just tripped on a piece of brush, too," replied Nate.

"Could be, but that isn't what it looked like to me."

The Border Patrol truck wound down the steep trails and then, high beams blazing, heaved its way out of a dry arroyo and drove towards them.

Ted stepped to the roadside, one palm out, the other hand cupping his eyes against the glare. The truck slowed and stopped a few feet back. He walked toward it on the driver's side. Nate approached the passenger side window and heard someone speaking from inside the truck.

"What's the problem, sir?" The voice was heavily accented, almost a parody of a Mexican accent.

"Sheeit!" Ted exclaimed. "What the hell do you pricks think your doing with this truck? What the hell did you do to the...?" He never finished the question. A flash illuminated Ted and the six occupants of the truck for a split second.

Nate heard a phfft, almost a pop, and then Ted staggered back, looking down at his chest in bewilderment. His rifle fell to the ground as he half-turned and then collapsed heavily.

"Ted!" Nate screamed as he started to run towards his friend. Then, as he realized what had happed, he stopped and drew his pistol from his belt. Two muzzle flashes from a silencer-equipped .32-calibre automatic were all he saw before the ground seemed to rush at him.

Pepsi sat in frozen disbelief as he watched his two friends fall. His shaking hands had hardly started to reach for the Navigator's ignition before the door flew open and rough hands dragged him from the SUV. He had no time to understand the depths of his misfortune before he too lay dead — two neat holes in his face and his glasses several feet away, one lens shattered by a bullet.

Minutes later the Border Patrol truck sat abandoned, its doors open and the feeble glow from its dome light faintly illuminating the corpses of the three vigilantes sprawled around it as the tail lights of their Navigator disappeared down the track and onto the blacktop, headed toward Sierra Vista and Interstate 10.

June 21.
Eastern seaboard.

The incessant rumble from the engines of the Olympic Airlines airbus altered note for the first time in hours. The captain announced, first in Greek and then in heavily accented English, that they were beginning their descent into New York's JFK. Dozens of travel-numbed passengers stirred, busying themselves with their own pre-landing rituals as the cabin crew started to clear up and get ready for arrival. The weather was clear but a little turbulent, causing the airbus to roll and yaw and clearly distressing some of its more highly strung occupants.

In his business class seat, middle-aged Greek entrepreneur Apostolos Zoupaniotis sat quietly, his dark eyes taking in the activity in the cabin. His neck prickled with anticipation of their landing. His seatmates on either side ignored him, rebuffed hours before by his curt manner and unwillingness to engage in conversation. Apostolos was normally a friendly and outgoing chap, but the real Apostolos Zoupaniotis was lying in the trunk of a rental car in a busy public parking lot in Athens.

The gentleman travelling with documents that included an elegantly forged Greek passport in Apostolos' name was known to his friends as Shojaa' Bala' Awi. He was born in Palestine and as a young child had learned how to throw rocks at Israeli soldiers. Later, rocks turned to Molotov cocktails and then to automatic rifles. He'd burst several Israeli scout cars wide open with homemade roadside bombs and completely destroyed a Mercedes SUV that belonged to CNN — unfortunately, he had always thought, without any Western journalists inside. For that job he'd used his favourite weapon, the RPG 7 rocket launcher. Awi proved quick-witted and resourceful enough to avoid capture by the Israelis, attributes that brought him to the attention of several well-placed fedayeen of Hezbollah. Several years of training in Hezbollah camps and three years in Athens developing Greek mannerisms, language and, most importantly, Greek-accented English had readied him for the mission on which he was currently embarked.

Below the airbus the waters of Long Island Sound glinted, pleasure craft and sailboats zigzagging across its brilliantine surface. A few thousand feet above the sound, Awi quietly rehearsed the hour that lay ahead, especially those moments he would stand face-to-face with a U.S. Customs officer. Five years of his life had been dedicated to the encounter and to the weeks that would follow, but no one would have known by his outward appearance the anxiety with which he faced their imminent arrival.

July 26.
Honolulu, Hawaii.

Four young men, suitcases in hand, exited the front doors of the arrivals terminal into the humid tropical heat that prevailed beyond the air conditioning of the Honolulu International Airport. Honolulu was a far cry from what they'd become accustomed to in the training facilities of North Korea. The four men, all originally from Indonesia, had been hand-picked because they had the colouring and facial attributes that made them appear more Japanese than Indonesian. To anyone who asked them a question, their replies would be offered in broken English with the halting nature of a Japanese man searching his mind for the next unfamiliar word.

They all spoke fluent Japanese and poor English, and they had a two-day layover in Hawaii before travelling on to San Francisco. When asked by Customs the purpose of their trip, they had excitedly answered, "Conquistador, the Conquistador car show in California." Their manner, their knowledge of Japan and of automobiles and their apparent enthusiasm for everything American belied their training and the depth of their hatred for the country they were entering — and their willingness to die for their Islamic beliefs.

These were among the last of a furtive army that had for the last two years been stealing into North America disguised as businessmen, tourists, honeymooners, students and immigrants. No one in this quiet band looked like or acted as if they were from anywhere that Islamic beliefs were common. In all cases they appeared to be from countries and cultures that, if not aligned with the doctrines and sharing the dominant beliefs of the United States, at least offered no threat or resistance to them or to American foreign policy in general. They had arrived singly or in small groups, had no knowledge of any other group and needed little to no direction or control.

Their missions were clear, they had backup plans and targets if their primary missions proved too difficult or dangerous, and they were not to endanger themselves or be caught or killed. This army was trained to be flexible, to go after targets of opportunity, targets that offered the least risk to themselves. Unlike the fodder of the Middle East who strapped on belts of high explosives to blow up marketplaces and weddings at the behest of their imams, these men were too well trained and valuable to waste in a flash of RDX. They were destined to be far more lethal. Their task was to bring down the crusaders' empire and to glorify the nation of Islam. Their missions were planned, refined and honed over the years since the fall of the World Trade Center. They were indoctrinated to the point where, to a man, they believed they were the Scimitar of Allah, a weapon designed to cleave the head of the Western world from its shoulders.

The great hero Osama bin Laden, despite the propaganda, had been dead for many years. A nameless but far more powerful and ambitious man had created, built and tasked this army. In all cases the only thing these soldiers knew as an organized military force was that they were not to strike any blow, break any law or draw any attention to themselves in any way until after the eighteenth day of the eighth month of their third year in operation. Aside from a lamentable episode in Arizona that, fortunately, the American press had blamed on organized drug smugglers, the infiltration had been smooth and bloodless.

A few members of the underground army who'd posed as immigrants had seen their applications disallowed, and a couple who were found to have expired student visas were picked up and deported. In those cases the instructions were clear. They were to go quietly and in no circumstance fight the deportation or expulsion. They were to react with disappointment but without any hint of aggression that could betray their training.

A first strike that would shake the entire world would signal the beginning of the campaign. The four men who were on their way to California after a brief stay in Hawaii, the only group with a strict timetable, were to accomplish this initial strike. After that, the timing of attacks was entirely up to each group or individual. Once they had, Allah willing, accomplished all of their set tasks, they would be free to strike anywhere and at any opportune target they wished. Their greatest goals would be to avoid capture and to strike blow after blow. Before their arrival, America already thought it was at war with Islamic fundamentalism. The nation and everyone in it were about to find out what war was all about.

CHAPTER 1

Derek James nosed his 66 Jaguar E-Type onto Highway 101 swinging around and past a group of tourist-laden cars that had been arresting his progress along State Street, Santa Barbara's main drag, for over twenty minutes. He was thinking he should have known better than to venture at midday into the tourist-ridden street with a vintage car that was prone to overheating, but he'd thought he could get away with it.

He had, but barely. The car's Smith's temperature gauge, the most important gauge on the dash, had risen steadily toward the red zone, despite the howling aftermarket cooling fans, as Derek had inched his way though town. Once on the highway and clear of heavy traffic, the needle started to fall and Derek accelerated southward toward Montecito. The growl of the Jag's twin-cam six resonated though the car's elegant cockpit and the lithe wooden steering wheel contorted beneath his grip as he joyfully swung from lane to lane around other traffic.

Derek was acutely aware that his Jag was nothing special to the tens of thousands of car aficionados who were gathering at Santa Barbara for the automobile concours at the Conquistador Golf and Country Club on the coming weekend, but it was at least not a rented Toyota or Chevy Cobalt. He'd been stuck with both those cars on his two previous visits to the concours, and he'd hated them. His reassignment from the FBI's Quantico, Virginia, headquarters to a post as liaison with Homeland Security in Southern California had few perks other than the proximity of his Los Angeles office to the one car event he never missed.

He, like thousands of other serious autophiles, was making the pilgrimage to the Conquistador Concours d'Elegance, a showing of the finest and rarest cars in the world. This extravagant affair was held at the exclusive Conquistador Golf and Country Club in the Balmoral Private Reserve, a huge and very exclusive gated community near Santa Barbara. The cars graced the exquisitely kept fairways behind the opulent Trocadero Lodge, and the Conquistador, as it was known by enthusiasts, had over the years become the foremost auto show in the United States and perhaps the world, attracting the rich, the famous and the powerful from all over the globe. As was once said by an entertainer who was himself a car enthusiast, the show behind the Trocadero Lodge was a place where the millionaires could watch the billionaires.

Derek decelerated, glorying in the Jaguar's snarl as it bled off speed through the gearbox and he threw the car onto the off-ramp for Montecito. He had just minutes to meet with Vanessa Leighton, a willowy brunette he'd been dating for almost four years and the very first serious relationship he'd been in. This was the first time Vanessa's schedule had allowed her to visit the concours with Derek, and he was looking forward to sharing it with her, indeed just looking forward to spending time with her after six weeks' abstinence. Due to his transfer from Washington to LA, theirs was now a long-distance relationship, but even distance seemed to pose no serious challenge to their love and affection. If anything, it put a finer point on it.

Vanessa had a pixie-like face and bright blue eyes that suited her often-mischievous manner. It was a manner that disguised a razor-sharp intellect. She'd flown in from Washington DC, where she was a freelance forensic analyst for various defence attorneys. Her job was to review and bring into dispute the forensics presented as evidence by district attorneys in Washington and other eastern seaboard locales. That she was very much in demand was testimony to how often she found flaws in evidence that, before her review, had seemed airtight. Many Washington forensic scientists had been keenly embarrassed when she brought their findings into question or disproved them outright, and Vanessa had found herself largely ostracized by that community, a fact that bothered her very little. That she made four times the money other forensic experts made did little to help her popularity.

Derek pulled into the lot of their hotel, one of the few built right on the beach, with a great view of the coast and of the city of Santa Barbara itself. While Santa Barbara was often cloaked in fog and low clouds, the nearby hotel was bathed in pools of sunshine, something Derek had noticed a few years before and took full advantage of each year.

Vanessa stood waiting in the lobby, looking out over the ocean through the enormous windows that lined the hotel's seaward side. Derek tried to sneak up on her, but she turned with a smile as he approached.

"Finally," she said. "I thought maybe you were stuck under the hood of the other woman. I know how jealous and temperamental she is." Vanessa's reference was to Derek's E-Type. She had always referred to the car as "the other woman," since she thought the Jag likely ranked about even with her in Derek's affections.

"Nope, the Jag's been running great, although I almost had a problem in Santa Barbara," Derek replied. "I got stuck in traffic and she almost overheated." He gripped Vanessa by the waist and kissed her firmly on the lips. Then he stood back looking at her. "God, now I know why I miss Washington so much. How are you, sweetheart?"

"I'm just fine…" She paused to look him in the eye. "Now."

Derek smiled. "The room's on the second floor with a great view of the sea otters fooling around in the breakers."

"Lovely," Vanessa replied. "I could use a few minutes to freshen up, and then I'd love to get something to eat. This view is just wonderful." She looked over the breakers that were crashing onto the shore. "It's been years since I've been to Santa Barbara. I'd forgotten how beautiful it is."

They stood together for a moment, arms wrapped around one another's waists, looking out at the ocean view, and then with a sultry smirk, Vanessa poked Derek in the ribs and said in her most fetching voice, "I think I would like to see your room now, sailor."

An hour later, as Vanessa finished dressing and Derek slid back into his jeans and buttoned his shirt, he asked, "Do you want to go up to Santa Barbara or just nip into Montecito, maybe to one of the restaurants on the esplanade?"

"The esplanade sounds good. Santa Barbara's too much work right now." Vanessa was weary from both the trip and their exuberant lovemaking. She slipped on an attractive red and white striped blouse and rummaged about in her suitcase for a pair of low-heeled pumps. Balancing on one foot while she righted the shoe and pushed her other foot into it, she asked complainingly, "So now I've done what a girl's got to do to get fed around here, can we get a move on before I waste away?"

Derek grabbed at her to pull her back onto the bed.

"Not on your life, mister. This femme fatale needs food," she giggled as she danced back out of his grasp.

August 15. 1:30 p.m. PST
Burlington, Wisconsin.

"So, Mr. Youngblood, do you know why I pulled you over?" asked the state trooper as he checked Jimmy Youngblood's licence, insurance and registration.

"No, sir," replied Youngblood. He struggled to maintain his composure as he considered his options should the officer somehow discover the two hundred and fifty pounds of military-grade explosives secreted behind interior panels and stuffed below the rear seat of his beaten-up and faded 1979 Lincoln Town Car. Just about the only thing he could think of was to kill the trooper and dump him back into his cruiser, although to accomplish that unnoticed was sheer fantasy considering how busy the road was.

"Well, Mr. Youngblood, you are not wearing your seatbelt," said the officer. "I should ticket you, but as you are from out of state," he added, referring to Youngblood's South Dakota licence plates and driver's licence, "I'm going to let you off with a warning."

"Thank you, officer," Youngblood replied, taking his papers back from the patrolman and then groping for and fastening his seatbelt.

"Have a good day, sir," said the officer.

Youngblood felt a surge of relief and started to raise his window.

"Just one more thing, Mr. Youngblood," said the trooper, leaning down to him.

Youngblood's hand froze on the window button.

"If you don't mind telling me, are you in Wisconsin on business or pleasure?"

Youngblood was ready for this. "Pleasure, sir. I have a girlfriend goes to college in Milwaukee, and I was visiting her. I'm on my way home now."

"Well, sir," replied the patrolman, satisfied, "you keep your seatbelt fastened and have a safe trip."

"I will officer. Thank you."

Youngblood put his car in gear, and making sure to signal, he edged into traffic, leaving the officer and his cruiser behind.

Jimmy Youngblood from South Dakota was actually Talal Abu Bakre, formally a Yemeni national but now posing as a Nakota tribal member of the Sioux nation. While he kept far away from South Dakota to avoid any possibility of detection, Bakre, with his colouring and high cheekbones, was well enough schooled in the Nakota and their culture to fool anyone who was not Sioux themselves. His job was to marshal explosives and weapons in designated caches and then post their locations so they could be utilized by others he would never see or know anything about if everything went to plan. He had been at this for two years, moving tons of materials all over the United States. While he was one in a long and very clever supply line, he had never met anyone else in the chain. His assignments were all sent to him in code over the Internet, disguised within porn or gaming websites. He used the same sites to post supply locations to an invisible army.

That these sites actually made money for the organization, mostly from pathetic Americans, amused him, especially considering the use those dollars were being put to. Bakre thought the sites disgusting but understood their value. There was little chance of their being discovered for the communication devices they really were. He'd gotten used to the images of females and males engaged in revolting acts and had learned to ignore even the faintest stirrings by reciting passages from the Quran in his head. As part of his training he'd memorized much of the holy book so he could still worship and keep strength. He missed fingering his own worn and faded Quran, left behind in another world, and he missed the mosque very much. But his mission dictated that he could never risk being seen taking even the slightest interest in Islam. Keeping a Quran could spell disaster if discovered. If he were ever found out despite all his precautions, he was prepared and equipped to commit suicide swallowing a cyanide caplet he kept in a packet of gum, a packet that was never farther from him than his shirt pocket.

A little more that a week before his brush with the Wisconsin state trooper, Bakre had been thousands of miles away positioning a huge cache of explosives and dozens of small well-padded vials containing a dirty brown powder in a secure drop near Santa Barbara.

August 15. 4:45 p.m. PST
Montecito, California.

Derek and Vanessa walked back to the hotel from the esplanade, where they had just enjoyed a great steak dinner in a nearby restaurant and poked around in several of the gift shops that lined the street. Like many summer evenings on the coast, the air was chilly and damp, so much so that Vanessa had bought a light jacket to ward off the cold.

"So what do you feel like doing?" asked Derek.

"This isn't my week, it's yours. You lead, I'll follow." replied Vanessa, zipping up her new jacket against the damp breeze.

"There are two car auctions within walking distance. Are you up to taking a quick peek at their inventory?"

"Sure," replied Vanessa, clearly invigorated by the meal. "Are you thinking of buying something else? A Ferrari perhaps? You'd fit in better in your new digs with a Ferrari."

"Contrary to popular belief, my dear, Los Angeles FBI agents don't make enough to drive Ferraris, keep a stable of starlets or own property on the beach, unlike some forensics examiners I know," Derek replied with a grin.

As the couple strolled down the mall toward the hotel that hosted one of the auctions, four Japanese tourists, digital cameras swinging from their necks, emerged from one of the hotel's side doors and jostled past them. Neither Derek nor Vanessa paid any attention to the four, their interest taken up by a vintage Maserati on display on the promenade. Even had he noticed them, neither Derek's suspicious nature nor his anti-terrorism training would have been roused by their passage, so perfect was their camouflage.

Gema Wulandari pushed past the American couple, followed closely by Liem Swie, Megawati Supomo and Abdul Haris Nasution. None of the four had heard these names, their real Indonesian names, spoken aloud for so long that anyone calling them by them would have been convincingly ignored. Wulandari was known as Inoue Nariaki, Supomo was Kato Kakerie, Swie answered to Sato Tadashi and Nasution's new persona was Ishikawa Chicao. Their Japanese identities were solid — each had belonged to real Japanese businessmen who were selected because they travelled widely and had few if any close personal ties in Japan. Those men had disappeared, their corpses completely destroyed so there was no chance, however slight, that any trace could be found that might raise questions about their replacements.

The four Indonesians had adopted the Japanese identities seamlessly and their impersonations had stood up through several Customs inspections as they made their way across the Pacific. Their travels had taken them from North Korea, where they'd been trained and where they'd received their new identities months before, to Beijing. In Beijing they were supplied with the appropriate documents to compliment their new identities, and to all intents and purposes, they became Japanese. From Beijing they made their way to Singapore, leapfrogged to Taiwan and then on to Japan, the litmus test of their facade, even though they only spent a few hours in the terminal waiting for a flight to Hawaii.

They spent four days in Hawaii, a small layover designed to familiarize them with a culture that until then they had only experienced in the abstract. Then they travelled on to San Francisco and finally a long car ride south on Highway 101. They were booked into one of the most expensive hotels in town, in keeping with the affluence of their personas. Now, years of training and indoctrination were to bear fruit. Gema Wulandari and his accomplices were to strike the first blow, which was to unleash a firestorm on the North American continent, and they had only three more days to prepare.

August 17. 2:35 a.m. PST
Eighteenth fairway, Conquistador Golf and Country Club.

Kato Kakerie and Sato Tadashi carefully picked their way along the rugged shoreline at the base of the fifteen-foot bluff that bordered the eighteenth fairway at the Conquistador. Carrying punishingly heavy packs, they had slipped down to the shoreline a quarter mile north, crossing a property on which a new house, its construction not advanced enough to warrant security or alarms, was being built in the woods bordering the beach. They'd made their way, deftly navigating their course over the serrated rocks and slick boulders revealed by low tide. Secreted behind the seawall, the sound of the breakers covering any small noise their equipment might make, they methodically scanned the area for guards, late-night workers or even errant revellers left over from celebrations in the lodge earlier in the evening. Although security at the golf club was almost non-existent, they were taking no chances. Even the slightest possibility of discovery would scrub the mission. Alternate targets for the contents of the knapsacks had been chosen, but none were as attractive as the Conquistador.

Clambering quietly up the embankment, they slipped across the fairways to a row of tents that were partially erected and would, on completion, house art displays, refreshments, souvenirs and VIPs. Stopping at each tent they removed pins from the upright supports and pushed a length of detcord, a ropelike high explosive, into each hollow tube, letting it hang to the bottom. They then poured in several pounds of a gelatinous liquid high explosive that firmed within a few moments of exposure to air. Following that, they stuffed cotton pads into each hole to insulate a series of plastic bags full of powder, which they inserted one by one on top of each cotton pad. Finally, they firmly anchored a tiny pre-set electronic timer-detonator, barely larger than a thumbnail, to the end of the detcord and gingerly pushed the end of the cord, complete with detonator, into the hole and far enough down the tube to avoid the steel pin when it was replaced. Kakerie and Tadashi repeated this procedure more than twenty times, preparing at least two poles in each of the large tents that covered the fairway from one end to the other.

The most anxious part of the process was sneaking to the main pavilion, which stood next to the clubhouse, and preparing four of the uprights there. This was the pavilion where all the judges and VIPs attending the ceremonies would be seated, and the charges installed there were specially designed for them. Along with the explosives and powder, Tadashi added several pounds of jagged roofing nails to the mix. This was not just to target the luminaries gathered under the tent but also to insure casualties above them, where scores of other public figures, celebrities and their families would line the balconies of the lodge itself to watch the cavalcade of rare and expensive automobiles as their drivers paraded them past on their way to pick up their awards.

By four in the morning the two men had retreated down to the shoreline, relieved to be rid of their excruciatingly heavy burdens. Now that they carried only empty knapsacks, they made much better time with far less labour on their way back along the coast to the building lot.

At 6:00 a.m. Sunday, the morning of the concours, they would meet Inoue Nariaki and Ishikawa Chicao in the parking lot of one of Santa Barbara's fancier hotels and depart to drive south along Highway 101 toward Los Angeles. Until that time, they would take a cheap hotel room in Carpinteria, a few miles south on Highway 1, and stay away from their companions and Santa Barbara.

CHAPTER 2

Inoue Nariaki and Ishikawa Chicao, disguised in work shirts and baseball caps, drove slowly past the mansions that border Balmoral Drive, headed for the tree-lined sports fields at Mathews Academy where owners and handlers were offloading and preparing the show cars that were to grace the fairway later in the morning. In their guise as enthusiastic Japanese car buffs, the pair had reconnoitred the sports fields the day before. From late afternoon until a little after sundown, they snapped pictures and spoke to show car owners and handlers about their plans for the coming day. By the time they departed, they'd picked out several cars that they were almost positive would be left unattended until about five in the morning. Each of them sat outside under car covers, unlike many of the show cars, which spent the night locked up in the dozens of car transporters that sat in neat lines across the field. Only one car was required for their purpose, but having several alternates chosen assured them of success.

They drove into the sports fields, and a couple of security guards, who sat in a small pavilion drinking coffee, waved them past. Their rented cube van was signed out from a small, disreputable and desperate rental agency near Santa Barbara Airport, a company where few questions were asked and cash was king. The white van bore a large vinyl sign, supplied in their arms cache and applied only hours earlier, that proclaimed in bold script Carson Classic Car Detailing, for Show or Go, a logo that also graced their baseball caps and the breast pockets of their work shirts. It was the same logo that several other cube vans already in the field sported, vans that had been buzzing around all week.

Driving down one of the aisles formed by the huge car transporters, they arrived at the end and were pleased to note that their first choice, a 1929 Pierce Arrow touring car, sat under a car cover, unmoved from where they'd first seen it in this fairly remote part of the polo field. It was parked in a quiet spot, quite isolated from the pre-show preparation that even now bustled in some areas closer to the entrance and the coffee tent. They were doubly pleased about this car's availability, as its owner, Bob Gentry, was an elderly gentleman in his early eighties, attending the show for the experience and not intent on a ribbon. In their chat with Gentry and his wife the afternoon before, Chicao had ascertained that Gentry had done all the cleaning and detailing he was likely to do and all that remained was to pull the car cover off before the old man, accompanied by his wife and several other family members, including a great-grandchild, drove the Pierce Arrow down to the show field.

Nariaki pulled the cube van alongside the car, blocking it from the view of anyone who might venture this far back, and parked. The van's interior lights had been broken so that they would not turn on when the doors were opened, decreasing the chance of arousing anyone's curiosity. Clambering out, the two men walked to the back of the van, pushed up the well-oiled rear door and pulled two large tool boxes, also emblazoned with the Carson logo, from the van's back bed. Chicao then wriggled under the massive old Pierce Arrow with a small battery-powered, hooded work light, and Nariaki pushed the first of the tool boxes to him. The car's immense ground clearance gave Chicao ample room to work, and he opened the tool box and started to remove several large bricks of high explosive.

The explosive was made to adhere tightly to any surface it was pressed onto, and it did not take Chicao long to mash lots of it into several deep recesses in the car's underbody. Finished with the first, he shoved the empty tool box out and waited for the second to be slid under the car. Nariaki pulled the first tool box out and was just bending to push the second under the car, when he froze. A man with a small flashlight emerged from between two tractor-trailers about forty feet away and walked towards them. Chicao remained under the car, motionless, as the man got closer. The small beam from the flashlight caught Nariaki in its shaft.

"Sorry," the flashlight bearer said as he swung the beam off Nariaki. "Just looking for a place to piss back here."

"It's okay," replied Nariaki, with the best American accent he could muster. He then turned his back on the man and made a show of noisily returning the empty tool box to the back of the van.

The man kept going, driven by the urgency of a full bladder, and disappeared beyond another row of parked trucks. Nariaki relaxed, thankful that he had not had to deal with the interloper. Someone disappearing from the sports fields in the middle of the night might not be noticed in time to change the events to follow, but it was better not to have to kill him and take the chance.

Nariaki slid the next tool box to Chicao. Chicao opened it and removed several more bricks of explosive. Finishing with those, he removed a small package of the same small preset detonators his associates had used in the tent poles on the fairway. He shoved two into each brick, building redundancy. A single detonator was likely enough to ignite the whole load, but he was taking no chances. Each detonator had a small button, which when depressed after the unit was inserted into the plastique initiated an anti-tamper program in the detonator's tiny brain. Trying to draw the detonator from the plastique would alert an O_2 sensor as it reached fresh air. If the bomb was discovered, even the most experienced technicians would ignite the forty pounds of military-grade high explosive as they tried to extract the detonators.

Finished, Chicao scrambled out, and the two men threw the second empty tool box into the van, closed and secured the rear cargo door and clambered in. They drove back past the two security guards, one of whom gave them a small wave and a nod, and then the pair turned left, leaving the sports fields and following the twists of Balmoral Drive southward and away.

6:00 a.m. PST
Ocean Rest Hotel and Spa parking lot. Montecito, California.

Kato Kakerie and Sato Tadashi pulled into the hotel parking lot and drove around the back to the loading docks where Chicao and Nariaki had parked the cube van. Access to the loading dock was normally forbidden, but a twenty dollar tip to the grounds and maintenance supervisor had convinced him to allow Chicao to park to one side of the dock on a day no deliveries were expected. They'd told the supervisor they only needed the space until early afternoon at which time they had to attend to clients and would move it. Nariaki placed a smiley-face sunscreen across the front window to block any view into the back of the van and then locked up, double checked the padlock on the rear door and circled the van to make sure that no casual inspection would arouse suspicion. Additionally he taped a handwritten note to the inside of the driver's window that stated that the van would be moved by 1:00 p.m. It would. These measures were all taken to allay suspicion. It would be inconvenient if someone were to discover the additional one hundred and fifty pounds of high-grade explosive and the remainder of the brown powder that now rested in the back.

The hotel explosion right in the centre of affluent and tourist-rich Santa Barbara was set for a full hour after detonation of the Pierce Arrow at Matthews Academy which would follow the explosions in the tent supports by just three minutes. This allowed time for the news of the attack at the concours to spread before the next blast, a measure thought to maximize confusion and panic. Tampering with the van doors or breaking a window would activate a vibration sensor and ignite the load prematurely. While not desirable, a premature explosion wouldn't really alter the course of the events. The hotel bomb was a fitting way to get rid of the excess explosives and biological dispersal agent they'd been supplied with. While none of the explosions would equal the strength or severity of blasts like Oklahoma City or the U.S. Embassy bombings in Africa, they'd be quite deadly on their own, and when associated with the biological agents, the effect, it was hoped, would be even greater and far reaching.

Chicao and Nariaki climbed into the rental car with Kakerie and Tadashi, and the four — Japanese tourists all — drove away from Santa Barbara southward on the 101, using the several hours remaining before the blasts to get as much distance between them and the Conquistador Golf and Country Club as a driver obeying all the laws and speed limits could.

August 18. 9:30 a.m. PST
Santa Barbara, California.

Vanessa finished the last of her western omelette and asked the waitress to refill her coffee. "I like this little place," she said to Derek, referring to the breakfast nook they'd discovered stuck down one of Santa Barbara's side streets.

"Yeah, it's not bad. It's about the only place you can get a simple breakfast around here," replied Derek through a mouthful of poached egg.

"So the plan is?"

"Well, I figure if we get there in the late morning, say about eleven thirty, we'll miss the opening rush. The awards ceremony will be starting around noon, so some of the crowd will move over to the awards grandstands and may thin out a little around the cars on the fairway."

"Grandstands and awards ceremonies. It sounds just like that cruise night at the White Castle you used to drag me to in DC," laughed Vanessa.

"No, not quite that classy." Derek smiled. "There are no Castle burgers to be had."

A few minutes later, they finished up, and Derek left enough on the table to cover breakfast and a considerable tip to the harried young waitress who'd been dealing with a rush of customers. They sauntered out into the morning mist and walked to the Jag, doing a little window-shopping along the way. As they strolled along the street, gazing into art galleries and store windows filled with antiques, they passed within a hundred feet of the plastique-filled cube van.

"Let's go up and down a couple more streets, and then we'll head over to the concours," said Derek.

"Good. And I'd like to pop back into that store across from where we left the Jag before we leave. They had a scarf I liked the look of, and I think I'll buy it."

"You're talking about the Bugatti scarf?" asked Derek, having noticed her examining it earlier under the watchful eye of a store clerk.

"Yes, I liked it."

"Well, take a look, but I'll bet it's going to be expensive."

"Don't care. I liked it, and I'm not going to buy too much else this trip. I made a solemn promise to myself before I left that I wouldn't spend the morning of my flight home scrambling around looking for a cheap piece of luggage to carry everything I didn't have when I got here."

9:30 p.m. Pakistan Standard Time (9:30 a.m. PST)
Islamabad, Pakistan.

The old man shifted his weight once again in a vain attempt to get comfortable on the thin rugs that graced the floor of this meeting room. His name was Muhammad al-Munajjid, and he was supreme amongst a dozen or more fundamentalist Muslim leaders, clerics, freedom fighters and businessmen that were gathering to await the events that would soon transpire on the American west coast.

A large, flat screen television, the only modern touch in the bare whitewashed room, sat on a simple table at one end, placed in such a way as to afford a view to all of the men seated along the walls. The television was tuned to CNN, but the sound was presently muted so as not to intrude on conversation. The room had an almost festive feel as a woman wearing a dark blue burka served strong teas and Pakistani sweetmeats to the guests. Her movements were quick and nervous, an indication of her fear of the men gathered in this room.

Al-Munajjid gestured at the woman to leave the room and cleared his throat to get the men's attention. The room fell silent. "My friends," he said quietly, "in just a few short hours we will finally answer this crusade the Americans have visited on our sacred lands. They will see their own blood shed on their own soil. They will learn that real war is far more than dropping bombs on woman and children from far up in the sky, and they will soon realize, as they see their comfortable lives crumble to dust, that this war is one they will all lament."

He paused for a moment and then, his voice rising, continued. "No longer will war be something to entertain them on their televisions. No longer will war be something their president can use to establish his power over the weak and rob them of what little they possess. No longer will war be a fruitful way to keep the nations of Islam under the American boot. They will, Allah willing, soon see the streets of their nation running red with the blood of their children. They will soon see their cities burn to ash."

Al-Munajjid spat the short sentences with venom, punctuating each one with a thrust of his clenched fist. "They will soon see the sword of Islam strike the heads from the shoulders of their leaders. They will soon see their factories razed, their industry stopped. No longer will they be safe in their towns and villages. No longer will they be safe on their beaches or in their markets or even at their sporting events. Indeed, the Americans will soon find they are not even safe in their own beds. We will school them in what the rest of the world has known for many years" — he paused for a moment for effect and then continued with a sneer, his tone dripping with revulsion — "that they are a scourge, a pestilence, a plague. They are a disease that we will wipe from the face of the world. Americans will soon know how weak they truly are — once they go hungry, once they hold the bloody corpses of their children to their starving breasts, once their government lies in ruins at our feet."

Al-Munajjid's voice dropped so low that the men in the room leaned forward to hear it. "My friends, I know this in my heart as surely as I know that Allah has blessed us and will look on us with his love and approval. This night will see the first blow fall. That first blow will be as the first leaf of a tree settling to the ground in autumn. Others will follow just a surely, just as relentlessly, and they will be just as uncountable. This war will be our war, fought on our terms, and our war will have them running in circles and snapping at their own tails like the rabid dogs they are. Their great weapons and their brutal soldiers will be powerless to stop us. Soon we will have them tearing at their own wounds in their blind rage and confusion. America will know what price their crusade against us exacts. America will soon know despair, and America will soon see the jubilation of the rest of the world as America shatters and falls to the earth. And when it has fallen, we will walk upon it, and it will know the remorseless tread of our feet. Then all men will be free to rejoice in the power and wisdom of Allah."

The room was silent, his audience rapt as al-Munajjid raised his cup to his lips, signalling an end to his soliloquy. He nodded to those around him and then rose stiffly and walked from the room, head bowed.

He was tired and wanted to rest for a couple of hours before the event. The truth was he would rather sit by himself alone and without a television. Years of careful planning hung in the balance, and his heart pounded in his chest, his palms grew slick, and he was dizzy with stress and anticipation as the moment of the first attack approached. He did no want the others to see or sense his nervousness. Indeed, they must not be allowed to sense the slightest weakness in him. He must remain the lion in a pack of vicious jackals. Soon enough he would see what his hand had wrought. He was unstoppable..

Behind him, the room filled with excited but hushed conversation.

10:00 a.m. PST
Eighteenth fairway, Trocadero Lodge complex, Santa Barbara, California.

It was another typical Santa Barbara morning on the lawn at the Concours d' Elegance behind the Trocadero. The lodge and the condos, pro shops and boutiques clustered around it were already buzzing with activity. Low clouds, almost fog, spawned by the cold deep waters that lay offshore, scudded across the brilliant green fairways behind the lodge, fairways that had been converted into the world's most expensive parking lot. Hundreds of classic and antique cars ran in lines along the golf course, their owners busy fussing with them, cleaning and wiping off dew drops one more time before the judging.

The judges were circling in teams, staring at tiny details, measuring, selecting and discounting, conferring in small groups and avoiding the owners' attempts to ingratiate themselves. Already hundreds of people milled about, studying the art of the car raised to levels of excellence that required hundreds of thousands, and in some cases millions, of dollars to achieve. In minutes, those hundreds of onlookers would swell to thousands as the gates opened at the top of the hill and the general public surged in, one hundred dollar tickets in hand.

By eleven o'clock, barely an hour before the first-class winners would start rolling across the winners' dais, the number of people crammed into the concours surpassed fifty thousand. Among that fifty thousand were a significant number of the world's richest individuals, ranging from industrial tycoons and dot-com millionaires to movie stars and Hollywood directors, all strolling about, seeing and being seen.

10:30 a.m. PST
Santa Barbara, California.

Derek glanced at his wristwatch as he and Vanessa strolled along the last few storefronts on the street where the Jag was parked. "We still have time, but not a lot," he said to Vanessa.

"I won't be long. I just want to grab that Bugatti scarf," she said, turning into the little boutique's doorway.

Derek remained outside, a smile playing across his lips as he watched Vanessa converse with the store clerk. Moments later she walked from the store, and Derek burst into laughter at her evident consternation. "Told you," he exclaimed gleefully.

"Three thousand dollars!"

"I know. As soon as you said it was a Bugatti scarf, I knew how much it would be."

"But three thousand dollars!"

"I suppose I should have warned you that it was probably an original from the 1930s," said Derek. "These days, collectors have them mounted and hung on the wall rather than letting their wives wear them."

"Well, it does prove one thing," said Vanessa.

"What's that?"

"I still have great, grand and expensive taste. Maybe I should dump you and spend the day at the show trolling for someone who can afford to support me in the manner to which I have yet to become accustomed." Vanessa vamped and then danced out of the way as Derek took a swipe at her behind and missed.

"Well, I guess it's time to head over," he said, checking his watch for the third time in the last five minutes. "By the time we get parked and take the shuttle in, it'll be around noon."

They climbed into the Jag, and Derek eased into traffic. He made a left turn onto State Street and drove down the hill through town and toward the beachfront. Making a right he followed a residential road past small but very expensive designer homes that crowded one another and hugged the winding road.

"God I love these houses. They are all so perfect and the gardens…" Vanessa's voice trailed off as yet another spectacular home came into view after a tight corner.

"They are beautiful," replied Derek, "but I'll lay you odds even the smallest of them is a couple of million dollars this close to the beach. One thing about this area is that no one can afford to live here except the filthy rich, even in a cottage of two thousand square feet. Wait until you see the homes along Balmoral Drive and in the Post Road area. Those are all probably thirty million or more." He reached over and squeezed her knee. "Tomorrow I'll take you for a drive along the coast, and you can see some of the houses and private clubs that have sprung up around here lately. The money is absolutely unbelievable."

At that the Jaguar rounded another bend, and the road opened up, forming lanes around two gate houses that contained Balmoral Estates security guards. Their uniforms resembled those of park rangers, hats and all, more than of a private security service. Derek waited in a short line and then waved his pre-purchased concours tickets at the gatekeeper.

The guard smiled and waved him on. "Enjoy the show, sir, ma'am," he said, tipping the brim of his hat.

"I wish the security people in Washington were that polite," said Vanessa to Derek as she smiled at the guard.

Derek nodded in agreement, engaged the clutch and accelerated away. The road was a series of sharp turns and curves that hugged the thickly forested hills. Every now and then they saw a shimmer of the Pacific Ocean or caught a glimpse of some of the immense homes that sheltered among the pines along the rocky coast. As they got closer to the lodge where the concours was being held, the traffic stopped dead.

"Damn," exclaimed Derek, "we still have about a mile to go, and then if last year was any indicator, it will be another mile or two before we get to the parking lots. I thought the traffic might be a little lighter this late."

"How far is the parking from the show?" asked Vanessa. "These shoes are fairly comfortable but they aren't for hiking."

"Shouldn't be a problem," replied Derek. "There's a shuttle bus from the parking lots to the showgrounds."

At that the traffic ahead started to move.

"Thank God. We're moving," said Derek.

Rounding another bend they saw that the hold up was due to a delivery truck making a turn into a narrow driveway. Traffic, while heavy, was moving along the narrow roads well aided by volunteers in orange and yellow safety vests. Twenty minutes later Derek was waved into a parking spot in a grove of tall pines by a young orange-vested volunteer who proudly sported a Police Auxiliary baseball cap. His dedication to his parking duties was evidenced by the severity of his bearing as he waved each car into its shady spot with about the same effort as a crewman waving an F-18 onto the deck of an aircraft carrier.

Derek and Vanessa climbed out of the car, and Derek opened the trunk.

"What are you getting?" asked Vanessa.

"I'm just grabbing my jacket. It may be cool next to the ocean." With that, he donned a light jacket adorned with Conquistador crests on the front and on the back an embroidered image of a car and the date of last year's concours.

"Oh, nice," said Vanessa.

"I'm starting to collect them. And they're almost as much as that scarf you wanted," Derek joked. "I'll buy this year's when we get down to the clothing concession tent on the lawn."

"So, why take this one if you are going to buy one?"

"I can't wear this year's jacket. That would be gauche," gasped Derek in mock horror. "Wearing last year's shows I'm not a newbie. Wearing this year's would prove I am."

"Oh, I see. Car show etiquette," smiled Vanessa, "like never use a Miller Beer can as a rad overflow in a hot rod if a Budweiser tallboy is available."

"Yep," replied Derek. "Same thing, and by the way, I am impressed. You've been paying attention."

"Some things just rivet a girl."

They strolled across the parking area, heading toward a knot of people who were clearly waiting for a shuttle to the showgrounds. A few minutes later a large shuttle bus pulled up, and they all squeezed aboard.

11:58 a.m. PST
Eighteenth fairway, behind the Trocadero Lodge.

Freddy Smith had been involved with antique cars for the better part of his adult life. Within one category he was considered an absolute authority, and that was the American luxury car of the late 1920s and early 1930s. His favourites were the opulently appointed Pierce Arrows and Packards, but it was his familiarity with all the U.S.-built pre-war luxury cars that ensured a prestigious invitation each year from the chief concours judge asking him to evaluate the American class that featured these cars and included, among others, Cadillacs, Peerless, Lincolns and Duesenbergs.

Smith had already finished most of his judging duties for the day and was in the middle of the final meeting with his fellow class judges to determine best in class. This year the decision was a difficult one, as each of the twelve cars in the class were so spectacularly restored and different from each other that in a fair world each would receive top honours. Of course, just being on the lawn at the Conquistador was a top honour for a car and its owner, but owners spent hundreds of thousands of dollars to win, and it was Smith and three other judges' duty to award first place in class. The winner in this class would then be in the running to win best in show against twenty or so other class winners It was the most prestigious award in the old car hobby world, where even a million dollars spent on grooming a car was more the norm than an aberration.

The judging was strict and impartial, although most of the forty or so judges at the event had received offers of dinners, vacations on private yachts and even money over the years from the odd owner or rebuild shop that was unscrupulous enough to stop at nothing to win. While Smith was very aware of these offers, as was every judge, he knew of no instance when a judge had ever accepted a bribe, which said a lot for the standards set by the concours and its judging staff.

It was just a few minutes to twelve, and he could hear the announcer on the PA warming up the crowd and announcing that the first cars were queuing near the podium to receive class awards for first and second place in each division. The awards would build until four o'clock, when the award for best in show would be announced with fireworks, streamers, confetti and all the pomp due the finale of such a major event.

One of Smith's favourite cars this year was one of the ones in his judging class, a grand 1929 Pierce Arrow. While the car was very nicely done and it was the closest in its fit and finish to what the car would have been like brand new, it did not stand a chance against some of the other cars that were so overrestored you could even see a reflection of your face on the flat surfaces of their nuts and bolts.

Smith had also taken to Bob Gentry, the car's owner, who plainly admitted he was content just to have been invited and was enjoying himself immensely. Pity, thought Smith, that so many other owners no longer had fun but had turned the whole thing into a source of nail-biting stress and into a money-dripping day where tempers often flared if a judging ribbon failed to appear on a given windshield. Bob Gentry, on the other hand, was just enjoying himself and his grand old car, a car he had built himself over many years. If there were an award for the true spirit of the hobby, thought Smith, Bob Gentry would win it.

As Smith turned his attention back to the other judges and their conversation, he heard a sharp cracking coming from down the fairway. The huge crowd obscured any chance for a view, aside from the sight of a small cloud rapidly billowing upwards. Damn, he thought, something's happened. His first thoughts were that a car had a very nasty backfire or, worse, caught fire for some reason.

11:58 a.m. PST
In front of the Trocadero Lodge.

Derek and Vanessa descended the stairs of the shuttle bus and sauntered to the end of a long line of people waiting their turn to pass through the show gates beside the lodge. "Boy, it's still pretty crowded. I'd have thought the lines would be a lot shorter by now, especially at over a hundred bucks a ticket," said Derek.

"The line's moving fairly well. We shouldn't be too long getting in," replied Vanessa.

At that moment Derek heard a cracking, a little like a shotgun blast, reverberate off of the buildings that framed the entrance to the fairway. "What the hell was that?"

Vanessa was turning to reply when a volley of explosive concussions rent the air in a staccato.

"That's not good," Derek said, his face betraying recognition of what he was hearing. "Vanessa, run," he said quietly.

"What?"

"Just run!" he yelled, grabbing her hand and almost pulling her off her feet.

The two raced back through the throng lining the walkway until they were clear of the crowd and away from the laneway between the buildings. Others in the crowd divided their attention between the cacophony of sounds coming from up ahead and the pair running past them. Many people just stood there confused and unsure of what was going on, while others started to run behind Derek and Vanessa. As the two raced away from the buildings, they glanced back to see multiple small mushroom clouds roiling upwards over the roofs of the buildings that separated them from the fairway.

Once across the road and well clear of the gates and the crowd around them, Derek slowed. "Damn, I don't believe it."

"What is it?" Vanessa asked, panting with exertion.

"It has to be a series of bombs."

"Shouldn't we see if we can help?"

"Yes, but not until it's safe. There's no point rushing to help and getting injured ourselves."

At that, others who were still at the gate and crowded into the narrow laneway between the buildings started running in panic. The reason was clear. Close on their heels, hundreds of screaming people burst into the lane from the fairway beyond, ramming into one another and into anyone else who stood in their way. Some fell and were trampled. Others stumbled over them, and soon the lane was paved with the fallen and injured while more and more people jammed into the narrow space. The clothing of some people in the crowd was blood-spattered and some were soaked in red. Many people were badly injured, and as soon as the adrenalin and shock wore off, they would collapse. The sound system, which had been playing classical music interspersed with show announcements, squealed with feedback, adding to the gruesome hubbub.

12:01 p.m. PST
Eighteenth fairway, behind the Trocadero.

Freddy Smith was incredulous as explosion after explosion crackled through the air. Down the fairway, he could see the tops of tents collapsing as fireballs shot skyward.

The sound of screaming started to grow, and the crowd around him bolted in all directions. Women in designer dresses and men in expensive suits gaped at the rising clouds and then scattered, some stampeding for the exits, others running in search of friends and loved ones. Compared to the piercing crump of explosions, the fairway seemed almost quiet despite the screams of the crowd.

Smith was standing in front of the 29 Pierce Arrow and ran to its side, clear of the throng that were pushing their way up the aisles formed by the parked show cars. Bob Gentry, the Pierce Arrow's owner stood on the other side of the car with his family, his mouth agape at the scene playing out around them. As thousands of people pushed toward them, Gentry opened the car's door and yelled to his family to climb up out of harm's way. Smith jumped onto the running board to avoid the crowd, which by now was dangerous in its panic. A wall of humanity surged around them, and from the vantage point of the car's running board, Smith could see that many of the show tents dotted around the field were collapsing or had collapsed and that some were on fire. Many people in the crowd were covered in a fine brown powder that drifted on the air and soiled their clothes, faces and hands.

Smith turned to look at the lodge and was horrified to see that many of the windows in the northern wing had shattered and that the reviewing tent and VIP area had been flattened. He could see bodies strewn all over the staircases and balconies, and flames flickered and grew stronger in several of the windows on the lodge's ground floor. The food tents, which were a little closer to him, were completely decimated when the initial explosions ignited the propane cylinders that powered their portable stoves. The injured, dead and dying were everywhere.

Smith turned back once more to see Bob Gentry and his family standing in the back of their massive car, hugging one another as they viewed the hellish spectacle that unfolded all around them. Suddenly the air rippled.

12:03 p.m. PST
Hillside across from Trocadero Lodge.

Derek and Vanessa watched in disbelief as the crowd trampled people underfoot in their mindless rush to safety.

"Oh my God," exclaimed Vanessa, "this can't be happening!"

Derek held her hand tighter, aware that for the moment there was nothing they could do. In the distance the first sirens could be heard moaning, and several police officers and security guards rushed toward the crowd and then stopped as they realized that they would be crushed if they tried to intercept the stampede. One policeman alone, either because brave or unaware of the mortal danger, stood his ground, holding his hands up to try to slow people before he too was gathered in the surging throng and then fell and disappeared beneath it.

Suddenly, the shock wave of an immense explosion threw Derek and Vanessa to the ground. Windows blasted from the Trocadero buildings, and a huge column of smoke that dwarfed all those previous billowed skywards. Derek threw himself over Vanessa to protect her as debris started to rain down. Chunks of steel, masonry and other less identifiable materials pelted from above.

One security guard who was just scrambling to his feet was smashed back into the ground as a chunk of the 1929 Pierce Arrow's cylinder head hit him squarely in the back, pulping his spine and internal organs instantly. Derek felt a sting as a tiny piece of shrapnel sliced though the flesh of his upper arm and buried itself in the ground. Finally the patter of falling objects ceased, and Derek looked up as he rolled off of Vanessa. The air was still full of smoke and light debris. The crowd had been knocked to the ground, hundreds of them cut down by the glass and masonry that had exploded from the buildings. The only sound now seemed to be sirens in the distance.

12:03 p.m. PST
Eighteenth fairway.

Freddy Smith, Bob Gentry and Gentry's family vanished as the air rippled upwards trying to escape the incredible power unleashed from beneath the old car. The car itself became tens of thousands of steel, iron and aluminum fragments, as did the components of several of the cars that were parked around it. Supersonic shock waves pulsated outward in a perfect circle from the explosion's epicentre, carrying those fragments forward like scythes cutting through everything in their paths.

While the initial explosions had killed dozens, the new blast killed hundreds and injured thousands more. The fairway became a carnal house of burning cars and dismembered corpses. Fires flickered everywhere and several cars started to burn. In no time, the fuel in many of the multi-million dollar cars caught fire and new but much smaller explosions dotted the fairway. At that moment the low scudding clouds above parted, allowing the sun to shine through and illuminate Dante's inferno below.

The smoke from the fires dotted about the fairway hung heavily on the still air. If there had been anyone who was not escaping from the fairway or rushing to help the injured, they might have noticed the floating brown powder as it crept sluggishly through the air and settled on everything and everyone who remained in the area. As the sun broke through the clouds, the air stirred, creating a gentle northwards flow that carried the airborne powder with it. Soon it would be drifting through the woods and into the multi-million dollar homes, county clubs, golf courses and equestrian facilities that dotted the Balmoral Private Reserve. Some powder might even make it beyond, to the city of Santa Barbara. The people touching and inhaling it were far too preoccupied to notice.

The ramifications were deadly. The apparently innocuous brown powder floating on the light breezes and driven upwards on the spiralling air from a host of large and small fires was composed of a specially engineered form of ricin, the deadly toxin of the castor bean mixed with a mutated hemorrhagic virus closely related to Ebola. The two agents had been developed and blended into an easily deployed airborne poison by former Soviet scientists who had been working in several very secret and well-equipped laboratories, first in Pakistan and then in Brunei when Pakistan came under scrutiny by the West and its intelligence services.

When the Iron Curtain fell in the 1990s and government programs were cancelled or simply went broke, the Russian scientists working on biological warfare agents went unpaid or became unemployed and their families went hungry. Given the opportunity to make hundreds of thousands of U.S. dollars in exchange for their cooperation in developing these toxins, three accomplished biological warfare scientists jumped at the chance. Years later they were successful beyond their wildest dreams. With the help of millions of dollars rerouted from the oil revenues of several Middle Eastern countries, they developed a highly advanced and stable form of weapons-grade hemorrhagic fever.

The three scientists, however, would not enjoy the wealth promised them or even get to see the fruits of their hard work. All three had long since become part of the food chain many miles out in the South China Sea. Their product, however, was still being manufactured and shipped around the world in small quantities, almost always disguised as cans of chocolate milk powder included in large shipments of the real thing. A small but very particular flaw in the label identified each toxin-filled can to their appointed receiver.

On the fairway almost all of the survivors among the fifty thousand people attending the show had breathed in the mixture, as would the rescue workers who would soon be arriving. Police helicopters and air ambulances would further ensure the toxin spread to many more people in the area in the coming hours, before the danger was fully recognized and the entire peninsula quarantined.

12:10 p.m. PST
Hillside across from Trocadero Lodge.

Security guards and police personnel had rushed to the gates over the last couple of minutes. While they were just as confused and panicked by the events, their training had kicked in, and they were blocking access to anyone rushing to see what had happened and doing whatever they could to help the injured and guide the remnants of the crowd to safety.

Dozens of people streamed past Derek and Vanessa, many injured and bleeding and all grim faced or sobbing with shock and fear. Many survivors, sensing relative safety, were collapsing on the lawn and under the trees that lined the walkway up the hill. People were on cellphones, either asking for help or contacting loved ones. Several reporters were using their cells to report what had happened. Derek and Vanessa both pitched in to do what they could for the injured who littered the hillside.

Derek was bent over an older, very well dressed gentleman. He was trying to staunch the bleeding from several large wounds in the man's left leg. He had already tied a tourniquet made from the man's expensive sports jacket around the bleeding stump of wrist, where a blast-borne piece of shrapnel had removed the man's hand with almost surgical precision. Vanessa worked beside Derek, ripping the jacket's silk liner into strips to make more impromptu bandages. The man sat up suddenly, looked right into Derek's eyes, mouthed something inaudible and then fell back to the ground, dead. Derek looked at Vanessa, whose eyes were red and full of tears, and nodded.

The couple moved on to the next injured person lying on the hillside, a young woman whose face was streaming with blood from several wounds in the crown of her head and whose non-responsiveness indicated she was in severe shock. Derek noticed the smudges of brown powder that soiled the woman's bright yellow dress, her shoulders and neck. "Vanessa, look at this."

Vanessa leaned forward to take a closer look. "It seems to be a powder, not dirt," she said, running her finger through it and examining the smudge on her fingertip.

Derek stood and took a closer look at several other people sprawled on the lawn. He grimaced as he realized what is might be that had soiled some of the people on the ground around them. "Oh my God," he exclaimed, "you don't think this could be a nerve agent or something?"

Vanessa stood. "I...I don't know she said hesitantly, unconsciously wiping her hands on her dress. She too looked at the people prostrate around her, and at the others who milled about. Many of them had brown stains on their skin and clothing. "Derek, I think we'd better tell someone that there could be more to this than just the bombs," she said.

Derek pointed at the temporary washrooms set up at the top of the hill, beside a hedgerow. "Let's get up there and wash, quickly, and hope to hell that if it is anything, we haven't absorbed it through our skin or breathed in any."

"Oh my God," muttered Vanessa as she looked at her fingers, some of them still stained by the powder she had wiped from the young woman's dress. She bent down and wiped them back and forth in the soft grass at their feet. Then for good measure, she dug her fingers into the soil below, trying to cleanse them of all traces. She stood and Derek pointed up the hill again.

"Let's go," he said urgently.

They both hurried up the hill.

As they half walked, half trotted toward the portable wash stations that accompanied the privies, Derek saw two state troopers, horror transforming their features as they took in the carnage in front of them. The officers were hurrying down the walkway towards them.

"Vanessa, you keep going and wash. I'll be there in a second. I just want to warn these two and get them to call for a haz-mat team." As he walked toward the troopers, he pulled his FBI identification from his pocket and flashed his badge.

12:30 p.m. PST
Highway 101, Thousand Oaks, California.

Kato Kakerie and Sato Tadashi strolled out of the convenience store tearing at the cellophane wrapping on their fresh packages of cigarettes. Both were inveterate chain smokers, a condition that did not seem to bother the other two occupants of the car at all. As they opened the back doors to climb in, chatting in Japanese to one another, Ishikawa Chicao yelled from the driver's seat to be quiet and turned up the volume on the radio. The newscaster was breaking the story.

"Ladies and gentlemen, this just in. We have an unconfirmed report that a series of explosions has rocked a large car show near Santa Barbara. We have few details at his time, but it is believed that there are several casualties. The cause of the explosions has not been determined, and Santa Barbara police and fire department officials have not responded to our calls. Stay tuned for continuing coverage of the explosion as details become available, and now back to our regular programming."

A Willie Nelson ballad played from the car's speakers as the four men glanced at one another, smiling ear to ear. Chicao backed the car out of its space and pulled into traffic, once again southbound, heading for downtown Los Angeles, a new weapons cache and the next in their series of strikes.

August 19. 12:45 a.m. PKST (August 18. 12:45 p.m. PST)
Islamabad, Pakistan.

Muhammad al-Munajjid swept back into the room with the large screen television. The two men who had fetched him from his quiet contemplation walked through the door first and took their positions framing the doorway, their eyes roving over the other men assembled in the room. While al-Munajjid trusted almost every man in the room, his two bodyguards constantly watched every movement and posture affected by those who were in close contact with their charge, vigilant for any sign of betrayal.

Al-Munajjid took his place of honour at the head of the room and watched the blonde CNN newscaster, who sat staring into the camera with one hand cupping her ear as she listened through her earpiece to her producers as they briefed her on the breaking story. Below her ran a video newstape repeating over and over that a series of bombs had rocked the car show at the Conquistador Golf and Country Club and that dozens of people were dead or injured.

"It's been confirmed," she said. "There are dozens of injuries and there have been deaths at the Conquistador Concours d'Elegance, a large car show being held near Santa Barbara. A series of small bombs followed by one major explosion reportedly ripped through a huge crowd of automobile enthusiasts who had gathered to view the event. The annual show was well attended by a public that normally includes major celebrities, successful entrepreneurs and financiers. It is not yet known whether any public figures are among the victims. We have our first live feed from our affiliate station in Santa Barbara taken from their news helicopter, which is currently over the showgrounds."

An aerial shot of the fairway appeared on the screen. The camera wandered from burning car to burning car, pulled back to pan the fairway, and then zoomed back in to focus on knots of people clustered around the bodies that littered the entire fairway. Many cars and several of the large tents were ablaze, and columns of thick black smoke rose from dozens of fires. The clubhouse itself was fully engulfed in a conflagration that belched flames from several of the terrace doors and from the shattered windows of its exclusive restaurant. It was quite evident from the footage that hundreds of people were gravely injured or dead and that firefighters and police were only now running onto the fairway in significant numbers as they arrived from nearby towns and stations.

In the white-walled room, al-Munajjid allowed himself a grin of satisfaction as his compatriots laughed and clapped one another on the back, revelling in the news and the scenes that were playing out on the American news channel. Al-Munajjid raised his hand, and there was sudden silence, although every man still smiled broadly.

"It begins. Allah be praised," exclaimed al-Munajjid. With that he rose and strode from the room. He needed to speak to others who had quietly supported him in jihad.

12:59 p.m. PST
Post Road, Balmoral.

"Hold on a second, Derek. Let me get these off," Vanessa said as she leaned on Derek and pulled her shoes off, stuffing them into her purse.

They were trudging along Post Road on their way to the parking lot where they'd left Derek's Jag. Hundreds of other spectators trudged along the road as well, all returning to cars that were parked a mile or more from the grounds. No parking lot shuttles were running. They had all been pressed into service as ambulances to take the injured to area hospitals. No one walking along the road was complaining though. They had seen first hand what could have happened to them had they not been lucky.

Derek's cell phone rang for the fifth time during the walk. He snapped it open. "Yes, I am on my way to the car. I'll get clear of the area and give you a call when I get back to the hotel. Yes, Susan, the receptionist has the hotel address. Check with her. I'll notify the hotel management that we'll be taking it over as a billet for the FEMA teams and Homeland Security. How many rooms do you want put aside for FBI and Homeland?" He waited for the response. "Okay, I'll block off ten, and FEMA can use the rest. There will be lots of rooms in both Santa Barbara and Montecito by tonight. I imagine tourists are going to leave in droves."

Derek listened again and then continued. "Okay, John, I'll wait for you and the rest of the team to get here. You can tell Washington that I'm sure it was a terrorist attack, and yes, I'm almost positive there is more to this than just the explosives. I'm betting the powder we saw on people was more than just residue from the blasts, but you're right. I can't be positive. It's just a guess." He paused. "I know Washington is going to resist sending in military biowarfare teams, but I think that waiting is going to make it a lot worse. At least get the haz-mat teams at Fort Dix ready to roll as soon as we know for sure. If it's not a problem, they can stand down with no harm done."

Derek's frown deepened as he listened. "If it were up to me, I would already have them in the air," he growled. Then he snapped the phone closed.

"God," he said to Vanessa, "Washington told LA that haz-mat won't arrive until a biological agent is confirmed. Someone is on the way up from Los Angeles by chopper to do that, but they are still half an hour out, and then it will be another hour until they can get set up, do their tests and confirm whether it's a bioweapon or not."

"In the meantime," replied Vanessa, "people are thrashing about in what may be a death trap."

"I know, but Washington doubts a biological attack is in progress and doesn't want to panic people until they get confirmation."

At that, two police cruisers, their sirens wailing, sped around the corner and then slowed as they met the road teeming with pedestrians. With sirens whooping they cleared their way through.

"It looks like the state troopers I told have a least started to get the word out," said Derek.

In both cars, the troopers were wearing tear gas masks, balaclavas and gloves.

Suddenly, the thunderclap of an explosion rolled through the tall pines of the Balmoral forest.

"What the hell," said Derek, looking in the direction of the thunderous blast. "It came from the north, like maybe Santa Barbara. It sounds like another one, a big one."

"Oh my god, oh my god," Vanessa cried, shocked at the ramifications of Derek's statement. Tears welled in her eyes. "What on earth is going on? Who is doing this?"

1:00 p.m. PST
Ocean Rest Hotel and Spa, Santa Barbara.

At precisely one o clock the timers in the van parked in the Ocean Rest's delivery area ignited the explosives. The van burst like a balloon, fragments of its aluminum and steel body carried on the supersonic pulse of the detonation. A young kitchen attendant was just about to open the steel fire door at the back of the inn to dump some kitchen waste when the door scintillated in front of him and gathered him up as it blew down the corridor. He was killed instantly.

Outside in the parking lot, a family from White Plains, New Jersey, were backing out of their parking spot when the concussive wave of the explosion hit their side windows and turned them into a shotgun blast of pebbled glass fragments. All four occupants — the parents and two teenage children — were killed. No one else died in the blast, but several people in their rooms were injured by glass fragments when windows in the back of the hotel shattered. Car alarms screamed in the parking lot, triggered by the explosion, and a mushroom of black smoke climbed skyward.

Carried within the billowing cloud, the remaining half quart of bioagent spread upwards and outwards. About half of it was immolated by the blast, but there was enough left to form a smudge in the air that eddied on the gentle breeze as it floated straight toward the downtown shops still packed with tourists before gently settling back to earth.

**August 19. 4:10 a.m. Japan Standard Time (August 18. 1:10 p.m. PST)
Air Force One, thirty-five thousand feet, eastbound from Japanese territorial airspace.**

"Mr. President, we have a communiqué from Washington regarding the explosion in California. It seems that it may be terrorist related and the target was a car show near Santa Barbara," said Henry Woeburn, one of the president's many and varied assistants on this, the last and homeward flight of a ten-day tour of the Asian Pacific region following the World Economic Summit in Melbourne, Australia.

"A car show. What kind of terrorist blows up a car show?" asked the president.

"Well, sir, it appears that this show is attended by a lot of VIPs, including very high-profile business people and celebrities. It is evidently well attended by the Hollywood set."

"Oh, great," interjected Dan Blomstrum, White House chief of staff, "just what this administration needs right now, more reasons for the Hollywood fraternity to muckrake."

"How many are hurt?" asked the president.

"Sir, we don't have definite numbers at the present time, but initial estimates indicate that perhaps as many as two hundred people have been injured or killed."

"Oh no," said the president quietly as the news sank in. "Well, for Christ's sake, get into the com room and get me as much information as you can. I will have to say something shortly, and I want to know what the hell is going on." He turned to his chief of staff. "Dan, we had better not wait until we land. It'd be best if I give at least some kind of statement in the next hour or two. In the meantime, make sure the press pool at the White House is assured that we are on top of this.

"Henry, keep on it and inform me as soon as you hear anything. Find someone on the ground in the area who can tell us what is happening without filtering it, and Henry, we had better stop in on the West Coast. Go forward and ask the pilots to change our destination to Los Angeles or San Francisco."

Woeburn turned to leave the office.

"Oh, and Henry," continued the president, "don't talk to anyone in the press corps on board, until I give my say-so."

"Mr. President, do you think landing on the West Coast is wise. We really don't have any idea what the continuing threat may be," cautioned Blomstrum.

"Dan, we have what, seven or eight hours to determine that risk before we hit American airspace? In the meantime, who do we have on board from CIA or FBI?"

"Really no one, sir. Just about everyone on board is Secret Service, media or economic and financial advisors."

"Well, get someone on standby from FBI or Homeland who can bring me up to speed on the satellite link."

The president swivelled in his plush office chair to gaze out the window. The aircraft's giant wing was gently moving up and down as if flapping to keep them airborne. At about a quarter of a mile away, two Japanese F-15 Eagles held formation with two U.S. Navy Super Hornets. The F-15s were an honour guard escorting the president from Japanese airspace. The Super Hornets were the first of a string of escort fighters that would rendezvous and accompany the presidential aircraft as it winged across the Pacific. As the president watched, the aircraft pitched slightly, right wing down as the pilots altered its heading to take up a new course to the California coast. The Japanese Eagles broke formation and turned away, banking through 180 degrees, and headed back home.

A moment later, the president was eyeing a new communiqué, a revised estimate of the casualties. While still preliminary, the new accounting was over two thousand, not two hundred, dead. His gut twisted.

4:20 p.m. Eastern Standard Time (1:20 p.m. PST)
NW 25th Street and NW 36th Avenue, Miami.

Miguel Ramírez parked his beaten up van in the alley next to the three-storey 1950s brick building. He had been listening to the radio when the first confused reports of the strike on the West Coast were announced. He had finished his hamburger, thrown the wrapper on the floor and headed to his task just two blocks away from where waited in the parking lot of a fast-food restaurant. He knew that today was the day and at what time to expect news on the radio. While he did not know what that news would be, he had been told he would know as soon as he heard it.

The van's paint was peeling and its rocker panels rusting, but new vinyl stickers on the doors proclaimed the New Cuba Air Conditioning Company, Sales and Service. It was a legitimate company, and Miguel had actually worked there for almost a year. Walking to the back of the van, he opened the dented cargo doors and pulled out a long heavy cardboard box from the clutter of old air-conditioning equipment and tools. The box was new and tightly wrapped with nylon packing straps. Stickers from a well-known heating and air-conditioning manufacturer adorned its sides, but in fact it contained something much more sinister.

Ramírez was twenty-four years old, American-born of Cuban descent, and he had lived his entire life in South Florida, where his mother and father struggled to make ends meet. His father worked in a cement factory, where he'd earned a chronic cough and poor health from breathing lime powder and other fine particulates at the jobsite. After years of faithful and uncomplaining service, he was still only paid a little over the minimum wage. Ramírez' mother had become a Hispanic stereotype, working as a cleaning lady for a maid service, and she often put in twelve-hour days. She had arthritis and was constantly harassed by her supervisor to speed up lest she be replaced by a younger, faster woman.

Ramírez had learned to hate America on the gang-ridden streets of Miami. As a teenager, he had turned his back on the Catholic Church after the local priest made several sexual innuendos culminating in a brief tussle in the church's recreation room. The priest suffered a bloody nose; Ramírez, another great disappointment. Two years ago he was converted to Islam by a Lebanese friend he'd met while working in a fish market. Ramírez worked cleaning fish, surrounded daily by the stink of entrails and his hands stained with blood. His conversion to Islam had been gradual, but by the time he finally quit the job, he had developed a burning hatred of America and all its injustices and saw Islam as a way to force America to change.

Ramírez shouldered the box and entered the old building. A security guard, a man in his late sixties seated at a rickety desk in the foyer, asked him where he was going. Miguel gave him a work order authorizing a Sunday repair to one of the air-conditioning units on the third floor. The guard glanced at it and passed it back, his gaze already wandering back to the soccer game playing on a small television. Ramírez made his way to the stairs and started up.

On the third floor, he walked past the offices mentioned in the repair order. At the end of the dimly lit hallway, he came to a shabby green door with a poorly lettered sign that read Roof Access, No Unauthorized Entry. Pulling a key from his pocket, he unlocked the padlock he had placed on the door's lock hasp just the day before to ensure that he would be the only one on the roof. Passing though the door, he padlocked it from the back so there would be no surprises, and then he walked up the short flight of stairs. The roof door creaked outwards revealing a flat gravel-strewn roof redolent with the smell of ancient sun-warmed tar.

He swung the door closed behind him and secured it with a metal rod made for the purpose and also set in position the day before, insurance against someone getting past the bottom door. He walked across the roof and checked the fire escape that ran down the east side of the building, making sure it was still unencumbered and useable. Looking down he saw the small orange Nissan Micra he'd borrowed from a friend and parked across the street awaiting his escape.

Returning to the west side of the building, he took a penknife from his pocket and slit the nylon straps on the box. After opening the lid, he reached in and removed a grey-green tube. The tube, originally marked with U.S. military stencils, was the disposable launcher of a Stinger ground-to-air missile. The missile had originally been a gift, one of five hundred Stingers given by the CIA to the Afghan mujahedeen. Never used against the Russians, it had been carefully stored and then smuggled back to its country of origin. Now it would finally be used but not in a way its maker, General Dynamics, or its first purchaser, the CIA would have wanted.

4:30 EST (1:30 p.m. PST)
Hold-short line, runway 08 L, Miami International Airport.

Captain Hans Weber was in a poor mood. Lufthansa flight 237, departing Miami for Berlin, had been held up at the gate for twenty minutes while a Transportation Safety Administration officer checked the paperwork on one of his 316 passengers, and then they'd had an interminable taxi from concourse F to the hold-short line for runway 08 left. He should have been in the air fifty minutes ago, and to make matters worse, he now had to wait for several small commuter jets and private executive-class twins to take off before his turn on the runway.

First officer Wilfred Hagler had handled the lion's share of the taxi and the com with the ground controllers while Weber made himself busy with some maintenance reports that listed several non-critical snags with the aircraft that in his opinion could have and should have already been repaired. The most irksome was an faulty light in the first-class washroom, a little problem that had given the cabin crew a lot of grief. More than a few customers had been in the middle of delicate things when the bulb flickered off and had ended up thrashing about in a tiny pitch-dark cubicle searching for necessities. That the light would then come on and show no further signs of disobedience until yet another critical moment made it seem as if an unseen jester were in charge of the switch. It was not something Weber found amusing in the slightest, even if some of the other crew had to hide their grins when the stewards reported each complaint to the flight deck.

Hagler acknowledged the Miami International ground controllers' hand-off to the flight controller and their clearance, and finally the lumbering 747-400 swung onto the runway, its nose pointed to the east. Hagler, who was still in control, pushed the throttles forward to the stop, and the giant aircraft's engines bellowed with full power as it began its take-off roll down the runway. Finally, with most of the runway behind it, the heavily loaded 747 clawed its way into the air.

4:36 p.m. EST (1:36 PST)
NW 25th Street and NW 36th Avenue, Miami.

Miguel Ramírez crouched on the rooftop, shouldering the thirty-five-pound Stinger missile and launcher system and gazing westward in anticipation of a target. If he'd been properly trained, Ramírez would have known that launching at an approaching aircraft would confuse the guidance system of the old heat-seeking missile, reducing his chances of a hit. But in the eyes of his Lebanese friend and mentor, Ramírez was expendable and not worth the investment of full training. After fifteen minutes of early morning instruction the day before, Ramírez was handed the Stinger and told to wait for the news that was sure to come soon after three o'clock the next day.

Aside from that and instructions to scope out a certain rooftop, secure its access and use its vantage for the launch, he knew little else of value. In the unlikely event that he was captured before the strike, or even after, he would be unable to supply the FBI with any useful information, especially not anything concerning the whereabouts of his "friend" who even now was on his way to another city, cloaked in another impeccable identity. Ramírez did not know that his friend and mentor, who had supplied the twenty-year-old missile, had little faith that it would perform flawlessly even though it had been well cared for. That was why he decided to leave his expendable protege the task of launching it rather than endanger one of his valuable fedayeen warriors.

On seeing an American Airlines 767 rise into the air from 08 right, the southernmost runway at the airport, Ramírez stood up, arming the ten-kilogram missile as he rose and, without any indication of a missile lock, pulled the trigger. The missile burst from its tube, launched by a single charge from a small primary motor. Once airborne and far enough from the launch point to avoid incinerating its operator, the missile started to falter and a larger motor kicked in, a tongue of flame lashing out from the missile's back end as it raced into the sky, accelerating to twice the speed of sound. Ramírez dropped the launcher tube to the rooftop and watched the Stinger corkscrew through the sky, searching for a lock.

The American Airlines 767 was in little danger — the missile arced upwards and then started to veer north. Ramírez spat with fury as he saw the missile's contrail arc away from his intended target. Suddenly the little missile jinked and turned earthward, having found the massive heat signature of the Lufthansa Boeing 747 as it climbed away from the runway. The missile sped through the air its nose pointed toward the 747. At the last moment, as the body of the leviathan eclipsed its starboard engines, the missile lost the signature emanating from them. For the 747 this mattered very little.

The tiny rocket slammed into the top of the Boeing, just four feet behind and above the cockpit windows. It cut through the aircraft's soft skin and slammed into the flight deck's armoured door, a tougher surface than the aluminum it had just sliced through. The three-kilogram warhead exploded. The flight deck, captain and first officer disappeared in a ball of super-heated flame, and the outer skin of the cockpit ripped away. Deprived of its control and critical systems, missing much of its forward fuselage, but engines still roaring, the immense airplane heeled over gently, careening to the south. As the roll increased, the aircraft stalled and slid sideways. For a moment, the inherent stability of the wings in their take off configuration seemed to right the plane. Then its tail dropped and the aircraft rose, gaining a few hundred feet and extending its death throes across a sky now peppered with its own fluttering debris. Suddenly the plane nosed down in a terminal stall and plummeted to earth — a scant two thousand feet below.

Ramírez couldn't believe his eyes. His fury at missing the first aircraft turned to elation upon seeing what the missile had hit. He had watched as the plane veered southwards from its easterly heading and started to drop. It screamed by his position so low he instinctively ducked. As it passed, he ran a few steps and then stopped, awestruck by what he had accomplished. He saw the aircraft tilt skyward, gain a few hundred feet and then plummet to the ground about three miles to the east of Miami International.

What Ramírez didn't know, nor did he care, was that the aircraft, brimming with cargo, fuel and 332 souls, slammed almost dead centre into the northwester face of Memorial Hospital. More than sixty-three thousand gallons of Jet A ignited as the mammoth machine plowed through the building. Propelled by the force behind them, flames, debris and aircraft parts sprayed outwards consuming anything and anyone in their path and spreading to nearby buildings, which also burst into flame. Within moments, a firestorm raced through the closely packed buildings that stood like dominoes behind the hospital.

Ramírez ran to the fire escape, down it and to the orange Micra while huge black clouds roiled into the sky. If anyone saw him, they paid him no attention as he started the car and rocketed off. In his mind, he was a successful jihadist on the run. Authorities would detain him within twelve hours, having found the launcher and easily connected it to the abandoned van and cardboard box that had carried it. While Ramírez would offer up lots of details about his Lebanese friend and other Muslim converts he knew, nothing he said would, in the grand scheme of things, prove very useful.

5:36 p.m. EST (2:36 PST)
1 West 72nd Street, New York City.

Lyndon Hersch, better known as movie star Linden Lane, fretted in the back of his Hummer limousine. He'd been held up on a movie shoot in Brooklyn, and if he didn't rush, he'd be late for a cocktail party being held in his honour by the mayor of New York City. In addition to the mayor, the governor of New York State and numerous other politicians as well as fellow celebrities from both Broadway and Los Angeles would attend.

Unlike many of his peer group, Lane was conscientious to a fault and hated to be late for any event. It was one of the many reasons he was well–liked, not just by his fans but also by almost everyone who knew him. Like many other celebrities, Lane was politically active, but unlike most, he knew his stuff. He was a left-leaning Republican, a conundrum he was able to make work, and was respected for his world and environmental views by both Republicans and Democrats. He also sponsored several worthwhile charities, all American based and dedicated to the poor and troubled of his country, as he believed that charity really should begin at home.

He counted among his close friends such people as Bill Gates, President Clinton and the incumbent president. While immensely popular in Hollywood and considered quite a prize by any party-throwing Beverly Hills host or hostess, he rarely appeared on the party circuit. He preferred to spend his private time on a four-thousand-acre ranch he owned in Colorado, where his ranch hands tended to the local wildlife and Lind's small herd of quarter horses and mustangs rather than to herds of cattle. No matter where he went, he was rarely bothered by the paparazzi, as his method of dealing with them was to walk over, shake their hands and have a chat. They'd ended up with so many pictures of him over time that the tabloids they stocked with sleazy images didn't consider him all that saleable an item.

His Hummer limo, chosen for him in New York by his producers — in keeping with the action adventure epic he was currently filming — and in Lane's opinion a detestable vehicle, pulled up to the curb in front of the famous Dakota Apartments. These too were quarters Lane would never in a million years have rented for the fifteen-week shoot but had been supplied by the producers who sublet one of the opulent apartments from an Italian clothing designer who was in Paris organizing his yearly fashion show. Lane detested all the fuss and bother, including the security that spun about him, but he considered it a small price to pay for the privileges that his life afforded him.

He started out of the limo and was immediately noticed by a gaggle of tourists who gathered daily in front of the Dakota to see the spot where John Lennon had been gunned down. As he stepped to the curb his driver came around the vehicle, once again too slow to arrive in time to open the door for his passenger.

"One day, Mr. Lane," the limo driver said, "I'll get around in time."

"Not while I have two good legs and two good arms you won't, Morty," said Lane.

As they spoke, the group of ten or so tourists surged toward them.

"Now ladies and gentlemen, let Mr. Lane through. He's on a tight schedule and can't be held up," proclaimed the limo driver as he put himself between the small crowd and Lane.

"It's okay, Morty. It'll just take a moment. Hang on, people." Lane turned and grabbed a handful of autographed pictures from a map pocket in the back of the limo. "I don't have time to personalize them right now — I am a little pressed for time — but if any of you would like to send these pictures to the address on the back, along with your name and a little bio about yourself and a return address, I'd be glad to send them back personalized."

In fact, he really would take the time to read each letter and personalize the photo before having his personal secretary mail them back. Numerous times he'd been urged to save himself the time and bother of answering fan mail by having his staff do it, but he refused, replying that it was these people who were responsible for his success and he owed it to them to answer their mail personally.

He passed out the glossy photographs to each waiting hand. As he chatted to the enraptured fans, he failed to notice two very un-fanlike workmen coming around each corner of the Hummer from the street.

His first inkling that something was wrong was when a woman gasped. Then she started to scream. He turned in time to see one of the two men in NYC sanitation coveralls level a small automatic weapon at him. Had he not refused security or bodyguards, he might have had a chance, but in all likelihood his protectors would have suffered the same fate as eleven of the people standing on the sidewalk, including Linden Lane himself.

There was an odd popping sound as the gun he was looking at bucked in the assassin's hands. Behind Hirsch an accomplice opened up from the other side. The knot of people was cut down, caught in the withering crossfire. From their vantage points at either end of the Hummer each gunman sprayed his victims with two magazines of thirty bullets each, methodically ejecting the first and snapping in the next before opening up again.

It took only a few seconds. The noses of the low-velocity bullets had been hollowed out and filled with a drop of mercury fulminate, an explosive salt of mercury prepared with nitric acid. Then each round was sealed with a drop of wax. These rounds exploded into splinters as they hit their targets, making them far more lethal. As well, each shell casing contained only about half a load of gunpowder. This ensured lower velocity and that few bullets would penetrate through and through. Instead they entered their victims and bounced around internally until they hit bone or something else hard enough to set off the fulminate if the initial impact had not already done so.

Moments later, the two gunmen ran from the carnage they had wrought and leapt onto two small motorcycles parked across the road. They took off, their small engines screaming, bobbed and weaved around cars and trucks, and disappeared into the New York traffic. Behind them lay the bullet-riddled remains of one of America's most-beloved film stars, hit five times, as well as ten other dead. Six more victims lay badly wounded, felled by the explosive bullets that had torn gaping holes in their bodies. Of the dozens of witnesses to the act, not one could give the police an accurate description of the two men. They said only that the perpetrators were white or perhaps Hispanic and that they were dressed as garbagemen.

4:56 p.m. Central Standard Time (2:56 p.m. PST)
Tulsa Convention Center, 100 Civic Center, Tulsa, Oklahoma.

The five-ton truck crept along Boulder Avenue, caught in the late-day traffic. On its doors a sign reading Springfield Convention and Display Supply Company accompanied a large vinyl photograph that graced each of the truck's box sides, showing an assortment of mundane-looking chairs, tables, desks and convention booth fixtures. Inside, the truck carried a hodgepodge of display booth flats, chairs and other trade show supplies, the cooling bodies of the truck's legitimate driver and his helper and, on a pallet, almost two tons of high explosives in boxes marked as blue and orange display curtains.

As it neared the convention centre, the truck pulled onto the wide pavement in front of the main entrance and the man on the passenger side got out and started to direct as the driver backed the truck toward the front of the building. A security guard inside saw what was going on and rushed out to intervene. "Hey, you. You can't bring that damned truck up here. The loading docks are around back," he yelled.

The man flagging the truck walked over. "I am very sorry, sir, but I have instructions to unload this special delivery through the front doors," he said with a heavy Indian accent.

"Well, you'd just better get that truck around back," replied the guard.

"No, sir," replied the man apologetically. "Here we have a written permission from the trade centre's office. Right here, sir." He showed the security guard a letter pinned to the clipboard he was carrying and had been using to wave the truck backwards.

The security guard took the clipboard from him and examined the letter, which was on convention centre letterhead and carried the general manager's signature. "Well, it looks okay," he said.

At that, the truck's driver got out and walked over. He too had a heavy accent, which the security guard thought was Russian but was actually Chechen. "We are going to go inside for a moment to get our helpers," he said.

"I can't let the two of you go in. One of you is going to have to wait with the truck," the guard replied.

"Please, sir," said the driver, "we have been on our way here for many hours without stopping and I need to use a bathroom."

"I do as well, sir," said the Indian man. "I have to go very badly and as soon as we finish, we will get our helpers to unload. We will be gone only a very short time."

"Okay, then," replied the guard, relenting, "but one of you comes back as soon as you're finished in the can. I'll stay with the truck until then."

The two men started off, walking quickly toward the doors.

Just as they opened the door, the guard yelled, "Hey, wait a minute."

The two men froze, the driver's hand slipping to a Sig Saur automatic he had concealed in the lining of his jacket.

"You guys didn't ask where the nearest shitter is. Walk in and take your first left. It's about fifty feet down the corridor and on your right."

"Thank you, sir," the Chechen replied as he continued on through the door. Once inside, the pair started to jog, heading deeper into the building and almost running down several people in the crowded hall. They and hundreds of others were filing into the centre to attend a World Wrestling Association grand slam event. Hundreds of men, woman and children waited patiently for the doors to the sports arena to open at six o'clock, only moments away. At one minute after six, the two men hurried out the back of the building, through the very loading docks the guard had mentioned, got into a red Dodge Caravan that sat idling just outside on the street and sped off.

At precisely 6:05, just as the guard looked at his watch and wondered how much longer the driver and his helper were going to be, the timers imbedded in the high explosives in the back of the truck went off.

2:56 p.m. PST.
Beach Resort Hotel, Montecito, California.

Derek closed the door to their room and leaned back on it. Vanessa sat, lost in thought, at the window desk, gazing out over the ocean and the waves breaking along the shoreline. She did not look away or acknowledge Derek's entry. Just beyond the breakers, two seals popped their heads up between swells and surveyed the beach before disappearing back into the beds of giant kelp that lay just offshore. The seals did not have much to occupy their attention. The beach was quiet, recently deserted by the usual mix of joggers, tourists and surfers.

North along the coast, black clouds were still rising into the air from Balmoral, proof that the fires at the Trocadero still burned. Small dark shapes buzzed around the columns of smoke — helicopters filled with reporters and photographers, always the first to respond. Several larger helicopters were coming and going, military or Coast Guard personnel evacuating the injured.

"All the arrangements have been made. The teams should begin arriving over the next few hours," said Derek. "Agents from Los Angeles should be here any time, and San Francisco is sending down reinforcements. Headquarters in Washington is also dispatching teams, so this place is going to get pretty busy in the next ten hours or so. They're talking about a suspicious plane crash in Miami as well. A 747 crashed while it was taking off, and Jeff at the LA office said it may have plowed into a hospital. There's a rumour it was shot down with a rocket."

"God, I hope it isn't connected to this," Vanessa said.

"I hope it's just an unhappy coincidence, but if it is connected, then we could be in a lot of trouble. Anyway, let's not panic yet. What do you want to do? Maybe we should get you back to DC."

"No, I can probably be more useful here, and besides, I'll bet travelling is going to be difficult in the next few days."

"I'm going to take a break. The hotel manager will call us if he needs any help. In the meantime, they're going to assemble an operations room for us, run phone lines and set up desks. We can refine it when the teams start arriving."

Vanessa turned away from the ocean view, her eyes filled with tears.

"Oh come here, sweetheart," said Derek, seeing her distress.

She rose from her chair, and he wrapped his arms around her as she buried her face in his shoulder and started to sob.

Before they arrived at the hotel, Derek had set wheels in motion by calling the management and asking them to begin evacuating the hotel and to secure desks, chairs and other requirements of the temporary command post the FBI would set up there. Once he and Vanessa had finally reached the parked Jaguar, the drive from the Trocadero Lodge to their hotel — usually ten minutes — had taken over an hour. They repeatedly had to pull off the road to make way for emergency vehicles headed to the disaster and then they were caught up in a nasty traffic jam. News had travelled quickly, and within a very short time, the picturesque winding roads were jammed with panicked tourists and locals trying to escape. Vanessa drove while Derek made and received phone call after phone call on his cell until the battery went dead.

Upon arriving at the hotel, both Derek and Vanessa rushed directly to their room and into the shower, where they scrubbed every square inch of their bodies with every kind of detergent, body wash, soap and shampoo that was available in the toiletries the hotel provided. As they undressed, Derek dumped all their clothing, including their shoes, onto a bath towel spread across the marble floor of the bathroom. Grabbing the four corners of the towel, he tied them together and stuffed the bundle into a large plastic suit bag. Tying the bag tightly, he put it by the door, ready to be either tested for contaminants or disposed of safely. Both prayed that the origin of the brown powder they were trying to scrub away was far more commonplace than the one they suspected — that the powder was from some benign source.

But Derek's training as well as his common sense told him that the odds were not in their favour. In fact, he'd already come to the conclusion that the last and largest blast may have just been set dressing, a dramatic conclusion to the attack, a graphic gift for the media. The smaller series of popping explosions was more deadly, if, in fact, it had been designed to spread a toxic agent.

"I'm okay now. It's just that things caught up with me," said Vanessa, letting Derek go, "I just keep getting images of all those people running and that old gentleman dying in front of us. Sorry."

"Sorry? Good God, sweetheart, the last thing on earth you need to be right now is sorry that you're upset. Is it okay if I turn on the news for a few minutes? Just to see if anything else has developed?"

Vanessa nodded her assent.

Derek reached for the remote on the nightstand and flicked on the television. The picture appeared but no sound, and he raised the volume. The television was set to a local and tourist information channel, so he scrolled looking for CNN. The familiar logo appeared with a news banner splashed across the bottom of the screen. Bold letters with flames behind them proclaimed "America under attack" as images of large buildings burning flashed in a square screen positioned in the upper right hand corner, above a fetching blonde news reader.

"Good God, look at this," he exclaimed.

Vanessa swung in her seat to look at the television.

The blonde, dressed in an expensive red suit with black velvet lapels held several sheets of paper in front of her. Her face betrayed the confusion and fear she felt as she scanned the hurriedly scrawled messages on the paper. She was unused to such primitive methods as news flashes on paper, but the teleprompter positioned over the camera lens was not keeping up with events as the news of fresh attacks poured in.

"This just in from New York City. There are reports that film actor Linden Lane has been shot by a gunman or gunmen outside of the Dakota apartment building near Central Park. Initial accounts are that Lane was killed along with several other people in virtually the same spot that John Lennon was assassinated in 1980. Lane was in New York working on a new action adventure film. He was scheduled to attend a fundraiser hosted by the city's mayor this evening and may have been on his way there at the time of the shooting. We will have more details as they become available."

The newscaster flipped to the next sheet of paper. "And from Miami, it has been confirmed that Lufthansa flight 237, a Boeing 747 Jumbo Jet bound for Berlin, crashed while taking off from Miami International Airport. Unconfirmed eyewitness accounts indicate the crash may have been caused by a missile launched from a nearby location. Several people say they saw a trail of smoke across the sky headed directly for the 747. It appears the aircraft was hit near the cockpit, which was torn from the rest of the airplane."

Aerial footage of burning buildings appeared again behind the blonde anchorwoman. "The plane crashed into a heavily populated part of Miami, setting fire to several large buildings and virtually destroying the buildings at the point of impact… Hold on a moment, ladies and gentlemen."

The newswoman cupped her hand to her ear. She looked up and continued. "This just confirmed. The building complex the Boeing 747 impacted was the Goodingham Memorial Hospital. At this time there is no firm estimate of the casualties, but they could number in the hundreds possibly thousands. In further news, casualties in the bombing on the West Coast in Santa Barbara are now estimated at over a thousand, and some of the victims are being airlifted to hospitals in Los Angeles and as far away as San Jose and San Francisco."

She stopped her narration for a moment, her eyes welling with tears. Then she attempted to speak again, but the words would not come. There were a few more moments' hesitation while she composed herself, and then she continued, her voice a little shaky but her professionalism reasserting itself. "There were at least a dozen explosions on the fairways behind the Trocadero Lodge at the Conquistador Golf and Country Club…"

As the woman droned on with her litany of disaster and death, the phone in the hotel room rang. Derek picked it up. "Hello. Oh hi, Tom. Yes, I heard. Miami and maybe an assassination in New York. You hadn't heard. It was just on CNN. Linden Lane, the movie star, was just killed. Yes, there wasn't much more than that. Hold on."

Derek grabbed a pad of paper and started taking notes.

Vanessa's gaze returned to the view of the ocean and the thick pillars of smoke rising into the sky from the golf club. The thumping of helicopter rotor blades had become almost constant, as many passed over the hotel on their way to various medical facilities.

6:10 p.m. EST (3:10 PST)
Sumner Tunnel, Mystic River, Boston.

Officer Colin Fitzpatrick, Boston PD, could just see the flashing lights ahead. They were the emergencies on what looked to be a tanker truck in the left-hand lane ahead, stopped dead and tying up traffic in the tunnel so that it looked more like weekday rush hour than late on Sunday afternoon.

There was little point radioing in. Even with repeaters, reception was awful on the worn-out radio set in his equally worn-out squad car. While this was a freeway and not really his jurisdiction, he figured he would stop and take a look, see if maybe he could help a bit, although he did not relish spending anymore time breathing the toxic air in this tunnel than he had to. He also got the heebie-jeebies thinking about all that concrete, rock and, most especially, water directly over his head.

He pulled to the right and edged past the cars that were jammed bumper to bumper. Pulling up behind the tanker, he set his roof lights flashing, got out and walked up to the cab. Fitzpatrick hauled himself up onto the running boards and looked in, but there was no one in the front. He opened the door, clambered up and in and poked his head around the corner into the sleeper behind the driver's seat.

"Hey buddy, what the hell do you think you're doing?" he asked the trucker who appeared to be asleep in the back. "Hey buddy, wake the hell up and get this truck out of here!" He gave the trucker a poke and got no response. "What the hell?" he muttered to himself.

He grabbed his flashlight from its holster and shone it on the man, grabbing his shoulder and rolling him over to his back. The driver was very dead, and a third of his face was missing — the exit wound caused by the large-calibre mushroom bullet that had entered through the back of his skull. He was killed when he stopped to relieve himself at a rest stop beside the turnpike a few miles south of Boston, several hours before.

Fitzpatrick jumped down from the truck and grabbed the mike of his walkie-talkie to report the truck and dead driver. At that second, the three improvised mines duct-taped to the underbelly of the petroleum tanker went off, almost in unison. Tens of thousands of gallons of high-grade gasoline exploded into the tunnel. Within a few minutes, the heat had become so intense the concrete started to crack and pop above the truck, and the wind rushing down the tunnel to feed the monster created an effect like a giant blow torch that little around it could withstand. The tanker's cab, what was left of Fitzpatrick's police car and all the cars in the surrounding traffic jam sagged as if they'd been thrown into a smelter.

Farther up the tunnel, those drivers and passengers who had not been killed by the initial blast fled their cars, running before the intense heat in a panicked attempt to flee the maelstrom behind them. Hundreds of cars were already stopped, and more were piling up at the rear of the jam, their occupants unaware of the problem until it was too late. When they tried to back out again, they found themselves hemmed in by the approaching traffic behind them.

Despite the designers and engineers' attempts to make the tunnel resistant to such a cataclysm — one of many nightmare scenarios they'd envisioned and tried to prepare against — they'd been let down by building techniques, maintenance and budgets. As the concrete heated and started to spall, it rained down in tiny flakes and massive blocks, exposing the rock beneath to the searing flames. Heat-induced cracks spread upwards to pockets full of water that had been meandering down through natural fissures for years, gathering above the tunnel and permeating the rock. In almost any other circumstance, this water would have never been a threat. At its worst, it would find its way though tiny cracks to make unsightly stains on the tunnel wall, but circumstances had changed. As this water started to trickle down through fresh cracks, it flashed into superheated steam, and as more water entered the mix, the steam's expansive power opened new pathways in the rock. These pathways raced upward like pressure cracks in ice, slicing through the various strata that separated the waters of the Mystic River above from the heavily trafficked tunnel below.

An immense cracking shook the rock wall, and in an instant the inferno in the tunnel was snuffed out as millions of gallons of water followed the collapsing rock to the tunnel floor. The whole force and weight of the river and the nearby ocean above rushed water up and down the tunnel in a cascading hydraulic ram that swept away every car, truck and person before it.

4:20 p.m. Mountain Standard Time (3:20 PST)
Shelley Oaks Family Restaurant, Highway 84 (old Route 66), a few miles south of Las Vegas, New Mexico.

Hank White was finished his day and heading home up Highway 84 on his way to his small ranch south of the tiny town of Las Vegas, New Mexico. He'd spent most of the day pissing around in Albuquerque, trying to find parts for a broken windmill-driven pump he needed to water the cattle on his ranch.

The pump was the better part of sixty years old, and while a lot of the castings were made of bronze and in fairly good shape, the pump rotor was attached to a steel shaft had become fused to the bronze and the dissimilar metals were now virtually inseparable. Hank had busted the rotor when he was trying to get it off the shaft to replace two worn bearings, and now he had spent a long hot day going from supplier to supplier trying to find a reasonable substitute that would fit the pump casing. He hadn't had any luck and was in a foul mood, knowing he was looking at several thousand dollars he couldn't afford to put in a whole new pump system. Either that or he'd be filling fifty-gallon drums at the house and carting them out to the cattle every morning. One thing about New Mexico summers was that not much, including cattle, could survive very long under its baking sun without a good supply of water.

He saw the Oaks diner up ahead and figured he would stop in for a quick coffee and see what was going on. The Oaks, as it was known locally, was a popular spot despite its relative isolation and was usually pretty busy with both county residents and tourists who were tracing the old Route 66. The Oaks had been around since the early fifties, so it was a bona fide historical stop for anyone making a Route 66 nostalgia tour. It didn't hurt that both the food and the coffee was good and there were two pretty waitresses serving it.

White pulled his old Ford pickup into the parking lot and parked it at the end of a line of cars in front of the restaurant. He strolled to the front doors and walked in. Despite the twelve or thirteen cars out front, there was no one to be seen. He thought that strange but nonetheless sat himself down in one of the window booths and grabbed a menu. He was hungry, and it was late enough to grab dinner before he went home and started the evening chores. His wife wouldn't be there, as this month she'd pulled evenings shifts at the small manufacturing plant in Las Vegas where she worked sorting and boxing components for the agricultural sprinklers the company produced.

White became aware of an underlying scent in the air, like the smell of a rifle just after it has gone off. It wasn't strong but lingered despite the restaurant's two gigantic air conditioners, which blasted away, dissipating even the smell of fried onions pretty quickly. Having seen no one still, he dropped the menu onto the table and stood up. "Hey, anybody here?"

There was no answer.

He walked toward the kitchen door behind the counter and gave it a push. "Hello? Where is everyone?" he called into the deserted kitchen. "Isn't this the damnedest thing," he said to himself.

He let the kitchen door swing closed and walked along the counter, skirting racks of souvenirs, Route 66 bumper stickers and the odd stuffed Area 51 alien doll. When he reached the end of the counter, he saw a pool of red on the floor. His first thought was that someone had dropped a bottle of ketchup. His gaze followed the stream that fed the pool toward the corridor leading to the washrooms. White got a rush of adrenalin. He leapt backwards, turned and ran three steps before he mastered his flight reflex. His heart pounding in his chest, he walked hesitantly back to the counter and looked down the corridor to a sight that would haunt him the rest of his life. In the beige and green corridor lined with joke postcards, their frames now knocked askew, lay the contorted bodies of eighteen people — eighteen men, women and children who had been herded into the dead end by three gunmen.

When the gunmen received the signal from a sentry stationed at the front doors to tell them the road and parking lot were clear, they opened up with their heavy automatic weapons. They used clip after clip of ammunition until many of the victims were unrecognizable. Satisfied, they walked out of the restaurant, got into a small van and headed off down 84.

Hank White had been lucky. He'd arrived ten minutes late to the affair and unknowingly passed the four killers on the highway as they made their way toward Albuquerque and beyond.

9:30 a.m. New Zealand Standard Time (3:30 p.m. PST)
Air Force One over the Pacific.

Air Force One had been running at full throttle since it left the Japanese coast. It had just cleared the Date Line and was now on the same calendar day as America. Inside the plane, a steady stream of reports had been barraging the communications room. The president sat behind two computer monitors in his office, scanning the reports as they became available and working alongside the other men and women crammed into the room to put the finishing touches on his first public statement regarding the events occurring on the mainland and to plan the military and governmental response.

The White House press corps members who were on the plane had just been given a bulletin outlining several of the attacks, and following the president's address, the press secretary was to keep them informed of any new attacks .

"Mr. President, would you like me to go in first and start the briefing?" asked press secretary William Carver.

"No thanks, Bill," replied the president. "I'll handle this one. You can keep them up on developments after I've spoken to them." He rose from his seat, tucked in his shirt and slid into the suit jacket held out to him by his aide. "Well, here goes."

The hubbub from the reporters hardly diminished as the president strode into the press compartment, one of the few areas on Air Force One with a seating layout like an ordinary airliner. Carver took the microphone set up on a small podium at the front of the compartment. "Ladies and gentlemen, the president of the United States." He then stepped aside as the president took his place. The room grew quiet; the loudest sound, the steady buzz of the 747's engines.

"Hello, everyone," he started, his voice low and grave. "By now you have all read the brief and know that we have a very serious situation developing at home. It appears that the United States is under terrorist attack and that these attacks continue. Since the briefs were circulated, several more incidents have occurred that can only be construed as forming part of a coordinated attack that spans much of the Continental U.S."

The silence burst as fifteen correspondents all started asking questions at once. The president held up his hand, gesturing for silence. "Please, ladies and gentlemen. The press secretary will give you details as soon as I have finished."

He went on. "In the face of this attack, I have requested that the FAA ground all flights into, out of and over the Continental United States, Hawaii and Alaska. This order covers both commercial and general aviation not engaged in authorized search and rescue or humanitarian assistance. All inbound commercial flights, if possible, are being turned back to their points of departure or diverted to Canada, Mexico or the Caribbean. Our borders with both Canada and Mexico are now closed to inbound surface traffic as well. Anyone wishing to leave the U.S. at any Continental border point will be allowed to do so, but only after being cleared by either Homeland Security or Customs and Immigration. The entire country, including Alaska, Hawaii and Puerto Rico, is on red alert, as are all U.S. embassies and consulates and government offices worldwide. Embassies will admit U.S. citizens but not foreign nationals, and no new visas will be issued. The visa waiver program will also be suspended until further notice. At this moment, National Guard units are being activated nationwide. White House staff has been in contact with the governors of all fifty states and with all the federal enforcement agencies, and state and municipal police forces are on high alert."

The president cleared his throat and took a sip of water from the glass an aide had just placed on the podium in front of him. "To continue, all military leaves have been cancelled, and as we speak, the air force is initiating combat air patrols over all major civic centres, and the Coast Guard will be increasing its coastal patrols. These patrols will be augmented by ships of the U.S. navy up to and including destroyers, frigates and cruisers. Any aircraft carriers currently in port or at sea and within range of the United States will aid in the CAP and maritime reconnaissance. For the duration of this emergency, no foreign shipping — aside from that moving strategic supplies — will be allowed to enter U.S. ports, and all foreign-flagged maritime traffic will be turned back from U.S. territorial waters. U.S.-flagged ships and approved foreign carriers of strategic supplies will be allowed to enter American ports but will be boarded and inspected before being escorted into dock.

"I would like the citizens of this great nation to fully understand that neither the U.S. government nor this office will tolerate this heinous attack, and we will not rest until the criminals responsible for these cowardly acts have been hunted down, whether they be the perpetrators within our borders or operators in other countries who may believe themselves to be safe from retribution."

He paused and looked at the stunned group before him. "I thank you for your attention. Mr. Carver will now take over the briefing."

Ignoring the calls of "Mr. President" and the reporters' questions he turned and strode from the compartment. As he returned to his office, chief of staff Dan Blomstrum passed him a new communiqué. He looked it over and his stomach roiled. It carried descriptions of the attack in Tulsa and the collapse of Boston's Sumner Tunnel. The report put the death toll at the Tulsa WWA match at over a thousand, many of them children. There were no casualty estimates for the Sumner tunnel, but preliminary reports outlined what looked to be a complete collapse and few survivors. Authorities had ordered all other tunnels in the Boston area and any major tunnels nationwide closed.

"It looks as if we're closing the barn door after the horse has fled," said the president.

"Yes sir, it appears that way," replied Blomstrum.

4:30 p.m. PST.
Dickinson Road, west of Seattle.

The forests around Seattle were as dry as tinder. It had been one of the driest summers on record in Washington State, and tight controls had been placed on campfires and barbecues, especially in the state and national park systems. These conditions were gifts from Allah, as far as Syed Atiq ul Hassan and Mohammed Ismael, U.S. citizens of Saudi origin, were concerned. They sat in a light blue Dodge Tradesman idling beside the road. The lightly trafficked road ran ahead in an almost straight line for a couple of miles, and they were waiting for it to clear of vehicles before they started their run. In the back of the van, three milk crates brimmed with wine bottles full of gasoline, simple Molotov cocktails with rags stuffed in their mouths.

Seeing nothing coming in either direction, Hassan clambered into the back of the van as Ismael shifted into gear and swung northbound onto the road. Hassan pulled the van's side cargo door open, and then, as they sped down the road, he lit bottle after bottle and hurled them into the dense underbrush past the shoulder. After a mile, he ran out of bottles and slid the door closed. Hassan accelerated, passing southbound cars that were already slowing as their drivers saw the flames leaping from the brush. The van turned left and disappeared, heading eastbound only slightly faster than the conflagration that its occupants had spawned.

A ten-knot easterly wind fanned the flames' progress, and soon a wall of fire a mile wide and growing wider by the minute sped through the forest towards the luxury homes and the commercial and industrial areas that lay across Puget Sound from the city of Seattle.

Ten minutes later the van sat abandoned in a busy home improvement centre parking lot, wiped clean of prints and any compromising items removed. Hassan and Ismael were in a small Jaguar sedan with tinted windows, headed to an area where huge stands of timber stood dry and unprotected. On the back seat, four more milk crates filled with Molotov cocktails sat covered by a child's Winnie the Pooh blanket and a few toys stacked on top. The pair drove south, intent on sowing the seeds of one of the greatest fires in U.S. history.

5:42 p.m. MST (4:42 PST)
Belden, Idaho.

Belden, Idaho, is a small town of a little over a thousand people situated approximately sixty miles northeast of Boise, a couple of miles off Interstate 90 along a well-tended two-lane stretch of blacktop. It is largely a retirement community, set in a green bowl between a series of low mountains and with breathtaking views in any direction one cares to face. One of the town's prettiest features is its wonderfully landscaped reservoir, which does double duty as a fine place to sit under aspens and weeping willows and read a good book on a warm summer's day. It is also storage for the water people use to water their lawns, wash their cars and, most importantly, drink.

While the reservoir was a popular spot among the local townsfolk, it rarely got visitors from farther away. Especially rare were young and not-so-touristy sorts, so James Borless, out walking his three-year-old Gordon setter, thought it a little strange when he noticed a dark-skinned man in his mid-twenties wandering along the reservoir's north bank, just a hundred yards away. His eyesight was not what it once was, and he'd left his glasses at home on the kitchen counter sometime during the frenzy between plucking the leash from the coat rack and exiting the house with the enthusiastic seventy-five-pound dog. He wasn't absolutely sure, but it appeared that the young chap on the north shore was dumping something into the water from what, with his poor eyesight, looked to be a large thermos bottle. He figured it was just the last of some old coffee or soup and dismissed the scene.

Had he turned on his radio or television that day or at least had a coffee himself at the local diner where the attacks on the United States were the subject of every conversation since the morning, he might have been more suspicious or given it more thought. A warning of any sort might have alerted Belden's tiny municipal office and its three full-time employees that their water purification plant had been broken into and tampered with so that toxins would pass unchallenged.

A few hours later James lay dying on his living room floor, one among three hundred dead in the small town and another three dozen critically ill. Most of those who survived incapacitation long enough to realize something was terribly wrong and try to seek help died on their way to the medical clinic. Not that help was there to be had. Both nurses and the town doctor had fallen ill within hours of sharing a pitcher of iced tea. Help from outside the town was on the way, but almost nobody who drank water from the reservoir survived long enough to see it, nor was any cure ever found for the toxin that had been dumped in it. The few who survived the poisoning soon realized that acute chronic pain and illness from severe damage to the kidneys, liver and other internal organs would be their new lot in life.

More than a week would pass before state authorities announced that the population of Belden had been poisoned by a new, virulent, incredibly fast acting and previously unknown strain of E. coli bacteria.

6:00 p.m. PST
Fourth floor meeting room, Beach Resort Hotel, Montecito.

Derek, as agent in charge and as the first Fed on the scene, had just finished outlining his eyewitness view of the attack on the greens at the Conquistador Golf and Country Club and its aftermath to a room full of law enforcement, FBI, Homeland Security, and Alcohol, Tobacco and Firearms officers and one CIA agent. Hotel management had equipped the room with a large screen television robbed from the downstairs lounge and with an overhead projector, a dozen phones and a switchboard, several desks and numerous chairs, drawn at the moment into a fairly intimate circle. The last of the team to arrive, two FBI officers and the CIA agent from Washington, were part of a small group currently dedicated to this particular incident.

With so many attacks recorded across the nation and with so few qualified federal officers to investigate them, the initial team assigned to the Trocadero Massacre, as the media had already coined it, had shrunk considerably in the past few hours as personnel on their way to Santa Barbara were diverted to new areas of concern. Already this bombing had taken a back seat on CNN as reports of new attacks poured in from all over the country.

"So my final concern," Derek said, "and the most important one is the nature of the brown powder released at the site. We're still waiting for the test results and that is really pissing me off." Derek looked at his watch. "We were supposed to have received results already, but so far we have squat, aside from a brief preliminary report we got at about 3:30 confirming that its origins cannot be explained as residue from either cars or any of the services or products for sale at the show. They suspect but they have not confirmed that it's a biological agent, and they're saying they don't know exactly what it is yet. So, I think it's prudent that we act as if we have a confirmed poisoning on our hands. In the meantime, I appreciate," he said nodding at the local law enforcement officers, "the efforts of the local police and Balmoral's private security companies, who have worked together to cordon off the lodge and the immediate areas until we find out what we're dealing with."

At that moment Derek's cell phone warbled from his shirt pocket. "Excuse me a moment, gentlemen."

He listened, his face darkening, and walked to a doorway and out to the balcony overlooking the ocean, where he paced to a fro as he listened to the lab report findings and the immediate and long terms effects of the brown powder. A few minutes later, Derek re-entered the room, and the buzz of conversation died as the men saw his face.

"We have a situation here that is a whole lot worse than we thought. As a matter of fact, the casualties we have taken already could pale in comparison to what we have in store. Gentlemen, the lab has found that the powder is a bioengineered weapons-grade blend of ricin — an exceptionally toxic and incurable poison distilled from castor beans — and what appears to be a stable and infectious hemorrhagic fever similar to Ebola. The lab doesn't know whether the fever is transmittable from person to person, as the virus is not exactly the same as its natural counterpart, but we should assume it is contagious. The toxicologists are not sure exactly how long it will take for symptoms to start showing, but their best guess is six to twelve hours, at least for the ricin. If the other compound is related to Ebola or Marburg hemorrhagic fevers, then it could be a couple of days before people start to get sick. This is a particularly devious mixture of toxins — basically, if the first one doesn't get you, the second will."

Derek pursed his lips and unconsciously shook his head before he continued. "Even individuals who did not ingest or breathe enough ricin for it to be fatal will likely be unable to fend off the fever. Their immune systems won't be capable of handling both toxins, and they will shut down. In the meantime, infected individuals may be able to spread the fever to others around them, so we are going to have to start rounding up everyone who was at the event immediately and isolate them until we know whether they are contagious or not."

A captain from the state troopers rose from his chair and asked, "What are the symptoms? I mean, we're going to have to tell people what to watch out for."

"What I have been told," Derek replied, "is that the people who are coming down with the ricin poisoning will get severe abdominal pain, vomiting and bloody diarrhea, followed by severe dehydration and falling blood pressure. It starts within a few hours and can go on for days. If an infected person lives longer than three days, their chances of survival start to improve and anyone living five or more days after contagion will likely recover, but just one milligram of ricin is fatal to almost any adult. Of course, that's not factoring in the hemorrhagic fever. This means that an awful—" Derek stopped for a moment as the image of Vanessa wiping the brown powder from her fingers assaulted him. Gathering himself he continued. "This means an awful lot of people who were in the area of the bomb blasts have breathed in or swallowed far more than a lethal dose."

There was complete silence in the room as the group digested the ramifications of that fact.

Derek continued. "Symptoms of the fever will take longer to kick in, and symptoms will parallel some of the symptoms of the ricin, but you can add severe chest pain, shock, delirium and hemorrhaging from eyes, ears and other cavities and, in advanced cases, even sweating blood. Some people have recovered from these fevers, but when I say some, it is only a tiny percentage of those infected. That said, this virus appears to be a manmade, biologically engineered derivative for air dispersal, and we really have no idea yet if it will run its course the same way as the natural virus.

"All I can say is that if the evil bastards who put this together are counting on a huge casualty list, they are probably going to get it. There were a lot of important and wealthy people at this show, and what is really terrifying me is that a lot of the ones who weren't injured left in their own private jets. If this compound is contagious and they were infected, then chances are it has now been spread across the country. We are going to have to get the records of departure from the airport and track down every single one of those planes. Some may have gotten home before the FAA's no-fly order, but what could make things a lot more difficult are the one who didn't get home and were diverted to the nearest available airport. We'd better get the FAA on this as soon as possible."

"On the ground here, our job is going to be horrendous. The military haz-mat teams are going to be here sometime tonight, and they'll help us deal with it, but for now, gentlemen, it is our job to keep the lid on. I have suggested the military expand the cordon well beyond the present perimeter and not let anyone in, aside from emergency response personnel, in case the wind took the biological agents farther than the lodge's immediate vicinity. No one, and I repeat, no one gets out no matter what the reason.

"The blast downtown is going to be an even bigger problem, because the powder may have blanketed neighbouring residential areas as well as the commercial downtown to the north of the blast. We may see the whole city locked down. Right now, people have been restricted to their homes, and police are enforcing a total curfew. The decision to maintain quarantine or initiate an evacuation is out of our hands. However, if it happens, gentlemen, we had better start to plan what the hell we are going to do with maybe a hundred and fifty thousand critically ill people who require immediate medical attention. So far, we have some military security on the ground, and they'll be taking over patrolling the perimeters. National Guard and regular units are also on their way. Their assistance is critical, as I am pretty sure there are not going to be enough of us to go around, especially when you consider the scope of the ongoing attacks. This means that we are going to have to work smart and efficiently with a minimum of backup."

Derek paused to take a drink from a bottle of imported water. He couldn't remember the last time his mouth felt so dry. He looked around at the grim-faced men and women in the room and imagined that his was not the only dry mouth. "And finally," he said, "for those of you who will be on the ground running forensics, the rescue and casualty work is largely out of the way, so you can get started on evidence procurement. I do not have to tell you that you are going to have to be very careful and wear full haz-mat suits as well as air tanks. Pace yourselves, keep an eye on your air supply, and for God's sake, don't rip your suits. You will be fully briefed by military personnel when you get to the site. Vans will be set up with the suits and supplies on each road at the final checkpoint. You will not be cleared into the zone until you have been issued a full haz-mat suit and have been briefed on its care and maintenance by military personnel, who will help you suit up."

Derek nodded at two army officers seated on his left and holding up a bright luminescent, lime green triangle with a row of numbers stamped on it. "You'll wear a pass supplied by the military at all times when in the zone. Wear them around your neck, over your suit. You'll hand them back and check out when you leave. Do not forget, or you may have an unpleasant meeting with the military security forces manning the cordons around the area and providing security on site. Also, if you need help with heavy lifting, call on them.

"Finally, the corpses of the dead are still on site. Only living victims have been evacuated. We'll be setting up a morgue on the outskirts of the zone, and the bodies will be transported by military trucks in the morning. For now, concentrate your investigation on the fatalities and the areas surrounding them, as unpleasant as that is, and secure the immediate vicinity prior to the bodies' removal. We have probably lost some evidence, but if there is anything out there that will help us get the bastards who did this, I want it found."

Checking his watch again, Derek finished off. "Each of you has your assignments. It is going to be a long night, so we'd better get started."

6:30 p.m. PST
Air Force One, over the Pacific Ocean.

"Mr. President, we have a new communiqué from Washington," said Bill Carver. He handed the president the notes, apologizing as he did so to Dan Blomstrum, who sat in the chair opposite the president at his desk, for leaning over him. Both the president and Blomstrum where in shirt sleeves and without ties, and the desk was covered in communiqués, messages and the paper clutter that builds so easily when serious work is being done.

"Sit down, Bill," said the president.

Carver pulled another chair up in front of the desk while the president read the latest dispatch.

"Christ almighty," said the president. "Barely six hours and they've started finger pointing and politicking on the Hill."

"Yes, sir," replied Carver, "it isn't like 9/11. The more unscrupulous in Washington have learned there's no long-term advantage to be gained from commiserating with the White House, disaster or not. They're going to try to put the blame somewhere, and judging from this sugar-coated turd from the senator and the emails from his cronies, it's already started."

"Bill, I really don't care about any of this shit right now, and I do not want to hear from the distinguished senator from Carolina, congressmen from New York or anyone else that's not directly involved in the emergency." He tossed the paper into the wastepaper basket next to his desk. "Anyway, let's get back to business. What about declaring martial law, Dan? It seems to me that it may be the only way to get a handle on this right now. We should talk to Admiral Irving at the Pentagon and see how long the armed forces would take to implement and enforce it."

"That's easier said than done, Mr. President. It's hard enough to declare martial law in a small area, but to try to declare it and then enforce it across the whole country could suck up an awful lot of resources. I'd be worried that we'd drain resources needed to track down the terrorists. I'd also be concerned that they might go to ground until we are forced to rescind it and then start up where they left off."

"Possibly," said the president. "But on the other hand it would deny them the freedom of movement they have now, and if they went to ground, we still might be able to pick up their trails. At the very least, it might break this cycle of attacks and give us some breathing room."

"I don't disagree, Mr. President," replied Blomstrum. "But there is no precedent for such a wide-ranging decree, and I'm just worried that, well, knowing what a lot of Americans are like, the cure might be worse than the disease. I've also been thinking we should fly straight on to Washington and not land on the West Coast. In the meantime, you can run things from up here."

"You may be right about diverting to Washington," replied the president. "But I want to spend as little time flying around as possible. Remember what happened to my predecessor on 9/11. It may have been smart to be on Air Force One during the emergency, but to the common man it appeared a little cowardly, and I do not want to come off as weak or cowardly right now. I need to lead, and I think that if we at least touch down in California, it will make people feel a little better."

At that moment another aide walked in with a communiqué and passed it to Carver.

"Well, Mr. President, there's no question about staying away from Santa Barbara now." He passed the president the note.

"Oh my God, this day is just getting worse and worse." The president looked at Blomstrum. "It's a chemical biological attack. They have no idea how many casualties we're going to take in Santa Barbara, but the governor is sealing the whole area off and wants to talk about a major evacuation."

The president leaned forward, keying his intercom. "Lieutenant," he said, addressing the Air Force One communications officer, "get me the governor of California ASAP." He looked at the men in the small office. "What the hell are we going to do with a whole city of people who may become critically ill within hours?"

"I'll contact the CDC and make sure they're up to speed and find out what the contingency planning is for this," said Blomstrum.

At that moment one of the phones on the desk rang. The president nodded at his chief of staff to pick up.

"No," he answered, "it's Dan Blomstrum." He listened for a few moments and then softly replaced the receiver in its cradle. "Initial casualty figures from the plane crash in Miami, sir. They think there may be as many as two thousand."

9:45 p.m. EST (6:45 PST)
Office of the chairman, Joint Chiefs of Staff, the Pentagon.

"Gentlemen, and lady, have a seat," said Admiral Allan R. Irving, making a sweeping gesture at the five seats arranged in front of his desk. Despite its opulent wood panelling adorned with historical paintings, Irving's office radiated an almost clinical, all-business feeling, as befitted its latest resident. The five officers representing all the U.S. armed services took their seats.

Admiral Irving, chairman of the Joint Chiefs of Staff, stood and walked around his desk, sat on its corner and folded his arms. He was the very picture of composure. Those who in the past had misinterpreted his relaxed style of command with being soft learned very quickly and to their detriment that Irving was as tough as old boots and completely comfortable with hard decisions. He had not become the top admiral in the U.S. Navy and gotten his four stars by playing politics. He had earned the stars and the position through a career filled with military adventure.

From his start in a plastic gunboat patrolling the Mekong Delta in Vietnam to his last shipboard command, a missile cruiser, he never flinched from putting himself and his command into the thick of things. As commander of the Ticonderoga-class missile cruiser Normandy, he was proclaimed a hero when he purposely ran his ship into the path of three French-made Exocet anti-shipping missiles that had supposedly been launched by terrorists but had come, in fact, from thinly disguised Iranian gunboats. The missiles were aimed at the nuclear-powered Nimitz-class supercarrier Harry S. Truman. Although Irving's crew shot down two missiles, a third slammed into the cruiser, which sustained heavy damage to the bridge and superstructure, and the admiral was wounded.

While some Pentagon staff accused him of grandstanding, a naval board of inquiry found that by his actions, the Truman had escaped the threat of severe damage and possible destruction. The carrier's decks had been crammed with ordinance, fuel and heavily laden fighter bombers about to be launched on missions in the Persian Gulf.

"So here's the situation," Irving said gravely. "As you all know, we are under attack by a seemingly well-coordinated group of terrorists who are spread across the nation. I've been in contact with the president several times to advise him of our posture and available assets within the country.

"Our biggest problem is the nature of these attacks. We're pretty sure they're implemented by either single individuals or small cells of three to ten terrorists. Groups like this are easier to combat using law enforcement agencies rather than resorting to the military, but law enforcement is going to be stretched to the limit, and as we all know, interagency and interdepartmental communications are almost nil. I have proposed to the president using military resources to transport law enforcement officers to where they may be needed and putting military personnel at their disposal to help in enforcement and in patrols as well as having them secure strategic targets like refineries or chemical storage or production facilities. We can also coordinate actions and communications between the various local state and federal agencies. I want to make sure that if some town deputy on a country road in the heart of Alabama finds out something that some other agency in New York State needs to know, that intelligence will flow unhindered.

"I want you people as a group acting as liaisons between your branches and civilian law enforcement. Your overall task is going to be making damned sure that the civilian authorities have every assistance and material they require when they require it. What I do not want under any circumstances is that we are seen to be flopping about without direction or, worse, that the United States appears to be occupied by its own military forces. We want to show Americans that they are safe, that we are on the job and that we are there to help out their local police forces, Homeland Security and the FBI. I would like to have our first workable plan ready by the time the president gets back to Washington or I meet him on the ground on the West Coast. Either way you should have about ten hours or so."

"Sir," asked Colonel Michael Pierce, "do you want us to include tactical response teams or Special Forces in the plan?"

"At this point, Mike, I just want a skeleton," Irving replied. "You won't have time to get lost in the details. Right now, a general overview of how military forces can be used to coordinate civilian communications and threat response and to secure important installations nationwide is required, and I don't mean monuments and court houses. I am very concerned about infrastructure, and I want to make damned sure it's secured. After that we can worry about other classes of targets. Once the president has approved the overview, we can start a more detailed plan and allocate resources."

He scanned the officers seated before him. "Anything else?"

No one replied.

"Then, people, let's get to it."

The officers rose and filed out of the office.

Irving walked around his desk and sat back down in his chair. Looking across the room at a painting of John Paul Jones on the bridge of his warship the Bon Homme Richard, he frowned and, paraphrasing, said under his breath, "We have just begun to fight...but who?"

6:50 p.m. PST
Compton, California.

Rajid Singh was walking north on South Alameda to get to the bus stop on East Compton Boulevard where the two streets intersected. He had just finished another twelve-hour shift in the convenience store where he worked, often seven days a week, for minimum wages. His shift should have ended at six o'clock, but the young girl who worked evenings rarely arrived on time and was even more rarely straight.

Today had been no exception. She'd clearly been under the influence of something when she walked through the door. Singh had given up complaining to her about tardiness, because whenever he did, she would start screaming, wag her finger back and forth and call him a motherfuckin' uppity raghead. Once, she had just glared at him, turned around and walked out of the store, leaving him to work until midnight. He'd learned his lesson and never made comment again.

This was all pretty hard for Singh, a U.S. resident for over fourteen months and an electrical engineer by training. His diplomas were issued by the Punjab Technical University in Jalandhar in his home province in northern India and broke very little ice in the Southern California job market. He lived in the hope that his lot would change and spent every moment of his spare time making applications and attending interviews, but so far the promised land had turned out to be a dangerous, dirty and poverty-stricken wasteland.

Singh had heard about the attacks that had started that day. Twice, young black men had accused him of being an Arab terrorist. His protestations that he was Sikh and had nothing to do with Muslims, extremist or not, fell on deaf ears — not for the first time. Singh had become acutely aware that many Americans had little knowledge of the world aside from a few inaccurate scraps garnered from action adventure movies. He'd reconciled himself to the fact that most of the people who came and went from the convenience store each day would view him, along with his turban, with suspicion and, in some cases, loathing. In this classless society riddled with class distinctions, he found himself at the bottom of the heap. He was dreadfully homesick and wistful for India, where at least classes were recognized and orderly and where his family held a position far from the bottom.

Singh was only a few steps from his stop and in plenty of time to make the next bus on the line's infrequent schedule when he was jolted by the scream of rubber on the road next to him. He spun around as six young black gangbangers leapt from the open doors of a beaten-up late seventies sedan sporting brand-new gold-spoked wheels and tires the thickness of rubber bands. For a moment, he didn't comprehend what was happening. He only grasped his situation when the first blows fell, the ring of the aluminum baseball bats strangely distant from the dull thudding he heard as the men rained down blow after blow.

Singh fell to the ground, bleeding and senseless from the repeated blows to his head. He was mercifully unaware when the beating abruptly ended and a young banger pulled a 357 Magnum from under his jacket and, aiming it at Singh's face, screamed, "Terrorist motherfucker!" He pulled the trigger again and again until the firing pin fell with a metallic click on a spent casing, the weapon's full load expended. The men jumped back into the idling car and, with a screech of tires, took off. What they left behind would have defied identification were it not for the green card the police found in Singh's slim uncluttered wallet.

His death marked the first of the many reprisals that increasingly angry and unreasonable mobs were to exact. Over the next days and weeks, America would become a very dangerous place for anyone remotely of Middle Eastern, South Asian or Southeast Asian origins.

7.:05 p.m. PST
Beach Resort Hotel, Montecito, California.

"I'm not feeling very well," said Vanessa, her voice strangely husky.

Derek froze, panic welling in his chest. He had just popped down to their room to find out if Vanessa would like to join the team members for a late dinner of take-out pizza and sodas that hotel management had arranged. The hotel's own kitchen was closed, as several of the staff had fled home to their families at the onset of the emergency. The manager had been challenged even finding a pizzeria that was open for business, but his persistence had paid off, and a stack of cooling pizzas had eventually arrived at the front desk.

Derek walked to the side of the bed and snapped on the bedside lamp, breaking the gloom occasioned by closed curtains.

Vanessa winced. "I've got such a bad headache," she said, shielding her eyes.

"I'd better get a doctor," Derek replied, his concern growing as he saw that she was drenched in sweat.

"No, just get me some Tylenol. I'll be fine. It's probably just a reaction to the stress of the day," she said, a wan smile on her lips.

"You're probably right, but it never hurts to be safe, and I just happen to have a doctor handy upstairs. I'll go and get him right now."

Derek hurried from the room, his calm exterior belying the panic he felt inside. He knew what was wrong, and he knew that Vanessa — a full medical doctor — also knew, despite her protestations. Only for a moment did he pause to think of his own well-being, and then, dismissing the concern, he hurried up the stairs to get the medical examiner who was right now eating pizza in the fourth floor meeting room.

7:30 p.m. PST
Hollywood Boulevard, Los Angeles.

"Hey, you can't leave that there," yelled Officer Fred Dawes. He was addressing the driver of a tour bus bedecked with banners that read, "Hollywood Tours, See the Homes of the Stars," who had clambered out of the vehicle after parking it right in front of the Chinese Theatre.

From the opposite side of the street, Dawes looked both ways and, raising his hand to ward off the oncoming traffic, attempted to cross the road after the bus's driver. By the time he succeeded, the driver had melted into the crowd of tourists and theatregoers who jammed the sidewalks and courtyard of the famous theatre. On this warm summer evening, scores of people lined the sidewalk in anticipation of getting good seats to the latest blockbuster, while others, mostly tourists, crowded the courtyard to compare their hand- and footprints to those of the stars immortalized in concrete in front of the venerable art nouveau building. Like millions of tourists before them, many were no doubt a little disappointed by the boulevard's rundown and tawdry appearance. Stores selling cheap and nasty souvenirs jostled with sex shops for the buyer's attention, but the grand old Chinese Theatre and the brass plaques and stars buried in the sidewalk on the Hollywood walk of fame still mesmerized.

On reaching the bus, Dawes ran around to the passenger door, still hoping to see its driver and praying that it was an unfortunate mistake. He made a frantic call for assistance on his radio nonetheless. Dawes and the rest of the LAPD were on high alert after the attacks that had occurred and they were all on guard for just this kind of circumstance. In his heart, he knew that none of the licensed tour bus operators would have parked in this restricted area. He pulled the folding passenger doors open and stepped up into the front of the bus.

He saw nothing unusual until he'd made it halfway down the aisle. Sitting on one of the seats on the curb side were a number of large dark blue backpacks, all identical and stacked on the seat like cordwood. Suspecting the worst, he ran for the door — and missed the lifeless body of the usual driver, stuffed between seats a few rows farther back.

As he leapt from the bus's step, Dawes started yelling at the crowd to run. "Bomb!" He screamed so loudly he could feel his throat ripple with pain. "There's a bomb on this bus!"

Many people in the crowd froze in disbelief, and some even thought it was some kind of Hollywood show. Others, more easily panicked, reacted immediately. Startled by their flight, the whole crowd surged in the primal mindlessness of the herd. In moments, over a thousand people were scrambling in all directions, pushing and shoving to get clear, many of them without knowing of what. Most of the crowd had not heard Officer Dawe's warning above the general hubbub of traffic, pedestrians and music piped from the theatre.

Several older men and women, unable to keep their feet, fell and were trampled by the mob behind them. The traffic on the busy street, the bus in front of the theatre and the theatre itself funnelled the fleeing crowd into a flailing mass. Anyone fortunate enough to run westward, cleared the theatre and reached the open area of the parking lot. Those who ran eastward found themselves hemmed into an area the width of the sidewalk — just twelve feet across. People burst into the street in front of oncoming traffic. Several were hit squarely, others clipped by cars that blared their horns as their brakes locked and tires shrieked.

Officer Dawes heard a siren start moaning as a nearby police patrol saw the panicked mob spilling onto the street. He bent to help an old man to his feet, and as he turned, he saw the front doors of the theatre open and a group of moviegoers start to exit from the theatre. With the dazed gait of people who have just sat for two hours in the darkness in front of a flickering screen, they blinked and stumbled onto the sidewalk.

Officer Dawes pelted towards them screaming, "Get back inside!"

At that moment the three hundred and fifty pounds of high explosives sitting in the bus, accompanied by another hundred and fifty pounds of roofing nails, erupted. The famous and ornate fascia of the Chinese Theatre dissolved in the blast, driven inward and through the crowd milling in its lobby. The bus evaporated, as did many of the cars and people, including Officer Dawes, whose fortune that day had placed him almost at the blast's epicentre.

Moments later, all that could be heard was a cacophony of car alarms and the oncoming banshee wail of sirens as smoke rose into the still evening air over Hollywood Boulevard.

8:15 p.m. PST
Beach Resort Hotel, Montecito, California.

"I'm pretty sure she has ricin poisoning," said Dr. Edward Kettel. Kettel was the medical examiner for Santa Barbara and had been attending the meetings in the emergency command centre set up in the hotel.

"So what can we do?" asked Derek, his concern palpable.

The two men leaned on the cement seawall outside Derek and Vanessa's room. Inside, Vanessa was lying in bed with a splitting headache. When Kettel examined her, she'd begun to display symptoms of respiratory distress, and she'd had a mild fever.

"There isn't a cure. We can treat some of the symptoms, but what we treat will depend on whether she ingested the toxin or inhaled it. Ricin exhibits differently depending on which route it took into the body."

"The truth is, doctor, she could have done both. I might come down with it as well. We were both in the same area, doing the same things, but Vanessa bent down over an injured girl whose dress and skin were covered in the powder from the explosions."

"How long was it before the two of you washed?"

"Just a few minutes. We both ran up the hill to a wash station next to some portable toilets. Vanessa actually scrubbed before I did, because I talked to a couple of troopers and made a phone call. When I got there, she was still washing her face and arms and hands."

"It's likely that she'd already inhaled or ingested the poison," said Kettel. "How about you? Are you feeling anything like tightness in the chest or a little shortness of breath?"

"No, I feel fine," replied Derek almost guiltily. "Well, I mean as well as can be expected."

"I'm going to see if we can get Vanessa into a hospital. There is virtually nothing I can do for her here, and the hours ahead are going to be very rough for her." Then Derek asked the question he'd been dreading asking and whose answer he dreaded more.

"What do you think her chances are, doctor?"

"I really don't know, but I would be less than honest if I told you that she isn't gravely ill. Ricin is very nasty, and if she survives the poison, hemorrhagic fever may still be waiting in the wings. It's still far too early to see that present, but I have no idea what the two of them will be like in concert."

"Thank you for your honesty, doctor."

An uncomfortable moment passed, and then Kettel excused himself to return to the command centre.

Derek slipped back into the room to lie on the bed and hold Vanessa in his arms.

8:30 p.m. PST
Air Force One, over the Pacific, one hour from landfall in California.

"We've made good time," said Bill Carver, looking at his watch. He was speaking to his aide, Amy Vandercamp, who sat in a plush seat across from him in the 747's staff lounge.

Amy, a short and plump twenty-three-year-old with a quick wit that belied her rather teddy-bearish appearance, put down the papers she'd been working on, glanced at a scrolling GPS-fed electronic map of the aircraft's progress that was set into the bulkhead and looked at her watch. "Yes, we have," she replied. "We're probably forty minutes or better ahead of a commercial flight. It proves that the new engines weren't a waste of taxpayers' money."

Vandercamp referred to a recent refit of Air Force One to replace its engines with newer mil-spec performance units not yet available to the airline industry. These were not only capable of pushing the aircraft faster, they also used only three quarters the fuel her civilian counterparts did, yet the president's opponents in Washington had howled long and hard over the supposed waste of taxpayers' money. In his defence, the president had pointed out that, unlike many former administrations, he had not given a damn about the colour of the plane's couches or the rugs in the office. All of the refits had been to upgrade performance, communications and — a new wrinkle — self-defence.

There were additional classified upgrades to the defence capabilities of the aircraft. In truth, despite her size she would make a good accounting of herself against almost any airborne foreign adversary. What she lacked in manoeuvrability and speed, she more than made up for in hidden long-range defensive clout. She packed six medium-range AIM 120 AMRAAM air-to-air missiles and a half-dozen short-range AIM 132 ASRAAMs in two weapons blisters added to the underside of her wings. These missiles could be used against aircraft posing a threat within a 360-degree radius from as far away as 130 miles to as close as 300 yards.

"At this rate, I guess we have an hour or so in the air before landing," Carver continued.

"Where are we landing?" asked Vandercamp, "Has the president made up his mind?"

"Yes. We're landing at Edwards Air Force Base, about seventy-five miles from Santa Barbara and protected by mountains. It's a good place to put down from a security standpoint, and it's close enough to Santa Barbara that the president can have meetings with some of the people working the bombing, if we get them choppered in."

As he spoke a staff member entered the lounge and asked Carver to join the president. Carver entered the office, and the president motioned him to take a seat. Henry Woeburn and Dan Blomstrum were already seated. "Gentlemen," the president began, "I've just received word of an attack in Los Angeles. A bomb detonated in front of the Chinese Theatre in Hollywood just as the early show was getting out and a crowd was lined up for the next show. Casualties are said to be high, but I have no word on how many people were killed or injured as of yet."

He took a breath and continued. "I have no room for error with these events. As a result, I've been agonizing for the last hour over whether I should declare not only a national emergency but a period of full martial law."

"Mr. President," Woeburn interjected, "there is no precedent. Do you even have the power?"

"Actually, Henry, there are several regional precedents, and of course, Lincoln declared martial law during the Civil War. That said, none of these — not even the suspension of liberties during the Civil War — can compare to martial law being declared nationally in this day and age. We are going to have to restrict not just movement but communications. That means we could be looking at cutting back cellphone and Internet communications or maybe even blacking them out completely for a period of time."

"Good God, sir, the country will be crippled. People will freak out," said Carver.

"I'm aware of that. In fact, I am acutely aware of it, and I'm torn between the damage that could be caused by curtailing telephone and electronic communications and the damage caused by allowing terrorists on American soil the luxury of unrestricted Internet access and communication among themselves or with others overseas. I've already addressed this issue and discussed the problems with Admiral Irving, and he is taking it to an emergency meeting of the Joint Chiefs."

"What about the question of authority?" asked Blomstrum.

"That's hazy, I have to agree. Congress certainly has the power to declare martial law, but by the time they implement it we may have lost control of the situation. The White House legal staff have offered the opinion that if I make the declaration, Congress can give tacit approval by either ignoring it and allowing it to stand, sanctioning it — which would be the best situation — or, if a majority is in favour, striking it down. Even if they voted to strike it down, it should allow us enough time to get things under control."

"Sir, what if this is a one-day wonder and they've shot their bolt?" asked Woeburn.

"I can't take that risk, Henry. First and foremost, we haven't caught any of them yet, and only one of them — the thug in Miami — has even been identified. We have to eliminate the threat at home, and it may take martial law to do that. Then, when we are back on an even keel, we'll root out the organizers and make them pay. And, gentlemen, when I say make them pay, I absolutely mean it, and I don't care who in the end is found responsible. Up until now, we've had to pretend that we were working with and making nice with foreign governments that hate our guts and are clearly on the other side.

"While they smile and stick out one hand for money from us, the other is busy passing out favours to the terrorists. Most of these governments are doing everything they can to screw us, short of declaring war. I would even lay bets that some of them are using our aid money to fund terrorist initiatives. It's time we abandoned diplomacy. Any country that we suspect is involved in this or even gives this attack tacit approval is going to get a kick in the balls."

He let that statement sink in for a second before continuing. "So far, we have no intelligence indicating or even hinting that this was going to happen. It's hard to believe there wasn't even a hint. Even the attack on 9/11 was easy to see in retrospect, and if they'd been at a higher alert, it might not have happened, but then hindsight is always 20/20. This has blindsided us far more, because we've been looking for trouble, although I'm sure there will be a few things that have been picked up that will start to make sense now — things that either the media or our honoured opponents on the Hill will delight in ramming down our throats."

"Once again, our intelligence services have let us down," said Carver.

"That's true, they have," replied the president, "But then both this office and Congress have insisted that they engage in street brawls using Queensberry Rules, so we shouldn't complain when they lose their teeth to a set of brass knuckles. I'll tell you this" — he stabbed the desktop with his finger, the stirrings of rage tingeing his usual calm and control — "and this will be going on the record as well. When we hunt these bastards, this time the gloves are going to be off. I don't care whose political or religious sensibilities we disturb. If we have to lay a beating on someone or pull out a few fingernails to get them to talk, so be it. Enough is enough."

8:38 p.m. PST
Beach Resort Hotel, Montecito, California.

Derek stood back to let two paramedics ease Vanessa onto a stretcher and secure the belts. She was clearly in pain and knew how serious her condition was becoming. Moments before the medical evacuation helicopter had alighted on the beach in front of the hotel, she had, with rasping voice and laboured breath, described to Derek the agonizing pains she was getting in her chest and stomach. He did his best to comfort her, stroking her hair and telling her she would get through this. He was torn. He didn't want the paramedics to take her away from him, but at the same time, he wanted them to hurry, to get her airborne and away, to get her to safety and to someone who could cleanse her of the evil compounds that festered within her body.

Dr. Kettel had used his weight to divert this chopper from the evacuation still underway in Santa Barbara. Vanessa, along with three other patients on board, was headed for the Community Memorial Hospital in Ventura. Primarily a heart institute, it was one of many medical facilities pressed into service in anticipation of the effects of the agents released at the Conquistador and in Santa Barbara. Already, advance teams from the Center for Disease Control and Prevention, in Atlanta, had arrived at various hospitals in and around Los Angeles to set up emergency medical clinics to treat casualties of both ricin poisoning and hemorrhagic fever, if it started to show up in the next few days. Vanessa, having been poisoned in the first blast at the lodge, was one of the first to be headed to the CDC emergency response clinics.

The U.S. Army was also going to set up medical facilities in the form of complete field hospitals, some of which were already in the air on their way to central California. The U.S. government and the Federal Emergency Management Agency had learned well the lessons taught by the various natural disasters that had plagued the country over the last decade. Of all the criticisms that were to be levelled at them over the next few months and years, none would suggest that the emergency response had been lacking in any way during the first days of the American War. Soon, Vanessa and hundreds of victims of ricin poisoning from the Conquistador blasts would be joined by thousands more, from the later blast in downtown Santa Barbara.

Derek held Vanessa's hand as the paramedics slid her stretcher into the Bell 429. Normally, the helicopter would have held only two litters, but the crew, with a bit of ingenuity, had jury-rigged a support that allowed them to place a third stretcher over the other two. It was into this position that they strapped Vanessa's stretcher, making sure after they did so that the blocks of wood that supported her litter above the others were secure.

The helicopter whipped up a stinging sandstorm, and Derek cringed. protecting his eyes and face with his hand. Then it lifted into the air and, nose down, accelerated over the water and southward. He stood on the beach watching its navigation lights merge with dozens of others blinking in the distance as the evacuations continued into the gathering gloom of night.

August 19. 9:00 a.m. PKST (August 18. 9:00 p.m. PST)
Islamabad, Pakistan.

Muhammad al-Munajjid sat back in the opulent leather seat in the rear of the new white Range Rover as it inched its way through early morning traffic on the northern outskirts of Islamabad. His three companions kept a close eye on the bicycles, three-wheeled delivery trucks and tiny cars that competed with one another in a chaotic scramble for progress along the packed roadway in front of the Rover.

Al-Munajjid thought it amusing that in an hour or less he would be free of these earthly bonds, winging his way westwards in a luxury jet, that iconic symbol of the very people whose destruction he had dedicated his life to. He'd received continuous updates on the progress of the attacks on America and was delighted. They'd succeeded beyond his wildest dreams. Of the four hundred freedom fighters he'd deployed in the United States, not one had been caught and the effects of their first day had thrown the United States into convulsions. CNN and all of the other American news services broadcast each wound repeatedly and in detail, compounding the effects and amplifying each pinprick far beyond its real tactical or strategic significance.

Al-Munajjid knew and understood that neither four hundred nor four thousand nor even forty thousand fighters in the United States could endanger the nation's security unless the Americans themselves, with their fascination — even obsession — with bad news and their belief in immediate solutions, created a panic that would make authorities lose control. He was confident that his pinpricks would so enrage the beast that eventually, seeing no clear-cut foe, it would turn in its rage and start consuming itself.

Within a few minutes the Range Rover, driven by one of three personal bodyguards, turned onto a lightly travelled roadway. Two of these hard men were from the Pakistan Military and the other from an American-trained elite Saudi military unit. They were all fanatical in their belief in and obedience to Al-Munajjid.

Al-Munajjid was tired, his age finally catching up with him after a sleepless night. He was now drained of the exaltation that had pumped adrenalin through his veins each time he learned of a new attack's success. At first, with news of the bombing in Santa Barbara, he'd sought seclusion and contemplation, praying for the triumph of his plan, but as cheers and laughter resonated down the austere hallways of the mosque, he rejoined his associates, revelling in the success of each strike and in the on-the-scene coverage the Americans media were kind enough to supply to the world.

The Range Rover turned at a laneway guarded by two Pakistani military police officers. With a nod, they raised a barrier and allowed the Rover down a short road that culminated in two Pakistani Air Force revetments, blast shelters for their American-supplied F-16s. One of the concrete walls hid a white Falcon 50 jet with a bright green tail adorned with the personal markings of one of the members of the Royal House of Saud. This secure area at the northwestern end of the Benazir Bhutto International Airport was well away from prying eyes, especially those of the American crews of the C-130 and heavy jet transports that came and went from the main terminals each day, dropping off supplies and personnel to support the combined U.S.-Pakistani hunt for terrorists in the northern mountains along the Afghan border.

This was one of the things that most delighted al-Munajjid about the Americans. They were, despite their immense power, almost childlike in their innocence and stupidity. For a decade now, they'd chased their own tails in the rugged Hindu Kush and in other mountain ranges of Pakistan, places no real terrorists would spend a single moment. He laughed to himself when he thought of how the U.S. forces had been chasing about after these fictional mountain terrorist organizations, based on information supplied by real jihadists and funnelled through friends in the Pakistani intelligence community. In some cases, the terrorists had even used U.S. military force to settle personal vendettas against tribal leaders and others with whom they were at odds. In effect, the Americans had been responsible for the deaths of many tribal leaders they could have enlisted as allies. Their unmanned attack drones were particularly useful in this respect. Once given the coordinates, they could be relied on to completely eliminate their targets.

The Rover pulled up next to the Falcon 50 and al-Munajjid's bodyguards clambered out, scanning in all directions for possible assassins or other trouble. As Al-Munajjid stepped out of the luxury SUV, a young man in a designer suit appeared at the door of the jet and walked down the steps, arms out in greeting, his diamond-studded Rolex glinting in the sun. "Welcome, my dearest cousin. It is so very good to see you, and congratulations on your success. Your family and friends await you at home," he said, embracing Al-Munajjid.

Within minutes, the steps were pulled back into the aircraft, its door sealed, and it rose into the air on a course for the Middle East and its home base in Riyadh.

9:26 p.m. PST
Air Force One, Edwards Air Force Base, California.

The president's 747 flared and gently touched down on the runway at Edwards Air Force Base and taxied to the main building complex, nestling itself into a flock of

Boeing C-17 transport aircraft. Portable stairs were already on the way as the huge aircraft glided to a stop, its engines spooling down quickly. The president and his staff, however, stayed on board. Air Force One was a far more effective and better-equipped base of operation than the air base's administrative complex, so work would continue on board. Nonetheless, the President was greatly relieved to be back on American soil.

Making landfall so near the first bombing and at the first available opportunity was a master stroke in leadership. Putting himself at risk, no matter how small, helped boost the morale of a desperate American public and dispel a little of the panic the media had whipped up in their mindless obsession with bad news and its associated ratings.

The base commander and a couple of staff officers were the first aboard to greet the president. In a quick businesslike meeting, the base commander outlined for the presidential staff the steps that had been taken to allow media access and bring in the various experts they had requested. The president's was scheduled to remain at the base for six hours before departing to Washington. A press conference would be held in two hours.

Twenty minutes after Air Force One touched down, three Gulfstream IV business jets in U.S. Air Force markings and escorted by F-16s touched down and taxied to positions near the 747. From them burst members of Cabinet, the National Security Agency, the CIA and the military, including the president's chief military advisor and head of the Joint Chiefs, Admiral Irving. Only FBI director Peter Archer was missing, stuck waiting for a military flight back from Italy where he was holidaying. As a group, they mounted the steps into the presidential aircraft and were shown to their seats in a spacious boardroom where they waited for the president to take his own seat at the head of the table. Among their number were the secretary of Defense, the secretary of the Interior, the director of Homeland Security, the director of the CIA, the secretary of energy and the attorney general.

The president strode into the room moments later, accompanied by Blomstrum and Carver. "Good evening, ladies and gentlemen," he said to the group seated along both sides of the conference table.

"I have called you all here for a number of reasons, so I'll get straight to the point. In the last few hours as these attacks have progressed, I've been at a bit of a loss as to how we are going to effectively combat them. In my consultations with Admiral Irving, it has become clear to me that the military and law enforcement agencies are going to have to work hand in glove to control this situation and ferret out and eliminate the terrorists. At this time, we have very little reliable information on how many have infiltrated the country, how they got in, how long they have been here or where they are from. My first question is addressed to Director Dowd," he said, looking at Allan Dowd, director of the NSA, the organization tasked with monitoring worldwide electronic communications for threats to the United States.

Dowd, a nerdish individual who cultured disarming affectations like his bowtie and his famous baggy brown discount suits, looked like a deer in the headlights as he waited for the presidents question.

Sensing Dowd's discomfort, the president held up his hand. "But first, ladies and gentlemen, let me clear the air. I am not looking for scapegoats. I'm looking for solutions. Right now the most important thing we can all possibly work toward is an immediate halt to this attack, followed by the arrest of its perpetrators. Following that, I want the organizers, who I am damned sure are sitting overseas somewhere watching TV and rejoicing, nailed to a cross. And I tell you this," he said, punctuating the last five words with his index finger on the desk, "I do not intend to play hide-and-seek with these pricks for the next decade. I want their heads on a platter — and fast. We've had over ten years to find out how not to fight these people. Now we're going to have to get smart about how to fight them. Now, let's get down to business.

"So, Allan," he said, addressing the director again, "has there been any intercepted communications that in hindsight look like command or control for these attacks?"

"No, Mr. President. We've been pouring over our intel, and if anything, our flow of suspicious communications both internally and externally has dropped off somewhat over the last few months. We haven't found anything the computers interpret as command or control — encrypted or not — even when we review records of communications in the areas of the attacks, both preceding them and afterwards. If they are in communication with each other, it isn't by cellphone or computer — at least not using any of the key words or sequences the computers are looking for."

"What about your department, Bob?" asked the president. He was addressing Bob Dutton, director of the CIA. Dutton had been a good friend of the president for many years and was considered, even by opponents, as competent, imaginative and resourceful, a good choice for the position he'd been assigned.

"We've had no clear indications of this attack, sir," he replied. "Since the attacks began, we've talked to British, French and Israeli intelligence, and none of them had any inkling that this was about take place. Whoever's behind this is not from the usual list of suspects. Very few known terrorist organizations are anywhere near sophisticated enough to do this without our getting at least a whiff, and to do it on such a large scale, to attack in such a widespread, coordinated and stealthy assault is well beyond their technical capabilities. Hell, most of them are just ignorant rabble whipped into froth by their religious leaders. They're almost always incredibly easy to spot because they can't get far enough beyond their rabid fundamentalism to operate in a Western society without bringing suspicion on themselves.

"Whoever's involved in this has got to have spent time in the States and been able to operate without causing a ripple. The other strange thing is no credible claims of responsibility have been posted. Usually, this bunch can't wait to jump around shooting guns in the air and bragging about how they've given their all to Allah. This time, nothing. It seems the mainstream terrorist organizations are just as surprised by this as we are. That's not to say these attacks haven't caused a stir. There are huge spontaneous demonstrations of support for them in almost every Middle Eastern country. It's like Christmas in Iraq and Iran, and even the Saudis are having trouble keeping their population's jubilation under control."

"There's something I'd like to add," said Dutton, who had paused to take a sip of water from one of Air Force One's emblazoned crystal glasses.

"Yes, Bob, go on," said the president.

"One of the things that has characterized just about all major terrorist attacks over the last few years is that they are suicide attacks. It seems, judging by what we've been able to determine so far, that not one of these is a suicide bombing. It seems they have in mind the conservation of their assets."

"Meaning?" asked the president.

"Meaning these attacks could continue until we've discovered every last one of them. Our biggest problem will be to determine how many there are in the country and how the hell we're going to track them down. So far, all these attacks have could have been accomplished by a couple of dozen individuals, so I hope they've shot their bolt, but we have no way of knowing how big this fifth column is nor what kind of schedule they intend to keep. If they've got a lot of sleepers, it's conceivable this could go on sporadically for years."

The room fell silent. The dull rumble of F-15s flying combat air patrol over the air base punctuated the insulated skin of the president's aircraft.

There was a knock on the conference room door.

"Come in," said the president.

Henry Woeburn poked his head in the room. "Sorry for the interruption, Mr. President, gentlemen, but sir, you had said to inform you of any significant news immediately." He passed the president a bulletin.

The president took a minute or so to read it while the others in the room spoke among themselves in muted tones. He finished reading and, looking up, addressed the room. "Well, as if we didn't have enough on our plates. People have begun rioting in New York, Miami, Atlanta and several other larger cities. Several mosques, Islamic centres, Sikh temples and even synagogues are burning, and this reports that Muslims as well as other religious and ethnic groups are being dragged from their homes and beaten to death.

"Admiral," he said looking straight at Irving, "I want the military to stop this and stop it now." He continued, "Gentlemen, I had intended to announce in an hour that I was seriously considering implementing marital law. That is one of the items I was going to discuss with all of you at this meeting. However, this forces my hand. I'm going to proclaim martial law immediately."

"Dan," he said addressing the White House chief of staff, "get the White House legal department busy."

"Bill," he said, addressing his press secretary, "let's get this ball rolling." He rose and, with Bill Carver following, headed from the room to ready his proclamation.

10:15 p.m. PST
Beach Resort Hotel, Montecito, California.

Derek wandered out of the fourth-floor command centre. Behind him the room buzzed in a controlled frenzy. Computers keyboards clicked, phones warbled, and several young assistants darted from desk to desk delivering phone messages, faxes and emails. Everyone was intent on their job, and motions were not wasted.

The rescue and evacuation of the injured was well over. Now the bustle was investigatory. Here, a dozen investigators compiled information that was streaming in from the white-suited forensics teams combing every inch of the fairway and poking through the debris of every burned-out car. Several forensics concentrated their search on the large hole blasted into the fairway by the vaporization of the old Pierce Arrow. They dug into the soil to unearth what the blast had buried in the hope of finding clues to the identities of the perpetrators of this mass crime.

Derek was at heart a field agent, his skills and nature far more suited to on-site investigation and to following leads than to acting as a glorified office manager. For a few hours he'd managed to put his worries about Vanessa to one side — not ignored, but the knot in his chest made tolerable by the minute-to-minute tasks that kept him busy. Now that the investigations were literally humming along and the immediate pressure was off, the worry came back like a iron fist squeezing his guts. He had tried phoning the medical centre several times, but the phone would either ring frustratingly unanswered, or a passing volunteer would pick it up who could not really tell him how Vanessa was or even if she was in the overcrowded emergency medical facility. He'd thought about driving down and using his credentials to get in, but that would be tantamount to going AWOL.

Derek stood on the balcony, watching white caps form on the incoming rollers and then break as the waves washed onto the beach, driven by the rising tide. They appeared iridescent in the floodlights that lit the beach and threw everything into sharp black-and-white relief. Beyond the breakers, the dark ocean merged with the clouded sky to obscure the horizon — an inky black bowl stretching out into infinity.

Far fewer blinking lights hovered in the distance over Santa Barbara. The hastily assembled fleet of medevac helicopters and aircraft had done their jobs, and now the residents of Santa Barbara were hunkered down behind closed doors, experiencing a curfew for the first time in their lives. For a few dumb teenagers choosing the wrong time for rebellion and the odd homeless person, the night had provided an exciting new experience. Insectile troops in camouflaged haz-mat suits and breathing gear and yelling muffled commands arrested them — their M 16 carbines levelled at the suspects — and trundled them off to emergency detention quarters set up in an abandoned glass factory.

"Derek, there's a call for you. She says she's a presidential assistant." One of the agents, a chap he knew from the Los Angeles Homeland Security office, leaned through the doorway onto the balcony to deliver the message.

Derek thanked him and walked in and took the phone. "Hello. Special agent James here,. May I help you?"

"Special agent, the president has requested a brief meeting with you. He understands that you were the first agent on the scene and that you are attached to Homeland Security as a special advisor," said Amy Vandercamp, Carver's aide.

"Well, yes, I was the first on the scene, but not in any official capacity. I was actually attending the show. I'm sure there are others here who would be better qualified to brief the president at this point. I've been setting up the offices and haven't spent any time on the ground."

"I understand, but there was a specific request for your presence," she replied.

"There's something else," Derek continued. "My girlfriend and I were both exposed to the biological agents. She is already sick and I may come down with it as well. I know that the medical people here are worried that it may be communicable."

"Yes, special agent, and appropriate steps will be taken during your visit. However, we've been told that the probability of infection is relatively low to non-existent."

"I hope you're right," said Derek.

"We can have you picked up within the hour, sir."

"Where am I going?" asked Derek.

"You're coming to Edwards Air Force Base."

"I'll be ready."

"Thank you, sir," said Amy, and the line went dead.

Thirty minutes later a Blackhawk helicopter landed on the beach in front of the hotel. Derek was met by two army non-commissioned officers as he walked towards the helicopter's open side door.

"Mr. James," yelled a corporal over the roar of the rotor blades.

"Yes," replied Derek.

"Please, sir, put this on," said the corporal as the private accompanying him passed Derek what looked like a painter's suit and a mask.

Derek pulled the white one-piece suit on. He had a little trouble getting it over his expensive English loafers and, in the process, filled one with sand. He jumped around trying to get his balance but got no help from the two soldiers, who stood well back from him. He got the suit on and zipped up the front.

The corporal yelled, "The hood as well sir."

Derek pulled the hood over his head and then donned the medical mask.

The private handed him a pair of yellow-tinted safety goggles. "If you would put these on, sir, they will protect your eyes while we spray you down with a decontaminant — just to be on the safe side."

The corporal grabbed a pump sprayer from the helicopter and passed it to the private, who sprayed Derek from head to foot, asking him to hold his arms over his head and rotate three hundred and sixty degrees as the private did so. "Good, sir. Climb aboard," the corporal yelled over the sound of the idling helicopter as the private finished.

Derek clambered into the large olive drab machine, settled himself on one of the canvas-covered benches and secured his seat belt. The Blackhawk lifted from the ground, swung out over the water and then, rising quickly, reversed course, passing directly over the top of the hotel and then eastward towards Edwards. Looking down, Derek saw his Jag in the parking lot and thought to himself how childlike and unimportant the day's events had painted his preoccupations with it and his interests. He kept trying to drive away the thought that if not for him, Vanessa would still be in Washington instead of lying critically ill in a hospital in California.

11:00 p.m. PST
Seattle.

Art Dodson, an eight-thousand-hour pilot, pulled gently back on the yoke of the twin-engined Cessna Skymaster and applied some left rudder, pulling the plane's nose up and away from the thick roiling smoke that billowed from the wildfires below. The fires lit the night sky, shimmering off the smoke and the overcast sky and reflecting the inferno beneath. He banked away from the raging fires that were now overwhelming both industrial and residential areas in the eastern reaches of Seattle's bedroom communities. Then he increased throttle and trimmed for the climb.

Art was the bird dog and fire boss for the drops of water and fire-suppression chemical made by a fleet of water bombers. His task was to direct each bomb run in the hope of cutting off the flames' rampaging progress. So far, neither Art nor the bombers he was coordinating were winning. A summer of drought had made for tinder conditions and turned each tree into a grenade ready to explode at the merest caress of flame. Driven by winds rising to fifteen knots, the fire leapt from crown to crown and immolated two-hundred-year-old trees in seconds. Dry underbrush went up in a second vicious conflagration that had already taken five fire and pumper trucks by surprise. Their crews had barely escaped with their lives as the trucks' fuel further fed the storm.

The monster bellowed with the combined roar of a thousand locomotives, and those on the ground vainly attempting to fight it were overwhelmed by the sound and their lungs seared by its breath. They communicated using hand signals and gestures, and they fought on, knowing that at any second they could fall victim to the capricious nature of the firestorm. Art couldn't help but worry about the brave men and women below protected from the dragon by nothing more than canvas coats and soot-smudged helmets. They were brave and hardy souls whose only weapons were handheld shovels and backpack sprayers. Their fight seemed as hopeless as a swimmer using a pen knife to battle a great white shark, and even more dangerous.

He set course eastward at five thousand feet, winging around the smoke columns that rose thousands of feet farther into the sky. The aircraft bucked and hammered as the writhing fountains of superheated air created updrafts and wind shears that could easily kill an inexperienced pilot. Clearing the front, he turned and dove to check the monster's progress. The forest was giving way to more highly populated residential areas, but the fire showed no sign of abating. Where the forest gave way to fields and meadows, it adapted to the new fuel source, racing across the openings like storm-driven waves inundating a beach. To the north, he could see an industrial area burning, the flames punctuated by brilliantly coloured explosions as heavy power lines, electrical equipment and chemicals of all descriptions ignited and added their stored energy to the cataclysm.

Art pulled the Skymaster from its dive, checked fuel and then radioed that he was bingo and headed back to base. He turned over his duties to another controller arriving on the scene in a Beech Bonanza. Looking down as he winged away, Art knew there was going to be no stopping this conflagration until it reached the shores of Puget Sound, the strip of water that, fortunately, protected downtown Seattle proper. Before that happened, there was very little that he or anyone else could do to stop it. In fifteen years of fighting wildfires, Art had never seen anything like this. The inferno was now thirty miles from north to south along a front created as six or seven smaller but still immense fires merged, fires that had been planned, implemented, and executed to be unstoppable..

Below the Skymaster, hundreds of thousands of cars were fleeing eastward by any route they could find. Art blinked back tears as he saw how many of them were not going to make it.

11:45 p.m. PST
Air Force One on the apron at Edwards Air Force Base

Derek sat watching the ebb and flow along the corridor on Air Force One from his vantage on a stowable leather-upholstered bench adjacent to the entry door. He'd had a couple of companions, but his pure white Tyvek coverall and mask had not endeared him to them, and they'd slid away from him as he took his seat. In short order and to their evident great relief, they'd been whisked away to meetings somewhere within the monstrous flying command post.

Alone for the first time in hours Derek realized how weary he was. It had been a truly horrendous day, but he'd had little time for reflection up until now. He was palpably worried about Vanessa, but he was not in the least worried about coming down with the poisoning or fever himself. He felt no physical distress aside from exhaustion, and he had a feeling that he'd dodged the bullet. That made his concern over Vanessa even more wounding. His mind kept returning to those moments when she'd leaned over the young girl who'd been dusted in brown powder. He berated himself with the thought that if he'd just been a little more on the ball, suspected it was a biological agent sooner, perhaps Vanessa wouldn't be in the throes of poisoning. The horror they'd witnessed at the Conquistador ran back and forth in his mind like a tape recording. He felt guilty that he'd not done more.

That he had really done everything he could and done it properly and sensibly never entered his mind.

A young air force lieutenant approached him. "Special agent James?" she asked.

"Yes," Derek said, stirring from his reverie.

"Please follow me, sir."

She turned and walked up the corridor as Derek gathered himself up. As he followed her, his plastic suit chafing at each step like corduroy, he couldn't help but marvel at just how big the aircraft was. The corridor was busy with earnest-looking people, a flood of activity that his progress parted like the waters of the Red Sea.

The lieutenant reached a doorway and opened it, gesturing for Derek to enter. He passed by her into a small room very much like the green room he had once occupied before an appearance on a New York talk show to discuss terrorism and the FBI. On a sideboard, there were two decanters, marked coffee and tea, as well as bottled water and a small assortment of pastries. As he sat in one of the comfortable waiting room chairs, he noted the coasters on the sideboard next to him. Each bore the presidential coat of arms and the motto "Air Force One" beneath it. A small plaque on the sideboard read, "Please feel free to take a coaster as a souvenir of your visit to Air Force One." Derek resisted the urge, but for the first time a sense of where he was cut through the fatigue, and he felt butterfly wings stir in the pit of his stomach.

He sat for twenty minutes before the same lieutenant opened the door and asked him to follow her. This time, two large dark-suited individuals, clearly Secret Service, took up positions behind Derek, escorting him down the corridor to another small room. He was ushered inside, and one of the men addressed him while the other stood at the door. "Just a final security check, sir. Could I see your identification, please?"

Derek opened his contamination suit and dug out his FBI credentials and passed them to the agent.

The agent donned a pair of latex gloves before taking the card and examining it. "And your personal ID, sir," he said.

Derek passed his wallet.

The agent quickly scanned Derek's license and his social security, medical and credit cards. Seemingly satisfied, he passed the credentials back and nodded to the other agent, who stepped forwards with a small metal detector.

"Arms up, please," he ordered, before passing the detector up one side of Derek's body and down the other. It squawked several times. As it did, Derek, who was familiar with the procedure, rummaged for the offending items and produced them. Satisfied, the agent withdrew back to his post by the door. Derek rezipped his suit.

"One last thing, sir. Your side arm, where is it?" asked the first agent.

"I don't have it with me," replied Derek. "I was on my own time when this happened. My issued gun is in my locker at the office. I have two other personally owned handguns, both at home in a gun safe."

"Thank you, sir," said the agent, opening the door and nodding at the lieutenant who waited outside.

"This way please, sir," she said.

Derek followed her along the corridor a few feet, and then they turned, passing two Air Force Security Forces personnel, and ascended a staircase past another Secret Service agent stationed at the top and to a spacious well-appointed reception room that ran full width of Air Force One, with portholes on both sides. At the forward end of the room a richly decorated wooden door carried the presidential coat of arms in marquetry, the soft hues of inlaid wood blending to form a perfect replica. Tucked inconspicuously in the left-hand side of the room was a smaller door with the sign "Crew only." Derek assumed it accessed the flight deck and engineering.

A gentleman sitting in one of the padded easy chairs, each of which had seat belts for use in flight, rose, tucking the papers he had been reading into the crevice between the seat cushion and the arm. "Special agent James?" he inquired.

"Yes."

"Hello. I'm Dan Blomstrum, White House chief of staff. Normally I would offer my hand, but in this instance…"

"I understand, sir. No need to apologize."

"Come on, then," Blomstrum motioned. He knocked lightly on the door with the coat of arms and started to open it even before the muffled response came from inside.

Derek followed him into the inner sanctum of Air Force One.

"Please, have a seat," were the first words Derek heard from the president of the United States, who sat behind his desk, shirt sleeves rolled up and looking a little haggard.

"Thank you, sir," replied Derek nervously, taking the offered seat, which had a plastic cover draped over it. Dan Blomstrum made himself comfortable in another chair beside the president's desk. Derek noted that both men sensibly kept their distance.

"Special agent," continued the president, "I understand you have had a very rough day, so we won't keep you long. You're probably wondering why you've been asked here, especially considering the scope of the problem this county has faced in the last few hours, so we will cut to the chase. Dan?"

Blomstrum shifted in his seat and peered at Derek over the top of his glasses. "We are going to have to act quickly and decisively to put a stop to these events," he said. "That's going to mean rooting out the organizers, not the perpetrators. To do this we're going to need a corps of dedicated people who have intelligence and anti-terrorism backgrounds. We understand that anti-terrorism intelligence has been your specialty at the FBI for some time, so it's not surprising that the director placed your name on a list of ten individuals within his department who are suited for what we have in mind. It was serendipitous that you were at the initial bombing, and that's why the president wanted to see you personally."

He continued, "In the last few hours, staff in Washington and at the Pentagon have come up with a plan to blend several services and departments into coordinated intelligence and strike teams. Initially, for the intelligence gathering, the teams will comprise two individuals responsible for the hunt, with special tactical units at their disposal who are capable of securing or eliminating any parties of interest. We're going to try to keep these teams' response time to within a couple of hours. The military will be handling the logistics of that. That means help will never be very far away, and physical action will be left to the strike teams, composed of Navy Seals, Green Berets and other special service tactical units.

"The intel teams will comprise agents from the FBI and the CIA and, in a departure from standard policy, we are going to allow the CIA to operate in country and the FBI to operate out of county. The idea behind putting together these teams is to improve the flow of intelligence and make available information from both departments as soon as it is required. In county, the team leader will be FBI or Homeland; outside, the CIA agent will lead. Both parties will share their departmental intelligence without reservation.

"The military will also be cooperating nationally with the law enforcement departments, making sure there will be no information bottlenecks. This should allow us to pool the resources of every agency and law enforcement department, hopefully enabling them to track down the terrorists who are in country and to supply the intel teams with anything of significance they discover. This information, along with anything gathered overseas by the CIA, Military Intelligence or NSA, may prove critical to getting at the people responsible for these atrocities."

"Derek," interjected the president, "it's unfortunate that you happened to be on site for what appears to have been the trigger attack, but that terrible coincidence may help us, and I thought I should ask you personally for your views on the attacks and on our preliminary response."

"Mr. President, what sticks in my mind is that these attacks resemble more a Special Forces style of warfare than they do standard terrorist practice. For instance, none of the attacks that I'm aware of have been suicides. That departure from normal terrorist methods may mean our opponents are far more dangerous and far better trained. If that's true, then we'll have our work cut out for us. They're striking at so many diverse targets that it's going to be almost impossible to predict or secure against further attacks without locking down the whole country. That task alone defies imagination. I think that if we are to have any chance of ending this quickly, we'll have to find the leaders and capture or kill them."

"That is almost point for point our thinking," replied the president. "We'd appreciate you heading one of the teams."

"I'd be pleased to, sir. My only hesitation is this." He indicated the suit he was wearing.

Blomstrum spoke. "Derek, we're pretty sure you are non-infectious, or you wouldn't have gotten in here. The suit and mask are just a further precaution. The blood they took from you back in Montecito so far indicates you are in the clear. However, we're going to put you up in the base hospital for further testing and observation, just to be on the safe side. Once you're given the green flag, you'll head to Washington to be paired up and assigned."

"Special agent James," said the president, "I would like to personally thank you for your actions today."

"Thank you, sir, but I just did what needed to be done."

"Yes, you did, and that's precisely the point," replied the president.

"Do you have any questions?" asked Blomstrum.

"Just one, sir. My girlfriend, Vanessa Leighton, has ricin poisoning, and I couldn't get through to the find out how she's doing. I was just wondering if someone here could find out for me. She was evacuated from the Beach Resort Hotel in Montecito."

"Consider it done, special agent," said Blomstrum. "We'll have someone contact you regarding her condition as soon as possible. Give her particulars to the lieutenant when she takes you downstairs."

"Thank you, sir. I appreciate that."

Blomstrum rose and opened the office door, ushering Derek from the room. Derek's guide, the young lieutenant, waited in the reception room, and Blomstrum spoke to her about Derek's request.

Derek looked back as the president's door swung closed. The president was already on the phone, head down and scrambling through the piles of paper on his desk.

August 19. 2:35 a.m. CST (12:35 a.m. PST)
Texas Industrial Complex, Gulf of Mexico.

Ben Garner walked along the fenceline adjacent to the stinking, oily, chemical-laden shipping canal. The canal ran into the heart of the industrial complex, serving the huge fleet of ships that came and went every day to off-load their cargoes of fuel oil, natural gas and other chemical and petroleum products from around the world. The Texas Industrial Complex was a huge facility tucked into Galveston Bay, along the Gulf Coast, and protected by its seawalls from much of what the Gulf of Mexico had thrown at it over the years. A few miles south, across the bay, glowed the city of Galveston, perched on a triangular sandbar, and to the northwest, Houston lit the sky.

Garner had been a security guard at the complex for almost fifteen years and knew the sprawling industrial facility by heart. Some of the younger guards would occasionally get themselves turned about and wander, lost in hundreds of acres of oil, gasoline and natural gas storage tanks and the maze of accompanying pipes and conduits, but Ben always figured you could drop him anywhere, and at a glance, he could tell you exactly where he was.

The night was overcast and a little dreary, with a soft drizzle that soaked your clothes before you were even aware you needed a raincoat. He figured he should head over to the guardhouse and grab his slicker before much longer, perhaps as soon as he'd finished walking the dockside. He passed under a spider's web of lines, power cables and pipes leading to a tanker that sat at berth. Several dock hands were about, and floodlights lit the area as the tanker gave up its cargo to the ravenous storage tanks that stood in ranks from the docks back for hundreds of acres. Work around the complex went on 24-7, although it was usually concentrated in small pockets, like the off-loading areas. The tank farms themselves were pretty lonely, even during the day shift.

Ben, now a couple of hundred yards past the tanker and well beyond the dock's floodlights, caught a furtive movement down one of the access routes. He aimed his flashlight, but aside from a jumble of pumps and a parked portable compressor, he could not make anything out. He walked up the narrow road, figuring he might as well check it out even though it was probably just raccoons or, at worst, a coyote. "Hey, anyone there?" he called.

There was no answer. Thinking he must be seeing things, he decided to keep on up and then turn left to head back to the guard station along Industrial Canal road. It was a crappy night to be on foot. After he dried off, he grabbed a cruiser to patrol the tank farms.

He was just passing the old Ingersol Rand compressor when he caught movement again and saw a figure slip furtively behind it in an attempt to hide. "Hey, what the hell? You, come on out here!" yelled Ben.

A figure dressed in black came around the end of the compressor and into the glare of Ben's flashlight.

"What they hell do you think your doing?" he asked. "Christ, are you supposed to be a ninja or something?"

The intruder was dressed in black from head to toe and had the hood of his black jacket pulled over his head and obscuring much of his face.

When Ben saw that the rest of the man's face was blacked out with camouflage makeup, he realized with a sinking sensation that this wasn't an ordinary intruder. When he stepped back, his progress was arrested by a thick muscular arm that wrapped itself around his face and pulled him off balance. He never saw and barely felt the well-honed commando knife that slit his throat deeply, so deeply that the only sound that emerged was a soft gurgle. His attackers hauled him into the maze of pipes servicing the nearest storage tank and continued with their work.

Half an hour earlier a small inflatable, crowded with six men, had paddled silently from the breakwater outside the harbour and up the canal to a tumble-down wooden wharf that was perfect for hiding the boat. Four men slipped ashore shouldering heavy backpacks and carrying two black canvas sacks each. Two of them headed inland while the other pair made their way along the docks toward the off-loading area and their inadvertent meeting with Ben Garner.

The men remaining in the boat waited a few minutes hidden amid the barnacled and ooze-encrusted wooden pilings that held up the remnants of the obsolete dock. Seeing the other four were clear, they paddled out, keeping close to the docksides. When they reached the end of the canal, they paddled across to the its southern shore, where numerous white natural gas tanks, each the size of a five-storey building, crowded together like ripe puffball mushrooms. At the same time, four other men slipped among the tanks on the west side of Highway 197, which cut the tank farm in two, lugging identical backpacks. They crept under poorly maintained fences and made their way from tank to tank, stopping for a moment at each one to lay a magnetic shaped charge before heading to the next. They also mined several of the largest of the myriad pipes and transfer valves that criss-crossed the farm.

An hour later the intruders had retreated to the low-income housing of Texas City, on the complex's northern and western boundaries. The men in the inflatable turned on a small electric outboard and returned to the old Dodge Minivan that waited for them next to a building on Dike Road where it ran out along the breakwater into Galveston Bay. Once, the pair had to hold their breathe as a Coast Guard cutter emerged from the gloom and drizzle and passed within fifty feet of them, but no alarm was raised.

As of yet America and her occupants had not learned the hard lessons of war on their own soil or the rewards of vigilance.

2:15 a.m. PST
USAF medical clinic, Edwards Air Force Base.

As he stepped from the staircase servicing Air Force One, Derek was met by a small blue four-door Chevy with USAF stencilled on its doors. The driver, a young private, opened the back door for him, and once he was inside, whisked him from the airfield apron to the administrative heart of the air base. Within minutes, they pulled in front of the base hospital, and Derek climbed out, opening his door before the private could.

"Have a good evening, sir," said the young man.

"Thank you," Derek replied. He walked though the front doors of the hospital and to the reception desk.

"May I help you?" inquired the duty nurse, eying Derek's Tyvek suit and mask.

"Yes, nurse. I'm Special Agent Derek James. I was told you people were expecting me."

"Special agent," a voice called from behind him.

Derek turned to see a portly staff sergeant walking across the foyer.

"Sorry. I was supposed to meet you at the curb. I didn't think they would get you here that quick," he said and reached out to shake Derek's hand. "My name's Fabricio González."

Derek started to reach out and then withdrew his hand. "Sergeant."

"It's okay," said the sergeant, holding up his hands to show that he was wearing latex gloves. "Come on, follow me. Your suite awaits."

Derek tailed the good-humoured sergeant down a brightly lit corridor painted the standard hospital green with cream trim. Near its end, the sergeant turned into a room on the left, flicking on the lights as he did so.

"Here you go. Private quarters and just as good as the Waldorf. Make yourself at home. I fancy you can't wait to get out of that suit."

"Your right," replied Derek. "I'm starting to pong a bit."

"I know," replied the sergeant with a facetious grin. He opened another door that led off the room. "Here's your ensuite." He indicated a small washroom equipped with a shower.

On seeing it, Derek suddenly felt that nothing else in the world mattered more than taking a warm shower, followed immediately by bed.

"I'll leave you alone," said the sergeant. "When you take off your suit and clothing, just toss them into this hamper." He pointed to a stainless steel container next to the bathroom door. "We'll supply you with a decent set of clothes. You look like a large shirt to me. Pants?"

"Thirty-four waist, thirty-six leg."

"Great. I'll make sure we get you something that doesn't fit," he quipped. "Have a shower, and then I'm sure the doctor will be in to see you." And was gone, the door swinging closed behind him.

Derek undressed and stepped into the small shower, adjusting the water to as hot as he could take. For minutes he just stood under its blast, leaning against the wall with his eyes closed and enjoying the heat. Then, after a quick wash down with a bar of soap, he was out and towelled.

There was a toothbrush wrapped in plastic and a new tube of toothpaste on the shelf above the sink. He took advantage and then stepped out, dressed in the light blue terry cloth bathrobe that had been hanging on the back of the door.

He was greeted by a middle-aged man sitting in the corner of his room, replete with greying hair, white lab coat and clipboard. "Special agent James?" he asked as he rose. "Good evening. I'm Doctor Walters. I'm just going to take a bit of blood, your temperature and give you a quick once over. Then I'll let you get some sleep."

"Pleased to meet you, doctor. You're not in a haz-mat suit," said Derek — part statement, part question.

"No. We leave that for Hollywood. Even if you have Ebola, it's not that infectious as long as proper precautions are taken. I will ask you to refrain from sneezing or coughing on me, however," he said with a grin.

"Deal, doctor, as long as you let me get some sleep soon."

"Hop into bed, then, and give me your left arm."

For the second time within twenty-four hours, Derek had blood taken. The doctor, wearing a mask and gloves, listened to Derek's breathing and heart, poked his abdomen and asked him a few questions about tenderness, shortness of breath and anything else that might be symptomatic of ricin poisoning or hemorrhagic fever. He made a few notes and then said, "It looks good to me, Derek. I think you're going to be in the clear. We'll know more when we get the results of the blood test back. In the meantime, I'll leave you alone, and you can get some sleep. If you have any trouble sleeping, take these." He offered Derek two pills in a small paper cup. "They're mild sleeping pills."

"Thank you, doctor."

"Good night."

"Good night, doctor."

Doctor Walters closed the door behind him and started down the corridor.

"Hey, doc."

Walters turned to see the staff sergeant making his way toward him.

"Yes, sergeant?"

The sergeant leaned close and said quietly, "We just got a message for special agent James. His girlfriend, she was evacuated to Community Memorial Hospital in Ventura with ricin poisoning."

"Yes?" asked Doctor Walter.

"She didn't make it, sir. Seems she passed away about an hour ago."

"Ah jeez," groaned Walters. "Thank you, staff sergeant."

"You going to tell him?" asked the sergeant.

"No, not tonight. He needs sleep. It will keep until morning."

"Good night, sir."

"Good night, staff sergeant."

4:45 a.m. CST (2:45 a.m. PST)
Texas Industrial Complex.

The dockworkers monitoring the pumping out of the oil tanker as it gradually rose in its berth with each passing hour heard an unusual cracking over the sound of the pumps and the mechanical gear they tended. For a moment, it sounded as if a thunderstorm was moving in, but the cracking became ever louder. Suddenly there was a massive whoomp and an immense ball of flame shot into the overcast above their heads.

Panicked, the workers broke to run along the quay, their clothing already starting to smoke, instinct screaming at them to get away from the storage tanks that loomed over the docks. Again and again, the deep whoomping reverberated, and fresh mushroom clouds of burning gasoline, oil and crude rose into the sky. Debris started to rain down, some of it flaming liquids, some of it riveted steel sections, one inch thick, of the storage tanks. Flaming petroleum bathed the ocean-going tankers tied up alongside the docks, absorbing the mammoth ships and their cargoes into the expanding maelstrom.

The shaped charges had done their work, bursting each tank and pipe on which they'd been laid. The devices themselves were simply made but effective, designed so a small primary shaped charge would burst into the tanks and vaporize a little of their contents. Next, a secondary charge, mounted piggyback, detonated. The delay was just the microsecond required for the proper introduction of its high explosive force. These secondary charges mated with the vapours released by the shaped charges, starting an expansive reaction. The charges, none much larger than a lunchbox, were merely tiny detonators, but the amount of energy they were designed to release was immense.

Within minutes, hundreds of millions of gallons of petroleum and chemicals merged into a raging inferno that brought a false dawn to the skies of Houston, melting the shingles of nearby houses and lighting the tarred roofs of industrial buildings on the outskirts of the complex. Tank after tank exploded and rivers of flaming fuel filled and then overran the dykes that had been made to contain much smaller spills. Then the natural gas storage vessels, scattered around the site like flightless blimps, detonated in a carefully choreographed delay. The gas containers blew flames into the sky that rained down again, igniting homes and businesses over a quarter mile distant. The heat near the inferno's centre was so intense that steel ran like water and miles of pipes laden with fuel or fumes sagged and burst. No force on earth could stop the rampage. The maelstrom of liquid fire and deadly smoke would burn for days, until it ran out of fuel.

Almost simultaneously, a few miles to the northwest near the centre of Houston, another smaller tank farm across the river from the Houston Industrial Complex erupted, raining fire onto the housing projects that bordered it. Fire trucks rushing from the city to the Texas Industrial Complex turned back, racing to contend with the other smaller, but no less deadly, inferno that threatened to engulf Houston's downtown core.

Around the United States, nine other major tank farms burst into flames. The Amoco refinery in Chicago went up in spectacular fashion, as did tank farms near Detroit, Savannah, New Orleans, Washington, San Francisco, Denver, Wichita and Atlanta. Within days America would have to decide just how far it was willing to dig into its strategic reserves in order to keep neighbourhood gas stations and continue day-to-day commerce. If there'd been any doubt in the minds of the American public as to whether or not they were at war, the huge palls of smoke rising into the sky, visible for hundreds of miles, put an end to it.

For many Americans their war had finally come home. For the first time, this was not just an electronic display in their living rooms of distant events under vivisection by an inexhaustible supply of self-important talking heads.

CHAPTER 3

Derek woke suddenly, a horrific dream casting him abruptly into wakefulness. His surroundings momentarily disoriented him, until the events of the day before came rushing back. Never one to laze, he immediately threw his legs over the side of the bed and rose, shaking off the grogginess of a deep but troubled sleep. Stepping to the small window, he opened the white venetian blind. He could see the bustle of the base outside, as cars, trucks and other less identifiable wheeled maintenance vehicles passed back and forth along the dusty roadway in front of the hospital.

He turned to see that at some time during the night new clothes had been delivered as the staff sergeant had promised. Draped over the back of the visitor's chair in the corner was a pair of black slacks. Socks and underwear were on the seat neatly folded, and there was a white shirt and plain black tie hanging from a hook next to the bathroom door. His shoes had been placed neatly under the chair and cleaned and polished almost to a shine — not an easy task with a pair of comfortable English walking shoes. He dressed in the unfamiliar and exceedingly plain outfit, omitting only the black tie. The room was a little close despite the hum of the building's air conditioner, which tried ineffectually to keep the desert outside at bay.

After slipping on his shoes, he decided to poke his head out and see what was going on. As he reached for the door handle, there was a knock that made him jump. "Come in," said Derek, stepping back from the door as it opened.

Doctor Walters stepped into the room.

"How are you feeling this morning?" he asked.

"Not bad, doctor."

"Good. So far we haven't gotten any indication that you've been infected. Preliminary findings on the cultures came up negative for hemorrhagic fever, and it seems that you were fortunate to have avoided contact with the ricin poison as well. That said, I have some very bad news for you."

"Vanessa?" said Derek, a feeling of dread overwhelming him.

"I'm afraid so. I'm very sorry to have to tell you that she passed away last night from the toxic effects of the ricin poisoning."

The doctor went on, but the sudden grief and shock struck Derek deaf as his mind raced over the news, back to the moments when he last saw her, held her and stroked her hair as she was loaded aboard the medevac chopper. To even earlier moments, when she kneeled beside a young woman in a saffron dress, trying to help her, and puzzled over the brown smudges on the woman's skin, hair and clothing. Then back, back to the hours before their fateful arrival at the Conquistador and the guilt-laden surge of what if? What if he had not begged her to come out to the show? What if they had just spent more time shopping? What if, what if, what if?

He stepped back and sat on the edge of the bed, collecting himself. Suddenly, his surroundings became crystal clear as a wave of hatred eclipsed his grief, rushing into his mind and body with an almost physical assault. His life had just been given irresistible purpose.

Chapter 4

August 20.
Andrews Air Force Base, Maryland.

Catherine Hunt had just returned from a six-week sojourn that had started in Belgrade, moved on to Istanbul and culminated with a day spent in Haifa meeting counterparts in the Israeli intelligence agency, Mossad. Catherine had serendipitously run into an arms supplier who specialized in selling sophisticated Eastern and Western European weaponry to fundamentalist movements all over the Middle East and Asia. Rumour had it that Joachim Schmitt, a former East German Stasi captain, was doing his best to add stolen Soviet-era nuclear weapons to his arsenal for sale. If that was the case, then there'd be any number of people in America, Europe and Israel who'd be very interested in his whereabouts.

Catherine had come across Schmitt by accident when he was introduced to her by a mutual acquaintance in Belgrade, an acquaintance that did not know she was a CIA field operative but did know that Schmitt dealt in arms. His was a profession that many people in the former Eastern bloc thought of as sexy and glamorous.

Catherine had been introduced as a successful financial writer and economist, a fiction supported by a website that listed her publishing history and her resume. She was supposedly in Belgrade to review the rising and falling economies of the newest Eastern European democracies.

Schmitt was almost as taken with her alleged celebrity and the interest she exhibited in him as he was with her stunning good looks, silky red hair and lithe five-foot-seven frame. He immediately invited her to a reception he was hosting at a palatial home overlooking the Dardanelles in Turkey. Catherine had put the invitation and subsequent visit to good use and collected the names of several of Schmitt's potential customers. Before Schmitt bade farewell to his guests, after which, incidentally, he'd planned on bedding Catherine, her "editor" called with an emergency meeting in London. Promising a quick return, Catherine said her goodbyes and arranged to meet Joachim in a week.

Her fictional departure to London actually led to a change of planes in Italy and an El Al flight to Tel Aviv and on to Haifa, an excursion extended courtesy of her superiors in the CIA to Mossad. Mossad spent a few hours debriefing Catherine. It was her opinion, after meeting with the businesslike but affable Israeli agents, that Schmitt's days were very much numbered. Her assignation with Joachim Schmitt, set for a week hence in Sarajevo, would certainly be kept, but not by Catherine.

Catherine was still in Haifa when news of the first attacks on America reached the world. She sat in a small hotel room watching CNN and the BBC, sick to her stomach as each vile incident was described and redescribed. Within six hours she had been called to the U.S. Embassy in Tel Aviv and issued orders to return to the States on the next available flight — a U.S. military airlift command C-130 Hercules, all commercial flights to the States having been grounded. It was the noisiest and most uncomfortable flight that Catherine had ever endured, despite the earplugs she'd been issued on boarding. She wondered how military personnel could arrive anywhere fit for duty after ten hours on one of these boneshakers.

The aircraft landed at Andrews Air Force Base, near Washington, and disgorged its ragtag collection of military and diplomatic corps personnel as well as a number of civilians like Catherine who were no doubt intelligence operatives, "spooks" in the common parlance. The group were cleared by both military and Customs officials, and Catherine boarded a minibus that took her to a waiting room near the base's gates where she could call a city cab. She was aching and weary and couldn't wait to grab a few hours' sleep in her little-used apartment near the bedroom community of Chevy Chase. She had a few hours before she had to report to Langley in the morning for what she could only imagine would be reassignment.

August 20.
Dulles International Airport, Chantilly, Virginia.

Derek stepped off the U.S. Air Force Gulfstream into a driving rain that poured down his neck as he raced for the access way to the terminal at Dulles International Airport, near Washington DC.

It had been two days since the attacks on the United States commenced. After the initial twenty-four hours, they had seemed to peter out, leaving a nationwide response to chase ghosts and founder. While no new attacks had been initiated, the effects of the opening assault were still ricocheting through the fabric of American society and its economy, which had been put on hold. Seattle was still dealing with raging fires, although part of the wildfire was now under control. Miami was grief-stricken over the downing of the 747 and the thousands of casualties from its impact and the subsequent fires. Tulsa was burying its dead, and Boston was trying to find a way to seal the rift in its shattered tunnel so it could start pumping out the millions of gallons of water that still covered an unknown number of corpses. The whole nation was looking over its shoulder. People were scared stiff of eating in restaurants or even drinking water that wasn't bottled.

The destruction of several of the largest fuel storage facilities and the firestorms they ignited, some still burning, had not only exacted a horrendous toll on people, neighbouring cities and the environment, but also caused gasoline prices to soar by a dollar a gallon at those gas stations that still had an adequate supply. Many stations were run dry by panic buying and could not get resupplied. The gas companies were too nervous to dispatch fuel tankers without escort by law enforcement or the National Guard, both of whom were already overstretched. Few regular deliveries were being made, and consumers were restricted to purchases of five gallons or less in most regions.

Military patrols in Humvees aided regular police patrols nationwide, and police officers, even those responding to domestic disputes, had at their backs companions in olive drab and carrying M-16s. For the first time since the American Civil War, the United States was rallying to enter battle on its own mainland, but against whom?

The president had declared martial law. However, in most parts of the country, citizens would not notice much of a change. There were no nationwide curfews in effect, but local governors in several states where violent anti-Muslim demonstrations and rioting had taken place had the power to impose curfews and use National Guard and even regular military forces to quell unrest. Despite these measures, there had been lynchings and murders all over the United States as a range of ethnic groups received the brunt of people's misguided hatred and vengeance. Military manpower was short everywhere because much of America's standing army and many of its National Guard were taken up with the never-ending commitment to the Middle East and, to a lesser extent, Afghanistan. The number of personnel required to ensure security along the Iraq-Iran border as well as patrol the rest of Iraq was a constant drain on an armed forces already strained by recruitment numbers that had dropped by the year.

While no politician had dared propose a draft, the Pentagon had sent memo after memo quietly begging for some kind of action to bolster its flagging resources. The United States had supposedly handed over power to the Iraqi government long ago, but a pullout of American forces would result in civil war and there was no doubt that Iran would sweep in to take over and put in place a friendly Shiite puppet. For several years, Iran had been steadily building up its forces along the border with Iraq, and it was commonly believed that they would invade the moment American forces were withdrawn. The Pentagon had also had to fill the gap in Afghanistan as one by one other nations in the alliance pulled out. Now ninety percent of ground forces in the troublesome region were American, and they controlled only twenty percent of the country. The rest was split among different warring factions, few of them with any affection for the West and its interests, although almost all of them were eager to profess cooperation as long as they were compensated.

As for the first attack on American soil at Santa Barbara, its true scope was just starting to be felt. Thousands had died both on the greens of the Conquistador and in the city of Santa Barbara, and while that in itself was horrendous, the strike had lopped the heads from many large corporations and companies as well as killing dozens of celebrity figures. The economic ramifications of so many highly placed fatalities could create long-term havoc. The hemorrhagic fever had not yet stricken many of those exposed to it, and epidemiologists hoped that the weapons-tailored virus might fizzle, but the ricin had been all too effective in its ability to kill and debilitate. Military and civilian authorities had set up special emergency clinics in warehouses and hangars to treat the hundreds of ricin victims as well as thirty or forty people who seemed to be exhibiting early symptoms of fever. Hundreds more were confined to special emergency observation areas where doctors, nurses and paramedics monitored them for any signs of illness.

So far, the state's response had been immediate and Herculean, but any further attacks on the same scale would seriously stretch medical and emergency services, perhaps to the breaking point.

Derek walked from the small plane toward a terminal complex devoid of activity. A U.S. Marine met him at the stairs leading from the tarmac to the companionway, checked his ID and allowed him to pass. Once inside, Derek followed the signs to ground transport, walking though empty corridors that had lost their familiarity along with their teeming hordes. The terminal building, its stores and eateries closed and barricaded, felt like a ghost town and put a fine point on Derek's mood, which bordered on depression.

He stepped out of the terminal and flagged one of the three cabs that sat at the curb. Not until they were well away from the airport did the roads take on some semblance of normality, the traffic light for the time of day but still fairly busy and comforting in its own way. The one discordant note was the number of military vehicles on patrol, mostly Humvees, whose crews included machine gunners standing in the roof hatches and manning light weapons. As of yet the military had seen no need to panic people with the introduction of armoured vehicles to city streets, but those, ranging from Stryker armoured cars to Abrams main battle tanks, were marshalled within striking distance of most points in Washington, a fact the Washington Post had trumpeted as military and civilian heavy equipment transporters moved the vehicles to their assembly points, hidden under tarpaulins.

Derek wasn't tired. Physically he was three hours behind, on Pacific Standard Time, and his respite in hospital, where he'd been kept under observation pending the results of a full spectrum of tests, had rested his body if not his mind. He was doing his best to continue functioning normally while in the throes of grief for Vanessa.

He'd been recalled to Washington to meet with other agents from the CIA and FBI on their new tasking, but the only home he had there was Vanessa's apartment. He'd dropped his own apartment when he was assigned to Los Angeles, with the intention of coming home to Vanessa's whenever he visited from the West Coast. They had both decided that, since he rarely used his own digs even when in town, it was silly for him to maintain them while he was away for an undetermined length of time.

It was the closest he'd ever come to a permanent commitment to a woman, but it felt so very right whenever they were together that neither of them had had doubts or reservations. After their relationship had gotten past the tempestuous, lovesick first stages, it had become comfortable and deeply loving. Despite leading incredibly busy, stressful and complex professional lives, they fit together like a pair of gloves and had become dependent on one another for shelter from the world when they needed it — an important consideration in professions that brimmed with all that is worst in the human condition.

Derek didn't want to stay at the apartment. It would be filled with ghosts. Instead, he asked the driver to take him to the Marriot on Pennsylvania Avenue, just a few blocks from FBI headquarters. He felt like a visitor in a city he'd called home for almost twenty of his thirty-two years. The sooner he was reassigned and the farther from anything familiar he was sent, the better. His one deeply held hope was that he'd be sent somewhere that would present him with the opportunity to take revenge, both for his nation and, more importantly, for himself.

August 20.
Ta'if, Saudi Arabia.

Muhammad al-Munajjid relaxed back into a fabulously expensive Italian recliner, a mystery novel by a famed English author close to hand and a fresh cup of tea on a small convenience table beside him. He was enjoying the cool breeze that brushed across the balcony of his luxury home perched in the hills overlooking Ta'if, the summer residence of the Saudi government.

Ta'if sat high on the slopes of the Al-Sarawat Mountains, near the Red Sea and Mecca, and was a popular escape among Saudi Arabia's ruling classes from the blast furnace Riyadh became during the summer. Ta'if had a long and turbulent history and was renowned as the place where the prophet Muhammad was stoned after city leaders had rejected his teachings. Driven from the city, his forces returned a decade later to lay siege. Although the siege itself was unsuccessful, city leaders negotiated a conversion to Islam, and Ta'if entered the fold. It had always been known for its fertile soils, cool climate and agricultural produce, which fed the populations that lived on the plains below. It was also a very secure city and largely free from Western intelligence gathering.

Al-Munajjid was very pleased with the progress and results of his attacks. The United States was in a state of confusion, and as he had hoped, much of the country had turned on itself with riots and civil unrest. The American media, hoping to relieve the situation somewhat, was trying to downplay these witch hunts, but to little avail. Dozens of people had been beaten to death or lynched, and in some places, the police had been powerless or even unwilling to intervene. Few mosques remained standing in the United States.

The nation's economy had ground to a halt, it had cut itself off from the rest of the world, its harbours and airports were idle, and much of the population spent their days at home behind locked doors. Just as al-Munajjid had instructed, his primary assault teams had backed off, leaving the Americans to panic and lash out at phantoms. In a few more hours, his warriors would begin a new round of attacks, none so dramatic as the first series, but designed to instill fear and panic and demonstrate to Americans that they would find no safe haven.

His sponsors were as pleased with their proxy attack as he. Two of their representatives had waited for his arrival at an office near Ta'if Regional Airport with news that the first monetary transfers had been made to his personal accounts, accounts skilfully hidden around the world. Those payments would proceed on an agreed schedule for the foreseeable future. The first payments alone covered all of al-Munajjid's personal expenditures for the years of planning. The next in the series would assure him of a handsome profit on his investment. If all went according to plan, al-Munajjid would soon rank among the top ten wealthiest citizens of Saudi Arabia and wield power that did not rely on religious fervour alone. Al-Munajjid was a clever man. He'd insisted that the payments all be made in Euros, not in American dollars. Never a trusting soul, not even in currencies, he had already instructed his bankers to convert most of his deposits to gold and silver bullion.

August 21.
J. Edgar Hoover Building, FBI headquarters, Washington DC.

Derek wound his way thorough the concrete obstacles littered around FBI headquarters, protection recently added to that already afforded by a small moat, lined by cement walls, that surrounded the building. Security was tight, tighter than he had ever seen before, and several two-man military teams patrolled the exterior. The main entrance was guarded by regular Washington police officers, and on entering the building, Derek joined a long queue of people waiting to pass through security. The building's foyer looked like an airport security area with its metal detectors, scanners, bomb-sniffing dogs and multitude of security personnel.

After a few minutes in line, he noticed there was a shorter, faster-moving one. A sign declared that it was for FBI agents only. He walked to the back of that line and within a few minutes had been processed and cleared. He was asked to wait in a ground-floor room while his arrival was announced. From there he would be picked up and escorted to his assignment meeting — all new procedure. He sat for fifteen minutes in a room that was usually an information and tour assembly point for the crowds of tourists who in normal times jostled one another for a look into the inner workings of the Federal Bureau of Investigation. In truly American fashion, even the FBI had its entertainment division.

Derek walked along the room's back wall, looking at a rogues' gallery of framed pictures displaying bootleggers, spies, Ku Klux Klansmen, serial killers, hardened criminals and, most recently, terrorists that the bureau had arrested over the years. He thought to himself how wonderful it would be when the wall could feature the bastards responsible for the latest atrocities. He was deep in thought when a friendly voice stirred him from his reverie.

"Hello, Derek," said Brian Good.

Derek turned and smiled. Good was an old friend in the bureau, and Derek had worked with him successfully several times in the distant past. He was exceptionally tall and thin and had always reminded Derek of Ichabod Crane from The Legend of Sleepy Hollow. Good, however, while appearing frail had proven himself a brilliant field agent and was well respected. He'd been assigned to the FBI's counter-terrorism department at almost the same time as Derek, although they had never been teamed together since their appointments.

"Hello, Brian. I see you have the same tailor," said Derek, smiling at Good's rumpled appearance. "Don't tell me we've been teamed up."

"No such luck," replied Good. "I've just been sent down to pick you up and deliver you upstairs. I've been put in charge of coordinating the teams we're assembling. It seems to be my lot to live life behind a desk while everyone else goes out to play."

"But you're probably going to make director before you're forty," laughed Derek.

"Well, I'm shocked and hurt that you, of all people, would think that I'm a political animal. By the way, could I interest you in a campaign button?"

The pair laughed as they walked to the elevator, where Good pushed the button and they waited side by side.

"I'm really sorry to hear about Vanessa," said Brian uncomfortably. "She's going to be missed."

"Yes, she is," said Derek.

As if by mutual consent, they said no more on the subject.

The elevator doors opened and the two men strode in. Good punched a button marked for the third floor, and the doors slid closed.

Derek sat by himself a couple of rows back in the briefing room, Good having excused himself to run another errand. There were at least forty people in the room, yet there was virtually no conversation and little noise aside from the odd self-conscious cough or the creaking of wooden chairs.

Through the windows, to the northwest, a thick column of black smoke could be seen rising into the air a few miles away. Derek, along with everyone else in the city, knew that the source of the smoke was the smouldering remains of the first mosque built in North America. Rioters had set fire to the Islamic Center of Washington DC, on Massachusetts Avenue, in the early hours of the previous day. The graceful building in Moorish style, which opened for worship in 1957, had burned for hours as the crowds that surrounded it gently but firmly kept firefighters from intervening, crowds that had cheered every time a wall fell or a new blast of flame shot upwards. Fortunately, no one had been killed either inside the building or out.

That good fortune had not accompanied the destruction of many other mosques across the United States. Followers of Islam had built dozens of mosques and Islamic centres across the country since this one's minaret first broke the Washington skyline. Now, almost all of them had burned or, if they were lucky enough to have escaped that fate, been cordoned off and closed by police in the interests of public safety. The public worship of Islam in the United States had come to a very sudden and, in many cases, violent hiatus.

Derek sat up straight in the uncomfortable wooden chair as assistant director of counter-terrorism Miles Nichols, entered the room along with the assistant director of the CIA, George Henry, and the director of the National Counter Intelligence Executive, Peter Hulling. The three men stood at the front of the briefing room, Nichols and Henry on either side of Hulling, who took his place behind the podium, placing a sheaf of papers on its desktop.

Hulling looked over his shoulder at the map of the USA that was projected on the wall behind him, held up a remote control and clicked it. Several red lights appeared on the map. "Ladies and gentlemen," he began, "you all know assistant director Nichols and assistant director Henry."

The two nodded at the assembled group, and Hulling continued.

"The illuminated points on this map show the attacks on the U.S. I am confident that all of you are current, but I will review them for clarity. As you can see they are fairly evenly spread over the map, but there doesn't appear to be any particular pattern to their distribution. We've found no pattern to the methods that have been used either. In only two attacks, in Santa Barbara and in Belden, were biological agents used, but they were distinctly different agents. For Santa Barbara, it was ricin, the toxin derived from castor beans, and it was mated with a hemorrhagic fever. In Belden, it was a form of E. coli. All of these agents were weapons-grade, not natural. The ricin and the E. coli were very effective. The hemorrhagic fever, we hope, is waning. So far, most of the victims in the Santa Barbara area who have succumbed died from ricin poisoning."

Derek listened, his face a stone, while Hulling's voice droned on with information that made him want to scream in rage.

"We can't assume, however, that the fever is not a threat. Over one hundred people contracted it. However, at this stage it does not seem to be as aggressive as the wild African varieties, and most if not all those effected show promising signs of recovery or have at least stabilized. It won't do to let down our guard, though. The CDC think it may have a long gestation period and present itself more aggressively later this week. I certainly hope that's not the case, but we're keeping anyone who may have been exposed and has not been cleared by testing under observation. That means that we have thousands of people literally incarcerated in the Santa Barbara area.

"The attack in Belden was on a tiny retirement town of absolutely no strategic value, but it seems that the terrorists are out to prove a point — the point of course being that Americans are not safe no matter where they are.

"The strikes on the refineries are a serious blow and one we should have all seen coming, but there's no point trying to place blame. We all knew how vulnerable those sites were, and evidently, so did the enemy. They were the only ones who did anything about it.

"Seattle was perhaps the simplest attack. We have evidence that it was implemented with nothing more than bottles full of gasoline. Casualties so far are in the hundreds, and property loss has not been determined at this time. Those fires are still raging.

"Boston, of course, is ongoing. We have no idea how many people died in the tunnel, but divers found the wreckage of a gasoline tanker at what appears to be ground zero. The tunnel is so unstable that further dives have been postponed until a plan for stabilizing the roof and walls can be engineered. In the meantime, the victims' remains will have to stay where they are, except for the few recovered so far. Based on missing persons' reports, we estimate that dozens perished. Of course the dollar value of losing that tunnel remains to be seen, but we all know what it took to dig it in the first place. The economic impact on the city is substantial. Every other tunnel there has been shut down or had its use severely restricted."

Hulling paused and took a moment to shuffle the pages in front of him. He cleared his throat before continuing.

"The truck bomb at Tulsa was sickening, because it appears that they targeted families, especially children, and we're sure the diner massacre at Las Vegas, New Mexico…" — he held up his hand — "yes, New Mexico, not Nevada, was a deliberate attempt, like the poisoning in Belden, to show the American public they are not safe anywhere. The bombing in Hollywood in front of the Chinese Theatre appears to have the same motives.

"So far, I am very unhappy to say, we have only one suspect in custody. He's a young Cuban American by the name of Miguel Ramírez who, we have confirmed by physical evidence as well as his own admission, shot down the Lufthansa airliner in Miami. It seems he was not even aiming for the 747, but misfired the rocket at an American airliner as it took off. It was just bad luck of the worst kind that it hit the 747. Rodríguez has revealed under questioning that he is a convert to Islam and that his handler was a Lebanese immigrant by the name of Adnan Awada.

"We have not been able to trace Awada. It seems he disappeared shortly before the missile attack and has not been heard of since. We have no state or federal records on Awada, so we have to assume that he was working under a false identity or identities and is currently laying low. I'm afraid Ramírez was disposable and they have protected themselves from his revealing any useable intelligence. All he spouts is anti-American gibberish. We will continue his interrogation, but I don't think it will lead anywhere. It does raise a very uncomfortable question, however. This Awada has been in the country for some time. Just how many other sleepers or radicalized American youth are out there who are willing to contribute to these attacks?

"As you all know, the attacks seem to have concluded. But since the people responsible have not been apprehended, we can only assume they are positioning for another series. In the meantime, we're bolstering security everywhere possible. Our biggest problem is manpower, which is stretched thin across the nation. The National Guard, army, navy and air force are doing what they can, but they've got serious personnel problems as well. Most of their forces are committed overseas. Many of our assets on the ground are tied up fighting vigilantism, so they're having a hard time providing security to the installations in their areas that may need it most. There is talk of bringing several battalions home from overseas to assist, but this has not been confirmed, and of course, their withdrawal from the Middle East and Asia will only serve to destabilize further already dangerously volatile regions.

"That may just be the objective of these attacks. At present no one, aside from a few fringe groups, has taken responsibility for the attacks or made any demands. That means we don't know what they want or even whether they want anything. As hard as it is to say, the best scenario would be that this is a revenge attack with no particular aim in mind.

"This is where you people come in. Your jobs will be to spread out not just across the U.S. but over the rest of the world and, using any intelligence you can find, to track down the bad guys. The president has told us we will have a free hand and whatever resources we require. You will be allowed to use any methods you deem effective to obtain information that will further your assignments. This is the first time we have been allowed to play using the same rules as the bad guys. Hopefully, that is going to be a real shock to them and an advantage to you.

"Most of you have already met your new partners and have your assignments. For those recent arrivals who have not, please see Brian Good at his office on the second floor. He'll pass out your assignments and make introductions. Are there any questions?"

A hand went up near the back of the room and agent Peter Todd stood.

"Sir, you didn't mention the shooting of Lyndon Lane in New York. Is it tied in with the rest of the attacks?"

"We suspect that's the case, and we're investigating on that basis. The assassination of celebrities is a new but certainly effective tactic, because it hits everyone with a sense of personal loss they may not feel when a refinery goes up or a tunnel is bombed."

"Are there any more questions?"

No one raised their hands.

"Good. Now assistant director Nichols would like a word."

Nichols took the podium, grasped the small microphone and pushed it aside. "I don't need this microphone to pass on what I want to say," he said, his voice unamplified but audible to everyone in the room nonetheless. "I just want to wish you good luck and Godspeed, and I hope from the very bottom of my heart that you'll all come home with a bag full of heads."

Someone at the back of the room yelled, "Yeah!" and the room broke into applause.

Derek did not applaud, but he certainly concurred with the sentiment.

Nichols turned from the podium, and he and the other two directors filed from the room.

Brian Good strode up the aisle from where he'd been waiting, leaning against the wall at the back, and took the podium himself. "Okay, people. Most of you know who I am. For those who don't, my name is Brian Good, and I will be the coordinator of this project. Most of you have your assignments and appropriate travel documents, so I want to see you get cracking. For those who don't I'll see you downstairs in fifteen minutes. That should be just enough time to grab yourselves a coffee."

As everyone rose and hustled out, Good grabbed Derek by the arm. "Hold on a minute, Derek. I want you to meet your new partner."

"Catherine," he called, "hold up a second."

Catherine Hunt, already on her way out of the room, turned at the door and made her way toward them. "Yes, Inspector Good?"

"Catherine, I would like you to meet Special Agent Derek James. Derek, Catherine Hunt."

Derek took Catherine's hand and shook it. Her grip was firm, unusual in a woman. Then he took in her appearance. She was stunning with her dark red shoulder-length hair and milk white complexion, but Derek's hollowed-out emotions were unreceptive to the appraisal of her assets most men would have subconsciously made. He took her hand with detached professionalism. "Pleased to meet you, Miss Hunt."

"Please," she said, "call me Catherine."

"Catherine," Brian Good continued, "is CIA. and has just returned from an assignment in Eastern Europe and the Middle East. She'll be your partner. I've already briefed her on your background and training. You'll have the next couple of days to get to know each other and get settled with the intel people and some of the special ops team. Derek, you haven't met them yet, but your special ops team is good. They're all Navy Seals, and they're going to be the tip of your lance. They can do most of the dirty work for you, should the need arise."

"You know, Brian, I don't think doing dirty work is going to be an issue," replied Derek.

"I understand, but if you get into a situation, use them, and that goes for both of you," he said, glancing at Catherine. "Your task and talents are investigative, and we don't want you in harm's way if we can avoid it. Leave the rough stuff to the pros. I have briefing packages downstairs that will supply you with all the information you'll need. These packages, by the way, are classified EYES, and they're not allowed to leave the building. As a matter of fact, they're not allowed to leave the second floor, so you'll have to memorize any information you need. You probably have lots of questions, but the brief will outline most of the procedural crap. I know this is likely a bit of a surprise for you both, especially the dual-agency teaming."

"I was aware of this operation. The president and the chief of staff told me," said Derek. He wasn't bragging; he was stating a fact.

"The president?" asked Good incredulously.

"Yes. Two days ago in California."

"Seriously," replied Good, maintaining a note of incredulity in his voice.

"Yes. I went on board Air Force One when he landed in California before I spent two days being poked and prodded in the Edwards infirmary. The president was interested in eye-witness accounts of the Santa Barbara attack. Of course, by that time there was a lot more going on than just the one attack, but the chief of staff told me about the formation of the teams, and they asked if I was interested, and here I am."

"Well then," replied Good, "let's get down to my office, and I'll give you the file with the most current information in it, and the two of you can spend a couple of hours going over it. Later on today you'll be introduced to the strike team coordinators. They're on their way in from Pensacola right now."

"I'm looking forwards to it," said Derek as the three of them grabbed an elevator for the short descent.

When the elevator doors opened on the second floor, they were met by a maelstrom of activity as people rushed up and down the corridor. A young man spied them and ran towards Goods waving a paper. "Sir, sir," he gasped, passing the paper to Good.

Good scanned the contents. "Oh shit!" he said.

August 21.
Cheyenne, Wyoming.

It had been a normal mid-week morning at the Minuteman Café on Del Range Boulevard near the Cheyenne Municipal Airport. The café was crowded with early risers there for the bacon and eggs special as well as commuters stopping in to grab a quick coffee and a pastry on their way to work. The café serviced employees from the Frontier Mall just across the road, several local industries, the airport, and the Francis E. Warren Air Force Base, home of many of the remaining Minuteman intercontinental ballistic missiles.

A long line of people waiting for take-out coffee further added to the congestion but most customers reckoned that the wait was worth it. Locals thought more of the Minuteman's coffee than they did of Starbucks', as evidenced by the virtually empty parking lot of the Starbucks nearby. If the Minuteman's parking lot had been a little less full, someone might have noticed the rusty, brown Chevy Citation that pulled into a parking spot immediately in front of the cafe's large picture windows. They might also have noticed that rather than coming in for coffee, the car's driver walked around the corner of the restaurant and climbed into a waiting van, which then drove slowly off the lot, turned east on Del Range and drove away.

A minute later, the abandoned car disappeared in a blinding blast from two hundred pounds of high explosive that blew the Minuteman Café from its foundation and slaughtered everyone inside.

August 21.
Albany, New York.

The traffic on the I-90 was typical morning rush hour stop and go where the 85 dead-ended, dumping its travellers onto the connecting interstate. A large red cube van, puffing clouds of blue smoke from a valve train that was years past its prime, pulled over directly under the overpass that brought westbound traffic from the 85 onto the 90 below, traffic that was headed for industrial and commercial areas in Albany and neighbouring Schenectady. The van's driver set his emergency flashers, climbed out and opened the vehicle's hood. Moments later a dilapidated tow truck pulled off in front of the van, and the van's driver got in. The tow truck drove off along the shoulder, passing the slow-moving commuter traffic in the 90's west bound lanes, and on reaching the Washington Avenue exit, took the ramp and disappeared into the city.

No one noticed anything unusual — not until the RDX high explosive and two and a half tons of ammonium nitrate, diesel fuel and powdered aluminum detonated. The force of the blast threw cars hundreds of feet, twisting them into unrecognizable burning scrap. It was strong enough and close enough to destroy the overpass's main structural supports so that the ramp above collapsed onto the I-90 in a rain of twisted rebar and shattered concrete.

Within the space of two hours, thirty-five other car bombs, some of them enormous, had detonated in crowded areas or beside congested highways along the eastern seaboard and in the Midwest.

Wednesday, August 21.
Fifth Street East, Cincinnati.

Officer Gordon Wojohowitz had spent eleven years on the Cincinnati police force and was still pulling traffic duty. Many in his position would have resented being in the same unit for most of their careers, but Wojohowitz was exactly where he wanted to be. He was a good cop, but his ambitions lay in other places — he was one of the best-known model railroaders in the eastern United States. His home was a wall-to-wall collection of model trains and all the paraphernalia that goes with them. Conservative estimates placed his collection at over half a million dollars, perhaps more at today's prices, but it was moot to Wojohowitz. His pay was adequate to his needs, and he would die before a single item in his collection was put on the auction block. His passion had excluded from his life many things including a wife and family, but he was content with his life even if it was not a truly happy one. In truth contentment had eluded many of his friends and fellow police officers.

He was in his patrol car, parked on the right-hand side of Fifth Street East, a one-way eastbound street in Cincinnati's downtown core, and he was about to move out after finishing a bit of paperwork. Suddenly a car, followed closely by a late-model black minivan, started a right turn the wrong way onto Fifth from Sycamore. Realizing their mistake, both cars' drivers swerved into a left-hand turn, cutting in front of other cars and setting off a concert of squealing brakes and blaring horns.

Wojohowitz checked his mirrors to see if he was clear to pull out and give chase, but oncoming traffic was thick. By the time he flicked on his emergency lights and found a hole , both vehicles had started a northbound turn onto Broadway, another one-way. Wojohowitz cut across the traffic and careened around the corner in pursuit. He saw that the van had pulled up on the right-hand side about halfway along the block. He just caught a glimpse of a dark-complexioned youth jumping into the rear seat of the accompanying car, which then sped off. A chill spread through Wojohowitz. Grabbing the mike, he broadcast his suspicions.

"Unit 324 requesting backup. A black minivan has been abandoned on Broadway between Fifth and Sixth. Driver has fled the scene in a white economy car, possibly a Nissan or Toyota. Unit 324 in pursuit." He toggled his siren and depressed the accelerator. In front of him, the traffic parted magically, giving him a free shot up Broadway after the white car.

His suspicions that the car's occupants were up to no good were confirmed as they sailed through a red light at Sixth, narrowly missing several vehicles in the intersection. He gained on them, and when he got within ten car lengths, the white car started to weave back and forth through the traffic. To Wojohowitz's horror, he saw a gun barrel poke out of the rear passenger side window. But instead of targeting the oncoming police car, the gunman started to spray the cars around it and pedestrians on the sidewalks.

Wojohowitz got back on the radio. "Shots fired, shots fired!" he screamed into the receiver. "Suspect car is firing automatic weapons into traffic!" He slammed the accelerator to the floor, aiming the car directly at the rear end of what he could now see was a Nissan Sentra.

The gunman, sensing immediate peril, changed his tactic. The rear window of the Sentra exploded as he took aim at Wojohowitz and fired through it. He was a moment too late. The bullets stitched the police car's hood, their paths diverted from their target, and across the right-hand side of the windshield.

The impact of the cruiser ramming the back of the much lighter Nissan threw the gunman off balance, and he stopped firing while the cruiser carried the smaller car along. The two cars careened into and across the New Street intersection. Suddenly the cruiser's engine seized, victim of the heavy-calibre slugs that had torn through it. The cars separated, as the Nissan accelerated away, flying into the next major intersection, at Broadway and Seventh, at almost seventy miles per hour. An eastbound straight truck was crossing on the green.

The white car, physics dictating its course despite the driver's attempts to swerve, slammed into the side of the truck just back of the cab. It slid under the truck's heavy steel chassis, a good section of the car's roof peeling back, and split open the truck's right-hand saddle tank, spewing diesel all over the road, the car and its occupants. Despite the spray of sparks as the truck dragged the small car forward, the fuel's low combustibility saved the area from conflagration.

As the truck ground to a halt, the gunman who'd been in the rear seat staggered from the wreckage and collapsed, the automatic assault rifle still in his hands. Dropping the rifle, he tried to crawl away from the wreckage, rising and then falling back to the ground as a badly shattered leg defied his adrenaline-induced attempt to flee. The car's driver had died with the impact.

Wojohowitz slammed to a halt and leapt from his crippled car, shattered glass pebbles cascading from him as he pulled his revolver from his hip. He ran toward the gunman, who scrambled crablike through the diesel fuel and debris on the pavement, blood streaming from a head wound and his left leg, which was clearly facing in the wrong direction, dragging. He was still trying to escape, but his attempt responded now to a mindless, undirected instinct. As Wojohowitz started to yell his warning to freeze, the gunman's head fell to the pavement, and with the onset of shock, he stopped moving.

Wojohowitz kicked the automatic weapon a safe distance away. He looked down at the semi-comatose man and then turned to survey the carnage that marked the white car's progress up Broadway from Fifth Street East. He took in wounded pedestrians lying on the sidewalk and cars skewed helter-skelter everywhere, many showing multiple bullet holes and some whose occupants were seriously wounded.

Then the air shimmered with a flash of light followed a moment later by an immense cracking. The explosives in the van three blocks away had ignited. The blast was powerful enough to bring down a good section of the nearest building, including a skywalk that connected it to the building opposite.

Wojohowitz stood there stunned, mouth agape, before a sight the likes of which he'd only ever seen on news reports from the Middle East. Consumed by rage, he looked down at the man at his feet and, summoning every bit of strength in his body, he kicked him. The man's hip shattered at the blow from Wojohowitz booted foot. But in his semi-conscious state, he could only groan.

There were many witnesses to this act, but not one ever complained — nor did anyone in the media or the police department when that kick, caught by a traffic camera at the intersection, was released and played again and again in the media and on the Internet. The incident's fame spread rapidly, fuelled by a revenge-hungry American population. America had its first important prisoner of the war, and its first hero.

CHAPTER 5

"The trouble is, sir, that we don't have enough available manpower on the ground," said Admiral Irving. He was seated at the conference table in the White House's underground situation room. Unlike its replica in Hollywood movies, the room had no glowing screens or noir lighting. In fact, it was bright and airy, despite lying sixty feet underground. The walls were decorated with historical paintings, a sink and buffet complete with coffee and pastries stood to one side, and as a concession to modern technology, flat screen computer monitors had been built into each place at the table. A very large flat screen TV and monitor hovered at the foot of the room next to the door, a position that afforded everyone in the room an adequate view.

Currently the image on it, and on the computer screens on the conference table, was of the continental United States. Round red circles indicated the sites of large attacks; smaller red pinpoints illustrated the locations of the car bombings.

The president sat at the head of the table, which was otherwise populated by the heads of American law enforcement and the U.S. military, several cabinet members and his own advisors.

"Iraq is a lot smaller," continued Admiral Irving, "and the armed forces have a lot more latitude for action, but we have found it almost impossible — no, actually impossible — to predict when or where terrorists will place a car bomb or stop them from doing it, and there are nowhere near the number of cars in Iraq that there are here. If we found a way to restrict car bombings, the terrorists could just change their approach and use improvised explosive devices instead. In Afghanistan and Iraq, those have ranged from donkey carcasses and other road kill packed with explosives to traffic light control boxes in the middle of intersections rigged with high explosives. Most of these are remotely activated, so the bomber just waits until a juicy target rolls by and detonates the bomb. If you think about the potential for creating these devices that exists in this country, the problem is staggering. I just don't know how we're going to get a handle on this other than tracking down the bombers and eliminating them. That's going to be a matter of good investigation techniques, not military action."

Irving sat back in his chair, his piece plainly stated.

"Mr. President, I have to agree with Admiral Irving," said FBI director Peter Archer. "We have to track down the enemy agents both here and, even more importantly, abroad who are responsible. To do that we're going to need one hell of a lot more information than we have now. In the meantime, however, a lot of our assets are tied up trying to control American citizens who are taking things into their own hands. On top of several riots, we've also had hundreds of murders, lynchings and beatings countrywide. In almost all cases the victims have been American citizens with Arab, Pakistani or Sikh backgrounds.

"These investigations are drawing away valuable assets we could use in other places. Troops could put a stop to the rioting and the mobs. I can't think of any other way to put a stop to the civil unrest. The military and National Guard has to control the populace while law enforcement goes after the bombers. I can't have valuable detectives and agents tied up investigating a bunch of hooligans who've decided to kill the local video store owner because they think he's a terrorist, not when we could be missing valuable forensics and eyewitness information. I know that local forensics investigators have been doing the best they can, but they just don't have the resources available to them that we do. The FBI has to prioritize and stay focused on just the enemy threat for the time being."

"The trouble, gentleman, is that you are asking me to suspend American freedoms, starting with the freedom of assembly," said the president.

"Mr. President," replied chief of staff Blomstrum, "we may not have any choice. In order to get a handle on this, we may have to apply full martial law, at least until we can make some headway on finding out who's behind the bombings and stop, or at least reduce, the number of attacks."

"I agree, Mr. President," interjected Admiral Irving. "A patchwork approach to the implementation of martial law is not going to work. I think most Americans are going to understand that until the emergency has passed they'll have to give up some of their freedoms. People are scared. A firm hand will dispel a lot of their fears and help quell the unrest. It will show them that we're serious about their protection."

The president sat quietly, head down, clearly reflecting on the conversation that had raged around the room for the past two hours. It all led to one conclusion, one no American president had ever had to make before on so grand a scale, and one guaranteed to become a cause célèbe among his opponents on Capitol Hill.

He looked up, a frown crossing his features. "All right, gentlemen, enforce martial law — curfews in all major cities and anywhere else necessary and," he looked directly at the directors of the CIA and FBI, "detention without charge for periods of up to a week, but no longer than a week. Do you understand?"

They nodded assent.

"Good. For now, let's wrap this up. I want you all here again in twenty-four hours. In the meantime, gentlemen, get me the pricks responsible for this."

August 22.
University Hospital, Cincinnati.

Awae Doloh woke racked with pain. Doloh was twenty-three years old, a Muslim from southern Cambodia. He had entered the world of extremism when a teenager, recruited by the radical Mujahedeen Islam Pattoni, a group intent on killing its way to a free Muslim state in southern Thailand. By the time he was nineteen, he'd been recruited by Jenmaah Islamiyah, an Asia-wide terrorist organization with strong ties to al Qaeda and Osama bin Laden's International Islamic Front. He spent time fighting in Afghanistan, where he was selected to train to enter the USA as a Philippine university student in an agricultural program.

His first attack had gone terribly wrong only in that he'd been captured. His handlers would be more than pleased with his actions, which had killed forty-seven people, destroyed most of a high-rise office complex and closed down the Cincinnati core for hours.

His head throbbed, and the nerve endings from his waist down screamed at the traumas they had endured. Unable to move more, he turned his head slowly, taking in his surroundings. As his eyes focused, the brilliance of the room made his head pound, and he felt as if his forehead would split open. The source of the agonizing light was a standard fluorescent fixture over his bed and a window that, from his vantage point, showed only sky. Once he'd come fully to his senses, he lifted his head enough to see that he was naked and firmly strapped to a hospital bed. For good measure, both his wrists were handcuffed to the bed's stout side rails.

With a surge of panic, he realized he was captive, and the events of the day before swam back into his mind. He remembered the flashing lights and police siren as his partner screamed at him to get into the Sentra. They left the bomb-laden van as planned and hurtled off in an attempt to elude the police car that had pulled out after them. He remembered the feel and sound of the AK-47 roaring in the car's close confines as he fired indiscriminately in an attempt to distract the police, perhaps make them stop the pursuit. He remembered the incredulous looks of the people who saw him fire. A vignette flashed into his memory of an elderly gentleman looking down at the fountain of blood that gushed from his stomach, just pierced by a heavy slug from the assault gun.

He remembered nothing of the accident or how he came to be in this bed. He felt hollow as he realized that unlike his fellow glorious freedom fighters spread out across the United States, he'd failed in his mission to avoid capture and now he was powerless even to take his own life as he'd been instructed and trained to do.

A woman's face appeared in the small rectangular window in the hospital room door and then disappeared. Moments later two large men, both wearing dark suits, strode into the room. The taller of the pair took a position at the foot of the bed while the other man, shorter but stocky, pulled the visitor's chair next to the bed and, with a flourish, spun it around so the chair back was facing Doloh. The man was in his mid-fifties and had dark brown hair, greying at the temples, and a relatively unlined face — interesting looking if not actually handsome. He swung one leg over the chair, saddle-style, crossed his arms and rested them on the chair back. Then he stared at the captive for a minute.

Doloh steadfastly refused to meet his gaze, but he couldn't help the occasional glance that flicked nervously at the imposing figure beside his bed. His apprehension was compounded by total helplessness and immense pain. He'd received cursory medical care, but his badly shattered leg had not been repaired or put in a cast, and he'd not been administered any painkillers.

Finally the man at his side spoke. "Well, son," he said softly, "you are in a world of shit, aren't you? I'm not even going to pretend to be your friend, but I will give you some friendly advice. You are going to tell us everything you know one way or the other. My advice is that you just tell us what we want to know, now, with no fuss or bother. If you don't, then what you're feeling now won't add up to a hill of beans compared to what you're going to feel. Do you understand?"

Doloh looked away, gazing out the hospital window at the leaden skies that promised rain. He missed the man's gently reaching over. He did not miss the excruciating pain as the man forcefully poked his finger into the swollen and discoloured swelling over Doloh's shattered hip. Doloh screamed at the bolt of pain.

"That, son," the man said, rising from the chair, "is just so you get my point. My friend and I are going to give you a little time to reflect. Say half an hour?" He checked his wristwatch. "And then we're going to come back and continue our little chat." He reached down and shook Doloh's broken leg on his way out, another blistering jolt.

The two men left Doloh alone to stare at the large clock hanging on the wall. Suddenly all the lessons learned from his handlers and spiritual leaders about Allah's blessings and the strength he could derive from his cause paled in comparison to the agony he felt and the remorseless sweep of the clock's second hand.

August 23.
On board a Cessna Citation, midway between Washington and Cincinnati.

Derek glanced at Catherine, who sat across from him on the small jet. She was busy with a sheaf of papers, mostly reports on the bombings that had occurred over the last two days. She was poring over them in the hopes that some of the attacks' signatures would correspond to techniques used in other places in the world and reveal something about the enemy's identity.

Derek had very little to say to Catherine. She was certainly very businesslike, which made it easy for Derek to interact with her with a minimum of effort. She seemed to have no need of small talk, preferring to busy herself with paperwork and research. That suited Derek well. He thought Catherine would make a good partner, but he was in no way interested in socializing or having to pretend interest in anything but the task at hand.

The pair had been assigned to fly to Cincinnati to take part in the interrogation of the terrorist in custody there. While the young man apparently had no specific knowledge about the organizers of these attacks, he was proving to be a wealth of information on some of their procedures and was giving insight into how the attackers got their explosives and firearms. Under questioning, he'd already revealed a good portion of his background and the organizations to which he'd belonged in Asia. It came as no surprise that Islamic fundamentalists were behind the attacks, but it had come as some surprise that he and his partner had belonged to a movement dedicated to the creation of an Islamic state in Thailand and in other countries in Southeast Asia.

Derek was lost in thought, many of them about Vanessa. He'd made numerous calls, sometimes using his position in the FBI as a wedge to get information, but to date he still had no idea when Vanessa's body would be released to her family or when or how she would be brought back to Washington. He'd spoken to her mother and brother several times over the last few days and knew that they were getting even less information than he was. They were grief-stricken over Vanessa's death, but neither of them blamed Derek. Vanessa's father, on the other hand, had answered the phone once and, on hearing Derek's voice, had very abruptly hung up.

He'd never liked Derek or what Derek did for a living very much, despite, or perhaps because of, the fact he'd been a Washington PD officer for twenty-eight years before his retirement. On the odd occasions when Vanessa had asked Derek to attend a family function in Virginia, where they now lived, some very icy silences had occurred when Derek and her father found themselves in a room alone. Derek assumed that now the old man was blaming him for Vanessa's death. But he couldn't possibly blame Derek any more than Derek blamed himself.

The Citation bucked as it hit some clear-air turbulence. A pile of papers Catherine had piled on the seat beside her slid to the floor. "Oh shit," she exclaimed, bending to pick them up.

"How's it going?" asked Derek as he unbuckled his seat belt to help her retrieve the papers that had slid under the seat.

"So far there doesn't seem to be any consistent pattern," she replied. "The techniques, explosives and procedures they're using are wildly different, and some materials may have been foraged for locally, while others are imported and have definite military origins.

"Forensics found chemical markers at some of the blast sites indicating domestic materials, and some of those have been traced to small amounts of explosives that have been disappearing from building sites and mining companies for over two years. Other bombs are homemade concoctions of ammonium nitrate, diesel, powdered aluminum and a number of other easily available and widely used materials, and some are high-grade military explosives from God knows where.

"The good news is that they may have blown their more exotic weapons in the first day's attacks. There hasn't been any bio or chemical attack since then. It's still pretty early to tell, but my guess is that for the most part they've been scavenging the country for their materials. Let's face it, you can get pretty well anything you want here, and a lot of the people selling are not curious or squeamish about how it will be used as long as they make a buck."

"What about the stolen explosives?" asked Derek. "I wonder if there are any leads?"

"These reports are pretty sketchy," replied Catherine. "But I doubt the investigations went much beyond local law enforcement and these reports filed federally. Thousands of pounds of explosives are stolen every year, and only a few hundred pounds are usually recovered. God knows where most of it ends up, but when you consider that a few years ago we lost over 350 tons of explosives in Iraq, where we're supposed to be paying attention, the disappearance of small amounts here wouldn't make much of a blip on the radar screen — not until now at any rate."

CHAPTER 6

August 24.
People's Liberation Army Naval Base, Zhanjiang, People's Republic of China.

The flotilla of destroyers and support ships was just slipping out of the harbour at Zhanjiang at quarter speed. Rear Admiral Hu Xiaofeng stood on the port bridge wing taking in the scene of sampans, ferries, tenders and tugs scurrying to get out of the way of the ten ships of his fleet. Most of his fleet was composed of the latest in missile and attack destroyers, the largest being the 8,800-ton Sovremenny-class destroyer that served as his flagship. Accompanying her were three more Sovremenny-class ships, three smaller 7,700-ton Chinese-designed and built Shenzen missile destroyers, two Jiangwei frigates and a Weishanhu supply ship.

Not attached to his flotilla, but spread out before it, was a group of nuclear-powered 093 attack subs and Ming- and Song-class diesel attack submarines. Over the last three days, these boats had slipped out of their camouflaged sub pens fully submerged. Although the submarines would eventually share the same patrol zones as his flotilla, the undersea predators would follow independent and solitary courses that had been set to avoid detection by American satellites and, more importantly, by the American attack boats that often lurked in the seas around Zhanjiang.

Hu was terrified of the American subs. He knew their capabilities, and he was also acutely aware that the Americans had been playing cat and mouse with the Russians for almost half a century while the Chinese submarine force, despite its Russian advisors, was still wet behind the ears, with very little experience in the arts of undersea deception. He also knew that a lot of the sophisticated electronic equipment on both his ships and the Chinese submarines was notoriously prone to failure, and he was not very confident in his fleet's ability to defend itself against or even to detect the U.S. hunter killers if they were intent on causing him harm.

Unfortunately, his superiors were blinded to the inadequacies of the flotilla's electronic warfare suites and instead enthusiastically denied that the new Chinese navy was no match for U.S. forces, especially the ones Hu was likely to meet up with in the area of responsibility he'd been assigned in the Persian Gulf. His steaming orders were to take the fleet to the new Chinese base in Pakistani waters, the Gwadar deepwater port in Baluchistan.

The Chinese had spent billions of dollars preparing this base so they would have a strategic foothold close to the oil reserves of the Gulf. It existed ostensibly to supply Pakistan with a deepwater container and oil depot, but its design accommodated the PLA Navy quite well and they kept a continuous but so far low-key presence there. China's original intention had been to a build a base in Iran, but after the American invasion and occupation of Iraq, it was decided that the U.S. presence would render a large base in the Gulf too difficult to defend from surveillance or attack.

The base in Baluchistan — close to the border between Iran and Pakistan — was almost as convenient and was well suited to extend the PLAN's influence into the Indian Ocean as well as the Persian Gulf. It was the final piece in China's "string of pearls" strategy, a string of strategic bases across the bottom of Asia and leading to the Middle East. Of these, Gwadar was the latest and most important. It gave the Chinese a base from which to observe and perhaps one day control the Persian Gulf as well as providing a convenient point from which to supply thousands of Chinese troops and armed civilian support workers in East Africa , something of a logistical nightmare from mainland China.

Hu had visited the base before and hated it. The location was a small peninsula, which jutted into the Arabian Sea southeast of the Strait of Hormuz. It was desolate and blisteringly hot. The neighbouring town of Gwadar was a primitive fishing village. The impoverished town was populated by various Muslim factions, most of them from Iran, and smaller groups of Hindus and Sikhs. These diverse and largely antagonistic factions agreed on one thing only — their resentment of the Chinese construction workers and naval personnel who had flooded the area. Hu had experienced enough discipline problems with bored and listless crew during his last visit, when he'd had only one ship to worry about. Now, with a fleet and hundreds of additional personnel, most of whom would be for the most part restricted to base in the punishing heat, morale and discipline were both going to be a challenge.

Hu Xiaofeng did not fully understand nor had he been made privy to why the PLA flotilla was being rushed to the Gulf, but his unvoiced opinion was, considering the crisis in the USA, he might be steaming into a hornets' nest of U.S. military might in the Gulf, one that was on full alert and feeling belligerent as well. He secretly prayed that this sailing was just an ill-timed strategic exercise, one that saner heads in Beijing would cancel while his fleet was en route.

August 24.
Outskirts of Fuzhou, Fujian Province, China.

Commander Tang Xu of the People's Liberation Army stood up from his desk, stretched and pulled his uniform jacket from the back of the worn wooden chair where he had draped it. His office and several others were perched in the rafters of a massive dockside warehouse, overlooking a scene of controlled chaos below. Dozens of technicians and supply personnel milled about, servicing a host of air-cushion landing craft in dingy grey camouflage packed into the huge building. These were small ten-man amphibious assault craft, but outside the warehouse, eight immense Zubr air-cushion landing craft sat covered in camouflage that was designed to persuade the American satellites above they were eight small warehouses. Other medium-sized hovercraft and amphibious assault landing craft were hidden in another twenty buildings that made up this supposedly civilian cargo-handling port facility.

No expense had been spared trying to deceive U.S. intelligence gathering while a massive amphibious assault force was assembled up and down the Chinese coastline opposite the renegade province of Taiwan. The plan had been gathering steam for five years, and military assets ranging from the huge Yuting and Yukan amphibious assault ships down to the ten-man landing craft and hovercraft waited for the day when Taiwan would, if needs be forcibly, returned to the fold. If not for the protection the Americans gave the island, that would have happened many years ago. Now, ironically, with American technological and industrial assistance, China was fast becoming powerful enough to do as it pleased within its sphere of influence, a sphere that included Taiwan as well as contested areas such as the Spratley Islands, claimed by both the Chinese and the detested Vietnamese, among others.

Xu was a rabid supporter of China's emerging military power and global influence. He was proud that China, long perceived as an unsophisticated pseudo-communistic feudal society was now a world leader that many Third World countries looked to as a partner in bringing down American imperialism. One of Xu's tasks was to interpret satellite photographs. These photographs came not just from military birds but also from agricultural and civilian satellites, some of whose images he'd sourced on the Internet. His job entailed examining photograph after photograph of camouflaged installations and equipment whose detection by the Americans might give away China's intentions. The moment he determined there was a chance of discovery, an alarm was sent out and the problem rectified. Even equipment as large as landing ships was cleverly camouflaged as civil shipping while civilian ships were dressed up in cardboard and plywood to serve as military decoys in an endless shell game aimed at concealing the gradual buildup of a huge concentration of military might.

In a world where it was assumed that American satellites could read the address on an envelope tossed onto the top of a heap in a garbage can, Xu's job was difficult and stressful. Even worse, he would never know whether the Americans had uncovered some or all of the deceptions despite his best efforts.

Xu descended the steep stairs to the concrete warehouse floor below. Mixing in with the workers, many of whom were leaving for the day, he walked to the door, where guards made sure that anyone entering or leaving had the correct papers and was dressed in civilian rather than military clothing. Xu, the originator of the rule, pulled a long grey shop coat over his uniform. While most of those coming and going did not effect military dress, wearing instead the blue or light green clothing of warehouse workers, he could not bring himself to run his command while not in uniform.

August 24.
University Hospital, Cincinnati.

Derek stood at the foot of the bed, staring at the captive. The young killer had received medical attention and now laid in a cast that extended from his belly, down one leg to his ankle. He was covered in cuts and bruises and one side of his face was badly swollen and discoloured. His injuries were all the result of the collision with the truck and the kick that had shattered his hip bone.

His interrogators had left no further physical damage but had managed to drain him of every scrap of important information that he knew after only a few hours of questioning. Far from a battle-hardened jihadist, his inquisitors had found a frightened and unworldly young man who'd quickly succumbed to their threats and his own fear and pain. It was good luck, really, to have had this one survive. Derek was under no illusion that others when captured would crack so easily. The CIA interrogator who'd grilled the young man offered the opinion that Awae Doloh wouldn't have been so easily broken if he'd been from the Middle East, where hatred was a way of life and instilled from the cradle to the grave.

Doloh had found his jihad in his late teens, with the temporary passion that blooms in the young but is quickly left behind as maturity and responsibility start to steer the course. The southern provinces of Thailand were only now becoming a hotbed of Islamic hatred, spurred mostly by agitators from other Islamic countries.

Thailand did not as yet have the deep generational hatred that was a fact of daily life in the Middle East. The agitators were working very hard to change that.

Derek turned to Catherine, who stood a few steps behind him. "Well, now we've seen the enemy, let's go and find out what they've managed to coax out of him."

A heavy-set nurse who looked more like a prison matron than an angel of mercy escorted the them from the room. She closed the door behind them and locked it with a key that swung from a lanyard at her belt.

Catherine nodded at the two uniformed guards, armed with automatic weapons, who sat on either side of the door. Her nod was not returned by the Special Forces men. They were bored stiff by the guard duty they'd drawn but still regarded each visitor to the injured terrorist as possibly hostile.

A few rooms down the hall, a meeting room had been set up. Aside from Awae Doloh, the floor was devoid of patients and medical staff. Derek and Catherine entered and were greeted by the two men who'd busily pumped out what little valuable information Doloh contained.

"So the world still thinks this creep is in a coma?" asked Catherine of the men, who were seated at a round table that dominated the small room.

"Yes, ma'am," replied one of them, rising. "And in a day or so, the world will hear that he succumbed to his injuries. "We'll ship him off to a secure detention facility on a restricted base in Nevada so no one will be the wiser."

"Good," replied Derek. "The less the enemy knows about what we've found out, the more chance they won't go to ground."

"I'm Bruce Edwards. This is Hank Rain," said the CIA interrogator, the same man who'd given Doloh's hip a poke and his leg a gentle shake the day before.

Rain rose from his chair and offered his hand to Derek. After a couple of minutes of introduction, the four sat down together at the table. "Can I get you a coffee or a soda, ma'am?" asked Rain.

"I'm fine," replied Catherine. "But thank you, and please, call me Catherine." She didn't want to sound rude, but "ma'am" was what people called her mother. She had a little trouble being called that herself.

"I'll take a coffee," said Derek.

"Sure, I'll have the fixings brought up. You sure?" he asked again of Catherine.

Derek twigged that Rain might be trying to make a little headway with Catherine. He doubted the man knew that Catherine was not only CIA but likely outranked him as well. He probably thought she was FBI, since she was introduced as Derek's partner.

"No, I'm sure," she replied.

Rain stepped out and Bruce Edwards began his report.

"So, when we got started, we had a few minutes of 'God is great' and 'Allah will protect me' before he decided that telling us his life story might be a better idea than waiting for heavenly help. I've never broken anyone so fast, and at first I was a little suspicious of how easy it was, but soon it became pretty clear that this guy was trained as a foot soldier. He's not too smart, but luckily for us, he has a good imagination. He spent a lot of time imagining all of the things I said we were going to do to him."

"So what have we found out?" asked Derek.

Edwards fiddled with a rubber band, expanding and contracting it between two fingers as he replied. "Well, he doesn't seem to know very much about the command structure. The guy that died in the crash was taking the orders, but Doloh did tell us that the instructions came by laptop computer. That's how they get their weapons and other resources. They receive the locations via the Internet and then pick up the goods."

"Do you believe him when he says doesn't know how to locate or decode messages?" asked Catherine.

"We're not sure. He's been singing like a canary though," said Rain, who'd returned to the room.

"Yes, but in my experience, singing like a canary can cover up a lot of what you really know," said Catherine.

"We haven't finished with him, yet," said Edwards.

"I'm sure you haven't, but remember, gloves are off. Do whatever it takes to wring everything out of the prick. I don't care if it kills him," said Derek quietly.

"Understood," said Rain.

"So what else have you got?" asked Catherine.

"They'd both been in the country for about six weeks and arrived together as students," continued Edwards. "Immigration says they entered on student visas and their papers described them as Buddhists from northern Thailand, but it seems they're both from the southern Muslim-dominated province."

"Turns out Doloh is from a good home," added Rain. "We've checked on his family, and they're upper-middle class. His father's a businessman, owns a string of small grocery stores, and they're not by any stretch fundamentalists. The Thais are still trying to dig up more for us. The dead one was known to them. They identified him immediately as a small-time organizer and troublemaker, and he's on their wanted list. Doloh was known to associate with fundamentalists and was a member of a pretty radical mosque but he isn't wanted for anything over there."

"What about their computer?" asked Catherine.

"We have it," replied Rain. "It was in the trunk of the car. It's pretty busted up, but the hard drive and everything else is just fine."

"And there's not much on it," said Edwards. "It seems that they spent a lot of time cruising porn sites though. It's full of porn-site cookies."

"What about email?" asked Derek.

"No email. In fact it wasn't even set up to receive email," replied Rain.

"So that means," said Catherine, "that they're getting their information from the Internet somehow. Maybe message boards or on some website?"

"That's what we're thinking," said Rain, "but aside from a lot of cookies from the porn sites, there aren't many visits anywhere else — at least anywhere that left indicators.

The techies are all over it, though," said Edwards. "If there's anything buried on the hard drive, they'll find it."

"Clever and effective," interjected Derek. "With disguised sites putting out coded orders, we can't shut them down, and the command structure can remain completely hidden. Plus, without email the soldiers can't give anything away."

"Or ask questions," said Catherine.

"Well, that's something else we've discovered," said Edwards. "These guys were getting info on how and where to pick up their supplies, but their list of targets was self-generated. Doloh says that he and his buddy got to decide targeting themselves, and they were free to wander wherever they wanted. Doloh says they were trained to deal with target selection and maximize civilian casualties."

"I can't believe the strikes on the West Coast and the refineries were left up to small isolated cells," said Derek. "They were just too well planned and implemented."

"That's my thinking, too," replied Edwards. "I think the first day was planned a long time in advance. All of the attacks since then have been small potatoes by comparison, and they've all been pretty standard terrorist fare like car bombings and machine gunning. The first day, almost all of the attacks were huge or, if not huge, particularly chilling. Psychologically, that set up the nation to expect the worst. Continuing the campaign using small teams and standard tactics just keeps the whole county off balance and people close to panic. Hell, in some cities the damage hasn't been caused by terrorists at all. It's been rioting locals or gangs of thugs burning down people's homes, businesses and mosques. In some places, it's made the Mississippi burnings and the KKK look like a pack of rank amateurs."

"Martial law should put a stop to that, for the most part," said Derek. "But it's also going to make it harder for the terrorists to move around."

"Well, that's a good thing, isn't it?" asked Rain.

"Not necessarily," said Catherine. "It will make it a lot harder for us to find them if they're forced into being even more careful."

"And we're going to have a hard enough time as it is," replied Derek.

August 24.
Ta'if, Saudi Arabia.

"Yes, it seems we have our first casualties," said Muhammad al-Munajjid to his visitor as he poured Shaye Bi Na' Na, a heavily sweetened green tea with mint, from an elegant and ornate Turkish teapot of solid gold. He expertly poured the brew from a great height above cups the size of shot glasses and finished with a flourish, secretly pleased at his own prowess. Al-Munajjid was dressed in simple Western garb — a turtleneck shirt and slacks — and wore an expensive pair of Italian sandals.

His guest, a tall gentleman with a noble bearing, rose from his place on a Western-style couch. He wore the traditional clothing of the Bedouin, the long flowing black robe called a bisht, and a ghutra, the white head dress, with a dark green and beautifully ornamented agal, or head band, adorning it. His bearing and posture gave away what his simple nomadic dress did not. He was a man used to giving orders and having them obeyed. That he met with al-Munajjid alone and in such familial surroundings bespoke al-Munajjid's standing in the underworld of the far-flung and populous Saudi nobility.

"Are there consequences?" the man asked.

"I shouldn't think so. One was reported dead at the scene, and the other was in a coma and then died in hospital. Their bodies will give up nothing, and there won't be enough clues in their belongings to reveal anything other than information we don't care about," replied al-Munajjid.

"I hope you're right. If the Americans get their hands on any of your valiant fighters and manage to extract information of note, things could go badly for you. Your 'new friends' would be the first to abandon you."

"I'm sure they would, but I have little to worry about. Virtually none of the men in America can offer much of value, and the Americans' interrogation techniques are soft and no match for the bravery of my soldiers. Their laws are weak and not suited to breaking men of spirit. Who can blame them. After all, they can only judge others by how they are themselves, and they have become soft and fat, accustomed to letting their machines doing the killing for them. They have forgotten what another man's blood dripping from their fingers can do to loosen his tongue."

"I will meet with my cousins," said the gentleman, "and express to them your confidence in this matter. If all goes according to plan, we shall soon be able to embark on our next joint venture and sweep from power those in our government who would still support the Americans. Then we will be free to aid our Sunni brothers in Iraq without risk of American retribution."

"I fear the Americans are finding themselves far too busy to meddle in our affairs any longer," said al-Munajjid smiling.

The gentleman drained the tiny cup of the strongly scented tea, pulled back the voluminous sleeve of his robe and glanced at his expensive Cartier watch. "I must go," he said. "I do not want to be late to my next meeting. There is much to do over the next few weeks and too few with the stomach to do it. I should not like to show disrespect to those who have the stomach."

August 24.
Scottsdale, Arizona.

Ashaq Mohammed and Khalid Alawasat sat patiently in their beat-up Honda Civic, impatiently waiting for the moment they would strike. The temperature on the retail strip of downtown Scottsdale had already soared to the high eighties despite the fact that it was only eight thirty in the morning. The temperature bothered neither man terribly. Both hailed from the searing wastes of Somalia where they'd led similar lives as youths, reluctantly serving the soldiers of warlords in the region and then enthusiastically fighting for the Islamic Courts Union.

The Union was an extremist Islamic group intent on taking over Somalia. They waged a fierce see-saw war against the Somali government as well as the warlords. Mohammed was recruited when he was just eight years old by a raiding party of seven men, underlings of a local warlord. They'd slaughtered almost everyone in Mohammed's village over the age of fifteen, including his mother, father, brother and two sisters. Before they killed them, the soldiers used his two sisters and several other girls in the village for some brutal entertainment. Mohammed had been forced to watch. As he tried to run to his sister's aid, he was beaten down and left in the dirt unconscious. Those that died that day were the more fortunate.

But five children survived, Mohammed among them. They were press-ganged and hauled from their homes. Mohammed's first duties were sexual, pleasuring the sadistic soldiers of the raiding party, who beat, robbed and killed their way across the destitute countryside, keeping only what they deemed valuable and laying waste to the rest. He also had to fetch water, wash their clothing and prepare their food, little of which he got to share. He was in all things their slave. After years of physical and mental abuse, he finally began to have his tormentors' trust, received his first firearm and was instructed in its use. He practiced for two weeks until he was sure of his own proficiency. When he was slapped in the head and scolded for wasting ammunition, he practiced with imaginary bullets.

One very early morning while Mohammed's captors lay sleeping around the remains of a small campfire, he found his revenge. He turned his weapon, an old British 303, on the men who'd made his life a living hell, men who were convinced he now shared their ambitions. He'd hidden well his seething hatred, which boiled from him now like pus from a long-infected wound. After killing four of the men and severely wounding and then mutilating the other three with a machete fashioned from the leaf spring of a truck, he fled into the wastes, headed for Mogadishu.

In Mogadishu he was taken in by a militia unit of the Islamic Courts Union. Rather than brutalizing him, they treated him well, fed him, clothed him, schooled him in sharia law and indoctrinated him in the ways of Islamic fundamentalism. When Mogadishu fell back into the hands of what he was told was a U.S.-backed Somali government, Mohammed fled westward to Kenya with a new friend, another Somali named Khalid Alawasat. They managed to slip past Kenyan troops, who'd attempted to seal the border, and made their way to Wajir in the east. Near the Dadaab refuge camp, they were taken in by a recruiter from a Kenyan-based Muslim organization with ties to al Qaeda. After months of hard training and instruction, the two had entered the United States, posing as Kenyan students taking economics at the University of Phoenix.

Both had just enough education and economic knowledge drummed into them to answer questions that might be asked by Immigration officers or other American authorities. Their thick accents and halting English were also considered satisfactory and to be all they would need to convince U.S. authorities of their bona fides as upper-middle-class Kenyans looking for an expensive American education.

This morning in the scintillating heat of Scottsdale, they were both dressed casually in T-shirts sporting NBA logos, stylish shorts, sneakers and baseball caps worn backwards. There was nothing furtive or suspicious about them as they sat drinking coffee in the family restaurant parking lot — certainly nothing that would cause a passerby to wonder what lay under the blanket in the back seat.

Checking his cheap digital Timex, Alawasat opened the car door and threw his cup of coffee, still half full, on the ground. Mohammed crumpled his empty cup and tossed it out the car window. Putting the car into gear, he drove onto the road and north to their destination just three blocks away. Mohammed checked his rear-view and nodded to Alawasat, who undid his seat belt and pulled the blanket from the Kalashnikov assault rifle and a string of hand grenades. He slid the rifle from the back seat, careful to keep it low to avoid anyone seeing it. After placing it, muzzle forward, on the floor in front him, he lifted the hand grenades and cradled them in his lap. Earlier that morning, he'd wired the six high-explosive fragmentation grenades together and wired their pins as well so that one pull would arm all of them and they could be tossed as a group.

Mohammed drove carefully. Neither man was a good driver, but Mohammed was marginally better than Alawasat. Their experience and training before arriving in the United States had been limited to a few hours on a beaten-up Hilux Toyota pickup in a desolate area of Kenya, so they found the traffic in Scottsdale and Phoenix to be especially intimidating. They were painfully cautious because their forged international driving permits would not stand up to the close scrutiny attendant on an accident or serious traffic violation.

Pulling into the left lane, Mohammed maintained a steady speed, a little under the limit. Ahead on the left-hand side was a busy driveway full of SUVs and minivans — mothers delivering their children to the Middleton Primary School summer daycare. He turned into the fray, carefully easing his way through the small children, mothers and daycare workers who streamed along the drive.

On reaching the school's jammed walkway, Mohammed stopped. He reached over and took the grenades from Alawasat, opened his door and stood, pulling the pins as he did so. Then, with a practised overhand, he tossed the grenades in an arc above the heads of the small crowd and toward the school's front door. Then he ducked below the car.

The grenades bounced off the shoulder of one woman, who yelped in surprise and pain. They hit the ground and slid a couple of feet. Only one woman, who'd once served in the military, knew immediately what they were. She turned, gathering up her eight-year-old daughter, and started to run, screaming a warning as she did so. Everyone else stood watching her, stunned and unsure how to react. The grenades exploded in a ragged howl, spraying blistering metal fragments that cut down everyone within thirty feet and injured, maimed or killed dozens of other people farther away with their windmilling shrapnel.

Alawasat, who had ducked below the Civic's window frame, opened his door and leapt from the car, Kalashnikov in hand and opening up on those lucky enough to have survived the grenades. He sprayed everyone within three hundred and sixty degrees as he walked around the car, changing magazines twice before jumping back into the passenger seat. Over three dozen men, women and children lay on the grass and driveway, felled by the blast and the hammering assault gun.

Other victims, many with blood streaming from their wounds, lay on the lawn in shock or ran about in confusion.

Mohammed pushed the accelerator to the floor, roaring across the yard and fishtailing inexpertly onto the road. He followed a much-practised escape route, driving quickly but not so quickly as to exceed his skills or raise attention. The car wound through subdivisions and down laneways before reaching a small shopping mall with a self-serve car wash. Mohammed parked the Honda beside the wash, and leaving the assault rifle behind, the two walked quickly to a waiting Pontiac Sunbird.

In the distance they could hear the wail of multiple sirens. Twenty minutes later they were on the highway and well out of Scottsdale, just passing Cave Creek on their way north. As Mohammed drove, Alawasat pecked on a laptop, surveying several pages of porn site advertising he'd downloaded the day before and making rough notes about a few that interested him. They had both changed into slacks, white shirts and ties. Carefully laid on the back seat to avoid wrinkling were their blazers, each emblazoned with the crest of a well-known cricket club in Kenya. The Sunbird itself carried a prominent U of P sticker on the rear window.

The pair were going to spend the weekend in Sedona and then return to Phoenix, just two good students having fun during summer break — until they chose their next target. Over the weekend, they would use the Holiday Inn's wireless computer service to access various porn sites Alawasat was now researching from his download. He'd glean from them the location of their next weapons' cache and make a reference to it in the margin of one of his school notebooks. By training, any notes during decoding would be made in water-soluble fine point marker. When he was finished, he'd soak the pages in the sink, inspect them and, satisfied the soluble ink scribbling was ruined, flush the notepaper down the toilet for good measure.

By the end of the weekend, they'd be directed to an online blog and learn the location of their next weapons' cache and its contents. With that knowledge, they'd start planning their next attack.

CHAPTER 7

August 24.
The Oval Office, the White House, Washington DC.

"We've gotten lucky, sir," said Dan Blomstrum to the president. "Phoenix PD found the car the terrorists used, and they were videotaped getting into a small dark-coloured late-model domestic, maybe a Chev or a Pontiac. The camera that caught them was a good distance away, inside a ma-and-pa convenience store, so the image isn't great and it's in black and white, but they think it can be digitally enhanced so we can at least pin down the make of the car and the licence number."

"Good," replied the president. "What else has been done?"

"Phoenix law enforcement and the National Guard have set up extra checkpoints in and around the city, but with the National Guard watching so many facilities and them and the police trying to maintain order, they're not able to put as many personnel on it as they'd like. They can keep up pressure for a while, but eventually they're going to get pretty tired. One of the problems is the sheer volume of traffic they have to monitor."

"Mr. President," interjected Admiral Irving, "I think we're going to have to put a ban on travel, at least non-essential."

"Just what the hell are we going to classify as non-essential," retorted Bill Carver. "The press are going to scream bloody murder."

"Bill, at this point, we don't have the luxury of worrying about media reaction," said the president.

"I think," said Irving, "in light of the Middleton attack, we should close schools across the nation, at least until we have the situation under control. I'm thinking children's activities like after-school lessons, clubs and sports should likewise be suspended. That'll take a lot of unnecessary traffic off the road. We should also order theatres and night clubs closed for the duration."

"Oh, that's just getting better and better," moaned Carver.

"Bill, he's right," said Blomstrum. "We're fighting a war on American soil against what I hope to hell is a foreign enemy. The American people might be a little spoiled, but they're just going to have to understand that these measures are being taken to shorten the duration of the emergency and defeat the terrorists."

"Order all unnecessary travel banned," said the President. "If people aren't going to work or shopping for food or on a health-related errand or appointment, then they'd better have a damned good excuse to be out and about. We'll have to publish guidelines and give people numbers to call for clarification."

"What's the penalty going to be?" asked Carver.

"Immediate seizure of their vehicle. We can impound them until the emergency is over," answered Irving. "My people worked this up, and we can store seized cars in school grounds and on sports fields, which won't be in use anyway."

"That's simple and elegant," said Blomstrum. "If they get their cars impounded, they've only got themselves to blame."

"So," Blomstrum finished, "that should rap things up for now."

"Just one more item," said Irving.

"Yes, admiral?" said the president.

"Mr. President, satellite intelligence as well as some of our assets in the South China Sea have reported a strong Chinese flotilla headed into the Indian Ocean. Nine warships supported by a tender. This force comprises quite a few capable destroyers and destroyer escorts, and ahead of them, we think, are an unknown number of diesel and atomic subs."

"Oh shit. Just what we need, the bloody Chinese acting up," said the president.

"Yes, sir. We're not positive, but they could be headed for the Persian Gulf," said Irving.

"What would they want there?" asked Blomstrum.

"They might be tempted to take advantage of our present situation, especially if they think it weakens our resolve internationally, sir. This might be a show of force with plans on using Gwadar, their new deepwater harbour in Pakistan. Until now, they've kept their official naval presence there to a minimum, maintaining the myth that they built it to aid the Pakistani economy, but with a naval force of this strength based there, they could pose a serious threat to traffic in the Strait of Hormuz."

"What can we do about it?" asked the president.

"I think we should beef up our assets both in the Persian Gulf and the Arabian Sea. We can shadow the Chinese force with elements of the Pacific fleet. Our thinking is that a carrier task force on their heels would put them in their place. If it were me, I'd think twice before I did anything stupid with a carrier load of F-18 Hornets or Strike Fighters milling about over my head. At the same time, we already have two Virginia-class hunter killers, the Virginia and the Texas, in place. One is shadowing the flotilla, and the other, we believe, is well ahead and in the baffles of a Chinese nuclear boat."

"In the baffles?" asked Carver.

"It describes the position a sub assumes behind another sub to avoid detection," Irving clarified. "Most subs can't detect something following immediately behind."

"Well, that about wraps it up," said the president, looking at his watch. "Admiral, stay on top of this situation, but remember, it's a sideshow compared to our other problems right now. Worst comes to worst, I'll give the Chinese premier a call and have a little heart-to-heart. The Chinese don't have the guts for confrontation so a few well-worded concerns should convince them that trying to take advantage of our present situation would not be prudent."

August 24.
Over Virginia.

The twin-engined King Air had been chartered by the government to transport officials quickly and safely from city to city on the eastern seaboard. Commercial and private flights were still not allowed over the continental United States, with the exception of emergency rescues and mercy flights, and even those had to have FAA permission and dial a special squawk code on their transponders. Legal flights were continuously monitored by air traffic controllers who for the first time in their careers had very little else to do. Failing to get permission for a flight could result in an immediate attack from air force, naval or Marine fighter aircraft that loitered thousands of feet above and whose pilots were not in the mood to give anyone the benefit of the doubt.

The King Air was descending from twelve thousand feet and starting its approach into Dulles International Airport, taking Derek and Catherine back to FBI headquarters. Derek gazed out the window distractedly, watching the lush Virginia landscape below roll past. He was weary from lack of sleep. Turning in early the night before, he'd fallen asleep the instant his head hit the pillow, but at one thirty he was jolted from sleep by a nightmare. By three in the morning, he'd given up trying to sleep and was watching television. All that was offered, aside from infomercials, on the three channels available on the motel's beaten-up TV was a poorly scripted and even more poorly acted early-fifties detective drama that proved inadequate to the task of distracting him from the horrors that raced through his mind.

Catherine, in the room next to his, had no such trouble and had banged on his door at six in the morning, bright-eyed and ready for breakfast. By seven thirty, they were on board the King Air, winging back to DC from Cincinnati.

Doloh had offered up little more, when Derek and Vanessa questioned him, than what he'd already told his other inquisitors. He was adamant that he did not know how his partner had received his messages on the computer. Derek doubted that. It seemed unreasonable and inefficient that the terrorists would fully trained only half their operatives. This group was many things, but inefficient was unfortunately not one of them.

Catherine was, as usual, skimming back and forth through numerous files downloaded onto her laptop from the terrorist's hard drive. Just about all of it was porn sites, porn-site advertising or downloaded maps of Cincinnati and surroundings. Nothing else was discovered on the hard drive, which had now been stripped of everything it contained, including information the terrorists had deleted but expert manipulation had salvaged. By now the files had been forwarded to the cryptologists and their immensely powerful computers at the NSA. If encrypted codes had been embedded anywhere on the hard drive, they would find it, or at least that was the hope.

Catherine turned her laptop off, snapped it closed, and placed it on the seat in front of her. "I don't know how they're getting messages from this crap, or even if they are, but I can certainly say that porn becomes remarkably boring after about ten seconds."

"Or less," replied Derek.

At that moment the aircraft's co-pilot turned in his seat, pulled his head set from one ear and addressed the pair, who sat a couple of rows behind the open cockpit on opposite sides of the narrow aisle. "Excuse me, but Flight Following has just asked us to give you a message to call FBI headquarters immediately. You can use your cell phone."

"Thank you," replied Derek, fishing in his pocket for the slim cell phone, a gift from Vanessa just two months before. He turned it on. The signal strength was excellent at the aircraft's altitude. Hitting speed dial, he called Brian Good, who answered almost immediately.

"Good," he barked into the receiver.

"Brian, it's Derek James."

"Hi, Derek. Listen, we have a lead. We have two of the fucks, the ones that bombed the school in Scottsdale, and we have their computer and the notes they were making."

"That's huge," replied Derek. "How did they get them?"

"Sons of bitches were caught on a convenience store camera when they traded cars. The images were blurry but we managed to get a partial plate and identify a college sticker in one window. Police in Sedona doing a drive-through check in a hotel parking lot in town bagged the car. A tactical team was dispatched from Flagstaff and caught them with their pants down. The suspects got the shit kicked out of them, but they're both alive, and they were taken before they had time to do anything about the notes they were making. We have the location of an arms cache where they were going to collect their next weapons."

"Who are they?" asked Derek.

In the seat across the aisle, Catherine watched Derek intently, trying to glean information from one side of the conversation.

"Hold on a sec, Brian." Cupping the phone, Derek said, "Cath, they got the Middleton School killers. There's two of them."

She smiled, clenched her fist and mouthed, "Yes!"

"Sorry, Brian. I just wanted to tell Catherine."

"No problem. Anyway, they got into the country posing as Kenyan students. They're probably Somali or Ethiopian, and they have definite al Qaeda connections. They're being questioned as we speak, but they're both tough nuts. It may be a while before we've wrung them out, but for now, we've at least got their cache location. We're preparing surveillance on it now. Hopefully it will lead to more terrorists or supply us with some more intel. Their computer had the same thing on it as the one in Cincinnati — porn sites — and they do use them to gather information. This is the first substantial break we've had."

"When you land, come straight in. I want to compare the information from Doloh with what we're getting out of these bastards, see if we can use what he's told us to give them the idea that we know more than we do."

"We should be there in ninety minutes or less," replied Derek.

"Great, I'll see you then."

"Bye," said Derek, but Good was already gone.

Derek turned to Catherine and filled her in as the pilots prepared to land.

August 24.
Skyline Drive, Kaysville, Utah.

Jimmy Youngblood, a.k.a. Abu Bakre, turned east on Skyline Drive, which wound up the highlands to the bluffs overlooking the bedroom community of Kaysville, near Salt Lake City. In the trunk of his Lincoln, he carried eleven fire extinguishers, most of them looking well used and all of them carrying recent certification tags. He was headed for a secluded cabin in the mountains off of Skyline Drive, a rundown little hovel, long abandoned, which would nonetheless provide a secure weapons cache. He'd been informed the shack was well off the road and surrounded by chain-link fence and large "stay out" signs sloppily scrawled in black paint years before.

Youngblood manoeuvred the ponderous Lincoln skilfully along the drive, which was proving to be a narrow dirt track with a grandiose name. He travelled its rutted surface for almost half an hour before reaching the almost invisible lane that led to the cabin. It had been marked weeks before by a reconnaissance team. The marking was simple, a torn plastic-weave cement bag securely wound into the branches of a roadside tree —to anyone else, just a typical and unremarkable piece of American flotsam.

The advance teams that had scoured America for secure places to cache their lethal contraband used a variety of markers. Youngblood knew them all by heart. Each had been cleverly chosen so as that it would look unremarkable but stand no chance of being compromised by any real litter. In this case, the cement bag was from a company in New Jersey, probably the only bag of its type west of the Mississippi.

He drove the car, ignoring the sound of the coarse, overgrown brush crowding the lane as it did its best to scour the faded paint on the once ostentatious luxury car. On reaching the old chain-link, he got out and opened a new but purposely beaten up and dirtied padlock. It was one of hundreds of artificially aged padlocks the terrorists were using across the country, every one of which had exactly the same key. He unlocked it and swung the rusty gate open, scraping it across the ground until it lodged on a rock and would swing no farther. The portal was wide enough to accept the Lincoln, so he got in, squeezed the car through and drove on.

He pulled up in front of the cabin in a puff of dust and realized immediately why someone would choose to build this primitive little retreat. It perched on a bluff overlooking a rugged valley in which not a sign of man could be discerned — amazing when one thought of the proximity of Salt Lake's urban sprawl. He wandered into the cabin, past a door that hung askew on broken hinges, his worn cowboy boots marking the undisturbed dust on the floor.

Inside, was the litter of disuse. A couple of broken wooden chairs, a pile of dried and brittle newspapers and magazines, all dated from the late seventies and early eighties, a couple of broken soft drink bottles, an ancient dried-out condom and whatever detritus the wind had stripped from the ground, trees and brush and carried past the broken door. There was no evidence of recent use; the cabin was just too remote to serve as a squat for the homeless or to attract teenagers looking for somewhere to conduct their clandestine assignations.

It was a great place to temporarily store the fire extinguishers as well as the twenty pounds of plastique explosives wrapped in cellophane whose labels claimed it contained modeling clay. Several small detonators were hidden inside the blocks as well. The fire extinguishers posed an even greater threat than the plastique. Inside each one was compressed sarin gas, one of the most toxic nerve poisons.

Youngblood did not know that, but he knew that whatever was concealed inside was unpleasant and bore careful handling. Likewise, he had no idea who would arrive within the next day or two to claim the package or to what use it would be put, and he did not care. He had his own problems now that travel had been restricted. He'd already talked his way through two checkpoints, telling the overwhelmed and inexperienced guardsmen that he was on his way to his estranged wife and kids, living in Tucson. His was one among hundreds of vehicles backed up at each checkpoint, and he was polite to the guardsman, something many citizens were not. As a result, they passed him through with minimal scrutiny. His chief concern was guaranteeing his constant and deadly migration from state to state, city to city, spider hole to spider hole continued. He was one of a dozen suppliers across the United States making sure the fedayeen were well stocked with the necessities of their trade.

August 30
Situation Room, the White House, Washington DC.

"Sixteen bombings in the last week, sir, thirty-seven dead and one hundred and fifteen injured by car bombs and IEDs. Ten are reported dead in the Seattle fire, and we still have no idea of the monetary loss, but conservative estimates put it into the billions. There are still a few hot spots burning, but the winds have died down and most of the fire burned itself out when it hit the shores of Puget Sound."

A nervous young White House aide read the report. He shuffled through his papers, cleared his throat and continued to read the damage briefing for the men seated around the situation room table. "As you know, sir, the mayor, two aides and three police officers were killed in an underground parking garage in Youngstown, Pennsylvania, when a car bomb went off as the mayor was arriving to work. That was two hours ago. There've also been numerous shootings across the country, but law enforcement thinks only a few of them were perpetrated by terrorist forces."

He faltered a bit, cleared his throat and started again.

"A number of them appear to be by citizens who are using the situation for payback or by psychotic copycats. Civil unrest is for the most part under control.

There have been some problems in Los Angeles with localized riots, and a lot of small businesses have been burned. Military patrols of the city have been increased and checkpoints set up, especially in South Central and East LA. There've also been some problems in San Jose, but the local police have it under control without military intervention. That's the end of this report sir."

"Thank you," said the president, his tone indicating that the aide was dismissed.

After a moment's nervous collecting and clearing papers into his briefcase, the young man left the room, the heavy door swinging closed behind him. The room was quiet for a moment, the men at the table digesting the long list of insults that had just been read to them. Finally, the silence was broken.

"Mr. President, we have to get the country up and running again. The economy is going to have a very hard time absorbing this as it is. If we don't loosen up some of the restrictions, it may not recover for years." The speaker was Gerald Billings, secretary of commerce. Billings was an accomplished businessman and self-made multi-millionaire as well as being a friend of the president, although he was another chosen for his talents rather than his relationship. He was astute and one of few bureaucrats in Washington who truly understood the vagaries of the global economies that drove the American standard of living. With air travel prohibited in U.S. skies and with severe restrictions on rail, ocean and road travel, the American economy, already reeling from the excesses of its banking and industrial collapse before the attacks, was in peril of a complete and catastrophic collapse.

Tens of millions of Americans had been temporarily laid off or unemployed and sat at home growing worried and impatient as they ran low on money. Far too many people were living from paycheque to paycheque and purchasing on credit. Cupboards were starting to empty, and families to go hungry as the emergency approached the end of its second full week. The second week had far fewer fatalities and significant attacks than the first, but lack of success tracking down the terrorists had demoralized the nation, and that demoralization was already showing signs of turning into a backlash against the government — or worse, against the police and National Guard who were trying to maintain order and security.

Overall, America had pulled together for the first week. There'd been several riots, scattered civil disobedience and violence targeting the immigrant population, but a combination of martial law and the National Guard had quickly quelled the unrest. While these events were troubling, for the most part the country had sat patiently waiting for results. Patience was starting to wear thin on day twelve of the emergency. With the start of the Labour Day weekend, the abnormality of the situation was underlined for every man, woman and child when local authorities and the media informed them that most holiday celebrations had been cancelled and long-distance civilian and commercial travel — aside from emergencies and critical supply — banned.

In truth, Americans were spoiled and unwilling to understand their changing circumstances.

"I understand the situation, Gerald," replied Admiral Irving. "But we can't open up air or surface travel yet. The absence of larger, more sophisticated attacks this week may prove that we've made it more difficult for them to organize more extensive and damaging strikes like the ones on the refineries."

"What about Seattle, admiral? That wasn't a big strike, just a few well-placed Molotov cocktails and dry summer weather," replied Billings.

"Gentlemen," interjected the president, "we'll have to allow some commerce over the weekend, especially if grocery stores are to remain stocked. And people will have to return to work and soon. We'd better announce that starting Monday, we encourage corporate America to return to work, but everyone will have to be on guard. I want commercial air travel back as well, but CAPs need to be ongoing. We'll let the public know that if any aircraft is hijacked, our only option may be to knock it down. That should reduce volume and travel to people who really need to be somewhere. For now the U.S. will remain on a war footing, but we'll have to let people take up their lives again. After all, this is our first time, but Britain, Spain, France and a host of other countries have been living with internal attacks for years. I hate to admit it, but this situation may well be with us for some time to come. I don't see any easy short-term solutions presenting themselves."

He paused and looked at Irving. "Admiral, how is the military doing?"

"Mr. President," replied Irving, "I know I keep harping on this, but we're overstretched. The National Guard and regular forces are doing a good job, but they're starting to wear out. I think we may have to reduce some of our troop commitments overseas, bring the men back here and use them. Right now, we have men on patrols and checkpoints who are pencil pushers, supply clerks and raw recruits with a minimum of training. We were already undermanned before the attacks. Keeping order at home as well as overseas is going to prove almost impossible in a few weeks, unless we act now."

"What do you propose, Admiral?" asked the president.

"We've taken a look at the situation in the Middle East and in central Europe, as well as at some of the larger bases in the Pacific. I think we may be able to sustain support to the Iraqi government with a phased troop withdrawal of sixty percent. I would withdraw twenty percent immediately, which means their own security forces and military would have to fill the gap. I propose that our secretary of state inform the president and government of Iraq of this ASAP so they can take over duty in areas presently under our control. We should just pull out of central Europe completely. Let the European Union look after its own mess."

"What about the oil fields?" asked Billings.

"We should use our remaining troop strength in Iraq to control and secure the fields, the pipelines and the ports against insurgents," said Irving. "Let the Iraqis look after the cities and areas outside the oil infrastructure."

"Could we ask the Brits to come back in, at least to southern Iraq? Maybe look after Basra again and the lower coast?" asked Blomstrum.

"I doubt that, Dan. The Brits have pretty much washed their hands of Iraq. You know that the Conservatives swept parliament because of their adamant rejection of Tony Blair's Iraq policies and our alliance with his government. There isn't a hope in hell they'd take the chance of going back in, and if I were in their place, I could think of two great reasons to stay out: first, the public would go berserk, and secondly, their new policies in the Middle East have kept them out of terrorist crosshairs. I don't think they'll jeopardize that, especially when they look at our current situation. Aside from the standard assurances of continuing moral support and grief over our losses, my feeling is that they'd balk at anything other than humanitarian support. ."

"What about the Canadians?"

"Their forces are already overextended and pinned down in Afghanistan and with other UN commitments," said Bob Dutton, director of the CIA. "The few remaining troops they have at home are busy patrolling the border between the States and Canada. They're tapped out."

"We don't seem to have many friends these days, do we," said the president.

"Sir, we're on our own," replied the admiral.

The president sat back, closing his eyes, his face tilted towards the ceiling. The last two weeks had taken its toll. He looked wrung out and his complexion, normally robust, was pallid under the situation room lights. "Pull them out," he said. "Bring them home, admiral — as many as you need as quickly as you need them. As far as Iraq is concerned, let them fight it out among themselves. Just secure the oil supply. No more fucking around with the pricks. We're done."

"Yes, sir," said Irving, closing his briefing notes and rising from the table. "We'll start a phased withdrawal immediately."

"You do that, admiral,"

Irving opened the door to leave.

"And admiral…" said the president.

"Yes, sir?"

"Cordon off all the largest oil assets in Iraq. Draw a line in the sand, and tell the Iraqis they're not welcome to cross it. Tell them we'll pay them for what we take, but make no mistake, we — not they — will control the flow of oil. The remaining forces we leave in Iraq should be more than sufficient for that. Get the Iraqis out of those production areas, and cordon it off. I don't want anyone who isn't American or an American-hired contractor within five miles of any Iraqi oil installation."

"Sir, what about the Iranians?" asked Irving.

The president thought about it for a moment, the fingers of his right hand rolling a gold pen back and forth across the desk. The pen stopped, and he looked at Irving. "Admiral, I want the Iranians informed that if they dare to interfere or try to take advantage of our withdrawal from Iraq in any way, our response will be immediate, using any of the weapons at our disposal we deem necessary. That means any weapons, admiral. Understood?"

"Yes, sir. Understood," said Irving as he left the room.

The other men in the room made no comment.

CHAPTER 8

September 1.
Dolly Dolphin Water Park, Salt Lake City.

Julio Sánchez rolled the barrel of chlorine across the damp pump room floor. The pounding of the immense pumps was deafening as it moved millions of gallons of waters through the water park, pulling it from the pool and thrusting it into the sky and down the long twisted fibreglass slides. His iPod, blasting Latino rapper Pit Bull's abusive lyrics into his ears, did little to relieve the din, and the almost intolerable humidity and oppressive heat in the room heightened his sour mood, a mood fuelled by having to work Labour Day weekend rather than spend it with his new girlfriend, Emma. He was crazy about her, the first non-Latino girl the twenty-two-year-old had ever dated. Even her parents seemed cool and were okay with his not being Mormon or having WASP roots. While Emma's family was Mormon, they were non-practising and seemed to carry none of the baggage of their background.

Although it was barely past eight in the morning, the day promised to be a scorcher. The park was open despite advice against it from the local authorities. The owners didn't want to miss the money they could generate on the last big weekend of summer, especially since they'd been closed most of August because of the emergency. To appease the local police, the company had hired extra security guards. Julio had seen some of them at the employees' gate. They looked as if they were smoking a joint while they leaned on the wall of the gatehouse and had barely acknowledged him as he drove past.

Julio rolled the chlorine barrel to several others waiting in line to be added to the system later in the day. There was a large chamber, a mixing reservoir available through a hatch in the floor. The chlorine was poured in and then metered into the tens of thousands of gallons of churning water that rushed through the building's piping on its way to the wading, swimming and wave pools and to fuel the towering waterslides and giant squirt guns in the amusement area. Julio had to hurry. The gates would open at nine, and he had to be finished here and on to his next chore.

He'd pulled lifeguard duty on the largest of three kiddy wading pools. He hated that post, his day consumed by screaming toddlers and pissy mothers. He wanted to lifeguard at the wave pool, which was usually full of cool dudes and, far more importantly, hot chicks in very tiny bikinis. It was, as one would expect, the most sought-after job at the park and one Julio had never done. The kiddy pool was at precisely the opposite end of the spectrum.

The door at the far end of the building opened, and a deliveryman in white coveralls came in and grabbed the chains that opened the large roll-up garage door. Julio continued with his chores. Once the door was open, a white van backed halfway in and another fellow, clad in white plastic coveralls, got out of the driver's side. The first guy walked towards Julio.

"Hey, how are you doing?" he called out over the roar of the pumps as he approached across the shining, wet floors.

Julio pulled the iPod bud from his ear. "Yeah, man. What do you need?" he yelled back.

The deliveryman leaned in to yell into his ear, "Where's the chlorine trap, bro?"

"Right there." Julio pointed to the trap door in the floor next to the waiting chlorine drums.

"Thanks, man. Hey, can you give me and my partner a hand with this delivery?"

"Sure. What have you got?"

"Just chemicals and some other stuff," the deliveryman replied. He was tall, about ten inches taller than Julio, who was five foot six, and in his white coveralls, he looked even bigger. But he seemed a nice guy, with a big smile and a thick Eastern European accent that made his Americanisms faintly amusing.

As they approached the back of the van, the driver, much shorter and swarthy, with an unpleasant complexion and greasy hair, opened the van's side cargo door. As Julio looked in at the stack of beaten-up fire extinguishers, he started to think there must be a mistake. He'd barely finished that thought when a crushing hard blow from a ball-peen hammer took his life. The men pushed his body roughly into the van and tossed a mouldy canvas tarp over him.

Then they grabbed a nearby cart and piled the extinguishers on it. They pushed the loaded cart across the floor to the trap door and opened it, revealing the water that swirled below in the mixing chamber. They pulled up their chemical-resistant coverall hoods, snapped latex gloves onto their hands and donned two full-face filter masks. Lifting each extinguisher from the cart, they pulled the safety pin, wrapped a plastic tie around the trigger and pulled it to open the valve and keep it open. Then they quickly tossed one extinguisher after the other into the chamber and watched as the metal canisters spewed their deadly contents into the water. Submersed, the sarin rushed into solution and transformed the roiling water into a deadly carrier.

Sarin in water remains odourless and colourless but just as lethal as when it's airborne. Its victims' symptoms take longer to manifest than when the poison is ingested in a gaseous state — anywhere from minutes to hours. The first indications are a suddenly runny nose and watering eyes. But after a while, there is blurred vision, eye pain, excessive sweating and drooling, followed by coughing, weakness, headaches, drowsiness, variable heart rate, nausea and vomiting. Finally, those most severely afflicted will lose consciousness, become paralysed or suffer complete respiratory failure. The onset of the milder symptoms is unremarkable, a matter for concern but not outright panic. Not until people realize that all around them, hundreds of others are coming down with the same symptoms and the weakest and youngest start to collapse will the panic begin.

Outside the public gates there were already long lines of excited park goers, many of them relieved to be spending a day away from the tragedies that had recently beset their nation and assaulted them day in and day out on the TV and radio and in print. In minutes, the gates would open, and they could spend the day having fun and escaping the unseasonably oppressive heat of summer's last holiday weekend.

September 1.
The Citadel, Allepo, Syria.

Muhammad al-Munajjid walked quietly through the ruins of the palace grounds on top of the Citadel, a medieval fortress that towered over the ancient city of Allepo in northern Syria. The Citadel had seemed a fitting place to meet with his supporters, especially this late in the afternoon, when the few tourists the fortress complex entertained had gone for the day. After closing, the ruins had been swept for stragglers by a team of Mukhabarat, the Syrian secret police, who then left the summit to guard the single entrance to the Citadel far below.

Al-Munajjid's connections to power in Syria were strong. He had called on them many times over the years, and they had frequently been helpful when support for his more radical plans scared off less-motivated adherents to the cause. Those contacts would make sure this meeting was secure, free from interruption or prying eyes.

The evening was coming on, the light taking on the rose of twilight, when he saw three men appear through the gates that led from the street fifty metres below. One of the trio, clearly overweight, was almost staggering from the exertion of having to walk the bridge ramp and stairs that ascended the Citadel's steep armoured flanks to the inner ruined city nestled behind the last vertical walls. All three men were Chinese and wore almost identical dark slacks and white shirts damp with perspiration.

Al-Munajjid approached them along a flagstone walk that had once felt the tread of Saladin and was now lined with the tumbledown remains of the once opulent twelfth-century buildings whose original purpose had been to provide secure homes for the nobility of ancient Syria. Here and there were string enclosures laid out by archaeologists. An abused bright lime green wheelbarrow added an incongruous modern note.

"I'm so very glad you have come," Al-Munajjid greeted the men in English.

Kuo Lin, the shortest of the three and the one who appeared to be suffering least from the residual heat of the day and his own exertions in climbing the embankment, offered his hand. "We are honoured to meet with you," he said, "although we have to say that we are not comfortable meeting in a place such as this."

"You don't have to be concerned," replied al-Munajjid. "I have friends who will make sure we meet in private. Come with me. I have some refreshments waiting in one of the buildings the archaeologists who are restoring the palace are using."

The Chinese followed al-Munajjid through a magnificent archway into the cool gloom of a stone-walled building. A large open portico on one side provided ample rosy light to illuminate a folding card table on which sat bottled water, two insulated flasks — one of tea, one of coffee — sugar in a small dented brass bowl and several plain porcelain cups. A plastic tray with a few pastries and breads from a local bakery offered a simple snack. In the corner of the room, various spades, shovels, trowels and handtools sat with other supplies among several soiled and beaten cardboard boxes, the debris of a German team that was excavating the Citadel grounds.

Al-Munajjid gestured in invitation at the refreshments, but none of the three men moved to take advantage of his hospitality. "I am sorry, my friends, that the amenities are not lavish as befits this occasion, but this is a fitting place for us to meet. The mighty Saladin once used this fortress to guard against the infidels, so I take some pleasure in using it for a similar purpose. And it is much harder for an enemy to eavesdrop here, for the Citadel's only approach is, as you know, closed and guarded, and the grounds were closely inspected for anyone who might have tried to stay beyond closing this evening."

"So, what is so important that you needed to meet with us in person?" This question was from Liang Peng, the heavyset Chinese man who mopped his brow as he spoke.

Huang Dong, the third in the group, was medium height and eerily unremarkable. He said nothing but his eyes darted around the room taking in everything in what seemed to be a constant appraisal of risk. He was feral in his mannerisms and posture and imparted to al-Munajjid a vague feeling of disquiet.

"I want your approval to move forward to the next stage of my plan. I have spoken to other supporters and have their blessing. All I need is yours, and I can start."

"We know things go well, but we hope that you are not becoming overconfident. Rushing now might harm our timetable, and we have too much invested to risk that," said Liang.

"There's a difference between rushing a plan and taking advantage of an enemy's weakness," replied al-Munajjid.

"True," said Kuo, "but what makes you so impatient to rush ahead?"

"Our success so far has been a dream come true. I think that starting on the second phase will sow more confusion than I had originally thought, especially if it strikes like a hammer, blows falling one after the other. If we act decisively and immediately, we can cut the last of America's supporters from her. I will make it too dangerous for anyone to support America's policies or adventurism or even to offer it aid. The isolation of the United States will further both our causes."

Al-Munajjid opened a bottle of water as he spoke and walked to the open portico looking out over the ruins. He continued dramatically. "This place was once a great seat of power, but now look at it, a ruin studied by little men whose only link to glory is through the dusty feces of long-dead warriors. Where we now stand is proof that no matter how powerful you think you are, you can be brought down. This seemingly impregnable Citadel was breached twice, both times by hordes from the east, daring warriors who were not afraid to tackle what must have seemed to them a power so great that any attack against it should surely perish. Our attacks may seem insignificant, but I think they will be sufficient to bring America to its knees. We spread fear and mistrust—"

Kuo raised a pudgy hand. "Yes, yes, yes. Please, spare us your rhetoric," he said tiredly. "We are not here to be propagandized. We are here to determine whether it is in our interest to have the timetable moved up."

"If I strike now, if I go to the next phase, the Americans will fall!" proclaimed Munajjid angrily.

"If you strike now, our aims may not be met satisfactorily, and we could lose a lot of money and years of careful planning," replied Liang. "But we will check with our superiors. If our timetable can be moved forward without risk, you may be able to expedite the next phase of your plan ahead of schedule. But hear me: without permission from us, you are forbidden to go outside our agreed timetable."

Al-Munajjid turned his back on the three Chinese. "Very well!" he spat as he looked out over the ruins and the city of Allepo.

The unexpectedly brief meeting over, the three Chinese filed out without another word.

Less than one hundred yards from the Citadel gates, Ben Levy and Ari Stein fiddled under the hood of a dilapidated Renault Dauphine, a relic of the sixties. While the car looked almost beyond repair, it was actually in quite good condition. It had been jury-rigged to break down and behave badly with the throw of a couple of hidden switches. Toggling these would stop the spark to one, then two, then back to one of the four cylinders, causing a violent and believable shaking of the motor and loss of power. The other switch activated a small electrode in the exhaust pipe that would cause the car to backfire alarmingly as the pipe filled with unburned gasoline from the dead cylinders. Today they were broken down on al-Kawakbi Street, a heavily policed road that ran in a ring around the Citadel.

A police officer stood watching their attempts to get the car running properly, offering the odd tidbit of advice despite the fact he'd never owned nor even driven a car in his entire life. The officer had checked the two men's papers and names and believed without a doubt that they were shoe merchants and beyond suspicion. To support their identities, the pair had stuffed the back of their car with used shoes of all types. It smelt terribly. Both men were fluent in an Allepo dialect of North Levantine Arabic, and their accents and usage of local slang were beyond reproach. Had the officer known they were Mossad agents, he would have shot them on the spot.

They had followed the three Chinese from the Nejrab Airport, on the southeastern outskirts of Allepo, curious as to where they might be headed. The Israeli agents were often assigned to the area around the airport to watch and report on the comings and goings of travellers, and their deep cover as merchants gave them credibility in the eyes of the ever-present police, many of whom they knew by name and bribed with lightly used American-made running shoes. To further their cover, they often made deals at the airport for black market merchandise that was not used shoes. Their covers regularly got them in trouble with the police, but not trouble deep enough that a well-placed bribe would not pull them out. No Mukhabarat officer would suspect small-time black marketeers of working for Mossad.

Levy and Stein watched the three Chinese as they got into a waiting cab, a cab that had been watched over by secret police officers and was parked right in front of the Citadel's imposing street-level gates. The early emergence of the trio told the Israelis that something funny was going on, especially since the Chinese had come directly to the Citadel from the airport, not an act typical of tourists. The fairly short time they had spent in the fortress, the fact that it was already closed for the day when they were let in and the presence of the secret police excited the Mossad agents. Finally they might have stumbled onto something that could get them some recognition from their superiors, perhaps even a transfer to a more interesting posting.

In a hushed conversation clear of the policeman, who was pacing up and down the pavement, bored with the broken-down car but reluctant to wander too far away, they decided to stay and watch to see who else came out of the Citadel. A few minutes after the Chinese drove off, an older Arabic man dressed in casual Western clothes emerged from the gates. The Mukhabarat officers treated him with great deference and, within seconds, a black BMW pulled up, and the man got in. As the BMW paused to pick up al-Munajjid, Levy toggled a switch under the hood and Stein turned the engine over. There was a tremendous backfire accompanied by a belch of black smoke, and the engine purred to life.

The secret police officer who was just then opening the BMW's door was momentarily startled by the backfire. He looked up at the Renault a hundred metres down the street and proclaimed it to be a piece of shit. Al-Munajjid did not hear the comment. He was sunk in anger with the arrogance of the Chinese, who had treated him as some kind of underling. He thought how delicious it would be to have the three Chinamen chained to a wall. As he drove off in the back of the BMW, the little Renault, puffing black smoke, pulled into traffic behind him and followed.

September 1.
J. Edgar Hoover Building, FBI headquarters, Washington DC.

"Saddle up, Cath. We're on our way to Salt Lake City," said Derek grimly as he entered the cubicle office the two had been assigned.

"Why? What now?" she said, looking up from her computer.

"There's been another attack, really vicious, at a water park in Salt Lake City. Something was put in the water that has affected hundreds of people. Lots of people are really sick, and the local authorities are terrified that a lot of the children will die from it."

"Oh God," said Catherine. She picked up an overnight bag that sat permanently packed under her desk and rose. "Let's go."

The two were driven from FBI headquarters to Andrews, where a small corporate jet waited for them. In the car, Derek repeated to Catherine the briefing Brian Good had given him on the attack and on the poison that was suspected to have caused the deaths.

"Sarin," she exclaimed. "Where the hell are they getting stuff like that? And in sufficient quantities to poison a whole water park?"

"Where and how they got it is what I'm hoping we can find out. What we know is that local police have found a number of fire extinguishers in a water treatment trap in the pumphouse. The also found blood spattered on the floor near the trap, and one of the staff members is missing. We're looking for him and running a background check. So far they haven't touched the extinguishers. They're waiting for a haz-mat team to recover them."

"Anyone see anything?" asked Catherine.

"Not from what Brian told me."

They spent the rest of the trip to Andrews Air Force Base in silence.

September 1.
Police headquarters, Salt Lake City.

The horrific events of the day had brought a rare quiet to the normally busy squad room of Salt Lake City's police department headquarters. Officers and detectives moved through the room or sat at their desks without the usual conversations, jokes or kibitzing common to a large, shared work area. News of the attack at Dolly Dolphin Water Park had come as a shock to many of the men and women in the room. They'd never dreamed their city would come under attack as so much of America had. Salt Lake's hospitals were brimming with the critically ill and dying, proof that America's war came without warning or mercy, and once again illustrating that no one was safe no matter where they were or want they were doing.

Over sixty bathers had died so far — the very young and the very old — and many more were in intensive care. Salt Lake's medical facilities and personnel were strained to the breaking point and relief workers, while on the way, had not yet arrived. One consolation was that emergency response depots stocked with medical supplies and personnel had been set up across the country to help in just such an emergency, but to the doctors and nurses, who saw children's lives slipping away and were powerless to help, it was little comfort.

Salt Lake's police were also demoralized and lashed out. When Homeland Security agents appeared at police headquarters demanding that all evidence be turned over to them, furious local police had refused and escorted them from the building. America's newest entrenched bureaucracy had long been considered just an expensive irritation to lawful and peaceful movement within and without America's borders. Now it had been found to be absolutely ineffectual as well, providing no security and no warning of the events that were unfolding across the nation. Its bureaucrats were fast becoming pariahs.

Tempers flared, and the federal agents narrowly escaped a beating — a scene caught by the omnipresent cameras of the media and flashed around the world.

September 2.
Fallon, Nevada.

Jimmy Youngblood drove his beat-up old Lincoln Town Car across the packed earth of the small lot and past the ramshackle Quonset hut with its sun-faded and weather-beaten signs proclaiming Wheeler's Car and Truck Repair — Tune-ups and Tires for Sale.

It had been many years since the Wheeler family owned and maintained a business here, and the property had long since gone to seed. An anonymous Los Angeles-based investment group bought it, and small signs were erected announcing the future home of a new auto supply store serving the city and farming communities of Fallon, Nevada. The fully fenced property was about five miles north of town, off the Veterans Memorial Highway, on Tarzyn Road. It was not remote, but there were no close neighbours, and the only passersby were Mexican farmworkers who wouldn't think twice about a casual visitor.

Almost a year earlier, two old shipping containers had been dropped off behind the building. They were themselves beaten up, with paint so faded that no one, not even the few that had noticed their arrival, had made comment or thought more about them.

Youngblood parked his car behind the building, out of site of traffic, and walked to the door of one of the containers. The door faced away from the road, but still Youngblood scanned the arid and unfriendly terrain behind the faded blue container intensely before he pulled a set of keys from his pocket and opened the two padlocks that secured the door locks. The padlocks were ordinary in appearance, but they were made of an alloy that would snap the blades of any bolt cutter, and even an oxyacetylene torch would have a tough time cutting them. They certainly denied the casual thief or snoop the fun of getting into the containers.

Youngblood had actually seen signs of a frustrated break-in on a container near Kingman, Arizona. Having found their attempts foiled, as evidenced by the scratches on the lock and the dents in the door, the would-be thieves had settled for adorning the container with graffiti, both comprehensible vulgarisms and incomprehensible gangland tags. The paint served to further camouflage the container, perfectly matching it to the rest of its environment.

Youngblood swung the door open and slipped into the blistering heat inside the metal box, pulling the door closed behind him. He much preferred visiting containers at night or early in the morning when the sun had not had a chance to raise their internal temperatures to 140 degrees.

Latching the door with a small hook, he pulled a flashlight out of his denim jacket and turned it on. The light revealed a wall of boxes of all shapes and sizes. On each box were large numbers scrawled in black marker. Many boxes had the same numbers written on them, while the numbers on other boxes were different from the rest.

Youngblood pulled three boxes from the stack, putting them on the floor of the container before digging into the wall to find another. One row back he found what he was looking for: a very small box, unreasonably heavy for its size, that was marked with a number unique to it. He smiled to himself as he looked into the box at the dull grey lead cylinder it contained. Heaving it to the floor by the sill, he unlatched the container's door and stepped out.

He walked around the container, checking in all directions for any unwanted visitors. Satisfied that he was still unobserved, he opened the door and removed the boxes, putting the small, heavy one in the trunk of the Lincoln, along with one of the others. The remaining two he jammed into the back seat. Opening one, he saw with satisfaction the whitish grey lumps of cellophane-wrapped high explosive they contained.

Fifteen minutes later, the locks secured on container and gate, Youngblood was driving back down the highway, southbound for Las Vegas.

September 2.
Situation Room, the White House, Washington DC.

"Mr. President, we are sure that the enemy agents are using porn sites on the Internet to exchange information and deliver orders and assignments," said FBI director Peter Archer addressing not just the President but Blomstrum and Carver who sat in at the meeting."

"So how do you propose stopping it?" asked Blomstrum, seated near the president at an ordinary desk in a small informal presidential office next to the Situation Room.

"I think we have to shut down the Internet," replied Archer.

"Good god, we can't do that!" chirped press secretary Carver. "The county — no, Christ, the world — will go nuts."

"I don't see any other alternative. We don't know their specific codes or how they are implanting the information, and it may not just be on porn sites. Different teams or groups may use different websites or even blogs to send and receive information. If we shut down the whole thing, we may be able to stop their command system," said Archer. "I don't like it any more than anyone else here. Hell, the FBI and almost everyone else, including the DoD, depends on the Internet and email communication for almost everything. These bastards have pretty much left us no choice, though."

"I'm not sure you're right, Peter," replied the president quietly. "Shutting down the Internet, or at least as much as we can get to without notice, will probably do more harm to the nation than the terrorist attacks. There's got to be some other way. Is it possible to shut down all the porn sites?"

"I don't know, Mr. President. We have people working on it, but so much of it originates from overseas that it may be impossible to control."

"The Chinese manage to control it," said the president.

"Yes, sir, they do. But they have special hardware, filters and routers that have been created for them, sometimes by U.S.-based companies, and installed progressively as they have allowed the Internet to grow. We would have to order the systems and then install them. It would cost billions of dollars and take months to implement, and then there'd be no guarantee that clever hackers couldn't get through it anyway. No, sir. I'm afraid that unless we just pull the plug, we're not going to be able to stop them."

"If we do decide to pull the plug, exactly how would we go about even finding it?" asked Blomstrum.

Archer replied, "We would have to go to the people who control the routers and servers. Most high-speed stuff would be pretty easy; it's controlled by the cable and telephone networks. Once they turn the service off, the system should grind to a halt. Low-speed is also carried on telephone lines. I'm pretty sure the phone companies would have some way of flipping the switch."

"Okay. Get me a plan for shutting it down. I'm not saying that's what we're going to do, but if we decide we have no other options, I want to know exactly what's going to happen...and to who."

September 2.
Dolly Dolphin Water Park, Salt Lake City.

Catherine peered into the access trap where the sarin-filled fire extinguishers had unloaded their toxic charges. The water was still, now that the huge pumps powering the park were turned off. The pumphouse echoed with the voices of forensic examiners, police officials and government and military personnel all milling about in a ballet of perfect futility. What few clues had existed were swept up long before. Catherine and Derek glanced at each other across the open hatch, both feeling more like morbid tourists than investigators.

"Not much to see here," said Derek quietly.

"No, there isn't," replied Catherine.

"Let's get back to the field office and see if the search for the white van has panned out," said Derek. "Maybe they've got more from the security cameras."

Thirty minutes later, the pair were approaching East 200 Street, where the FBI regional office was located. Ten minutes earlier they'd been informed that special agent in charge Blake Peavey wanted to see them and had urgent news.

"We've caught a huge break here," said Peavey as he passed Derek a small pile of colour copies on glossy paper. Peavey was fair haired, middle aged and average height. He had the weather-beaten complexion of a man who spent almost every moment of his leisure time outdoors. "In the first three stills taken from the security cameras at the water park guard station, we can see the van but no good images of its occupants. They were both leaning back and turned away from the cameras."

Catherine, who sat beside Derek and across the desk from Peavey, leaned forward to see the pictures as Derek took them from the agent.

Peavey's office was Spartan, a reflection of his recent appointment to this post, which since the sarin attack bore a huge responsibility and almost unbearable pressure from both the media and Washington. Small and furnished by government contract, it had a nice view of the mountains surrounding Salt Lake City, a fact that was currently lost on the three agents sitting there.

"So they were aware of the camera and its position," said Catherine.

"Hard to miss," replied Peavey. "It was one of those huge white clunkers dangling from the side of the guard house. It wasn't even aimed very well, the lens was filthy, and the resolution's crap. We did get the van's licence tag, but it's a stolen plate. Belongs to a Ford Taurus laid up outside a small repair shop west of town. The shop owner says the car's been there about four days waiting for parts. He didn't notice when the tag disappeared. The owners are a Mormon couple with a small butcher's shop and delicatessen. No connection. The theft was probably opportunistic and I'll bet the bad guys made it on their way past, figuring they could use a new licence plate."

"Wow!" exclaimed Derek as he reached the fourth colour photocopy.

"Got them," said Peavey, smiling. "That picture was taken by a red-light camera about four miles south of the park. The great thing is they were stopped at the light. The camera's set up to take a picture of a car's rear end, to get its plate number. The photograph was snapped because of a young kid in a Camaro zipping through."

The picture showed in great detail the two occupants of the white van, which sat in the right lane as the Camaro zoomed past going the opposite way. Both men were gazing out the van's windshield and almost directly into the camera lens.

Derek stared into the faces of two cold-blooded monsters and said. "We can find these guys with this."

"Damned straight," said Peavey. "We're blowing up the image and doing portraits of both men. Our photo department is working a computer sim to give us their facial profiles and a 360 view as well. Every TV station and newspaper in the country is going to have this in the next hour. My only fear is that whoever sees these pricks first might beat them to death before we get there."

September 3.
Highway 95, Amargosa Valley, Nevada.

Brian Rees was on an Iron Hand patrol, military code for aerial radiation survey. He turned north once again, looking at his watch and doing a quick mental calculation of the fuel remaining for the two thirsty Pratt and Whitney engines in the Eurocopter EC135 he was flying. He had just enough for one more patrol up and down Highway 95 before heading back to the field for Jet A and a much-needed break.

The landscape around here was high desert and resembled nothing so much as a barren moonscape. Even the usual desert scrub had a hard time in this parched and infertile hell. Death Valley lay just ten miles to the west. The stretch between Indian Springs and Beatty included Amargosa Valley Junction, a grandiose name for a crossroads that boasted nothing more than a rundown gas station, a diner, and a casino. The junction marked the halfway point of his assigned patrol area.

Rees's usual duties were to fly the expensive twin-engined Eurocopter for geophysical survey work, but right now the sensitive equipment in the helicopter had another mission. The sodium iodide scintillator installed in the rear compartment was capable of detecting even low levels of radiation, and it was connected to a computer that could analyze the source and type of radiation recorded. In order for his crewman and equipment operator, Jim White, who was nestled amid the wires and electronic boxes in the back compartment, to monitor the passing traffic, Rees had to fly fairly low, as much as possible keeping the helicopter at an altitude of less than a hundred feet and just twenty yards or so from the edge of the tarmac.

A few times, his huge rotors had kicked up a minor dust storm. He could imagine how pissed some of the drivers got in the sparse traffic below as they drove into the clouds of swirling desert sand, but he had no other option if the equipment was going to detect any unusual radiation — something he fervently hoped it would not do. He kept his ground speed to around forty knots, allowing a fairly low closure rate for oncoming traffic and giving the equipment and computers time to do their thing.

His patrol was aimed at a choke point on the highway south to Las Vegas. Similar radiation sweeps were being made across the country in the hopes that any nuclear weapon the terrorists tried to deploy might be discovered before they could use it. It was the search for a needle in a haystack — a needle that might not even exist — but better than nothing. This was the fourth time today Rees had flown up and down the road, and he'd to shake off a certain amount of boredom, something he would never have dreamed possible when he began flying helicopters ten years before. Now it had turned into just another job, and patrolling up and down a highway was even more tedious than his usual work, which at least took him out over the beautiful, rugged and, often, remote terrain of the Southwest.

His aerial survey company was one of dozens across the country that had been enlisted to help with national security, and the three choppers in his fleet were all on government contract to watch out for unauthorized radioactive materials being moved on highways.

He was just about at the halfway point to Beatty when White came over the headset, "Brian, I have a hit. It just peaked, and now it's receding in intensity."

"Shit," exclaimed Rees.

He swung the Eurocopter around and identified the only vehicle on the road ahead of him as an old Lincoln, maybe a Cadillac. He could tell any helicopter of any make and variant instantly, but with cars he had trouble distinguishing a station wagon from a Ferrari. As the helicopter pulled even with what was now clearly an old Lincoln, White announced from his monitor in the back,

"Yup, that's it all right. I have a strong source signal coming from that car."

Rees could see the car's driver, who looked like a Native American, glaring at them. "Jim, I'm going to accelerate ahead of this guy slowly and then come around.

I'll turn east and fly up the canyon ahead, get some altitude and then we can keep an eye on him from a distance until help arrives. Can you give him a friendly wave. He looks like the cat that just ate the canary. It might calm him down."

As the helicopter started to outpace the Lincoln, White waved and smiled at the driver from his spot in the chopper's back seat. The driver waved back and forced a smile.

Once he had gained a quarter-mile lead, Rees gradually banked to the right and flew into a canyon, gaining speed and altitude as he pushed the throttles and collective. He started his radio call to the flight monitoring station as the helicopter cleared the canyon's walls and rose into clear air starting a turn back towards the highway.

"Flight Guard, Flight Guard, Flight Guard. This is november niner four six niner sierra tango."

The Air National Guard watch station based at Nellis Air Force Base near Las Vegas replied. "Sierra tango, this is Flight Guard."

"Sierra tango is an Iron Hand EC135 on Highway 95, currently eight miles north of Amargosa Valley. We have a solid hit. The containing vehicle is a late seventies possibly early eighties Lincoln. The driver appears to be Native American. We have a very strong return, repeat, a very strong return. We are approximately four miles behind him and climbing to three thousand. We will continue to pace him, however, we are nearing a low-fuel condition."

"Roger that, sierra tango," replied the watch. "We will dispatch ground and air. Hold for an ETA."

Rees waited a minute.

"Sierra tango, Flight Guard."

"Flight Guard, this is sierra tango."

"Sierra tango, airborne support currently eight minutes out. Ground approximately thirty."

"Flight Guard, roger that. Thank you. We have fuel to stay with him until the cavalry arrives. Sierra tango out." Rees kept the Eurocopter well back of the car and stayed off to one side hoping that the Lincoln's driver wouldn't spot him, a faint hope at best.

Jimmy Youngblood, his heart racing, had spotted the chopper as soon as it took up position a couple of miles behind him. The stocky little helicopter made a recognizable spot in the sky despite Rees's efforts to be stealthy. As the old Lincoln surged ahead, southbound on 95, Youngblood nursed the adrenaline-drenched fear that began to claw at his guts as soon as he realized he was compromised.

Now, he thought, in his favourite of the Americanisms he had learned during his training and indoctrination, the shit was about to hit the fan. He hoped he was mistaken and the helicopter was not onto him, but he doubted it. There was not much flying these days that was not security related. Private and general aviation was still banned from American skies.

Las Vegas was sixty miles away, an unattainable distance. Youngblood grabbed a map off of the seat next to him, glancing at it as he mashed the accelerator even more firmly toward the floorboards. He looked at nearby towns. The closest was Pahrump, about twenty-five miles away, still too far and much too small to provide cover. The nearest place that even had a name, Amargosa Valley, was just ahead, its few buildings just visible in the haze of heat. With no particular plan in mind, he headed for it and whatever it might bring.

The lingering hope that he was just being paranoid was erased a few minutes later when one and then two olive drab Blackhawk helicopters flashed overhead and then started slow lazy turns. He couldn't see any external weapons as they roared by, but he did glimpse what could only be troops framed in their open doors. He hoped he would have time to get at the two Kalashnikovs and ammo he'd stashed under the car's rear seat — and perhaps even get into the trunk for what lay there.

He wished he had a Quran.

September 3.
Mossad headquarters, Herzliya, Israel.

Herzliya, located a few miles north of Tel Aviv, Israel, boasts beautiful Mediterranean beaches, huge holiday resorts, modern shopping centres and the headquarters of Mossad. American-born Israeli Lee Horowitz had spent years working for Mossad and never once gotten more than fifty feet away from his office desk while engaged in any assignment. He didn't really care. Picking through reports filed by field operatives let him live vicariously with no threat to his personal safety. His middle-aged paunch and nerdish looks did not conceal a brilliant mind, but he was bright enough for his job, which was selecting the reports of relative importance from the avalanche that washed into Mossad every hour of every day.

Horowitz's special area of expertise was Syria, Jordan and Turkey. He knew the agents who worked those countries and had gotten good at analyzing the intelligence they passed him. Three times he'd been instrumental in the early detection of plots aimed at harming the security of Israel. Right now, he fingered the pages and photographs describing the three Chinese who had visited the Citadel in Allepo while it was closed. He scrutinized the photographs of the lone Arabic man who exited the Citadel soon after the Chinese had left, but failed to recognize him.

The report stated that he'd been tailed to the airport and photographed as he boarded a private jet with Saudi registration. Horowitz recognized the markings on the jet. It belonged to a charter service fleet owned by one of the hundreds of relatives of the Saudi royal family. The old Arab was clearly a VIP of some sort. He'd been accompanied by Syrian security people who dropped him at the plane. Then three large bodyguards met him at the bottom of the aircraft's steps, two plainly Arabic and one a middle-European Caucasian with a distinctly Slavic look to him. These men accompanied the Arab as he boarded, one turning to pull the steps up and dog the door before the aircraft started to taxi. The last photos were of the tail number of the jet as it taxied past the photographer.

The report was filed from Allepo, normally a fairly quiet place — at least from an intelligence-gathering standpoint. Horowitz didn't think it was a code-red dispatch. The Chinese were crawling all over the Middle East these days. No surprise there. And he didn't recognize the old Arab as a person of interest. He put the report into a file case, marked it with a yellow sticker and tossed it into a bin for further processing and examination. At some point in the next couple of days, someone would go over the report in fine detail, but until then there were dozens of seemingly more important documents piling up on his desk.

Twenty minutes later, an office boy came by and picked up the piles of low-priority dispatches and loaded them onto a cart. He pushed the cart into the hallway where he left it for the next day. He checked his watch, smiled and sauntered off to the staff room to get his coat and go home for the day.

September 3.
La Belle Epoque, Berne, Switzerland.

Al-Munajjid visited Berne often. It was one of his favourite cities and such a relief from the sweltering blast furnace of Saudi Arabia in late summer. La Belle Epoque was a wonderful little hotel, beautifully decorated in deco and art nouveau, and while it did not boast as many stars as some of Berne's other hotels, it suited al-Munajjid well.

He had spent the last few hours relaxing, eaten an above-average lunch of steak & eggs and taken a walk down to the banks of the Aare River. This followed a morning spent organizing his personal funds and a breakfast meeting with two European bankers, men who supplied cash from an investor group to a host of supposedly profitable companies in the Middle East, all of them controlled by al-Munajjid.

Right now the bankers said they had a great deal of liquidity as their investment group was pulling funding from the United States as quickly as possible. Both men would have been very surprised to learn that those profitable Middle Eastern companies they were funnelling their money into were, in fact, in some part responsible for their devastating losses in the United States and producing nothing more substantial than a very efficient way to launder and disperse funds that would go to al-Munajjid's personal accounts and his international adventures. Soon, the two would not be so happy. All the money they had invested today in a new hotel development in the Emirates would disappear into thin air, as would all their holdings in al-Munajjid's shells.

The room phone rang. Al-Munajjid rolled off the bed and walked across his suite, picking up the phone and plunking down in an overstuffed thirties armchair that provided a great view of the busy street in front of the hotel. "Hello," al-Munajjid answered in English.

"Muhammad al-Munajjid?" queried a voice in English with a trace of an Asian accent.

"Yes."

"The timetable has been moved up. You have our permission to proceed with Morning Star."

Al-Munajjid paused and then thanked the caller before hanging up.

Leaning back into the folds of the plush chair, he took a deep breath. The excitement he felt was making his head swim just a little. He sat quietly for a few minutes before picking up the phone and placing a call, a call that would initiate a new string of assaults and isolate America from the rest of the world just a little more.

CHAPTER 9

September 3.
The Oval Office, the White House.

Dan Blomstrum walked into the president's office mindful that the president had just moments ago asked for a half hour without interruption, just so he could gather his thoughts and take a few minutes to try to relieve the acute stress that had been building hour after hour since the emergency began.

"Yes, Dan?" the president asked. He wasn't angry, knowing that whatever he was about to hear trumped his need for a half hour's respite.

"Mr. President, I'm sorry for the interruption, but you need to see this."

Blomstrum laid a memo on his desk.

The president picked it up and read it quickly.

"Fuck!" he yelled. "Those pricks, those fucking pricks!"

He threw the memo into the garbage can beside his desk and rose. He was fuming. "Get me that little fat-fuck ambassador of theirs. I want that son of a bitch wetting the carpet in front of this desk in an hour — or less! Get the secretary of state here, and Admiral Irving. I want that little Chinese cocksucker to tell his bosses in Beijing that we consider their actions to be a threat to our national security and that the Pentagon may well be involved in our response."

The chief of staff withdrew from the office wordlessly, leaving the president of the United States shaking with rage.

Fifteen minutes later, Blomstrum was back in front of the president's desk. "State just got off the phone with the Chinese Embassy. They're saying the ambassador's staff sends his great regret, but he is indisposed and can not possibly get here until tomorrow morning at the earliest."

The president was incredulous, his face flushed with anger.

"What the hell are those sons of bitches up to?"

September 3.
Amargosa Casino, Inn and Restaurant, Amargosa Valley, Nevada

Youngblood prayed that the two helicopters roaring up from behind him were not armed with hellfire missiles. Luckily for him, they were not, but they did contain a squad of fourteen well-armed National Guardsmen itching for a little revenge.

Youngblood yanked the Lincoln's steering wheel and the unwieldy car lurched sideways, swaying as much as turning off of Highway 95's hardtop. Clouds of fine dust burst into the air as the car raced across the wide dirt parking lot of Amargosa's largest establishment — the gas bar, casino, hotel and restaurant, a faded and peeling sixties monstrosity that sat beside the junction of Highways 95 and 373.

One of the Blackhawks slammed down into the parking lot just yards behind the fleeing car, the Guardsmen hanging from its doors firing at the Lincoln as it fled toward the nearby building complex. Several men jumped from the chopper, racing after the car. A corporal screamed a ceasefire as he saw the rounds kicking up dust and debris and stitching holes in the side of the restaurant. The shocked faces that appeared behind the restaurants windows brought the Guardsmen to the sudden realization that there were civilians at risk, and they hesitated.

It was what Youngblood needed. He slammed on the car's brakes, sliding in the dust, into and through the glass doors of the casino-restaurant combination. He plowed through a young couple who were just exiting the building, throwing them through the air along with spinning shards of glass and twisted aluminum framing. The Lincoln ground to a stop with a good portion of the front counter and a cash register adorning its long hood. Searing steam from a crushed radiator jetted into the air, adding to the noise and mayhem. The pungent smell of antifreeze and the more menacing smell of leaking gasoline assaulted the people who sat in shock at their tables or who had fled toward the back of the room.

Youngblood, his chest tight with pain from the shoulder belt that had kept him from flying out of the car, hit the belt release and threw the car door open. He saw the Guardsmen running toward the building. Spurred on, he threw the driver seat forward, grabbed the rear bench seat and lifted it up, along with the boxes of explosives that rested on it, revealing the concealed weapons and ammo. He grabbed one of the Russian-made assault rifles, pulled it from the car, pointed it out the restaurant's shattered doors and pulled the trigger.

Several of the approaching Guardsmen, taken by surprise, dived to the ground. One was wounded in the leg. They crawled for shelter behind the vehicles in the parking lot, took position and waited for orders.

Youngblood saw that his quick burst had sent his opponents to ground. He scanned the restaurant, taking in for the first time the terrified people who huddled at the back of the room. His car blocked their escape into the casino or to other doors in the building.

The casino itself, with its handful of decrepit one-armed bandits and a couple of craps and poker tables, was not even a shadow of the great gambling palaces sixty miles south. It was almost always sparsely populated, even on a Saturday night, but now it was devoid of even the most diehard senior-citizen gamblers. Its occupants had fled out the back emergency doors as soon as the Lincoln crashed through the front doors and they saw Youngblood tumble out and grab the Kalashnikov.

Youngblood pocketed several rifle clips and yelled at the people in the restaurant to get down. Almost as one, they hit the floor.

There were eleven diners and two waitresses. The diners were mostly locals, although two older couples were passing through, on their way to Vegas, and had motorhomes parked outside. There had been a couple of cars at the gas bar. One had left in a swirling cloud of dust; the other remained, its owners the young couple run down in the restaurant foyer as the Lincoln crashed through.

Looking into the casino, Youngblood eyed the rear glass doors, painted black to keep out daylight. He looked around, and seeing a nylon rope strung through some toppled stanchions, he pulled it free and ran for the rear door, turning as he did so to send a brief burst of fire out the front windows and keep heads down. He wound the rope around the quick release bars on the doors, from one side to the other, securing them against being opened from the outside.

Hurrying back to the steaming car, he scrambled over the body of the girl he'd hit as he had plowed in. He jumped over the hood of the car in time to notice a large fellow, clad in grey coveralls, trying to sneak along the side wall next to the serving counter, partially shielded by clouds of vapour still streaming from the Lincolns twisted radiator. In his hands he carried a barstool brandished as a weapon. Without a moment's hesitation, Abu Bakre, soldier of Allah once again, turned the automatic rifle on the man and fired.

It was a short burst but well aimed. The first round caught the man in the chest, slamming him back and upwards. The next ripped through his throat and the last hit him full in the face. He was dead before his fingers could loose the stool.

Two other men, dressed in coveralls like the victim, stood up as if they might try to help. They died a moment later. The acrid smell of cordite eddied around the room, joining the other aromas of smoke, dust and steam.

The other customers and staff, still on the floor, whimpered and wriggled closer to each other, instinctively trying to herd together to escape danger. Bakre yelled at them to stay put or be killed, before he opened the Lincoln's passenger door and, pushing the front seat forward, started to pull the boxed explosives out of the back seat, sliding them across the polished floor. Once again, pushing the rear bench out of the way, he grabbed the other rifle and a Browning 9-mm handgun. Securing the rest of the ammo and stowing it in various pockets, he slammed the car door.

The rear of the car was too exposed to the outside for him to attempt to get at the trunk. The explosives and weapons he had with him would have to do. To underscore that point, a burst of automatic fire from an M-16 outside clattered into the Lincoln and the wall behind it. The high-velocity rounds made an odd hollow tapping as they punched through the car's thin sheet metal and the wall behind the counter. Many passed right on through the kitchen on the other side and out the rear wall into the parking lot behind the building. One round perforated the grey lead canister in the Lincoln's trunk, a canister made to safely contain the radioactivity of its cargo but not to protect it from high-velocity military ball ammunition. A small amount of the container's contents puffed into the trunk. Had Brian Rees and his helicopter still been close by, the instruments would have pegged as the deadly radioactive isotope plutonium-241 was released inside the Lincoln's trunk.

While the 241 was fissile and not weapons-grade material, it was highly radioactive and was effective in a dirty bomb. It had been smuggled out of Russia in 1995 and hoarded for all the years since. Many people would have been greatly disappointed to know that it had been released in such an isolated spot after so many years. Their dream had always been to see it detonated in the heart of a major U.S. city, a city like Las Vegas.

The other helicopter had landed on the building's blind side, disgorged its cargo of soldiers and then, with a pounding roar, flown right over the building's rooftop. Several of the soldiers from the Blackhawk crawled to the restaurant's side window. While the others kept low, one peeked in, hoping to see what was going on inside without being noticed. His attempt failed.

A torrent of AK bullets smashed through the windows and over their heads while others punched right through the block wall beside them. Three of the five men were wounded — two fatally — as pieces of concrete and the steel slugs from the rifle ripped through them. The last two jumped up and opened fire, pouring their entire magazines into the restaurant. Bakre returned fire and fell to the floor to avoid the hail of incoming bullets. Troops out front opened up as well, the civilians inside no longer a consideration in the heat of battle.

The fuel tank of the Lincoln was pierced and more gasoline poured to the ground. Another burst of automatic fire came from out front, the steel-jacketed rounds glinting off the undercarriage. The sparks lit the gasoline beneath the car, and flames erupted. Bakre got up, ignoring the searing heat, and fired again, but this time he aimed carefully through the plate-glass windows at the fuel pumps out front. To his immense disappointment, nothing happened. Just a small hole in the pump and some shattered glass. Exploding gas pumps, it seemed, were a fiction of the American movies. Under his Lincoln, however, things were perking along well. The intense heat vaporized the fuel remaining in the car's gas tank, and it exploded with a loud whump. Flames and smoke roiled through the building.

The explosion spread plutonium-241 throughout the building and into the column of smoke and heat. As more and more of the building caught fire, the updrafts carried the isotope into the sky above. The containment canister melted and dripped though the Lincoln's rusty trunk floor. The genie was out of the bottle.

Bakre stood up, flinching from the heat of the inferno. The people in the restaurant were throwing themselves out the shattered window, over the bodies of the two Guardsmen. He opened fire on them, satisfied to see several fall. He sprinted for the window himself, driven on by the rising flames and leapt through.

A Guardsman saw him, gun still in hand, and opened fire. Most of the burst missed its target, but one round caught Bakre high in the chest and deflected upwards, blowing out his shoulder joint. He spun from the impact, the Kalashnikov flying from him, and fell to the ground. As he spun he saw the package of gum containing his suicide capsule fly out of his top shirt pocket, and a knife of despair stabbed him.

A moment later, his head swimming from the pain of his shattered shoulder, he tried to rise and scramble for cover. A booted foot slammed him to the ground. Within minutes he was secured and four soldiers were roughly manhandling him into one of the Blackhawks. As they pushed him headfirst into the chopper, the aircraft shuddered. The burning building had ignited the primers in one of the boxes of explosives, which in their turn ignited the plastique. The building disintegrated, its flames extinguished by the mammoth blast that shot upward, carrying the rest of the lead canister's contents into the hot Nevada sky and a lazy southeasterly breeze.

Just ahead of the breeze, the helicopter with Bakre on board flew on to Las Vegas with its prisoner. Many of the National Guardsmen and a handful of onlookers remained behind, none of them yet aware of the deadly veil descending over them.

On Highway 95, approaching from the south, a column of fast-moving police cars and military vehicles rushed toward the column of smoke that soiled the bare desert vista, new fodder for the deadly genie.

September 4.
Arabian Sea, near the Strait of Hormuz.

Half of Rear Admiral Hu Xiaofeng's flotilla was tying up alongside the docks in Gwadar's brand new harbour facility. The other half, including his Sovremenny-class destroyer, the flagship Hangzhou, were still underway, making ten knots northbound toward the Strait of Hormuz. Hu's intention was to follow his orders, and his orders were to sail into the Persian Gulf to waters off of the coast of Dubai, turn and steam slowly back toward Gwadar. At that time, the rest of his flotilla would leave port, bound for a brief patrol to the African coast and back. They would zigzag across the Gulf of Oman and the Arabian Sea, hugging coastlines and threatening the commercial sea lanes by their presence.

While the African patrol was out, Hu's remaining ships would scatter to individual patrols of the Gulf of Oman, monitoring U.S. and British naval traffic. He was instructed to get as close to the U.S. carrier group as possible without endangering his ships and dog them — far enough away to avoid outright American action but close enough to keep their commanders on edge.

Hu expected to be seeing a lot of U.S. military aircraft in the coming days. His battle centre would enjoy painting them with their target and acquisition systems, hopefully testing both the crew and the anti-shipping and anti-aircraft systems. He just wished he had the sophisticated over-the-horizon capability the Americans enjoyed with their airborne, carrier-based surveillance systems. He was going to have to make do with several small, fast patrol boats that wandered to and fro miles ahead of the fleet ships and with intelligence fed to him by Iranian aircraft and their fishing and patrol boats. The system might be primitive, but it was surprisingly effective, and he was rarely without some idea of the American fleet's movements.

Hu was leaning back in his flag chair, watching the bridge crew going about their duties. Only minutes earlier, they had received intelligence that the American carrier group was outbound from the Persian Gulf. The bridge was in a bustle. Hu knew that the combat control centre a couple of decks below would also be a scene of frenetic activity. The Hangzhou's captain was out on the port flying bridge and was clearly nervous about the U.S. carrier group's proximity to the small flotilla. He was sure U.S. submarines must already be close by.

The Chinese anti-submarine capability was poor, but hopefully better than the American's thought. To help out, two Chinese submarines were in the area, both of them rigged for silent running, and were listening for any American submarines that might be stalking the destroyers and missile frigates of his group.

Hu looked out over the port bow at the Dalian, a Ludo III-class destroyer leading them by several hundred yards. She was old, dating from the seventies, but still packed a wallop with her Sea Eagle anti-shipping missiles, and she looked wonderful against the great foaming wake spreading out behind her.

Radar alerted the bridge crew. They were painting what could only be two U.S. Aegis-class destroyer pickets, lead hounds of the carrier group emerging from the strait. One, he suspected, would be the relatively new USS Lassen, a ship more capable in many ways than his. Still, the Sunburn sea-skimming missiles the Hangzhou carried were potent anti-ship weapons, having a range of over sixty miles, and were at this moment quite ready to launch should the need arise. Their presence alone would force the Americans to keep their distance.

The captain walked back into the bridge, glancing at Hu and then stopping for a quick look at the navigational radar.

"Captain," said Hu, beckoning him over.

"Yes, admiral" replied the captain.

"Perhaps we should lay to." His tone and words sounded like a suggestion rather than an order, but the captain knew better. "As the Americans clear the strait, they will have to manoeuvre around us. They will not want to get too close and will be forced to adjust their course to keep their distance. It should prove quite inconvenient."

The captain looked perplexed. Despite commanding the flag destroyer, he was not privy to the orders from Beijing to put pressure on the U.S. fleet in the area. "If you wish, admiral, but it may annoy the American commander, sir. He will have to go well out of his way to avoid us."

"I'm counting on it, captain."

September 4.
FBI regional office, Salt Lake City.

Derek put down the reports on the interception of the terrorist in Nevada. It seemed that the cloud of radiation that travelled from the restaurant had a fairly narrow footprint across almost completely desolate and uninhabited land in the Desert National Wildlife Refuge. The light southeasterly winds that at first looked as if they would blow it into Las Vegas had veered northeast. Still, the area around Amargosa and that section of Highway 95 would be unusable for the next ten years at least, and twenty-four people would soon sicken from radiation poisoning.

If not for the lucky detection by the helicopter crew, things would have been worse, far worse. If the plutonium had been set off in Las Vegas, hundreds of thousands might have been afflicted. The terrorist himself was being interrogated in Las Vegas, and the results seemed promising. They'd already wrung his identity from him. Now they were working on getting the rest. Things were looking up.

As Derek put the reports from Las Vegas down, ready to continue his own report on the water park investigation, Catherine rushed into their temporary office. "Derek, they have them. They're holed up in a rest centre washroom on Highway 80, between Green River and Rock Springs in Wyoming."

Derek's frown of concentration turned to elation as he realized she was speaking of the Salt Lake City poisoners.

"An off-duty Wyoming highway patrolman identified them and called it in on his cell. They saw him making the call, got suspicious and tried to make a run for it, but the patrolman rammed their car with his pickup truck. They got out and made it into the rest stop washroom. There are no hostages, and so far no one's been hurt. The place is surrounded, and they have no chance of getting out."

Derek grinned. "That is good news."

"Even better, they had a small arsenal in the car but had to abandon it. All they may have are handguns."

"So, my guess is we're on our way to Wyoming. Christ, if we had as many leads as we have travel miles we could have stopped this terrorist army single-handed."

"Yup," she replied as she opened the door and held it. "And just to prove your point, there's a car waiting for us in the motor pool."

September 4
The Oval Office, the White House.

Dan Blomstrum rapped on the office door and entered. "Mr. President," he said, "the Chinese ambassador is here and waiting in the Diplomatic Reception Room."

"Good. Send an aide to get him and drag his ass here. No fanfare."

Blomstrum turned to exit the room.

"And Dan…"

Blomstrum turned.

"Give it fifteen minutes or so."

Blomstrum smiled, "Yes, sir."

When the corpulent ambassador arrived, the president, Secretary of State Warren Clyde, Secretary of the Treasury Ken Potter, Admiral Irving, Blomstrum and several aides were seated in the Oval Office. A junior aide, looking very uncomfortable, ushered in the Chinese ambassador, who was alone, his aides cooling their heels in the Diplomatic Reception Room.

He was led to a spot in the centre of the semicircle of seated men and, sizing up the situation, hesitated. The president wanted the Chinese ambassador to know that he was not the only one able to indulge in the diplomacy of measured rudeness. There was no chair for the ambassador, who would be forced to stand in front of the assembly of hostile men.

Before the ambassador could speak or raise objection, the president nodded at Secretary Potter, who cleared his throat. "Mr. Ambassador," he said, "it has come to our attention that China has began selling blocks of American bonds that it holds, bonds so far equivalent to over 130 billion dollars at face value. Our concern, Mr. Ambassador, is that China has been selling these bonds at less than their face value, and these actions are devaluing the American dollar. Further," he said, glancing down at his notes, "the sale of these bonds has been used to finance the acquisition of natural resources from sources that, until now, have been the exclusive partners of the United States and her closest allies.

"The continued sale of U.S. bonds at less than their value must stop immediately, as should the Chinese undermining of American natural resource supply chains and interests."

The president held up his hand to stop Potter. "In short," the president said forcefully, "if China does not stop the sale of bonds immediately, the ramifications will be grave indeed."

"Mr. President," the ambassador said, "it is not China's wish to irritate its good friends, but we find ourselves in an uncomfortable situation. We are in dire need of resources for our population, and to be frank, sir, with the very unfortunate troubles that you are currently experiencing, confidence in the U.S. economy is eroding rather quickly. China finds itself holding over a trillion dollars in U.S. capital funds and we have been, to our great sorrow, forced by market conditions to purchase at inflated prices what we can before the value of our holdings decline even further. We are afraid we cannot take the chance of greater losses, especially since, until now, all we have been guilty of is aiding our American friends by financing their budget deficits. China regrets that, through no fault of its own, it is now forced to take this action."

The president smiled at the ambassador and said quietly, menace colouring his words, "Listen, you son of a bitch. You tell the premier that we are not about to put up with this provocation. As far as we're concerned, Chinese actions — both financial and military — are tantamount to a declaration of war with this country. Do you understand the gravity of what I am saying, Mr. Ambassador?" He paused. "Do you?"

The ambassador, prepared for this display of brinkmanship, waited a moment before answering. "Mr. President, threats can do neither of us any good now. You must understand that China wishes its American friends and allies no ill will, but we must act to protect our people and our struggling economy. I will speak to the premier, but I fear that he will feel even more strongly than I that we must take advantage of what value remains in your dollars before they become worthless."

"You son of a bitch," exclaimed Potter. "It's your manipulations that are devaluing the American dollar."

"No, sir," the ambassador replied, turning to face Potter. "I am afraid you are mistaken. My superiors feel that it is your own financial conduct and policies, combined with the unfortunate terrorist activity within your borders and your response to the attacks, that have caused this calamitous decline in your nation's worth. We are just taking emergency measures to protect our economy and national interests."

The president interrupted, pointing his finger at the ambassador. "You tell the premier what I said. And Mr. Ambassador, I want you and your diplomatic staff to get the hell out of my country on the next available transport unless Beijing complies with our request to halt the sale of American treasury bonds immediately."

"Very well, Mr. President," replied the ambassador, smiling. "I am overdue to spend time with my family at home. I look forward to our next meeting, when perhaps times will not be quite so interesting."

"You arrogant shit," snorted Admiral Irving as the ambassador was escorted from the room, the door closing behind him.

The president rose from his place behind the Oval Office's magnificent desk. "Fat little prick's got balls. You've got to give him that."

September 4.
Highway 80, Wyoming.

By the time Derek and Catherine pulled up to the police cruiser that blocked access to the rest centre parking lot on Highway 80 in Wyoming, the two terrorists lay dead in a funeral home in Rock Springs that did double duty as the morgue. Attempts to talk them into surrendering had come to nothing, and after a short shoot out — a brief exchange in which no one was hurt — the pair had killed themselves with the last two rounds of the single 9-mm handgun they had with them when they ran into the washrooms. Most of the police units that had responded were now gone, but several cars belonging to local investigators were on the scene, and the terrorist's car, along with the washroom where they'd taken shelter, were cordoned off with bright yellow plastic tape that fluttered in the hot breeze.

After showing identification, Derek and Catherine were allowed onto the lot.

As they got out of their car, a short, stocky fellow in a dusty grey suit, a Western string tie and a well-broken-in stetson walked towards them, a question written on his face. Derek pulled his FBI badge from his pocket.

"Hey, how are you." the man said, extending a hand to Derek with a firm dry grasp. "I'm Lieutenant Stiles, Wyoming State Patrol." Then Stiles turned and took Catherine's hand, not quite shaking it but holding it and smiling at her. "Haven't had the pleasure of meeting FBI people before. Welcome to you as well, missy. I'm afraid our little shindig is over, but we do have a carload of interesting toys and other stuff that should interest you."

"Pleased to meet you," replied Catherine, smiling at Stiles' Western manner and cowboy drawl. She took no offence at his use of "missy." "I'm Catherine Hunt, and I am actually not FBI," she said, pulling out her CIA identification.

"Well, I'll be damned," said Stiles, eying her credentials. "Never met anyone from the CIA either. Hell, the captain's gonna be mighty pissed that he left already. Come on. We've been expecting you. Haven't touched anything aside from moving the bodies out. Nothing on them, mind you. We were pretty careful about that, but if you want to see them, I can take you to the morgue."

"I don't think we'll need to do that, lieutenant," said Derek. "But thanks for the offer. We'll need a copy of the medical examiner's report, but I'd bet that the Bureau has already been in touch asking for it. If not, Wyoming State Patrol should be up on the emergency protocols." He waved his hand toward the rest centre. "So, let's see what you've got."

The lieutenant walked them to a rusty red Plymouth Horizon, a relic of the eighties, with Kansas plates. Gone was the white van the terrorists had used during their attack. Both the car's doors stood open, testimony to its hasty abandonment. The trunk had been opened, and inside were several automatic weapons, accompanying ammunition, a laptop and a notebook.

Catherine leaned in and picked up the notebook, flipping it open to reveal several pages of scrawled notes. "Damn," she said. "Derek, look at this." Inside there were notes, directions and references to various websites scrawled in an untidy hand. There were also doodles and several things written in an unfamiliar language.

"Jeez, I think we may have discovered the Rosetta stone," said Derek, taking the notebook when Catherine offered it. As he surveyed the writing, his face lit up. "It looks like some of this fills in the blanks left by the notes seized in Sedona from the schoolyard bombers."

Flipping pages, he saw a rough floor plan of the pump buildings at the water park, directions to the park and notes about traffic in the area. Taped to one of the pages was a section cut from a larger city map, featuring the water park in the centre and then what was surely various escape routes highlighted.

"We need to get that to Washington," said Catherine. "Same with the laptop. Lieutenant, we'll need to take these two items."

"No problem, ma'am. We'll just need to get you to sign a receipt, and they're all yours."

Derek looked around the desolate landscape adjoining the highway. "We're going to have to make tracks with this stuff. We'd had better see if the military's got any choppers in the area. Are there any military bases nearby, lieutenant?"

"Closest would have to be at Ogden — Hill Air Force Base. That's about a two-hour drive, more or less."

"Good," said Derek, taking out his cellphone and dialling the Salt Lake FBI office.

As the waited for their lift, Derek and Catherine had a quick but enjoyable dinner with Lieutenant Stiles, who regaled them with stories of modern-day cattle rustlers, teenagers trying to break land speed records racing down the state highway in homemade jalopies and master criminals who once tried to make off with a cash machine outside a bank by tying a chain to it and then around the bumper of their car. They were caught when they sped away, but their bumper didn't. It had come off and was left — complete with their current licence plate — still firmly chained to the cash machine.

As twilight deepened, the unmistakable sound of a heavy helicopter assaulted them. It was a Blackhawk and landed in the lot outside the restaurant at the crossroads of Highway 80 and Highway 373 southbound. Minutes later, Derek and Catherine were on board with the laptop and notebook on their way to Hill Air Force Base and a waiting jet transport.

Lieutenant Stiles watched the huge chopper disappear into the gathering dusk, its blinking navigation lights growing smaller with distance. He turned to a state patrolman and the sheriff, who stood with him watching the helicopter disappear. "Well, don't that beat all, Benny," he said, addressing the patrolman. "You'd better get Sid, and the two of you ferry that FBI car back to Salt Lake. Here's the keys. I'm going to go home, apologize to Dorris for not bringing those two for dinner and then turn in. This has been about the busiest day I've had since Christ was a kitten. I'm beat."

He got into his ten-year-old Chevy Blazer and drove off.

Forty minutes later, the Blackhawk flared for a landing at Hill AFB, touching down on a helipad adjacent to a taxiway at the end of which sat rows of F-16 and

F-18 fighters. A helicopter crewman opened the chopper's door, and Derek and Catherine stepped out. An air force major waved them over to a Humvee that sat parked a safe distance from the helipad. As they ran, they instinctively crouched to avoid blades that spun too far overhead to pose any real danger. A pair of F-15 Eagles on their way to a combat air patrol taxied past on a nearby runway, their roar mixing with the ear-splitting racket already washing over them.

Once in the Humvee, they could at least shout introductions.

"I'm Bruce Thorn," said the major, yelling over his shoulder at the pair in the back seat.

Derek noticed he dropped his rank from his introduction.

Thorn continued. "The base commander, Major-General George Hillborne, extends his regrets that he could not greet you himself. We understand you are in quite a hurry, so I will be driving you straight to your next ride. I'd suggest a quick pit stop though."

Derek and Catherine both nodded in agreement. Nothing like the vibration of a helicopter to arouse the call of nature.

Ten minutes and a rest stop behind them, the Humvee pulled up to a hulking black shadow on the apron. Derek jumped out of the truck, followed by Catherine. He looked up at the aircraft that towered over them.

"Geez," he exclaimed, "it's a B-1B."

"Sure is," said the major. "It was the next plane out and headed for Florida, so a side trip to Washington is no big deal. The aircraft commander will get you in, strap you down and brief you. It won't be comfortable, but it'll be fast. Here he is."

The pilot was tall, greying and had a nose a little too large to be called distinguished. But he had a pleasant smile. "Evening, folks. We have never carried civilian personnel before, so you'll have to forgive the poor amenities and lack of in-flight movie." He addressed a crew chief standing behind them. "Sergeant."

The sergeant walked up and offered the agents a pair of flight suits and headsets.

"They'll probably be a bit big on you," he said to Catherine, "but they'll keep the chill off. The plane has pretty good heaters, but up where you're going, the cold sort of creeps into it and can chill you right through after a couple of hours of sitting cramped up."

After they were in and secure, Derek could make out just a little of the scene through the cockpit window from his jump seat tucked into a recess in the maze of electronics that filled the aircraft. Catherine was in another cramped seat behind a bulkhead, and he could not see her. The aircraft commander had asked that they keep conversation to a minimum until the plane was airborne and at cruising altitude but said they could listen in on the intercom to the cockpit chatter as the pilots went through an extravagant check list, rhyming out items and checks that were totally incomprehensible to a layman.

Derek leaned back, making himself as comfortable as possible in the surroundings. The acceleration and noise when the bomber started its takeoff roll was nothing like anything he had experienced. The bomber climbed, it seemed to him, almost vertically upwards until it reached its cruise height, fully twenty thousand feet higher than a commercial airliner would ever dare go. Sixty thousand feet above the earth, with the continuous roar of the bomber's huge engines adding to the discomfort, Derek sat with his eyes closed, going over the last weeks in his mind, resentful that, to date, his accomplishments seemed to be nothing more than those of a glorified errand boy.

Perhaps this time they'd caught a break. He knew that none of the investigative teams had done any better, but maybe now that they had a couple of the bastards in custody and several computers and now this notebook, they could at last start getting somewhere. The computers could be cross-referenced to see what sites were common to both, and then, if commonality could be determined, code breakers might start unravelling the enemy's communication system.

He was glad to be on his way back to Washington. Before he left Salt Lake City, he'd learned that Vanessa's body had been released and was travelling by train back to her family's home in Virginia. He wanted to be there to say goodbye.

CHAPTER 10

September 5.
Lacroix Coffee Shop, New York City.

Shojaa' Bala' Awi, whose papers identified him as the Greek businessman Apostolos Zoupaniotis, had been lying low since his arrival in New York on June 21. He'd spent the last three months getting to know the city, which — aside from the assassination of the American actor by Awi's cell — had not experienced any other attacks. This was intentional. The absence of strikes was designed to put the city on edge, and it had worked well. It was New York's own population that had made the city unsafe. Riots, street demonstrations, looting and murder had all raised their ugly heads, but vigilance had decreased marginally with each day that no new terrorist attack occurred.

Gone was the warm, pulling-together feeling New Yorkers had shared since their recovery from 9/11. Now the climate was one of distrust and dread. Troops guarded city intersections and patrolled Fifth Avenue and Hell's Kitchen alike. The city was now operating, its financial districts reopened following Labour Day weekend. This was what Awi had been waiting for.

Awi ran one of the few larger cells in al-Munajjid's army. Most of America's assailants were organized into groups of three or fewer — in some cases a single soldier acted alone — but there existed several groups of four or more, such as the ones that had initiated the first attack in Santa Barbara, blown up the refineries in Houston and would now strike New York.

Group leaders had total discretionary power to pick their targets, although they had been given a list of suggestions. It was up to them to measure the risks on the ground and implement an attack plan or move on. Awi had a short list of three sites he really wanted to target, but after studying them, he realized that two were out of the question.

One was the Statue of Liberty. While not a target that would offer many casualties, its destruction would wreak havoc with American morale. Awi was not alone in his assessment. City Hall had realized the statue's value as a target and taken steps to protect it. Heightened security combined with the sheer mass of explosives needed to do significant damage and the logistics of delivering them made a successful attack almost impossible. Awi had also thought of attacking the tourist-laden ferry boats that serviced the statue, but deemed it not worth the risk. In these days of continual car bombings and terror attacks across the nation, Awi's ego couldn't accept an attack that would only get press for a day. He considered attacking Ellis Island but, once again, found it too difficult to pull off and lacking the Statue of Liberty's significance.

The next logical choice was the Empire State building, but it was not one that excited him. He doubted he could do any substantial damage to the building, which was well guarded and whose owners had pestered the city into placing concrete barricades around it.

That left him with the only target he felt met his requirements. An attack on it was feasible, would realize numerous casualties and would demoralize if not America, then certainly New York.

The Rockefeller Center. Famous for its fountains, statues and Christmas tree and home to Radio City Music Hall, it combined so much American culture into one target that it was irresistible to a man who hated America as fervently as Awi did. That it also housed the Bank of America and an American television network made its appeal overpowering.

Today was the day. He had thought of waiting for 9/11, but he did not want the great achievement of his philosophical mentor, bin Laden, sullied in any way — especially if his attack were to fail, a possibility that had struck him sleepless many nights as hour after hour he rolled details and plans around in his mind.

Now, his plan was about to be realized. Awi himself, cellphone in hand, was to coordinate the attack. Early in the morning, two tour company buses and two delivery trucks were stolen, their drivers killed. The terrorists hoped the vehicles would not be noticed missing for a few hours, maybe not until the end of the working day. In either case, it would be far too late to stop Awi.

The vehicles were driven to an industrial area and into a large vacant warehouse where they were loaded with hundreds of pounds of stashed high explosives and tons of ammonium nitrate. In the end, each vehicle carried more than three tons of explosives. Unlike the other attacks, Awi's was designed, against orders, to be a suicide mission, and his four drivers were all prepared. Their sacrifice would still leave him with a cell of four men, more that enough to keep going with further bombings later.

Awi fidgeted in his seat. He was several streets away but had a marginal view of Rockefeller Plaza from his perch in the window of a small coffee shop. He nursed a large black coffee, a pale imitation of the syrupy, bitter coffees he knew and loved from home.

It was only moments away. Minutes earlier, he had made four phone calls, one to each of the drivers, making sure their watches were synchronized and then giving them the go-ahead, telling them quietly that heaven awaited. With a rush of anticipation, he saw the double-deck tour bus drive past him, its huge vinyl posters advertising soft drinks and New York attractions. Awi grimaced at the advertisement promoting a Broadway play featuring a sluttily dressed American whore.

The bus's deadly load was packed onto the open top deck, under a huge green and white striped tarp. The fact that the vehicle was empty except for its driver would engender little curiosity. New York hosted few tourists these days, and those that remained were probably trying desperately to get out. Tour buses, on the other hand, had become such a fixture of downtown Manhattan that their presence would be ignored.

As it passed, Awi knew that the two delivery vehicles and the other, single-deck bus would also be approaching their go points through traffic that was heavy, but still far lighter than normal for New York. Awi had arranged that the three drivers whose targets were on Rockefeller Plaza would rendezvous before making their final charge. The other driver, whose target point was on the Avenue of the Americas, would wait until hearing the blasts and then drive up and detonate.

Awi could barely contain himself. His hand holding the coffee cup began to shake, and he realized that it had drawn the attention of a woman seated a couple of stools down. He put down the coffee, smiled at the woman, who turned her head away quickly, and held his hands on the countertop to still them.

He could see the bus inching through traffic toward the target. It halted. He even heard the blaring horn of a taxi behind it before it surged forwards, making the turn into the pedestrian-filled walk off the Avenue of the Americas. He stood up and glimpsed the other bus and the stolen delivery truck turning in from the other direction to follow the double-decker. The three disappeared around the corner, and then the window in front of him and the ground beneath his feet shook. Another, bigger blast followed, its power cracking the coffee shop window. Clouds of smoke and debris rose into the sky above and rolled, as if in slow motion, onto the street. People panicked as huge chunks of masonry and glass rained down.

Awi glanced back as he started for the door and saw the woman. He realized she had watched him and knew. He saw it in her eyes. He reached into his jacket and pulled out a tiny .32-calibre Beretta. The coffee shop was a melee as people tried to get out, desperate to see what was going on, while others tried to scramble in for cover.

In the confusion, no one saw the woman slump to the counter, a tiny hole over the top of one ear, and certainly, with all the yelling and car horns, the crack of the small-calibre pistol went unnoticed. As she slumped, another blast rocked the café, and the front of Radio City Music Hall evaporated, as did hundreds of people inside watching a matinee performance of a state-sponsored travelling Chinese circus.

Awi couldn't help himself. He grinned uncontrollably as he realized he'd hit all four targets: the Time-Life building, the General Electric building, the Bank of America and Radio City Music Hall. He walked from the coffee shop into air thick with dust, smoke and the pungent smell of burning fuel and rubber. He hurried into the crowd, an even mix of those running away from disaster and those running toward it.

September 5.
Roosevelt Room, the White House, Washington DC.

The White House aide, panting from his run from the West Wing, knocked lightly on the door of the Roosevelt Room. A Secret Service agent opened it and issued the aide in.

"Yes?" the president asked. He sat at a long conference table with members of the transportation and commerce departments. They were desperately trying to get the country's economy moving again, and the president was listening to and considering various plans.

"Mr. President, New York has been attacked. It's on the news. It's the Rockefeller Center."

"Thank you," the president replied in a flat monotone that disguised the wrench to his stomach the news had caused. He had been a councilman in New York. He loved the Rockefeller Center in a way only a New Yorker would understand.

"Gentlemen, I'm afraid I have to leave you." He rose and, with his Secret Service bodyguard in tow, headed for the Oval Office and its televisions.

Within minutes of his arrival, the office was filling with his closest aides and advisors. They all sat transfixed as the TV screens brought them images of the irreparable damage done to the Rockefeller Center. Right now the cameras were trained on what had been Radio City Music Hall.

A gaping black maw filled with tangled debris stood in its place. The blast had been so great that buildings across the road also sustained enormous damage, their bottom stories caved in upon themselves. Hulks of cars still burned and smoked, many of them thrown by the blast. like shrapnel, at the surrounding buildings. Around the fifty-foot-wide crater that had consumed the sidewalk in front of the music hall and much of the street, the shattered remnants of vehicles formed a crazy, smoking mosaic. On occasion the camera would catch grisly human remains and then quickly flick away as the cameraman took in what was in the viewfinder. He had to do so many times.

The scene changed to views of lines of ambulances and fire trucks arriving and then on to the carnage of Rockefeller Plaza, where the three vehicles had exploded. There, the damage was even more horrific than in front of Radio City. What had been, until minutes ago, one of the great prides of American commerce and culture looked like a street scene in Berlin in 1945. No buildings had collapsed, and while some small fires burned, there was nothing on the scale of the inferno when the World Trade Center fell. Nonetheless, the television images made it abundantly clear that what remained of Rockefeller Center's most important buildings was beyond repair, that their internal structures would never be safe again.

It would take days to tally the human cost, but when rescue workers finished scouring the area, it would be found that this attack had taken fifteen hundred lives, either dead or missing, and injured almost three thousand people.

The president asked for the television to be turned off. He had seen enough. The Oval Office was filled with powerful men whose frustration was reaching critical levels. Their power had been rendered virtually impotent by the unfolding events and this enemy that behaved like a cancer in the bloodstream of its prey — tiny, concealed, almost impossible to stop and ultimately fatal.

September 5.
Office of the chairman of the Joint Chiefs of Staff, the Pentagon, Washington DC.

Admiral Allan R. Irving sat at his desk with his head cupped between his hands, rubbing his temples with his thumbs. He'd spent the last hour receiving reports on the Rockefeller disaster and watching televised coverage. He was running on a mixture of caffeine and sugar, and for the first time in his life, he felt drained and old. He needed sleep but had not even attempted to go home in the last four days, bunking instead in a small room off his office suite where his restless naps were too often disturbed by unfolding events. His only trips out in the last week were his frequent visits to the White House.

Those trips, in themselves, were stressful, conducted like a chess game, his exact location in the convoy of eight to ten vehicles concealed. Several times he had actually ridden in the escort Humvees instead of one of the three armoured limos or several accompanying GMC Denali SUVs. He figured he now knew what it was like to be a drug lord or the dictator of a tinpot tropical county, always on the run and surrounded by anxious guards.

His phone rang.

"Irving," he said into it gruffly, a little annoyed that his moment's peace had been shattered.

"Allan, we have a flashcom on the Chinese flotilla in the Persian Gulf," reported Admiral Ryan Armstrong, chief of Naval Intelligence and an old shipmate of Irving's.

"What now?"

"Five F-18 Super Hornets from the carrier strike group Abraham Lincoln were fired on as they passed within six miles of two Chinese ships, a Hangzhou-class, perhaps the Hangzhou herself, and a missile frigate that were approximately thirty miles north of the Strait of Hormuz. There was only one missile loosed, and it originated from the frigate. It missed, but it evidently filled the flight pants of two of the pilots."

"Shit on a stick. Who's commanding the Abraham Lincoln?"

"Admiral Percival, sir. He's scrambled five more F-18s and two E-2C Hawkeyes."

"Okay, get him and tell him to keep them at least twenty-five miles away from the Chinese ships, and they are not to radiate. Passive only. I don't want any provocations. We don't need to escalate this before we know more. Have we heard from the Chinese?"

"Yes. The captain of the destroyer radioed almost immediately to apologize for the launch, put it down to an overzealous crew member. And then he proceeded to lecture Percival on the dangers of overflights. Percival is ready to blow the little prick out of the water."

"I can't say I blame him. First they fuck with the strike group as it's clearing the strait, and now this. Those bastards are up to something."

"Allan, we've had several subs shadowing our assets in the area, as well, and they are undoubtedly Chinese. The two Kilos the Iranians have operational are still dockside and haven't moved in six weeks. The third is still sitting on the bottom after sinking when it caught fire at the dock a few months ago. This kind of activity is unparalleled in the Gulf. Shit, they must realize it's our pond. Pissing in it without our permission is just plain stupid."

"Who have we got that can reinforce the Lincoln group, put on a show of overwhelming force?" asked Irving.

"Not sure right now, but I can check with PacFleet. But even with just the Lincoln group, we outgun them and have air support as well."

"I know, but another strike group in the area would drive home that the People's Liberation Army Naval forces' most significant foray into blue water so far can be overwhelmingly outmatched by just a fraction of our blue-water fleet and that they had better learn to give us the respect we deserve. I'm not about to let the Chinese navy or anyone else for that matter think they can push us around. I don't give a shit what's going on at home!"

September 5.
Lancaster House, London.

Ambassador Clements was enjoying himself immensely. The ornate interiors of Lancaster House, many of them as beautiful now as when they were built in the early 1800s, never failed to impress him. He was passionate about architecture and revelled in his ability as America's representative to Britain to gain entry to palaces, mansions and grand estates that only people of nobility, even in modern-day England, would ever have access to. Lancaster House, a part of the St. James' Palace complex, was strikingly beautiful and a special pleasure. In comparison to some of these British buildings, American historical structures were just poor cousins.

Today he had lunched with several senior British government officials, including the minister of defence and the foreign secretary. Of course, America's troubles were the agenda, with the British offering to provide troops to aid in homeland security. Clements relayed the message from the president that as kind as he considered the offer, it might hurt American morale to have foreign troops, no matter how friendly, on U.S. soil. Clements' suggestion, however, that the British military might make their way back to Iraq to relieve U.S. forces there was met with a polite, but firm, rebuff.

The lunch was superb and had included delicately spiced cucumber sandwiches.

After lunch, he'd been taken on a tour of the building by the minister of defence and Shelley Morgan, the house manager. He was then treated to a coffee, a wonderful brandy and some very tasty French pastries in a small buffet set up in the green room. By three o'clock he was already almost half an hour overdue to get back to the embassy. Reluctantly, saying his goodbyes, he and his aide were escorted to their limousine.

The small convoy led by two police Range Rovers and followed by the ambassador's armoured Cadillac, a Ford Victoria Sedan carrying two U.S. Marine Corps guards and two motorcycles pulled out of Lugsmoor Lane, which led away from the rear of Lancaster House and turned onto Pall Mall. As the limousine was making the turn, a city maintenance worker raking the grass under a copse of small trees reached into his equipment cart, pulled a canvas bag off a small rocket launcher, aimed it and fired point-blank at the car.

The rocket-propelled grenade hit the thick armoured glass, which was bullet resistant but not up to the task the grenade presented. It bounced a couple of inches back from the rear window before detonating with a resounding crack. The blast struck down the motorcycle police officers immediately behind the car, killing one instantly and wounding the other in the face and torso.

The Marines in the Ford Victoria reacted quickly and swerved toward the lone gunman. He started to run but then he stopped, turned and, putting his hands on his hips, smiled broadly as the car slammed into him. It threw him ten feet to land, moaning, his two legs and jaw broken. The Marines jumped out of the car, brandishing pistols. At that moment, the first and second police Range Rovers backed up and slammed to a halt beside the broken and smoking limousine.

The first officer to the car looked through the window into the back seat as he tried to open the buckled door. He promptly threw up. Inside, the ambassador and his aide had received the full benefit of the shrapnel from the thick bulletproof glass as well as from the grenade itself.

Ten minutes later, the area around the ambassador's car was teeming with police, and Secret Service agents were just arriving from the U.S. embassy. Despite his broken legs, the gunman had been thrown roughly into a police car, where he sat waiting in agony for medical attention.

Another police Range Rover, light flashing and siren ululating, approached from up Pall Mall, but as it got closer, it picked up speed and then veered straight at the knot of people and vehicles. Too late, the officers realized something was wrong. The speeding Range Rover ploughed into several of the parked police cars and government vehicles, including the one containing the terrorist who had launched the grenade. The Rover detonated with a blast that blew out all the windows from the neighbouring buildings and left the cluster of vehicles a blazing ruin.

The message was abundantly clear: the American war would be expanded to those who dared help the Americans. Similar bombings occurred in Helsinki, Prague, Geneva and Naples over the next three hours. In each case, U.S. interests and citizens were assaulted by guns, grenades and explosives, and then, a short time later, anyone seeking to help them were targeted by much larger devices in vehicles driven by suicide bombers. In all cases, there were far fewer American victims than there were casualties among the police and medical aid workers. By the end of the day, over a hundred and fifty Europeans had died and many more were injured at the hands of suicide bombers while trying to assist U.S. casualties.

September 6.
Ta'if, Saudi Arabia.

Al-Munajjid was glad to be back home. Once, when he was younger, he enjoyed travel, but as his sixties wore on, the constant leapfrogging from one place to the next, even in the luxurious aircraft provided to him, wore him down. He looked forwards to a few days rest in his palatial summer home.

He was very pleased that the next phase of his operations had started so smoothly. The first day of attacks in Europe went astoundingly well, with all targets achieved. Soon the campaign would spread to America's friends in Asia and the South Pacific. He was especially looking forwards to the strikes planned in Australia. The Australians had proven themselves not just supporters of American policies but intolerant and abusive towards true believers in their country. Time they learned a lesson.

He was a little annoyed at losing some of his operatives in the United States, although, he thought to himself, he should be grateful that so few had been caught. Still, he was disturbed by the blatant flaunting of his orders not to sacrifice men in suicide attacks, at least not yet. This Palestinian, Shojaa' Bala' Awi, would bear some watching, especially because the results of his bombing — whether despite ignoring orders or because of it — had been so dramatic. He would raise his concerns to Awi personally should Awi survive his American holiday. It would not do for the puppets to start cutting their strings.

Each morning, al-Munajjid had dozens of international newspapers delivered to his door. He relished leafing through them while enjoying coffee and orange juice and seeing what his plans were accomplishing and what the world had to say about it. The world of late was divided into two camps: those countries that saw his war as just and righteous and were taking delight in America's bloodying, and those American puppets that screamed about atrocities and the evil that was being visited on the West. It amused him greatly that the same writers who screamed "atrocity" when a car bomb went off were quite content to file long-winded discussions extolling the virtue of the air attacks that killed men, woman and children with equal abandon while rarely achieving their declared aims or killing their intended targets.

While al-Munajjid looked forward to the wealth and power that even now he could feel gathering around him, he still felt blessed to be both achieving his personal goals and furthering the cause of Islam. He was also clever enough to remain hidden in the shadows. He wanted no part of the fame that would send him rushing from spider hole to spider hole, cave to cave, always on the move in a never-ending quest to elude his pursuers. He had noticed with some satisfaction that there were people in the world who were standing up to take credit for his war. He was content to let them do it and reap the rewards of becoming prey.

Perhaps he should actually find a way to encourage false claims. The more such assertions were made, the more confused his enemies would become and the less likely they would chance on him. The people who knew his identity and his importance to this war would never turn on him. They had as much to lose as he did.

Taking a sip of his coffee and a bite out of a marvellously fresh cinnamon roll — an addiction he had picked up in his travels in the West — he leafed through yesterday's Wall Street Journal. He surveyed the financial sections, noting that the financial world was ablaze at perceived Chinese duplicity in their sudden and unprecedented sale of the American debt. The Chinese had also moved to nationalize many American-owned factories in China, claiming that the unfortunate move was necessary if China was to regain some of the financial losses and hardships that the plunging American economy had brought to the People's Republic.

It was reported that the seizure of assets might bring several large American corporations, including several car manufacturers, crashing into bankruptcy. Just as well, he thought. They probably wouldn't have been able to get enough steel anyway. In the last few days, China had announced contracts signed with steel mills in Korea, India and South America and with dozens of Third World steel producers over the rest of the globe. China now controlled over fifty percent of the world's steel supply. The American president was largely silent about the Chinese acquisition of world resources, but his government was not. Politician after politician railed against the Chinese and their sudden and rapacious moves that, despite Chinese protestations to the contrary, clearly corresponded to plans hatched long ago.

Al-Munajjid's great joy was that America was just as toothless in stopping this new economic war for which they had supplied the weaponry as they were in stopping his attacks within their own country. In short order, he thought, America and its allies would find themselves in a depression that would make their Great Depression of the last century look like a minor financial blip. He wondered, smiling to himself, how much a Malibu beach house might sell for in five years. He had always liked California.

September 10.
Situation Room, the White House.

"Gentlemen, we are up to our asses in alligators. It's time we started pulling some of their teeth," said the president in his opening remark of the meeting.

A smatter of polite laughter followed from the men assembled around the Situation Room table.

"The internal attacks on this nation have had an extremely disruptive effect on our population, our way of life and, most importantly, our economy. Every American in the country has been hit, and hit hard, by this. Gas stations have no fuel, grocery stores are understocked and what schools remain open do so only with the help of an incredibly expensive security or police guard. We've had civilian unrest and rioting, and while much of that is behind us, there are many naturalized Americans who don't dare appear on the streets outside their homes for fear of retribution for something they've had nothing to do with.

"Now we have another, much graver threat than our internal problems, and that is the one posed by what amounts to China's declaration of financial war. The financial measures that China has taken have put us in an untenable position, and while there is nothing illegal in their actions, they are nonetheless heinous, especially when considering the attacks on America. I know that some of you are of the opinion that China may know more about the attacks on America, which have now spread to American assets, citizens and our friends and allies around the world, than they let on. We have no proof that China is behind these attacks in any way, and on an official level, they continue to offer aid and condolences. However, their actions worldwide speak far louder than their words. If, indeed, they have no prior knowledge of or culpability in the attacks, they certainly haven't let the grass grow under their feet in taking advantage of our weakened situation.

"The seizure of American-owned factories and property in China is inexcusable and the same can be said of their sale of American treasury bonds and the transfer of debt to third parties in exchange for resources worth sometimes only a fraction of the capital — our capital — used to back the transaction. The list of resources they now have access to or control is a significant threat to the continued prosperity of this nation. We must find a way to regain full access to resources that the Chinese are currently controlling or seek to control."

The president paused to take a drink from a Waterford pinwheel glass filled with Perrier and continued. "The last decade has seen an explosion in the Chinese economy, and they have spent the last few years buying up resource-based companies. They even control much of what we have long considered a strategic reserve of oil, to the north of us in the tar sands of central Canada. At the present time, companies owned by or with assets leased or heavily financed by the Chinese control over thirty-five percent of the tar sands, and they control over seventy-percent of the companies that have the technology to extract the oil from the sands economically.

"They have also cemented ties with Venezuela for their oil and are currently mounting an aggressive diplomatic drive to extend their influence across the Middle East. Iran and Pakistan have both benefited from Chinese development and trade agreements, and we know that our friends, the Saudis, have had talks with Chinese representatives.

"So, it would appear that the Chinese have outsmarted us at our own game and have just been waiting for the right moment to strike a decisive economic blow that, if successful, would catapult China to the peak of the world economy while reducing the United States to has-been status."

He looked around the room, at each of the men seated there. "Gentlemen, I am not about to sit idly by and let that happen. What we need are solutions, and we need them quickly, and we need them to be implemented easily and very, very quickly. Now, I know that Admiral Irving also has something to say about the Chinese," he said in conclusion.

"Mr. President, gentlemen." Admiral Irving rose from his seat to address the room. "As you know, Chinese naval forces in the Gulf of Oman and in the Persian Gulf itself have been running a series of exercises that seem calculated to interfere with our own activities in the region. To date, they have blocked our egress from the Strait of Hormuz to the Gulf of Oman, causing a carrier strike force to slow and divert many miles from their planned course shortly after one of the Chinese frigates accidentally fired a Gadfly ship-to-air missile at a flight of passing F-18s. No one was hurt, but the missile came very close to two aircraft that had to take exceptional measures to avoid being hit. It appears the Chinese have submarines in the region, including nuclear boats and diesel electrics. These have been shadowing our surface forces. There are also various Chinese surface ships involved in that practice.

"At present, the Chinese flotilla is split into two groups. Several ships are presently patrolling the eastern coast of Africa while the others are scattered around the Persian Gulf or the waters immediately south of the Strait of Hormuz. They've been running in on oil tankers as well as other cargo ships and are quite literally a nuisance to navigation. We have protested with their people in charge of naval operations and with the highest levels of their government, but their response is that the Chinese ships are on a goodwill tour of the area to visit their many friends and that their commanders must be excused for their relative inexperience, as this is their first visit to the area.

"With the president's consent, I've recalled the Abraham Lincoln carrier strike force back to the Gulf. The Lincoln had been on its way home and was, incidentally, the force that was both blocked by Chinese ships and had its F-18s fired on. The Ronald Reagan, which was to relieve the Lincoln strike force, will continue into the Gulf of Oman and Persian Gulf and will serve as back up. Further to that, I've ordered the Eisenhower carrier strike force, presently in the Coral Sea on its way to Japan and Taiwan, to steam for the Gulf of Oman instead and to take up a position south of the Strait of Hormuz. That will bring three very powerful battle groups into play against the relatively insignificant Chinese flotilla. We are going to put a very fine point on the fact that they've bitten off far more than they can chew with their ten toy boats."

Irving sat down, indicating he had finished.

Taking his cue, Warren Clyde, secretary of state, rose and looked over his notes before speaking. "Mr. President, we have been engaged in a constant dialogue with Beijing concerning these events and are demanding that they explain their actions and cease and desist any actions that are overtly injurious to our economy and well-being. Each time we threaten, they tell us that they will do their best to help us out of our unfortunate situation but that they must protect their own interests first. It's like punching a bag full of jelly. They just give in to every demand or take it under advisement or refer it for consideration, all without any intention of doing a damned thing. We're getting nowhere.

"I have no idea how to go about rectifying this diplomatically, and since the provocations aren't illegal, we can't justify any kind of military solution even if we could see one. Each time we lose our temper, they cluck and tell us they don't blame us for being irritable, given the heinous attacks on our people we are presently enduring. After an hour on the phone with them, I would, quite frankly, like to drop a freakin' nuke on their heads.

"In short, they have been condescending and are constantly lecturing us on our international behaviour and policies, and referring to our nation's relative youth in world affairs. Our expulsion of their ambassador and his diplomatic staff has not been met in a tit-for-tat expulsion of our people from Beijing. Instead, our ambassador was called in and they explained to her that they understood how our tempers must be frayed because of our internal terrorist activities and they forgave us for expelling their diplomats. They continually apologize for their financial actions with the line that they feel terrible, but they must put their own interests first. We are being stonewalled. We know it and they know we know it. Hell, the world knows it, but we can't fight it without coming across as the bad guys."

September 10.
Riverside Cemetery, Hopewell, Virginia.

Derek's drive to Hopewell from Washington had been a study in frustration. Traffic had not been heavy, but the security around Washington and its suburbs meant stop after stop at roadblocks and checkpoints and long queues behind tractor-trailers and delivery trucks. Each truck was opened and inspected by National Guardsmen and regular military, and almost every checkpoint had a backlog of twenty or thirty vehicles. Some checkpoints were impromptu affairs, set up by roving security teams in Humvees and deuce-and-a-half troop transports. Others were complex semi-permanent affairs set up with guard huts and concrete block mazes that had to be negotiated slowly.

Derek's identification did not pull much weight with the troops. He flashed it but was still required at to get out of the car, open the trunk and stand by while some twenty-year-old Guardsmen tumbled through its contents, pulled the carpets up and lifted the trunk side covers off, all while another post-pubescent soldier kept him in the loose focus of the business end of an M-16 rifle.

The day did not lend itself to cheer. It was exceptionally cold for mid–September, and a steady rain fell from glowering dark skies. Strong winds drove the cold and wet right into Derek's clothing. He thought it unfair that Vanessa's burial couldn't have been on the kind of warm fall day that she had so desperately loved in life.

He pulled into the parking lot of the Tapscott Funeral Home, which was conveniently right across the road from the Riverside Cemetery. He hurried in, entering the memorial room just as the service was beginning. People turned to see the late arrival, and Derek caught a brief smile from Vanessa's mother and an "it figures" sneer from her father. He took a seat at the back of the crowded room. Vanessa's coffin was closed and sat front and centre in the room, almost invisible beneath a huge pile of flowers. Behind it, too, a virtual wall of flowers made a backdrop, camouflaging the maroon velvet curtains and silver cross that adorned the small stage behind the podium at which the minister stood.

"Ladies and gentlemen," he began, "we are here not to grieve the passing of Vanessa Leighton, but to celebrate her life. I did not have the pleasure of knowing Vanessa personally but…"

Half an hour later, Vanessa's service, including a truly bizarre speech by an old high school boyfriend and a tearful but eloquent farewell from one of her best friends, was finished. The funeral director approached Derek as he stood. "Derek James?"

"Yes."

"Mrs. Leighton has asked if you would be willing to serve as pallbearer for the walk across the road and to the graveside."

Derek saw Vanessa's mother looking at him through the sympathetic knot of mourners that surrounded her. He accepted.

A policeman in a bright yellow raincoat and a crinkled clear-plastic cover protecting his uniform hat held up traffic on the avenue in front of the funeral home as the procession made their way across. Derek couldn't believe how heavy the coffin was, even between six pallbearers. After a long, slow and drenching walk to the graveside, the men gently dropped the casket onto a low stand. Three raincoated cemetery workers quickly positioned it on the hydraulic drop over the yawning grave and retreated. Derek watched as rivulets of cold muddy water trickled from under the faux grass mat covering the mound of earth that would soon entomb the love of his life. Tiny rivers cascaded over the edge of the grave in cataracts, pooling in the dank clay below.

The minister, now with a cheap clear-plastic raincoat over his jacket, read several passages and then said a brief prayer as the casket descended, irrevocably, into the ground. In the background, a few rows over, the cemetery workers lounged around a bright yellow back hoe, sheltered from the downpour by a huge maple tree just being kissed by its rich fall plumage. They were smoking and waiting for the mourners to leave before denying Vanessa a view of the sky. Derek thought how ordinary it was for them, just a brief chance to grab a cigarette before going back to work.

At the reception held at her parent's house, people drank and ate, laughed at jokes and offered their condolences to family and friends. Vanessa's mother and brother came to Derek and asked him how he was, and her father pushed through the crowd to offer his hand. He formally thanked Derek for attending, as if he was a casual acquaintance.

It was with regret, poignant grief and some relief that Derek took his leave of Vanessa's family, undoubtedly for the last time, despite mutual assurances to the contrary. As he walked from the house, Vanessa's mother hurried after him onto the porch. She grabbed him by both elbows, raised herself on tiptoe and kissed him on the cheek. Then she stood back. Wordlessly, she turned and walked back into the house, the screen door spring squealing before the door itself banged shut behind her, a final requiem.

Climbing into his car for the laborious drive home, he backed out of the drive and bid farewell to the life that might have been and a woman that he missed so very much. He cried in the privacy of his car on his way back to Washington, sobbing and beginning to cleanse himself of some of the torturous emotions that had racked him since that horrific day in August.

CHAPTER 11

September 10.
Malibu, California.

Inoue Nariaki, sitting in his rented Chevy Cobalt, turned to Sato Tadashi and raised his eyebrows. Tadashi spoke into a small handheld walkie-talkie no bigger than a cellphone, initiating their plan. They were observing the comings and goings outside a popular Malibu restaurant, one frequented by movie stars and other Los Angeles area luminaries.

Nariaki, Chicao, Kakerie and Tadashi had been relatively inactive since their attack on the concours that had heralded the war on America, although they had been responsible for a couple of small car bombings and three shootings, all of California highway patrolmen alone in their cruisers. Lawmen had become a favourite prey of the terrorists across the United States.

The restaurant had its own newly hired security, but Nariaki, over a two-week reconnaissance, had noticed that the security personnel had started to be become lax as they grew accustomed to their jobs and the ebb and flow of the many celebrities. The place was owned by a small investment group of well-known actors, and it was their celebrity that attracted so many others. It was unadvertised and very low-key, its clientele protected from locals and tourists seeking to rub elbows with celebrities or petition them for their autographs. Here, the rich and famous were safe from excited Midwesterners wanting to snap cellphone pictures of them posing with overweight grandmothers and acned adolescents.

Nariaki had come across the restaurant quite by chance as he walked the streets of Malibu in his quest for an interesting target. Now, with the evening rush of Ferraris, Bentley Continentals, Hummers and hybrid Prius, the stars were coming out. He put the Chevy Cobalt into gear and drove off around the corner to wait for his accomplices.

A new Lincoln Navigator, recently stolen, with custom wheels, a fancy pearl paint job and throbbing music pounding from within pulled up to the valet area of the restaurant. The two security men, who looked and dressed more like Chippendales than security guards, glanced at the truck and dismissed it. One of the valets approached. Kato Kakerie and Ishikawa Chicao climbed out, closing and locking the doors of the truck behind them.

"Excuse me," Kakerie said to the valet, "would you mind if we left it here for a moment. We want to go in and see if our friends have arrived yet."

"Well sir, we are not supposed…" The valet paused when he saw the crisp new fifty dollar bill Kakerie held out between two fingers. "I suppose a few minutes will be fine, but I will have to have your keys."

"No problem" said Kakerie, smiling and passing the young man the keys and the fifty.

He and Chicao made their way into the luxurious foyer of the eatery. A well-dressed and breathtakingly beautiful young blonde looked up from her floor plan and asked if they had a reservation.

"Yes, this is Mr. Chicao. He has a dinner appointment," said Kakeri, indicating Chicao, who stood in the middle of the foyer looking around self-importantly from behind a dark pair of sunglasses.

"Yes, sir," she said, confirming the name and the table the reservation had been assigned. A pretty brunette walked up to them. "Maria will take you to your table," said the blonde.

Kakeri and Chicao followed Maria through a restaurant packed with many of the who's who of Malibu society, arriving finally at their table. "Excuse me, but where are your washrooms?" asked Kakerie.

"Right down that hallway, sir," replied the girl, indicating a hall at the rear of the room.

"Thank you." Kakerie then turned to Chicao and addressed him briefly in Japanese while pointing at the hallway.

"Your welcome," replied the girl. "I'll just leave your menus on the table."

"Thank you very much," replied Chicao, pretending to labour in broken English as the two men headed toward the hallway and the exit door they knew was at its end.

A few minutes later, the valet became concerned that the two men had not returned for their truck. He took the Navigator's key off the board, deciding to move it a little farther out of the way. But when he put the key in the lock, it wouldn't turn. He took it out, looked at it and tried again.

"Move that friggin' truck out of the way," one of the other valets said from the window of an Aston Martin he was taking to the valet parking lot.

"I can't. The key doesn't work."

The other valet jumped out of the car and approached, putting his hand out to take the key and try himself.

On the walk in front of the restaurant, a very influential and famous director and a well-known and successful producer waited for three studio executives to get out of their limo. Two starlets, both more famous for their off-screen antics than for their onscreen work, were just climbing from their Maseratti. One was whining about the strap on her expensive designer shoes that had just snapped. At that moment the two hundred and fifty pounds of explosive in the Navigator went off, sweeping much of the restaurant from the expensive land that it occupied.

Chicao and Kakerie had gotten into the Cobalt with Tadashi and Nariaki and driven off scant seconds before.

September 11.
The Oval Office, the White House.

"Not one?" asked the president, incredulous at the news.

"No, sir, not one," replied Dan Blomstrum. He had just imparted the news that there had not been one attack all day — September 11. No one thought it was because of their increased security, though they had tried to prepare for whatever eventuality the anniversary of 9/11 might bring.

"The arrogant bastards. If that isn't a kick in the face, I don't know what is," said the president, realizing the implications and helplessness of his situation. This war was being fought on the enemy's terms, and only the enemy had the power to halt or prosecute it. He realized the media's pundits, already very critical of his performance, were going to have a field day with this — much of it at his expense.

No president in history had as low a popularity rating as the one he now enjoyed. It mattered little to the American public that no one — not even Roosevelt himself —could have done any better in his position. He had, in fact, done remarkably well in an untenable situation, but in America the buck stopped at his desk.

September 12.
Port of Key West, Key West, Florida.

Lieutenant-Commander Alistair Goodhale groaned to himself in response to a light knock on his cabin door. He was in the middle of a series of performance reports that were going to be overdue if he was not left alone. "Come in," he barked.

A petty officer second class opened the door. "Sir, we've just had a request from the harbourmaster's office in port. There's an old, derelict cabin cruiser that's drifted in and wedged itself between a cruise ship and the dock. They don't want to approach it without us checking it out first."

"No one saw it coming in?"

"No, sir. They didn't notice it until after first light this morning."

"All right. Tell Lieutenant Anderson to come about. We'll head in."

The 110-foot Island-class Coast Guard cutter Archer had sailed from Key West a short time before on a drug interdiction and anti-terrorism security patrol off the western reaches. Its current position was only ten nautical miles northwest of Wisteria Island, which stood off the port's entrance near the large commercial docks where the cruise ships tied up.

"Come and get me when we're approaching the port. Until that time, instruct the Lieutenant that I don't want to be disturbed, even if he thinks we're sinking."

"Aye aye, sir," replied the petty officer, backing from the room.

"And close the goddamned door behind you."

"Sir." The petty officer reversed course in midstep and apologetically pulled the door closed.

Seventy minutes later the Archer was laid to about sixty yards behind the stern of the American-flagged cruise ship American Vista. The Vista was only a couple of years old, weighed in at a little over a hundred thousand tons and was one of only a couple of American-flagged cruise ships in existence. It was a floating pleasure palace that bobbed about the Caribbean in the winter or visited Alaskan waters in the summer and offered everything from a comprehensive casino to health spas and all-you-can-eat gourmet buffets. Today it was slated to head across the Atlantic from Key West pass, by the Pillars of Hercules and into the Mediterranean, with calls to Rome, Venice, Athens and the French Riviera on the agenda. The Vista was a wonder of modern ship design and had fully automated computer control systems that looked after everything from the temperature and humidity of the staterooms to the ship's position — to within five yards — and heralded any threats to navigation within fifty miles.

Despite all of the sophisticated hardware, no one had noticed the sixties-era thirty-foot cabin cruiser, all peeling paint and rotted wood, that had drifted in overnight. It nestled now between the concrete dock and the curved steel wall of the Vista, bobbing back and forth in the narrow confines, banging against both the ship and the sea wall. It would not be moved too far, and the harbourmaster had scotched an effort to throw a line on it and pull it back and out, citing rules that obliged him to involve the Coast Guard. He'd also asked the Vista to stop boarding until the problem, if there was one, was cleared up, but the cruise ship company had insisted that boarding continue as planned. They'd lost a staggering amount of revenue in the last four weeks, their ships prohibited from entering U.S. waters and many of them tied up in port. This trip was almost three weeks late, having originally been scheduled to leave port August 20. They told the harbourmaster in no uncertain terms that the American Vista would depart on schedule. He later regretted his own response. "It's your funeral," he'd said.

A midshipman and two seaman from the Archer clambered into an inflatable-hull speedboat the Coast Guard cutter's crew had lowered on its port davit. They had instructions to board the cruiser, inspect it and then secure a line and drag it out from the space in which it floated. Lieutenant-Commander Goodhale watched from the Archer's bow as the three men sped off. He turned and started back to his cabin to finish up his paperwork. "Give me a yell when we're ready to get underway again," he said to his lieutenant.

Midshipman Benjamin Wallace carefully heaved himself over the stern of the old Chris-Craft onto the small rear deck. He and his two companions had been warned to be especially cautious during their boarding and to secure every compartment of the boat before they prepared it for a tow. On the stern, the name Sexy Saturday and the homeport Key Largo were etched in faded gold vinyl that was in only marginally better shape than the dry, rotted stern planks. His first view of the rest of the boat showed it to be in no better condition. It was clearly a derelict whose glory days were years behind her, and he considered it a miracle that the boat was actually afloat. The midshipman thought his biggest problem might be finding a cleat sound enough to tie off the tow rope.

He entered the cabin, the smell of mould and spoiled gasoline assailing his nose. The gentle sound of water slapping in the bilges confirmed that she was not completely watertight. There seemed to be nothing amiss, and he almost turned to leave, but he thought to himself that he had better take a quick look at the forward compartment. The two seamen were on the deck above. He could see the legs of one passing the cabin windows as he made his way forward along the narrow starboard walk, and he could hear the other moving around on the flying bridge above.

He gave the narrow door separating the main cabin from the forward sleeping berth a good pull. It was not locked, but years of humidity and neglect had warped it against its frame and the floor. He looked down and noticed signs that it had recently been forced open. A long fresh gouge marred the flaking and brittle battleship linoleum.

"Hey!" yelled the seaman who had gone forward. "This thing has been anchored. I can see a taut line attached to a clevis fixed on the bow under the surface."

Midshipman Wallace pulled the door open at the same time as he yelled an acknowledgment to the seaman's announcement. He looked in at a pile of dirty white sheets and old blankets that rose to the cabin's low ceiling. He entered the compartment and grabbed a handful of stained and yellowing bedding, pulling it back to reveal a stack of boxes that filled the berth from front to back and floor to ceiling. He realized too late that he had also, in yanking back the cabin door, pulled the pins from several grenades that had been fastened to the door.. The grenades proved adequate to the task of detonating the stacked explosives eight minutes ahead of the time set on the electronic detonators.

Lieutenant-Commander Goodhale's pen flew from his fingers as the Chris-Craft exploded, blasting like a shot gun from the aperture between the concrete dock and the ship's hull and washing across the deck of his cutter. Two seamen on deck were blown off of their feet: one broke his arm, the other sustained extensive injuries to his face and neck. The Archer escaped with little more than singed paint and a deck littered with debris. The American Vista, however, had a hole blown though her hull the size of a compact car. The blast occurred at the waterline and, compressed as it was between the unyielding concrete of the pier and the ship, stove her in like she was made of tinfoil. Several people on deck who'd been looking over the side were killed immediately.

On board, the whole ship shuddered and alarms started screaming from the public address system. The hundreds of people already aboard, who had not even had the benefit of an emergency briefing, panicked and headed as one for the narrow gangway that connected the ship to the terminal. Bloody chaos ensued as senior citizens and thirty-somethings alike mowed each other down in the stampede. Many people were cast over the side, falling three stories to the water below. Others, not so lucky, hit the unyielding concrete and metal cladding of the pier.

Fires broke out in several places. One that ignited in the galley was quickly brought under control by the automatic fire suppression systems, but not before a cook sustained third-degree burns on his hands and arms as he tried to extinguish the flames with a kitchen towel. Severed fuel lines and a compromised natural gas storage tank were feeding another, far more serious blaze that was developing into a steel-slumping inferno impervious to the ship's high-tech fire-containment system. Within an hour the blaze had raged through all the compartments above water level. Mortally wounded, the Vista started to settle to the bottom that lay just twenty feet below her keel. She listed over to rest her superstructure on the dock, grating and rasping on the pier as she shuddered in her death throes.

Ten hours later she was a giant smoking hulk, spewing toxins and bleeding diesel into the harbour. Soon the pristine waters of Key West scintillated with the deadly rainbows of a catastrophic fuel spill.

September 12.
J. Edgar Hoover Building, Washington DC.

Derek walked into the small office he and Catherine shared. "There's been another major attack. They blew up a cruise ship in Key West."

"Are we going?" asked Catherine.

"No, no," replied Derek. "No, I just saw it on the news."

"Just I thought…"

"I know. Every time I come in here, it's to tell you we're heading out. Not this time."

"Good," replied Catherine, "because I just got a call to say that we're to attend a meeting at the NSA. It seems they finally have a breakthrough." She smiled. "It was the notebook combined with the laptops that did it. They know how the information is being transmitted. Now they have to figure out who's sending it and who's getting it."

"Hey, anything is better than nothing."

"Yeah, and so far almost all we've had is a whole lot of nothing."

Three hours later they were in a plush windowless boardroom buried in the heart of the gigantic National Security Agency building at Fort Meade, Maryland. They had been offered coffee, tea and some very stale Danishes with gummy lemon-curd centres while they waited, seated at an immense boardroom-style table, fully thirty feet long and made from highly polished and highly abused rosewood. Fifteen other agents from various departments, as well as military personnel, waited with them, some of them inhaling the ancient Danish pastries with great relish. A few minutes later, an intern, two NSA code breakers and a supervisor walked in. The intern shuffled around the table, handing out thin spiral-bound reports stamped, in very bold letters on the pale blue covers, TOP SECRET. The other three took their place at the head of the table and laid various folders and notes in front of themselves.

Derek opened his copy as the three men prepared. The first page contained little other than several arcane references to numbered files, long strings of numbers and a brief paragraph listing the names of the people who prepared and supervised the report. The second page was a summary of contents. As he leafed through, the NSA supervisor cleared his throat and addressed the room.

"Ladies and gentlemen, my name is Richard Landry. With me is Daniel Morris on my right and Glen Fulton on my left. Daniel works in computer cryptology here at the NSA and Glen works in signals."

He took a pair of glasses from the pocket of his suit jacket and put them. Then he opened a folder and began to read. "On September 4th, the NSA received a notebook kept by the two terrorist suspects thought responsible for the Salt Lake poisoning who were apprehended in Wyoming. FBI agent Derek James and CIA agent Catherine Hunt" — he nodded at them — "were on the scene shortly afterward and brought to us a notebook containing several pages of notes and maps concerning the Salt Lake attack. It appears the terrorists were well trained in target evaluation, including ingress and egress techniques. These people are not the sloppy, poorly trained suicide bombers we see around the world. These notes show that these men were carefully studying not one but several targets of opportunity in Salt Lake. It now seems clear that they exercise relative autonomy in picking their targets and implementing attacks, something that, understandably, makes our job of tracking them more difficult than we had previously thought.

"Until this time, we'd assumed that a controller, probably out of country, was picking the targets and issuing orders. That is not their method. The notes, however, have revealed an Achilles heel. I am positive the instigators of these attacks would be horrified to find that this notebook has fallen in our laps. All indications are that anything written during decoding should be destroyed immediately. The Salt Lake terrorists, for reasons known only to them, apparently ignored those orders. Their notes have revealed a code, arranged by colour and image, that they refer to when viewing certain porn sites, most of which originate, we think, from servers in Africa and Asia. Objects in the background of pictures on these sites send them to other web addresses that appear harmless but in fact give provide information that allows them to locate previously emplaced weapons and supplies.

"In the Salt Lake attack, the notes indicate that the terrorists had visited a porn site. We also have their laptop, which showed us that they had then visited several pages that used blue frames around the pictures. This particular site has about two hundred pages and uses about ten different colours for its picture frames. In no instance does a page display more than one colour of frame. The laptop shows that they had visited three pages, each with a blue frame. This is where we got lucky, because the fellow making the notes was a doodler. He scrawled the Arabic and English words for blue several times and doodled around them on his notepad. The notes are in a shaky hand, indicating that they were probably made in a moving car. Viewing the web pages he listed, we looked for embedded codes, number strings and a host of other possible digitized data. The notes once again came to the rescue. A reference to one of the girls in the pictures said that she was from Salt Lake City.

"With that, we had our first substantial clue. We examined the one particular picture on the page describing a girl from Salt Lake. In the background of her picture, on the wall of her bedroom, was a calendar with dates picked out in blue. These formed a very simple code the decryption computers took care of. The numbers represented letters in the Mesopotamian Arabic dialect. The letters gave the address of a reputable travel blog on which we found a posting that looked as if it was written by a Swiss family describing their American vacation. In the blog were maps of the Salt Lake area and a description of how to reach a scenic view that featured a cabin. It also mentioned that litter had spoiled some of the area, citing as an example an ugly cement bag.

"A police team sent to follow these instructions found that a cement bag had been firmly wedged in the brush and that this bag marked the laneway to an abandoned cabin. Judging from recent disturbances and vehicle tracks, we think this is where the terrorists picked up the sarin-filled canisters they used in their attack as well as the explosives that remained unused in the trunk of their car.

"So now that we are starting to understand how they operate, we can make some sense of what we've found on several other laptops that have come into our possession. These confirm that other teams are using porn sites — not all the same porn sites, but in all cases the colour framing around the photographs is the same. In only one other case did we get some paper notes. These were written on hotel paper in a water-soluble ink. In those notes was the location of an arms cache written in plain English. Police secured them before the terrorists had time to destroy them, but aside from the written location of the cache, the rest of the notes seemed insignificant scrawl — incomprehensible because we didn't have the source. These notes originated with the pair who were posing as foreign students and were taken in a hotel in Sedona, Arizona — the two responsible for the attack on the Middleton Primary School in Scottsdale. So far, interrogators haven't been able to get much out of them, and it was assumed they'd cached the weapons themselves. Now it seems we were wrong. It looks like there are pre-positioned weapons caches spread across the United States. We don't yet know who positioned these caches or when, but we're working on that, and we're working under the assumption that the same kind of embedded Internet location system is used in each case.

"Our key to the command and information structure of the enemy, or at least a portion of it, is the colour frames around the porn gallery pictures. Computers are culling all similar sites and marking those that use framing, but as it's a relatively popular method of posting graphics, we have our work cut out for us. We're working on the supposition that only sites that use one colour frame per page are of interest, but that still leaves us in a very large pond. We have to examine each one frame by frame to determine if there is intel or not, and to complicate things, we're finding that the calendar trick is not used in all cases. In some pictures, other items in the background will hold the key, or there is no information at all. It may be that different teams use different coloured frames or other information sources, such as background signs or even descriptions of the girls in the text, to receive directions to the appropriate websites. New pictures are downloaded almost every day while others disappear.

"In this froth, spread across hundreds of sites, lies the key to the command and control of the enemy. It's an ingenuous method for supplying fresh intelligence. The first laptop we secured, from the bomber in Cincinnati, shows the pages they frequented, but on those pages, none of the pictures features a calendar in the background. Instead, there were bulletin boards and handwritten signs in the background. We're working on those to determine if they represent code strings, like those on the calendars. We just started that process this morning, but it shouldn't take too long. On the signs, various colours are featured, and some are the same colour as the frames around the pictures. It looks like a strike to us, now that we know something about their methodology. Now the trick will be to realize the intelligence at the same time as the terrorists do and perhaps beat them to the punch."

Taking off his glasses, he closed his notebook. "So, are there any questions?"

Derek and Catherine discussed the briefing on their short trip back to Washington. The trip itself was made along uncongested roads with only a few checkpoints. While many of the restrictions imposed on daily travel by martial law had been lifted to enable people to get back to their lives, traffic on the roads was still very light. Gasoline prices had tripled, and many stations were closed from lack of supply. Gasoline tankers moved across the nation warily and had to be heavily guarded against roadside bombs. They were a popular target for the enemy, as were tanker cars on the rail lines. In more unpopulated areas, they had also been shot at with small-calibre explosive rounds by snipers secreted hundreds of yards away.

Moving most chemicals and dangerous industrial supplies — the most targeted objects in America — was a difficult and risky task. Unfortunately, there was not anywhere near enough military or law enforcement personnel to escort every tanker truck and freight train that the country needed to maintain its economy. Even though the number of carriers targeted and blown up was a tiny fraction of the nation's supply, the spectre of gasoline tankers ablaze in villages, towns or cities or on desolate country roads was a powerful and sobering inducement to caution. As a result, many Americans found themselves thrust into an ecologically friendly world where they appropriated their children's bicycles and scooters to get to work and out shopping. In one month, American culture had been shaken to its roots, and Americans were thrust headlong into a very new reality.

While they were waiting for traffic to clear a checkpoint, Catherine's cellphone rang. She answered, "Hunt."

The call was from Brian Good.

"Hello Brian," she said. "We're on the highway about halfway back." She looked at Derek over her sunglasses as she listened to Good on the other end of the phone. "Great, we'll be back ASAP," she said, snapping the phone shut almost on top of her goodbye.

"More good news," she said in answer to Derek's raised eyebrow. "Brian says they just got some interesting intel from overseas. We're doing the follow up. He wants us back as soon as possible to brief us on our next trip. He didn't say where we're going, but he did say we'd need our passports."

"That is good news. Maybe things are starting to break in our favour," said Derek. He revved the car's engine impatiently as the line of cars inched forwards once more. He knew better than to try pulling around and jumping line. Everyone in America did now. The checkpoints around Washington were manned by troops hardened in Iraq whose checkpoint duties there had trained them to shoot first and ask questions later. Derek had no desire to add to the growing list of injuries and fatalities that had occurred over the last couple of weeks at checkpoints.

CHAPTER 12

"Sir, we're painting a force of three ships, one destroyer and two destroyer escorts. They're entering the straits and will be passing the Reagan when we're positioned due north of the Musandam Peninsula. That'll give us about two miles of separation," reported the combat control officer three decks below the flag bridge where Captain Glen Billings and Admiral Foster Cook presided over the aircraft carrier Ronald Reagan and her escort group, currently entering the strait, inbound to the Persian Gulf.

"Damn, those sons of bitches. Two miles is not enough," said Billings, "especially if they decide that a couple of escorts and a tin can are worth exchanging for a carrier."

"We aren't at war yet," replied Cook. "Just make sure every radar in the strike force is turned on and every gun trained on them. I want low- and high-level CAPs as well, and make damned sure the Chinese commander knows they're hot. Get some more Sea Hawks in the air. Spread them out to the north of us and get them dipping as close to Iranian waters as we can go. Let's make damned sure there aren't any subs sitting on the bottom using those Iranian islands as cover. If they find one, I want the helos parting their hair. Their sub commanders need to know that if they sneeze in the wrong direction, we'll have their asses."

"Maybe we should slow, avoid passing in the choke point. The strait's only twenty miles wide," Billings replied, concerned. "They couldn't have planned it better if what they're trying to do is run us out of manoeuvring room."

"Captain, I appreciate your concern for the welfare of your ship, but I'll be damned if I'm going to let a couple of pissy little Chinese toy boats push this strike force off its course. And I'm sure as hell not going to change speed to accommodate them. Bad enough that the Lincoln group had to go out of their way to avoid them, but that was before we knew they were playing games with us. They're not going to win this one. I want escorts all over them like flies on shit, and I want so many aircraft overhead they won't be able to hear themselves think."

"Yes, sir," Billings replied.

September 13.
Aboard the Sanming, Straits of Hormuz.

Captain Serik Manai was a rarity in the People's Liberation Army Navy. He was not ethnic Chinese. His family were Kazakhs, originally from western Mongolia near the Altair Mountains. His father, a devout follower of Mao Zedong, had settled his family in Bayan Obo, a town on the Chinese-Mongolian border, when Manai was a child. Manai came from a place that was as far from the ocean as is possible in Asia. And yet as a small boy, he dreamt of nothing other than going to sea. He left home to join the People's Liberation Army, and after two years as a regular infantryman, he achieved his goal and won a transfer to the navy.

He fought racism and prejudice from his peers and his superiors in the navy, but he finally earned both respect and rank with his perseverance, quiet efficiency and adroit political savvy. Over twenty years later, he commanded the bridge of the PLAN Jiangwhei-class missile cruiser Sanming, breathing the humid, sweltering air of the Persian Gulf and still as in love with the sea as when he was a small boy.

Just visible in the ribbons of heat, two nautical miles behind him, the larger Wenzhou followed in his wake. The Wenzhou was a more modern and more capable Jiangkai-class missile frigate that had just arrived on station along with three other warships. Manai considered the trailing Wenzhou a beautiful ship, and he envied some of her advanced weaponry, but he would not have traded the Sanming, his first command, for her. Out of sight, one of the old Shenzen-class missile destroyers brought up the rear of the three-ship patrol. With the addition of the Wenzhou and three other frigates, the Chinese flotilla in the Persian Gulf and Arabian Sea numbered fourteen surface ships, the largest long-range blue-water deployment in the history of the Chinese navy, but a force that was still far outnumbered by the American naval forces in the area. Still, Manai thought to himself, a wily flea can make an elephant go mad.

His patrol had been waiting for the American carrier and its escorts to arrive at the strait. It was no accident that the three ships were going to pass the Americans in the narrowest channel, between the tip of the Musandam Peninsula and the Iranian islands and coast to the north. It was a good chance for the Chinese crews to see their American adversary at close quarters and would drive the American escorts wild with worry. Nowhere else but in the strait would the Chinese vessels get within two miles of an American carrier without being forcibly warned off or blown out of the water.

"Sir, we have a high-speed contact approaching from 026 degrees, range ten miles and altitude five thousand feet, closing at three hundred knots!" said one of his junior officers, tension already apparent in his voice. Every man on the bridge knew what was going on. — one of the reasons Manai was popular with his crew but sometimes in conflict with the navy's political officer. The men were excited and, if they were smart, a little afraid.

"Good, good," said Manai. "The first buzzings from a hive of angry bees. Read off the contact as it approaches."

"Five miles, three thousand feet, sir. Two aircraft," said the operator seconds later. "Four miles and descending. Increasing speed."

Manai motioned to his first officer. "Shall we go out and enjoy the show?"

"Yes, sir."

Manai walked out onto the gangway accompanied by his first officer. He looked westward in the direction from which the aircraft were approaching.

The radar operator's voice issued from the speakers above the small deck. "Two miles and closing. Zero altitude."

On the decks below, Manai could see the automatic close-in anti-aircraft systems swivelling to pick up the incoming fighters that were now racing across the ocean at the height of the waves.

"There, there they are!" yelled a sailor on watch excitedly.

"One mile."

Two tiny dots had appeared, low on the water. In fractions of a second they grew into two F-18 Super Hornets that rose just high enough to clear the frigates' radar masts, thundering overhead in a stirring display of power. The men on the frigate covered their ears as the roar of the fighters' engines and afterburners washed over the small warship. The two fighters nosed up vertically and, with their afterburners streaming exhaust, they assaulted the ship with a sonic boom and then went vertical and in the blink of an eye were lost to sight in the hazy skies above. Their engines were still audible, however, a continuous rumble that for the next few hours would be the Chinese ship's companion as flight after flight of F-18s made their presence known, although none as dramatically as these first two.

It was a great exercise for his combat command centre. They were busy painting the aircraft with all their systems, including ship-to-air missile acquisition and the close-in acquisition radars that were slaved to their 30-mm chain guns.

Manai thought of how nervous the fighter pilots must be with all of their threat displays lit up and flying so close to ships that they could not be entirely sure would not blow them from the sky. Of course, he shared their trepidation. He knew that any one of the Super Hornets carried enough weaponry to turn his ship into a series of diminishing ripples on the water's surface.

September 14.
Riyadh, Saudi Arabia.

Al-Munajjid was issued through the extravagant wrought-iron and ceramic-inlaid gates into a private walled garden. The heat of the midday sun was oppressive, and al-Munajjid wished he was wearing traditional clothes rather than the stylish Western clothing he had on. By noon in Riyadh, even the most expensive and lightweight linen Italian suit looked as if it had been dragged along a muddy road for an hour.

He walked through the garden to a small pavilion at its centre. An older gentleman, the same man who'd met him in Ta'if, was bent over a row of potted seedlings with a set of secateurs, snipping small branches from each one. His name was Bandar id bin Abdul Aziz. The open-sided pavilion was set up in such a way as to force al-Munajjid to stand in the blazing sun while its occupant, well shaded and under a palm-bladed electric ceiling fan, finished with the last plant in the line before finally, without turning from the task at hand, addressing him.

"Dearest cousin," he said quietly but with venom, "I am well aware of the success of your endeavour, and I wholeheartedly support your actions both in heart and in purse, but I cannot ignore the fact that the Americans are not leaving the Middle East in any significant numbers. Not only are they not leaving, but the actions of your friends have actually inspired the arrival of two more carrier fleets. So instead of one, we now have three. Just how does this encourage my own unimportant plans? I think to myself. In my ignorance of world events, I had anticipated less, not more, American influence in this region. Your plan and my purse," he spat, his voice rising with anger, "was supposed to draw the Americans out of Iraq, not fill the gulf from top to bottom with their ships."

Al-Munajjid, unaccustomed to occupying a servile position, bridled inwardly but knew better than to let the contempt he felt show. "Yes cousin, it is unfortunate, but the slow withdrawal of the Americans only demonstrates that they are a slow-moving and cumbersome opponent and unused to having to be fast on their feet. Their media, even their congress, are screaming to bring their troops home to deal with their internal problems. A major withdrawal is just a matter of time. They are begging their allies to send reinforcements so they can pull men out. In time, they will realize that no one is coming, and they will leave."

"And what about the fleets?" Aziz turned from his plants to look directly at al-Munajjid for the first time, his steel-hard gaze underscored by his distinguished, raptorial features. "Their fleets will have no place in quelling the attacks in America."

"No, they will not," responded al-Munajjid, "but they will find it hard to justify the huge expense and fuel demands of maintaining these fleets while their economy crumbles and their people go without gas and without jobs. When the troops leave the Middle East, so will their fleets. The American government will be looking for any way it can to save money and concentrate on their internal problems. They may not want to dig into their strategic reserves or uncap internal oil production, but those assets exist and will encourage them to perhaps focus inwardly for a time while they try to establish order at home. By the time they re-establish order, our plans will have borne fruit, and the world will be a very different place — one in which the Americans will have lost their influence."

"What about Europe?"

"Europe is not America's friend. They never have been. Only the English are willing to stand by the Americans, but not at the expense of a war within their own borders. We have made it quite clear by our actions in Europe and Britain that any support of America will bring retribution. After an explosion yesterday near Brussels, the ambulance and police refused to help a vanload of American employees of Chase Manhattan Bank. Emergency services stayed well back until the bomb squad got there to see if there were any other bombs. As the bomb squad arrived, my people detonated two car bombs remotely."

"So, it was not successful?"

"On the contrary, it showed how successful we have become. It has literally become too dangerous to help Americans. Stay away, you live. Rush to help, you will die. The media themselves have made such figurative comparisons: Help an American, and you could end up dead. Help America, you could end up embroiled in their war. Very few governments have the stomach for that or a population that would tolerate having their children killed to prop up American interests. My dearest cousin, I just ask that you be patient. The American fleet will be powerless to effect our plans for this nation."

"It is good to talk with you, cousin," Aziz replied quietly, "but for your sake, I hope you are right. If not, well I am not the only one who will be disappointed if our desires do not come to pass as planned."

He turned back to his plants and waved his hand as if brushing away crumbs.

Al-Munajjid stood for a moment, his eyes narrowing, stunned by the dismissal, and then he withdrew wordlessly, rage as well as the searing sun colouring his cheeks. Here is another one, he thought to himself, that will be made to pay. The arrogant old piece of dung actually thought his money was being used to elevate him to power.

September 15.
The Oval Office, the White House, Washington DC.

The president sat, his eyes focused on an elaborate pen and holder set his father gave him when he graduated from college. His old man, who passed away many years ago, had joked that he expected his son to keep enough refills for the pen so that he could still use them when he took over the Oval Office. He had.

There were at least six others people in the office and aides coming and going in a subdued chaos. Each man seated on the comfortable couches in front of the president's desk were taking his turn briefing the president on the events of the day before as well as on current situations. The undersecretary of the Department of Commerce had just finished his report with a dreary summation of the country's slide into recession and figures that showed rampant inflation. The New York Stock Exchange had recently re-opened, but it was moribund. American stock markets were dragging the global economy down and then down again.

While no one in this room wanted to use the word, the media had no such qualms and screamed "depression" in their headlines. On one of the TV screens set in the Oval Office wall, a ruggedly handsome and clearly self-possessed reporter revelled in showing pictures of the dirty thirties and the dustbowl, while a banner ran across the bottom of the screen asking, "Are soup lines next?" Pundits claimed that America's industrial might had been sold off to their would-be enemies and heaped abuse on the president's administration even though he'd been elected on a platform of bringing U.S. heavy industry back from the brink of extinction. That he had not been able to do so in the three short years of his first administration now seemed to his critics an impeachable offence. They chose to ignore that for twenty years or more, U.S. corporations had been fleeing to foreign producers in their never-ending quest for higher quarterly profits while Americans regularly passed over more expensive American-made goods to get deals at their neighbourhood big box stores. America had sold its soul and its technologies for cheaper gas, cheaper goods and Saturday blue light specials. Now it appeared the entire fragile mess was crumbling, and it was time to pay the piper.

Dan Blomstrum rose and passed the president a memo detailing the casualties of the day before. Sixteen civilians had died in car bombings. Three tankers — two gasoline and one concentrated boric acid — were blown up by roadside bombs. A train was derailed in South Dakota, resulting in three dead and a large chemical spill that would have to wait as there were no trained resources or suitable equipment available for cleanup. Six police officers were assassinated while on duty. One piece of good news, if it could be called that, was that a large bomb had been discovered before it detonated near a police station in Selma, Alabama. No lives lost. Not true of a National Guard truck blown up by an anti-tank mine attached to the bottom of a manhole cover in Cleveland. Eight troops in the truck died as well as eleven bystanders.

It was a fairly light day in America's war. Total casualties for September 14 were forty-four dead and sixty-two wounded, down by twenty-four casualties from the day before. These were pinpricks in a population of almost three hundred million spread across such a vast country. Nonetheless, their persistence had a dramatic effect on the nation's morale. A note at the bottom of the memo stated that nineteen people who were exposed to the radiation cloud loosed northwest of Las Vegas, including the terrorist himself, were critically ill and not expected to recover.

Finishing the memo, the president addressed Warren Clyde, secretary of state. "How is State doing? Are we getting anywhere with the Chinese?"

"Mr. President," replied Clyde, leaning forward on the couch, "they are intractable. They will not respond to either our requests or our threats and their constant lecturing of our people as if they were schoolchildren is starting to fray nerves. Every time someone loses their temper, the Chinese cluck and tell us how understandably upset we must be. They are as large a pack of condescending jackasses as we have ever come across, but as a tactic, it's working well. It's really hard to threaten anyone who refuses to acknowledge the threat. They aren't asking for anything, so there isn't even a platform to base negotiations on. Short of embroiling us in a shooting war with them, we just don't know how to go about making them see things our way."

"What about our request for allied troops to fill the breech when we pull our forces back in the Middle East?"

"Not one, sir. The Germans, Italians, Dutch and, of course, the French have refused outright. The Brits say they are considering it but think they could only do it with support from their populace, which is a polite way of saying no. The Canadians can't. Their two guys are busy, and their naval rowboat's leaking."

The tension eased just a little as the listeners, including the president, chuckled at the mild jibe.

"Our good friends the Russians have said they'd be willing to send troops, as has the League of Arab Nations — exactly what we don't want. The Iranians have actually been pulling troops away from the border with Iraq, but this is likely a ruse to encourage us to leave, and strangely enough, both Iraq and Afghanistan are incredibly quiet and peaceful. There are small incidents between Shiites and Sunnis but no substantial attacks on U.S. personnel.

"It's as if the whole region's holding its breath, waiting to see what happens.

Once again, this could be a ploy to lull us into pulling out more quickly, but I have to say if it is a tactic, it's a bloody good one, because the media have been picking up on the lack of activity and are using it to beat us over the head and demand an immediate withdrawal. The implications are terrifying — that whoever is attacking us at home has enough power to quell the unrest of an untold number of warring factions across the Middle East. That kind of influence is unprecedented. More amazing still, we have no real clue of who's behind this. So far, every terrorist organization that has laid claim has been proved wrong.

"The final point, returning full circle, is once again the Chinese. Their naval forces have been very active in the Gulf of Oman and the Persian Gulf, and they have reinforced their fleet, which now numbers fourteen surface ships and an indeterminate number of subs. They will not tell us what their ships are doing other than to say that they pose no threat to the U.S. Navy or our interests in the region and are engaged in peaceful pursuits that are none of our business. They have been in and out of Iranian waters with total impunity and, on occasion, they have conducted small exercises with Iranian gunboats and patrol ships. They will not comment on any of these exercises or even acknowledge them."

"Admiral?" inquired the president.

Irving responded, "Mr. President, we are having the same problems as State. We can't get them to acknowledge that there is a problem or give us any clear indication of what they are trying to accomplish tactically. They are all over our ships in the Gulf. Their units have been blocking us by simply getting in the way. When we demand they move, they apologize and either dither about or withdraw slowly or site mechanical problems. Yesterday three ships timed their entry to the Strait of Hormuz to coincide with the entry of the Reagan, which was arriving from the Gulf of Oman to take up station in the Persian Gulf. The strike force kept aircraft over the ships all day, and two destroyers intercepted them. During the intercept, the crews of the Chinese ships came on deck and waved at our ships. One Chinese frigate moved to within one and a half miles of the Reagan before one of our destroyers, the Decatur, and the Aegis cruiser Lake Champlain physically blocked it from moving any closer. The Chinese crews were behaving like tourists on a passenger liner.

"Short of firing on the Chinese ships, there seems to be no answer to these provocations, and they damned well know it. If they are sabre rattling, it's the weirdest form of it I have ever seen. They are intentionally antagonizing forces that outnumber them, have full air support and are their technological superiors in every way. It's hard to understand what they think they can gain aside from our enmity."

"We could say the same thing about their fiscal policies," said Dan Blomstrum. Their economy is being hurt just as badly as ours, a point that they keep raising. And yet, they continue to sell at huge losses. They have certainly secured a much wider resource base, but it doesn't come close to representing the amount of money they are losing."

"Yes, but if this is a war," said the president, "you always expect to take casualties. Their nation's economy and their population's well-being have never been Beijing's first concern. I think we've been living with the dragon in our backyard for so long that we've forgotten that it's red. China is not a capitalist state. They can and do play from a different rule book, and what we have to do is figure out what game they are playing and what they hope to gain from all of this."

"I think that is quite clear, Mr. President," said Secretary of State Clyde. "The Chinese are waging a financial war with us that is dedicated to cutting off our access to world resources, most especially Middle Eastern oil, as well as to crippling our economy. I think they're using the terrorist attacks on our nation to promote their own interests, if, indeed, they aren't behind those attacks in the first place." He looked around the room at the men and read the looks on their faces. "Oh, look, I don't for a minute think there isn't one of you who hasn't thought that the Chinese are probably behind this."

The president spoke. "He's right. None of you would be in this room if the thought hadn't occurred to you. What we need to do is get some kind of definitive answer one way or the other. If it is the Chinese, and that thought scares the shit out of me, then we will have to act swiftly and with a ferocity that completely stuns them."

"There's one problem with that, Mr. President," said Admiral Irving. "We may not have the ability to strike a decisive blow against China or her interests right now. The way we're strung out all over the world and with so many resources needed at home, we need to focus on just one or two specific areas of interest. As far as I can see, they're after oil at our expense. They've built the deepwater port. They're building ships as fast as they can, and they're building up naval and land forces in and around the Gulf."

"I hardly think a few thousand civilian workers in East Africa and a few small ships in the Gulf constitute a substantial threat," said Blomstrum.

"I hardly think it is a threat we can afford to ignore," replied Irving, raising his voice. "We're only guessing at how many of those so-called civilian workers are sitting in the Horn of Africa. There could be a lot more than we think, and we're not talking about a bunch of Chinese Peace Corps workers here. All of them carry guns and have significant military training, up to and including time in the

Chinese Special Forces. Even the Somali warlords are scared of those bastards. It wouldn't take much to assemble them as a strike force using East Africa as a staging area. They could hit and control a lot of small but critical areas in the Middle East, especially if they're cooperating with the Iranians and the Pakistanis. Pulling our forces out of Iraq could seriously endanger our access to the oil reserves in the Middle East."

"We've lived without Iraqi oil before, admiral," said the undersecretary of commerce. "If we need to, we can always fall back on Saudi oil plus our own strategic reserves until we can re-establish our influence in Iraq. The Chinese won't have an easier time of it in the Middle East than we've had."

"That might be true, but would you be willing to bet your life on it, Mr. Undersecretary?" Irving snapped.

"Gentlemen," said the president, taking back control of the room. "I have some very hard decisions to make here and much too little information to base them on. That said, I'm forced to roll the die and make them anyway. The way I see it, we're going to have to bring a substantial force back from the Middle East.

"Admiral, I hate to keep beating the same drum, but it's time for a major withdrawal. I need to see a plan from you outlining a quick and substantial reduction in ground forces in the Gulf region. We need them at home. You can maintain enough reserves in men and material in Iraq, Kuwait and the Emirates to persuade the locals that we are not abandoning our interests or the interests of our allies. Using those forces, I want a military cordon built around the oil fields, pipelines and ports in Iraq. I don't give a shit if there's not a single Marine or Ranger in Baghdad or any other Iraqi city. Abandon them. If the Sunnis and Shiites decide to kill each other on mass, I don't care. It's time they took responsibility for themselves. If you need to move more naval units and air support into the Gulf to back up the ground forces around the oil fields, then do it, but get my soldiers home and get them home now."

CHAPTER 13

September 15.
Mossad headquarters, Herzliyya, Israel.

Derek was glad that Catherine was with him. She was a natural traveller and seemed as at home and composed in the crowded streets of Tel Aviv and Herzliyya as in an American town. They were stuffed into the back of a scruffy ten-year-old BMW 320 taxi replete with torn seats and an overly effusive Palestinian driver. He gabbled on at great length on subjects ranging from the weather to his moderate political views, which Derek thought were modified for their benefit and not likely his real beliefs. That his captive audience seemed completely uninterested in his thoughts on world events had completely escaped him and, in fact, encouraged him to make his points by turning in the seat and gesturing while the car continued to careen through the congested thoroughfares as if it had a mind of its own.

The cabbie had picked them up from their hotel, the Dan Panorama Tel Aviv, where they had grabbed a few hours sleep after arriving late the night before. The trek to Israel had been arduous. They were booked on one of the few international commercial flights currently operating from the States to Europe. There was to be a stop in Paris and then on to Rome, where they would connect with an El Al flight to Tel Aviv. There were no commercial flights direct to Israel from the United States right now and only a few to destinations in Europe. Even with the greatly diminished volume of air traffic and available airliners since August 18, the waiting lounge in Washington's Dulles was bereft of passengers.

The government was allowing commercial airliners to fly, but flights were very tightly controlled and restricted to routes that took them over only the most thinly populated areas of the United States. If an airliner pilot were unlucky enough to wander from his flight plan, before long he would find a fully armed F-16 on either wingtip. Airport security had also grown in magnitude since August. Gone were the minimum-wage security personnel. Now it was military police or federal agents who cleared people through, and it took over two hours to perform the check, even with the reduced number of travellers.

Unlike in earlier times, Derek and Catherine's badges and identification did not make their passage any easier nor did it illicit a more friendly reaction from security, whose demeanour ranged from detached professionalism to downright belligerence. Having endured all that, they were just settling themselves in the lounge to wait the forty minutes until boarding when the PA system announced an immediate evacuation of the terminal, and black-uniformed security guards along with regular military police swept through the building driving everyone before them.

A bomb threat had been phoned in, closing down operations. These threats were becoming commonplace and were almost as effective as a real bomb at halting the flow of what little commercial air traffic currently existed. While everyone knew that the threats were probably toothless, no one dared take the risk of ignoring them. The flight was cancelled, and when they finally found an airline representative who would take the time to speak with them, they were informed that even if things went well, their flight would not leave until the next day. Derek phoned headquarters and informed them of the situation. Twenty minutes later, he got a call back from Brian Good. After Derek informed him that they were stuck in an airport parking lot during a security shutdown, Good asked them to wait a few minutes while he looked into alternative transport.

Three hours later, following yet another security check, they were sitting on canvas jump seats on board an air force C-17 Globemaster III lifting off from Andrews and headed for Ramstein Air Force Base in Germany. The C-17 was the antithesis of a modern airliner. It was bulky, incredibly noisy and almost impossibly uncomfortable. Adding to the general charm of the no-nonsense cargo plane was a sign on the bulkhead over the toilet in the tiny washroom: "Take time and aim. That's an order. Piss rots aluminum."

The spacious interior of the aircraft was almost devoid of cargo aside from a couple of pallets of aircraft parts that were tied down near the centre of the largely hollow fuselage. The loadmaster, a pleasant airman in his mid-twenties with a twangy Georgia accent, explained that they were bringing ground personnel back from Ramstein, Germany, and that the American part of the base would soon be working with only a skeleton crew. Hours later Derek and Catherine, still partially deafened by their transatlantic journey despite using ear plugs, were on a small, crowded Lufthansa commuter jet headed for Rome, where they would try to catch another El Al connection to Tel Aviv.

It took them almost twenty-six hours to reach Israel. Derek had never thought a journey where you nothing but sit could be so completely draining. Dragging himself out of bed the next day after only four hours sleep was one of the most difficult things that he'd ever done. They had a quick breakfast of stale scones, fresh orange juice and thick coffee in the hotel's atrium and then walked out and hailed a cab. The cab driver's incessant monologue during the journey north to Herzliyya did little to lighten his mood, and he marvelled at Catherine's ability to look so fresh and relaxed and to be so patient with the driver, who was clearly taken with her looks and trying to impress her.

As the taxi approached Mossad headquarters, they were stopped at a security checkpoint at the base of the hill leading up to the modern buildings that housed Israel's world-famous secret service. Three soldiers in combat fatigues and carrying automatic weapons watched as a security officer in a white shirt and tie asked Derek and Catherine to get out of the taxi and checked their identification and documents. The taxi turned and left, and a white van pulled up to carry the agents the short trip up the tree-lined roadway that led to the Mossad complex.

In the first gesture of welcome they'd received on this trip, a young Mossad employee met them at the main doors and rushed them past the security check and up a flight of stairs to a hallway lined with offices. The floor was carpeted a rich blue, and the walls were sky blue, a cheery combination that belied the gravity of the work that went on there. Three quarters of the way down the hall, they were led through a double door into a large reception office.

A middle-aged woman sat at a desk thumbing through a pile of papers. On seeing them she rose. "Good morning. I'm Gilda Fein, Mr. Halevy's assistant. Mr. Halevy is expecting you. If you could take a seat, I'll inform him that you've arrived."

"Thank you," replied Catherine. Derek and Catherine took seats on a black leather couch behind a glass-topped coffee table covered in periodicals ranging from National Geographic to a Jane's Defense Weekly, as well as newspapers in both English and Hebrew. Derek was just reaching for the Jane's when the door at the back of the office opened and a short black-haired man burst into the room as if riding a wave of raw energy.

"Welcome, welcome," he said, striding across the room and presenting his hand to Derek, "I'm Jacob Halevy." He was short, but what he lacked in stature he more than made up for in build. He was in shirt sleeves, which were rolled up, displaying thick muscular arms. On one forearm he sported a tattoo of the Star of David with crossed swords behind it. His torso was massive, and Derek thought he wouldn't like to go one on one with him. In place of a tie, Halevy had left the top button of his shirt open and wore a gold Star of David nestled on a thick matt of jet-black hair.

He turned to Catherine. "And Agent Hunt, it's so very good to have you back."

"Hello, Jacob," she replied smiling. "It's good to be back."

"Come in." He gestured toward his office door. "I've had coffee, tea and some very good pastries brought in. Isaac Mesulam…" He looked at Catherine. "You haven't met him, have you?"

She shook her head.

"Well, Isaac is the one who put this briefing together. He has a wonderful grasp of minutiae. If not for him, I'm afraid this little golden egg we are about to serve up might have escaped us entirely."

Halevy's office was a working space, and in stark contrast to the outer office, which was as neat as a pin, Jacob's inner sanctum was certainly not a showpiece. Stacks of file boxes lined one wall, and papers, books and framed family photographs rested on the window sill. The view outside was of a parking lot bordered by scrawny palms with a few tongues of mown grass intruding into the asphalt. One picture, a mass-produced painting of a Mediterranean coast, hung over his desk at a ten-degree list. His desk was cluttered with three stacks of papers eight inches tall, memos and reports and a number of items that had a white cloth thrown over them.

Seeing Catherine eyeing the cloth, Halevy shrugged his shoulders. "I hope you don't mind. It's a little security precaution. You understand. Please, sit. Let's have a coffee, shall we?"

There were five wingback chairs set in a circle next to the windows. At their centre was a small round table that held both coffee and tea pots, milk and sugar, pastries and an assortment of plastic spoons and plain white serviettes. The trio sat, and Halevy poured a coffee for Derek, a tea for Catherine and then a coffee for himself and took a sip.

For the next few minutes he regaled the pair with stories of his military service and, in response to a question from Derek, described how he and Catherine had met four years earlier at an Austrian Embassy affair in Belgium, an affair, he said, that featured many more spies than diplomats. He laughed, saying he'd spent the whole evening expecting James Bond to put in an appearance. Instead of an urbane Bond, he'd been introduced to a British foreign office worker named Wally Bumby, who'd had a great big mustard stain on his lapel and bad breath. He finished by saying that the entire evening had not gone badly. He'd also been introduced to Catherine. "Too bad I'm a married man and scared of my wife," he laughed.

Catherine chuckled and poked back. "Jacob, if you aren't careful, I can arrange for your wife to find out about your philandering ways."

"And then I'd be finished. You'd have accomplished in a second what the Palestinians have not been able to do in twenty years."

At that moment, a middle-aged fellow in a dark suit, with a corona of white fluff surrounding his otherwise bald pate, a hawkish nose and a small greying beard, walked through the door.

"Ah, Isaac," said Halevy. "Isaac Mesulam, I would like you to meet Catherine Hunt and Derek James. I'm sorry. It's James, isn't it?"

Derek nodded as he rose to shake Mesulam's hand.

"Catherine is with the CIA and Derek is a special agent with the FBI."

"Pleased to meet you," said Mesulam.

Derek and Catherine sat back down after rising, and Mesulam fell onto one of the wingbacks, clucking under his breath as he organized an armful of folders. He placed two on the table and the remainder on the floor beside his chair.

"So, Isaac, let's tell our friends what we've discovered."

Mesulam opened the first of the two folders and passed copies of a series of photographs to the two Americans. "I was reviewing an assortment of low-interest files when I came upon these," he said. "They're photographs taken in Allepo, Syria, on September 1st of a Saudi by the name of Muhammad al-Munajjid. They were taken shortly after what we think may have been a meeting with three Chinese businessmen at the Citadel, an old historic ruin in the centre of the city.

"Interestingly, the meeting took place while the Citadel was closed to the public, and it appears that the Mukhabarat, the Syrian secret police, were involved or at least providing security. That's what aroused our interest. Unfortunately, we have nothing on the three Chinese. They arrived on a flight from Geneva — we think — had the meeting and left, boarding a flight that took them to Damascus and then on to Beijing. We've run their pictures but come up empty."

Derek leafed through several photographs taken of the three Chinese men at the airport.

"Have you sent copies to Langley?" asked Catherine.

"Yes. We forwarded them to the CIA. So far they've had no more luck identifying them than we have. Muhammad al-Munajjid is a different matter, however. On him we have the dirt, so to speak. He's a Saudi national and very loosely related to the royal family."

"Ha!" snorted Halevy. "Who in that cursed country isn't related to the Saudi royal family?"

"Now then," admonished Catherine sarcastically, "You are referring to an honoured and trusted ally of the United States."

"With allies like that, you spend all your time removing knives from your back," replied Halevy.

"Al-Munajjid," Mesulam continued, "is an interesting character who flies below the radar much of the time but may, in fact, wield a lot of power through his connections both to certain groups on the fringes of Saudi power and to various religious groups, including some very hard-core fundamentalists. On the surface, he operates as an entrepreneur, and his interests vary from importing cheap desalination equipment from China to buying and selling Swiss chocolate, but we have strong evidence that he acts as a go-between to channel money from rich Muslim businessmen to various extremist organizations all over the world."

"So, are you saying he may be part of the attack on the U.S.?" asked Derek.

"We haven't drawn that conclusion," said Halevy, "but the interesting thing is that this man is well placed but relatively unknown and has not been under our scrutiny or anyone else's as far as we can determine."

"I was very lucky, actually," said Mesulam, "I thought he looked familiar, so I went back through our photographic files. These next pictures came to light. Even then, if it weren't for the date the pictures were taken, I doubt they would have stuck in my mind."

Mesulam held up a glossy of al-Munajjid, dressed in traditional garb, getting out of a Range Rover with a group of bodyguards. In other shots, he was walking toward and boarding a private jet. As he approached the plane, a younger, well-dressed man, swarthy in complexion, descended the steps to welcome him.

"These pictures were taken of al-Munajjid in Islamabad the day the attacks began in the United States. What is very interesting is that the aircraft he is boarding belongs to a member of the second circle of the Saudi royal family and a black sheep, as well. His name is Bandar id bin Abdul Aziz, and he has been hostile to the government in Saudi Arabia since he was deposed from a profitable ministry portfolio in the 1980s. Ostensibly, he was charged with corruption, although in Saudi Arabia that is like charging a fish for swimming. Rumour has it that he was shorting more senior members of the family on kickbacks from some pretty major building and development projects, and that's what got him into trouble."

"Whatever the reason," interjected Halevy, "he's been leading a fairly reclusive life in Riyadh and travels only occasionally to London or Paris on shopping expeditions. His children are not so reclusive, and it was one of them who greeted al-Munajjid on the aircraft."

"We purchased these photographs," continued Mesulam, "from a fortunately placed local source who thought it interesting that a private jet with Saudi markings was parked in the military area of Islamabad's airport — well away from civilian aviation and prying eyes. It was just plain luck that they happened to see it and be in a position to take the photographs just as al-Munajjid was boarding."

"Normally," said Halevy, "none of this would ring any alarms, but these are not normal times, and we've been following up on even the unlikeliest clues. Israel's enemies have been emboldened by the attacks on the United States, and it's in our interests to see them stopped as quickly as possible."

"This al-Munajjid, do we know what he's up to now?" asked Catherine.

"We've only just located him at his primary summer residence. He has a villa in the hills of Ta'if, and that poses a bit of a problem," said Halevy.

"How so?" asked Derek.

"Ta'if is a very secure area. It's a lot cooler that Riyadh, and many members of the Saudi royal family and government spend the summer there. Al-Munajjid's villa is in the middle of a very high-end group of residences. Getting an agent into the area will, I'm afraid, prove almost if not completely impossible. The Saudi security forces are very good when it comes to looking after their benefactors' privacy. If we're going to find out what he's up to, our only opportunity will be when he's on the move."

"I have to admit, I'm a little confused," said Derek. "I mean, you're telling us about this al-Munajjid at the same time you're saying you really don't know much about him or his activities. All you have is that he was in Pakistan in August and Syria a little later and that he may be passing out money. I mean, couldn't this meeting with the Chinese have something to do with buying and selling Chinese goods? I don't see enough to suspect him."

Halevy replied, "Mossad is very well connected and has reliable contacts in almost all the militant Islamic groups, including al Qaeda. While some of them have claimed the attacks on America as their own, we haven't been able to find a shred of evidence supporting their claims. On the whole, the extremists are stupid, uneducated and unsophisticated people incapable of the planning required to implement a terrorist war like the one in America. It's one thing to blow up a bus in Israel or Baghdad, quite another to put a force into the U.S. to do the same thing. We've heard rumours for months about a successor to bin Laden, a man who would lead the extremists to victory. Even though these stories are forever circulating, and we've rarely had occasion to take them seriously, we have to theorize that if none of the regular cast is responsible for the attacks on U.S. soil, the source must be elsewhere. It is for that reason that al-Munajjid's actions strike us as interesting.

"We are very good at sniffing out, how would you say it, the skunks in the woodpile, and it is the protection and attention that al-Munajjid is receiving all out of proportion to his station that makes us think that perhaps something is going on. The Syrian secret police are not in the habit of escorting ordinary businessmen to and from their meetings, and the private jets of cast-off royal family members are not usually put at the disposal of ordinary import-exporters. We suspect he could have been meeting with the Chinese to beg funding, maybe buy weapons or further some aim that we as yet do not understand. If al-Munajjid is tied up with Bandar id bin Abdul Aziz, then he is no friend of the ruling House of Saud or, by extension, America. You can assume then that there may be more to his activities than meets the eye."

"Besides," interjected Catherine, "there's not much else to go on. It can't hurt to follow this up."

"I suppose you're right," said Derek. "The worst it could be is a dead end."

"This villa in Ta'if, I assume it's a modern home?" asked Catherine.

"I don't know, but I could find out," replied Halevy.

"Why don't you."

"And we should see if he has any offices, what companies he runs or owns and what mechanisms he might have at his disposal for funnelling or laundering money," said Derek. Perhaps we can determine whether he has a computer system we can hack into."

"Next would be getting someone next to him," added Catherine.

"That would be difficult," said Mesulam.

"That would be my specialty," said Catherine quietly.

September 15.
Special Portable Emergency Radiation Burn (SPERB) unit,
Nellis Air Force Base, Las Vegas, Nevada.

Only eleven of the original twenty-six victims of plutonium poisoning were alive — several of them just barely — despite the best efforts of the team of specialists who staffed the SPERB unit, which had been formed to deal with just such an emergency as a dirty bomb. The doctors that manned it were the best in their field, assembled from all over the United States, but their patients had received far too concentrated a dose of plutonium for their treatments to have any effect. The clinic was housed in a row of negative-pressure-sealed portable buildings pulled from the back of a C-130 Hercules and situated beside an inactive taxiway at the western border of Nellis Air Force Base, far removed from the main buildings and hangars.

They were glorified tents really, but well suited to the confinement of radioactive materials. Pumps drew air through specially designed airlocks that kept pressure inside the buildings slightly lower than outside. The air passed through a series of intricate scrubbers, and the last screen in the high-tech exhaust stack of each building monitored it as it was evacuated. The moment the screen detected radiation in the plume, computers would arrest the passage of air out of the facility and lock it down. The fifteen fatalities were held in a separate portable freezer unit nearby waiting for disposal. Their remains were highly radioactive, and they were quite literally hazardous waste requiring special handling and long-term storage.

Abu Bakre, the author of the disaster, was still alive, but he was often delirious and flip-flopped between his true identity and his assumed persona, Jimmy Youngblood. He was dreadfully ill, the plutonium eating him from the inside out, and past the ability to scream from the pain that wracked him. The doctors were surprised he still survived. Other victims who had been exposed at the same time and to lower levels of radiation had already succumbed.

Bakre's interrogation had been relentless. His inquisitors cognizant of the limited time they had to wring his secrets from him. They used his rapidly developing sickness as a weapon to extract information that, if he had been healthy, he would have died to protect. Their methods would not have been condoned by the signatories of the Geneva Convention, but the inquisitors could not have cared less. This was a primitive war, one of survival, not of gentlemanly rules. The men conducting the questioning, their superiors and their superiors' superiors, on and on up to the president, were to a man interested only in results. Bakre's rights and comforts, fabrications of a gentler climate, were of no consideration.

Bakre was housed in one of the portable buildings, its sole occupant despite the presence of other beds. Unlike the other victims, he was given only enough painkillers to keep him from slipping into unconsciousness. It was the promise of painkillers that got him to talk. Even when, as the toxins consumed him, he slipped in and out of delirium, he was useful, a sponge to be wrung out. By the time he hovered between life and death, he had given up his heritage, his recruitment, training, arrival in America and many of his travels. He had for the promise of morphine scrawled maps of the locations of twelve containers filled with weapons as well as his personal codes, which allowed him to access websites to locate further arms caches as they were required. Finally, the key to trap an unknown number of terrorists, he turned in his lock. Interrogators documented the instructions for weapons distribution and the methods of telegraphing that information to the end-users and passed the intelligence gleefully to those agencies so desperate for it.

His inquisitors were satisfied with their efforts, but they didn't know that Bakre role in the war represented only ten percent of the arms supply. It was a figure he had never been party to so could not divulge. The terrorists he had been supplying were now at risk — a good beginning. And national security and police forces were instructed to be on the lookout for and search any transport containers, especially ones that appeared abandoned, across the nation.

September 16.
The White House.

"Sir, it seems the Canadians have just had their first episode." White house staffers had started to refer to attacks as episodes, an effort to arrest ever-sagging morale.

The president motioned to the West Winger delivering the news to drop the bulletin on his desk. He was working in a small office situated off the Oval Office, one that had been set up for the real paperwork of the presidency rather than the formal signings and declarations so often photographed in the Oval Office proper.

Henry Woeburn, in his role as presidential advisor, was in the office as well. His duties now included briefing the president on the Pentagon's withdrawals worldwide.

The president read that a bomb had been set off at an automotive and motorcycle trade show in Toronto. A famous motorcycle customizer and television personality from the United States had been killed along with six people in the crowd. Thirty-seven more had injuries ranging from life-threatening wounds to minor scrapes and shock. A further seven people were killed by a massive car bomb that was detonated amid the ambulance and emergency vehicles scrambling to the exhibition building. It was fortunate that more people had not died in the explosion, but sadly the dead were all emergency personnel. The formula of attacking U.S. citizens and then targeting the people who tried to help them was holding true.

"God, these bastards are really well organized." The president offered Woeburn the bulletin to read. Then he picked up the phone.

"Betty," he said, speaking to his office administrator, "get me the Canadian prime minister...Yes, ring me through as soon as the connection is made. Thank you."

He looked at Woeburn. "I'll phone and offer my condolences personally. As much as we joke about the Canadians, they're family. I don't want them getting gun shy."

Just as he said that, the lights dimmed and went out for a moment before flickering back to life as the White House's emergency generating system came on line.

"What the hell?" said the president. "That's never happened before." The phone on his desk rang, and he picked it up. His face twisted as he listened to the caller, and then he slammed the phone back onto its cradle.

"Shit!" he exploded. "The powers off in the city'. I just hope it isn't another goddamned attack."

Two hours later, the president had learned the extent of the hydro cut. Two generating plants — one in Toledo, Ohio, and another in northern New York state — had been hit almost simultaneously at a peak hour of usage. The resulting domino effect had taken out power along most of the eastern seaboard as far south as the Carolinas and across the American midwest and parts of Canada. Over twenty percent of the population of North America was without power.

"How the hell does this happen? Those jackasses have had years since the power failure in 2003 to fix the grid and prevent this kind of thing. The loss of a couple of power plants shouldn't black out the whole goddamned country," the president said to Dan Blomstrum.

"Yes, sir, but most of the grid is privately owned and operated. They've fixed some of the problems but rarely at the expense of their bottom lines."

"How the hell did the terrorists get past security? I thought we had all the power stations covered nine ways to Sunday."

"We haven't heard yet. All we know is that it's a confirmed act of sabotage. Other than that, nothing. Phone and computer systems are pretty much buggered, the roads are gridlocked, and people are walking home."

"Where the hell is Irving? I want to know how they got past the military cordons around the power plants."

"Sir, Admiral Irving radioed to say that he's stuck in traffic and will be here as soon as possible."

September 16.
Hydro generating plant 16, Ohio Energy Corporation, Toledo, Ohio.

Lieutenant-Colonel William Boyce walked around the bodies of the five men sprawled on the driveway, men who had been in his command. He felt sick to his stomach. He had always been an administrator, not a combat soldier, and the presence of war where it should not exist came as a physical as well as mental shock to him. These were just kids, playing at the arts of war, and the terrorists had taken lethal advantage of their trusting natures and willingness to help.

The sole survivor of this National Guard detail assigned to guard the rear entrance to the generating station had told him the grisly details of the attack before he was loaded into an ambulance. The six militiamen, of a unit of fourteen stationed on the grounds, had been guarding the rear gates that led to the hydro station transformer field when a car and a five-ton straight truck collided near the end of the driveway. One of the car's occupants fell out, his face covered in blood.

The Guardsmen ran to help, their orders not to abandon their post forgotten.

As they neared the wreck, the truck's rear door rolled up and two men holding automatic weapons opened fire. Their assault was complimented by fire from the driver and passenger, miraculously recovered from their wounds, who now brandished a shotgun and an AK-47, respectively. Five soldiers were dead before they knew what hit them. The very lucky survivor was momentarily knocked unconscious by a round that glanced off his helmet. After massacring the guardsmen, the terrorists backed the truck up and drove through the gates, followed by the car. Moments later the truck sat abandoned in the midst of the transformers and the five terrorists were fleeing in the car. Two guardsmen who, having heard the gunfire, were running to help were vaporized by an immense explosion that demolished almost every transformer and toppled the high-tension wires leading away from them. The back wall of the coal-fired power station received extensive damage and two of the steam turbines inside were beyond repair.

An attack on a generating station in New York state a few hours later employed very similar tactics, and while the damage was not as extensive and only three members of a private security company had been injured, the plant had to remain closed for days while repairs were made. The end result was a devastating loss of power and a ripple effect that tore through decades-old carrier equipment, burning out transformers and shattering corroded connectors. The surge would knock out electrical power to a large part of North America for several hours.

In Toledo, power would not return for almost a week.

September 18.
San'a, Yemen.

Al-Munajjid detested Yemen and had for years. It was not his first choice for this meeting that among other things would celebrate one month since the War on America began, but it was a place that several other attendees felt offered both security and anonymity. He was dressed in simple Arabic garb as befitted his identity as a devout believer whose greatest ambitions and motives were the glory of Islam.

After his borrowed private jet, to which he had almost unlimited access, had touched down at San'a International Airport, he'd climbed into the luxurious back seat of a large black Mercedes 600 that waited on the tarmac and sped off. The route from the airport avoided the city of San'a, the capital of Yemen, to the south. Instead, the driver and his escort, a Toyota Landcruiser filled with bodyguards, left the paved roads near the airport and drove westward along dirt roads that were once camel tracks and today were little improved. The Mercedes' suspension

226

smoothed out some of the roughness, and the air conditioning was effective respite against the ninety-seven-degree heat outside.

The journey was far worse for the men in the heavily sprung Toyota, which followed in a cloud of dust the consistency of icing sugar kicked up by the Mercedes' passage. The drive lasted for almost an hour, until they finally arrived at a large well-tended farm in the hills west of San'a. The farm had been a coffee plantation at one time, founded by English expats who'd left Yemen after the British pulled out of Aden. It had struggled along for several years until severe droughts finally put an end to the crop. Khat trees now stood in carefully tended rows where coffee plants had once thrived. The leaves of these small evergreens produce a mildly addictive stimulant that, when they are chewed, imparts an amphetamine-like high. Khat is popular over most of Africa and the Middle East,. and had become a major cash crop in Yemen.

The Mercedes pulled up in front of a large colonial-style house nestled between three towering rocks that rose from the craggy hillside. The building's imposing backdrop sheltered it from the worst of the midday sun as well as making it far more secure from spying. In addition to the natural security afforded by the soaring rock faces, several well-trained soldiers on loan from the Yemeni Armed Forces stood vigil on the craggy peaks above the plantation buildings.

Al-Munajjid got out of the car, which drove off to park alongside several other Mercedes and BMWs. He was among the last to arrive. Only fitting, he thought to himself, that they should wait for me. While they had all been useful tools, supplying either manpower or money to help accomplish his ends, he was the architect of the greatest disaster that had ever befallen America. Even the accomplishments of Osama paled in comparison.

He walked up the steps onto the front porch of the old house. The magnificent front doors lay open, two guards — once again, Yemeni regulars — standing at attention, one on either side. He hesitated for a moment in the doorway before catching sight of a slim, salubrious man in his mid-thirties who hurried from an magnificent hallway into the main entranceway. "I am Muhammad al-Munajjid," he said imperiously.

"It is an honour, sir, to receive you into the home of my uncle. I am Abdul Rashid."

"Ah, servant of the rightly guided one, a strong name." Al-Munajjid's charisma and the personal observation immediately touched the young man.

"Yes, sir. Thank you, thank you, sir," replied Rashid fawningly. "Do you have luggage? Perhaps you would like a few moments to rest from your journey and freshen up?"

"No. As much as I would enjoy your hospitality, the weight of my task makes great demands of my time. I must see to the business at hand and then return to the airport. I have pressing business elsewhere."

"Yes, sir. Please, follow me," requested Rashid. "The others are waiting in the library. There is mint tea or coffee prepared."

Rashid led al-Munajjid down the hall and through a pair of carved oak doors, themselves a rarity on the southern Arabian Peninsula, and into a library that would not have looked out of place in an English manor house. Fourteen men waited for him, standing about in small groups chatting. When he strode into the room, they all turned and, smiling, applauded him. Al-Munajjid was taken aback for a moment and his face flickered, betraying the pleasure he felt, before he reasserted a stern demeanour.

"Thank you, my friends. Few men have been as blessed as I to have friends such as you, who have made the dreams of Islam a reality." He made his way into the room and the men surrounded him. He spent about half an hour chatting to them, making sure he spoke to and gave each one attention. Al-Munajjid utilized all his skills and his remarkable ability to manipulate people. Had he been a politician or a cleric, he could have held huge numbers of people under his sway, so powerful were his talents of persuasion. But al-Munajjid's aspirations were not about fame or political position. In the Middle East, as elsewhere, these could be fleeting and, indeed, deadly. He preferred his power — real power — and financial success from controlling what went on behinds the scenes. Better to control a small room full of the rich and powerful than to hold sway over tens of thousands of the poor and ignorant.

The men made their way into an adjoining room, a large dining room that featured a long Western-style conference table. It was a far cry from the pillow-lined whitewashed rooms of their last meeting place in Pakistan. Al-Munajjid took his place at the head of the table, waiting for the other men to settle before addressing them. He turned slowly from man to man, making sure he looked directly into the eyes of each one before he spoke.

"My brothers, because you are as surely my brothers as any bound by blood, we have accomplished much since our last gathering. On that great day, when we, together, struck our first blow, we dared not dream that God would bless us with such great favour. But now we know we are truly blessed and that his will is worked through us. Our enemies quake with rage and impotence, thrashing about at ghosts while they bleed from many tiny cuts. It is not these insignificant wounds that will topple the beast. It is the beast's own talons that rake and tear at its flesh as it strikes at the tiny desert gnats that torment it. In these last thirty days, the beast has felt the very scourge it has for so long visited upon the Prophet's children."

He paused for a moment and then, his voice rising in a tried and true oratory style, he spat, "Soon neither its politicians nor its people will have the stomach to meddle in the affairs of others. Soon its tentacles will have withdrawn into its leprous body. Soon, each one of you will realize your dreams, and soon each one of you will assume your rightful places — places of power and influence." He paused, looking about the room at the men, who sat mesmerized, and then he continued. "Soon the true believers, the faithful of the one true God will be free to enjoy a world in which we do not have to cower from the infidels. Soon we will achieve what we have worked eight hundred years to accomplish. Soon! Soon! Soon!" He punctuated each "soon" with a clenched fist.

There was silence around the table for a moment, and then once again the men applauded his short but stirring soliloquy, rising from their seats as they did so. Al-Munajjid allowed them their applause, bowing his head in feigned modesty. He then raised his hand, motioning for quiet.

"My brothers, soon all your desires will be realized," he said so quietly that his listeners had to hold their breath to hear it. "But we have not finished our task. Your talents and power are still required. I must ask that your unwavering support continue, without hesitation or question, in the understanding that not all things can be known to you."

He balled his fists slowly and with noticeable drama. "Some of you or those that you represent have questioned what I do." He looked straight at Rashid, Bandar id bin Abdul Aziz's nephew, while others in the room murmured.

Aziz's nephew appeared flustered before the questioning glances of the other men in the room.

"I cannot have intrigue and threats conjured behind my back. I cannot and will not suffer interference in my activities or have my motives questioned by those who judge me by judging their own petty desires. I work for all Islam." This last sentence he said slowly, delivered with all the venom he had pent up since his brief audience with Aziz in Riyadh. Let Aziz's cronies seated in the room deliver that back to him and his supporters, he thought to himself. The remonstration delivered in front of many of Al-Munajjid's devout, powerful and self-interested supporters would muzzle that old and scabrous cur.

An hour later he was on his way back to the San'a International Airport, enduring the dusty track and having once again consolidated his hold over the men who fuelled his plans and ambitions. He smiled as he thought how skilled he'd become at avoiding snakebites while dancing in a pit filled with vipers.

September 18.
City Hotel, Tel Aviv, Israel.

The City Hotel in Tel Aviv was certainly not a five-star affair, but at least it offered free breakfast. Unfortunately for Derek, the liberally spiced and very greasy sausages, which contained a meat whose origins were unclear, had sat heavily in his stomach for most of the day and brought on a violent bout of indigestion. He was still fatigued from his trip, and now he was bored as well. His mood was a little depressed, occasioned by the date and the horrendous events of the last month as well as his inactivity. While Mossad and CIA contacts in Riyadh looked for al-Munajjid and a way of getting close to him, he and his partner waited.

Catherine, who had a room down the hall, was not indolent. She spent much of her time on the balcony, sheaves of paper pinned under ashtrays and books to keep them in place against the Mediterranean breezes. She seemed to relish being buried in paper and was busied herself going over reports about al-Munajjid and reading tomes and classified papers supplied by Halevy regarding the backgrounds and recent activities of many of the terrorist organizations so prominent in the countries ringing Israel's borders. These organizations were all merciless and could have aided or had a part in the attack on America.

Derek had offered to help, but Catherine had a way of reviewing the documents and compiling pertinent elements that disallowed a team effort. She did brief him on points of interest, and he read her notes and conclusions, but for the most part she was happily ensconced in and required the quiet of her room alone.

Derek looked at his watch and noted the time. It was six thirty, and he knew he should get something to eat even if he didn't feel like it. He was still not on Israeli time, which was hours ahead of his bodily rhythms. He was just contemplating phoning Catherine to see if she wanted to go downstairs and get a bite, when there was a knock on the door. He took a look through the peephole and saw Catherine in the hall.

As a break they had been the night before to a beachfront restaurant for dinner and taken a brisk walk along the beach. But a westerly wind, unusually cold for the region, had cut through their light clothing, forcing a return to the sheltered streets and avenues for their walk back to the hotel. It was the longest purely social interaction the two had experienced in their three weeks of partnership. By agreement, they hadn't spoken about work or the war, and both had shared their pasts, their childhoods, their family backgrounds and even some amusing tales of their teenage romances. While far from a romantic evening — something neither one desired — it was a human one and had for the first time allowed each a glimpse into the person they were teamed with.

Men spying the couple were clearly envious of Derek and what they assumed was his relationship with a stunning woman. Woman smiled knowingly as Catherine laughed or Derek guffawed at the punchline of a story.

Derek was impressed at Catherine's credentials. He'd thought, churlishly, that her employ at the agency was based more on her striking looks than on her intellectual abilities. He discovered that she held an engineering degree from MIT, spoke French, Italian and Hebrew — a fact she asked him to keep under his hat, especially around the Mossad people — and she had a pilot's license, both for fixed and rotary wing. She'd been recruited by the CIA while a student at MIT. Instead of taking up a promising and highly remunerative career in the private sector, she'd opted for a low-grade pay scale and the chance to chat up greasy third world diplomats and politicians the world over. It was a decision she said she'd never regretted.

He, on the other hand, had told her of his childhood dream of being a G-man, which started when an uncle gave him a collection of vintage Junior G-man badges, secret code rings and storybooks from the fifties. He lacked the fedora so prominent in the pulp magazines and comics, but in most other ways, he'd accomplished that childhood desire. He described his love of antique cars and told her of his Jaguar and its many eccentricities.

She knew virtually nothing about old cars but marvelled at his patience with a vehicle that, in her opinion, did not seem to be very good at what it was designed for. His explanations to the contrary amused her no end, especially when he described how it felt to drive the Jag on a winding road, as long as it didn't break down.

There was one uncomfortable moment of silence when she asked where his Jag was now. When he explained that he hadn't seen it since leaving Santa Barbara and that his office had made arrangements to store it for him, Catherine quickly and effectively changed the subject, to their mutual relief.

He opened the door to Catherine standing in the hallway. She said, "Come to my room. We have company."

"Sure," he replied. "Just let me get my shoes on, and I'll be there in a second."

Jacob Halevy sat at the small writing table in the corner of Catherine's room. The sliding glass doors were closed, the curtains were pulled, and the room's lights were on. Catherine had her small clock radio turned on and had placed it so that it touched the glass of the door, a precaution that would hopefully foil anyone trying to spy on them with a laser that could translate the vibrations of the glass into the conversation held in the room.

"Hello, Derek," said Halevy jovially as Derek entered. Catherine locked the door.

"Hello, Jacob," replied Derek.

"We have a location on our very busy and well-travelled friend, and it confirms that there is far more to him than meets the eye. Today he's been in Yemen. We know this because a very bad fellow we've been shadowing, one of the leaders of a powerful Lebanese militia, is at a meeting in Yemen, a meeting at which al-Munajjid has popped up. We don't know what the meeting's about, but there are quite a few individuals attending that we recognize, individuals, I'm sad to say, who could not be described as supporters of either Israel or the United States.

"He has since left the meeting, and my people could not follow him without fear of being discovered, but luckily, another asset picked him up again at San'a airport, where he boarded a private jet. We lost him again when he departed, but there was an American AWACS plane near enough to monitor his flight and your Naval Intelligence Office in Bahrain was kind enough to share that information with us. He appears to be on his way to Riyadh. If I were you, I'd head there myself. Catherine, you know the territory."

"Yes, I've been to Riyadh plenty of times," she replied.

"Will you need any assistance?"

"No. Thank you, Jacob. You've already been of more assistance than I can tell you. We have some good people in Riyadh, and even better domestic assets."

"I know you do, but if you should need any help, any help at all, you know how to get in touch with me. In the meantime, if you don't mind, I shall retrieve all of my top secret papers with which it appears you have wallpapered your room."

"Be my guest," laughed Catherine. "They should all be there, well, aside from the ones that the wind blew off the balcony."

"Ah, that will at least give Tel Aviv's esteemed sanitation department something to do."

After Jacob left, Derek turned to Catherine. "Are we sure this guy is a viable interest? I mean, just because the Israelis don't like him doesn't mean he has anything to do with the attacks on the States."

"True, but the spy game is a game of hunches, and Jacob is damned good at hunches. He doesn't give the fruits of that talent away lightly. He knows, and so does the whole Israeli government, that if the attacks go on for much longer, Americans may be inclined to abandon the Middle East and hang Israel out to dry. Without our support, they'd soon have to deal with a horde of jackals who won't be satisfied just nipping at their heels. I'm sure they've been poring over every single piece of intelligence they can lay their hands on trying to find the culprits, and their assets in the region are truly impressive. It's pretty obvious that giving us information that would stop the attacks or flush out who's responsible would not only pay us back for years of assistance, in some minds, it would put us in their debt."

"So, I guess were on our way to Riyadh."

"Yup, but first we'll have to fly to Rome, visit the Saudi Embassy and get some documents and then book a flight. You can't get there from here. I'll phone Langley and advise them that we need some Saudi wheels greased. Hopefully, our visas will be ready when we land in Italy."

CHAPTER 14

September 19.
Situation Room, the White House.

"Mr. President, the large-scale withdrawal of American troops from the Middle East and Afghanistan has begun," said Admiral Irving, his voice filled with gravity.

Every man in the room knew what this meant — that America was in retreat. Irving stood at the end of the room with a pointer, which he aimed at areas of interest on the map of the Middle East displayed on the room's largest screen.

"Military Airlift Command is using all available assets to pull our men and material out of Iraq through two main debarkation points: the International Airport in Baghdad and the Kuwait International Airport. Heavy equipment, including Abrams tanks, armoured personnel carriers, military construction and security equipment and key command and control systems are being moved to safe storage areas behind a military cordon or, if possible, airlifted out. Heavy equipment that is surplus to our needs and not air portable will be marshalled at Khar az Zaubayr and readied for debarkation on U.S. naval ships or contracted foreign-flagged vessels.

"We'll be leaving equipment earmarked for Iraqi security and military forces, including sixty-five Abrams tanks, one hundred and twenty-four Bradley fighting vehicles, eighty wheeled armoured cars, the Rhino armoured buses, cargo trucks, Humvees and assorted large- and small-calibre weapons and ammunition. A lot of the equipment has GPS tags incorporated in it so that in the event that anyone tries to use it against us, its location can be dialled in, and it can be destroyed. The Iraqis do not know of the tags' existence, and the tags cannot be disarmed without crippling the command-and-control or engine-management systems of the units.

"The control zones are as follows: the Kurkuk oil fields in northern Iraq and a corridor encompassing the Iraq-Turkish pipeline and the northern oil production facilities of Bayji, Al Qayyarah and Mosul. We have the co-operation of the local Kurds, and the Turks are allowing us logistical-support access through Turkey in return for pipeline security up to their border. In eastern Iraq we'll protect the oil fields of Abu Gharab, Jabal Faqi and Buzurgan on the Iran-Iraq border, along with the southern pipeline, the smaller field at Majnun and pipelines leading to the oil production facilities in Basra. Finally, the southern fields at Al Rumaylah and Az Zubayr will remain controlled areas, along with the oil terminal at Kawr az Zubayr.

"Remaining American divisions in Iraq will bar all Iraqi and other military and civil organizations from these areas. Iraqi oil workers will be allowed to retain their jobs, but tight control and security measures will be enforced. These areas will be under strict military law. There are numerous smaller oil fields and oil production facilities that will remain under Iraqi control, and we are abandoning the Iraq strategic pipeline that runs through the country from north to south. Control of the smaller fields and pipelines was deemed too difficult to maintain from a logistical standpoint with the forces remaining at our disposal. The Iraqis have promised their co-operation, and these areas will be under their control and supervision."

Irving drew a number of reconnaissance photographs from his papers and passed them to an aide. A moment later they appeared on the large screen and on the desk screens in front of the men assembled around the table.

"Our most immediate concerns are focused on the fields on the Iraq-Iran border. These photographs show that the Iranians still have a strong force in the border region closest to this controlled area. That makes their intentions suspect. They've made large withdrawals of troops and material from the rest of the border region with, as you all know, great fanfare. The third photograph shows that they have also moved what appear to be anti-aircraft missile batteries into the areas immediately adjacent to the border near the Iraqi oil fields. Those units have all been target tagged, and if we need to, we can send drones in to take them out. To sum up, this plan allows a seventy-percent withdrawal of our military personnel on the ground."

"So, admiral, are you confident the forces that remain in Iraq can maintain control of the zones you've laid out?" asked the president.

"Yes, sir, as long as they are provided with adequate air support. There are three carrier task forces in the Gulf region, as you know, and I'm sure this has encouraged the Chinese to lay off with their shenanigans for the last few days. Several of their ships are in harbour in Pakistan, and there are only two missile frigates still in the Persian Gulf, both in harbour in Iran on a visit. This allows us some flexibility, so I've had two carrier strike forces, the Reagan and the Abraham Lincoln, moved to the northern end of the Gulf to provide cover and assistance to the withdrawal. The Eisenhower is nearing the Gulf of Oman, and the Lincoln will be rotating home as soon as the John C. Stennis strike force arrives. The Kennedy is also on her way to the Gulf, and the George Washington is headed for Afghanistan.

"We have one group left in the Pacific, the George H. W. Bush, which is on station just southwest of Japan. Remaining carrier strike force groups at port in San Diego, Hawaii and Norfolk and quite a few of their personnel are supporting land-based security operations, and their aircraft are on CAP. I'm sure with six carrier strike forces in the region, no one, not even the Iranians, is going to consider an incursion into Iraq — for any reason — a viable option."

"Very good, admiral. Thank you," said the president wearily. "Mr. Dutton, has the CIA anything to report?"

"All I can say, sir, it that we are presently following up on several leads. Along with our regular intelligence-gathering operations, we also have three of the special operations teams overseas — one in Oslo, one in London and the last in transit from Israel to Riyadh. The most promising lead so far seems to be from our team in Oslo. They are investigating a splinter terrorist organization that has been quietly building strength in several European cities and could be responsible for some of the anti-American bombings in Germany, France and Portugal."

As the meeting wore on, the president, exhaustion clear on his face, nodded off, the consequence of averaging less than four hours — four troubled hours — of sleep per night. The men assembled at the table looked at each other in perplexity, before Chief of Staff Blomstrum rose and quietly proclaimed the meeting over.

September 20.
Waigaoqiao complex, Port of Shanghai, China.

The brand-new super container ship CSCL Great Wall was the largest of her kind. She was capable of carrying over 9,200 twenty-foot containers with a payload exceeding fifty-two thousand tons. Its mass was equivalent to that of several Titanics and its ranking as a leviathan of the oceans was secure. Very few ports could handle her length of 364 meters and her beam of forty-two. She was presently tied up at the Waigaoqiao complex, Phase 5, the only ship at the dock and warehouse facility. Waigaoqiao was so new it was not yet open to commercial traffic.

Some workers in the harbour area had thought that odd, although none would have expressed their opinion. Living under a totalitarian regime bred a sixth sense in people for what should or should not be discussed publicly. What aroused the unspoken disquiet was that Phase 5 had been completed five months before, yet its gates and warehouses remained locked. The Great Wall had arrived just two weeks ago, straight from the shipyards at Guangzhou, but had yet to sail on a commercial voyage. This was definitely a departure from standard procedures. Ships, especially ones of this size and expense, were usually run twenty-four hours a day, seven days a week, year in and year out, until they died of old age and ended up at the breakers. A brand-new ship sitting dockside, completely inactive, was, to say the least, unusual.

When the first of thousands of trucks arrived carrying multicoloured commercial containers, the locals viewed the occasion with a sense of "it's about time." Finally, the odd silence at Phase 5 had ended, and it looked like things were starting to happen. One after another, the trucks entered the grounds, disappearing into the huge warehouse buildings that adjoined the dock and emerging a short time later having offloaded their containers. Within three days, the warehouses were jammed with over nine thousand containers and yet, and this was strange too, not a single one had been lifted to the holds or decks of the Great Wall.

September 21.
Ventura County, California.

Inoue Nariaki and Sato Tadashi pulled their rented Toyota SUV up to the padlocked fence that enclosed the old gas station. The station had been slated for demolition to clear the land it sat on for access to an industrial park development that was pegged to begin building in the next three months. Tadashi got out of the car and unlocked the gate, opening it for Nariaki to drive through, and then closed it again, carefully replacing the lock on the chain. After Nariaki opened another padlock that used the same key, the two men made their way into the old station, opened one of the bay doors and drove the Toyota in.

Tadashi pulled the door down and they looked around the dirty building. Tadashi was in the office-cum-showroom, where people in an earlier time had waited for oil changes and tires while mechanics with dirty nails and calloused hands scratched their heads and scrawled simple math on blotters to figure out bills and charges. The filthy picture windows, caked from years of oil-laden fumes and California dust, denied a view either in or out, but a warm brown glow lit the room. Tadashi was just about to force the door to the restroom when Nariaki called from the shop. "Tadashi, here," he said in Japanese. They still assumed the identity of Japanese nationals, but now they carried papers identifying them as businessmen on special visas.

Nariaki stood next to a pile of boards and garbage that he had pulled off a mechanics pit. In the pit rested a cache of seven boxes of high explosives, ammunition, machine pistols and four American-made M-16 assault rifles. They quickly loaded the back of the Toyota with all the material from the pit, and within ten minutes of their arrival, they were ready to leave.

A musical chime sounded from Tadashi's pocket, and he answered his cellphone. "Oh God, oh God," he said, snapping the phone closed. "Ishikawa says there are Americans outside and more arriving. He and Kato have wished us peace and good fortune. They are leaving."

Ishikawa Chicao and Kato Kakerie had been half a mile away, perched on a road that wound along the Ventura hills, high above and overlooking the old gas station. They had seen, too late to do their accomplices any good, the column of dissimilar civilian vehicles that streamed towards the station. Heavily armed men jumped out, surrounding the station, and a moment later a column of police cars and military support vehicles hidden in a nearby industrial mall joined them. A light armoured car rammed through the padlocked fence, backed up and then drove along the fenceline, ripping it from the ground and opening up a larger field of access. Within minutes, over two hundred men, backed up by three light armoured cars equipped with thirty-calibre machine guns, ringed the station, maintaining a distance of one hundred yard and taking whatever cover was available. A bullhorn mounted on one of the armoured cars screeched for a moment with feedback and then delivered a command to the terrorists to emerge with their hands up.

Nariaki looked at Tadashi, jammed a clip into an M-16 and took shelter behind the column of blocks that separated the two overhead doors. Tadashi was furiously emptying the Toyota's cargo back into the mechanics pit. Then he scuttled across the floor, staying low, and started to push the boxes of explosives up to the each wall of the garage, sliding two in front of the glass doors of the overheads. He jammed small electronic detonators into each one, synchronizing the timers for fifteen minutes, a period he felt might be an little extravagant as far as his and Nariaki's life expectancy was concerned.

A moment later, the nose of an armoured car smashed through the glass of the overhead doors, the debris flying across the floor. Tadashi jumped into the mechanics pit, shouldering an M-16. He pulled the trigger as black-uniformed SWAT team members swarmed around and past the armoured car. Nothing happened. He looked at Nariaki, who was retreating backwards across the shop, slapping the side of his rifle in frustration. Six or seven troopers slammed him to the ground. Tadashi spun about, frantic to grab one of the machine pistols that he'd placed on the pit's edge in preparation for battle. He was met by a fast-moving combat boot that stove in his nose and knocked him into unconsciousness.

The two men were dragged into an armoured paddy wagon, and a deputy slammed the door behind them. Inside the building, the SWAT team, soldiers and sheriff's deputies stood around chatting and joking. A SWAT team member opened one of the boxes of explosives, grabbed a grey putty-like block and tossed it, digital primer and all, at a friend. He laughed and dropped the block on the ground, discarded. Seconds later, the timer on the block and all the other primers in the garage ticked off fifteen minutes.

At a command from outside, the men started to move out, having swept up the weapons and ammunition that lay in the mechanics pit. They left behind the boxes filled with grey blocks of modelling clay but secured the embedded timers and removed their detonation caps. The blocks were left as a souvenir for the demolition and construction crews that would arrive in a few days to tear the old place down. Several members of the SWAT team had pocketed dud bullets as souvenirs themselves.

On the mountainside above, Chicao and Kakerie drove at reckless speed along the dirt road that hugged the hillside. They rounded a sharp corner, skidding on the packed dirt despite reducing speed to a little less than thirty miles per hour. Chicao was just reprimanding Kakerie for cornering too fast when he was thrown forwards into his shoulder belt. Kakerie had jammed on the brakes as an armoured car appeared on the apex of the hairpin, blocking the narrow road. He started to back up, the front of the car flopping back and forth as he fought to master the dynamics of driving a car quickly in reverse. Another armoured car lunged onto the road from a dense copse of bushes behind him. As he jumped onto the brakes again, Chicao leapt from the car screaming, "Allah is great," and fired his Kalashnikov at the approaching vehicle, its rounds tinkling and sparking on the armoured front end.

The gunner behind the shield mount on top of the armoured car's hull had prayed for a moment like this, and opened fire. The stream of bullets from the thirty-calibre machine gun almost cut Chicao in half. He spun from the impact, his assault rifle describing a perfect arc in the air as he loosed it. He was dead long before he hit the ground. The bullets kicked up geysers of dust from the road and then tracked over the car with devastating effect. Joining the heavy rounds were lighter-calibre but equally devastating fire from over twenty gunners stationed on the hillside above the road. In less than ten seconds it was all over, the car a smoking colander holding the wafting fragments of the burst interior and the pulped remains of Kakerie.

The four Japanese impostors, authors of the first strike against America, were the first to fall to the intelligence gathered from Abu Bakre, a.k.a. Jimmy Youngblood. The one great advantage the Americans now held was the independence and isolation of each terrorist cell. Law enforcement could use the same techniques of entrapment against them over and over again as long as the details of each apprehension remained out of the media and under wraps.

September 21.
Riyadh, Saudi Arabia.

A Buick from the U.S. consular fleet picked up Derek and Catherine at the airport when they finally arrived from Rome. After deliberation, the State Department and the CIA had decided to have them operate in Saudi Arabia with the knowledge and assistance of the Saudis. The Saudi rulers, terrified the Americans might turn on them, were anxious to offer any aid they could, especially since the shift in American perceptions following the rise of bin Laden, the fall of the World Trade Center and the implication of so many Saudi nationals in the plot.

The consulate's driver, a young chap from Baltimore, chatted with Derek on the way from the airport to the Four Seasons Hotel, a luxury for which the Saudis were footing the bill.

Catherine sat quietly, taking in the scenery. She was wearing a black head scarf and an ankle-length black dress with a high collar that she'd purchased in Rome. They were acceptable apparel for a female foreign national visiting Saudi Arabia. She had grave doubts about the assistance she and Derek would get from Saudi intelligence or their police forces. She knew that Saudi internal security services were staffed largely by agents with anti-American sympathies who were more closely tied to al Qaeda than to the United States.

It was an open secret that several departments in the Saudi bureaucracy had in the past assisted al Qaeda in its efforts. Saudi intelligence and police services were influenced by a religious police force called Mutawwa that was strictly Wahhabi, a devout and unforgiving form of Islam that numbered among its enemies any other religion as well as other Islamic factions. They most especially detested American involvement in Iraq. She suspected that enlisting Saudi help might benefit more their opponents than the United States.

Catherine, who could not move about alone in Saudi Arabia, was posing as Derek's wife. To that end, the U.S. Embassy in Rome had issued them a marriage certificate and other documents identifying her as Mrs. Derek James. Without these documents, she and Derek stood the chance of being harassed or even arrested on the street. Under Saudi law, women were not allowed to fraternize with men other than a blood relative or spouse. She couldn't go out alone either, and for the duration of their stay, she would be considered Derek's chattel. While her abilities to conduct fieldwork might be limited by the country's laws, neither her organizational talents nor her instincts would be compromised. In addition, she and Derek could, if required, get the help of CIA assets the Saudis did not know existed.

As their car pulled up in front of the Four Seasons, a tall, slight and immaculately groomed Arab strode to the front doors and watched. Derek and Catherine clambered out of the Buick and waited while a bellman and the young chauffeur emptied the trunk of their bags and suitcases. The bellman piled the luggage onto a brass cart and started off through the front doors, headed for reception. The tall Saudi held the door for the bellman and then approached the couple.

"Mr. James?" he said, addressing Derek.

"Yes?"

"I am Abdullah Abdulaziz Ibrahim Alluwaijri of the Justice Ministry. I have been sent to greet you and make sure you are comfortable and have everything you may need." He reached to shake Derek's hand. "If you would be so kind as to follow me, I will take you to your suite. The hotel staff will bring your bags up. There is no need to check in. I have to say, Mr. James, that I am very excited. It is not every day that have someone from the world-famous FBI visiting us."

"Well, I have to say that this is my first visit to Saudi Arabia. From what I've seen so far, it's a very beautiful country. This city is spectacular."

"Ah, you are too kind. I must agree that Riyadh is a beautiful city. Perhaps if you get time, I can take you to see some of the sights, such as the Masmak fortress."

"That'd be great, but I'm afraid this is a business trip, and my superiors in Washington might get a little annoyed if they found out I was touring about rather than working. I'm afraid I won't have too much time to myself."

"A great pity, Mr. James. A great pity. Riyadh has so much to offer."

Derek noted that Alluwaijri never once looked at Catherine or spoke to her. He also saw that Catherine had assumed the role of a subservient and obedient wife. She stood several feet away and had become, to Alluwaijri at least, almost invisible.

A few moments later, they were in their suite on the sixth floor. Alluwaijri had left them alone after asking if Derek would be amenable to a meeting in two hours, perhaps in the hotel's restaurant, with a gentleman from the Saudi anti-terrorist squad. Derek agreed to the time and locale.

At the agreed hour, Derek sat in the Tea Lounge on the hotel's ground floor, fingering a cup of coffee that had left a number of rings on the glass table in front of him. He was rather nervous, especially without Catherine, who had informed him that her presence at such a meeting would be ill advised. He sat near the back of the almost deserted room while he waited. Few hotel guests were around at this hour of the day.

Finally, ten minutes late, Alluwaijri walked in accompanied by another Saudi who was dressed in a traditional white tobe, the loose-sleeved floor-length robe prevalent in Riyadh. Accompanying the two men were a pair of very muscular individuals wearing identical dark suits who took station a few feet away and scanned the entrance as well as the other tea room guests.

Alluwaijri greeted Derek as he approached. "Mr. James, it is my pleasure to introduce you to Rhaman al-Tuwaijri."

Derek rose, taking al-Tuwaijri's offered hand.

"Mr. al-Tuwaijri is head of the Justice Ministry's anti-terrorism department."

"It is a great pleasure to meet you, Mr. James," said al-Tuwaijri.

"A pleasure to meet you, sir. Please, join me."

"Thank you, Mr. James," said Alluwaijri as the three men sat.

A waiter started towards the table, but the two bodyguards cut him off and, after a brief word, sent him away.

"So, Mr. James," began al-Tuwaijri, "we have been told by your embassy that you would like to investigate the affairs of a Saudi national."

"Yes, sir, we would. We have intelligence that this individual, a Muhammad al-Munajjid, lives in Saudi Arabia and may have knowledge of or links to terrorist organizations that may be involved in the attacks on the U.S."

"How did you happen to come upon this intelligence?" asked Alluwaijri.

"I'm not privy to that, sir. I'm just following orders to come to Riyadh and see what information I can ferret out about the gentleman in question."

Al-Tuwaijri responded, "We have had some time to investigate al-Munajjid since your embassy informed us of its interest, and we have found that he is a successful businessman with interests and companies all over the Middle East and Europe. The man is a devout follower of the lessons of the Quran and has never given any indication of terrorist affiliations or tendencies. We Saudis keep a very strict and accurate list of everyone within our borders who may be sympathetic to causes or groups that both our governments would consider of concern, and we can assure you that neither he nor any of his close associates has ever been under suspicion."

Derek could sense that Catherine's reservations about involving the Saudis were going to be proven entirely accurate. He decided not to force the issue. "Well, sir, I hope we're not wasting your time, then."

"I assure you, Mr. James, our time is yours for the taking," said Alluwaijri. "We are very concerned about the heinous attacks on the United States, which we consider our greatest ally and friend —"

"And we certainly understand, after the unfortunate events of 9/11, why you would cast your nets in our direction," interjected al-Tuwaijri.

"But we can both personally assure you" — Alluwaijri glanced at al-Tuwaijri, who nodded in agreement — "that since those awful events, we have redoubled our efforts to track down and neutralize anyone within our kingdom who might give assistance or succour to the thugs and criminals who serve al Qaeda."

"So, you don't think this al-Munajjid could be involved?" asked Derek.

"We are not saying that, Mr. James. And we assure you that we will take another very good look at his movements and assist you in any inquiries you care to make," replied Alluwaijri. "We are currently looking into his reported trip to Yemen and would very much appreciate it if you could find out how your FBI acquired that intelligence. It might aid us in our inquiries."

I'll bet it would, thought Derek. The two Saudis engaged him in idle conversation about the vagaries of international law enforcement for a few minutes, and then al-Tuwaijri, glancing at his very expensive Ulysse Nardin watch, rose and excused himself with the pretext of another pressing engagement. Alluwaijri assured Derek he would get back to him within the next few hours and thanked him for his patience. Both men, accompanied by the guards, made their exit, leaving Derek with the definite feeling that little co-operation was coming their way.

Derek opened the door to their suite and was about to say something about the meeting, when Catherine walked into the living room from the bedroom with her finger pressed against her mouth. "Hello, honey. How was your meeting?" she asked.

Derek caught on. "Very informative."

"Good." She walked over, pecked him on the lips and grabbed his hand. "You just have to see this view. It's wonderful." She led him to the balcony and once outside, nuzzled him with her lips, her face buried against his neck. In a faint whisper Derek could barely hear, she said, "There's three bugs and two wide-angle cameras I've found so far. There are probably more, but I can't appear to be looking for them. Don't say anything. They can't see my lips because of my hair, but if someone is videotaping us from a nearby building, they'd see yours."

She pulled back and said, "Sweetheart, I'm getting a little hungry. Why don't we go out for a bite to eat."

"Sure. That sounds good. We can take a walk. Mr. Alluwaijri said he would get back to me in a couple of hours, but until then, I don't have anything to do."

"Great. I'll get ready."

Once outside, walking along the street, Catherine said, "Don't look, but there's a tail across the road and half a block back."

"Great. It's good to be among friends," said Derek. "You were right. They didn't even seem to care if they were convincing. They said they'd look into al-Munajjid and his travels, but in their opinion, he was not a threat. Reading between the lines, they seemed a hell of a lot more interested in where we got our information. Alluwaijri asked for our source outright."

"I'm sure he did. They probably suspect Mossad supplied it. It drives them nuts that the Israelis have the Middle East so well wired. I think we should listen to their report, act as if we half believe it and then leave the country."

"Leave the country," said Derek. "We just got here."

"We aren't going to be able to accomplish anything with their security service trailing us and bugging our rooms, and I can't take the chance of contacting any local assets and compromising them. Mind you, it's not a completely wasted trip. We've confirmed that the Saudis are not interested in helping us investigate al-Munajjid, which indicates he may be complicit in the attacks."

"How so?" asked Derek.

"If he were an innocent, they'd have already put his severed head on a spear outside our hotel room just to prove what great allies they are."

"Boy," said Derek, "I can see why they were so ready to put us up in a fancy hotel at their expense. I'd bet you that room is permanently rented to the Saudi security service."

"If nothing else, this has confirmed my belief that there is no real help here, at least from the Saudi bureaucracy."

That evening, Derek received a call from the front desk. Alluwaijri had arrived and waited in the lobby for him. Derek arrived in the lobby and shook Alluwaijri's hand. The two men took seats on a pair of overstuffed settees separated by a glass table. Alluwaijri put a file folder he'd been carrying on the table, opened it and passed some of the papers it contained to Derek.

"Mr. James, this is the latest information we have on al-Munajjid. He has travelled extensively in the last two years, but in every case his travels seem to be related to his import-export business and other holdings in various countries in both the Middle East and Asia. He is a devout Muslim and could be considered opposed to American policies in the Middle East, but if that were a crime, we would have to imprison almost everyone who lives here. There is no hint of terrorist affiliation and no hint that he has funded any terrorist groups. We don't know who or what you came across to arouse suspicion, but it would certainly be helpful to know exactly what was in those accusations. Perhaps that knowledge would help us further our own investigations."

Derek leafed though the papers he'd been presented. Most of them were copies of airline itineraries and a compilation of the destinations and time spent out of Saudi Arabia. As an investigative tool, they were almost useless. Derek already knew that al-Munajjid had the use of private jets, which meant the airline paperwork had been concocted in an attempt to disguise the man's real comings and goings. Derek was quite sure that Alluwaijri was cognizant of that.

"Quite truthfully," Derek said, "I have not seen them. My orders were to come to Riyadh and discuss with you a joint investigation of this al-Munajjid guy. Once again, I have to say that I don't know anything about the specific reports or their origins, but I can certainly ask the Bureau if they'd be willing to furnish you with them."

"That would be most satisfactory. In the meantime, we can tell you that al-Munajjid is not presently in Saudi Arabia. As far as we know, he is somewhere in Europe on business."

"What about that trip to Yemen he reportedly took and his meeting with at least one known terrorist leader?"

"We do have that information for you. It seems that Mr. al-Munajjid was in Yemen purchasing khat for export to Africa. We Saudis do not approve of the trade but as long as he does not bring it here, he is free to sell it to those countries that find its use acceptable."

"So, what you are telling me is that this guy is squeaky clean — except for his drug dealing, that is. What about the terrorist?"

"The sale of khat is a popular way to raise money for many organizations. I am sure that the terrorist was there for the same reason as al-Munajjid and was likely a competitor for the product."

"Well, then, it looks like our intelligence was faulty, doesn't it?" Derek said, looking Alluwaijri right in the eye.

"It would seem so, Mr. James. It's a shame you and your lovely wife have wasted your time coming to Riyadh, at least as far as this investigation is concerned. But please, let me arrange a personal tour of the city for you."

"You're very kind," said Derek, "but I really wouldn't feel right about holidaying while my country is under attack."

"Certainly understandable," said Alluwaijri. "If I can't be of assistance in any other way, perhaps I can at least arrange your travel to Rome or anywhere else in Europe you would like to go."

"That's good of you," said Derek, who couldn't keep an edge from appearing in his voice. "But I'm sure the embassy already has that covered for us. Thank you."

"Mr. James, you are quite welcome. If I come across anything of interest, I will call you immediately. Here is my card, as well. Call if you require any assistance at all. Please, do not hesitate."

"Thank you," said Derek, rising.

"I wish you and your wife a pleasant trip."

The men shook hands, and Alluwaijri left the lobby. Derek waited a moment and then walked to a window that overlooked the hotel carriageway and valet station. Alluwaijri did not notice or perhaps did not care that on the other side of the heavily mirrored glass Derek saw him drop the file into a garbage can before stepping into the white Bentley Continental he'd left at the curb. "Asshole," Derek said under his breath before turning and heading for his heavily monitored hotel room.

September 21.
Ta'if, Saudi Arabia.

Al-Munajjid's cellphone rang, the vibration making it dance on the heavily ornamented copper table that was the centrepiece of the garden room in the Ta'if villa. He plucked it from the table and snapped it open. "Yes," he said brusquely.

"Sir, this is Abdullah Alluwaijri. I have some news for you."

"What is it?"

"The American FBI agent is leaving Riyadh, and I believe he will have little further interest in you. He seemed somewhat satisfied that you were not a threat."

"Somewhat?"

"The American is a policeman. He will probably never be completely satisfied, but what can he do. He answers to men higher up. I am sure that the Americans are grasping at straws."

"Yes, but in this case the straw was made from gold. I don't want them getting this close again. Do you hear me? Did you find out how they came across my name?"

"No, sir. He said he hadn't read the reports. He'd just been assigned to make contact with us to determine whether you played a role in their problems."

"So, you believe he doesn't know?"

"Yes, sir."

To himself, al-Munajjid said, "I would dearly like to know who told the Americans about me." Then he had another thought, "What about al-Tuwaijri?" he asked.

"That old fool's not interested. He met with the American, made some accommodating noises and then went back to his fat wife. He's left me in charge and didn't even ask for reports."

"Just make sure he stays disinterested. It would not do to alert loyal members of the government to our movements."

"You have no worries there, sir. I know everything that goes on, and even the Americans' interest in you did not ring any alarms. Al-Tuwaijri is far more convinced that you are not of interest than the Americans are."

CHAPTER 15

September 22.
George H. W. Bush strike force, East China Sea.

The George H. W. Bush was the newest, most sophisticated and last of the U.S. Navy's powerful Nimitz-class carriers. She'd only just finished her lengthy sea trials and was on her first operational tour. To date, she'd steamed across the Pacific, rounded the top of Japan, cruised south through its northern sea and passed through the channel separating Japan from Korea. She was now in the East China Sea just north of the Ryuku Islands.

Two of her ninety aircraft, F-35 Lightning IIs of the new Joint Strike Fighters, were doing public relations and air show duties in Japan and were slated to rejoin the carrier in a couple of days. The rest of her compliment of fixed-wing and rotary aircraft were on board and fully operational. The Bush was the first carrier to be completely equipped with the Lightning II strike fighter, which she carried in two versions. The first was the F-35B, which was a fighter with short takeoff and vertical landing fighter and replaced the Marine Corp's Sea Harriers. The second was the F-35C, which replaced the Navy's F-18 Super Hornets and used conventional takeoff and landing techniques.

Admiral Donald Gibson was in charge of the Bush and her escorts and was mightily pleased that his first seaborne command as an admiral was to head up America's newest and most powerful carrier group. He didn't miss his last post, which had been a desk at the Pentagon, but it was that desk and his adroit political skills that had earned him his present placement. While at the Pentagon, he'd curried many favours and racked up even more debts from men higher up the chain and more powerful than he. In some ways, it was a relief for those men to see the back of Gibson and his Machiavellian machinations. In exchange, he'd gotten what he really wanted — a carrier fleet command.

Gibson had spent most of his life smitten with the aircraft carriers that were such an integral part of the U.S. Navy and the country's force extension. When he was a kid, he'd had models of almost every major U.S. carrier from World War II and the atomic carriers that followed. When he graduated from high school, it only followed that he would work his way into the U.S. Naval Academy and then on to becoming a successful officer, if not always a gentleman. In all the years he'd served, he'd never lost sight of his deeply held desire to command an aircraft carrier. He narrowly missed captaining one a few years before and had almost given up hope — until the Bush's keel was laid down. From that point on, he'd waged a ruthless campaign in the hallways and backrooms of the Pentagon to get the command he now enjoyed. Today, he presided over a fleet of ships that could have won World War II in the Pacific single-handedly.

Accompanying the Bush, there was a Ticonderoga Aegis cruiser, named the USS Chosin after the Korean War battle, three guided-missile destroyers, five anti-submarine destroyers, two attack subs and two supply ships. Usually the Bush would have had two Ticonderoga-class cruisers but in her maiden trip across the Atlantic into what was presently considered a low-risk zone of operations, her other escort had remained in San Diego receiving some much-needed upgrades to her software programs.

Captain Lewis Harding, the Bush's skipper, ran the carrier's day-to-day operations from the ship's bridge, one storey up from the admiral's flag bridge. Both bridges were ensconced in the towering island that was the Bush.

Suddenly the quiet of the flag bridge was shattered.

"Sir, the combat information centre reports a bogey at thirty-four thousand, 125 miles out and inbound from 220 degrees, a possible Chinese snoop."

"How the hell did it get so close? demanded Admiral Gibson.

"One moment, sir. I'll ask," replied the bridge officer who issued the warning. "Sir," he said after listening a moment to his headset, "the bogey was mixed in with standard commercial traffic before it deviated to its new course. CIC says it's a possible Tu-154, B 1438. It's a Chinese commercial airliner adapted for reconnaissance."

"Jet?" Gibson asked.

"Yes, sir."

"Vector CAP to intercept, and get the alert aircraft up. I want that thing turned away."

"Aye aye, sir."

After a moment the bridge officer said agitatedly, "Sir, CIC on the Chosin reports an identical signature, bogey inbound from eighty-five degrees, presently at fifteen thousand feet and climbing. One hundred and sixty out."

"Get me four more 35s up, now!" The admiral addressed the officers on the bridge, "Gentlemen, the strike force is going to battle stations. Request Captain Harding to join me on the flag bridge. This is not a drill. I repeat, gentlemen. This is not a drill."

Within moments, the carrier along with all of her escorts were hives of activity as their crews rushed to don their battle dress and assume their stations. Air crew rushed from the ready room to clamber into their cockpits and hurry through pre-flight checks while the two ready-alert aircraft surged off the carrier in a cloud of superheated steam from catapults that hurled them into the sky.

A little more than one hundred miles away and closing fast, the crew of the inbound Tu-154 was aware of the stir they were causing. Their airborne interrogation and surveillance systems were humming, and now they planned to monitor the approach of the stealthy new American fighters, accumulating whatever data they could as well as recording the Bush's electronic signals and countermeasures.

An identical aircraft almost three hundred miles southeast of the first was climbing to thirty thousand feet in an effort to reap as many important signals from the carrier strike force as they could before they were intercepted. Both aircraft had been instructed to maintain an offensive inbound course for as long as they could before breaking off. Their presence would stir up lots of activity that could be turned into very useful intelligence for the Chinese navy and air force.

Moments later, two grey blurs flashed past the Tu-154. The large jet rocked in the turbulence caused by their supersonic flypast. Their arrival was a surprise, as they had remained invisible until they were within a very short distance of the surveillance aircraft. The co-pilot looked at the pilot in shock. Surely China's most advanced surveillance aircraft should have more warning of the American fighters' approach than a scant two seconds. If the Americans had come out shooting, the 154 would never have known what hit it.

The Chinese pilot doggedly maintained his course until the two Lightnings appeared on his wingtips. The pilot of the F-35 on the right wingtip made a slashing motion across his throat and then balled his fist. The three aircraft flew in formation for the next few minutes, and then the sleek and menacing fighter aircraft on the left wing tip veered right over the top of the big plane, buffeting it with its exhaust flow. The pilot of the Lighting on the right wingtip made the throat-cutting motion once again as he shook his head, and then he rocketed away on a sweeping left turn, accelerating to Mach 2.

The threat displays in the Tu-154's cockpit lit up like a storefront at Christmastime as the missile and weapons systems of the other Lighting, now trailing the massive surveillance aircraft, locked on the engines. The Chinese pilot, recognizing that he'd pushed hard enough and that the operators in the back had acquired as much information as they were likely to get, abruptly dipped his left wing and brought the yoke back hard into his stomach, commencing an immediate turn, away from the ships that were now less than twenty miles ahead. He did not know it, but the pilots of the F-35s were awaiting instructions to splash the Chinese aircraft if it penetrated a ring whose outer border was ten miles from the flagship's flight deck.

And if the Lightings had somehow failed in their mission, there was a guided-missile destroyer less that five miles away to the north that would have picked up the gauntlet, its anti-aircraft systems hot. It was one of a halo of defensive ships that ringed the Bush at all times.

A similar scenario played out to the southeast as the other spy plane was intercepted. Its crew was not quite as daring as the first, and they described an arc away from the Bush as soon as the first fighters flashed past the spy plane's lumbering form.

September 23.
Hunan, East China Sea, north of Taiwan.

Lieutenant Zhi Yang looked down into the hold from the inspection platform fifteen feet above four midget submarines nestled on purpose-built cradles in the bowels of the dredge and recovery ship Hunan. This ugly, slow and utilitarian vessel was, in fact, never intended for such mundane tasks as dredging and salvage, although it could do both to maintain its cover. The reason for its existence was those four small subs. Yang was the commander of one. Each carried a crew of four men.

Unlike midget submarines of the past, these were exceptionally sophisticated machines that could remain submerged for up to sixty hours. Their range and crew comfort, both superb considering their size, were further augmented by attached but disposable hydrodynamic pods that contained supplementary batteries and stores of breathable compressed air and air conditioning that were piped into the subs' hulls with breakaway connectors. Once the pods were emptied of their supplies or the subs were going into combat, they could be jettisoned quickly and, more importantly, quietly.

The submarines and their pods were constructed of advanced composites that returned a sonar signal little more significant than that of a small fish. Little metal was used in the construction of these highly classified boats, and they were covered in a secret anechoic material which demanded that anyone walking on their top surfaces wear special protective footwear. If the crew needed to communicate while submerged or sense the world above, they could deploy tiny sensors and transmitters tethered to the sub by thin but tough transparent optical fibres. Any information was transmitted by the sensors along the fibre to the sub below.

These tiny floating computers designed to look like the ordinary flotsam so common on the oceans of the twenty-first century assumed the role of the periscope. Unlike the subs of the past, these midget submarines didn't need targeting periscopes. The torpedoes didn't work that way. Instead, targeting information on selection and range was downloaded to the commander's computer and, once approved, transferred to the torpedoes themselves. In an ironic twist, the targeting information system was actually carried on the surface in what appeared to be a beaten-up economy-sized plastic bottle of a famous American detergent.

These little submarines were to the silent underwater world what stealth aircraft were to the skies above — invisible to detection by normal means. They existed for one simple purpose: to kill Nimitz-class American carriers. To do this, they employed two special torpedoes, weapons that had as much in common with tank-killing munitions and autonomous robots as they did with classical torpedo design. Each was almost forty feet long and housed in special flared recesses in the bottom of the sub. When fired, they dropped silently from the sub's bottom and then either proceeded on their way or hovered on a time delay. The delay could last for hours or days, depending on their programming. As they sensed their targets coming within range, their on-board computer and targeting systems kicked into high gear.

The torpedoes stalked their prey, their speed and acoustic signatures responding to their target's position and speed. They were capable of sixty-knot sprints, over two times faster than the Nimitz carriers' thirty-four-knot maximum. They could close from any angle but would only greyhound toward their targets if they had no other alternative. Their on-board control systems much preferred to stalk like a cat than charge like a bull and did so far from the surface — often two hundred to three hundred feet below their target —relying on an array of passive systems that monitored the noisy super carriers above. Only when the torpedo was positioned almost directly underneath the carrier's hull would it choose to abandon its stealthy ways. At that moment, the electrical motor unit was jettisoned and four rocket motors ignited, accelerating the torpedo vertically to over one hundred knots to deliver its hammer blow.

The Nimitz carrier's thick twin hulls, designed to withstand standard torpedoes were no proof against these. They had a three-stage warhead, similar in artillery terms to an amour-piercing sabot shell. When the torpedo was close enough to its target, a shaped explosive charge peeled open the ship's outer hull. Then a high-speed depleted uranium slug almost a foot wide and four feet long blasted into the second interior hull followed by the torpedo's main shaped charge — almost a ton of high explosives whose detonation took advantage of the breech cause by the sabot when it entered the bottom of the ship. The resulting explosion, coupled with the immense cavitation of the water under the ship and its associated shock wave would cripple or fatally wound any carrier it was used against. In testing, it had bested every combination of hull design and armour its developers had thrown at it.

The U.S. Navy had no inkling of either the nearly invisible mini-subs or their sophisticated weaponry. Indeed, most high-ranking officers in the U.S. Navy would have been incredulous that the Chinese were even capable of developing technology on this level. The subs would have shaken their long-standing belief in Chinese technological ineptitude to the core. The fact that the Chinese had over sixty of these vessels encapsulated in the holds of innocent-looking but specially designed trawlers, junks, work ships and coastal freighters would have caused U.S. Naval planners and tacticians many sleepless nights.

Suddenly red strobes flickered to life in the hold above Yang's head, the silent signal that the crews were to man their stations and make ready to launch. He hurried to his vessel, happy that the long wait was finally ending and his intensive training might soon be put to use. Soon the first of the Hunan's four subs was dropped into the waters of the East China Sea, beads in a string of thirty pearls to be positioned between the Bush carrier strike force and areas of special Chinese interest.

September 26.
Situation Room, the White House.

The president readied himself for the next meeting with his conflict advisors while trying to ignore the severe indigestion that had plagued him for the last few days. It first jolted him from a troubled sleep at three o'clock in the morning, and he'd thought he was having a heart attack, so severe was the pain and pressure. A sensation like a dozen knives piercing his chest left him frightened and gasping. A hurried visit from the staff doctor assured him that it was not his heart but severe indigestion caused by stress. It hurt no less, but at least the panic from the fear of imminent death was assuaged.

He was now on a steady diet of prescription antacids, none of which seemed to help that much. If they were working, he thought, what indescribable agony would he be suffering if he weren't taking them. In a time of such severe emergency, he felt as if his own body was letting him down when he needed it most, providing another miserable distraction from the already miserable work at hand.

He arrived at the door to the Situation Room, which was filled with troubled-looking cabinet members and department heads. Once he'd sat amid the sixteen men seated at the table, the president called the meeting to order. "Gentlemen, your reports please — starting with yours, admiral."

"Yes, sir," said Irving. "The withdrawal of our forces from the Middle East and southeastern Europe as well as from Afghanistan is on schedule. Already we have a strong number of troops back in the country and deployed to assist law enforcement agencies and bolster ongoing security patrols, roadblocks and guard duties. To support our withdrawal, U.S. naval carriers in the Persian Gulf, joined by two more strike forces in the Mediterranean, are supplying an increased number of aircraft to provide combat air patrols and patrol the borders of our restricted zones in Iraq. We have also upped the number of patrols along the Iraq-Iran border in both number of aircraft and frequency lest the Iranians get any stupid ideas.

"The Chinese fleet in the Persian Gulf is still acting with more respect. It seems that our display of overwhelming force has cowed them, but none of their forces have withdrawn from the area. In a separate incident we had two Chinese surveillance aircraft take a run at the George Bush carrier group in the East China Sea, no doubt collecting as much intel as they could on the new carrier or on the new F-35s she operates. Both were driven off by fighters from the Bush, and there has been no further activity. The carrier group is presently on station about five hundred miles north of Taiwan.

"Our withdrawal in Iraq into the no-go zones has been almost flawless, and I am pleased to say that we currently have all the oil fields and pipelines outlined in our strategic plan covered. There has been light but unorganized resistance from the locals. We lost three troops to a car bomb at a checkpoint, and there have been several rocket-propelled grenade attacks on perimeter patrol vehicles — all with fatal results for the perpetrators — but all in all, resistance has been inconsequential. This could mean they are taking time to assess our positions before continuing with their attacks or have begged off because our current strategy makes us a much harder target. For the first time since the initial invasion, our troops have the upper hand tactically and know that everyone behind them is on their side and everyone in front can be viewed as hostile.

"In another bit of good news, the Turkish government, despite domestic pressure to the contrary, has allowed us two air corridors though their airspace to access the northern parts of Iraq with aircraft from the carriers in the Med.

"That's it, Mr. President. Internationally, things are going quite well, and the

Middle East is quieter than it has been for years."

"Thank you, admiral."

"Peter," said the president to the FBI's director.

Peter Archer cleared his throat and began. "Well, sir, we have some very good news. So far, we have captured or killed twenty-six terrorists with only one of our own injured."

The room broke out in spontaneous applause and cheers, and for the first time, everyone — even the president — smiled.

"Peter, that's outstanding," he said.

"Yes, sir. Thank you. The interrogation of Abu Bakre before he died of radiation poisoning gave us a lot of information. We're pretty sure that our efforts have cleaned up most of the terrorist cells operating in the southwest. We have, as you all know, captured alive two of the men responsible for the first attack in California, and two others responsible were killed. Since then, using the same tactic of arranging the weapons cache pickups just as Bakre did, we have captured a further twelve and killed fourteen. One marshal's deputy in a sting near Austin, Texas, was shot in the leg before killing the terrorist with his nickel-plated forty-five. Mind you, as good as this news is, we believe there may still be active cells in the southwest, and we are currently working to entrap them as well."

"So, the information we have relates only to cells operating in the southwest?" asked the president.

"Not just the southwest, sir. We nailed two cells in the Midwest as well, but it seems that Bakre's routes took him in an oval that extended as far north as Illinois and as far south as Southern California. We know there must be several of these weapons suppliers operating, and we now have a pretty good idea of how they work. We've located three other containers whose locations we did not get from Bakre.

"In fact, we think they may not have anything to do with him. They were filled with weapons, explosive materials and even fake IDs. One was found in an old rail yard near Bethlehem, Pennsylvania, and two, in St. Louis. So far, no one has turned up to claim them, but when they do, we'll nail the bastards. We have around-the-clock surveillance on all three sites, so when someone turns up to make a withdrawal, we'll get them, and hopefully, we'll be able to take down another series of cells."

"If you don't mind me asking," said Dan Blomstrum, "how exactly are we issuing information to the terrorists?"

"Well, that's really pretty good," said Archer smiling. "We have a list of about two hundred blogs that Bakre could use to supply information. What he would do is go onto a porn site that was readied with certain information directing cell members to a specific blog built into it."

Noticing that many of the men around the table looked a little lost, Archer explained. "These pages were individually coded for different cells. So take, for example, a cell member who looks on several specific porn sites for one, two or three colour combinations. Say, Red cell is looking for a site that features red-framed pictures featuring girls from, say, Phoenix, which would be Red cell's area of operation. The specific info they want is contained in a picture of a girl who may be wearing something yellow or lying on a yellow blanket. Then they check that specific picture for signs, posters or calendars that feature numbers in the image, say, outlined on a calendar in the background. The numbers equate with a simple code in Arabic that the cell members work out and that gives them the address of a blog page. They go to that blog, where they get specific directions to a pickup site. The directions are usually disguised as a posting about a recent trip or, perhaps, describing a route to a relative's house. We took Bakre's place and wrote our own blogs, which led the cells directly into our trap."

"That all seems pretty complicated to me," said one of the cabinet members.

"It does at first, but it's quite easy once you're used to it. It's all pretty simple low-tech stuff that these guys could easily decipher from memory and that was designed to be almost impossible for computers to decode because each cell has its own specific information triggers. Without the triggers, we would never find our way through all the layers, and since it is a visual system of pictures and prompts, the NSA's computers weren't likely to recognize it as a code.

"Even with what we know, it's proving almost impossible to find any other cells that are not dependant on supply from Bakre. But we are working on it, and we may soon have a good computer model that can ferret out what we need. One problem we have is that there are literally tens of thousands of porn sites on the Internet, each with hundreds of pages, and every cell has a number of sites they use that no other cell uses. It makes a needle in a haystack look like a slam dunk."

"So, if we did just shut down the Internet, we could stop this immediately," said the president.

"No, sir. I don't think so. We would dry up their source for weapons temporarily, but the terrorists would still be on the loose and still pose a grave threat. I think all we'd do is slow them down a bit while losing our one good chance to stop them using their own system."

"Point taken," said the president. "Hell, I just wish we could spread some of this good news to the American people."

"So do I, sir, but we can't afford to have the terrorists find out that we're onto them, or they may revert to a secondary plan we know nothing about or just abandon their standard procedures of supply and forage for weapons. That's certainly not that hard to do in this country."

"So listen up, everyone in this room," interjected Dan Blomstrum sternly. "This is not to be spoken about to anyone — not your wives, mothers, fathers or your madams."

Most of the assembled men smiled at the small jest.

"We can't afford a leak. If we leak, it means lives lost, and anyone I find responsible for a leak, no matter how innocent it seemed at the time, will find themselves inside the walls of the most uncomfortable federal prison I can find, if not in front if a firing squad. And that is not a joke."

Director Archer waited for Blomstrum to finish his warning and then continued his report. "Finally, and on a sadder note," he said, reading from a page of statistics, "we've had over one hundred and thirty fatal casualties this week and almost four hundred serious injuries from bombings and shootings nationwide. Several incidents involved the shooting of law enforcement officers, most of them off duty, and three civic politicians were assassinated this week, including the mayor of the small town of Briar, South Carolina.

"Another very nasty fire was set using Molotov cocktails. It was in Vermont and destroyed thousands of acres of woodland and reduced much of the ski resort town of Killington to ash. It's still burning in places but is under control, more due to a very lucky storm front than to the efforts of the local firefighters who are terribly undermanned."

He turned a page of his notes. "Six gas tankers were attacked and demolished, and we had four improvised explosive devices target military convoys. Fortunately, while there was material loss, there were no military casualties resulting. That's all I have right now."

"So, whose next?" asked the president as Archer finished. "How about you, Ken?"

"Sir," said Ken Potter, leaning forward and opening his treasury department folder. "I'm afraid I have very little but bad news."

"Go on," said the president.

"The economy is in a shambles. We have thousands of large American corporations in very serious trouble, and the number of small businesses that are teetering or have already closed is staggering. With the Chinese having very effectively stabbed us in the back, the federal government does not have the resources to help them, especially considering the enormous expense of internal security plus our overseas commitments.

"There are many areas of the country that have no gasoline either because of shortages or because they are in areas deemed too dangerous to supply at this time. There is also the very nasty problem of home heating as we get into the colder days of fall. Of course there is already a healthy black market in gasoline and other fuels as well as in other hard-to-get items."

"Christ, that didn't take long," moaned Blomstrum.

"I think we should start shooting black marketeers," said Admiral Irving.

"I have to admit to a similar sentiment," said the president, "but I think throwing them in jail and tossing away the key is as far as we might want to go right now."

"The ports are open to shipping once again," continued Potter, "but the backlog of goods is huge, and unfortunately, tight security has slowed normal operations significantly. We are presently opening every container and inspecting each one carefully, which means that materials leaving port have been reduced to a trickle and secure storage for uninspected containers is getting scarce. In the meantime, there are hundreds of ships piling up out on the ocean that can't get into port, and the navy and Coast Guard are having to use more and more resources just to monitor the waiting ships."

Admiral Irving nodded in agreement.

Potter continued. "The stock market has fallen more dramatically than it did during the Depression, and despite federal safeguards, I'm afraid there are going to be a lot of banks closing their doors." Potter's report lasted another forty-five minutes, outlining just how badly wounded the great nation of America had become in the scant month and a few days since August 18. The men in the room started to comprehend for the first time just how fragile a hold America had on its way of life. They also started to realize just how fundamentally different American life would soon become as it lost its grasp on the brass ring.

CHAPTER 16

September 27.
People's Liberation Army headquarters, Beijing.

General Liao Xilong, chief of staff of the People's Liberation Army, read the last of a deskload of reports, satellite scan interpretations and intelligence files. In the last six hours, he'd reviewed stacks of photographs and fingered dozens of reports from all over the world. He was confident that the timelines and objectives set years before had been realized.

He read one more report and not for the first time that evening. It was the shortest and most succinct of all the papers he had pored over that day. It read, "All 7th Fleet forces in harbours in Japan, aside from carrier battle group Bush in China Sea. Attached U.S. Marine Corps units of 7th Fleet withdrawn. No other viable U.S. seaborne threat within seven days' striking distance." The plan had, to date, been flawless. He hoped that it would continue to be so.

He let the paper flutter to the desk as he picked up his cheap ballpoint and, with a tired flourish, penned a signature on the bottom of a set of orders. That signature, the second to last in a long string of signatures, would awaken the carefully assembled machinery of war.

September 27.
London, England.

"I have to admit I like London a lot better than Riyadh, Tel Aviv or even Rome," said Derek. "At least I can almost speak the language."

He and Catherine were grabbing a quick breakfast in a secluded stall in the back of a grubby little London restaurant a block from their hotel. A nondescript and rather battered file folder lay on the table between them.

Catherine smiled and finished her coffee, an inglorious black tar poured by a young Turkish immigrant who was plainly far more interested in tucking himself behind the register and playing Internet games on his cellphone than he was in waiting on customers.

"Well, I certainly can't disagree," replied Catherine, "at least about Riyadh. The Saudis have never been my favourite people. Despite their money and decadence, they still hold dear a lot stone-age values. I'm glad we may not have to return there. I hate being hamstrung by their prohibitions against my sex. Besides, I think this plan will get us closer to al-Munajjid than we could in Saudi Arabia and without arousing any suspicion in him. As a matter of fact, if this Muhammad ibn Ya'la al-Dabbi al-Muffaddal knows enough, we may not have to get to al-Munajjid at all."

"How the hell do you do that?" said Derek incredulously.

"What?" asked Catherine.

"Just rattle off those great long-winded Arab names as if you've known them all your life."

"I don't know. I don't think about it. Once I read them, they just sort of stick."

Derek was looking at a photocopy of a photograph taken at the Islamabad airport following the first attacks on the United States, part of a file folder that contained a report on al-Munajjid. The photo showed al-Munajjid and al-Muffaddal greeting one another next to the private jet stairs and showed the younger man to great advantage. "So, how are you going to get close to this young globe-trotting cousin of al-Munajjid's. I mean, won't he suspect something's up if all of a sudden a beautiful woman latches onto him?"

"Probably not. In his case, I imagine I'll have a few things going for me. For a start, if we have to get close to al-Munajjid, coming in as an acquaintance of his jet-setting cousin is going to be a lot more convincing than trying to feign an interest in the old man. The cousin, on the other hand — well, he's one of those spoiled rich kids so used to having people fawning all over them that they come to expect it, even crave it."

"But still, won't it seem a little odd when you appear from nowhere and suddenly start showing an interest in this guy?" asked Derek.

"Not if I'm careful about it. You have to remember that there are an awful lot of young, good-looking women who aren't afraid of prostituting themselves to get close to that much money. And his background is hardly one that puts women on a pedestal. It doesn't matter how he dresses or how many Rolex watches or private jets he has, he is still a product of a society that treats women as property. That makes him particularly vulnerable. There is no advantage greater than that of being underestimated."

"I suppose you're right. Judging from what we know about him already," Derek said, absentmindedly tapping the file folder that contained a thin Mossad report on al-Muffaddal and his family.

"The file the Israelis supplied doesn't paint a glowing picture of either his work ethic or his smarts," said Catherine. "His father is the smart one, made all his money importing Palestinians, Turks and Pakistanis to do the jobs that Saudis wouldn't. He'd charge them a fortune to bring them in officially and then take a kickback on their wages, all state sanctioned. Lots of competition now, but when the old man started, he was one of the first — unless you count the actual slave traders. He isn't too far removed from them in practice or intent.

"He has several daughters but only one son, Muhammad, and he dotes on the boy. The kid's thirty-four and has never held down a job in his life, just jet-sets around and spends dad's money. He has luxury apartments and country homes spread across Europe. Here in London, he lives in Mayfair, and he's a regular at the Yorkshire Rose, a fancy little eatery near his apartment. According to the brief, he takes at least one or two meals a day there, usually breakfast and lunch. We'll see if we can snare him there."

"And exactly how are we going to do that?" asked Derek.

"Simple. You're going to be my prick of a boyfriend and dump me over breakfast tomorrow morning."

"Great. Now I'm the bad guy."

They finished the rest of their breakfasts, discussing the latest news from the States. After paying the bill, Derek finished his coffee and looked out the window of the restaurant at the unfamiliar buildings and even more unfamiliar European and English cars that inched past on the congested street.

"Boy, this is all such a long, long stretch from my training with the Bureau," he said to no one in particular.

September 27.
Port of Shanghai, China.

The first trains arrived as twilight started to descend over Shanghai. The super container ship the Great Wall was still empty and floated high in the water, but around her on the quay and in the adjoining warehouse complex, the first stirrings of an immense exercise in military planning and discipline were becoming apparent. As the sky darkened the first train slowed on tracks that led up to the huge main warehouse building. The great doors opened, and the train disappeared like a worm into an apple.

Inside the building everything was ready. Hundreds of containers stood on massive conveyers and on the forks of gigantic tow motors that would soon whisk them though and out of the building into the Great Wall's holds or to the crowd of stork-like loading cranes waiting by its decks. The first train disgorged its load. Thousands of crack army troops in full combat gear ran to meet a line of men, each waving a different coloured flag. Each unit found and then followed a flag of a particular colour until they arrived at their containers. These were equipped with rows of seats, internal lighting, fresh-air units, food lockers, air conditioning, chemical toilets and enough reserve power to last five days. They were not by any stretch of the imagination comfortable, but they were survivable, and that was enough to satisfy most military minds.

The first containers to load did not carry men. They were orange or dark blue in colour, and the holds of the Great Wall filled with them as the other containers in the warehouse filled with men. These containers contained logistical support supplies and heavy weapons, up to and including tanks and mobile missile launchers, that would supply the army after the target port was fully secured.

Despite the Great Wall's immense capacity, she was almost full by midnight. This was largely due to clever port construction, conveyer systems that fed her though large access doors in her sides and the expertise of the crane operators who swung the containers skywards and then lowered them like children's blocks to the gargantuan ship's deck in stacks. By dawn, her decks were stacked five high with containers that carried a complete army.

This was the most vulnerable part of the plan. The Great Wall, if discovered, would be a very easy target. Her strength lay in her enemy's total ignorance of her cargo. Her loss would create the largest single-day fatality list in the history of warfare, but her safe arrival in port would be a masterstroke, trumping the allied invasion of Europe. A coordinated assault from the sea and the skies would pave the way for her safe unloading.

The Great Wall sailed on her maiden voyage at a little after nine in the morning, September 28.

September 28.
Mayfair, London.

Muhammad ibn Ya'la al-Dabbi al-Muffaddal took the sleeping girl's arm by the wrist and threw it carelessly from his chest before dragging himself upright in the large satin-sheeted bed. The girl was Eastern European, either Romanian or Hungarian. She'd told him, but he didn't remember and didn't care. She was very pretty, with large green eyes. Her naturally brunette hair had been dyed a brassy blonde in a dirty sink in the tiny washroom she shared with the other residents of the boarding house she roomed in far from Mayfair. Her make up was carefully and skilfully applied to make her look older than her seventeen years, but in the first light of day, with the paint fading, she looked a child. Al-Muffaddal wanted nothing more to do with her. He'd let his personal assistant deal with it.

She'd be woken, given a half hour to get washed and dressed in the guest bathroom and then unceremoniously shown the door, without having seen al-Muffaddal again. Since she had no money — one of al-Muffaddal's security men had quietly searched her purse after his employer had led her to the bedroom — she might get a couple of pounds for bus fare.

Al-Muffaddal spent the next hour seeing to his toilet in the opulent granite-floored private washroom of his fabulously expensive Mayfair apartment. For a moment, as he washed and then slid into his Jacuzzi, he thought that if the girl was still in the apartment he should have her brought in. A quick blow job might be good. He didn't even know her name, having never been formally introduced at the art gallery cocktail party where he'd picked her up. She was just one more piece of the human flotsam that flowed across Western Europe and Britain looking for an escape from the poverty of Eastern Europe, flotsam he was quite prepared to use and then discard. He thought for a second and then changed his mind. This morning he'd service himself. It was less trouble.

By eleven o'clock al-Muffaddal had made his way onto the street and walked briskly toward the Yorkshire Rose. He had a couple of errands to run for his esteemed cousin today, but not until the afternoon.

He spent a few hours a week engaged in odd jobs, mostly banking transactions and transfers his father and al-Munajjid requested of him. He bridled at this sometimes, despite the lightness of the load, but he had to admit that his much older cousin had hatched and delivered up a brilliant plan. Al-Munajjid's inner circle was sure to reap great profit and power if America lost its stranglehold on the Middle East. It seemed entirely natural to al-Muffaddal that he share in the glory. So much so that he was prepared to make small sacrifices like running errands and taxiing al-Munajjid around the world in his Falcon jet, an aircraft that carried the colours of his family's branch of the House of Saud.

The traffic crawled past him, as London traffic was wont to do. On occasion, it would stop and he would gain, passing cars that moments before had passed him. In one of these cars were two American agents who'd been keeping track of his progress since he left the apartment. It was quite clear where he was headed. One of the agents opened his cellphone and dialled.

In the Yorkshire Rose, Catherine's cellphone jittered on the table. She answered, thanked the caller and then snapped it closed. "That was the flower shop," she said to Derek, who sat across from her perusing the menu. "They're going to be able to deliver today."

Derek grunted in reply.

"The flower shop" meant that their gamble on time and location had blossomed.

The Yorkshire Rose was one of those small, chi-chi restaurants that are all chrome and crisp white linen. The walls were devoid of decoration, lined instead with handmade textured linen wallpaper and deco-inspired chrome light fixtures. The silver and white was offset dramatically by the odd splash of vibrant ruby red. It looked very designer and very expensive and was both.

Derek and Catherine sat at a table a few feet from and in full view of the window table that restaurant staff kept reserved for al-Muffaddal's daily visits. There were even a couple of tabloid papers rolled up and waiting for him on it. The female waitresses, who all fervently despised him, would watch with great amusement and a little disgust as he flipped from page to page in his quest for the bare-bosomed girls that graced many of England's less prestigious dailies.

Five minutes later, al-Muffaddal walked through the door, headed for his table and plunked himself down, sprawling in the chair, his legs splayed across the aisle so the waitresses would have to carefully step over his two-thousand-dollar loafers. Within a second of taking his seat, he had his cellphone out and was talking on it. This ensured that the waitress, who had hurried to the table at the urging of the restaurant manager, would have to wait while he finished his call. This morning he wore an expensive pair of tailored slacks, an Italian silk shirt, fabulously expensive designer sunglasses — worn indoors and out —and a gem-encrusted man's Rolex. The top three buttons of his shirt were open, and a thatch of thick black hair thrust through the triangle at his throat together with three heavy chains — two in gold and one in platinum.

Derek murmured to Catherine, "Geez, isn't he the greasy asshole."

"Isn't he," she replied.

"I don't envy you your job."

"Don't worry. I have experience manipulating his type. They're easy. It's the smart ones who respect you that are tough."

"So?" asked Derek.

"We'll leave it a few minutes. Let him settle in. Oh, here we go. He doesn't let any grass grow. He's noticed me." Catherine leaned forwards, her plunging neckline showing to good advantage, and adjusted one of her high heels. At the same time she displayed a long and shapely leg.

Her conversation with Derek, held in low tones, had been engineered. She was to look at him intensely while he leaned back in his chair, his body language conveying boredom, even distraction.

Derek was enjoying himself in his role as actor.

Al-Muffaddal postured, trying to get Catherine's attention, even dropping his sunglasses to look over their tops with a look he'd practised in the mirror and thought of as smouldering. Most women viewed it as creepy.

Derek and Catherine continued to talk in hushed tones that could not be overheard. But the intensity of their conversation alerted anyone looking that there was something wrong. Suddenly, Derek stood, slamming his chair backwards into the chairs at the table behind.

"You fucking bitch. You're not my wife. If I want to see someone else, and you don't like it, it's your fucking problem, not mine. I'm out of here!"

He threw his napkin onto the table, spilling Catherine's coffee across the white linen, turned and stamped toward the door. Halfway there he paused and turned back. "And do not, under any circumstance, call me again. Ever!" He strode from the restaurant, the door swinging closed behind him.

Catherine remained at the table, coffee dripping to the floor from the linen. She sat bolt upright, but her head was down, and her shoulders shook as she sobbed gently. It was masterful.

Al-Muffaddal looked from Catherine, her long legs extending from a short skirt as she swung away from the dripping coffee, to the door and then back to Catherine. Sensing that Derek was not about to reappear any time soon, he rose and walked over to her table.

"Excuse me, miss. Please, let me help you with that spill," he said with as much concern as he could convincingly muster. He patted at the spreading pool of coffee that inundated a third of the table.

"No, no," said Catherine, "Please, don't bother. I'll get it." Catherine swished at the coffee ineffectually with her own napkin.

"It's no bother, please." Al-Muffaddal turned and snapped his fingers at the manager, who was already on his way with a stack of cloths. "Please," al-Muffaddal said, "get this mess cleaned up for the lady."

"Yes, sir. Right away," said the manager.

Al-Muffaddal missed the irritation that creased the man's face as he bent to attend to the spill. "Miss, please, come to my table for a moment. Let me get you a fresh coffee."

"No, it's all right, thank you very much. I'm fine."

"No, you are not," he replied, "and you should not be. No woman as lovely as you should be treated that way. The man is a boor."

A waitress walking up behind al-Muffaddal rolled her eyes.

Catherine smiled wanly and said, "I'm flattered, but really, I don't want to bother you."

"I insist. Waitress, bring this lady a fresh coffee. Or would you prefer wine?"

"Oh, no, not wine. A coffee will be fine," said Catherine to the waitress.

The waitress smiled at her sympathetically, wishing she could give Catherine the appropriate warnings.

The three could hear the conversation in the restaurant. Catherine was wired, although in this day and age, there was no wire. Instead, a very sensitive microphone and tiny transmitter was secreted in the butterfly pendant that nested in her cleavage. Al-Muffaddal's voice issued from a small receiver sitting between the car's two front seats.

"So, do you live in London?" he asked.

"No," replied Catherine. "I live in New York, but I'm here for a couple of months researching my next book."

"Book? Ah, so you're an author."

If the eavesdroppers had been able to see the couple, they would have been amused at just how much trouble al-Muffaddal was having keeping his gaze from straying to the butterfly.

"And what do you write? Romantic novels?"

"No," said Catherine, "I'm an economist. My books cover financial business."

Al-Muffaddal was slow to respond, and when he did, it was with some discomfort. "I see, I see. So, you are American?"

"Born and raised," replied Catherine, "and by the way, my name is Melissa Turner."

Al-Muffaddal, back in familiar territory, relaxed a bit. "And mine is Muhammad al-Muffaddal."

"I'm pleased to meet you," said Catherine.

"Likewise."

"So, Mr. al-Muffaddal."

"Please," he said, holding up his hand, "please call me Muhammad."

"Muhammad," replied Catherine smiling. "So, tell me where you are from."

"I am Saudi. My family is from Riyadh."

"That is exciting, and very romantic. Are you in London on business or are you vacationing?"

"Actually, neither. I have an apartment down the road. You see, I'm very fortunate to come from a family that is quite wealthy, and I look after their interests in Europe and here in England."

"Wow," said Catherine in a totally convincing manner. "What business is your family in?"

"We supply skilled and unskilled labour to corporations and governments in Saudi Arabia and several other countries in the Middle East. I suppose you would call us professional headhunters."

"What a great business. I suppose you get to meet all kinds of interesting people. How do you go about finding them?"

"Well, I don't. We have many offices and professionals for that. My tasks are much simpler. My job is to monitor the financial transactions and various investments that my family makes in Europe. I really don't have anything to do with the daily running of the business. I'm afraid my duties leave me with much spare time on my hands, so it can be very lonely."

"Oh, that's too bad, but I suppose it would get lonely being so far away from home all the time," Catherine said, her concern apparent enough to make al-Muffaddal wriggle, inwardly gleeful that his next conquest was going to be so easy.

He reached across the table, taking her hand.

"I must admit that the odd period of loneliness pales in comparison to the joy of meeting someone like you."

In the car down the road, Derek and the other two agents looked at one another with big grins. "Oh, brother. This guy really makes you want to puke," exclaimed the agent behind the wheel. Derek, who sat in the back seat, was surprised at his own reaction as a little knot of concern worried at his gut.

As al-Muffaddal pulled her hand halfway across the table, Catherine looked down at her wristwatch and exclaimed, "Oh my goodness, is that the time? I'm late."

She reached and put her other hand on top of al-Muffaddal's and gave his hand an affectionate little squeeze as she withdrew her other hand from his grasp. "I'm so sorry. I have an appointment across town, and I'll be late if I don't get going. I feel badly. You've been so kind."

Al-Muffaddal's face flashed annoyance before his practiced smile returned and he asked, "Can I offer you a ride to your appointment?"

"I couldn't put you out like that, and I need my own car as I have a fair bit to do this afternoon. If I don't get it done, I'll catch hell from my editor."

Al-Muffaddal felt his conquest slipping away. "Dinner tonight, then?" he asked a little too desperately in an effort to save the situation.

"Oh, I'm sorry. I can't," she replied, rising from her chair.

Al-Muffaddal sat back disappointed.

After a pause, Catherine said, "But I'm free tomorrow evening."

"Wonderful, wonderful. Can I pick you up, say, around seven?" he asked, immediately cheerful.

"That would be great." Catherine rummaged about in her small bag before withdrawing a hotel card. She pulled a pen out of the purse's side pocket and scrawled a number. "This is my hotel, and this is my room number. I'll see you at seven." She smiled at him and then turned and walked from the restaurant, purposely putting a little swing into her hips as she went.

Al-Muffaddal was so busy inspecting her legs and rear as she left the restaurant that he didn't even think about the bill for the coffees and Catherine's breakfast with Derek until the waitress brought it to him and asked if he was covering both. He grumbled a little as he paid and then thought about the favour he'd been done. This one was nice, very nice, and American. Perhaps he would keep her for a week or so.

He even fantasized about having her abducted and taken to Saudi Arabia. He could always sell her when he tired of her, and with her creamy skin and flaming red hair, he could probably get a pretty penny. American woman were worth so much more than the Eastern Europeans that had flooded the market for the last few years.

September 29.
Strait of Hormuz.

The Qin Shi Huang, an atomic-powered Type 93 Shang-class attack submarine, had slipped very quietly into the Strait of Hormuz two weeks before — so slowly and quietly, in fact, that it had eluded detection by the American-laid Sound Surveillance System lines that crisscrossed the strait listening for just such an incursion. The submarine hugged the northern shore of the strait, seeking out a trench that lay in Iranian waters. Once the narrow chasm was found, the Qin Shi Huang went to ground, its machinery stilled and its crew living in whispers.

The Iranians had supplied the PLAN with the trench's location. Its orientation, depth and proximity to the Iranian coast made it very difficult for U.S. Navy airborne magnetic detection devices to pick up a submarine resting on its bottom. Any magnetic anomaly was more likely to be attributed to the rusting old coastal freighter that lay on the trench's southern edge.

The Qin Shi Huang was named for the first emperor of China, and she was the first in a class of attack submarines that had kept the Americans guessing since their inception. No one outside of a few high-ranking Chinese government officials, Chinese navy brass and the sub's builders even knew how many existed or how capable they were. The Americans assumed, from intelligence they'd acquired, that there were only three or four, and those were fraught with problems that left them tied up in port. They'd had satellite surveillance of the subs with black smoke issuing from their hatches on more than one occasion. What the pictures did not reveal was that the submarines and their crews were great actors.

Small, portable smoke generators were set up below the subs' hatches and ignited, giving the impression that the boats were in trouble. To add to the effect, the crew would scamper around on deck, breaking out firefighting equipment and readying lifeboats, and the subs' ballast tanks were rigged to provide lists of up to thirty degrees. The crews thought they were involved in realistic drills when in fact the whole scene was engineered to play to the American satellite cameras. The closing scene, repeated on more than one occasion, was a rescue and tow back to port. Another misleading feature of the sub was its markings: the Chinese had twenty examples of the class, but they shared only three sets of numbers and markings. Chinese misinformation had also convinced the Americans that the new class was at best the equal of the older Russian Victor-class and, as such. no match for U.S. surface or subsurface forces.

At all times at least fifteen Shangs wandered the oceans available to do Beijing's bidding, and if any risked compromise while on patrol, a small and cleverly designed blister mounted to the aft decks would telegraph the signatures of an older and far less capable class of Chinese submarine. If a skipper thought he was at risk of being detected, he'd switch the unit on and its synthetic symphony of machine and propeller sound would cleverly rise and mask the real and very insignificant signature of the Shang-class sub, a signature that U.S. sonar operators had no record of.

The deception had been working for five years, since the first Shang was launched, and unlike the Soviet submarines of an earlier period, the Chinese submarines avoided the U.S. Navy at all costs and played no games with them.

The captain of the sub allowed a tiny buoy and receiver to be released. It rose to the surface seven hundred feet above, where it floated disguised as a discarded fishing net float. At precisely nine hundred hours local time, the receiver in the sub displayed an incoming message on its computer screen. It translated to "terracotta," a reference to Emperor Qin Shi Huang's famous terracotta army and addressed to this sub. The submarine's commander ordered the float retracted. He expected no more messages. His job, one of sowing the seeds of mistrust in the region, had begun.

Twenty minutes later, the Qin Shi Huang slipped out of its spider hole and headed south toward the busy shipping lanes. There it quietly and efficiently lay two dozen sophisticated non-ferrous anti-shipping mines. They were of French design, and if one ever happened to be recovered, no one would suspect they were perfect imitations created in a weapons facility two hundred miles west of Hong Kong. While incapable of sinking the armoured carriers and cruisers of the American fleet, they were imminently capable of sinking lesser destroyer escorts and, more importantly, the great bloated single-hulled monsters that bulged with crude oil and passed through the strait in huge numbers.

Less than two hours after the mines had been sown across the shipping lanes, the crude oil tanker Arthur Van Kindross, owned by Boron Oil, struck one, tearing a hole in her starboard hull just forty feet back from the bow. The mine not only ripped a thirty-foot hole in the hull ten-feet below the surface, it ignited the crude inside the forward hold. Tens of thousands of gallons of burning oil spread across the calm waters of the strait as the ship foundered and started to break up before beginning its inevitable plunge to the seabed.

A small patrol boat from the United Arab Emirates saw the black clouds tinged with flame rising on the horizon and heard the tanker's call for help. Its captain rang up full speed, setting course for the stricken giant. Five nautical miles from the mortally wounded tanker, it too hit a mine. The 120-foot patrol boat was lifted clear out of the water, it's back snapped, and plunged down in two pieces. Of its twenty-four-man crew, only one survived the blast. He was thrown bleeding and broken through the air and clear of the wreck, but within minutes, his instinctual struggle to remain on the surface attracted the attention of several sharks.

September 29.
Atlanta, Georgia.

Mohammed al-Tayeb had been in the United States legally for years. He'd been instrumental in supplying information to various terrorist organizations on American legal, military and civil procedures. He'd earmarked thousands of possible targets for attack, and he'd even recruited and brainwashed the young and disenfranchised Miguel Ramírez, who knocked down the Lufthansa 747 with such devastating results.

Recruiting Ramírez had been more a source of entertainment than a necessity, and he was sure some members of his organization would have disapproved, but it had worked out in the end. The risky attack with the old Stinger had been a resounding success, and Ramírez knew nothing that would compromise the mission, so his capture did not matter. Even if the Americans had broken him, which al-Tayeb was sure they would within an hour of Ramírez's capture, all they would learn was the misinformation he'd implanted in the young man's head.

That all seemed so long ago. The America he now manoeuvred through was not the America of a month and a half ago. Today she was a vicious creature whose people were scared and dangerous. Civil liberties were rapidly dwindling, and although freedom of speech remained, uttering anything the slightest bit critical of the U.S. government or any of the new and often draconian security measures was fraught with peril. Americans were having a hard time adjusting, but to al-Tayeb, who was born and raised in Lebanon, America felt a lot more like home.

This morning he was driving past the CDC, the Center for Disease Control and Prevention, on Clifton Road in northeastern Atlanta. It was a target he would have loved to hit, but massive security ringed it, making only a suicide attack viable, and al-Tayeb was not by nature suicidal. He was cautious and calculating, although he enjoyed the thrill of testing himself and his skilfully wrought personas. He was a true chameleon and blended into the landscape seamlessly. Anyone talking to him now would think he was Mexican American. His looks, dress and accent reproduced that of a boy raised in Brownsville, Texas, to the core. The boy-turned-man whose identity al-Tayeb had adopted was long dead, an unidentified and partially consumed floater in an alligator-infested Miami swamp, but his identity survived, drawn over the terrorist like a second skin.

He turned off Clifton Road, stopping briefly at a security checkpoint where he showed his papers, which included a worker's badge from Emory University, near the CDC. He'd just finished his night shift, mopping halls in the Candler School of Theology. It amused him no end that a devout Muslim whose greatest ambition was to fell Christianity moved among its young acolytes without suspicion or notice. He was even more entertained that the cross he wore around his neck as part of his disguise was viewed with scorn by a few of those young people, who considered him a dupe of evil papists and tried to bring him into their perversion of the sacred light.

There was no time to sleep off a night of work this morning, so he downed two white pills — mild stimulants — to fend off the tendrils of weariness that could affect his performance this day. He was on his way to meet with the two other members of his cell, and today they were to strike a massive blow.

In the last few weeks the three men had been responsible for a number of improvised explosive devises that had left several people dead and shocked residents in the Atlanta area, but today they were after bigger game than the odd truck or police car. After a forty-minute drive through Atlanta's much-reduced rush hour traffic, he pulled into the parking lot of a small rundown industrial mall in the South End. He walked to the back and looked around to make sure no one was showing any interest in him before he unlocked the main door to unit six and entered, pulling the door to behind him and relocking it.

The unit was empty except for a large green military six-by-six transport truck. The vehicle had been purloined from a military park the night before by the two men who now hovered around it. "This is very good. The truck is perfect," al-Tayeb said to his accomplices. "You had no problems?"

"No, no problems at all. Our papers were accepted without question," replied one of the men, an East Asian with a slight frame.

His companion, a tall black man with ebony skin and the refined features of Northeast Africa, joined them. He was Eritrean. Both men wore National Guard combat uniforms. They looked polished and were immaculately groomed — not the picture of sloppy terrorists that most people harboured.

Within minutes al-Tayeb had changed into the dress uniform of a lieutenant-colonel of the National Guard, checked his papers and identification and made himself ready. "The truck's fully loaded?" he asked as he raised the tarp from the rear tailgate and peered into the gloomy interior.

"Yes, it's full," replied the two men almost in unison.

"We loaded it before we changed into these uniforms. We used it all," one of them added.

"Good. And the timers and remote are prepared?"

"Yes," said the Eritrean, passing al-Tayeb a small black box with two hooded buttons on it — a remote detonator.

"Then we're ready. If we leave now, we should be downtown in half an hour and to the target a few minutes later, so let's get started. Have you both prayed?"

The other men nodded.

The oriental clambered into the cab as the other man opened the tarp and climbed over the tailgate to sit in the cargo box and nursemaid the load. His companion in the back was six tons of high-grade explosives and a further two tons of truck parts and equipment that had a two-fold purpose. One was to camouflage hundreds of grey bricks that lined the truck bed, and the other, lesser purpose, considering the weight and power of the explosives, was to serve as shrapnel.

The truck fired up, its big diesel rattling as al-Tayeb opened the overhead door. He climbed into the passenger side of the cab and took his seat, brushing from his dress jacket the dust he'd picked up from the chains of the door as he raised it.

Soon they were in traffic, following a route carefully chosen to take them through the fewest security checks. There would only be one roadblock, which al-

Tayeb knew to be manned by disinterested Guardsmen who bridled at the amount of work they had to do checking the stream of tractor-trailers that flowed along this route into Atlanta to keep the city's pulse steady even in these troubled times.

His instincts were good. As they slowed for the checkpoint, he flashed his military ID to a group of Guardsmen who stood on the side of the road. One of them, a sergeant, waved them through and saluted al-Tayeb, who returned the salute correctly. Ahead of them, the city centre beckoned.

CHAPTER 17

September 29.
The White House

"Who's responsible? Is it the fucking Chinese?"

"We don't know, Mr. President," replied Admiral Irving. He and the president were alone in the president's working office. "One of our minesweepers has identified the mines as French made. They are equipped with both magnetic proximity detonators as well as contact detonators and are very hard to detect because very little metal is used in their construction. The French say they aren't missing any, and they're adamant that their mines have not been sold to any counties in the Middle East. Their list of customers for these is Norway, Belgium, Spain, Greece and Brazil. We're checking with those countries to see if they're missing any or to find out if they've sold them to a third party."

"So, what's your best guess, admiral?"

"I don't think it's the Chinese, sir. It serves them no purpose, and besides, they use cloned copies of old Soviet-era anti-shipping mines. Iran comes to mind, but that would be fouling their own beaches, and again, what would be the advantage? I have to think that it's a terrorist attack, probably aimed at our forces in the Gulf. I know there are a lot of people pretty pissed off that we've strengthened our naval presence, even though we're pulling out our land-based force."

"What's the danger to our carriers?"

"Negligible, sir. The mines are powerful but not enough to sink a carrier or any of our cruisers, although a contact would certainly rattle some teeth. Some of our smaller escorts and the supply ships are at risk, but hopefully, we'll have located all the mines and cleaned them up pretty soon, and whoever laid them will not get the opportunity again."

"So, they just got the two, then," said the president. "What are the ramifications of the oil tanker's sinking?"

"We've closed the strait for now. The Emirates are cooperating fully. They're pretty pissed off about losing one of their shiny new patrol boats, but Iran, as can be expected, is screaming. That comes under the heading of 'who gives a shit.' The strait is a mess. The tanker split in half as the oil weakened her back, and the bow is under, but the aft two thirds is still afloat and spreading burning crude. The slick is already four miles across and growing. A lot of it is on fire. Emergency cleanup vessels are on the way from the Emirates and Saudi Arabia and should be there soon, but they're going dead slow, looking for mines. Hopefully, when they get to the wreck, they can boom the slick and contain it before it gets much farther. Fortunately, the weather is cooperating, and the seas are calm, or it could have been a lot worse. On the other hand, forecasters are predicting increasing wind from the northeast by midday tomorrow, so we've got to get things under control pretty quickly."

"And what are the Chinese doing?"

"They've offered assistance and have two frigates in the area patrolling for mines. They offered further assistance, which we respectfully declined. They've got four other ships in the Persian Gulf, but those have been steering clear. Their remaining surface ships are tied up in port in Gwadar or at sea to the south, just off Pakistan's shore. We know there are at least four Chinese diesel subs in the area, as well. We've seen them on the surface recharging their batteries or taking supply from the tender. We suspect there are also a couple of Han-class nuclear attack boats, but they're shit boxes and probably more dangerous to their own crews than to our boats. We have two Los Angeles attack boats on station just off Gwadar, keeping track of things. Either is capable of taking out the whole lot of Chinese subs before they know what hits them, so we're not too worried. They seem to have done a quick rethink about their antics after a few days of being in the crosshairs of so many carrier groups."

"Admiral, do you think we have to keep so many carrier strike forces in the region?" asked the president. "It's getting pretty expensive, and to tell you the honest truth, we really can't afford it with conditions as they are. The Chinese are really screwing us financially, as you know, and if we don't husband our resources carefully until this crap is all behind us, we risk weakening ourselves too much to curtail any real Chinese adventurism in the Middle East."

"Well sir, we've cut back some. We have six of our fifteen carriers in port, and the Lincoln is headed home now the Stennis is on station in the Gulf. We could recall one group from the Med, and if we needed to, we could cover our withdrawal from Iraq with two groups in the Persian Gulf instead of three. We still need the Washington on station in the Gulf of Oman to cover our withdrawal from Afghanistan, but we could pull the Eisenhower and let the Washington split duties between Afghanistan and the Gulf of Oman. That leaves just five groups out, including the Bush, which has just started to patrol the area between Taiwan and Japan. We're spread pretty thin, but it's manageable, and we can still have at least three groups on standby in home ports, keep their crews close by and the ships ready to sortie."

"Could you support the Gulf with just two groups? One in the Persian Gulf and one in the Mediterranean?" asked the president.

"That would leave us pretty vulnerable, sir. I don't think it would be a good idea," replied Irving.

"It may not be a good idea, but I don't know whether we have much choice. I suggest it would be prudent to make plans to operate with two groups as soon as the lion's share of the withdrawal has been implemented."

"What about the Chinese fleet, sir?"

"Admiral, are you telling me that if it came to blows, one carrier force along with, what, five or six of our attack subs in the area is not sufficient to make short work of a dozen or so Chinese destroyers and a motley crew of old subs?"

"Well, no sir. It's that we generally keep the bad guys at bay with a show of overwhelming force."

"Well, admiral, I propose that you convince anyone interested in becoming an opponent that one carrier strike force constitutes overwhelming force."

Admiral Irving rarely disagreed with the president, but as he left the White House, he had the uneasy feeling that the president's judgment was becoming impaired by the overwhelming stress he was under.

September 29.
Spring and Marietta streets, Atlanta, Georgia.

Mohammed al-Tayeb returned the salute of a group of regular soldiers standing at the intersection of Spring Street and Marietta. His target was only one block away, and he could hardly breathe from anxiety. His driver got into the left lane, easing the truck carefully in so as not to cause a problem nor draw attention to them. He indicated a left turn half a block before the next intersection of Techwood Drive and Marietta.

The target building thrust skywards, crowned by large red letters that spelled CNN. This was the palace of the self-proclaimed kings and queens of the modern world media. The driver made the turn onto Techwood and swung over to the right-hand side of the road. He stopped the military truck when it pulled level with the centre of the multi-storey building. The truck's door opened, and al-Tayeb stepped down. Approaching from the other side, the driver rounded the front of the vehicle, and the third of the group hopped down from the back and tied the tarpaulin tightly onto the tailgate.

As he finished, a National Guard corporal walked toward them from his security post. He stiffened when he saw al-Tayeb. "Sir," he barked, snapping to attention.

"At ease, corporal," said al-Tayeb in a masterful Mexican American accent. Before the soldier had time to think, he added, "Corporal, I want you to keep an eye on this truck while we're in the building. I have to give a quick interview to the news network, and I'm hoping I'll be back out here in half an hour at the outside. There are valuable classified government-owned materials in the back of this vehicle, and I do not want anyone seeing or stealing them. Do you understand, corporal?"

"Yes, sir."

"Very well." Al-Tayeb turned and walked along the sidewalk toward the main entrance of the building, his two companions in step behind him. He stuck his hand into his pocket and thumbed the two safety hoods that cloaked the buttons on the remote. Then he pushed both buttons, starting a countdown of sixty seconds. There were no pulsing lights or beeping sounds. The countdown was silent and imperceptible.

Once the three terrorists had ducked into the alcove formed by the massive entranceway and were out of the corporal's view, they stepped up their pace, jogging through the lofty inner atrium of the building and out through doors that opened on the Andrew Young Parkway. Behind them, the corporal was having second thoughts about the truck and its occupants and radioed his lieutenant for advice.

The three terrorists dashed across the wide parkway and made good time, breaking into a full run along Marietta, their feet given wings by the adrenalin that coursed through their systems. Al-Tayeb was just unlocking the door of a white Dodge Neon parked in a lot two blocks away at Foundry and Marietta when the air cracked with manmade thunder and the ground shook beneath them. They jumped into the car and blasted out of the lot north along Marietta and away from the cloud of dust and debris that was rolling up the road behind them.

In Atlanta, a city that had suffered few attacks, the huge CNN complex caved into its immense atrium. The news network the whole world was watching suddenly disappeared, the flash of startled faces a televised requiem before they were replaced by grey, speckled television screens and white noise.

September 29.
London.

Catherine sat in the lobby of the Dorian Hotel waiting for al-Muffaddal to arrive. Derek was nowhere to be seen, because he would be recognized. He was several blocks away cooling his heels in his and Catherine's real accommodations. He was to take no part in this phase of the operation, and he felt both impotent and very worried about the danger Catherine could be exposed to if their suspicions were correct.

The Dorian was a quaint, family-owned hotel a few blocks from Buckingham Palace that had been open to business since the last decade of the nineteenth century. It still held close many of the features of its original design, and the rich Victorian furniture, decorations and embellishments in the lobby wouldn't have raised an eyebrow among real Victorians. The only incongruous feature of the room was the shifting blue light illuminating the desk clerk from her otherwise hidden computer screen.

Catherine had met the clerk earlier in the day when she checked in, hauling several bags filled mostly with newspaper to provide weight. The room number she had provided to al-Muffaddal was, in fact, incorrect. That room had been unavailable, but that was of little consequence, attributable to a lapse in memory or to a woman being cautious about a man just met.

At about ten after seven, a dark metallic blue Aston Martin DB9 pulled up in front of the hotel, and al-Muffaddal got out, leaving the car idling on the curb. He swept into the lobby flourishing a single rose, which he presented to Catherine as she stood up.

"Ah, Catherine, you look beautiful," he exclaimed, taking in her form, his gaze lingering for a moment too long on her bust before rising to her face.

"Thank you, Muhammad."

She did look stunning. She wore a tight saffron yellow dress, split to near the top of her leg on her left side. The neckline was plunging but not too much so, and a stunning faux-emerald necklace accented the simple dress, expensive costume jewellery that was sufficient in its quality to pass for the real thing. Matching saffron pumps with a sensible high heel finished off her outfit. She'd left her hair long and flowing so that it framed her face, highlighting a masterful application of makeup and ruby red lipstick. She looked every inch a nineteen-thirties movie star. She knew how to play to her strengths and to the weaknesses of men.

"I have a surprise for you, a wonderful surprise, a wonderful place," he said.

"Where are we going?" she asked.

"Oh, now that would ruin the surprise, wouldn't it?" he replied, laughing. Al-Muffaddal took her by the hand and escorted he though the hotel's entranceway and opened the front passenger door of the Aston with a flourish.

"Nice car," she said, sinking into the sumptuous leather and taking in the woodwork and elegant dashboard. He closed the door and walked around to the other side. After getting in, he revved the motor and threw the car into the London traffic with little regard for the motoring rights of others. While blazing through the city at speeds too high for his driving skills, he talked about himself and Catherine let him, making appropriate and seemingly awestruck comments designed to stroke his ego and encourage him to run on.

By the time they arrived at a fancy modern restaurant that hung above banks of the Thames and gave a scintillating view of the city, Catherine had heard about the man's conquests, business acumen, jet aircraft, multiple homes and a host of other topics he felt impressed her. She was not as effusive as he was used to, but then, he thought to himself, he'd gotten rather used to the Eastern European tramps that usually graced his bed, ready to say or do anything to bathe in his money and power for just a few hours. This woman was an American. She was well travelled and sophisticated, but in the end, he thought, she was just a woman and would succumb to his charms.

They were met at the door of the restaurant by the maître d' and the restaurant manager, who escorted them through the hubbub and onto an enclosed patio that looked over the Thames and the awakening lights of London at twilight. There was only one table on the patio, set for two and adorned with all the trappings of fine dining as well as a fabulously expensive centrepiece of rare orchids. Next to the table, there were two bottles of champagne cooling in ice. One was a bottle of 1995 Krug Clos du Mesnil, and the other a bottle of Cristal Brut 1990.

The Krug was worth a mere four hundred pounds; the Cristal, over ten thousand, but al-Muffaddal had no intention of opening the Cristal. He would treat it with practised disdain, his glowing recommendation — like the wine steward's — would be the Krug. The wine steward's preference was heavily influenced by the hundred pound tip he'd received along with instructions earlier that day.

"I've arranged so that we will not be disturbed while we dine," al-Muffaddal proclaimed as they were ushered to the table.

"I can see that," said Catherine. "My goodness, isn't this view breathtaking."

"Yes, it is." He looked pointedly at Catherine's figure. She smiled and hid her face in her hair, an endearing schoolgirl mannerism and the perfect way to disguise what she really thought.

As they settled, a waiter dressed in formal attire arrived, not to take their order but to outline the previously selected foods and beverages the chef was already preparing. It appeared that al-Muffaddal was not a great believer in women making their own decisions. By the time they'd finished their meal — a platter of small appetizers and salad, a main course of pheasant with a sliver of venison, a host of exotically prepared vegetables, all topped off with a deliriously rich crème caramel and coffee — Catherine had managed to sip only a half glass of Krug and a half glass of wine while al-Muffaddal, pointedly ignoring the teachings of the Quran had finished the bottle of Krug, the wine and the first of several shots of single-malt Scotch. He was well into his cups.

As he drank, his boasts grew more vociferous. Catherine guided the conversation, careful not to raise any red flags. Her questions seemed innocent in content yet encouraged al-Muffaddal to ever-greater heights of braggadocio. After their meal, while al-Muffaddal was having another Scotch, Catherine mentioned how lucky she was to be in Europe while America was having so many troubles. When she commented further that U.S. policies might finally have brought retribution, Al-Muffaddal immediately perked up. "Well, I have to admit that many people in my homeland hate America and its policies, especially its support of the Jews," he said.

"What about you, Muhammad? How do you feel about America?"

"I have met many Americans that I like very much," he replied, not wanting to endanger his chances of bedding Catherine by offending her nationality.

"I agree, most Americans are good people," replied Catherine, "but I don't know. I think that in the last twenty years, the American government has become a bully that ignores ordinary people. I think that corporations run America now. What other reason would there be to invade countries, if not for their oil?"

Al-Muffaddal lit up. Slurring from drink, he picked up the thought and ran with it. "Yes, yes, yes, you are right," he exclaimed, leaning over the table and taking her hand. "It is not Americans who run America anymore. It is the Zionist pigs who run the companies. America has been taken over by them, and now they want to take over the rest of the world."

"My goodness," responded Catherine, "do you really think so?"

"I know it," he said, "and every person in the Middle East knows it. It is the Zionists who are behind everything. I know this for a fact. A fact. My cousin has fought them for many years, and he has told me stories of how they spread their corruption. They are ungodly, a blight. Americans should throw them out the same way we fight to throw them out."

"If you're right, I certainly agree. Sometimes when I am researching my books, I come across things that are hard to explain. If Zionists have, in fact, infiltrated America, it would explain many things," Catherine said reflectively.

"You see," he said. "If you think about it, you will see I am right. You are a very clever woman Catherine, a jewel."

"This cousin of yours," she asked, taking a risk but reluctant to let the opening he provided go to waste, "you say he fights them. That sounds interesting."

"We all fight them, but my cousin, he is a great man, a man of great power, and I will stand at his side." Then he reigned himself in himself despite his inebriation.

A moment of silence ensued and then he changed the subject abruptly.

"Catherine, would you like to take a walk?"

"That would be lovely," she said, instinct telling her not to push further. They left the restaurant and walked along the banks of the Thames. Their conversation did not touch on Zionism or America again, but al-Muffaddal had no dearth of things about himself he wanted Catherine to know. He was now drunk enough to start bragging about his sexual exploits and how good he was in bed.

Catherine fenced with him brilliantly, letting on that she was interested but also that she was still upset about her breakup. She put it to him that she needed a few days to get over it. He became a little sullen once he understood she would not be returning to his apartment that night, but her talents and beauty were such that he took the bait. Now she would reel him in. The evening's conversation was a good start. He'd come close to telling her things he perhaps should not. His comments about this cousin were intriguing and suggested they were on the right track. With a little more enticement and perhaps a little more booze, she felt confident he would open up, especially with his tendency to brag in an effort to impress.

Once back at the restaurant, Catherine managed to persuade al-Muffaddal to leave his car behind because he was too drunk to drive. The valet's assured them it would be safe overnight, and they took a cab instead. They stopped at the Dorian first. Asking the cabbie to wait, al-Muffaddal jumped out of the cab, opened the curbside door for Catherine and then walked her to the entranceway, stumbling in his drunken haste to beat the doorman to opening the heavy bronze door for her. "May I call you?" he asked.

She pecked him quickly on the cheek. "Of course," she said, giving him a fetching look and passing him a card with her cellphone number on it. Then in a swirl of saffron and the scent of expensive perfume, she was gone.

Al-Muffaddal fell back into the cab, cursing his luck and frustrated the evening had not ended the way he'd planned. Still, she was a rare beauty. Perhaps with just a bit more patience, he would take his prize. The cabbie had to wake him up when they arrived outside the Mayfair flat. Weaving across the pavement, he tried several times before he could get the key in his door lock, and then he set off the alarm while stabbing ineffectually at the alarm pad. In the morning, he would think that perhaps Islam's ban on alcohol was not such a bad idea.

Derek had been pacing in his hotel room all evening, worried about Catherine and unable to concentrate on television long enough to keep the thread. He'd repeatedly called the team that was shadowing her and listening in on her conversations. His four calls were met with the same answer from the two agents, who, knowing Catherine by reputation, were amused at his concern. "Nothing doing. No cause for concern."

It did not make him feel better. Those two agents were now ensconced in a room right next to Catherine's and would maintain a watch in case al-Muffaddal decided to pay a late-night call.

Catherine called at two in the morning to brief Derek on the evening. The phone call meant he could finally go to bed and get some sleep.

CHAPTER 18

September 30.
Jianggezhuang, China.

Jianggezhuang was a natural harbour positioned on a peninsula that jutted into the Yellow Sea south of Beijing. Despite providing a natural refuge from the pounding waves, no junks, sampans or fishing vessels took advantage of it. They'd been driven off long ago. Now, in an elaborate underground facility, Jianggezhuang harboured most of China's top-secret nuclear-powered ballistic and attack submarines.

The huge subterranean shipyard could be reached from the ocean by two tunnels thirty-three feet wide. These were equipped with giant blast doors that could be closed in less that five minutes and would protect the underground installation from anything but the most powerful hydrogen weapon. The Chinese were also very aware of American technological advances in espionage. Both tunnels' exits and the channels scooped out of the seabed leading from them were equipped with cold-water generators that produced vast amounts of frigid water, an artifice aimed at cloaking the comings and goings of the subs from satellite detection by creating a thermal layer impenetrable to infrared cameras.

Black dye could be emitted at the same time to muddy the water and reduce visibility to less than three feet, further concealing the subs' movements. The submarines had over eighty feet of water above their hulls to hide them as they left. The top thirty feet received the full array of deceptive measures. A few thousand yards out, the subs could drop into an abyss, safe from detection.

The sudden appearance of these anti-surveillance devices every time a boat was coming or going would be almost as telling as encountering the vessels themselves, so the base's staff were careful to turn them on periodically whether a sub was in the channel or not. Their superiors did not want the Americans to twig to the deception and hoped that the changes in water temperature and clarity, if noticed, would be attributed to upwelling or currents. At other times, no special effects were used, and subs just departed on the surface or sat tied up at piers in plain view along the bayshore. It was all aimed at supplying the American navy with confusing and misleading information. American intelligence analysts and pundits thought they knew far more about the Chinese base and submarine movements than they did.

It was three o'clock in the morning when the fifth Han-class boat of the night slipped furtively from its nest. Within hours, seven Han and four new 093 Shang nuclear-powered attack boats would be in position to sit quietly on the seabed as a second string of defence between Taiwan and the American carrier strike force, which had no inkling of the powerful web being prepared to ensnare it. Two weeks before, several 094 ballistic submarines — called Boomers in the slang of the cold war — all carrying missiles with a range of five thousand miles had sortied from Jianggezhuang to lay a few hundred miles off the U.S. coast. All of them had now reported they were on station.

September 30.
Fuzhou, Fyian, China.

Commander Tang Xu was delighted when the last of hundreds of hovercraft and assault boats of various sizes was finally checked off as fully provisioned. All of the smaller craft had been loaded on their carriers and departed hours, even days ago. Their carriers were disguised as civilian shipping and steamed for scattered hold-short points near the target, a stressful procedure that was timed to elude the frequent passes overhead of American spy satellites. The huge assault craft which had masqueraded as small buildings were teeming with troops and nearly ready to embark on their high-speed ocean journey. In a few minutes, the facades would be pulled down and the craft fired up.

Xu paced in his office, start-time jitters clawing at his insides as he imagined the U.S. satellite that was just now passing overhead and away. Below his office, the great warehouse stood empty aside from a few small assault craft that had been struck off due to last-minute mechanical issues, the teeming workers gone. Checking his watch, he realized there were only minutes to go before the giant hovercraft would depart at high speed. This was the riskiest part of the upcoming operation, as the hovercraft would be easily detected by airborne reconnaissance radar if the Chinese special electronic warfare units had not done their jobs.

He sat back at his desk, distractedly shuffling the few remaining papers that that begged his signature. Excited as he was at what his nation soon stood to accomplish, he couldn't expunge a nagging sense of dread. Silly, he thought, these emotions are no different from those felt by military men throughout history the world over. It was the eve of battle.

September 30.
Keelung Harbour, Taiwan.

In the Keelung container port in northern Taiwan, east across a narrow band of mountains from Taipei, capital of the Republic of China, the Great Wall sat quietly alongside her designated quay, a port facility specially built to support the new class of super container ships that both the Chinese and Koreans were building. The Great Wall had been met in the early evening by bands and waving crowds of Taiwanese as she shouldered her way alongside the dock. Politicians gave speeches about a new era in Chinese and Taiwanese cooperation and how projects like this could put the differences between the Chinese nation and her errant province behind them. A representative from Beijing gave a short speech thanking the Taiwanese for participating in the Great Wall's maiden voyage and extolling the virtues of the new container facility.

The last revellers had left just an hour ago. Now the great access doors in the ship's side started to slide open, and the first of its deployable container-conveyor system was made ready. Along the dock, the crane operators prepared to load the containers they thought the Great Wall was in port to pick up despite her already voluminous load. Those preparations would end, however, with a sudden and unanticipated shift change shortly after the stroke of midnight.

September 30.
Situation Room, the White House.

Admiral Irving had arrived a full half hour before anyone else and sat now in the situation room by himself, reflecting on the events that tortured him every hour of the day. The United States was in a bad way. He would never in a million years have thought his country's system as delicate and vulnerable as it had proven to be. He had always laughed at the Soviet Union's rapid downfall and the chaos that followed. It looked as if the United States might soon follow in its footsteps, and while he was head of the Joint Chiefs, as well.

The constant tension and the unrelenting stream of officers, bureaucrats and politicians who demanded his attention day in and day out were starting to affect his health. His uniforms, once crisp and perfectly tailored, had started to get a little baggy, and his complexion, often described as hale and hearty, was sallow and waxen. He wondered if a younger, healthier man should take his place, but he dismissed the thought. He was no quitter.

His reflections were soon interrupted by the arrival of staffers and the first of the president's inner circle. Soon the room was brimming with grim-faced men. Finally, the president himself entered the room, his practised stride and air of confidence belying the fact that, like Irving, stress and lack of sleep were taking a very real toll on his health. More and more often over the past few days, the two men who were once almost always in step had found themselves in discord. The president kept on demanding, Irving's protestations notwithstanding, a severe reduction in the U.S. force extension around the world. Irving thought an extensive military presence was necessary despite the hardships and financial penalties to their teetering economy it entailed. Sacrifices would have to be made to keep America a force to be reckoned with globally.

Increasingly, the president focused on the internal problems, ignoring what Irving considered, in the words of Winston Churchill, the gathering storm. He was rapidly losing his chances of persuading the president as well as his cronies that the U.S. military had to maintain its role as an international police force, or other countries — China and Russia being the most likely candidates — might step in to take their place. So far, Russia had been strangely quiet concerning world events and the plight of America. That made Irving nervous, but nowhere near as nervous as the Chinese were making him. They kept on doing weird and irrational things militarily, especially in the Persian Gulf. Terrorists had been blamed for laying mines in the Gulf, and the French for covering up lost mines, but Irving still nursed an uneasy suspicion that the Chinese were, in fact, responsible. He just couldn't figure out what their motives might be. And with the constant flow of emergencies, he did not have that much time to dwell on it.

"Gentlemen," said the president.

The men in the room acknowledged his greeting.

"So," he continued, "what is our first order of business today?"

"Mr. President," replied Dan Blomstrum, "I think that CIA should have the first word."

The president nodded to CIA director Bob Dutton. "So, Bob, what have you got for me?"

"Well, sir, three hours ago the U.S. navy seal strike team assigned to our intelligence team in northern Europe were called in to eliminate a terrorist cell that was operating in Denmark and the rest of Scandinavia and northern Germany. We took out six of them after our intelligence unit confirmed their involvement in several bombings in Europe."

"Are they connected directly to our internal problems?" asked Blomstrum.

"We don't think they were a direct link. It's more likely they were hired guns."

"What is the reaction from the Danes?" asked the president.

"Nothing yet, sir. It all went off pretty quietly. Hopefully, when the remains are discovered, the Danes will chalk up their elimination to a squabble between factions. There was enough intelligence and bomb-making equipment left at the scene to persuade the authorities that these were very bad guys.

"The team that visited Riyadh and is investigating a lead from Mossad are in contact with a close relative of the suspect and currently in London. We don't have much from them yet, but if anything interesting comes of it, we'll circulate it immediately. The other teams both in the States and overseas are investigating leads but most are of groups we don't think have any involvement in the attacks here. Some are wannabes and others are established terrorist organizations that have been buoyed by world events."

The president leaned back in his chair, idly wiping at a condensation ring left by his water glass on the table. "So that's it, then," he said to Dutton.

"Yes, sir."

The president sat for another few moments before looking straight at Dutton. He spoke quietly. "It seems to me to be a pretty pathetic report considering the vast sums of money the intelligence community has sucked out of this country for the last fifty years. Can you tell me why the only credible leads that we are developing to date come to us from foreign intelligence services, despite the fact that the NSA, the CIA and every other intelligence service in this county are running around like chickens with their heads cut off?

"This is the first time what you people do, or more to the point, don't do effects the taxpayer directly, and I wonder if any of you have taken your heads out of your asses long enough to look around at what the taxpayer is saying about having to live in a police state and under siege. They want and deserve results. They don't care that you can read the name off a post box in the middle of Kazakhstan when there's someone blowing the shit out of their country and you can't even come up with a credible list of suspects.

"Gentlemen, I suggest you get your asses in gear. Forget the fancy hardware and get some goddamned assets on the ground that can find out who the hell is screwing us over. Do you understand?"

His gaze fell on each of the men responsible for some branch of U.S. intelligence services, the heads of the NSA, the CIA, the Information Analysis and Infrastructure Protection Directorate, Homeland Security, the Defense Intelligence Agency and several other agencies. "If you don't, then maybe it's time to streamline."

Leaving them with that thought, he continued, "Admiral?"

Irving cleared his throat. "Sir, as you know, our troop and resource pull back is well over halfway accomplished. Most of our ground forces, aside from those covering areas that will remain under U.S. control, are out of Iraq. There's been a marked increase in internecine fighting between the various religious factions, and the government and local authorities are hard pressed to respond. As a result, warlords and radicalized religious militias are appearing. If this continues the government will cease to exist within a matter of months. We are sure the Iranians are fuelling these conflicts with logistical aid to the Shiites. The border between Iraq and Iran remains quiet although the Iranians still have troops and tanks stationed within striking distance of the oil fields north of Basra. We've noticed some troop deployments by the Saudis along their border with Iraq, and when questioned, they responded that they have positioned forces for war games and as a persuasive way to stop any incursions by terrorists into Saudi territory.

"Syria has not bolstered their troop strength along their border and says that it has no intention of doing so. That said, they are actively supplying Sunni factions with weapons and materials to counter Iranians supplies to the Shiites.

"The Chinese have been making regular sweeps into the Persian Gulf with their naval units, but they stay close to Iranian territorial waters. Their comment is that with the destabilization of Iraq, they need to assist the Iranians with security issues. What they're really doing is making sure their supply of Iranian oil is not compromised. They haven't been interfering with U.S. naval units, and when overflown by our patrol aircraft, they haven't been turning on their weapons systems. Since the mine-laying incident and the loss of two ships, they have stepped up their patrols in the Gulf and are now trying to convince the locals that they are a viable alternative to U.S. naval forces, and we know they've contacted several Gulf states to inform them that they're willing to cooperate in any joint exercise aimed a strengthening security in the area, especially as U.S. priorities are perceived to have shifted…"

Irving gave his summation. "We currently have two carrier task forces left in the region — one in the Mediterranean and one in the Gulf of Oman, which is also supporting the pullout from Afghanistan. Our other carriers have sailed for home port, leaving only the Bush on patrol in the western Pacific region."

He paused to take a sip of water and then, clearing his throat, continued. "American land forces arriving back into the States have been immediately dispatched across the country to bolster security and continue the hunt for the terrorists. We believe the increased number of security troops has had some effect nationwide, as the number of bombings and other forms of attack has fallen about twenty percent, but with targets ranging from hydro electric transformers and propane supply yards to bus shelters and shopping mall food courts, it is difficult, even impossible, to predict where or when the next attack will be. Increased security just might be running these guys to ground and making them even cagier and harder to find. We are experiencing a lot of resistance from the public, and there have been some unfortunate incidents sparked by both security forces handling people too roughly and citizens objecting violently to the security checks. These incidents have been increasing as people are becoming more frustrated at what they see as the government's failure to win this war quickly.

"We have reduced the number and frequency of combat air patrols, restricting them for the most part to large population centres. We do have alert aircraft stationed across the country that can be airborne in ten to twenty minutes if required, but it seems a waste of resources to keep the aircraft up, especially with the fuel situation and resupply problems some bases are having. Jointly with agents from the FBI, we have" — he nodded at the Bureau's director and then stopped to leaf though his papers and pull up a list — "ah, here it is. We have killed fifty-six terrorists and captured eleven since the beginning of the war."

There. He'd said it, he thought to himself. He'd twice proclaimed it a war not a terrorist attack, and no one around the table was disagreeing with him.

"We have to date captured sixteen explosives and weapons caches. Good news is that we dispatched nine of the terrorists as a direct result of following their own procedures and ferreting out weapons caches we did not learn about from Abu Bakre. So we're making some headway. The volume of attacks has decreased substantially, to almost zero in the southwest and north into the plains. Those are the areas where Bakre's activities were centred, and we're hoping we got most if not all of the operatives in those areas.

"News blackouts have hopefully kept other terrorist cells operating in the rest of the country ignorant of the fact that we have started to rake some of them up. Every soldier at every roadblock has been told to look out for single men who cannot produce proof of local addresses and who are travelling long distances. We're hoping to net more of their weapons deliverymen, which could lead to another dramatic series of takedowns. We still don't know how many terrorists we're up against, but it could be as many as a thousand. If it is that high, or even half that, then we still have a long way to go."

Two hours later the meeting broke up, and its participants scurried away to berate their own staff and pass on some of the pressure the president had exerted on them. Irving had made several attempts to bring his concerns about the worldwide withdrawal of forces to the conversation, but no one, most especially not the president, was in the mood, and his attempts had been curtailed by a glower from his commander-in-chief.

He'd also wanted to raise some of his misgivings about the Chinese, but once again he'd failed. He left the meeting, if anything, more depressed and worried than he'd been before it commenced. He said a little prayer that his fears would not be realized and that the president was correct in his decisions.

September 30.
Politburo bunker and command centre, north of Beijing.

Six men sat in a bare cement-walled room four hundred feet underground. The room's only ornamentation was a red flag with yellow stars — the flag of communist China. Two of the six men wore the grey suit common to high-ranking party members and four generals sat in military attire. All six were stone-faced and spoke little. Several were sipping tea. They were at this moment the most powerful men in China, and they were about to make a final and irrevocable decision.

A knock on the door was followed by the entry of a young officer smartly dressed in the uniform of a major in the People's Liberation Army. He stepped forward and placed a dispatch reverently in front of the old man who sat at the head of the table. He then stepped back against the wall and stood rigidly at attention.

The six men, each in their, turn took the dispatch, read it briefly and nodded. It was a report on the current tactical and strategic position of U.S. forces in the Pacific region. When it arrived back to the gentleman at the table's head, he passed it to the young major and nodded. The young man left the room, dispatch in hand and with the order to commence the invasion of Taiwan.

October 1.
Keelung, Taiwan.

It was twelve minutes after twelve midnight, less than five minutes after the code word "Taiping" was flashed to every participating unit commander in the Chinese military. Eleven crane operators in the port of Keelung lay dead and their replacements had started lifted containers from the Great Wall's holds. At the same time, thousands of men clambered from the stacked containers on her immense decks. When the night shift of dock workers arrived to start the Great Wall's unloading, they were killed or bound with plastic ties and thrown into containers that had moments before been full of military vehicles and light tanks. A steady stream of forty-foot containers spewed from the guts of the ship, filled with supplies that would sustain the first day of the invasion and support the assault troops that were already fanning out across the shipyard.

The troops' job was to protect the heavy weapons that the Great Wall carried until both airborne and seaborne assault troops from China made their landings on the northern beaches and areas surrounding Taipei. Taipei was to be the centre of a blitzkrieg attack. Once the capital and its strategic resources were secured, the massive Chinese army could easily sweep through the mountainous little island from one end to the other. Across the northern part of Taiwan, Chinese special forces teams moved to destroy power, radar and communications structures, and saboteurs and assassins struck at military and political leaders as they slept. Within an hour, the 6th Corps of the Taiwanese army, dedicated to the defence of Taipei, was in disarray, its commanders dead and most of its communications systems destroyed. In barracks, many of the troops needed to defend Taiwan's independence slumbered on.

As the shock troops from the Great Wall established and secured the container port as a bridgehead, hundreds of paratroops started to descend from the skies over Taipei. Taiwanese fighter aircraft scrambled to repulse the transports, but the fighter and bomber aircraft that escorted them were knocked from the skies by sophisticated shoulder-launched missiles by the PLA Special Operations Forces concealed around their air bases.

Immediately after the special forces units withdrew, waves of YJ-83 and YJ-63 Cruise missiles were launched from Xian heavy bombers. Chinese copies of the venerable Soviet Badger slammed into dozens of Taiwanese military command and control installations, air bases and barracks, finishing off what special forces had begun.

Not long afterward, the first wave of hovercraft-borne amphibious shock troops started hitting the beaches. The largest transports, the 555-ton Zubr-class, tore across the sand and rocks and then, behind walls of automatic weapons fire provided by the shock troops, mounted the coastal highways of northern Taiwan and set off at high speed towards their objectives. Armoured fences mounted on the leading edges of the largest hovercrafts' inflated skirts threw civilian traffic out of their way as if brushing away annoying flies. Behind them, like puppies following their dam, smaller hovercraft trailed in procession. These spread in rings from the beachheads, cutting them off from the Taiwanese military, which was now starting to respond in desultory fashion. The task was to secure bridgeheads on Taiwan's west coast to compliment the seizure of the container port on the east coast.

Even now, ten more container ships loaded with troops and supplies were headed across the Straits of Taiwan to join the Great Wall. The rest of the amphibious task force of landing ships and barges that was steaming toward the island would find their landings virtually unopposed. Within hours, Taipei would be cut off from the rest of Taiwan, and an almost impenetrable steel fence of arms and machines would be erected to prevent help from either the 10th Corps, tasked with the defence of central Taiwan, or the 8th Corps, far to the south, from reaching the city. Sixth Corps, Taiwan's finest, still held on in some areas of the north but had been rendered impotent by the scale and ferocity of the attack.

Several years of conciliatory negotiations with what had seemed a gentler and more cooperative Beijing had not just lulled Taiwan's population but had served to take the edge off the Taiwanese military.

September 30.
Geneva.

Al-Munajjid was sitting at a small outdoor café, enjoying a strong cup of coffee and nibbling on a croissant. It was a lovely late September evening, pleasantly and unseasonably warm. He'd taken a walk to clear his head and relax a little and then had decided to pay the penalty an evening coffee might exact from his sleep. Two bodyguards sat at a table a few feet away keeping a sharp eye out.

Today he had pocketed a vast sum of money, the latest in a series of payments from European investors who believed they were taking control of several Saudi companies that serviced the oil industry. Once the money had appeared in his accounts, he'd converted it into gold and deposited that into several of dozens of special accounts and strong boxes he maintained in Swiss banks.

Despite the lack of breaking news, he was aware that his largest underwriters, the Chinese, were right now engaged in their own pursuits, and once these were fully underway and their aims achieved, they would have little more interest in his endeavours. On the other hand, his Middle Eastern intrigues were just about turn exciting, now that U.S. troop strength in the region was so thin and only one battle group floated in the Persian Gulf. The conflict to come would be short, sweet and decisive, and largely restricted to the urban areas of Saudi Arabia, so one carrier group's aircraft would be of little advantage even if the Americans had the resolve to use them.

Overall he was very pleased with himself and the carnage he had wrought, but his grandest designs were not quite realized. There was no telling how those might go over the next forty-eight hours, but whichever way they swung, al-Munajjid would come out just fine. If his associates in Saudi Arabia won the ensuing battle, he'd walk into a power base that just a few years ago he could only have dreamed of. If, on the other hand, they were unsuccessful, well, he was still a very rich man and his role largely anonymous. He'd been very careful in crafting his participation, giving credit for his schemes to others who were more than happy to accept them as their own. When he denied any role, he would be believed. Plus, he had one more card he could play, one that could see him succeed even as his associates, with his help, failed.

Al-Munajjid was not inclined to lead from the front. He was, instead, a consummate puppeteer with a high regard for his own skin. That was why he was in Geneva at that moment, instead of Ta'if or Riyadh. He had intimate knowledge of the timetables and events that would soon engulf his homeland.

He looked at his watch, thinking he should get back to his hotel. He was feeling his age, the years of hard work and, especially, the last weeks' stress. He knew this night would be a restless one. Tomorrow morning he would head into La Belle Epoque. It was from this safe haven he would sit back and watch the results of his machinations.

CHAPTER 19

September 30.
Canada Place Mall, Canary Wharf, London.

Catherine had agreed to meet Muhammad al-Muffaddal at a small coffee shop in Canary Wharf's Canada Place Mall. She'd told him when he phoned, his voice still groggy from the previous evening's libations, that she was going to be at the wharf doing some shopping and asked if he would like to meet her there for a coffee around four o'clock.

Derek, Catherine and the head of operations for London had met that morning in a private flat in the South End. During that twenty-minute meeting and after reviewing the transcript of Catherine's date, they felt they should just bring him in and wring whatever information he had out of him. Al-Muffaddal's slip and, more importantly, his reaction when he realized he may have said too much made them think that a few hours spent with a professional interrogator could bear fruit and quickly.

Catherine sipped a black coffee and waited for al-Muffaddal to appear. True to form, he was already ten minutes late, not, she thought, because he'd been held up, but because he'd think being late made him somehow seem important. Catherine was used to boorish behaviour in men — women who looked like her generally were — but she put al-Muffaddal in a class all his own.

The small coffee shop had a couple of tables in the aisle of the mall, and she had a good view up and down it. Shoppers were sparse today, but even if the mall had been packed, al-Muffaddal would have stood out like a sore thumb. She saw him while he was still six shops down the mall, and she had to choke back a laugh. He looked like a refugee from a 1970s disco, with a touch of Miami golfer. He wore a shiny satin shirt, open at the neck and halfway to his navel. That was bad enough, but it was a brilliant orange as well. Over this he wore what on a more conservatively dressed individual would have been a mark of style and wealth — a wonderfully expensive and well-tailored sport jacket — but when combined with the shirt and skin-tight white pants that were positively see-through and revealed, to her horror, the hint of a G-string, any pretence of good taste was quickly and firmly dispatched. He only wore one gold chain today, choosing to accent instead his copious jet-black chest hair, which, it appeared, he had combed and moussed for maximum effect. The last touch was yet another jewel-encrusted Rolex, which hung loosely from his wrist so that it could be seen dangling below his cuff.

It took all the skill Catherine had to rise and greet him, even pecking him on the cheek, without breaking into a spasm of giggles.

"Ah, Catherine, you look such a vision today," he said as she sat back down.

"Well, thank you, Muhammad. You look wonderful yourself," she replied, biting her lip just a little.

"So, I see you have started without me," he said, indicating several shopping bags that leaned on her leg.

"Yes, I didn't want to bore you by dragging you from one woman's store to another. I thought we could just enjoy an early dinner. I passed a great little place earlier. Maybe we can make our way there."

"That would be wonderful. Perhaps afterwards I can show you my flat. I have very many beautiful things there I would like you to see."

Catherine smiled coyly. "That would be interesting Muhammad. I'd love to."

Emboldened by her response, he put his arm around her waist as they walked from the café. In five store lengths, he'd already let his hand slip twice from her waist to the top of her buttocks. Catherine giggled each time and twisted away, not so much to discourage him but to tease him. She wanted him focused on one thing and one thing only in a few minutes. To that end she started a light banter with a faint sexual overtone. His responses had no overtone. Buoyed by her quips, he was bragging about his prowess and describing in lurid detail his version of what makes a woman aroused and satisfied. Catherine thought scabies would be preferable to any sexual contact with this lout.

She forced a turn down a long and quiet corridor lined with pay lockers and entrances to ladies' and men's washrooms. Al-Muffaddal hardly noticed so intent was he on his tryst with the beautiful redhead. As they passed the washrooms, the corridor took a turn, becoming an accessway for the rear doors of the mall's stores on one side. Finally, al-Muffaddal noticed that they were well off the beaten track. "Catherine, where are we going?" he asked.

"Muhammad, I thought maybe we could find a quiet place right here in the mall. You know, somewhere where we can get to know one another just a little bit better before we eat. I was down here earlier and that door at the end leads into a room that is just perfect. It will be so exciting. I like exciting." She rendered the last three words in an evocative and syrupy purr.

Grinning from ear to ear, al-Muffaddal practically dragged her the rest of the way down the corridor. He grasped the door handle and gave the door a good push, ushering Catherine through and taking the opportunity to run his hand across her buttocks.

The room was dark, and he was completely inside, the door closing behind him, before he realized they were not alone. Derek stood illuminated by the last light from the disappearing corridor. Then an arm encircled his neck and a gloved hand covered his face with a foul-smelling rag.

Al-Muffaddal slumped, nearly unconscious, as the two CIA operatives grabbed him on either side and rushed him through one more door to a white van sitting at a loading dock with its back doors open. They threw him unceremoniously into the back where he landed hard on the corrugated metal floor, opening a deep cut over his left eye.

Derrick and Catherine walked back into the corridor, checking to see that no one had overheard the snatch. They sauntered back into the mall and headed for the restaurant that Catherine had earlier told al-Muffaddal about to have a quiet but enjoyable celebration, their task complete. The rest of al-Muffaddal's day would not go well.

September 30.
The White House.

The president had retired to the small sitting room off his bedroom to spend a few minutes catching his breath and taking more antacid pills to quell the vicious and relentless heartburn he lived with. The doctors had prescribed all manner of antacids and reflux medications, but none seemed to work. The only thing that offered some respite from the pain was Tums, one of the cheapest and oldest gastric medications on the market. He ate them like candy.

He was just starting to feel the relief that sitting quietly after popping a few of the chalky pills could bring when there was a rap on the door and he heard the now-dreaded words "Mr. President, we need to see you."

He rose and opened the door.

Outside the room stood Dan Blomstrum and Lieutenant-Colonel Silas Woodhill, the military officer permanently attached to the White House and responsible for the Situation Room and the communications systems that fed it.

"God damn, couldn't this have waited for just a few minutes?" he asked, his agitation clear.

"Mr. President, I'm afraid not," replied Blomstrum. He nodded at the lieutenant-colonel.

"Sir," replied the man confidently, "we've just received intelligence that the Chinese have begun a full-scale invasion of Taiwan."

The president stood for a second, no emotion whatsoever playing across his features. "When?" he asked, the stomach acid already rising into his gullet.

"Around twelve midnight Taiwan time, eleven hundred hours our time, sir. It appears they are landing at Keelung, a container ship port on Taiwan's northeast coast, and we have an unconfirmed report of amphibious assault hovercraft landing in strength on the east coast. They are also bombarding Taiwanese military installations and airfields with cruise missiles."

The president looked at his watch. It read 11:39 a.m. "So, they've been at it for almost forty minutes."

"Mr. President," said Blomstrum, "both the Taiwanese president and the Japanese prime minister have phoned, and I told them you would get back to them immediately."

"Dan," he said to Blomstrum, "give me a minute, and then I'm headed for the Situation Room. Assemble the troops." The president closed the door on the two men and headed for the bathroom, his need pressing as his bowels turned to water.

September 30.
Woodland, California.

Lucy Montgomery was headed into Sacramento in her ten-year-old Ford Taurus. As usual at this time of the morning, she had her three kids with her. She would drop them off at their grandmother's in Rio Linda before heading to work at the State of California land registry office in downtown Sacramento. She was on shortened hours because of the emergency and worked a three-day week, starting work at 9:30, rather than her usual nine to five, five days a week. It was 8:40, so she had plenty of time to drop off the kids, pick up a coffee and get in.

Ahead on the eastbound 5 into Sacramento, there was the usual traffic jam, the backup exacerbated by the military checkpoint that straddled the highway where it passed over the Tule Canal. On either side of the highway, workers were out in the fields picking the last crops of garlic and artichoke for this season.

The traffic seemed to be moving well despite the checkpoint, and the children were all absorbed watching cartoons on the screen her husband had installed on the back seat. Montgomery considered it the best three hundred dollars they'd ever spent. In no time at all, she was pulling up to the checkpoint. There were about forty soldiers and their civilian helpers — a newly formed citizens militia who wore red, white and blue armbands. Montgomery pulled up to the soldiers, who flagged her to stop on a grid they'd marked out on the pavement. Cars were allowed forward ten at a time and were attended to at once. A similar queue of ten occupied the lane to her left and another queue handled buses, trucks and other heavy traffic on the paved shoulder to her right. She grabbed her licence and identification, ready to hand it out even though she recognized the soldier and had spoken to him many times. They were sticklers, although Montgomery doubted that a mother of three on her way to work would ever be considered a serious threat to national security.

She was wrong. As she rolled down her window, a seventy-five-pound charge of RDX ignited under the car. Montgomery and her children were vaporized immediately, taking with them fifty-four soldiers, militia members and the occupants of several surrounding cars and buses, who died immediately or shortly thereafter. Another eighteen bystanders were badly injured.

The terrorists were on to a new tactic, one that could render every car on America's highways suspect. In the middle of the night, a man had slipped into the dark shadows surrounding Montgomery's Taurus, which was parked in her driveway, a lane sandwiched between her house and the neighbours' and difficult to see from the street. He had securely attached the satchel charge to the undercarriage of her car and activated a remote-control detonator.

That morning as Montgomery pulled up to the checkpoint, the terrorist was standing in one of the adjoining fields, dressed as a farm hand. When he saw that her car had reached the attending soldier, he pushed a tiny remote switch. Work stopped in the fields. As the workers watched the billowing black clouds rise from the wreckage, the terrorist calmly walked from the field, got into an old pickup truck and slowly drove away.

September 30.
London.

Muhammad al-Muffaddal came to strapped into a heavy steel chair, the most uncomfortable device he had ever sat on. The room he was in was very dim, lit only by a distant street light whose rays had managed to pass though a filthy translucent window with wire reinforcement that sat just below the ceiling of an equally dirty room. The room was about twenty feet by ten, its most distinguishable feature in the gloom a dark door directly in front of him. Still groggy, he tried to call out before he realized that the lower half of his face was wrapped in duct tape and he had something wedged in his mouth that forced it open and made his jaw ache terribly. He sat there becoming more and more uncomfortable as time wore on and the ether with which he'd been anaesthetized wore off.

His rear started to ache, but he was so tightly secured he couldn't move even a fraction to alleviate the pain, which radiated upwards. It didn't help that many years before he'd broken his coccyx during a game of soccer, and it still bothered him on occasion — more so, now.

After what seemed like hours but was less than one, he heard a snapping, and a searing light appeared from several large bulbs in hanging fixtures spaced evenly down the centre of the ceiling. Peeling paint water stains and the silhouettes of old machinery long removed marked the walls, and accumulated dirt and debris lay heavy over everything. Bare wires and torn tubing stuck out from every surface. It was very apparent that this space was long neglected and rarely visited. He took in what he could by rolling his eyes, since his head was as immobile as the rest of his body. He realized suddenly that he was completely naked. He started to panic. He was not now and never had been a brave man. Beating the odd woman because she displeased him or just for the fun of it was the closest he had ever come to conflict. His life until this moment had been one of privilege. He was ill prepared for the hours that lay ahead and for his first meeting with men who were more sadistic and cold than he, although, in their defence, they were motivated by a higher cause than their own pleasure.

With a screech of dry metal, the door swung open, and two large men strode briskly in and past him, engrossed in an almost comforting bustle as they bashed and clanged behind him. One was black and one white, although al-Muffaddal gauged this only by their hands. Both men wore black balaclavas. Suddenly, a large dry hand grabbed him on the shoulder and gave it a friendly squeeze, and one of the men came into his field of vision.

"Well, then, aren't you a sorry sight. I suppose our accommodations are a little ruder than what you're used to. I have to apologize for that. But if you cooperate over the next while, well, we'll give you back your things and send you on your way. First, however, I'm going to ask you a few questions just to get started. I'll expect answers."

He continued, looking directly into al-Muffaddal's eyes for the first time, "Now Mr. al-Muffaddal, or can I call you Muhammad?"

Al-Muffaddal stared back, trying his best to conjure a threatening and hateful look, but the result was too tinged with fear to be convincing.

His inquisitor paused for a moment. "No, I suppose that would be disrespectful after such short acquaintance and with you being so important and all," he said. "Mr. al-Muffaddal it remains. My name is Mr. L and my friend here is Mr. J, and we are both very pleased to make your acquaintance."

"Mr. al-Muffaddal, suppose you tell me what it is you are doing in London," said J from behind.

L waited for a moment and then clucked. "Dear, dear, not willing to answer. Mr. J, could you pass me the small ball-peen, please." He reached over al-Muffaddal's shoulder and retrieved a hammer so small it looked like a toy. "Silly little thing, isn't it?" he said, showing it to al-Muffaddal, "but it has its uses. Just watch." Mr. L bent down and with a quick flick of the wrist struck the very end of al-Muffaddal's big toe, impacting his nail and driving it back into the flesh.

Al-Muffaddal's eyes bulged, and he choked on the wooden plug taped into his mouth, but aside from a gushing whimper, he was unable to make any other sound.

"Well, you are brave, aren't you? I've been told that hurts quite a bit. Let's try again, shall we?"

Al-Muffaddal tried in vain to move his foot away, but it was securely taped to the chair leg, and all he could do was twitch it a bit. The second blow made the cords stand out on his neck, and he spasmed.

"Well, that looks as if it hurt just a little more. Mr. J, could you bring the tools around here where I can get to them a little easier."

J came into Al-Muffaddal's line of vision, pushing a stainless-steel lab cart that had a range of handy man tools laying on it. Muffaddal's eyes grew wide as he took in the implements, which ranged from ordinary well-worn screwdrivers to a small cordless grinder and a cordless drill.

"I'm terribly sorry. I know you were probably expecting all manner of shiny surgical equipment. Unfortunately, we don't have that kind of budget, so we're forced to use whatever we find lying around." He picked up one of the screwdrivers and looked at it. "It doesn't look like these have ever been washed. I suggest that when — or if — you get out of here, you get yourself a course of antibiotics and a tetanus shot. You could catch some very nasty things from these tools."

He picked up a sizable claw hammer from the cart. "Let's try hammer that's a bit bigger, shall we?" The man knelt once more in front of al-Muffaddal and swung the hammer with force into the top of al-Muffaddal's foot. Bone cracked, and a scream escaped al-Muffaddal despite the binding around his mouth. He passed out only to be snapped back to this new world of agony when one of the men simply threw a bucket of icy cold water over him.

"Well, that's better," said L. "I think he might be ready to answer a few questions now. Mr. J, would you be so kind as to remove the tape from his face? And Mr. J, do be careful, you know how painful removing tape from skin and hair can be."

J reached forwards and ripped the tape from the Arab's mouth. Al-Muffaddal howled in pain and spat out a plug of wood that the tape had bound in his mouth. He was trembling and gasping for breath.

Within two hours and with little more coercion, al-Muffaddal had told the men everything he knew about his family business interests and practices, their contacts in the Saudi government, several terrorist organizations and, most importantly, a good deal of information on the movements, inclinations and pursuits of his much older cousin, Muhammad al-Munajjid.

September 30.
London.

Derek placed the hotel phone's receiver back into its cradle. A voice on the other end, with a Jamaican accent, had told him that Mr. Bryson had been very cooperative and willing to talk about selling his company. In fact, the voice had added, Mr. Bryson had said his company came with the expert advice of its long-term president and founder.

Derek turned to Catherine with a broad smile. "Got him! It's al-Munajjid. He's the top man."

"Perfect!" exclaimed Catherine. "That's the best news I've heard in a long time. The best thing about it is that he was stupid enough to let the cat out of the bag so quickly. I was dreading having to take our relationship any further. To tell you the truth, even mild flirting with him made me nauseous. I can't imagine having to pretend to fall for him."

Derek looked at Catherine nervously, his eyes slipping away from hers in discomfort.

"What?" she asked.

"Nothing."

"No. There's something." She looked at him quizzically before her face softened. "Oh, wait. I know. No, Derek, I wouldn't have slept with him. That's not part of the job description. The art is in getting a subject to think you're going to sleep with them. I've known agents who've used their bodies as tools, and I know it's the public perception, but once you do that, you lose their interest, especially with a lot of these Middle Eastern pigs. To them a woman is a disposable item. I seriously doubt I would have had a second date with al-Muffaddal if I'd gone to bed with him on the first. If I can't find out what I need by the first couple of dates, I have to change tactics."

"So, I'm really a fish out of water here. What do we do next?"

"Next we have to talk to al-Muffaddal's interrogators and get the details."

"What's going to happen to al-Muffaddal?"

"They'll wring him out. Once he has nothing left to tell, he'll be disposed of."

Derek thought he'd be ready for anything after what he had been through, but the sudden realization of just how brutal this world was and how comfortable Catherine was in it shook him.

Hours later, al-Muffaddal's body would be found, run over by a commuter train. His foot was found a few yards from his body, caught and crushed between two rails. He'd apparently become trapped when a switch was thrown and a train changed tracks at the South London rail yard. He was partially clothed, the rest of his garments strewn across a dirty old blanket, and a half-open condom wrapper lay near his left hand. All traces of duct tape adhesive had been cleaned from his body before it had been so artfully abandoned. As a further red herring, a cheap evening purse was found nearby. All it contained were a few cigarettes, ticket stubs, some inexpensive perfume and two photographs taken in a small Eastern European village. There was no ID in it. Police investigators, after looking into al-Muffaddal's character, would close the case, writing it off as an unusual but accidental death during a hasty and ill-planned encounter with a prostitute.

CHAPTER 20

October 1.
Western Beachhead, Hsinchu City, Taiwan.

Lee Pan was scared, but he drew some comfort from his position in the column of seven tanks — third instead of first. At twenty-two years of age, he commanded one of China's newest main battle tanks, the Type 99. The T-99 carried a 125-mm smoothbore gun and AT-11 Sniper anti-tank missiles as well as heavy machine guns and optional weapons pods, depending on the mission profile.

Today, a boxy pod containing dozens of small anti-personnel rockets filled with shrapnel was fixed on the turret. The T-99 was considered a match — at least by the Chinese general staff — for anything the Taiwanese defence could throw at it, even if they were equipped with U.S. Abrams, a tank Chinese intelligence maintained was not in Taiwan's inventory.

So far they'd faced only small arms fire and the odd rocket-propelled grenade, and they'd radioed the location of each enemy firing position to the attack aircraft that circled overhead. Using tactics similar to the ones the Americans had used in Iraq, the Chinese were sprinting across Taiwan, ignoring a lot of enemy concentrations in order to achieve an overlying strategic objective. But the Chinese also had secondary units follow behind to mop up and secure lines of communication, protect resupply and widen these corridors. Unlike the rabble the Americans had faced in Iraq, the enemy facing the PLA was well trained, well motivated and well armed, and the Chinese knew it. The momentary confusion the invasion had caused would soon be shaken off, and the Taiwanese forces would take advantage of the smallest errors in judgment.

Lee's unit was already one shy, having left one tank on the beach that had run long enough to clear the hovercraft transporter but died halfway up the embankment to the highway. Its absence would increase the demands made of the remaining battle tanks. Lee also worried about the new odds of his tank being hit — one in seven instead of one in eight. He, like many of his countrymen, was an inveterate gambler and acutely aware of how the smallest shift in percentages made a loss more or less likely.

His column was escorted by several armoured troop carriers. They were making a dash to secure a major intersection that allowed access to a highway that cut across Taiwan from east to west and joined with the main highway in the northeast, Route 7, which ran south along the spine of the central mountains. His column was racing to support airborne assault troops who might soon be under heavy fire if the Taiwanese military got their act together.

Suddenly the ground around his column blossomed in huge fountains of earth, concrete, asphalt and debris. Somewhere an artillery unit had this stretch of highway zeroed in. The tank immediately in front of his received a round square in the centre of its back deck behind the turret. Spare fuel tanks, ammo boxes and metal shards from the tank's armour spun through the air in a ball of searing heat and deadly projectiles. Lee was lucky. While his tank was pelted, he escaped injury. The stricken tank slewed to the left and stopped dead. Lee ducked into the hatch and ordered his driver to swing around and past the stricken tank at the same time the column's commander radioed instructions to spread out and accelerate.

At that moment, Lee popped his head back out and saw a shoulder-fired missile arc away from the roof of a nearby industrial building. It slammed into the lead tank and was followed immediately by four more. Lee dropped into the interior of his tank's turret, pulling the hatch closed over him, just as another smoke contrail headed right for him. He screamed at his driver to spin left harder, partly to avoid the crippled number two tank and partly to avoid the oncoming rockets. The tank lurched as it dipped into one of the fresh holes dug by the 105-mm shells that rained down on the column.

The first rocket to hit Lee's tank impacted its skirts, slanted slabs of armour that protected the bogeys and road wheels. Three more hits came in quick succession on the tank's right side as Lee's gunner swung the massive turret to engage what must have been at least a dozen rocketeers hidden on nearby rooftops. The inside of the tank rang like a bell as blow after blow hit it and the reactive armour was blasted off. So far none of the strikes was fatal, but the crew was becoming disoriented.

The driver reversed direction and slammed into the dead tank ahead of him before spinning left once again and mounting the road's median strip. The concrete divider threw the vehicle into the air, and it descended with an impact that sent Lee's head into the gun's breechblock. He reeled backwards, hitting his head again on a radio junction box, and tried to shake off the blows as blood poured down his face. Finally, his gunner let loose a round, and the tank's own gun added to the blasts. Slowed by the concrete divider, the tank was the target of a new volley of missiles. Several struck in areas already stripped of the T 99's reactive armour.

A blistering sphere of plasma and molten steel pierced the interior Kevlar coating in the crew compartment, killing the gunner instantly and blowing Lee's right leg off. He yelped, not in pain but in confusion, puzzled at the loss. Suddenly the whole tank lifted into the air as a 105-mm high-explosive round hit its left track. It rose high on one side before hammering back to earth, its engine dead and a fire just starting to glow in its interior, sparked by the blast that had taken Lee's leg. Lee slid to the battle compartment floor, his tank rapidly turning to wreckage around him. As his life trickled across the rubberized floor, he wondered where the flag-waving crowds were that his commanding officers had promised would herald their arrival in the People's province of Taiwan.

Three minutes after the last of Lee's column of T 99s died on the highway, a detachment of Chinese paratroops holding the military air base in Hsinchu City to the north attacked and overran the ROC battery of mobile 105 artillery pieces positioned east of the airport.

The Taiwanese rocketeers retired from their rooftop positions to regroup and retreat to another predetermined ambush point farther down the highway. There they would await the next wave of invading armour. They had an ample supply of American-made Super Dragon and Javelin anti-tank rockets whose effectiveness had cheered their users no end. This time they'd been lucky. Not one man had been lost. Even so, every one was sure their good luck wouldn't last.

September 30.
Situation Room, the White House.

Once again, the Situation Room was crowded, but this time uniforms outnumbered expensive tailored suits. Among the men seated at the table were all of the Joint Chiefs, the secretary of Defense and the secretaries of all the military services.

The president sat listening to a very confusing situation report on the ongoing invasion of Taiwan. So far, the United States was not embroiled, but two of their AWACS aircraft that normally patrolled the area around Taiwan were missing and assumed downed. Only one got off a mayday, and that shed no light on the cause of the aircraft's disappearance. The crew, had they survived, would have been very surprised to learn they were the first casualties of a new seaborne laser anti-aircraft system the Chinese had been developing.

Of little use against fighters or small nimble aircraft, the large and cumbersome lasers, mounted on the decks of commercial ships, were just what the doctor ordered when it came to downing airliner-sized aircraft like the American AWACS on their predictable racetrack courses. Unlike missiles, the lasers struck with no warning and were virtually undetectable by their unsuspecting prey. The lasers silently severed a plane's fuel and hydraulic lines and pierced its tanks, causing hydraulic problems and making the aircraft unresponsive. Then, after the leaking fuel was superheated to combustion, it exploded.

"So, Admiral Irving, what actions does the Pentagon recommend at this point?" asked the president.

"Sir, normally we would have far more strength in the region, but as you know, current events have forced us to change most of our strategic posture. At this time, we have only one carrier strike force in position — the Bush. Most of our troops at bases in Japan have been withdrawn, and operations by our air bases in the region are hampered by reductions in personnel , budget allocations and supplies. We have few options here, Mr. President, short of threatening the Chinese with tactical nuclear strikes."

"What can the Bush do?" asked Dan Blomstrum.

"She's close enough to offer some aid to the Taiwanese, perhaps in support of their ground units. It's a pretty hostile sky over Taiwan right now, though. The Republic air force never got off the ground in strength, and the mainland Chinese have almost total air superiority at this time."

"Can we make a dent in that superiority? Perhaps long enough for the Republic's air force to get airborne?" asked the president.

"We can try, sir. The Bush is almost entirely equipped with the new Joint Strike Fighter. There is nothing in the Chinese inventory that can match it. Our boys should be able to bloody their noses if nothing else."

"Sir," the Air Force chief of staff said, "we also have a few F-22 Raptors on Okinawa. With aerial refuelling, we may be able to get them into the fray effectively."

The president digested the information he'd received. The room was quiet. "Admiral, scramble the Bush's air wings. And general," he said to the Air Force chief, "get as many Raptors over Taiwan as is possible. I am so fed up with the fucking Chinese, it'll be really nice to finally strike back at them, even if it only bloodies their noses.

"Dan," the president continued, "when we get to my office, I want the Chinese premier on the phone. Perhaps it's time I threatened him with a bit more than a couple of wings of naval aircraft.

"Admiral, I want our task forces in the Persian Gulf ready to sink every Chinese war ship in the region on my order. If the Chinese don't back off, they'll soon find all their shiny new toys in the Gulf sitting on the bottom."

"Sir," replied Irving, "I suggest we sink any Chinese subs we are tailing in the Gulf right now, before they get any warning and can slip away. I would also like permission, once you give the order, to attack their base at Gwadar in order to deny them its use and sink any Chinese naval units tied up there."

"Can you do that without killing Pakistanis?" asked the president.

"I think so, sir. The Pakistanis and the Chinese have not been getting along that well in the region, and their resources at Gwadar are not integrated. I believe we can take out the Chinese navy and their warehouses without any collateral damage to Pakistan. The Pakistanis will scream blue murder, of course, but I'll bet you behind closed doors, the locals will be pretty happy about the strike."

"Then do it, admiral." The president turned to Blomstrum. "Dan, get my staff to start calling our closest allies, and I mean allies. No Middle Eastern or Asian countries aside from Japan are to get any warning at all."

"Sir," said Irving, "I suggest we speak to the British Admiralty immediately. They'd better be put on alert in case any of their naval units are in harm's way."

"Good idea, admiral. I will now order the United States to move to DEFCON 2, gentlemen." This was the second-highest military alert in the United States, and although the U.S. defence posture had been at DEFCON 3 since the first week of the terrorist attacks, this was the first time since the Cuban Missile Crisis that a president has ordered DEFCON 2. The only higher alert, DEFCON 1, was only called when there was danger of imminent foreign attack — most likely nuclear — against the United States. Its implementation could unleash the U.S. nuclear arsenal.

"I'll be staying right here, but I want the vice president and his staff airborne and ready to run the show if something happens to me. Make sure he is fully briefed. Admiral, implement Looking Glass, get those aircraft up ASAP. I want the Chinese to know that if they even think of using a nuclear weapon against this country we are ready for them." He addressed Blomstrum. "Dan, let's get the government moved out of Washington."

Addressing the room, the president said, "Well gentlemen, I'm sure you are all going to have a very busy day, so you'd better get to it." He rose, and as he walked from the Situation Room, he said quietly to Blomstrum, who followed, "Dan, get the First Lady and the kids out of here. I don't want my worrying about them staying in DC to colour any of my decisions."

Blomstrum understood his meaning exactly. He looked right at the president and replied with some gravity, "Yes, sir, consider it done."

October 1.
East China Sea, sixty miles east of Okinawa, Japan.

The Bush was at full alert. Battle stations had been ordered minutes after a flash message from the intelligence unit on Okinawa reported the Chinese landings in Taiwan. Now, three hours later, Admiral Gibson sat on the flag bridge anxiously waiting for instructions from the Pentagon. On the flight deck far below his perch, a pair of F-35 Lightings were on the catapults, ready to go, and overhead two more circled on Combat Air Patrol. In the distance, Gibson could see anti-submarine helicopters rushing out to dip with their sonar into the ocean in front of the Bush and her entourage. The deck behind the ready aircraft was crammed with fully armed Lightnings, lined up and ready for their turn on the catapults. Below, the hangar decks were frantic with activity as F-35s were configured for both air-to-air and ground-attack roles. The Bush was getting ready to fight.

If orders arrived to help repel the invasion, then the air base at Okinawa would be contributing to the effort. They had already scrambled several Boeing E-3 surveillance aircraft to replace the missing AWACS. These would stand off Taiwan to the north and east, hopefully out of harm's way, to monitor events on the island. KC-135 aerial tankers were also being prepared to fuel both the Bush's Lightnings and the Naval F-18 Super Hornets flying out of Okinawa. The U.S. Air Force F-22 Raptors based on Okinawa would use their own KC-10 Extender, as their refuelling techniques were different from the Navy's.

Gibson sat on the darkened flag bridge watching the staff compiling what information could so far be gleaned. He was as uncomfortable as he imagined the captain on the ship's bridge and the air boss responsible for the aircraft wings would be in their own command stations. For each man, the clock's hands seemed to crawl as they awaited the command to action or — but this was unimaginable — orders to stand down and depart the region.

A lieutenant monitoring flag communications turned and addressed him. "Sir, flash message. Back stop, back stop, back stop."

"Thank you, lieutenant." Gibson spoke to his staff. "All right, men. Let's go."

Seconds later the news was flashed from the flag bridge to the ship's captain and the air boss, and only heartbeats after that, the first of the Lightings leapt into the sky, followed by successive pairs of fighters. None of the aircraft waited for the others to catch up to create formations. Modern tactics and technology suggested their odds were better if they went in stealthily and fought in teams of two using their standoff weapons. The first dozen or so aircraft on stage would engage the Chinese air force, while the next waves would look for and engage ground targets.

A priority message from the Pentagon to the ROC high command fighting on the ground was supposed to inform the Taiwanese that U.S. forces were coming. Despite this warning and the friendly ID codes they squawked, the U.S. Navy pilots knew they would be no safer from friendly fire than from the invading Chinese. They would put their trust in their aircraft's stealth technology instead.

In the air, three hundred miles to the west and cruising at thirty thousand feet, a Chinese reconnaissance aircraft, one of the two Tu-153s that had charged at the Bush on September 22, noted the increased level of electronic activity emanating from the carrier and her escorts. It was very clear that the Bush was starting to engage offensive operations. The 153's signals officer typed in a numbered code to alert the Chinese high command that the Americans were coming.

September 30.
Underground command facility, the White House.

"Mr. President," said Henry Woeburn as he came through the open door, "this just came in from Langley. The CIA thinks one of their teams in Europe has turned up the terrorists' head man. His name is Muhammad Al-Munajjid. He's a Saudi national, and he appears to be both a spiritual leader with fundamentalist leanings as well as a successful entrepreneur with diverse business interests in the Middle East and in Europe."

"How did we turn him up?" asked the president.

"A tip from Mossad. They suspected he might be involved at some level. We were even luckier in getting to a fairly close relative of his, a Saudi rich kid by the name of Muhammad al-Muffaddal who seems to have been his personal bumboy as well as an outstanding prick. Our team picked him up in London, and a special interrogation team questioned him for a few hours. The guy knew a lot, not in great detail, but enough to incriminate this al-Munajjid and place him at the top of the heap."

"So, where is al-Munajjid?"

"We aren't sure, but al-Muffaddal placed him somewhere in Europe, probably Switzerland. Al-Muffaddal's family jet carted al-Munajjid around the world, and the last place they dropped him was at the airport in Geneva."

"This is the best news I've had in a while. Let's pick him up."

"We're working on that, sir. The team that turned him up is on their way to Switzerland and we have a special tactical team en route to back them up."

"Do the Swiss know about any of this?"

"No, sir."

"Keep it that way. Who's in this team?"

"Two operatives, sir, a Catherine Hunt who is CIA and FBI Special Agent Derek James."

"Derek James. I met him. He was the poor bastard whose girlfriend died in the Santa Barbara attack. My God," the president said reflectively, "that seems a long time ago." Brightening, he continued. "Good. Get me a complete report as soon as it's available. I want to savour this one for a while."

"Yes, sir. I'll do that."

"And Henry?"

"Yes, Mr. President."

"Send my personal congratulations and express my gratitude to Hunt and James."

"Consider it done, sir."

October 1.
East China Sea.

Lieutenant Yang and his three crew members had been sitting at two hundred feet below the calm waters of the East China Sea for almost twenty-six hours, and while they were a little bored, they were quite comfortable. The mother ship, Hunan, had dropped its flock of mini-subs at ten-mile intervals to wait quietly for targets. All the subs sat at around two hundred feet, just below a cold upwelling caused by the spine of an underwater mountain range that broke the surface in places in a string of islands between Japan and Taiwan. The cold current made their detection even more unlikely than it already was.

The Hunan's four submarines were farthest east of all the small subs that waited for the Bush. Farther out, several atomic subs — Chinese hunter-killers — sat at much greater depths waiting for their remote sensors to pick up their quarry should it happen their way, something that would only occur if the Bush was fleeing the region.

Two hundred feet above Lieutenant Yang, a bright orange "Giant Size" plastic detergent bottle, one end encrusted with goose barnacles, bobbed on the surface. Inside the bottle was a range of sensors and a communications relay. It was tethered to the mini-sub by incredibly strong but thin and neutrally buoyant optical fibres that relayed information from the surface to the waiting sub below.

The sensors could pick up and give accurate range and course information on ships moving in waters as far away as fifteen miles and alert the sub's crew to shipping much farther away than that. This information was relayed to both the command console in the submarine and to its two torpedoes, whose computers were constantly updated with the position of enemy surface units, water conditions and the sea floor's topography. The sonic profile of various U.S. and British ships and submarines and their priority as targets were all embedded in the torpedoes' efficient minds.

When readied for firing, the torpedo would relay to the command console the list of shipping nearby and wait for the target list to be checked and prioritized by the submarine commander. In the event that a prioritized list was not provided before firing, then the torpedo was programmed to search out the largest and most valuable target available, stalk it and attack — all autonomously. The communications gear in the floating bottle allowed the mini-subs to stay in contact with friendly surface units, satellites and reconnaissance aircraft and to pick up special military messages from naval headquarters.

Suddenly, the sub's interior was washed in a pulsing green light. A message was being received. Yang leaned forward and punched a button to illuminate the screen. All systems on the small boat remained in power-saving standby mode until keyed. On the screen, there was one word — Titanic — a story well known and much beloved by the Chinese since the blockbuster movie, and a very appropriate code word in this case.

Yang smiled, flipped the monitor to the course-and-navigation screen and engaged the autopilot. His was the boat closest to the target's present position, and he was almost in line with it's present course. He presumed all the other boats in the string that traversed a good section of the East China Sea were doing the same thing. The navigation computers on board each sub recorded the location of their quarry, part of the download that had accompanied the word "Titanic." Like a huge purse seine, thirty mini-subs began their furtive stalk toward the Bush carrier strike force, drawing the ends of the net together on their noisy and so far oblivious target.

CHAPTER 21

October 1.
Red Sea, off of Jeddah, Saudi Arabia.

Captain Nawaf Basnan ordered full stop to the helmsman and the 3,700-ton French-built Royal Saudi Navy frigate, al-Riyadh, slowed gently and coasted to a stop, her sleek hull rolling a little from side to side in the light moonlit swell. The Lafayette-class frigate had been commissioned in the year 2000, and she was now the oldest of the four in her class that patrolled the coast of Saudi Arabia from the Red Sea to the Persian Gulf.

All of the other Saudi frigates were currently on station in the Gulf. Basnan's was the only one in the Red Sea. She was currently just over a mile from the shoreline and almost immediately abeam of the Royal Palace at Jeddah. Basnan glanced at his watch, noted the time and ordered the forward gun readied for action. An hour earlier, several officers of the ship's crew, accompanied by armed sailors, had rounded up and locked away over half of the ship's compliment. Most went peacefully and without question, having been told their incarceration was part of an exercise to train a Special Forces rescue team. The only men left on deck were the crew and officers who were rigidly loyal to Basnan and his ideals.

He looked down from the bridge at the 100-mm gun on the forward deck and watched it swivel to port. The barrel rose slightly, and the ship's first officer reported the gun ready for action. Basnan looked at his watch again — less than a minute until twelve. He gazed at the lights that flickered in the waves, reflections from the nearby city of Jeddah, and smiled. As the minute hand made contact with the top of his watch, he said simply and quietly, "Fire. Fire at will."

The first officer yelled the command into his headset microphone, and the gun went off, sending the first of dozens of high-explosive rounds sailing through the air towards the palace. Ten minutes later, Basnan ordered ceasefire.

On the shore, the palace was a flaming ruin. Several fires in the city marked where a few salvoes had hit police headquarters and military buildings, but the lion's share of the ordnance had destroyed one of the most beautiful royal palaces in Saudi Arabia, and several members of the royal household as well.

A lookout alerted them to a small patrol boat that was approaching at high speed, the flower of machine-gun fire blossoming on its bow. Chain guns on the deck of the frigate opened up, sawing the coastal patroller almost in half before it exploded, its fiery light joining that of the burning palace.

Basnan ordered al-Riyadh to full speed and on a course southward and away from retribution. No aircraft rose to chase it. The few Royal Saudi Air Force fighters that had escaped sabotage and gotten airborne had more pressing targets than one fleeing frigate. In Jeddah, as in most of Saudi Arabia's cities and its major towns, radical Sunni rebels were attacking key government buildings and the homes of the royal family itself.

October 1.
Riyadh, Saudi Arabia.

The first sounds of explosions echoed through the city at precisely twelve midnight and radiated from the royal compound, where radical Muslim insurgents allied to Bandar id bin Abdul Aziz had fired the first shots of a coup d'état that spanned Saudi Arabia.

Aziz represented a wing of the royal family that had been thrust into the back eddies of Saudi Arabian power and had long resented it. They'd formed a perfect marriage with radical Sunnis in several ways. One was to promise continued support for the attacks underway against the United States and her possessions, which had compelled the Americans to withdraw their military from the Middle East. Aziz's relationship with al-Munajjid had accomplished that, and it had won Aziz and his allies support from the radicals. Another was to promise a devout Islamic state, free of American influence, and finally, he had promised to take Iraq from the Shiites and turn it into a Sunni-run protectorate of Saudi Arabia. To that end, several generals in charge of Saudi land forces had joined the coup. The generals had made sure military units loyal to the ruling family would either be in barracks, where they could be bottled up and eliminated, or out in the field, conducting a major exercise near the Iraq border.

At the moment the coup began, the units along the border were issued orders to cross the frontier and head for Baghdad. As justification, they were misinformed that covert Iraqi forces had attacked Riyadh, and Iraqi commandos had attacked palaces and seats of government across Arabia. Iraqi forces had also been reported near Mecca. The aim was twofold: to keep the loyalists out of communication with the rest of the country so that news of the coup, if it did leak to them, could be put down to Iraqi disinformation and actions; and to keep them too busy with the Iraqi defence forces to do much about the coup even if they did discover the truth.

The invasion would weaken loyalist forces because they would be the fodder used to breech the Iraqi defences. Once the coup had succeeded — a matter of hours if everything went according to plan — the conspirators could take advantage of the gains made in Iraq. Military units loyal to the royal family would be given the option of either joining the war against Iraq in support of their new government or facing down hostile Iraqi forces on the one side and the military of the new Saudi regime on the other. At best, survivors could look forward to imprisonment, but elimination was far more likely. The rebels wagered that almost every soldier would change his allegiance — even without such an ultimatum — once he knew a new government had taken power.

The United States, which had its hands full at home and in the Far East and had few resources left in the Middle East aside from the oil field guard, would be powerless to intervene. It served the plotters well that U.S. forces would keep the vast oil reserves in Iraq free from harm so they could be plucked by the Saudis later on.

The invasion of Taiwan had preceded the coup in Saudi Arabia by five hours and signalled the beginning of the rebellion, at the stroke of midnight, Riyadh time. The coup would surprise not just the Americans but the Chinese as well.

October 1.
Over France.

Derek stared out the window of the Gulfstream IV at the twinkling lights that spattered the French countryside thirty-five thousand feet below. It was a few minutes past midnight. Catherine was fast asleep in a reclining chair across the aisle and, much to Derek's amusement, every now and then a light snore would escape her lips. Something to tease her with, he thought to himself.

He didn't kid her very much, something he'd always done with his male partners, and he wasn't sure if it was because she was female or because at some deep level he was attracted to her despite Vanessa's recent death. Maybe, he thought, he was keeping it all strictly professional because he was afraid that being more familiar might open him up when he thought he should still be mourning. He wasn't sure what kind of man would appeal to Catherine. She didn't give any feedback about her personal likes and dislikes. But then again, their conversations — aside from the one during the dinner they'd shared in Israel — rarely wandered from their assignment and the discussion of current events.

He'd been horrified to hear about the Chinese invasion of Taiwan and the Saudi coup, news he'd saw on a television in the airport lounge as they'd passed through on their way to the plane. It had really shaken him, especially because they'd just been in Riyadh. Catherine, staring at the newscaster as he read, said, "interesting times," a reference to the old Chinese curse, "May you live in interesting times."

Now they were on their way to Geneva to track down the Arab dirtbag behind the heinous attacks on the United States and ultimately responsible for Vanessa's death. He hoped the CIA in Geneva had located al-Munajjid already, but Derek wanted to be there when the Navy Seals kicked in his door and, with any luck, beat the shit out of him.

He drifted off to a disturbed sleep from which he was awoken by the steward for the landing an hour or so later. He glanced over at Catherine, who was already wide awake and smiled at him as she snapped her seat belt in place and moved her seat back to vertical.

Passing through Swiss customs in the expensive passenger reception lounge for private aircraft was a cursory affair, the customs agent warm and courteous. He studied their passports for a moment, asked each of them whether they were in the country on business or pleasure — to which Catherine replied pleasure — and then passed them back. Smiling, he wished them a pleasant stay, nodded and then retreated through a doorway to a room in which a television's light flickered and the voices of reporters with English accents could be heard talking about Taiwan. Now that the American media was so heavily muzzled and the largest American international news service in Atlanta destroyed, the world had turned back to the BBC for its up-to-the-minute news.

When Derek and Catherine emerged from the terminal, a white Mercedes sedan waited at the curb. The driver, stationed just inside the terminal doors, introduced himself and showed his U.S. embassy identification as they made their way through the door. He explained that he'd been instructed to take them to the Bristol Hotel, where they could check in and meet their CIA contact in the hotel lounge. The Bristol, he said, was on the lake and as near the centre of Geneva as possible, making it a convenient place from which to do business.

Geneva was a pretty city at the tip of a spur in southwestern Switzerland that penetrated France and situated on Europe's largest body of fresh water, Lac Leman, or Lake Geneva on some maps. Like many European cities, Geneva was ancient by North American standards, and Derek found himself starting to appreciate how new and, in many ways, pretentious and hollow much of North American culture was. In Europe, people lived in houses that were built before American independence and thought nothing of it.

The driver of the white Mercedes was good and got them from the airport well north of the city to their hotel in short order. Even in the deep of night, when most sane people were in bed asleep, Geneva was beautiful, many of the stunning buildings lit with floods that rendered them faintly unreal, as if drawn from a children's storybook.

On arriving at the hotel an hour later, Catherine and Derek barely had enough time to throw their bags in their rooms and splash a little water on their faces before the front desk advised them that they had a visitor waiting in the lobby. Derek entered the elevator, but just as the doors were closing, he saw Catherine emerge from her room. He held the elevator.

"Thanks," she said, hustling in.

"You're welcome."

"God, what I wouldn't do for a night in my own bed," said Catherine.

"I would settle for a night of sleep that didn't include bouncing around at thirty thousand feet."

When the elevator doors opened on the lobby, Derek spied a grey-haired middle-aged and slightly paunchy man dressed casually in a golf shirt and blue jeans and wearing a pair of slightly flashy adidas running shoes. He was sitting in one of the lobby's wingback chairs, was leafing through an old copy of National Geographic, a staple of lobbies and waiting rooms the world over.

Noticing them, the man stood, revealing that he was of above-average height. "Catherine," he exclaimed, "great to see you!"

"Hello, John, how are you doing?" she replied, genuinely pleased to see him and giving him a hug.

"I'm just fine, but as you can see," he said, pointing to his paunch and grinning, "life as a station chief in Switzerland is hard, very hard."

Catherine patted his belly and laughed. "So I see," she replied. "Derek, I'd like you to meet John Kopriva. John was my field trainer at Langley when I was just starting out. He was such a miserable instructor that I think they made him station chief in Switzerland just to get rid of him."

"Like I always said, Cat, you rise to your level of incompetence."

"Well, you must have been very incompetent then to land a plum like this one," she teased.

"My incompetence knows no bounds," he replied laughing. "Derek, pleased to meet you." He took Derek's hand in a firm, dry grasp.

"Pleased to meet you, as well," replied Derek, feeling a little left out by the pair's warmth and familiarity with one another.

"So, I read in the email from London that you are FBI. This must all be a bit strange," said Kopriva to Derek.

"The amount of travel is. I'm used to having the same desk at least four days in a row, but the scum we're chasing are all too familiar."

"Derek's an anti-terrorism specialist. He was attached to Homeland Security in Los Angeles before the attacks stateside," said Catherine.

"You're the guy that was at the Santa Barbara attack," exclaimed Kopriva. "I read about you in some of the reports. I guess that was pretty tough."

"It was," said Derek.

"Well, I'll tell you one thing, if it's any consolation," said Kopriva by way of changing the subject, "you're working with one of the best students I ever trained, and I hear she hasn't done too badly for herself since she's been in the field."

"You're too kind. What do you want?" asked Catherine and smiled.

"Right now, I want to get a coffee, and I guess we'd better start making some plans."

"Coffee sounds good," said Derek. "I could use a little caffeine kick around now."

"There's a little all-night café a couple of blocks away. The coffee's good and they have some really good pastries," Kopriva said, looking at his watch, which read a quarter to four. "This time of the morning, the pastries will just be coming out of the ovens."

Fifteen minutes later, they were sitting under the café's fluorescent lights with steaming coffee in front of them. The room was so narrow that a row of small tables barely fit between the glass-fronted counters and the wall, but the aroma of fresh brewed coffee and the sweet and enticing smell of fresh and expertly baked pastry made the place homey and welcoming rather than overlit and austere.

They sat near the back at the only four-person table in the place. At this time of the morning, there were only two other customers, both seated near the front. A uniformed city worker, grabbing a cup before going to work, read the paper while another fellow, clearly recovering from a night of drinking, nursed a coffee and, judging by his wincing demeanour, the beginnings of a monumental hangover. Neither was in earshot, and the café's staff was busy bashing and clanging about in the kitchen, from which wafted the delicious aroma of baked bead.

"So, we've been trying the local hotels and inns in Geneva for this al-Munajjid fellow, so far with no luck."

"What's the process?" asked Catherine.

"Mostly showing one of the two pictures we have of this guy to doormen and desk clerks."

"The hook?" she asked.

"We're saying either he was the driver of a car that might have sideswiped our parked Range Rover or he might be the witness to a hit and run."

"How many people have you got on it?" asked Derek.

"Everyone I can lay my hands on. Langley informed me that this has the highest priority. I have the word out to the other station chiefs in Europe that I need grunts, and I expect several more agents to come in from Berlin and Amsterdam later this morning. Hopefully, there will be more we can get our hands on. I'll make some calls a little later, when all the smart people get up."

"So, what are our chances of getting this guy quickly?" asked Derek.

"Quite frankly, I don't know. It depends on his lifestyle, where he stays and who he stays with. It could be a long search, especially if he has a safe house or stays with associates. Switzerland is small, but it's a dammed difficult place to work in. The Swiss guard their neutrality with great passion, and there's no way we can ask them for assistance and get it, especially if they suspect we're running an operation in country."

"I thought Switzerland was full of secret agents," said Derek.

"Sure, during the Second World War maybe, but these days not much goes on here. Diplomacy and UN delegations have replaced spies and espionage as staple fare. It's a great place to be a station chief — lots of cocktail parties and galas and not much spying and paperwork...well, that is, until now.

"So what can you two tell me about this bastard? London said you could fill in the blanks when you got here. They didn't want to relay anything online."

Catherine stirred her coffee and started to repeat to Kopriva the information they'd received on al-Munajjid from Mossad and from the interrogation of al-Muffaddal in London. Thirty minutes later they said their goodbyes, and Derek and Catherine walked back to their hotel to grab a few hours of uninterrupted sleep.

October 1.
Geneva.

Al-Munajjid walked from his hotel lobby into a light drizzle. Low scudding clouds threatened the city despite weather reports that had insisted the day was going to be overcast but warm and dry. Switzerland's weather was notoriously hard to predict, a result of its mountainous terrain and deep valleys, but that never stopped people from having their hopes dashed when the forecasts proved to be false. Even al-Munajjid was a little disappointed. He'd been looking forward to the scenic drive. He was a man who could never get enough of bright green countryside.

He'd hired a private limousine and driver to make the trek to Berne. His bodyguards, highly trained and discreet, would follow behind in a Mercedes SUV, keeping an eye out for trouble and for any cars that might try to tail al-Munajjid's car. The precaution was not due to any suspicion that American agents were looking for him. Al-Munajjid had many enemies and had lived like this for years.

As he got into the back of the limousine, a long silver Mercedes 600, the doorman, just returning from a visit to the toilet, caught a glimpse of him and remembered the two men who'd been to the hotel a couple of hours ago shopping around a picture of a man who looked surprisingly like the one getting into the limo. He walked to his small kiosk and rummaged through some odds and ends, finally coming up with a plain white card with a name and number on it. While not stupid enough to believe that the two big men with American accents would be looking at six in the morning for an Arab driver because of a minor hit and run, he didn't care what their real business with the man was. He did care about the reward they'd promised if he called them with any information.

As the large silver Mercedes pulled from the hotel drive followed by a black Mercedes SUV with two men inside it, he dialled an outside line from his kiosk phone and left a message on an answering machine. He gave his name and the hotel and said he was on his way home shortly but would be back at the hotel for his next shift at twelve that night. As the silver Mercedes drove off, he jotted down its registration number and that of the black SUV.

October 1.
Baltimore.

Shojaa' Bala' Awi had found getting around the eastern seaboard of the United States increasingly difficult. The Americans had learned a lot about internal security in the past month and a half. He was also fairly sure his weapons courier had been compromised or was being too cautious to make a drop. He checked his computer and the porn sites almost hourly looking for a posted message indicating that a weapons cache had been positioned for his team. Nothing. What he did not know was that U.S. forces had discovered many of the containers holding weapons intended for the terrorists and had captured most of the weapons distributors.

The caches had always been the plan's weakest link, but they'd served very well for the first three weeks. Weapons for the embedded terrorist army were now rapidly becoming scarce. Mind you, Awi was inventive and did not rely on securing arms from the caches, but they did make his plans easier. Since his destruction of the Rockefeller Center, his cell had been involved in several car bombings and shootings. Two of his men, specialists, ranged the countryside looking for vulnerable police officers, National Guardsmen or regular military, on duty or off, to assassinate. They actually preferred to trail an officer home and kill not just the policeman but his entire family. Awi's men checked in with him twice daily to see if there were any changes in their orders or if Awi had new targets for them.

On the rare occasions when they met, always in a secure location, they would regale him with stories of their cunning, daring and close calls. They certainly seemed to enjoy the hunt. His other two men, specialists in booby traps and roadside explosive devices, were running out of things to do. They'd used up their stock of explosives, and scrounging for materials had become difficult if not impossible. These four men were all that was left of his original cell, the other four having martyred themselves in the destruction of the Rockefeller Center.

Awi looked at his watch and decided it was time to get up. He was staying in a small room in a boarding house provided to him by the American-Arab Friendship Society. The federation comprised intellectuals and business people with Arab backgrounds who lived and worked in the USA and existed to promote peaceful and mutually beneficial American-Arab cultural relationships. Since the attacks began, what it did more of was to provide refuge for Arab-Americans who'd been driven from their homes or otherwise caught up in the events of the day.

Awi had long ago abandoned his alias, Apostolos Zoupaniotis, the Greek businessman who'd arrived from Athens. Now he had the papers of a Turkish citizen in the United States with a green card. He often thought about the irony of his protectors' harbouring in their midst the very threat they continually cried they did not represent to Americans.

He was going to meet with all four of his men today. They were tired of waiting for new weapons. It was time to go out and get some of their own. That would be more difficult than it once was. Gun shops and suppliers of any ammunition or explosive devices were closed for business, their wares under lock and key, tightly controlled by a government that had never before denied Americans their right to bear arms. Now that Americans, motivated by fear or loathing, killed more Americans a day than the terrorist attacks did, the government had implemented dozens of new emergency bans on firearms and the right to carry them.

Cruising the Internet, however, had provided a wealth of information on weapons and explosives hobbyists. On gun club websites and gun collector blogs — most of them posted before the attacks began — Awi had located the addresses of collectors who had exactly what he was looking for. Today he was going to lay out a plan to hit two or, if they were lucky, three of these collectors in the Baltimore area and secure weapons and ammunition up to and including .50-calibre machine guns. He had already prepared several places to hide them. Now he had to assemble his team.

An hour later, Awi sat in a coffee shop frequented by many middle European and Middle Eastern customers. He sat at a table at the back of the shop. One by one his men arrived, ordering coffee and doughnuts at the front counter before sauntering to the back and greeting one another amiably, just some friends meeting for a quick coffee before their working day began. It appeared so normal that everyone in the shop ignored them, focused instead on their own day's beginnings.

Awi was in the middle of outlining his plan to the others when two young black kids, neither more than fifteen years of age, walked into the coffee shop and up to the front counter. They were waiting for service when the younger one looked down the shop and poked the older boy in the ribs to get his attention. He pointed at Awi and his men. That action rang feint alarms in Awi's head, but he dismissed the youths as children until they were almost halfway down aisle, their attention riveted on the five men.

As they strutted into earshot, Awi motioned to his men to be quiet. All five men at the table looked around at the boys as they stopped next to the table. They were dressed in the loose fitting and faintly clownish apparel of the local street gangs, complete with baseball caps worn sideways and at unlikely angles. The larger of the two boys, the one wearing a Chicago Bulls sweatshirt, spoke. "Hey, you mofuckers. You lookin' like fuckin' sand niggers. You sand niggers or what, mofuckers?"

Awi was a little taken aback, and one of his younger men rose to confront the boys. His chair slid backwards and then toppled over, clanging to the floor and alerting the other coffee shop patrons that something was amiss. Awi also rose, but to stop his man, the unwanted attention and visions of discovery turning his mouth to dust. His man told the boy to fuck off, his Middle Eastern accent punctuating the English phase.

It was the trigger the two young boys had been waiting for. The smaller boy pulled a tiny machine pistol, a Beretta 93R, from under his voluminous Mighty Ducks shirt. At the same time the bigger boy brandished a similarly hidden American Mauser M2 .45-calibre pistol.

Time slowed for Awi. Neither he nor his men were armed. He'd deemed it too dangerous to carry unless they were on a mission. All they could do was dive for cover. The machine pistol spat the first of its twenty rounds before the boy had levelled it, so the fist three 9 mm slugs ripped holes in the floor and table. The Beretta was a burst-fire automatic that fired three rounds at a time. The next mushrooming rounds tore into Awi's two men on the side of the table closest to the boys, spinning one man in a circle as the bullets crashed through his knee joint and taking the other man in the groin. The final burst of three exploded into his chest.

With time slowing to fractions of a second, Awi marvelled at the sophisticated weapons the two boys brandished as the first slug from the .45 Mauser hit him in the sternum, where the bone deflected it downward, though his stomach and then, in pieces, out his back an inch to the left of his spine. The gunfire slammed him into the wall behind his seat as if he'd been hit with a battle-axe instead of a tiny piece of steel-jacketed lead. He saw his men dance with the bullets' impact and the grim, emotionless faces of the two little boys who were laying low the architect of one of the most magnificent attacks on the United States in history. The next two rounds, one from the Beretta that had grazed one of his men and another from the .45, tore though his body, taking pieces of him with them as they ripped through the dry wall and into the women's washroom behind.

He wondered if his family would ever know that he was the one who'd toppled the Rockefeller Center in New York or that he'd killed one of America's most popular movie stars. As life slipped from him, he could no longer remember his accomplishments. All he saw through the gathering mist were the two boys, their guns finally quiet, the muzzles smoking. He realized then that the Middle East was not the only place that bred child warriors, and that he wanted his mother.

The shooting in the coffee shop didn't make headlines. It was lost in a sea of censored news events that filled this and every other day. The two children calmly walked out the rear door of the coffee shop, back to their lives as gangbangers. They left five dead men in their wake and had wounded a woman who was in the washroom during the shooting.

Police investigators would not realize the significance of the event for several days, and although they eventually discovered that the dead men had formed part of the terrorist army, investigators could never directly connect them to the Rockefeller Center bombing.

CHAPTER 22

October 1.
East China Sea.

Lieutenant Yang could almost hear through the mini-sub's hull the distant vibrations of the American carrier fleet. His weapons specialist, hunched over a computer behind Yang, punched a key on the keyboard that activated a flashing message on Yang's command console screen: the weapons had detected their quarry and were ready to start the hunt. Yang cleared the protect flap from his firing button and pushed it, his prerogative as the submarine's commander, although any one of the four-man crew could have launched the weapons once the initial release was authorized.

The result was anti-climactic. Unlike the torpedoes of the past whose whooshing launch was accompanied by great clouds of noisy bubbles, the mini-sub's two smart torps fell gently away from their nests in the sub's hull and then quietly left on their course toward the oncoming battle group. They angled downward, moving at no more than five knots, to gain another hundred feet in depth, and then they levelled, travelling almost side by side and within thirty feet of one another. They navigated passively, listening intently to the clamour created by the ships' churning propellers ten miles ahead. Their computer minds studied the wall of sound, searching, separating, comparing and prioritizing their target lists.

Within ten minutes of their launch, they'd pinpointed both the George Bush and her largest escort. The ships were put into a one-two ranking. Torpedo number one accelerated slightly to eight knots, a speed still stealthy enough to avoid detection until it was too late for the target. The second torpedo would continue on its course more slowly, waiting for the outcome of number one's attack. If, judging from the sounds it heard, its programming deemed number one's attack successful, then torpedo two would attack the second target. This arrangement was an effort by frugal programmers to maximize weapon effectiveness.

A miss by both torpedoes would offer no relief to the Bush, however, as there were still thirty clever torpedoes — and if those failed, another thirty — in the East China Sea with her name recorded in their tiny minds. Only if they could not find her or were confident she'd been destroyed would those torpedoes seek an alternate target. Already six were on their way toward her.

October 1.
George H. W. Bush flag bridge.

Admiral Gibson sat nervously waiting for news from the first air wings into hostile airspace over Taiwan. His flag staff had very little to do aside from monitoring events, despite the frantic activity on deck and in the combat information centre. His attack order had launched an initial wave of thirty-six F-35s headed for Taiwan, and now it was all about the aircraft and protecting the carrier. The Bush's destroyer escorts and anti-submarine helicopters scoured the undersea with sonar, looking for hostile craft, and the Aegis-class cruiser and missile destroyers patrolled in rings around the carrier for airborne threats. Commercial airliners were being warned away, and air traffic to and from Japan or bound for other areas of Asia was fleeing the area lest they be targeted.

Suddenly, a flag lieutenant asked for Gibson's attention, "Sir, we have a shadow almost directly off the bow, six thousand yards."

"Sub?" he asked.

The lieutenant was listening intently to the voice in his headphones from the combat information centre, CIC. "Unconfirmed. sir. It's coming and going. Sonar's saying it may just be a reflection from the thermals. They're routing a copter to the area to dip just in case."

"Sir," a chief petty officer chimed in, "CIC is reporting our F-35s have had their first contact with hostiles twelve miles north of Taiwan. Splash two bogeys."

"Great, this will be a great chance to see what our new toys can do," said the admiral. "First contact, two kills. That will give the Chinks something to think about." Years of official political correctness had drained away, and Gibson, without thinking, reverted to the name for the Chinese so popular with GIs during the Korean War.

An ethnic Chinese seaman first class, monitoring a computer screen on the flag bridge, looked up in shock for a moment before averting his eyes.

October 1.
Under the Bush, East China Sea.

Almost five hundred feet below and less that four hundred yards directly in front of the George H. W. Bush's onrushing keel, the Chinese torpedo dispatched by Lieutenant Yang waited, hovering, its neutral buoyancy compensator allowing it to hang motionless in the water and its anechoic stealth design making it virtually invisible to the Bush's sonar sweeps, even at this range. A sensor in the torpedo, alerted by the proximity of its main target, activated four tiny bow thrusters in the nose of the torpedo. It angled upwards, its snub nose tracking the bottom of the approaching carrier like a bluetick coonhound nosing its prey.

Nearby, three more torpedoes just arriving from other submarines coasted to a stop and imitated the first, their on-board computers instructing them to wait until the ship was in the best position for a hit. Their only movements were the constant attitude adjustments they made as the carrier came ever closer. Other torpedoes over a mile out still crawled towards the Bush. Her Ticonderoga-class Aegis cruiser, the Chosin, was also being stalked.

"Sir," cried the midshipman to Admiral Gibson, "one of our attack subs has a target. Says its small but could be a bogey of some sort. They're going to active sonar!"

"How far out?" demanded Gibson.

The midshipman spoke into his headset and then answered, "Five thousand yards, sir. The attack subs are engaging."

Great, Gibson thought, the U.S. Navy's most expensive hunter-killers are probably engaging a sperm whale in an effort to keep the Bush safe.

Lieutenant Yang heard the launch of a conventional torpedo. It was their first warning that an American hunter-killer was nearby. The mini-subs' detection systems were passive and not very sophisticated. Having loosed all their weaponry, they were unimportant to the outcome of events. If they survived, great, but only their crews cared about that. Neither Yang nor his crew had any idea what the torpedo's target might be, but he and his men prayed as one that it wasn't their sub.

After an eternity, the torpedo's sound signature altered, starting to diminish as it swept by their position almost a quarter mile off their starboard beam. Apparently, it wasn't after them. The American sub had detected a mini-submarine — the last of the group — that was in the middle of unleashing its torpedoes and had been moving at more than sixteen knots to arrive at a firing position, a speed that caused discernable cavitation. The sounds created by its propeller and the water rushing over its hull had alerted the American sonar operator to its presence.

The mini-sub was still a long way out — a testimony to the sophistication of the American sensors — and the American torpedo buzzed through the water for what seemed an interminable time. Suddenly, a detonation sounded. The torpedo's proximity detectors had triggered the explosion and annihilated the light mini-sub and its crew, but not before its two torpedoes made a clean get away. It was the only Chinese mini-sub to be lost in action.

"Sir, CIC reports objects in the water. No ID," relayed the flag lieutenant to Gibson.

"What they hell do you mean objects, for Christ's sake?"

"They don't know, sir. They might be mines, but they're too deep. They're over four hundred feet down."

"Shit," yelled Gibson. "Unless they're nukes. Nukes would work from that far down. Tell the captain to go to flank speed."

The ship was already accelerating as Gibson shouted the order, the captain having reached the same decision at the same moment as Gibson did. Down on the carrier's flight deck, another pair of F-35s, loaded down with ordnance, waited to take position while an E-2C Hawkeye surveillance aircraft was launched.

The Bush was almost directly over Yang's torpedo when its computers decided it had optimum firing solution. Four explosive bolts detonated, blowing away its underwater propulsion system and battery packs. A second later, the solid fuel booster ignited. In the Bush's sonar room, two sonarmen winced, one of them tearing off his headset at the roar telegraphed to his ears from the sensitive underwater array.

The torpedo, now a missile, accelerated to over a hundred knots, its four powerful rocket engines muscling it upward despite the water's resistance. Only inches from the supercarrier's speeding keel, the torpedo's nose dissolved in a vicious blast. The steel of the ship's hull spalled as the torpedo's depleted uranium slug shot into it, ripping an irregular hole twelve inches wide, right though the ship's armoured belly, and continued upward, its kinetic energy still not expended.

On the heels of the first blast, the torpedo's main chemical charge went off. The explosion blew upwards into the ship and, outside the damaged hull, formed a mammoth ball of gases that pushed the water away at supersonic speeds. As the gases dissipated, the water returned, tearing through the Bush's armoured bottom of layered steel and Kevlar as if it was soggy tissue.

Inside the Bush, the sabot found one of the ship's ballast tanks, where aviation fuel was stored. It came to a stop within the bunker, almost molten, its energy spent.

The chemical blast that followed it, seeking the easiest path through the Bush's gut, met the vaporized cloud of Jet A that sprayed from the perforated bunker. The fuel ignited in an inferno that threw crewmen from their feet on the flight deck high above. That blast occurred just as the water pushed away by the initial explosion came crashing back into the hull. The combined force actually lifted the carrier, despite her 102,000-ton displacement.

Up on the flag bridge, it felt like they'd hit a large speed bump. The torpedo's talons had ripped a hole twenty feet wide in the bottom plate and the sea rushed in, tearing at the already buckled and weakened ribs of the stricken leviathan. Admiral Gibson sat stock still as his mind raced through the list of possibilities before returning to the one he knew was most likely. He prayed that his brand-new ship, the most powerful vessel ever built, had not just received a mortal blow.

The second of Yang's torpedoes, sensing its companion's successful impact above, raced away, accelerating to its top speed, sixty knots. Its programmers knew that for the second torpedo the jig would be up and stealth not as critical. It raced for the USS Chosin, angling upward and tracking the cruiser as the ship began to turn toward. the Bush. The Chosin's crew had seen the burst of spray that broke from the carrier's side amidships and fountained into the air, and her captain had heard the reports of explosions from his own CIC.

The next lurking primary torpedo, launched from another mini-sub, was still concentrated on the carrier. Its propulsion unit blew from its bottom, but one of the explosive bolts failed to fire properly, and the unit remained attached on one side, skewing the torpedo sideways. The torpedo's rockets fired anyway, and the torpedo dragged the propulsion pod a few feet though the water before it broke away. The missile's course was altered, and it raced upward, missing the carrier's bottom and glancing along the hull.

After skittering along the side of the ship, the wayward torpedo impacted the bottom of one of the carrier's aircraft elevators. On the platform was one F-35 on its way to the flight deck, and, despite standing orders to the contrary, several carts weighed down with ordnance that was being taken up to reload the first wave of Lightnings as they returned from their sorties. In their rush to position weapons on deck, the armament officer decided to use the aircraft elevator as well as the smaller ordnance lifts. The elevator evaporated in the ensuing blast, a fireball racing thousands of feet into the sky. The sleek aircraft, its fuel and guns, as well as the cluster, smart and tank-busting ordnance caught in the blast added their combined energy to the event. The elevator was halfway up when it was hit. As a result, the explosion scoured much of the Bush's flight deck, knocking the Hawkeye from the catapult halfway along its launch. The aircraft broke up as it was thrust from its trajectory at right angles.

The F-35s waiting in line behind blew away like toys swept from a table by a petulant child. Worse, below the flight deck, the fireball hurtled into and through the hangar deck, immolating crewmen who laboured to arm and ready for combat the ship's remaining fighters. From every opening shots multicoloured flames, so that the carrier looked to the nearby escorts like one of those little red schoolhouses children have been igniting on the Fourth of July for decades.

Five more torpedoes ripped into the blazing carcass of the Bush over the next few minutes as she started to list to starboard and slowed in the water. The crew of the Chosin stood frozen in disbelief as watched the destruction of the huge ship now barely a mile from them. Suddenly the bow of their own ship rose almost ten feet into the air, as if they had just hit a huge North Atlantic wave. Falling back to the ocean's surface, the bow split open, and water crashed in.

The Chosin looked like a submarine performing an emergency dive as she sliced towards the depths. Her propellers were still whirling at flank speed as they disappeared under the waves. Two more torpedoes slammed into the submerged ship, breaking her corpse into small pieces that skittered back and forth and spread across a mile of sea bottom.

Admiral Gibson lay bleeding from dozens of shrapnel wounds on the floor of the Bush's flag bridge. Through numbness and shock, he felt the sting of salt water as it washed across the stump at the end of his left arm and then rose to cover him. The Bush had rolled over and vanished, leaving only burning aviation fuel and scattered debris as her memorial. Less than eight minutes after Yang's torpedo had blown a hole in her bottom, she was gone from sight. She'd agonized on the surface a full two minutes longer than the Ticonderoga-class USS Chosin.

Despite the carrier's mortal wounds, her reactors, as programmed, had shut down and sealed themselves during the emergency and now lay submerged in the twisted wreckage, intact and issuing only tiny amounts of radioactivity. They were about the only part of the ship that had lived up to their designers' expectations.

The remaining carrier escorts, the three missile destroyers and a handful of anti-submarine destroyers had no time to mourn the carrier's passing. They had their hands full trying to avoid a menace they did not understand. With the Bush and the Chosin out of the way, the tiny brains in the remaining sixteen torpedoes that still cruised the East China Sea reviewed their target lists, listened for new acoustic signatures and set off to stalk new prey.

By the time they were finished, only two anti-submarine warfare destroyers and one missile destroyer survived. All three had been well north of the Bush, at the outer limits of the torpedoes' range, when they were detected. The three ships were now racing at flank speed for the safety of Okinawa. They'd eluded their pursuers, which one by one slowed from sixty knots as they depleted their electrical power and then, unable to continue their pursuit, detonated their warheads to ensure that not one would fall into enemy hands.

The only American vessels to have escaped unscathed and unstalked were the two hunter-killer submarines. The Chinese torpedoes had blithely ignored both. The subs were not part of their programming.

October 1.
President's office, emergency underground complex, the White House.

"Henry, I wouldn't admit this to another living soul, and don't you ever breathe a word of it but I am at my wits' end. I feel like a checker player in the middle of a grand masters chess tournament."

"Mr. President," replied Woeburn, "it's natural to get down about this. Who the hell could have foreseen this shit storm? But sir, you have it in you to stand and react decisively. If you don't, sir, the country risks losing everything it's stood for and achieved over the last hundred years."

The president glowered at Woeburn and snarled, "Henry, I didn't bring you in here to mouth rousing platitudes. I want you to do your fucking job and offer me some advice I can take into the Situation Room in half an hour."

The president's rebuke was interrupted by a knock on the door.

"Come in," the president barked, his irritation evident.

Dan Blomstrum walked in, nodded at Woeburn and said, "Sir, we have a grave situation in the East China Sea."

"What now?" snapped the president.

"Sir, the carrier Bush has gone down together with all but one hundred and thirteen of her crew. The Aegis cruiser Chosin was lost as well, as were several other escort ships in the strike force."

"Oh my God," the president said, leaning back into his chair. "How?"

"We don't know yet, sir. They think it was a massive attack by Chinese submarines, but that is unconfirmed. There were no reports of aerial activity, and they were not attacked by silkworms or any other anti-shipping missile system. Reports are hazy. The only ships that survived were too far away to receive reliable intelligence."

"How many men have we lost?" asked the president quietly.

"The survivors from the Bush are in radio contact from their lifeboats, but we are having trouble picking them up because we can't risk a search and rescue ship. Air refuellable Sea Stallion's are on their way from Okinawa but won't arrive on the scene for a while. It is unconfirmed a this time, but if those one hundred and thirteen are the only survivors, then we've lost over six thousand on the Bush, including Admiral Gibson and his flag staff.

"Over half of the Bush's aircraft were airborne at the time of the attack, so at least those crews are safe. We have no reported losses of aircraft due to enemy action. Most are on their way to Okinawa, and we've scrambled aerial tankers to help them get there."

"What about the other ships in the group? Their crews?"

"There are no reports of survivors from the Chosin. The AWACS said one minute she was there, the next she was gone. We're receiving scattered reports of survivors from some of the other destroyers. Crew lifeboats are equipped with satellite phones and locator beacons, so if there are men out there, we'll find them."

"Son of a bitch," said the president to himself. Then his eyes narrowed, and his voice grew cold.

"Dan, tell Irving to sink those fucking ships in the Gulf and wipe that base off the face of the earth. Inform the Chinese that if they do not cease all hostile actions against Taiwan immediately, they will face dire and perhaps fatal consequences."

"Yes, sir," replied Blomstrum. "One question. How are we going to make good on that threat, short of going nuclear?"

"We'll discuss that in the Situation Room in half an hour. You two get the staff ready."

"Yes, sir."

"And Dan," said the president as Blomstrum and Woeburn hustled out of the office, "we will not rule out the use of nukes."

October 1.
Geneva.

"Son of a bitch, we just missed him," Derek cursed, cradling the hotel room phone on his shoulder as he made a grab for stationary and a pen. The pen wouldn't write, and he ground it into the pad in his frustration.

Catherine tossed him another from the coffee table.

He took down the names of the doorman who'd reported al-Munajjid's whereabouts and the hotel he'd been staying in. Thanking the embassy staffer who'd phoned them with the information, he put the phone down and grabbed his jacket. "Come on, we have a lead, but the bastard's left the hotel he was in. The doorman saw him checking out this morning and he took down the plate number of his car. The station staff may be able to get an ID and address from the plate number."

Half an hour later, they stood talking to the doorman at al-Munajjid's hotel. He explained to them that the message about the hit-and-run driver must have originated with the night shift, as he did not know a thing about it. Derek asked where the night doorman might be found. He was advised to speak to the front desk.

The front desk clerk would not give them the address but did phone the doorman, who, groggy from being awoken but anxious to get a reward, agreed to speak to Derek and gave him his street number. They took a taxi to a rundown block of row houses that, like lower-income areas the world over, was rife with trash and graffiti. The graffiti was almost identical to what Derek was familiar with in LA, and it was scrawled over every flat surface — a sad testimony to America's cultural influence in the world.

Walking up a short path bordered by overgrown weeds, Derek knocked on the door. Catherine stood behind him a couple of feet, and the taxi driver waited on the curb, unconcerned and happy that the meter was still ticking over while he sat and read the paper.

The door opened, and the doorman peered out, first at Derek and then Catherine. He was dressed in a string T-shirt and dirty track pants that may have been light blue at one time but were now stained and soiled to a blotchy grey. On seeing Catherine, he grunted unconsciously and straightened. He stood in the door, blocking Derek's view of the hallway behind him, but judging by the smell that issued from it of stale cabbage and body odour, Derek was just as happy to chat on the stoop.

"Hello, I'm Derek James. I was the one who spoke to you from the hotel."

"How are you Mr. James? How can I help?" asked the doorman in lightly accented and perfect English.

"Well, this is my sister, and she's the owner of the Range Rover that asshole clobbered. She's pretty upset about it. She's only had the truck a few days, and we would really like to find the guy who smashed into it."

"I was informed by the two men who came by this morning that there was a reward."

"Yes, there is, depending on the information we get." Derek pulled an envelope from his jacket and opened it, revealing mixed bills amounting to two hundred euros.

The doorman's eyes lit up. "Just a minute," he said, disappearing back into the hall and closing the door.

Derek turned to Catherine and shrugged.

A moment later, the door reopened and the doorman stuck a piece of paper out. "Here. It's the plate number of the Mercedes limousine. It was a local service, I think. The driver looked familiar. There were two big guys in a black Mercedes SUV following. I took down both licence numbers."

"That's great," said Derek, handing the man the envelope.

The doorman snatched it, balling it up in his greasy hand, and started to withdraw into the house. He hesitated as Derek turned to walk back to the cab. "So, tell me. You two coming here and the other two asking questions…" he paused and continued, "And a reward? Who is that fellow, anyway?"

Derek turned, smiled and said, "He's just a very poor driver who hit the wrong person's car."

The doorman smirked and closed the door.

An hour later Derek had tracked down the limo service and was speaking on the phone to a bubbly receptionist whose accent and rapid speech made understanding what she said rather difficult. Derek had to ask her to repeat herself after every sentence. He'd endured the whole limousine service sales pitch before he was able to ask about a particular Mercedes limousine he'd like to rent that he'd seen at a hotel.

She told him it was unavailable but they had another nearly identical car, except it was black. Derek thanked her but said he'd much prefer the lighter-coloured car, for as long as two weeks. She replied that she could talk to her boss and ask, but as far as she knew, that car was in Berne with a good client and would not be back for a few days. Sensing that no more information was forthcoming, he thanked her, promising to phone in a few days, and hung up with sigh of relief.

"He's in Berne," said Derek happily.

"Right, then. We'll get him there. I'll tell the station chief and get us a car," said Catherine.

October 1.
Situation Room, the White House.

"All right, gentlemen, we have multiple and very, very grave problems now, and I want solid well-thought-out ideas for solving them. It's time to earn your pay," said the president as he took his seat. "Mr. Blomstrum, would you review them for me, and then I want ideas…from all of you!"

"You gentlemen know about the loss of the Bush and her escorts," Blomstrum began. "Now the president and I would like to know how the Chinese managed to sink the most powerful naval force in history in just under half an hour, and we need a suitable response to that loss!"

Blomstrum slowly scanned the table of gathered military and intelligence community heads. "Next, the invasion of Taiwan by the mainland Chinese. The Taiwanese are screaming for help. We need ideas on how to accomplish that.

"The Saudis — as if we didn't have enough on our plate — have taken this opportunity to have a coup. I know they're far from our closest friends, but on paper the government of Saudi Arabia is still our ally. Do we attempt to prop up the royal family or throw the chaff to the wind and see were it lands?

"Our situation at home is critical and ongoing. Last, but not least, our allies are all very sympathetic but, in almost all cases, completely unwilling to give us anything but lip service. Even the British prime minister told our secretary of state that although personally he'd like to support us militarily, the people of Britain feel we are getting payback — comeuppence was his word for it — for a lot of our foreign policy and for the military incursions of the last few years. He maintains it'd be political suicide to jump in, and he's told us he has no intention of doing that with elections coming up next spring.

"These are the problems we need to solve," finished Blomstrum. "Admiral Irving, your take?"

Irving leaned forward, shoulders hunched and his palms flat on the table as if about to stand, then he straightened and began. "We are almost sure the Chinese used submarines, but we have no idea how or what kind. Their nuclear boats are just not quiet enough to take us by surprise, and the diesel electrics don't have the ability to stay under long enough to sneak in, lay in wait and then attack. This attack had to be carefully orchestrated, and the area the Bush was in had been under intense surveillance for days. Maybe one diesel boat could have snuck in, but one boat could not sink the Bush. This loss has almost completely defanged our force extension in the region of Taiwan. The 18th combat wing, based at Kadena, is one of our largest combat air wings, but it doesn't have the personnel to maintain twenty-four strike operations for any length of time as well as sustaining a credible defence.

"On top of that, the Japanese have made it absolutely clear that they do not want operations against the Chinese run out of Kadena. Their fear, and a quite legitimate one, is that we'll invite retaliation from the Chinese, which could result in air strikes on Okinawa or, even worse, an invasion by Chinese ground forces. If the Chinese got a foothold on Okinawa, the Japanese doubt they could politely be asked to leave when it was all over. In short, gentlemen, while we may be able to shake our fists at the Chinese right now, the loss of the Bush and the vulnerability of Okinawa to attack mean that's about all we can do in the region."

"What about the Persian Gulf?" asked the president.

"That, Mr. President, is another story. We still have one carrier group there and one in the Med, and they're both on high alert. We are" — Irving looked at his watch — "less than forty minutes away from sinking every single ship and destroying every asset the Chinese have in the Gulf. B-1B and B-2 bombers are already en route to the Chinese facility on Gwadar. We'll inform the Pakistani government in Karachi about the attack precisely five minutes before the first bombs drop. Our hunter-killer subs are locked and loaded and have located almost all of the Chinese submarines operating in the region. They're already in the process of eradicating those submarines.

"We think we're only missing the location of one, and we really don't know if it's still in the Gulf or has headed back to China. Our subs' skippers should have finished off the Chinese submarine fleet at approximately the same time the first bombs fall on Gwadar. Carrier-based aircraft along with U.S. Air Force planes stationed in the Emirates will then mop up the Chinese surface ships with the exception of two that are currently tied up at port in Iran. However, those will not be allowed to leave Iranian waters intact.

"While we have so far maintained a total news blackout on the loss of the Bush at home, we've told the crews of the carrier strike force in the Gulf. My guess is that to a man they will want revenge."

"Good. Now we can give those sons of bitches what's coming to them," said U.S. Air Force general Mike Olden.

"Small consolation for the loss of the Bush strike force and her men," replied Irving.

"Bob, what about the Saudi coup?" the president asked CIA director Dutton. "I know it's just started, but do you have any solid information on what the hell is going on?"

"Sir," he said, "armed insurgents backed by elements of the Saudi armed forces have taken several small cities and towns at this point. We think they control about a third of Riyadh as well, but there's no clear intelligence. It's pretty sketchy right now. The king and his closest family members have fled and are en route to their palace in Spain. The king's brother and the defence minister, a first cousin, have remained in Saudi and are coordinating loyalist military units fighting the insurrection.

"From our perspective, what is most disturbing are reports that Saudi military units have crossed the Saudi-Iraq border and appear to be heading toward Baghdad. It's a rather ragtag push and doesn't appear to be well supported or organized, but it could still be more than the Iraqi military can handle."

"When the hell did that happen?" asked the president.

"Shortly after the coup started, sir."

"Does this incursion pose any threat to our ground forces in Iraq?" asked Dan Blomstrum.

"Not at this time, but if they alter course, the southern oil fields may be at risk."

"Do we have enough assets to stop them if they attack our no-go zones?" asked the president.

"I think so, sir, but we have a feeling this may be spurred more by rival religious groups than by any attempt to secure oil pipelines or wellheads. Air Force and U.S. Navy aircraft can offer any support our ground forces need, but they will be a little busy the next few hours finishing off the Chinese."

"And do you think, Admiral, that we should support the Iraqi government?"

"Sir, it's a squabble between two of our supposed allies who both really hate our guts. I think that as long as the Saudi forces don't make an end run for the oil fields, we should just keep our noses out of it."

"Duly noted, Admiral Irving, and I have to say I agree." The president continued, "Gentlemen, I am trying to get in contact with the Chinese premier, but so far he is avoiding my calls. The message I want to relay to him is that if the Chinese do not stand down on Taiwan, he risks going to war with the United States — total war. I am not talking about a limited war, gentlemen. I am talking about all-out war.

"So far the Chinese have been evasive and uncommunicative. I'm hoping that sinking their fleet in the Persian Gulf and destroying their base in Pakistan will bring them to their senses, but if they still refuse to talk, then I need a bigger stick. Admiral Irving, General Olden, I would like to discuss the possibility of a limited nuclear strike against appropriate Chinese military targets."

The room went quiet, every man struggling with what the president had just said.

"Sir, they have boomers. They can fight back," said Irving, referring to the Chinese nuclear missile submarines.

"I know that," snapped the president. "You will have to nullify them and any threat they offer to the U.S. mainland. I have read in the reports. Admiral, that Naval Intelligence knows how many are within striking distance of the States and their approximate positions. Eliminate them."

"Mr. President, we think we know to within a half mile where they are, and when and if they move, SOSUS can pinpoint them. But we'll have to account for drift on their last known positions. They've been sitting very quietly for the last few days."

"So, can you kill them?"

"We can, sir, but if we miss one or more, and they get the opportunity to fire, we won't have a lot of time. Most of their ballistic missiles have a flight time from their present positions of less than fifteen minutes. If just one sub survives, we could find ourselves looking down the barrel of sixteen ballistic missiles, each with a range of five thousand miles." Irving sat back thinking about the problems associated with killing the boomers.

"What about nuclear-tipped torpedoes, Admiral?"

"That would eliminate the guesswork, Mr. President. A nuke would get them even if we missed by more than a mile."

"Do you have any attack subs carrying nukes right now?" asked Blomstrum.

"No, sir. We could equip a couple that are in port, but deploying them would take too long, and we wouldn't be able to attack more than a couple of the boomers. I recommend launching the nuclear torpedoes from the air, sir. We can have Super Hornets and P3 Orion maritime patrol aircraft that could be armed with nuclear torpedoes and in the air within eight hours."

"Admiral, arm those aircraft, and put them on standby."

"Yes, sir."

"So that leaves us with the war at home. Director Archer?" The president looked at Peter Archer.

The FBI Director's voice trembled a little bit. The talk about releasing nuclear weapons, discussed in what he took to be an almost blasé fashion by the men in the room, had unnerved him. He was, at the core of his being, just a policeman, and he was psychologically unprepared for the decisions he'd just heard these men making.

"Sir, we have to date captured and killed over two hundred terrorists. I would say that we are winning, but we still have no idea how many terrorists may still be in the country. We've managed to reduce the number of attacks by more than seventy percent, but we don't know if this is because we've eliminated most of them or if they're just lying low. We've captured a huge stockpile of weapons from pre-positioned containers as well as the men whose job it was to distribute them. This has reduced the severity of the attacks that are still taking place.

"We think that most of the remaining terrorist cells have to forage for weapons, and with tight controls on both guns and explosive materials nationwide, getting effective offensive weapons is getting increasingly harder. I'm hoping we won't see any more massive attacks. We may have to live with roadside bombings and assassinations for some time to come, but over the course of the next few months or a couple of years, maybe, we should be able to get almost all of them."

"A couple of years? Fuck a couple of years, Director Archer," screamed the president. "We need these assholes cleaned up in the next few weeks! For crying out loud, I've given you every single fucking tool you've asked for to fight these pricks, and you have the fucking nerve to tell me you could still be a couple of years away from getting them? Americans can't survive a couple of years of martial law while you blunder around. Get the fuck out of my sight!"

Archer, his mouth hanging open in shock, sat absolutely still for a moment and then began to organize his papers and put them in his briefcase. Everyone around the table held his breath.

"Get the fuck out!" The president repeated this slowly and vehemently, his eyes narrowed.

Archer rose and stumbled from the room. The president sat still, seething, waiting for his rage to subside before he continued the meeting.

CHAPTER 23

October 2.
Gulf of Oman.

Rear Admiral Hu Xiaofeng lay in the cot in the small cabin behind his destroyer's bridge, trying to grab a few minutes of sleep. His day had been full of dispatches, alerts and warnings, byproducts of the tensions the invasion of Taiwan had created even this far from the battle theatre. He had an epiphany once the invasion was reported, and for the first time, his mission to the Gulf and his often-puzzling orders became clear. He'd been the court jester, occupying the emperor's attention while the assassins crept up from behind.

His radar men had been fully occupied with U.S. naval aircraft passing in close proximity. Several had overflown with weapons hot, his threat displays recording the weapons' lock-on. The stress of literally keeping his finger on the firing button all day had gotten the best of him, and he was exhausted, yet his system, still flooded with adrenalin, would not let him sleep.

He heard a commotion up the short corridor to the bridge and levered himself from the cot, cursing as he tipped his dinner plate and leftovers from a small bedside table in the process of jumping up and grabbing his uniform jacket. He hurried onto the bridge into a maelstrom. Radar was painting two more American fighters inbound. Its sensors had detected active weapons radars.

Hu was wondering when the Americans would tire of this game when suddenly the radar operator yelled that weapons had been released. The two Super Hornets had unleashed their Harpoon anti-shipping missiles. Two more Hornets appeared on screen, and the operator yelled that two more Harpoons were inbound, their target perhaps the smaller Shenzen missile destroyer that accompanied his larger Sovremenny-class destroyer.

Hu yelled the order to open fire, his finger finally pushing the button it had hovered over for so long. The Shenzen destroyer four hundred yards to port also lit, a fraction faster on the draw than Hu's Sovremenny, as it fired anti-aircraft missiles and all its anti-missile defences sprang into action. The decks of Hu's destroyer lit then, the smoke from repeated missile launches — illuminated by the rockets' bright tails — creating odd pulsing orbs of fire in the night.

The communications system was crackling with activity. He realized that his fleet was dying. He could hear them, their radio men screaming as other ships near and far were hit with missile after missile. Suddenly, his destroyer's close-in missile defence system, Chinese-made chain guns that were a loose copy of the American Phalanx defensive system, burst into life. Their muzzle blasts lit up the sides of the destroyer. The sound was like tearing fabric.

Hu knew his time was up. The close-in system was his beautiful ship's funeral dirge. The first Harpoon, travelling at over six hundred miles per hour, slammed into the bow. Hu caught a glimpse of it disappearing under the ship, and for a moment frozen in time, he thought it might have missed. Then he saw the blast issue from the other side of his ship, a tumbling ball of flame, smoke, steel shards and debris. He never saw the missile that followed it and struck the destroyer not ten feet below his feet. He barely had time to realize he was dead before he too was part of a mushrooming ball of steel shards and debris.

A half hour later, the Sovremenny-class destroyer, pride of the Chinese fleet, was a raging inferno floating listlessly across the waters of the Gulf of Oman, her crew dead or dying in the flaming oil that rode on the ocean's surface. There was no trace of the Shenzen-destroyer, which had disappeared in a spectacular blast when one of the Harpoons found her magazines. An hour after the attack began, the Chinese navy both above and below the waters in and around the Gulf was gone. A few twisted and burning wrecks still defied the pull of the depths, and the deepwater port of Gwadar sat, a twisted and smoking pile of rubble, damaged beyond repair by the attentions of the U.S. Air Force.

October 2.
President's office, emergency underground complex, the White House.

The President sat in the small functional office, his desk surrounded by five chairs. In them sat Dan Blomstrum, Admiral Irving, Secretary of State Warren Clyde, NSA director Allan Dowd and Henry Woeburn. Behind the five men sat three more, all expert Chinese translators and authorities on Chinese culture. They were schooled not only in the languages of China but also in the pauses and rhythm of the speaker, which could on occasion be even more telling than the words spoken.

The phone on the president's desk rang, and he punched the speaker phone button. "Mr. President, the Chinese premier is on the line. Should I connect you now?" asked the chief White House operator.

"Yes, Shirley. Thank you," replied the president. "Mr. Premier," he began. "I am very glad that you've seen fit to answer my call after being indisposed for so long."

The reply was in the singsong of the Hakka language. The premier was a noted linguist, fluent in Cantonese, Mandarin and Hakka. That he chose Hakka instead of the official language, Mandarin, was in line with the odd Chinese recalcitrance that had coloured their relations with the United States leading up to and after the invasion of Taiwan. The premier's choice further irked the president because the man shouldn't need translators; he was fluent in English.

The translation followed. "I am glad as well, and I am sorry for the indisposition that has prevented me from speaking to you."

"I'm sure you are, sir, but my guess is that you've been pretty busy planning and executing the invasion of Taiwan as well as ambushing an American fleet on the high seas, an act, I may say, that violates international law better."

The singsong was again overlaid by the translator's voice. "Mr. President, no laws were broken. Our forces dealt with a pirate fleet that was attacking lawful elements of the People's Liberation Army in pursuit of re-establishing order in a rogue province of the People's Republic."

"Premier Lichang," replied the president, "I don't want to hear this crap, nor am I in any mood to play along with your bullshit. As you are probably already aware, we have dealt with your forces in the Gulf of Oman and the Persian Gulf as well as your deepwater base in Pakistan, and we haven't finished with you. The United States has no intention of allowing the invasion of Taiwan to continue. A refusal to halt your military adventurism in the Republic of China and immediately withdraw your forces from the island will result in severe consequences. We also expect payment of reparations for damages caused by your blatant and unlawful invasion, and the government of the United States demands reparations for the sinking of the George W. H. Bush and her fleet."

"Mr. President, we have no idea what you could possibly mean by severe consequences, as you have no forces of any consequence in the region. Our police action in Taiwan is a long-overdue internal matter, and your interference will not be tolerated."

"Mr. Premier, we have more than enough power to deal with the People's Republic."

"I certainly hope, Mr. President, that you are not hinting at the use nuclear weapons. I am sure you are aware that we have ballistic missiles aimed at and capable of hitting every major American military target and civilian population centre. The People's Republic will forgive you the sinking of its eastern fleet and the destruction of its base, a trade for your task force, if it makes you feel better, but we will not allow any further meddling in our affairs, and you will find that our resolve in this matter is unshakeable. I believe we have a stalemate — what you used to call mutually assured destruction — the same stalemate you shared with the Soviet Union.

"The one difference is, Mr. President, that the United States was not fighting a war on its own soil when it was facing the Soviet Union, and it had allies as well. Mr. President, I believe that you no longer have the ability to affect our affairs, nor do you have any friends or allies left who will support you in your meddling. I think you will also find that my nation is quite a bit more popular around the world than yours, and many of your allies have special financial and trade relations with us that I am sure that they would not want to jeopardize. Perhaps, Mr. President, if you had read Sun Tzu's Arts of War, you would be in a better position to make good on your threats. That is all I have to say." The translator finished well after the line went dead.

The president, realizing he'd just been hung up on, sat open mouthed.

"Son of a bitch," spat Irving.

"Mr. President," said the chief translator, "I think he gave away something important."

"What's that?"

"His reference to the terrorist attacks on the United States seemed self-satisfied, as if he was gloating, and his last comments about the Arts of War were delivered in the same tone. Arts of War advocates the defeat of an enemy by subterfuge instead of direct military action. It also promotes fighting a war by proxy. Do you agree?" he asked the other two interpreters.

They nodded.

Allan Dowd spoke up next. "I've always been pretty sure the Chinese had something to do with the attacks, considering how quickly they took advantage and what they have gained. But most especially in light of the premier's attitude, I am dammed sure they are behind it, or at the very least privy to how and when it was going to happen. It all reads like a playbook: the attacks here, the dumping of our debt, the weird aggressive-passive behaviour in the Gulf and, finally, the invasion. Hell, for all we know they could even be behind the coup in Saudi Arabia. The Saudis have trillions of dollars invested in the U.S. Who's to say what the hell will happen if the insurrection is successful."

"Gentleman, give me ten minutes," said the president, "but don't go far."

The men excused themselves and shuffled from the room. A few minutes later, he called all but the translators back into the small office.

"Admiral Irving, get the colonel in here with the football." The football was a specially built briefcase — in effect, a computer — that, when activated by passwords only the president had access to, relayed the release of nuclear weapons from the U.S. atomic arsenal. It was always within a few feet of the president, carried by an officer specially selected from the U.S. military. The admiral opened the door and motioned for the officer to bring the football in.

"Admiral, take out those boomers. Use the nukes," said the president.

"Yes, sir," replied Irving gravely.

The officer with the football held it open for the president, who punched on the keyboard a code copied from a small laminated card that hung from a light chain around the president's neck and hidden under his shirt. He received a new code card every day, spit out randomly from a machine that created it and then spoke to the football and to which only the president of the United States, or his successor should the president be killed, had access.

Every man in the room felt some nausea from the decision that had just been made.

"I want a short list of Chinese military targets, ones small enough to be obliterated by a tactical nuke. I know I'm letting the genie out of the bottle, but it will be a small genie. Hopefully, it will persuade the Chinese that their ambitions have failed, and we are still the power. I want that list within the hour, admiral."

"Mr. President, if you want this package delivered, how would you like it done?"

"What do you mean, admiral?"

"Well, sir, do you want a ballistic launch, cruise missile or bomber?"

"I want the least amount of warning possible. I would like to contact the Chinese premier about five minutes before the strike, but I also want the option of cancelling at that time."

"I'd suggest a B-2 Spirit then, sir," said Irving. "It'll take longer to get there, but they'll never see a stealth bomber coming. It can also be recalled right up to the moment before the drop."

"That sounds right. Let's go with a Spirit, then."

After the president had been left alone, he noticed that his hands were shaking, and he couldn't stop them, not even when he concentrated.

October 2.
Berne, Switzerland.

Derek had butterflies in his stomach. The thought of catching the son of a bitch responsible for Vanessa's death excited him in an unfamiliar way. He supposed it was the primal anticipation of revenge. He and Catherine had made good time and were just entering the outskirts of Berne. John Kopriva, the CIA station chief in Switzerland, had given them the names of the limousine driver and the hotel he was staying in and had advised them that it was a cheap economy hotel and not likely to house their quarry. The driver, however, should know exactly where al-Munajjid was staying.

Derek had seen some sights in the last couple of weeks, but Berne, the capital of Switzerland, was absolutely stunning in its beauty and quaint charm and by far his favourite city so far, at least from what he had seen of it. The limo driver's hotel might have been economical, but there was nothing rundown about it. It was on the eastern outskirts of the city, a good distance from the old centre and the river Aare that meandered around the core, but it was neat and tidy.

Derek spotted the Mercedes limousine as they drove up. The hotel had it parked just to one side of the front entrance. Derek parked behind it and got out. He sauntered past the car, looking inside as if interested in the Mercedes rather that what it might contain. He saw a driver's log on the front seat with the limo company logo on the cover. Satisfied it was the right car, he palmed a small transmitter and gently tucked it under the front wheel arch, its magnet grabbing the metal and holding it there securely.

"Kann ich helfe Ihnen?" asked someone in what sounded to Derek like German.

A young man with a hotel employee pin on his chest was having a smoke outside the front doors. For a moment, Derek thought the employee had seen him placing the locator. Seeing Derek's reaction, the young man switched to English. "Can I help you, sir?"

"No, just looking at this car," replied Derek. "Boy, this is something else. It'd be nice to be able to afford a car like this. Do you know the owner? Man, he's got to have some money, huh?"

"No, this car is for hire. It belongs to an agency in Geneva. You can rent it. If you'd like to speak to the driver, he's staying here. I could get him for you."

Derek realized he hadn't been seen placing the locator. The chap was just being courteous. "No, that's ok, I'm sure I couldn't afford to hire it, and I already have a rental, this Volkswagen — what do they call it here? — a Golf. Boy, that sure is a doozy of a car. Is the guy renting it staying here?"

"No, just the driver stays here. Are you checking in, sir?"

"Well, I wanted to check your room rates."

"I'm sure the front desk would be pleased to answer any questions you have, although I'm not sure we have any vacancies tonight."

"Oh, that's too bad."

"I could suggest the Swiss Manor. It's a small hotel down the hill. If you take this road down four blocks and then turn right, it is a small brown building with a timbered front just three doors along on the left side. You cannot miss it."

"Well, thank you very much," said Derek as the young man butted his cigarette on the rim of a cast iron waste can and headed for the hotel doors. They bade each other good day, and Derek got back into his car, where Catherine waited.

"It's the car, so I guess we just have to do some old-fashioned police work. We'll park up the road, grab a couple of coffees, and wait for the driver to lead us to al-Munajjid."

After they'd parked a ways down the road, and Derek had popped out to get them a couple of coffees, Catherine called the embassy. Her cellphone was equipped to scramble calls to CIA numbers on special secure lines in the various embassies. Her scrambled call could then be transferred to other secure cellphones. She contacted the U.S. embassy in Berne and in moments she was talking to Kopriva, who was still in Geneva.

"Hello, John. It's Catherine. We've found his limousine, and we're sitting on it. Has the strike team landed yet?"

"Yes, they're already in Berne and are just getting sorted out. How do you want to use them?"

"Maybe they could take over here, and then we — wait. Hold on, John."

Derek was walking back to the car from a small café, but she saw him drop the two coffees he was carrying into a garbage container. Jumping in, he said, "We're rolling. The driver just got into the car."

"I see him," said Catherine as the Mercedes nosed out from the front of the hotel.

"John, we're on the road. Alert the team, and get them into transport. If their cells are active, I can give them our location, and they can get on the way."

Three minutes later, Kopriva called back and gave Catherine the Seal team's secure number. The Mercedes proceeded at a leisurely pace. Derek had no trouble staying well back and following it. Less than an hour later, the big limo pulled up in front of La Belle Epoque in the old city. The driver sat inside waiting.

Derek checked his watch and noted that it was about ten minutes to eleven. At five to eleven, a tall, heavy-built man dressed in a conservative, grey pinstriped suit walked out the front doors and looked around carefully. Derek felt the man's gaze as it stopped on their car, which was parked in a no-parking delivery zone across the narrow street, the only place available.

As the man looked at them intently, Catherine, looking annoyed, raised a street map into view and slapped Derek with it as she unfolded it. She slammed it onto the dash in front of the steering wheel and stabbed her finger onto it. Under her breath she said, "He's a pro, probably one of al-Munajjid's bodyguards."

The bodyguard took note of Catherine's performance with the map. She was hoping he would assume they were lost tourists — a man who disdained maps and a wife pissed because of it. His careful examination of the hotel's surroundings continued. Then he opened his cellphone and made a call as he walked back and forth in front of the hotel entrance.

Yuri Gregovich hated the little prick he shepherded around. He didn't care how important the Saudi was, or thought he was. In Gregovich's mind he was just another camel jockey. Al-Munajjid's arrogance and the way he treated his two bodyguards annoyed Gregovich no end, and he fantasized about snapping the Arab's neck and watching his body dance. But Gregovich was willing to put up with the abuse in exchange for the huge paycheques that appeared like clockwork in his bank account. Gregovich and his partner were always on call for the frequent occasions al-Munajjid left the Middle East. In the Middle East, al-Munajjid travelled with a gaggle of Arab bodyguards.

Gregovich knew most of them and considered them undisciplined, loud-mouthed rabble incapable of stopping a well-planned assassination. He'd been Spetznatz, the Soviet Union's version of the American Special Forces. His partner was a Catholic from Northern Ireland who had, despite his religion, made it into and excelled in the British Special Air Service, the vaunted SAS. Gregovich begrudgingly agreed that Sean Flannigan's training was, if anything, even better than his own, and Flannigan was one of the few men Gregovich would trust with his back.

Gregovich had taken note of the couple pulled up across the street. Their presence set off his alarms. The woman, a beautiful redhead, had grabbed a map and made a fuss, but Gregovich was not convinced. While clever, it was too little, too late. He casually took his cellphone and called Flannigan, who was with al-Munajjid and just getting ready to come down. "Sean, I think we might have trouble. I have a couple in a car across the street that I don't like the looks of. Hold him up there for a few minutes until I see what they're doing."

"Roger that," replied Flannigan, slipping into radio parlance.

Gregovich snapped the phone closed, stretched and swung his arms back and forth as if he was bored.

"I think we've been burned," said Catherine.

"Right. We'd better head out, then. Hopefully, he'll see us leave and relax," replied Derek.

"Okay," said Catherine as pantomimed throwing her hands up in disgust and acting pissed.

Derek scowled at her and then screeched the tires as he pulled into traffic. She could be heard calling him an asshole as the car zoomed past the front doors of the hotel.

"How long until the team gets here?" asked Derek.

"I'll find out and warn them about the bodyguard," answered Catherine. She had a brief conversation on her cell, ended the call and said, "First two are five minutes out in a small car. They should arrive in time. The rest of the team is in a van five minutes behind them."

Gregovich saw the couple leave and thought for a moment he was being paranoid. But that was what he was paid for. He studied the area carefully for any other suspicious-looking individuals and walked away from the hotel front to gaze up at its windows and see if anyone was spying on them from above. Everything looked innocent enough, but just in case, he was going to bolt.

Fifteen minutes later, al-Munajjid was out a side service door with Flannigan, into the limousine, which had pulled around, and off to a rendezvous. Gregovich took the Mercedes SUV's keys from the valet and waited ten minutes to see whether al-Munajjid's departure caused any ripples. Everything looked normal. He loaded the bags the other two had abandoned into the back of the Mercedes and drove off, on his way to the rendezvous, before dumping the limousine and heading on to al-Munajjid's Swiss bolthole, a safe house in the mountains to the east of the city.

He was unaware that the limousine now had a transponder on it, and so did one of the bags, placed there by a Seal team member in the elevator as they'd been brought to the lobby by a bellboy. He was not the only one who could use entrances and exits other than the front doors. If he'd been in less of a hurry, he might have noticed the tiny rip in the bottom of the Louis Vuitton bag, a bag the Seal had correctly assumed would not belong to a bodyguard. Now, even if the Mercedes limo was abandoned, chances were good the bag would stay with al-Munajjid. The noose was drawing tighter.

Now all Derek and Catherine needed was a quiet spot, free from police and official Swiss interference, to take their quarry. Neither gave a damn about the tenets of Swiss neutrality. Neither did the president of the United States, who at this moment had his hands full with other, more pressing issues.

October 2.
The Xia, 350 miles off San Diego.

The Xia was the only boat in her class and had the distinction of being the oldest Chinese ballistic missile submarine. While she had teething problems originally — a fact purposely disseminated to Western intelligence — by the early years of the new millennium, she'd become an efficient and deadly machine. But her reputation as a useless prototype — of never having met operational status nor left Chinese waters — remained intact.

Three weeks earlier, satellites had seen her enter the underground sub pens at Jianggezhuang, but they had not seen her leave a few hours later. Now she was the closest Chinese sub to the American heartland. Her position was not because her JL-2 ballistic missiles couldn't reach America from much farther out, but because from there her missiles would reach Denver and targets farther west quickly. The Chinese had reasoned that if the Americans had a viable anti-missile system they were ignorant of, the sub's proximity to the coast might allow penetration and a successful attack before the Americans could respond. They were hedging their bets. All her missiles were targeted at American nuclear installations and air bases housing nuclear-capable bombers.

Her larger and newer cousins, the Type 94 Jin-class boats were much farther out, their targeting concentrated on U.S. cities. The Xia had one other advantage, one her commander and the chiefs of the Chinese navy knew nothing about. She did not share the 94s' acoustic flaw, a noise the United States had long since identified and its SOSUS system was able to hear and track. The Americans were unaware of the Xia's presence.

At precisely eighteen hundred hours, the 92's sonarmen, who were hunched over their waterfall displays, heard a succession of ear-shattering blasts, one after the other in a symphony of white noise that lasted almost four minutes. All over the Pacific Ocean, cetaceans ranging from blue whales to porpoises were struck deaf or stunned by the magnitude of the noise. Many were killed instantly when their sensitive hearing organs burst. Others, farther away, were not so fortunate. Deaf and unable to echolocate to find food or even other members of their pods, they were condemned instead to a lingering death.

In that four-minute wave of raw energy, China lost all but one of her ballistic missile fleet. Nine boats ceased to exist with little or no warning, and plumes of vaporized radioactive water and seabed rose into the sky to mark their passing. In the Xia, it took commander a moment to understand what he was hearing. His orders were clear. In the event that he detected any nuclear detonation or was hunted or otherwise compromised, he was to launch.

"Planesman, take us up to launch depth," he ordered. He followed with the commands that would prepare and unleash his flock.

October 2.
USS Seawolf, 340 miles off San Diego.

"Skipper," a sonarman yelled, "I've got a target. It sounds like tubes being flooded, big tubes. We're picking it up on our waterfall, and SOSUS confirms."

"Where?" snapped Commander Brent Reid, skipper of the Seawolf.

The Seawolf was one of a class of hugely expensive attack submarines destined to replace the Los Angeles–class boats. The program was cancelled due to budgetary cutbacks at just three boats. The nine additional Seawolf-class submarines planned were replaced by much less expensive Virginia-class attack boats. The decision had nothing to do with the Seawolf's competence. She and her two sisters were still the most deadly underwater hunter-killers in the world.

"Seventeen thousand yards, sir, bearing two six zero."

Hearing the distance, Reid's concern that his boat was the target of an unseen hunter was diminished, but the flooding of large tubes could portend something even more ominous. Reid knew that time was of the essence and that at a range of over ten miles, they could not possibly attack the enemy with conventional Mark 48 torpedoes. He needed something faster, especially if the enemy sub was preparing a missile launch.

The whole sub's crew was aware that something huge was going on. They'd heard it through the hull as well as on their passive detection equipment. They'd submerged after receiving a flash message from Pacific Fleet headquarters in Hawaii and were at full battle stations. Those orders, read to them by Reid on their receipt, had been simple. They were to sink any and all submarines they encountered in their patrol area. Reid had never believed he would have the opportunity to follow his orders and engage an enemy. Lady Luck was indeed smiling on them when, with an entire ocean to navigate, a bogey turned up right in his little patch.

"Crap, we'd better take her out before she fires. Weapons, prepare to fire both T-lams."

"Preparing T-lams, sir."

The weapons officer relayed the order to the torpedo room. Two of the Seawolf's eight 30-inch torpedo tubes contained these, the newest U.S. Navy cruise missile, the T-lam E. It was a derivative of the land-skimming sub-launched Tomahawk cruise missiles used against land targets, but the E had a different and more sophisticated targeting ability. It was designed to fire from a torpedo tube, take to the air and then re-enter the water near its intended target.

To accomplish this feat, the approximate range and bearing was fed from the sub's fire-control computer to the T-Lam's on-board computer. These coordinates got the missile close enough to the target for its magnetometers and infrared systems to pinpoint a splashdown point near its quarry. Then, with its powerful sonar blasting, it pinpointed the enemy and its powerful secondary submersible propulsion system kicked in, driving it towards its prey. Once close to its target, proximity sensors would detonate the enormously powerful chemical warhead, designed to cave in any submarine hull no matter how tough.

"T-lam ready to fire, sir," yelled the weapons officer, excitement apparent in his voice. This was no exercise, and the precision and energy of the crew's responses showed it.

"Fire," Reid ordered.

"Firing, sir!" The weapons officer punched two buttons in quick succession. The whole boat reverberated to the thump of the compressed gas driving the two missiles from their nests. The sounds of their ignition and of their rise into the air were clear and met with silence by the crew, who during practice firings had always cheered as the missiles went up. Like a scene from a 1950s sub flick, every face in the boat was pointed upward as the men imagined what was occurring over their heads.

October 2.
The Xia, 350 miles off San Diego.

"Commander, we've detected a missile launch."

The Xia's commander, in the middle of monitoring the ballistic missiles' launch regime, took a moment to change gears. "Is it one of ours?" he asked.

"No, sir, it's not a friendly," replied the sonarman, panic colouring his voice.

"Distance?"

"Perhaps sixteen or seventeen thousand yards, sir. I'm not sure, but I heard two launches."

"Missile control, are we ready to fire?" asked the Commander.

"Almost, sir. The last two missiles are finishing their diagnostics."

"Open doors, and ripple fire as soon as all twelve lights are green."

There were still two yellow lights on the missile control panel. One winked to green, and after what seemed an impossible length of time, the final missile indicator flashed green. All twelve birds were ready to go.

The missile man looked once again at the commander, despite his orders to fire. The commander, understanding the man's hesitation, nodded. The missile control operator cleared a clear acrylic button guard away from a large oval button and, taking a deep breath, stabbed it.

Nothing happened for a moment, and then the missile silo door flew open with a reverberating clang, and huge volumes of roaring gas shook the boat from one end to the other as the first missile popped from its tube in a cloud of compressed nitrogen. With the second roar came another, louder sound. It was the first missile igniting a few feet above the sub's submerged decks as it broached the ocean's surface, shook as if to shed the water that fountained around it and exploded skywards.

The second missile's firing masked the plop and splash of the first T-Lam arriving from the Seawolf. As the number three missile ejected from the Xia's tube, the first T-lam detected its mass and ignited less than four feet from the missile's side as it cleared the subs deck. The combined explosions of the U.S. warhead and the stricken Chinese missile's fuel load slammed into the Xia hovering fifteen feet below and spun her onto her side.

The crew was thrown against the unyielding, control-encrusted walls of their compartments. Many were badly injured and lay screaming in shock and surprise as the salt water from scores of small ruptures washed over them. The commotion did not last long. The second T-Lam E exploded against the Xia's side just aft of the conning tower. As the fourth missile popped from its tube, the Xia broke in half. The missile spiralled lazily away from the broken submarine, heading towards the sea bottom far below, as the air and gases freed from the broken hull whooshed up and away. Soon, relieved of their buoyancy, the two halves of the Xia followed the missile to the bottom, dragging her crew and the rest of her deadly load into the deeps with her.

October 2.
The Seawolf, 310 miles off San Diego.

"Sir, she's breaking up. We got her," yelled the Seawolf's sonarman"

The men in the control room cheered, and even Reid smiled for a fleeting second before his features clouded and the room was silenced by the sonarman's next words.

"Sir, she got two away," he said.

CHAPTER 24

October 2.
Home of Bandar id bin Abdul Aziz, Rhiyadh.

Abdullah Alluwaijri knocked with the butt of his 9-mm Browning automatic on the massive iron gate that guarded Aziz's home compound. The barrel of the gun was still warm, and Alluwaijri took some pleasure from the fact that the first person the gun killed was the self-important al-Tuwaijri, his boss in the Justice Department and a piece of camel dung who had always put personal gain before his duty to Islam and country. Alluwaijri had taken no pleasure from subsequent killing during the takeover of the Ministry of Justice buildings but was satisfied that their plans had gone like clockwork.

That was until royalist guard units had burst from the building's underground parking lot, sweeping all the unsuspecting revolutionaries from their conquest. Alluwaijri was one of the few to escape, and he'd made a beeline to Aziz's headquarters to report on the incident and to get information on what was happening in the rest of Saudi Arabia.

He was worried. The men who had cleared his forces out of the ministry building came from nowhere, as if they'd waited in ambush. He'd had reports of similar things happening in other places in the city before his cellphone went dead. His walkie-talkie, a fallback he and the other insurgents carried, were either defective or the frequency had been jammed. He had a sinking feeling that the exultation of the rebellion's first hours might be short-lived.

An aggressive voice challenged him, calling from above, and he looked up to see a Bedouin perched on top of the wall, his face wrapped in a black ghutra so that only his eyes were visible.

Alluwaijri gave his name and the password that identified him as friendly, a co-conspirator. The gate creaked open to reveal at least a dozen more hardened desert nomads in the compound, their automatic rifles levelled at him. "I am here to see Abdullah Aziz," he said to a stringy looking fellow whose eyes darted nervously past him to the open door at his back.

"Who are you spat?" the Bedouin.

"I am Alluwaijri, the new minister of justice. Tell him. He will see me."

A runner disappeared into the house and then reappeared a few minutes later waving at them to bring him. Alluwaijri was escorted by two of the men, their guns still aimed at his back, into a large room filled with blinking computer screens and bustling people. Here was the heart of the rebellion, and at its heart, Aziz. He waved the Bedouin away.

"You have to forgive my Bedouin. They are enthusiastic in their duties," said Aziz without taking his eyes off a computer screen that displayed a Google map of Riyadh.

On the screen were marked in grease pencil the positions of both rebels and loyalists. Alluwaijri noticed that the areas controlled by rebels looked a lot smaller than he had assumed them to be a few hours ago. He also noticed that a similar monitor perched next to the first had streaming video from the BBC Middle East desk reporting on the insurrection. It was an efficient way of getting intelligence not forthcoming from Aziz's forces now that they had communications troubles.

"We lost the Ministry of Justice buildings," said Alluwaijri when Aziz offered nothing else.

The man's eyes crinkled with displeasure, but his voice remained calm as he replied, "We have lost many of our conquests in the last few hours. I sense that there is a traitor in our midst. It seems that neither your ministry building nor your new title as the minister of justice will be as easily won as we thought."

His eyes flashed with anger as he said quietly, "My position as Saudi Arabia's new ruler may likewise be in jeopardy unless we marshal our forces and take back the initiative. We must do this before military reinforcements can arrive from the northern frontier. Even now, the forces loyal to the king that we sent charging into Iraq are returning without firing a shot. It seems that the Iraqis were waiting for them not with guns but with a white flag. They offered information about the coup and convinced the commanders that Iraqi forces were not to blame for the fighting."

"Perhaps they showed them the cursed BBC." Aziz gestured at the computer. "I have bled off forces to bolster the fighting in Riyadh, to position them as pickets between us and the army."

"These setbacks reek of a traitor. We must find this pig and dispatch him. Right now, I need you to command our defences to the north of Riyadh. You must stop any military units from arriving until we have the situation in hand here. I rely on your talents to do that task and do it successfully."

"It will be done," replied Alluwaijri solemnly, although he had no intention of going to the northern outskirts of Riyadh. He realized that things were even worse than he had imagined. On the BBC video behind Aziz, a column of tanks and armoured personnel carriers were arriving to bolster the defences around the royal residence in Riyadh.

At this point, Alluwaijri's thoughts regarding the uprising were not about its success or failure, but how to escape it.

October 2.
Combat Information and Command Center, underground complex,
the White House.

The Combat Information and Command Center was the White House facility that most looked like the public perception of the Situation Room. It had a wall covered in flat screen displays of world and regional maps dotted with blue flashing icons and trails representing U.S. ground forces, aircraft and ships. Numbered icons and flashing symbols depicted foreign military activity and units. These were either white for allied, green for non-aligned or red for hostile. The island of Taiwan and the oceans around it were covered in flashing red icons.

One larger screen showed a blown-up image of Taiwan and surrounding waters. Fully one third of the northern part of the island showed red. There were two small ROC-held pockets in Taipei identified by small white icons.

The president sat in a high-backed chair on a raised platform overlooking the room. Admiral Irving and Dan Blomstrum sat on either side of him. A small table in front of them held several unfinished cups of coffee and bottles of water. As the president watched the image of Taiwan, one of the white icons in Taipei winked out and a red icon moved over its location.

On the flat screen that depicted the Pacific region, there were a number of flashing blue icons. These were the U.S. naval aircraft that were launching at the Chinese submarines, represented by small silhouettes. One by one the pilots announced that their nuclear-tipped torpedoes were away. The flashing icons of the aircraft moved in arcs that described rapid 180-degree turns. Shortly afterward, symbols denoting radioactivity, each surrounded by a heavy black octagon, appeared over the sub icons — nine of them one after the other — the grave markers of the Chinese ballistic missile fleet thousands of miles from America.

"All targets have been destroyed," announced a U.S. Air Force major who coordinated the controllers in a redundant confirmation of the information on the display.

Then one of the controllers who were hunched over their computers yelled and punched a button transferring his computer image to a larger display screen.

Two icons flashed incredibly close to the American coast, icons that struck everyone in the room with dread.

"Sir, reported missile launch. Repeat, missile launch three-zero-four nautical miles due west of Southern California."

"What?" yelled the president, rising. "We got all of them! You said there were only nine!" he screamed at Irving.

All three men stared in horror at the display as the tiny red missiles crossed the map.

"Peterson Air Force Base confirms ballistic missile launch. Patriot batteries are alert and targeting," reported the major in the same even tones he'd used previously. "Initial computer analysis on projected ballistic track one identifies Denver or possibly Colorado Springs and Peterson itself. Waiting for final analysis. Track two, positive track identification Warren Air Force Base, Wyoming. They're after the Minuteman IIIs."

Peterson AFB was on the outskirts of Colorado Springs and had taken over almost all the duties once performed two thousand feet underground in the old NORAD Cheyenne Mountain complex. It was the command and control centre for much of America's land-based offensive and defensive nuclear capability. Warren AFB housed the Minuteman IIIs, the last in the family tree of American intercontinental ballistic missiles and also the only fully operational land-based long-range nuclear missiles left in the U.S. arsenal.

The rest of America's active nuclear weapons were designed to be delivered by stealth aircraft, cruise missiles or by virtually undetectable ballistic missile submarines that could sit on the seabed anywhere in the world and with equal ease deliver their payloads to Beijing, Moscow or Tehran.

"Mr. President, Admiral Irving, Peterson confirms Colorado Springs is the track one target," said the major.

Admiral Irving stared at the status screen for the newest of the Patriot missile systems, the Mark 5 high-altitude ballistic missile interceptors with a range of two hundred miles and an effective ceiling of seventy-five. There were five active batteries on the California coastline but only two in range of the Chinese missiles' flight paths. He scowled when he saw several amber lights marking the two closest missile batteries. Amber meant not all the missiles were yet prepared to fire.

The Chinese missile tracks diverged as the missiles headed for their separate targets.

"Patriots in the air," announced the major.

The president couldn't help noting how cool and collected the man remained despite the horrendous ramifications of the events he was monitoring.

On a screen that showed a close-up of the California coastline and the western United States, five blue darts rose from points on the coast. Two were headed straight for the missile that had targeted the Warren AFB complex; the other three, for the missile that had targeted Colorado Springs and the obsolete NORAD Cheyenne Mountain command centre.

The major's voice droned, describing trajectories and approach speeds like a bored announcer at a pre-season football game.

All eyes in the room were riveted on the flat screen that displayed the West Coast as the blue tracks approached the two red tracks. Time crawled until finally the paths of two of the missiles converged on one of the Chinese ICBMs.

"Kill confirmed, kill confirmed," said the major, his voice rising a little for the first time.

On the screen, the icon representing the missile headed for Warren AFB winked out, replaced by a flashing black bull's eye — a clean kill. The missile and its single warhead were nothing but shards and debris far over the earth.

The other ICBM was still very much alive.

"Patriots intercepting track one. One miss," said the major.

On the screen, the leading blue track winked out an inch or so from the red track.

"The second missile has detonated. It's another miss," said the major, stress entering his voice.

"One Patriot still tracking." The major paused, listening to the voices in his headset.

On the screen the two tracks — one red, one blue — converged.

"We have a hit," he announced.

For a moment the black bull's eye appeared, and a cheer went up. Then suddenly, it winked out, replaced by the red ICBM icon and track. The line extending before the missile was dotted, indicating its calculated course. The red icon still crept along its dotted highway.

"Can we fire more missiles?" asked the president.

"No, sir, the ICBM is beyond the batteries' range," replied the major.

"Shit. What the hell can we do now?" the president asked Admiral Irving.

"Nothing, sir. There are no other anti-missile systems available."

"What about that freakin' expensive laser-equipped 747? Where the hell is that piece of shit?" asked the president. He was referring to the still largely experimental Sky Ray anti-missile laser system carried on a specially adapted Boeing 747, a system that had caused him grief with Congress and citizens groups when its cost came out at ten times the original budget.

"The only operational Sky Ray is on a track over the East Coast, sir, covering the area from Washington to New York, sir," replied Irving.

"Shit," said the president quietly. "Shit".

October 2.
Sixty miles over California.

The Chinese JL-2 ballistic missile soared 337 thousand feet above the earth. Its first stage was long gone, and its second stage was running out of fuel, committing it to a powerless ballistic course that would take it plunging into Colorado Springs or, more accurately, Peterson Air Force Base. Its designers had equipped it with an accuracy of less than an eighth of a mile, but the missile would not need to be that close to effectively decimate its target. Its 700-kiloton single warhead was programmed to detonate two thousand feet over Peterson, destroying the base's satellite uplink capability. The side effect of destroying the civilian population of Colorado Sprigs as well as all the military personnel at Peterson had not factored into the equation.

The only people likely to survive the blast were the personnel still stationed in the bowels of the mothballed NORAD Cheyenne Mountain complex, a small staff that just kept the facilities from outright decay.

The last of the Patriots, its fuel expended, had almost caught up to the JL-2 when its computer sensed a loss of inertia and detonated its warhead. It was within thirty feet of the speeding ICBM when it exploded. A fragment of the Patriot's carcass — a chunk of aluminum shrapnel the size of a grape — accelerated along its intercept track and clipped the bottom of the JL-2's fuselage. The impact tore a patch of the missile's skin and caused a tiny, almost imperceptible wobble. Lacking the ability to correct its flight path, the ICBM began to drift ever so slightly from its programmed course. Other than that, it had escaped unscathed.

October 2.
Combat Information and Command Center, underground complex,
the White House.

The president fell back into his seat, his full attention on the screen that portrayed the bright red track of the Chinese ICBM. It was the first time in his life that he felt absolutely helpless. His stomach was a knot of pain, like someone had punched him in the gut repeatedly, and every muscle in his body was as taut as a bowstring.

The room in front of him was largely silent aside from the major's murmuring litany of distance and time to impact. The voice resonated in the chamber of flashing lights and glowing situation maps like some strange Gregorian chant.

The major interrupted himself. "Mr. President, Peterson has determined that the missile has been damaged and is wandering from its original track. The newest calculations estimate an impact short of the original target zone that may put it into a lightly populated area in the mountains, approximately twenty miles west of Colorado Springs."

The president and his two companions, Blomstrum and Irving, broke into smiles. At least they would not lose a military base and a city today.

"Dan, I think I need to speak to the Chinese again," said the president to Blomstrum.

"Yes, sir. I think you do," replied Blomstrum, leaning for one of the phones on the table in front of them and calling the White House switchboard.

"Admiral Irving, let's review that list of Chinese targets and make a decision."

"Yes, sir." Irving grabbed a valise that was nestled on the floor next to his chair, placed it on the table and opened it, drawing out a plastic-covered folder with the U.S. Space Command coat of arms on it.

"Let's call the secretaries in to the Situation Room and alert the vice president."

Blomstrum nodded and rang the Situation Room manager, asking him to summon the secretaries of state, Defense, Homeland Security and commerce as well as other critical members of the president's cabinet. The next decision was not his alone.

"It's funny," said the president.

"What's funny, sir?" asked Irving.

"Oh, it's funny that we never thought the Chinese were enough of a threat to put in a red phone like we had for the Soviets.

October 2.
Forty miles over the southeastern tip of Utah.

The damage to the JL-2 was rapidly getting worse as aerodynamic forces started to rip at the missile's injured outer skin. As the hole widened the wobble increased, and the missile started to nose down ever more steeply from its original ballistic trajectory. At twenty miles above the mountainous terrain below, a large section of the rear fuselage ripped away, and the missile started to tumble.

With all aerodynamic stability lost, it slowed its arc dramatically and started a free fall. The plunge wrenched the warhead from the main body of the missile but did not deactivate its arming and detonation sequence. The warhead plummeted to earth, shedding bits and pieces of the missile's inner trusses and bulkheads as it went but still a mass of lethal machinery.

It shot past the mountaintops, careening earthward into a valley. Its altimeter, unperturbed by the tumble, did its job and when the warhead reached the altitude its programmers had calculated was two thousand feet above Peterson AFB, the 700-kilton weapon exploded. In fact, the device was 487 feet above the valley floor and almost directly over the tranquil mountain town of Durango.

CHAPTER 25

October 2.
Near Rothenbach, Switzerland.

"Looks like he may have dumped the limo. It's on the way back from a small town ahead, a place called Rothenbach," said Catherine. She was juggling a coffee, now quite cold, with her cellphone as she received up-to-the-minute information from the NSA satellite that was tracking both al-Munajjid's limo and the Louis Vuitton bag the bodyguard had placed in the Mercedes SUV. The NSA was relaying the information from Washington to a European-based U.S. computer server that translated the information and digitally forwarded it to Catherine's phone. It passed on the information in a quite human-sounding voice that agents referred to as Gladys.

"How about the SUV?" asked Derek.

"It's still on the road and headed toward Rothenbach. Looks like he's on his way to pick up al-Munajjid and the other bodyguard."

Derek was driving a bit over the speed limit with the Seal team close behind in their car and van.

Derek and Catherine had made the Seals' acquaintance during a hurried tactical meeting as they prepared to tail al-Munajjid. Lieutenant Don McLean was the team leader, there was recon unit of two men, Andy Turner and Chip "String" Garret, and the rest of the team comprised five men: Conner Ash, who was McLean's second; Brian Far, Sam "Hobbit" Wilkes, whose nickname referred to the size of his feet; Peter Swiggart; and finally, Gary Cypher. They were all mission-hardened, and even in an organization as elite as the U.S. Navy Seals, they were considered the cream of the crop.

The slow pace on the road was driving Derek crazy. He just wanted to mash the accelerator against the floorboards and catch up to al-Munajjid, but Catherine had cautioned him about the strictness of Swiss speed limits. They were five minutes behind the Mercedes SUV and ten minutes from Rothenbach.

The driver of the black SUV must have been cautioned the same way, as he rarely made any gain on his lead over them.

Within a few minutes, the Mercedes limo passed them going the other way. The driver was in shirt sleeves, arm hanging out the window with a cigarette in hand. He had all the windows, even those in the back, rolled down. The limo was otherwise empty. Catherine's instinct had been right.

Derek fretted that they would get to Rothenbach too late or that the transponder might fail or be compromised. The primitive juices released into a male's system just before a hunt or a fight to the death were flooding into him now making him fretful and impatient. Catherine seemed to have the opposite reaction. In fact, she appeared quite relaxed.

Almost twenty minutes later, after slowing for some construction on the narrow, winding road, they reached a sign that announced the village of Rothenbach im Emmental. Beyond the sign, a cluster of quaint buildings marked the outskirts. Feeling that they might be conspicuous in such a small settlement, they opted to have Andy and String, the Seal's advance recon team, take the small car into town and look around for their quarry.

Just as the recon team was reporting that they'd discovered the Mercedes SUV empty and parked beside a small grocery at the south end of the hamlet, Catherine told them that the bag with the transponder was on the move again.

The two Seals in the village looked about and saw an old green Mercedes sedan, paint faded and belching diesel smoke, head away from the front of a small inn. Four men were inside the car.

"Reconnaissance reports that they have a probable contact," a voice announced from a small walkie-talkie suspended in a cup holder in the console between Derek and Catherine. It was McLean reporting to them from the van behind.

The Seals had parked their van about ten feet back of Catherine and Derek in a laneway off the main road leading out of town. Now, their quarry in range, the team leader flashed his lights at Derek and put the van in gear. Derek turned right onto the main road, gunning his engine just a little as he headed into town. At the village's main intersection, the two recon men waited in their car. They were pointed north, up the road taken by the old green Mercedes.

Derek pulled up next to them, the Seals behind. The Seal team leader got out of the van and walked up and squatted on the driver's side.

"What do you think?" Derek asked the team leader.

"We should probably put recon on their tails and let them report back, sir," he replied. He looked through car at the two men on the other side. "Get to it," McLean said to his recon men.

Nodding at him, the recon team leader engaged the transmission and grimaced at the slight grinding of gears as he edged out onto the tarmac and headed off after the green Mercedes. A little less that a mile from the village, the two men passed a steep wooded slope that fell abruptly to the roadside, interrupting the hillside pastures of much of the surrounding area.

As the two Seals drove past, one of them thought he caught a glimpse of someone in the woods. The man's position had been compromised when he put his cellphone to his ear.

"Sir, the two men we saw in town are on the road just passing me." Ali Mustafa spoke to Gregovich from what he thought was a fully concealed position in the woods. He'd been dropped there to keep an eye out for anyone who looked suspicious. The area was not one frequented by tourists, and newcomers stuck out. Mustafa knew that from personal experience. After five years of living in the district, he'd been accepted by the locals, if not as a native, at least as a resident.

He was an employee of al-Munajjid, tasked with tending to his safe house, and had brought the green Mercedes to Rothenbach to pick up his master. Mustafa owed al-Munajjid much and was unfailingly loyal. His position of trust was his greatest pride, and he took every precaution to ensure that his master's wishes were carried out to the letter. He was not militarily trained, however, and had no idea that he had alerted his master's pursuers to his position.

Gregovich snapped his phone closed and turned to al-Munajjid, who sat in the back of the Mercedes. "Sir, I think we do have a tail. Perhaps we should keep going."

"Do you?" replied al-Munajjid, "Are you so sure we have a tail that the inconvenience of wandering around the Swiss country with no particular destination is justified?"

Gregovich caught the warning in al-Munajjid's voice. "No, sir, I am not completely sure."

"Well, until you are, let us assume that my expensive state-of-the-art safe house, one organized by you, I might add, remains uncompromised. Pull off the road, and see if our followers pass."

"Yes, sir" said Gregovich, all the while thinking just how much he would delight in failing in his mission to protect the arrogant little Saudi. "Sean," he said to his partner, "find a place to pull into that will hide the car, and then we'll see what happens."

The Irishman drove another quarter mile before spying a laneway that led between two old stone farm buildings. Turning cautiously so as to not disturb the gravel on the roadside, he drove up the lane and hid the car behind the larger of the sheds. Both Gregovich and Flannigan got out of the car. Al-Munajjid remained in the back reading a magazine, one of several that Mustafa had thoughtfully provided for his master.

"Sean, you get down to the road and have a good look at these two, but hurry. They're only three or four minutes behind."

Flannigan hurried off. Gregovich was pleased when he saw that after crossing the road, his partner apparently disappeared into thin air. That SAS, he thought. He is good.

Mustafa had decided that now the two men were gone, it was safe to walk back to the village and perhaps get a coffee at the inn while he waited. If no one came to collect him in the next couple of hours, he'd phone the housekeeper, who lived in town, and get her to drive him home. As he walked briskly along the shoulder, a blue van appeared rounding the corner. It was unexceptional, and he thought nothing of it until its squealed to a halt beside him. The sound just about made him jump out of his skin, but he was still unprepared for the shock of seeing three huge men leap from the back of the van.

The men grabbed Mustafa and threw him through the air into the back of the van, where other men pinned him to the floor. A rough hand rummaged through his pockets and grabbed his cellphone. These men were all speaking English, one language Mustafa had not added to his lexicon, which included German, French, Arabic and a smattering of Italian.

Andy and String knew they'd been compromised, so they proceeded along the road at a leisurely pace, giving no sign that they were looking out for anything other than the commonplace hazards of driving a country road. They did not see Flannigan as they passed the farm lane where the green Mercedes was concealed.

Flannigan did see them, and immediately flipped open his phone. "Yuri," he said in his Irish lilt, "they were both pretty big fellows, and they have the look of hard men, but they were giving no sign of being on alert. It could be they are just a couple of locals."

"Is that your opinion?" asked Gregovich.

"Locals, you mean?" said Sean.

"Yes."

"No, sir, my own opinion is that they're as professional as a pair of Dutch whores."

"Have they slowed?" asked Gregovich, knowing that Flannigan would be able to see a considerable distance along the road from his position before it bent away and rose into the local glen.

"No. They're just disappearing now. You know, Yuri, if they are a tail, then they might have another way to track us. They didn't seem in much of a hurry for men who needed to catch up and maintain a visual."

"I was thinking the same thing," said Gregovich. "Perhaps I should have a look at the luggage."

"Perhaps you should," replied Flannigan.

Five minutes later, Gregovich had the tiny GPS transponder in his hand. Flannigan rejoined him by the car.

"They know exactly where we are," Gregovich spat.

"Let's see," said Flannigan. "Ah, American," he said as he examined the electronic bug. "Very nice. I assume we picked this up in Berne. Or do you think earlier?"

"I don't know, but if they had it earlier, surely they would have moved on us already."

"They may be getting ready to do that right now."

Gregovich rapped on the back window, and al-Munajjid rolled it down.

"Sir, we have a tail. We, as well as this area, have been compromised," he said, showing al-Munajjid the bug. "I suggest we go to the house, leave this in the garage with the door closed and head out the back laneways. We should get to Zurich and fly out of Kloten airport."

Al-Munajjid was already absolutely seething, so much so that when the stupid Russian told him his expensive safe house was anything but, he was speechless. He held his tongue, smart enough to realize that he shouldn't risk arousing antipathy from the two men he must now rely on to get him out of danger. He would give his stupid cousin in London, Muhammad al-Muffaddal, a call and demand that he get the jet to Zurich. In a few hours, he could be safe in Syria or Pakistan — really safe, where no American or anyone else for that matter could get to him — at least until he could figure out just how badly compromised he was.

Al-Muffaddal's cellphone was off, doing nothing to soothe al-Munajjid's savage mood.

October 3.
Joliet, Illinois.

Sam Barstow had been a trucker all his life, aside from a stint in the Marine Corps, and he couldn't think of a job he would rather have. Not bad for a guy who was headed for his sixtieth birthday. Mind you, he thought, trucking had been a lot easier before martial law and all the checkpoints that burned precious diesel, which now cost almost four bucks a gallon and was often unavailable at even the largest truck stops.

Barstow was lucky compared to tens of thousands of other truckers who had not put a wheel to the pavement since the emergency began. The sudden and severe economic depression, fuel shortages, spiralling costs and strict emergency measures made life pretty difficult for any trucker still lucky enough to be carrying loads, but at least he was still on the road and making just enough to get by. He took stock of how fortunate he was every time in his travels he passed scenes poignantly reminiscent of the Great Depression. Thousands of men stood beside the roadways of America holding signs begging for work in exchange for money or food to feed their families.

He was on his way into south Chicago, carrying a load of chemicals and raw plastic bead from a plant in Sioux Falls, South Dakota, and had made reasonable time despite the checkpoints that dotted Highway 80. A Shania Twain song played on the radio. He liked the look of her but considered her music just a little girly for a real country music fan. He was just coming up on the Des Plaines River Bridge in Joliet when his low-fuel alert sounded off. He'd hoped he could get clear of Joliet before needing to fuel but decided to get off here rather than take the chance of running his tank dry.

Barstow got off on the cloverleaf just west of the river, with a mind to head to a gas station he knew on Railroad Street, an industrial parkway that followed the river's shoreline. As he edged his two-year-old Volvo tractor onto the surface streets, he spied an old blue Ford Econoline van pulled up under the bridge that carried Highway 80 across the river. He noticed the late-sixties Econoline only because he had an identical one at home he'd been tinkering with for years. It was almost completely restored now, but he could remember vividly the dilapidated state it had been in when he got it.

The one under the bridge was far from restored, and while it looked to be the same year, it was probably in even worse shape than his was when he first started working on it. What really arrested his attention, however, was that the van under the bridge had the complete chrome Econoline script on the back door, a trim piece he'd been looking for as long as he'd been gathering up the bits and pieces missing from his project.

Barstow saw someone sitting in the van, so he decided to pull over and see if the guy would be interested in pulling the trim piece off and selling it to him. He jumped out of the cab and rounded the back of his trailer, walking toward the van, which had a stick-on magnetic sign on the side that said, "Spanner and Kinnear" and, below that, "concrete inspections, sewers, supports and structural." The van was nestled well under the bridge next to the two main columns that held the span as it crossed over the water. Barstow called out to the fellow wearing a bright yellow construction hat who was sitting in the van, but then he realized he'd already been seen, and that seemed to be causing some concern.

As Barstow scrambled around a pile of garbage and old 45-gallon drums that someone had dumped there, his angle relative to the van changed, and now he could see that the side door was open and another guy was busy unloading a bunch of cardboard boxes. The man was stacking them in a semicircular wall around one side of the bridge support. Barstow noticed that the other main pillar, a few feet away, had a blue plastic tarp covering what could only be a similar pile of boxes. Barstow didn't need to be a rocket scientist to figure out what was going on.

He yelled, "Hey!" Then common sense took over, and he started to back away just as the man in the van directed a 9-mm pistol his way and started firing.

Barstow was lucky the shots all went wild, the man's aim hampered by the large West Coast mirror hanging on the driver's door.

"Son of a bitch," Barstow screamed, heading out at the fastest run he'd managed for years. A bullet crashed into the trailer right beside his head just as he grabbed the trailer's tail-light assembly and used it to swing around the corner and out of the line of fire. Pelting alongside the trailer, he reached the cab and started to clamber up, but his left foot was knocked away from him, and a blistering pain blossomed. The gunman had kept firing at what little he could see of Barstow under the belly of the trailer and tractor and gotten in just one lucky shot as Barstow leapt for the cab. It blew two of Barstow's toes off his left foot and left jagged metal shards from his steel-toed boot embedded in the wounds.

Despite the pain or perhaps because of it, Barstow was galvanized into action. The Econoline was rolling now, and all Barstow could think off was getting the bastards that were in it. He slammed the truck's clutch pedal to the floor, his foot almost slipping off it as the blood from his wound poured over the rubber. The pain was nauseating, but he persevered as he slammed the rig into gear and started it rolling forward. The driver of the Econoline had not been able to get far enough forward to clear the front of the truck. His choices were the river or a possible collision. He chose the collision, which he must have thought would be glancing, but Barstow, an excellent shot and a master of leading a target, did just that, swinging the rig to the left even though his quarry was still to his right.

On seeing the tractor turn away, the van's driver pulled over even harder. He realized too late that even though the tractor was moving more slowly, it was gaining enough speed on him to cut it close. Had he been a better driver, he would have braked hard, spun around and headed back the way he'd come, but he was not. His panicked reaction was to jam the accelerator to the floor in the hopes that the wheezing six-cylinder between the seats of the old van would have enough left in her to clear the front of the oncoming juggernaut. It did not.

Barstow's calculations proved accurate. The Econoline had almost made it onto the road when the front of the towering Volvo gathered up the old van, slamming it from its course. Barstow dragged the tractor into third gear, screaming in pain as he threw the clutch pedal to the floor and mashed the accelerator. The big rig's diesel bellowed and then shook like a rat in a terrier's mouth as its rev limiter kicked in. The Econoline and the two men in her were hammered into an eight-foot-high concrete abutment that rose beside the road. The momentum and inertia of the fully loaded tractor-trailer — and Barstow's foot hard on the accelerator — were more than enough to pulp the van and its occupants into a slim mass of twisted metal and flesh.

Thirty minutes later, Barstow was in hospital, and a horde of reporters jammed the hallways waiting for a description of his exploit. The massive bomb, which would have knocked the bridge from its lofty perch, was safely disarmed. It had been set to explode during the height of rush hour. More important than the averted catastrophe, two more of al-Munajjid's elite terrorists met a timely end.

October 3.
Riyadh, Saudi Arabia.

Reports of a rapid succession of failures, missed opportunities and lost positions continued to flow into Aziz's command centre. It almost seemed as if the government had been tipped off and waiting for the coup. Aziz wracked his brain for possible traitors in his midst. He could think of no one who wouldn't be risking death if they'd betrayed his plan to the authorities. And then it hit him: al-Munajjid. Clever, conniving, power-hungry little al-Munajjid, whose contacts and associations had helped pave the way for Aziz's quest for power.

Suddenly, gunfire and explosions erupted near the compound, and every head in the room snapped up. Just as suddenly, every computer terminal in the room went dead, and the lights went off, leaving just a dribble of illumination from a small window set high in one wall. Aziz turned to one of his Bedouin bodyguards, who looked at him and said, "Sir, I think it's time to go."

A few minutes later, Aziz and four of his Bedouin supporters made a break through a small service door on the opposite side of the compound from where his men engaged government forces on the street in a firefight. Around them they could see and hear the rebel forces in the area marshal to protect their headquarters. As they hurried down the street, there was an immense flash in front of them. A rocket from a government attack copter had found a knot of rebels where the street intersected with another. Two of Aziz's Bedouin fell, mortally wounded by spinning shrapnel.

Aziz felt a warm buzzing in his side and put his hand to the spot. It came away covered in the warm blood that was spreading across his torso. Panicked, he pulled his clothes away to reveal a bloody but minor flesh wound.

Now gunfire from both small arms and heavy weapons resounded all around them, echoing off the walls of neighbouring compounds and channelling along the narrow streets so that it was almost impossible for Aziz and his men to determine exactly where they were. Their headlong flight was interrupted when an armoured car, a brand-new American-supplied Stryker, roared across the intersection ahead.

Aziz wondered if it was crewed by his men or the government's. An answer came in the form of an anti-tank rocket launched from the same attack chopper that had wounded him. It caught the Stryker in the rear as it was passing from sight. A trail of fire and smoke followed the mortally stricken armoured vehicle as its own momentum took it down the street and out of sight.

As Aziz and his two remaining men got to the intersection, they almost collided with a group of men hurrying toward them. Aziz thought for a moment it was another group of his rebels, but then, as one of them raised his rifle, he realized his error. His lifeless body spun in a macabre dance as a stream of 9-mm bullets stitched across his chest, neck and face. The Bedouin bodyguards suffered the same fate, although one lived long enough to have his throat expertly cut by a member of the crack troops of the Royal Palace Guard.

CHAPTER 26

October 5 (west of Date Line).
Highway 21, Taiwan.

Corporal Tian Lam was weary beyond anything he'd ever experienced. His squad, a Dragon anti-tank missile unit, had been on the go for almost fifty hours now, nonstop, with only a twenty-minute nap before they were forced to press southward by the advancing PLA tanks.

Only once had the squad seen anything they could celebrate. On the first day, they'd engaged a column of main battle tanks and armoured troop carriers. Their battalion was getting the worst of it when suddenly a cloud of explosions rolled from one end of the enemy column to the other, leaving tanks and carriers burning and popping as their ammunition cooked off. A few seconds later, two of the most beautiful aircraft Lam had ever seen winged low overhead, fighter bombers that carried American naval markings. They rose cheering and jumping for joy, thinking salvation was at hand, the Americans had arrived. But that was the first and last time they'd seen U.S. forces, and their joy had gradually turned to anger and despair as the seemingly inexhaustible wave of the PLA pushed them back and back again.

Lam was in charge of the remaining six men in his platoon. His sergeant had been lost the day before while running for cover during an artillery barrage. Since then, the six men, their supply of Dragons exhausted and with no chance of resupply, had been on the run, with little thought of doing anything but escape the withering fire that met them every time they tried to fight back against the onslaught.

They were presently slogging along the mountainsides paralleling Highway 21, just south of the Sun Moon Lake in the central mountains of the island. Highway 21 followed the river valley and was the only main road running down Taiwan's mountainous spine. It was still hotly contested. They'd been losing ground, but at least they'd slowed the Chinese advance from the north.

It was not the same story to the west. The top two thirds of Taiwan's west coast, the area most heavily populated, had largely been lost as more and more Chinese troops arriving from the mainland pushed their way southward and accompanying leapfrog amphibious assaults cut into the defenders from the side. The smooth, sandy beaches of the coast had proven as indefensible as many military planners had always believed. To make matters worse, the mainland Chinese thought nothing of filling the skies with airborne assault troops no matter if they fell into deadly fire. Even with ten times the troop losses among the lightly armed Chinese, the defenders were losing far too many vital positions to them, positions that could have helped stem the flow from the north.

Lam heard a shouted challenge from in front as he trudged around a rough outcropping about two hundred feet above the road. Two troops rose from a concealed position, wearing the shoulder flashes of Taiwan's 102 Infantry, 8th Corps. They stood with their weapons aimed at his squad. Lam answered their challenge wearily, indifferent to whether he got shot or not. His password was still valid, and the squad was let through.

A few feet on, a sergeant grabbed them and issued them instructions to report to a bustling field headquarters a quarter mile down the highway. Eighth Corps was the military command charged with defending the southern parts of Taiwan. Its commanders were sweeping up the remains of the central defence — 10th Corps — which was fleeing southwards and organizing a line of resistance across Taiwan, running from Hsia-Lun on the west coast, passing just south of Sun Moon Lake and across to Hua-Lien on the east coast.

Lam's squad was to be re-equipped with the new American-made Javelin rocket launchers. Lam was cheered by the prospect. The Javelin, on which the squad had also trained, was far more capable than the old Dragons they normally carried. It rarely missed and, even better, rarely failed to kill what it hit. A squad firing a Javelin could also bug out as soon as the rocket left the launcher. It was a fire-and-forget system. That improved the user's chances of survival, because they could get the hell away from their compromised firing position.

An hour after reporting in and being assigned to a new command, Lam and his men were sleeping soundly on the hard ground in the shelter of a rocky outcropping a half mile behind the front. The cacophony of distant battle punctuated their dreams but didn't have the power to wake men so thoroughly exhausted. Lam did not know it, but his steady retreat to the south was over. The PLA would not manage to gain another mile of Highway 21.

October 4.
President's office, underground complex, the White House.

It had taken twenty minutes spent completely alone for the president to come to terms with the extinction of the town of Durango, Colorado. He'd paced the small office, sat listlessly in his office chair with his head in his hands, fighting back tears, and wished fervently that his wife was by his side so there would be another person whose hand he could hold and who would understand that his grief and depression were signs not of weakness but rather of his humanity. Breaking down in tears in front of the Joint Chiefs and cabinet was not an option.

He finally emerged from his office to a pool of anxious faces in the reception area. Everyone knew about the blast, from the lowliest intern to his personal assistant Amy Vandercamp, and all of them were looking to him for leadership. He'd vowed not to disappoint them. "Amy," he said, "I want the Joint Chiefs, pertinent cabinet and White House staff in the Situation Room right now. Get me the NSA, CIA and Homeland directors as well."

She nodded and picked up her phone.

The president headed to the Combat Information and Command Center to view the current world situation and, most especially, Taiwan and Saudi Arabia. As he strode along the hall, an intern caught up to him and delivered a sealed flash message.

He opened it and read that the Israelis had detected a large-scale buildup of Syrian armour infiltrating the Baka Valley. Terrorist incursions into northern Israel as well as rocket barrages from Hezbollah launchers had reached a ferocity without precedent. It was a reflection of the Arab world's perception that the United States was no longer a threat. He intended to prove them wrong on that count, but not right now.

The president thanked the intern and proceeded up the hallway, thinking that Israel was on its own with this one, and he really could care less if they nuked the Syrians back into the Stone Age. He would have an apologetic dispatch prepared stating that he was a little busy but would support the Israelis in any action they deemed necessary to alleviate the situation and, further, he would sign any requests for new weapons purchases or a lend-lease, even for weapons that until now the United States had been reluctant to sell the Israelis for fear of a negative world reaction.

Twenty minutes later, with a few late arrivals still filtering in to the room, the president called the meeting to order.

"Gentlemen, as you all know, a nuclear device has exploded on American soil and caused at least three thousand casualties. While it would have been much worse if the weapon had reached its target, we cannot fail to react as if we had lost a major city. The Chinese must know at a gut level that Americans consider every life precious and that the loss of one American life in our homeland due to enemy action will be punished as if they had killed a million. The Chinese may consider life cheap, but they must not believe that American lives come cheaply."

A murmur of assent rose from the men, who were as furious and as hungry for revenge as their president.

"So, using a list that Admiral Irving has provided of possible strategic and tactical military targets in China deemed to bring the greatest losses to their nation, I have selected one — one that I feel is fitting, considering the situation. Admiral," he said to Irving, "I would like the naval base and underground submarine complex at Jianggezhuang annihilated."

To the rest of the room he said, "For those of you who may not know, Jianggezhuang is the Chinese navy's main base of operations for their nuclear sub fleet, or what is left of it, and may still contain submarines capable of sortie and nuclear launch. The Chinese JL-2 ICBMs are reputed to have a range of eight thousand miles, so taking out the base, where they might have others subs in reserve capable of launching an attack on the U.S., is I believe prudent.

"The icing on the cake is that Jianggezhuang is within fifteen miles of their Qingdao naval base, which is the headquarters and training facility for their North Sea Fleet. Fifteen miles is close enough to put Qingdao out of business, as we will have to use a specially designed high-yield warhead to break into sub pens that are hardened against nuclear weapons. Taking out the sub base will provide Beijing with quite a fireworks display and telegraph a clear message that we are the meanest motherfuckers that they can possibly imagine and that their Arts of War bullshit only works when you are stabbing your friends in the back.

"The strike will be carried out by three stealth bombers. Two will be redundant and only launch their weapons if the primary aircraft is incapable of completing its mission. So, gentlemen," said the president, looking around the table, "if there are no objections, I would like to order that the strike against Jianggezhuang be implemented immediately."

There were no dissenting voices.

"Good. Then I will arrange to break the news to the Chinese five minutes before detonation. At that time, I will be telling them that unless they withdraw from Taiwan and stand down their forces worldwide, they risk a further escalation. I will not make the same mistake we made with the Russians in the late forties, letting them become an overwhelming threat. Now that we have taken care of their ballistic missile boats, the Chinese have a very limited ability to launch a nuclear attack on the United States. Should they choose to try a land-based launch, we will make it quite clear that we have the capability to knock their land-based missiles from the skies and reduce their largest cities to rubble."

A light started to flash on the phone in front of the president — an urgent call.

"Excuse me for a moment, gentlemen," he said, picking up the receiver. "Yes," he said gruffly. He listened for a moment before hanging up.

"Well, a small piece of good news, at last," he announced. "The Muslim extremist coup in Saudi Arabia appears to be over, and its organizers have been captured or killed. Apparently the king and his family are making plans to return to Riyadh."

October 4.
Outskirts of Rothenbach, Switzerland.

Derek and Catherine watched from the safety of a hedgerow as the Seal team slipped through the darkness toward the modest house. Al-Munajjid's hideout was a nicely restored 1920s gentleman's farmhouse — very nice but not grand or opulent. The grounds were wide and open with tidy, trimmed lawns and dotted with small formal gardens. There were several well-maintained outbuildings as well. Cameras were visible on all four corners of the house, but several others, which hung in trees, were much harder to locate.

Mustafa, tied up, blindfolded and gagged in the back of the van, had given away many of the house's security measures with very little persuasion from Peter Swiggart and Brian Far. They specialized in quickly acquiring from enemy detainees information critical to a mission.

A scan of the area had revealed that Mustafa had divulged many but not all of the security systems in place. Another short conversation and he'd proven eager to give up almost everything he knew about the house and where in it his benefactor might be. Once the Seals knew the lay of the land, they decided to wait until dark, but not too late, since the later the hour, the higher the state of alert professional bodyguards were likely to maintain. As darkness fell, the Seals crept up, dealing with various sensors, cameras and trip wires as they advanced.

Derek, who was briefed on the plan, was watching through a pair of borrowed night-vision glasses, yet much of what was transpiring escaped him. He was very glad these guys were on his side and not the enemy's. When he mentioned as much to Catherine, her quiet and sobering rejoinder was that the other team was probably cut from the same cloth.

Derek saw figures emerge around the building, standing alongside windows and doorways. Suddenly they sprang into action. He was blinded momentarily when one of the Seals kicked the front door open and his night-vision goggles received the full benefit of the house's entry hall lighting. He saw some bright flashes of light accompanied by loud bangs as the Seals tossed flash-bang grenades ahead of sweep through the house.

A few minutes later, one came outside and waved them in.

"Shit, I thought we had him," said Derek disappointedly as he walked through the empty house.

"No, it appears they found the bug," replied McLean. "It was tossed on the floor in the garage. They're smart. Rather than crushing it, which would have tipped us that they'd found it, they figured we'd waste time preparing an assault — time they could use to get away. We'd better move out of here soon in case someone has alerted the authorities. It might be hard to explain to the local gendarmes why a fully armed Seal team, along with the FBI and CIA, are busy kicking open farmhouse doors in their scenic countryside."

"Sir, we have something, out back on the lawn," called one of the team from the open back door.

"What is it?" McLean asked.

"Tire tracks, sir," said Cypher, "leading across the lawn to a laneway out back of the house."

"You two," said the team leader, pointing at his two recon men, "follow the tracks and see where they lead. I'll take the rest and go to ground at assembly point A, somewhere along the road, until I hear from you."

"What about the captive?" asked Derek.

"He'll have to endure our company a while longer. We can't risk letting him go."

Derek got on the phone to John Kopriva immediately. "John, it's Derek James. We got close, but they discovered our transponder and slipped away."

"Damn," replied Kopriva, "do you know which way he went?"

"We're not sure, but we know he didn't slip past us and back towards Berne, at least not by the route he came. I suspect he's headed for Zurich. We have an associate of his who claims he doesn't have any more boltholes in Switzerland. His opinion is that al-Munajjid will try to get to a Muslim country."

"I'm sure he offered that opinion freely," said Kopriva wryly.

"Well, it was a couple of Seals doing the asking. So what are our chances of finding him again? You know the country."

"Without the help of the local authorities. he'll be pretty hard to locate, even with the increased manpower we have available. What we can do is cover the logical places he can leave from, like airports and train stations. But even then, now he knows we're on his tail, it'll be a long shot. If he were in Germany or Italy, we could enlist the locals, but the damned Swiss would need to have ten committee meetings first to decide whether or not helping out violates their neutrality."

"But he's a suspected of criminal terrorism, for God's sakes. He's not the ambassador from little bum fuck," replied Derek viciously.

"Let me see what I can do. I'll see if I can speak directly to the Swiss minister for justice and find out if there is any angle on this thing that will allow us to enlist their help."

"That would be great. Thanks," said Derek.

"So, what are you and Cat going to do now?"

"Not much we can do. We figured that heading to Zurich and hoping that's the direction he went might be the most sensible option."

"Right. Well, let me get to work on this and see if there's any hope of finding the prick. I'll call you as soon as I know anything."

"John, we have one more problem," said Derek. "The captive. It makes me nervous to have to carry him along, and he'll drain resources. McLean doesn't want to leave him here in case he can call in reinforcements or contact al-Munajjid."

"Tell you what. Leave him there hog-tied. I'll have him picked up."

"Great," said Derek, relieved to solve the problem so easily.

October 4.
The Swiss countryside.

Al-Munajjid sat in the back of the green Mercedes feeling a little carsick. The rolling of the car on the winding country roads combined with a suspension that had softened with age to make the last couple of hours very uncomfortable. He had no idea where he was. His two bodyguards had not once used a major highway in their drive to Zurich, staying instead on back roads that seemed like twisting goat paths. He'd been frustrated and annoyed that he hadn't been able to contact al-Muffaddal, until he contacted one of his London associates and was told that al-Muffaddal had been found dead in a rail yard. The news terrified al-Munajjid and his irritation with his bodyguards over what he'd thought was a false alarm drained in an instant.

He'd received some good news on his BlackBerry. The revolt in Saudi Arabia was over. He'd only emailed the information his close contacts in the government were waiting for a couple of hours before the coup began. He'd intentionally sent it late, with the explanation that he'd only just gained access to it. No one other than Aziz knew that al-Munajjid had masterminded almost every detail of the coup, and had Aziz won, the old hawk would, with al-Munajjid's blessing, have taken full credit. His government contacts believed that al-Munajjid was a royalist and, now, a hero who had worked to substantiate rumours he had heard. Although late, the government had used the information well, and the royal family knew who they had to thank for their last-minute salvation.

Aziz had been dealt with, and all the money he'd invested with al-Munajjid or lent to him would no longer have to be accounted for. Plus, al-Munajjid was promised he could look forward to the largesse of a grateful monarch. Had events gone the other way, and Aziz and his rebels won, al-Munajjid would have had the gratitude of the new regime. Either way, al-Munajjid came out the winner.

The only disturbing thing was that somehow, someone knew about him, and that someone was on his tail. Now the coup in Saudi Arabia was over, al-Munajjid thought it might be in his best interest to run home. Saudi Arabia was a very tightly controlled country in normal times. Post-uprising, controls would be even stricter, making it an even safer place to go to ground. The master of smoke and mirrors desperately needed to know who was after him and what they wanted or knew.

Flannigan drove quickly and efficiently, using a Garmin GPS portable map system to navigate the mountainous countryside while Gregovich phoned several executive jet services to find out if a charter jet was available in Zurich. He was often frustrated mid-call when the twisting roads put him beyond range of the nearest cell towers. Finally he got both a connection and a company that had a jet, a new Learjet 45XR available on the tarmac in Munich that could be in Zurich within three hours. They requested destination and reason for travel as well as passport numbers and credit card information.

Gregovich supplied them with the information complete with a cover story: The flight would be to Aswan, Egypt, for a well-to-do and very eccentric gentlemen who, after reading a National Geographic article, had a hankering to see the Aswan dam and the monuments at Abu Simbel. There would be a scheduled refuelling stop in Cairo, and then they would proceed to the airport in Abu Simbel. Gregovich did not tell them that as the aircraft approached Aswan, which was near the western limit of the Arabian Peninsula, the jet's crew would be persuaded to change the flight plan. He calculated that they should have more than enough fuel for the diversion to the airport near Mecca and al-Munajjid's home in Ta'if.

CHAPTER 27

October 5.
Fifty thousand feet over the Yellow Sea.

The three B-2 Spirit stealth bombers had been armed, readied and hidden in a large hangar ready for their mission long before the orders to take off were finally issued. They'd been forward positioned in Hawaii at Hickham Air Force Base, far from their home base in Missouri, a measure aimed at expediting their attack more quickly and efficiently. All three crews were nervous, but none as taut as the crew in the lead aircraft, the primary attack bomber. Now, having almost reached their target area, the crews became too busy to think about the ramifications of the actions they were about to take.

The man piloting the lead Spirit was Lieutenant-Colonel Jordan Defoe, who had transferred from flying B-1B Lancers three years ago and had been, in his opinion, the happiest man in the U.S. Air Force ever since. There was something about the Flying Wing that he had always found incredibly appealing. His fascination had found its seed in a movie he'd seen as a kid, the first Hollywood rendition of the War of the Worlds. In that movie, a Northrop Flying Wing had dropped a nuclear weapon on the invaders from Mars. Although the strike against the Martians was unsuccessful, Defoe had been smitten with the Flying Wing bomber.

His life had now come full circle from that moment when, as a child, he'd sat in a darkened movie theatre watching the Flying Wing deliver the nuclear weapon. Now he was the pilot at the controls of an aircraft very similar in concept, but he knew that there would be one difference. The attack he was going to make would leave a much greater impression on his enemy than the Hollywood attack had done on the war machines of the Martian invaders.

The stealth business was a lonely one where formation flying and the support of your squadron mates was an alien concept. The three B-2 bombers were spread miles apart and their crews had no idea where their other planes were. Nor did they have any need to. The only communication they might receive from one another was a special computer read from their transponders if an aircraft was in trouble or breaking up and incapable of fulfilling its mission. The computer in the next aircraft in line would inform its crew that they were at the plate.

The sensitive instruments and passive systems, which utilized incoming data from both satellite and airborne surveillance, painted a vivid picture of enemy air activity far to the south, over Taiwan and the Chinese coast adjacent to the island. There was little or no traffic in front of them over the sea between China and the southern tip of Korea, which they'd passed over on their way to their destination. If their luck held, the Chinese would never know they'd visited until their bomb load impacted the target. At this point, they were marginally in range, and even if they were detected, they could launch with a reasonable expectation of success. The pilot in the lead plane alerted his crew that they were nearing their launch point. The other B-2 two crews, having reached viable launch points, entered racetrack holding patterns to await the results of the first aircraft's launch.

The lead B-2 sent a coded transmission by an undetectable laser messaging system to a satellite overhead that in turn relayed it to the military command and to the president in Washington. The message: the weapon is hot. The weapons, one in each of the Spirit's weapons bays, were high-speed cruise missiles, each armed with a 1.2-megaton B83 warhead specifically designed to take out deeply embedded and hardened targets.

Unlike most nuclear weapons, which exploded in the air above a target, these particular weapons dove into the ground, using their high-speed flight as a battering ram. Special nose cones made of exotic, hardened materials achieved maximum penetration of rock or steel-reinforced concrete before the warhead exploded. Because of the debris it kicked up, the explosion was very dirty. If there was an easterly wind, the radioactive cloud and debris would smother and destroy Qindao naval base, fifteen miles away along the coast, as efficiently as if the base had been directly under the warhead. The same could be said for any towns, cities or villages that lay in the fallout's path.

October 5.
President's office, underground complex, the White House.

"So, the remaining White House staff are all volunteers?" asked the president.

"Yes, sir," replied Blomstrum, "but almost every one of the critical White House staff has volunteered to stay. We've sent mothers with younger children and younger men with families home despite that, but for now the White House is to all intents and purposes fully staffed."

"And the vice president is refuelled and airborne?"

"Yes, sir. He changed planes at Edwards almost two hours ago and departed. He's at altitude and safe. ."

"Good. So that means that all our ducks are in order. We're in as good a shape now as can be expected of a country about to go to nuclear war."

"Yes, sir, we are."

"Then its time I spoke to the Premier."

Eight minutes later, the phone in front of the president rang once, indicating that the premier of China was on the other end of the line. The president locked eyes with Blomstrum for a minute before picking up the phone and said, "So, Dan, when we were wet behind the ears sitting in that little coffee shop in New York, and you suggested I run for the nomination, did you ever dream we would end up here?"

"No, Mr. President, I didn't. But can I say one thing?"

"Sure."

"I am very glad that you're the man behind that desk right now and not the guy you ran against."

"Thanks, Dan."

The president snapped the phone off of its cradle and said without a pause, "Premier Lichang, I am phoning to tell you that within the next few minutes, the United States will attack and obliterate a military target in China. This is in retaliation for the nuclear strike on the United States, which resulted in the deaths of over three thousand Americans. Our retaliation will be limited for the moment at one strike but—"

"Mr. President, this is unacceptable," Lichang bellowed into the phone in English. "China will not—"

"Shut up," yelled the president, "I am not finished, and I am not in any mood to hear your crap. I've been putting up with your crap for the last two months. Now you are going to listen to me and you are going to do exactly what I say or what remains of your nation will still be digging themselves out of the rubble with wooden sticks in a hundred years."

"Mr. President," the premier tried again to interject.

"Mr. Premier, perhaps you were not listening. I have no more patience, and you have no more time, so once again I advise you to shut up and listen to me because your nation's survival depends on your listening very carefully." The president took a breath. "First, you will halt your invasion of Taiwan immediately. A withdrawal will be discussed once things have calmed down, but right now not one more PLA soldier will take one more step forward on the soil of the sovereign nation the Republic of China."

"Mr. President, Taiwan is ours. It is not a sovereign nation. It is a province of—"

Once again the President raised his voice over the objection. "Next, Lichang, you will cease your military adventures in the Middle East and you will cease to supply Iran, Syria and other nations that are responsible for terrorist activities with nuclear technology or weapons of any kind. You will also cease immediately the financial attacks that we both know have been aimed at undermining the U.S. economy."

Suddenly, the president heard an excited hubbub at the other end of the phone.

October 5.
Fifty thousand feet over the Yellow Sea, 208 miles from Jianggezhuang.

Lieutenant-Colonel Defoe pressed the launch button on his control stick, triggering a rapid succession of events. Underneath the B-2, the bomb bay doors snapped open and just as quickly the cruise missile, itself of very stealthy design, fell away. Almost before the bomb had cleared the doors, they snapped closed once again. The bomb was released at maximum speed because the stealth's cloak of invisibility was broken as long as the bomb bay was open. To minimize this risk, the whole launch process had been refined to take place in under four seconds.

As soon as the weapon left the bomb bay and the doors snapped shut, Defoe put the B-2 into a sharp right bank, turning through 180 degrees to flee back the way he'd come. The Spirit was not a street brawler. It was the master of the sneak attack, and once that attack had been implemented, it could do little but get the hell out as quickly as its crew could make it go.

The cruise missile fell about fifty feet before its rocket motor kicked in. Its nose tilted upwards, and within seconds, the missile was at eighty thousand feet and shedding its rocket pack. As it levelled off, its pulse jet took over. With a cruise speed of almost three times the speed of sound, it was the fastest of the cruise missiles and classed ultra-secret. As a further party trick, when it nosed over, an additional propellant pack accelerated it another 150 miles per hour for its terminal dive. Even if detected — and its very low radar signature made that only a slight possibility — its speed and angle of attack made it a very difficult foe to defeat with existing technology.

At twenty miles from the target, the missile's computer identified and designated its impact area. It computed the steepest angle of attack and cruised for an additional eight miles before it altered direction abruptly, pointing its nose earthwards. The tertiary and final drive system ignited, and the missile screamed downwards. Not a single person on the ground below saw or heard their incoming fate. The missile smashed into the ground about fourteen feet from where the U.S. military estimated the centre of the sub pens was located below ground. It was moving so fast it penetrated the pens' thick armoured ceilings, and its warhead triggered just as it emerged into the manmade cavern above two submarines that were in the final stages of being prepped for an armed patrol.

One submarine carried JL-2 missiles and was getting ready to make for a location where it would have a free hand to launch at the United States. In a nanosecond, the pens filled with the heat and light of a blazing artificial sun, and in an unexpected twist, one of the nuclear warheads stored in the facility exploded, adding its 700-kiloton fist to the conflagration. An immense cloud rose into the sky, a death pall announcing the end of a large part of China's nuclear offensive capability. The ground shook for miles around, and even in Beijing, several hundred miles to the northwest, the ferocious noise of the blast and the quiver in the earth below their feet made millions of people turn as one to look in the same direction.

The combined radioactivity of the U.S. and Chinese warheads and over forty other weapons stored in the facility rose thousands of feet into the sky and began a trek aided by light westerlies near the bottom of a huge high-pressure system that would create a lethal footprint across the breadth of China, southern Mongolia and even into Pakistan, northern India and the Lake Balkhash region of Kazakhstan.

October 5.
President's office, underground complex, the White House.

Another voice, not that of Premier Lichang, came on the phone. The speaker did not know English as well as Lichang and was hesitant and unsure. "I am sorry. The premier is called away. He would be to you talking later hours."

In the background, the president could hear urgent conversation just before the line went dead.

"Well, I guess they got the news," said Blomstrum, who'd been listening in on the speakerphone.

"I guess they did," said the president. "Now that it's hit the fan, we'll have to see what happens. I sure as hell hope that Irving's intelligence estimates are right about China's reluctance to raise the stakes any higher."

October 6.
Highway 21, south of Sun Moon Lake, Taiwan.

Lam had killed four main battle tanks in the last few hours. Now the PLA were being far more cautious and no longer tried to bludgeon their way past his position. The rout of the Taiwanese forces had finally been transformed into a stalemate. The defenders now had the terrain and the technology on their side. Overly conservative Taiwanese commanders at first held back on the use of their newest weapons, hoping perhaps to repel the PLA without having to dig into their precious reserve of the latest technological wonders. Weapons like the Javelin were not just high tech but also high priced. Only after older weapons like the Dragons were seen to be largely ineffective had the more capable Javelins been supplied. Many other weapons in the Taiwanese arsenal had also been held in reserve until it was almost too late.

Lam's team had scouted out six firing positions on the steep hillsides. As soon as they fired a Javelin anti-tank rocket from one, they would scamper to another. Twice their old firing positions had come under withering fire from the highway below, but each time Lam and his squad were well clear before the fusillade began. Lam was one of hundreds of men hidden in the hills. To dislodge them the PLA had organized three infantry charges, but each time the Chinese ran into well-prepared defences that combined lethal artillery, mine fields, withering cross fire. The steep and rocky terrain offered limited routes upwards, and these were the ones the defending artillery zeroed in on.

The valley floor was a charnel house of dead and dying whose twisted and rent remains were illuminated by the blazing wrecks of dozens of armoured vehicles. The Taiwanese forces were starting to realize that the poorly trained troops they faced were not the juggernaut they'd originally feared. The invaders' strategy seemed to be to prevail by force of numbers, but times had changed, and the Taiwanese weaponry was just as good at taking out a thousand as it was at taking out ten. The war of attrition was becoming very one-sided. Low, early morning clouds that hung just over the peaks of the mountains had also been a great help in warding off attacking aircraft. On the odd occasion that a pilot broke through the cloud bottoms to brave the rocky incline of the mountain pass, a swarm of shoulder-launched anti-aircraft missiles would rise to devour it. The mountainsides were strewn with the tinsel of unsuccessful but daring young pilots.

Lam ducked as a barrage of artillery shells started to rain down on the hillside from PLA artillery positions a few miles up the road. These barrages were the harbingers of renewed attacks, and from their positions all along the valley floor, the defenders steeled themselves to repel the next advance. Suddenly a cavalry charge of massive Chinese tanks appeared from behind a wall of smoke created by the artillery and supplemented by the tanks themselves.

Lam's team was preparing to unleash its next fusillade when he called to cease fire. Something inexplicable was happening. The tanks had stopped mid-charge and were now reversing back into their own clouds. As they hurtled backwards through the roiling smokescreen or swivelled on their tracks to flee in the direction from which they'd just come. some of them even ran over supporting infantry who were not quick enough to avoid them. As the smoke dissipated and the valley floor could once more be seen, the roar of the retreating tanks' engines was the only sound that reverberated along the valley walls.

Lam radioed the forward command post to request information. One of his men, always prepared to offer a negative opinion, suggested that the PLA was retreating because they were getting ready to nuke them. Lam snapped back angrily that he thought that highly unlikely. The mainland Chinese didn't want to reduce Taiwan to glowing rubble; they wanted it for themselves.

Two hours later, the first Taiwanese reconnaissance units drove cautiously northward up Highway 21, past Lam's position, looking for the invaders. They would not find an entrenched line until they were just north of Sun Moon Lake. It looked as if the enemy had spent themselves and was digging in to the north, at least temporarily.

October 6.
Schupfheim, Switzerland.

Derek had been out of touch with world news during their pursuit of al-Munajjid, but on seeing the screaming headlines, he grabbed a copy of a London newspaper off a rack in the small café where he and Catherine were snatching breakfast. They were both weary. A night's sleep had been a luxury they had not been afforded as they raced across Switzerland hoping and praying they were making the right guesses about al-Munajjid's flight.

The Seals had broken into two units, and each was taking a different route to Zurich on the long shot that Kopriva's agents, racing to fan across Zurich, would see al-Munajjid and either Derek and Catherine or one of the Seal teams might be close enough to pick them up once more.

Derek was horrified when he read about the Sino-American nuclear exchange and the other colossal events that were rocking a world that thought the fall of the Soviet empire had eliminated the threat of all-out nuclear war. On reading of the nuclear attack on Durango and the town's total annihilation, he felt sick to his stomach. Even Catherine's usually cool and controlled demeanour was shaken when he passed her various sections of the paper to read. Speculation was rife that the Americans would respond in kind.

Derek noticed that the café, which was bustling when they had walked in, had gone strangely quiet as they ate. Catherine suggested it was because they were Americans. Seeing the contemptuous looks that some patrons shot them as they left, Derek could only concur.

Catherine offered to drive awhile, but Derek said he was fine for an hour or so. Knowing that she knew Zurich well, he wanted to let her drive as they entered the outskirts. They avoided Highway 1 between Berne and Zurich, while the Seals Turner and Garret had taken the most direct route. Derek's route wandered along secondary roads, like Highway 10, mapped out by their GPS, and they would enter Zurich from the south along the lake. Catherine had suggested using different routes. She figured that al-Munajjid's bodyguards would not know how many vehicles were in pursuit, so they would likely try to take as evasive a course as they could, thinking that the major highways would be under intense scrutiny.

Of course, it was all guess work. They still did not know if he was even headed to Zurich.

Derek was just opening his car door, and Catherine was on the other side about to climb in, when he saw her staring incredulously. Derek turned to follow her gaze. In one of those surreal moments that life sometimes offers up, the old green Mercedes with its three occupants rounded a corner down the street and headed toward them. Derek made out the hulking Russian in the passenger seat at the same time the bodyguard saw him.

Gregovich recognized the pair instantly and told Flannigan to floor it. Flannigan instantly stomped his foot to the floor. The old Mercedes engine, never built for high performance, rattled a bit as it absorbed the flood of diesel rushing through its injectors but pushed the car forward smartly nonetheless.

As Derek fumbled the key into the ignition of their car, the Mercedes swerved around a corner and was lost from sight. "Shit, I don't believe it. I don't fucking believe it," he yelled as he lurched onto the road and sped after the fleeing Mercedes. As they rounded the corner, there was no sign of the car. It had already disappeared around the next bend.

Catherine fired up the GPS and impatiently stabbed the buttons as it offered up its menu. "This is Highway 10. They can't get off it for the next four or five miles when they get to Hasle, the next small town. If they get off there, they might be able to lose us in the network of roads that run north, but eventually, they'll have to emerge at Highway 2 near Wolhusen. That's where 2 and 10 meet. Until then, they don't have many options. We could lose them on these back roads though, if they decide that making a run for Zurich is out of the question. Of course, they could try to lose us on foot in the mountains," Catherine finished with a smile.

"I don't think that's al-Munajjid's style, somehow," replied Derek. "I guess we have a good old American car chase on ours hands."

"I'll phone the Seals and see if they can get to Wolhusen ahead of our friends and intercept them at the top of 10 before they can head out in other directions."

A couple of minutes later, she had her answer. "The recon team might be able to head him off if they get lucky, but the van with the rest of the Seals is too far north and bogged down with bad roads and construction."

Derek flogged the hell out of the little Volkswagen Golf. Initially, he'd detested it, but he was starting to view it with some respect after the abuse it seemed willing to absorb. It looked like the car would be putting up with significantly more in the next little while as Derek slammed it around the cornered, tires squealing, and kept the accelerator nailed as far as he dared. Coming up on Hasle, just a short drive along the road, they saw the Mercedes ahead. Its brake lights flared, and it started to make a left turn where Catherine had thought it might, but whether the driver changed his mind at the last moment or the car had been moving too fast, it wallowed and then resumed its headlong flight along 10 and into the small village ahead.

The green car dashed through the hamlet at high speed, taking the twists and bends as if on a Grand Prix track. A woman walking her small dog was almost run down but managed to scramble out of the way at the last moment.

Derek, although feeling guilty about it, also tore through the town to the stares of the open-mouthed townsfolk. He was terrified he would lose their prey, although he really didn't know what they would do if they caught up. Both he and Catherine were armed with handguns, but Derek was quite sure the men in the car ahead were armed with far more powerful weapons. Derek's game plan was to stay with them, hoping to keep the pressure on and keep them running into the arms of the two men of the Seal recon team who were racing to cut them off.

Derek lost sight of the Mercedes as it rounded one of the sharp bends in the road just past the village. As he rounded a second curve, the road straightened out and proceeded to the large town of Entlebuch. The Mercedes was not ahead of them. "Shit," he yelled, jamming on the brakes, the anti-lock braking system juddering in torment. He slapped the car into reverse and floored it, spinning the wheel in a sliding rearward turn, assisted by the parking brake.

"Nice," was all Catherine said as she hung on to handle that Volkswagen had thoughtfully provided on the right-hand windshield pillar. Balancing the portable GPS against the forces at work, she saw where their quarry had turned off. "It's an intersection back there on the second bend. We were so busy cornering, we missed it. It runs on an angle back off the road."

Rounding the bend again, they saw it, and Derek screamed onto the smaller road, which immediately curved around a cluster of farm buildings and then straightened out. The Mercedes was nowhere to be seen. As they sped past a second group of buildings that bracketed the lane, Catherine yelled a warning. There was the Mercedes tucked into the side of a shed and facing away from the road. Both front doors were open and the two bodyguards out and standing on either side of the car.

"Keep going, keep going!" Catherine shouted as she saw the two men level evil-looking machine pistols. Both spouted flame simultaneously.

Derek had hesitated and actually started to brake before accelerating again at full power, spurred on by the sounds of bullets impacting on the car's coachwork. The rear window dissolved, and the car resounded with thuds. Catherine almost slid under the dashboard as rounds punctured the roof above her head and glanced off the front pillar. The front windshield turned into a maze of cracks and then opaque. Derek smashed at the glass with his fist but was unable to break a hole to see though. He stuck his head out of the window, but he had already started to lose control.

The car roared across the thankfully level verge and smashed through a wooden fence and into a cow pasture. Despite the Golf's bouncing and hammering across the rough ground, Catherine had seen the problem and grabbed her gun, using its butt to smash at the windshield in front of Derek. A large piece broke away and flew back into the car showering them with pebbled safety glass. Now able to see, Derek continued the headlong flight across the field as more bullets impacted.

They were getting farther away now, and the compact, close-range buzz saws the bodyguards were using were fast losing their accuracy. Despite that, a bullet grazed Catherine's scalp and she yelped.

Derek hit the first major obstruction, a small drainage ditch that meandered across the pasture. The car leapt into the air and its front end impacted the opposite bank. Then it half-rolled onto one side. Furiously spinning the steering wheel away from the impending rollover, Derek managed to put the car back on all fours, but it was plain it had received a critical blow. Its front wheels fought one another as their supporting systems bent and twisted, and the steering wheel shuddered and spun from Derek's grasp. A agonizing pain lanced up his arm as the steering wheel spoke snapped at his thumb and dislocated it.

The car slowed despite the engine's banshee wail, and at last it ground to a halt, the two front wheels almost facing one another and snapped front-end parts furrowing the dirt beneath it. Derek and Catherine both flew out of the car, rolling across the ground to avoid the stream of bullets directed at them. Suddenly they realized the ripping sound of the two machine pistols had ceased, replaced by the agonized rattle of a diesel engine at full RPM. Looking over the grass, Derek could see the Mercedes fleeing along the road and away from its two pursuers. He stood and could see the man sitting in the back seat of the car — al-Munajjid!

Despite the growing distance, he locked eyes with the stony-faced Saudi. "I'll get you, you fucking prick," he yelled in frustration.

Al-Munajjid's reptilian gaze never faltered, and his icy demeanour remained unchanged until distance stole the detail.

Derek turned and saw Catherine as she wobbled to her feet. "Oh my God," he exclaimed, seeing that her face was covered in blood. "Sit down," he yelled as he ran to her. She collapsed back on the grass, and he took her by the shoulders. "Are you okay?"

"I think so. It burns, and I have a hell of a headache coming, but…oh dear." Her hand came away from her face, and she saw it was covered in blood. Her eyes rolled back and her head lolled forward as she slumped in Derek's grasp and slipped into unconsciousness.

In the distance, Derek could hear the ululating warble of approaching emergency vehicles. Their little adventure had not gone unnoticed. In a moment of panic, he remembered the Seal-supplied pistols they carried, in Switzerland very illegal weapons. He grabbed his from his pocket, thanking God that he did not have to dispose of a shoulder holster as well. He scrambled to the car and found Catherine's pistol on the passenger-side floor.

Hurrying back to where she lay unconscious on the ground, he checked her breathing. Then he dug with his fingers into the soft soil and pulled a stout weed from its mooring. When the hole was large enough, he shoved the two guns in, pushed soil back over them and threw the excess dirt under the car. He finished up by replanting the weed and, he hoped, eliminating any sign of the small excavation. He phoned the Seals to tell them what happened and then flopped down exhausted next to Catherine, who showed signs of stirring.

There was nothing he could do now but hold a pocket flap he'd ripped off his jacket to Catherine's wound to staunch the bleeding and wait for the Swiss authorities to arrive.

October 6.
Entlebuch, Switzerland.

"Why did you not kill them, you incompetent curs?" spat al-Munajjid from the back of the Mercedes as it raced along Haldenstrasse, the pretty country road on which they'd laid their ambush. Derek and Catherine had ceased to be a threat. Catherine was in the back of an ambulance headed to hospital in Entlebuch, and Derek was in the back of a police car waiting for a police inspector to arrive.

"It did not serve our purposes to kill them, sir," replied Gregovich.

"And why is that?" asked al-Munajjid, his eyes gleaming with hostility.

"Because killing them would have put the entire Swiss police force on our trail," bristled Gregovich. "Leaving them alive with a bullet-riddled car will create a distraction that, if we are lucky, will occupy the police long enough for us to get clear. Whoever those people are, and I suspect they are Americans, they'll have a tough time explaining what they were doing to get themselves shot up. And I have my doubts whether they'd want to describe us to the Swiss police, or they would have already done so. Besides, we're almost at our car exchange. Any information they have about our car will soon be another red herring for the Swiss police to chase."

Partially satisfied but, as always, unwilling to congratulate his guardians on their efficiency, al-Munajjid sat back into his seat and watched the bright green hills roll past.

Gregovich shot a glance at Flannigan, whose return look and slight shake of his head said it all. In truth, both men would have relished turning their guns on their charge rather than using them to get him out of trouble. Then again, they were not paid to like the man, and nice people rarely needed the service of men with their skills.

Twenty minutes later, the green Mercedes sat in a dark padlocked garage down an obscure country lane. The three men continued their journey to Zurich in a two-year-old Jaguar sedan with deeply tinted windows, one of several different cars al-Munajjid's security apparatus had dotted about the Swiss countryside. The cars had been intended to serve as transport to the Swiss safe house, but the Jag was now just as useful as a getaway car.

CHAPTER 28

October 6.
The Rose Garden, White House grounds.

"Sir, the Chinese premier is on the phone," said a young White House aide.

The president had decided he needed, after days spent underground, a few minutes in the fresh air to clear the cobwebs. Around him, but trying their best to keep out of sight, was a virtual army of Secret Service agents and military. On the roof of the White House, the profiles of anti-aircraft Phalanx Gatling guns and ground-to-air missile launchers and their crews altered the famous roofline, and less than sixty feet from the gardens sat one of several much larger anti-aircraft missile systems that ringed the president's home. It was very hard to forget, even for a moment, that the United States was in crisis.

Just inside the French doors leading into the West Wing, Dan Blomstrum stood and fretted about the president's exposure, but his concerns had been overruled when the president told him in no uncertain terms that he needed to feel the sun on his skin and a breeze in his hair, if only for a few minutes. It had been over ten hours since he'd given the premier of China his ultimatum — ten very stressful hours.

The U.S. military had been on its highest alert, and fingers had hovered over the launch buttons, clearances having already been given, in case a Chinese retaliatory attack was detected. So far, everything had been unnervingly quiet, but two hours earlier, the president had received unconfirmed reports that the Chinese assault on Taiwan had slowed or stopped. Activity in the skies over Taiwan had also declined dramatically. The waves of heavy bombers, attack aircraft and their escorts had been reduced to pairs of patrolling fighter bombers over the areas held by the mainland Chinese forces. There was still fierce fighting in some areas, but in most of the island, Taiwanese forces had reportedly gone on the offensive in an attempt to recover lost ground.

The skies over the Yellow Sea to the north were another matter. They were filled with an armada of aircraft that made both the Japanese and the South Koreans very nervous. After the nuclear strike, dozens of fighters had risen into the sky like paper wasps from a damaged nest, and they were to be found at all altitudes. The two remaining American B-2s, with their weapons on board, beat a hasty retreat from the holding positions where they'd been stationed in case further strikes against China were called for. Despite their stealth capability, the Chinese M1 Eyeball still had a chance of discovering them, and with so many Chinese fighters in the air and the mission accomplished, discretion was called for.

The president headed into the West Wing and into the Oval Office, plunking down behind his desk as he picked up the phone. After a moment, the call was connected.

"Mr. President, my government and the people of China have determined that despite the American government's reprehensible attack on our peaceful country, it is in the interest of the innocent Chinese people and their equally innocent American counterparts that our two governments work together to ensure our dispute does not ascend to a higher level."

"Premier Lichang, if you remember, it was your country's sneak attack on a U.S. battle fleet that started this."

"Sir," replied Lichang, "that fleet was engaged in offensive operations against the orderly recuperation of Taiwan as an integral province of the People's Republic."

"No, sir!" the president said vehemently. "I do not intend to get into an argument with you that neither of us is going to win or even come close to settling," replied the president sternly. "You well know that the United States considers itself a friend and ally of Taiwan, and our fleet was responding to a request from its elected leader for help stemming an unprovoked attack by your forces."

"And you, sir, you sank our naval forces in the Gulf and bombed a harbour port of a neutral third party nation and then, using nuclear weapons, destroyed nine of our submarines while they were engaged in peaceful activities."

"Yes, nuclear submarine with weapons aimed at the U.S., and the only one we didn't get in time launched two nuclear weapons, one of which landed in America and killed thousands outright and possibly many more with its lingering effects!" The president paused, breathless for a moment.

The line was quiet. Lichang did not rebut with the U.S. nuclear attack on Jianggezhuang.

The president was willing to bet that the premier was far more upset about the material losses than he was about civilian casualties the American attack and the huge fallout pattern had caused. "We can go around and around this particular bush all day long, Lichang, but recapping events and making recriminations is going to get us nowhere. What we need to talk about right this instant is how you are going to comply with my demands."

"Mr. President, the Chinese People's representatives have been considering your requests and have agreed to comply, at least temporarily, with several of them. To improve relations between our nations during these hours of peril, we have halted our advance in Taiwan. We will not remove our forces at this time, and we do not consider that point negotiable, but as a concession, we will suspend naval activities in the Gulf region."

You have no naval forces in the Gulf region, the president thought to himself.

"Although we positively deny that our financial activities were an attempt to destabilize the American economy, we have suspended any further sale or seizures of American corporate holdings in China, and the sale of American bonds and debts has been halted. You have to forgive us. We may have acted in haste in an attempt to protect our own fledgling economy, but you must remember that our financial leaders lack the sophistication and experience of yours. Despite that, they have been severely reprimanded for any troubles their mistaken policies may have caused you."

Dan Blomstrum, listening in on the speakerphone and familiar with the financial slaughterhouse of Hong Kong, rolled his eyes and exclaimed almost loud enough for the premier to hear, "Oh brother, what a crock of shit."

"It has also come to our attention," Lichang continued, "that members of your government may have put forward the idea that the People's Republic had a part it the heinous terrorist attacks on the United States. I would like to say that this proposition is completely untrue. My government would never give council to or support any illegal activities, especially against a country that, until these unfortunate incidents, we have considered our friend and business partner.

"We have, however, suspended all financial aid and weapons shipments to any country that might misdirect those weapons to criminal forces anywhere in the world. Furthermore, the People's Republic will without hesitation do everything in its power to aid its American friends in apprehending the parties responsible for the egregious attacks on your nation. Our intelligence services will be tasked with providing such support immediately."

"Premier Lichang, I will take what you've said and the concessions you've proposed as a first step in improving the dangerous relations between our two nations. I will meet with other members of my government, and we will discuss this conversation. I will have our secretary of state contact you after our considerations."

"Mr. President, can I take this to mean that you will downgrade your present alert status?"

"You can take this to mean we will consider a reduced DEFCON status."

"I look forward to further contact from your government and the resolution of this matter."

"As do I, Premier Lichang."

"Thank you for your time, Mr. President."

"You are welcome, sir."

With that, the president hung the phone very gently back upon its cradle.

"Son of a bitch, you did it. You backed them down," said Blomstrum.

"That was surreal. It was if we were discussing a neighbourly disagreement instead of a conflict that has cost thousands of lives," the president said in consternation. Despite the calm and authoritative manner he'd used with the Chinese premier, his hands were still shaking from the tension he'd been under.

October 6.
Entlebuch Police Station, Entlebuch, Switzerland.

"Yes, inspector, I am FBI and I have been in Europe, and I have been making discreet inquiries, but neither my partner nor I have done anything illegal, and I assure you, sir, that if we'd known that the individual we were trying to speak to was going to react in this fashion, we would have called you immediately."

"So, you deny that you had any idea that these men you were following were armed and considered your 'inquiry' dangerous enough to ambush you and fill your car with holes."

"Yes, that is the case, inspector."

Middle-aged and slightly paunchy, Police Inspector Joachim Rader was far more comfortable with investigations that concerned drunk and disorderly than he was with gangland style-shootings. He leaned back in his chair tenting his fingers and pressing them against his bottom lip as he hmmmed. He clearly disbelieved Derek's story but was just as clearly unsure of what to do about it. Relief from his dilemma arrived in the form of a knock on his office door.

The young duty officer leaned into the room and said, "Inspector, there are two men at the front desk. One is from the government, and the other is American. They would like to speak to you."

With a scathing look at Derek, the inspector left the room. A few minutes later, he returned. "You are free to go," he announced. "I can wash my hands of you and your unbelievable little story. Now you are someone else's problem."

"Thank you," said Derek rising. He was quite uncomfortable with the situation and the need to lie about it. He had great sympathy for the inspector and was unused to being on the wrong side of the desk.

Rader already had his head down and a pen poised over a pile of paperwork. He was plainly finished with and apparently relieved to be rid of Derek.

Derek strode into the station lobby, and there was John Kopriva and a tall, gaunt, well-dressed man Derek had never seen before.

"Ah, Derek, I'm so glad to see you are safe," said the amiable Kopriva as he took Derek's hand in greeting.

"Thank you, John. I am little relieved to be safe. How is Catherine? Have you heard?" Derek was clearly anxious.

"Cat's fine," Kopriva replied. "She's waiting at the hospital for us to pick her up after we've collected you. She was lucky, the bullet passed through the back of the seat before it glanced off her forehead. I always thought she had a thick skull. Now there's proof." He chuckled. "Anyway, aside from a mild concussion and a headache, she's fine."

Kopriva continued. "Derek, I'd like you to meet Felix Petitpierre. He's with Foreign Affairs and has been very helpful in assuring the police that you pose no threat and should be released."

"Good to meet you," said Derek.

Petitpierre took his hand and shook it, nodding but offering no verbal salutation in return.

"I have explained our situation to Felix," said Kopriva "and he and his government understand — although, as can be expected, they don't condone — your little adventure. In order to get rid of you, they will assist in looking of the gentlemen who shot up your car and almost killed the pair of you. They would not have been so accommodating had you not been shot up. It makes clear that we are after the bad guys."

Kopriva gave Derek a look, raising one eyebrow in question, which Petitpierre could not see. "If you or Catherine had been armed, they would take a very different tack."

"Neither of us had any inkling the fellows we were attempting to interview were armed and dangerous. We were just following up a lead given us in London that this Saudi fellow might have information about the U.S. attacks he was willing to sell." Derek hoped his off-the-cuff explanation would convince the rather hostile Petitpierre.

Kopriva smiled, which heartened Derek, who felt very much out of his depth with the whole OO7 shtick.

Two hours later, Kopriva, Catherine and Derek were hurtling towards Zurich. Kopriva travelled in style, manhandling a big BMW 760i along the twisting Swiss roads. When Catherine pointed out he was getting far too many perks, Kopriva replied that Uncle Sam owned no part of his Bimmer. Derek, sitting in the spacious back seat, was fascinated with the little refrigerator in the centre armrest.

Catherine had been waiting for them to pick her up in the hospital lobby and left the hospital with a bandage wrapped all around her head, but as soon as they were on the road, she'd asked John to stop at an apothecary. Derek nipped in and bought a package of flesh-coloured Band-Aids and a strong headache remedy. He gingerly unwrapped the dressing for her and replaced it with the store-bought bandage. She winced several times during the process but made no complaint. The wound was small and had been closed with four stitches, but the area around the stitches was inflamed and looked very sore.

"At least I won't look like a fife player from the War of Independence now," she laughed.

Kopriva asked them to give him a detailed account of what had happened. He drove and offered no comments as the two briefed him on their adventure, starting with al-Munajjid's escape from the safe house and ending with Kopriva's arrival in Entlebuch.

"Well, we got very lucky," Kopriva said. "The Seals are on their tail again. They followed them to a cheap hotel near the airport in Zurich. We're pretty sure they're waiting for a private jet. Al-Munajjid doesn't fly economy. Right after they shot you up, they changed cars and kept going for Zurich."

"How did the Seals pick him up if he changed cars?" asked Catherine.

"This has to be our little secret. Okay?" said Kopriva, glancing over his shoulder at Derek.

Derek nodded. Kopriva knew he had no need to warn Catherine.

"The NSA managed to manoeuvre a satellite close enough to pick them up. They'd been watching them since they left the farmhouse."

"Son of a bitch!" Derek exploded. "You mean to tell me they knew where those pricks were the whole time?"

"Well, yeah. The NSA did, but we didn't, and satellite intel isn't usually in real time. This intelligence, however, was, and this is what you can't tell anyone, because of the way they got it. The CIA, acting on NSA intelligence, put up a specially modified and very stealthy Global Hawk variant based at Ramstein, Germany, and flew it into Swiss airspace. That is, by the way, a severe breach of their neutrality. It pinpointed the car exchange and followed the bad guys all the way to Zurich, where the Seals picked up their trail. The Swiss cannot under any circumstances find out that we had an unmanned recon platform in their airspace, or the small amount of cooperation we get from them at the best of times will evaporate. Plus, the UN will have a conniption fit."

"Speaking of cooperation. How did you get the cheerful corpse to clear us so quickly?" asked Catherine, referring to Petitpierre.

"I have intelligence about some recent banking transactions that involved profit from uncontrolled diamonds, and there are a few senior members of the Swiss foreign affairs department who would rather it didn't become common knowledge. A favour in exchange for a memory loss."

"Uncontrolled diamonds?" asked Derek.

"Blood diamonds," replied Catherine. "A lot of terrorists and rebels in Africa finance their operations with illegally mined diamonds. Some banks deal with them because they like the cash flow and are prepared to turn a blind eye, but they are not supposed to. The Swiss banking system got a black eye when people found out they'd been hoarding illegally gotten gold and riches banked by the Nazis and stonewalling the families that had legal claims on it. If the world found out their banks had been dealing with illicit diamonds, it would blacken the other one."

"So, what now? Can we pick him up in Zurich?"

"The Swiss are not prepared to let us pick him up. Petitpierre made that quite clear."

"Not even for questioning?" asked Derek.

"Not even," replied Kopriva. "In fact, they want him desperately for shooting up you two. Shootings are unfortunately de rigueur in the States, but here they are very big news. We don't want him wrapped up in the Swiss legal system, and if he didn't personally pull the trigger, the chances of him getting bail and disappearing are just too good. If they don't give him bail, and he sits in a Swiss prison, we can't question him anyway, so it's still no damned good. We need to pump that old prick for everything he knows, and that's not going to happen during a pleasant conversation in a Swiss police station. We're going to have to snatch him right from under their noses."

October 6.
Bridge of al-Riyadh, Gulf of Oman.

Captain Nawaf Basnan knew the game was up. The two U.S. destroyers that had been tailing him had been replaced by two Royal Saudi Navy F-2000 class frigates. Although lighter than his ship, they were still capable. He entertained the thought of engaging them, but that option was laid to rest when a new silhouette appeared on the horizon.

Al-Riyadh's sister ship the Lafayette-class Makkah steamed toward him at flank speed. He was low on fuel and had only one third of his ship's compliment. The rest of the crew, who'd remained loyal to the kingdom were still detained in the seamen's mess under armed guard. He could choose to fight and lose or spare the lives of his men below, men he respected and really had no quarrel with other than their refusal to join the rebel forces.

In hindsight, that perhaps was an intelligent decision. The elation of the first few hours after the shelling of the Royal Palace at Jeddah had worn off quickly as he listened to reports of rebel-held towns and villages quickly succumbing to government troops. When he lost contact with headquarters in Riyadh, he knew that he would not be the new head of the Saudi Navy and that all was lost. With nowhere to go and running low on supplies, he'd steamed into the Gulf to meet his fate. It had come in the form of a U.S. Navy patrol aircraft followed by the rapid appearance of the two U.S. destroyers, both far larger and more deadly than his frigate. They were just escorts, however, and never contacted him or made any threat aside from that of their presence, stalking two thousand yards behind.

During the ten hours they'd shadowed him, he'd felt like a mouse in the middle of a large empty room with two cats just waiting to pounce. The reason they did not pounce became clear when two Saudi frigates appeared on the horizon. Now the Makkah had joined them, he knew a fight was just stupid, an empty gesture that would only kill good men.

The Makkah steamed right up his starboard side until the two frigates were even and only two hundred feet apart. All her guns were trained on al-Riyadh. In fact, he noticed, they were all aimed at his bridge. Al-Riyadh's guns were pointed straight ahead or at the sky. He wanted them to know that he posed no threat.

The Makkah ordered him to heave to, and he complied immediately, reducing power until he barely maintained steerage in the rough sea. Several small boats full of Royal Saudi Marines departed the Makkah, forging across the six-foot swells to al-Riyadh's side. He ordered ladders thrown over the side for the borders and then spoke to his second-in-command. "Ayad, you've been a good friend and a useful ally, but now I think our paths will part. I want you to go down and release the men below."

Then he addressed the rest of the bridge crew, who were watching the Makkah's boarding party scramble onto the deck below. "Gentlemen, please clear the bridge."

One man hesitated, and Basnan met his eye. "Now!"

He was left alone on the bridge of his ship, the one thing that had almost meant more to him than his quest for power. He pulled his sidearm, a 9-mm Browning, from its holster and sat in his bridge chair. As the Makkah's marines slammed open the bridge door and stormed in, he put the barrel in his mouth and pulled the trigger.

Al-Riyadh was the very last rebel-held possession and Basnan the last rebel leader at large. Now both had been reclaimed by the Kingdom of Saudi Arabia.

CHAPTER 29

October 7.
The Welcome Suites, Schaffenhauserstrasse, Zurich, Switzerland.

Al-Munajjid was bored, and his boredom was quickly turning to frustration, and his frustration, to petty anger. He had been cooped up in this plebeian hotel for hours. His bodyguards did not want him going out in public. He had to rely on them to bring him food, and for dinner the evening before, they'd had the audacity to deliver a sloppy muck of veal and fried onions that had a nauseating aroma he could still detect whiffs of in the room. He'd sent them out once again on a quest for decent food, which seemed very hard to accomplish this close to the airport. The tawdry hole of a hotel offered no room service, and the only food it provided was a continental breakfast of stale croissants and oversweetened American cereal flakes.

Their anticipated stay — a mere three or four hours — had turned into more than twenty, with no end in sight. The charter jet that was supposed to be waiting for them when he got to Zurich was still on the tarmac in Munich with an engine problem. The woman who represented the charter service was apologetic but had claimed there were no other aircraft with a long enough range available at such short notice. She said the problem was minor, and the repair would take very little time as soon as they got the required part. He'd already paid in full, which infuriated al-Munajjid even more. He fantasized about plucking the out the eyes of the woman who had the nerve to offer him so many feeble excuses for the charter company's inefficiency.

Al-Munajjid greatly regretted the death of the stupid al-Muffaddal in London, which had made his father's jet unavailable for al-Munajjid's use. He was sure by now that Aziz was dead at the hands of the royal family's troops, and if his son had not been killed, he would be enjoying a direct pipeline to Aziz's fortune. Al-Munajjid was confident he could have stripped the Playboy of his father's fortune — the idiot worshipped him — and left him destitute within months. Al-Muffaddal's death was proving terribly inconvenient.

Al-Munajjid's reveries were broken by a loud knock on his door. He looked out into the hallway through the peephole and saw the Irishman standing there. He opened the door and snapped irritably, "What?"

"The aircraft is on the way, sir. It should be landing in the next forty-five minutes, and we can board as soon as they top off their tanks."

Al-Munajjid had left the travel arrangements to his bodyguard after a frothing conversation with the charter company that ended with the company threatening to cancel the flight. In order to smooth things over, Flannigan had evolved seamlessly from bodyguard to travel agent and made peace with the charter company. They had alerted him once the repair, a faulty fuel-flow sensor, had been made and the aircraft dispatched.

"We can leave in half an hour, sir," he said.

"Very well," al-Munajjid replied, shutting the door in Flannigan's face.

He sat at the room's small desk and flipped open his laptop. He had one more thing to do before he went to the airport. Opening an Internet browser, he connected to an online bingo site. He tapped a few keys, bringing up the image of a bingo card from within his laptop's memory. Attaching it to an email, he poked the send button and delivered it to the site. Seeing that the transfer was successful, he turned off the laptop and prepared to leave Switzerland for good.

October 7.
Swiss Bear Café, Schaffenhouserstrasse, Zurich, Switzerland.

Derek stared through the Swiss Bear Café's plate glass window at the hotel a few hundred yards down the road where al-Munajjid was holed up. Kopriva had dropped him and Catherine at the café and then cleared the area. McLean felt that too many Americans milling about posed a risk. He did not want the surveillance blown if the suspicious bodyguards did a recon and saw a disproportionate amount of idlers hovering about. He knew now that al-Munajjid's handlers were well-trained professionals who were cagey and ruthless.

McLean was sitting with Derek and Catherine, sharing a coffee and briefing them on the stakeout. So far, al-Munajjid had kept to a room on the top floor of the economy hotel. His two bodyguards had taken turns over the last twenty hours patrolling the hotel and its grounds and walking the street in both directions, looking for anything that might be a threat. The Seals, also highly trained in surveillance, had taken positions covering the hotel and its exits. Wilkes had taken a room at a nearby hotel with an overview of al-Munajjid's room but that had not panned out because the Saudi never drew his curtains.

"So we're sort of screwed then," said Catherine.

"Yes, ma'am. There's no way we can grab him for from the hotel. Well, we could grab him, but keeping him would be the problem. We just don't have enough preparation or assets on the ground to be able to zero his guards and lift him without making a pretty big fuss. His guys are good. They've set everything up exactly the way I would do it. I'll bet one is always in the room or in the hallway near his boss and the other is out on recon."

"If they've been doing this for well over twenty hours, the two of them have to be exhausted," said Derek.

"Yes, they probably are," replied the Seal, but I'll bet they're trained to work though exhaustion the same way we are, and they probably have stimulants to help out. It will take a lot more than twenty-four hours without sleep to make them less wary."

"Who do you think the bodyguards are?" asked Catherine.

"Probably retired Special Forces or Spetznatz, certainly ex-military turned for-hire. The one guy looks Slavic. He could be Russian or from one of the middle European countries. The other guy looks like a Brit or a Scot. We've taken pictures and sent them out to get IDs but haven't heard back yet."

At that moment, the Seal leader's cellphone warbled quietly. He took it out of the breast pocket of his Ralph Lauren shirt and answered. "Right, we'll get ready," he said.

Snapping the phone closed, he looked at Derek and Catherine and said, "They're on the move."

"Finally," said Catherine.

"Kopriva has two men at the corporate jet terminal. We'd better alert them. I'll bet that's where he's headed," Derek said.

"You're probably right. I can't think of anywhere else they might head for unless maybe the heliport," said the Seal.

"Kopriva has that covered," said Catherine, "but I can't see it. Al-Munajjid is going to want to get the hell out of Dodge farther and faster than a chopper can take him. A private jet is his only realistic option. He can't take the chance of getting bogged down with a commercial flight, especially now that he knows someone is on his tail."

"We'd better find out if there are any jets there waiting for him," Derek suggested. "If there is, can we get him before he gets to it and, if not, find out where it's going or maybe stop it."

"It depends on what you want to do," said McLean. "If you want him dead, we can do that here on the ground. It would be risky, but not as risky as snatching him. If he gets into the air, the air force or navy might be able to knock him down. We've got to have capable planes somewhere in Europe, but if he gets away, then we stand a real chance of losing him — maybe forever — like we did that bin Laden prick."

"He's a bad guy," said Catherine, "and as much as I would like to see him dead, we have to get him alive. We need to pump him of everything he knows about the attacks. I don't want to take the chance of putting a bullet into the head of the only guy who knows how to track down all the terrorist forces in the States, as appealing as that idea might be."

"Plus," said Derek, "he might not be the biggest fish. He has to have had other supporters. He's rich and as slimy as an eel, but is he rich enough and smart enough to have organized, planned and implemented the attacks all by himself? We have to know. As much as I like the idea of killing him, it isn't an option, at least not right now. Too much is riding on what he might have in his head."

October 7.
Washington DC.

Mahad Hussein had been in the United States for three years. He had a legal green card and a responsible position as the lead man in a team of twelve cleaners who worked for a janitorial service. Hussein was a long-legged black Somali, a Christian refugee whose immigration to the USA had been assisted by a Washington-based church group. Over the last few years, the janitorial service had won several major contracts that included the cleaning of government buildings, one of which was the U.S. Treasury complex that housed the Office of Terrorism and Financial Intelligence.

His employers were delighted with him, a go-getter with a superb work ethic who never slacked or took sick days. In an industry filled with underachievers, he was considered quite a prize, and his abilities eventually put him in charge of the team that cleaned one of the service's biggest accounts. He was of above-average intelligence and very resourceful. He was also one of al-Munajjid's prides and joys, a deeply imbedded agent whose credentials and background had been researched and checked time and time again by Homeland Security and a number of other investigative agencies without result. He had not been involved in a single attack, and he was the last infiltrator left who had not attacked or attempted to attack his assigned target.

His task was to penetrate the Treasury Department and attack the data system's computer hardware and the office staff who handled enormous amounts of sensitive information and had been instrumental over the years in thwarting many cash-building enterprises by Muslim extremist groups. Given time and just a few clues, al-Munajjid worried that they might get lucky and pinpoint his financial manipulations, or perhaps those of his backers.

Al-Munajjid had fed the Treasury Department's anti-terrorism wing many red herrings in the last three years in an effort to keep them too busy to make a chance discovery of his financial machinations. In some cases, he'd even fed them real information that compromised other terrorist networks. But now that the Americans might be on to him, he felt an intense investigation could reveal too much for comfort. And the Americans would not be his only concern if they found out what he'd been doing. Many of his friends would be just as eager to talk to him if they knew how much of their investments he'd arranged to keep for himself. He probably would not survive those conversations. He needed to shut down any investigation before it could begin. Al-Munajjid had a contingency plan for almost everything.

Hussein had closely monitored the Internet websites since the assault on America had begun, eagerly anticipating the picture code that would release him to strike his target. Unlike most of the websites used by al-Munajjid's men to receive information, Hussein's was not a porn or gambling site. Given Hussein's cover as a devout African Christian, those were deemed too likely to raise security eyebrows if his laptop was examined, especially if the Americans were already aware of the terrorist intelligence relay system.

His specific Internet contact was on a Christian online bingo site that would offer him a specially numbered bingo card when it was time to commence his attack. He'd waited patiently for that card, checking the site twice daily, and inevitably felt a little disappointed every time. When he received the special card this morning, he couldn't believe his great fortune. Finally, he would join the struggle against the Americans. His instructions were clear. He was to implement his attack as soon as possible after receiving the code.

Hussein worked alone. None of the other men in his cleaning team had any inkling that he was more than he seemed, a nice guy who was overly conscientious. They had no idea that every day for the last few months he'd been bringing in tiny amounts of plastic explosive and that he'd devised a way to get it past the security desk at the building's back doors. Had he been required to enter though the front of the building, he would never have made it past the chemical sniffers. The security desk he passed near the loading dock entrances had no such device. The sniffers there were used to examine the interiors of trucks arriving with deliveries and were kept up on the receiving platform, no threat to anyone coming in the staff door with security clearance and ID card.

Hussein had long ago determined that, given the nature of his task, only a suicide attack could succeed. Al-Munajjid's intention was never to have him commit more than one attack, so his survival was unimportant. Of course, Hussein thought he was sacrificing himself to the greater good of Islam. He would not have been quite so eager if he'd known his task was to ensure the safety and security of al-Munajjid's purloined fortune.

He arrived early, nodding at the security guard, who was not surprised to see him. He frequently arrived an hour or so before his shift commenced. He made his way up to a second-floor storage room, the largest janitorial storage locker in the building, where many of the larger machines like floor polishers and big industrial vacuums were kept. Along the back wall were a number of large lockers that contained janitorial supplies and were kept locked at all times to avoid pilfering. There were nine, and they all had identical padlocks, except for one. It had a key that only Hussein carried, on a string around his neck. It was this padlock he opened each morning to add the next small slab of explosive to his collection. This morning he would not add any.

He would spend the next hour carefully packing the largest wheeled mop bucket available almost to the rim. When he was finished and had a small watertight radio detonator in place, he added two inches of dirty soapy water to it and placed a big mop over top of the whole bucket, hiding most of the water and all of the explosives.

As he wheeled the bucket into the hallway, the first three of his day-shift workers ambled along the corridor and greeted him. He snapped at them to get to work, and one of them gave him the finger. He ignored the man and continued on his way to the service elevator that would take him up two floors to the computer centre that serviced the investigative wing of the Treasury Department.

When the elevator opened, he noticed a small knot of people down the hall. His heart jumped when he saw who was visiting. It was the secretary of the Treasury himself along with other highly placed bureaucrats from Treasury and Homeland Security. It looked as if an early morning visit was in progress. Head down and carefully pushing his bucket so no water would slop, he passed by the chatting men who ignored his passage. He turned into the computer centre alcove that led off the main hallway and showed his ID badge to the security guard, one he knew well. The guard looked up and smiled as Hussein pushed the glass doors open with his back and dragged the mop bucket in.

The computer centre was a large room filled with dozens of work stations, each with its own computer screen and keyboard. The mainframe and server were at the back in their own climate-controlled glass-walled room. Hussein pushed his mop bucket carefully down the centre aisle, headed for the back of the room. His pulse was racing and his mouth as dry as sand.

For the most part, the people at their stations ignored him in the way most office workers ignore janitorial staff. A couple of them raised their heads, and one young woman with freckles and a winning smile gave him a warm look. The room was full, the workers beginning their day, and there was the nine o' clock bustle of an office staff preparing the day's tasks. The secretary of the Treasury and his entourage entered the room through the glass doors, and two supervisors left their stations to greet them.

Hussein knew that the power of his bomb would likely have taken out the computers from the hallway if he had not been able to get any closer, but he manoeuvred the bucket right up alongside the glass wall anyway. Suddenly content and feeling an odd sense of calm and peace, his lifelong goal realized and his journey nearing its end, he fell to his knees and slipped the detonator from his pocket. He saw the freckled girl looking at him, her smile turning to concern. He recited a prayer under his breath and pushed the button.

October 7.
Private jet terminal, Zurich Airport, Zurich, Switzerland.

Al-Munajjid's mood was even blacker than it had been at the hotel. His bodyguards, fearing the Swiss police or others might have staked out the private terminal, had paid a shifty-eyed little Macedonian who drove for an airline catering company a lot of money to taxi them the last two miles to the terminal. Al-Munajjid was forced to abandon his comfortable back seat and was hustled into the back of the catering truck. His Jaguar was left abandoned behind a rundown air freight warehouse, his one and only ride in it over.

The Arab bristled when he saw enough money to rent a brand-new Rolls Phantom for two weeks change hands. He would like to have slit the greasy little Macedonian's throat, but instead he was condemned to sit for the duration perched on a cardboard box whose top sank ever lower as his weight compressed the goods inside. The truck stank of warm airline food tinged by the slightly sour odour of things that had escaped their containers and gently turned to mould. The truck swayed back and forth, and the Macedonian had a habit of mashing the accelerator until the truck was careening towards the traffic in front and then slamming on the brake. Al-Munajjid was forced to grip a greasy rail that ran along the van's inside wall. He passed the time by giving his bodyguards hate-filled looks.

Gregovich sat across from him in then back of the van, his attention riveted to the small back door glass as he searched for possible trouble outside. Flannigan sat in the passenger seat in front, also on the alert for trouble. They reached the service gate to the terminal just as the sun was starting to set. Security was far more lax here than it was at the commercial carrier terminals.

The guard took a quick look at the Macedonian's company credentials and waved him through. The driver slowed and parked in front of a small office that stuck out from the back of the terminal. He walked in, got a location for the charter jet and clearance to drive across the apron. A few minutes later, he pulled the van up alongside the leading edge of one wing and opened the van's back doors. Gregovich helped al-Munajjid down, and the three men mounted the jet's boarding steps and entered.

Al-Munajjid swept past the flight crew who were busy in the cockpit and seemed a little taken aback by the men's unorthodox arrival. Gregovich, following him up the stairs, saw their faces and smiled at them, shrugging his shoulders and spinning his finger around his ear and then pointing at the old Arab. The cockpit crew smiled and turned back to their pre-flight ritual. Al-Munajjid missed the exchange. He'd plunked himself down in a luxuriously padded seat and glared impatiently out the window.

The captain of the aircraft came back to greet the men. Al-Munajjid, without looking, waved his hand in dismissal at the pilot. Flannigan picked up the slack and accepted the man's corporate greeting.

One pleasant surprise was that the aircraft was a Gulfstream II and not the smaller jet they'd anticipated. The problems of the original plane had not been solved satisfactorily, and the charter service had substituted the Gulfstream to replace it. This aircraft had the range to make the flight to Abu Simbel non-stop. Flannigan reviewed the flight plan with the captain and then took his seat. A few minutes later, the engines were run up, and the crew fiddled with checklists and waited for taxi clearances from the ground controllers.

Derek and Catherine watched the gleaming white jet taxi towards the runway. McLean was in the van in the parking lot on his satellite phone trying to arrange a tracking, and perhaps an intercept, and transportation for the team. They'd almost had al-Munajjid when the Jaguar's occupants stopped to make the exchange for the catering truck. Dan and Catherine, following close on the heels of the recon team, had seen the Jag turn into an industrial area, and then the Seals reported that it had disappeared behind a warehouse. They waited patiently, praying that the rest of the strike team would turn up in time with their weapons. It looked like the perfect opportunity, as the warehouse was tucked in an industrial cul-de-sac, as unobserved a location as they were likely to get.

Their opportunity was wasted by, of all things, a mundane traffic tie-up. The Seal team in their van had been about a quarter mile back, as was prudent for a larger, more visible vehicle during a tailing operation. Unfortunately, they were right behind a limousine when a taxi in the next lane suddenly and without warning swerved in front of the limo, cutting it off. The taxi clipped the limousine, and the limo driver, in an attempt to avoid the accident, ran into the adjacent lane, smacking into an old oil-puffing Peugeot. Traffic ground to a halt as drivers jumped out of their cars and started to scream at one another.

The Seals were caught right in the middle lane, directly behind the accident. The team leader's jaw was so tightly clenched in frustration that a tooth cracked. He realized that perhaps their one and only opportunity to take al-Munajjid alive was slipping through their fingers.

"Well, that's it then," said Derek dejectedly as he watched the air ripple behind the Gulfstream as it rose from the runway and disappeared into the darkening skies. Its only trace was the navigation lights that twinkled as if mocking them.

"Right now, maybe," said Catherine, "but I suspect we're not done yet." She pointed at the Seal team leader running across the parking lot towards them, a big grin on his face.

"We've got transport, and it's at this airport. We can be in the air in ten minutes."

"What kind of transport?" asked Derek.

"A goddamn 767, man, a Boeing three-hundred-passenger freakin' 767. They're dumping the passengers off the plane as we speak. We have to get to the main terminal building, but we don't have to go through security. They'll conduct us right to the plane, weapons and all. Some sweet-thinking bastard in the State Department's think tank did an IWWI. They thought a situation might arise where we'd need immediate transport, although I think it was probably so we could get the hell away if we were caught bending international laws. They've been monitoring U.S. flights in and out of Europe and were ready to appropriate aircraft at a moment's notice. Kopriva figured out the bad guys were headed to Zurich, so he got one there."

"What the hell is a IWWI?" asked Derek.

"That's an 'I wonder what if'" answered Catherine. "God, I could kiss that man. He makes a better station chief than he did an instructor," she exclaimed, referring to Kopriva and his behind-the-scenes machinations.

Derek smiled at the first-class accommodations he shared with his fellow travellers. The cavernous interior behind them was empty, aside from the team's duffel bags loaded down with weapons and equipment, which were strapped into the seats in the cabin-class area. They had no flight attendants to help them, but there were three urns of fresh coffee, soft drinks, bottled water and a selection of sandwiches wrapped in plastic. The Seals, all big chaps, seemed to appreciate this more than Derek and Catherine and had already made a sizable dent in the sandwich platters.

The big jet's engines barely felt the aircraft's weight as it hurled heavenwards. Its paying passengers had been bound for New York, almost all of them business people or government employees. Tourists coming from or going to the United States no longer existed. The passengers had been hurriedly evacuated, and their luggage lay strewn across the tarmac as the strike team made their way aboard. The Seal team leader had a hurried chat with the captain and first officer, both men very fortunately members of the American Air National Guard and comfortable with the instant conversion to military jurisdiction.

Less than half an hour later, the 767 was winging its way southward, hot on the heels of the Gulfstream. The pursuers' advantage was that the occupants of the private jet had no idea the chase was on, and its pilots were flying with fuel conservation in mind. The 767 was pouring on the coals, its two massive Pratt and Whitney PW 4000s kicking out almost sixty-three thousand pounds of thrust each, and with the light load, the raw thrust was being converted to Mach 0.8 rather than to payload capacity. The pilots kept the nose pointed skywards, throttling for the best rate of climb, before levelling off at altitude and dashing after the Gulfstream.

U.S. agents on the ground were working on obtaining the Gulfstream's flight plan from the Swiss authorities, but for now, U.S. Air Force AWACS based out of Germany were tracking it from forty-thousand feet over the Alps. The Gulfstream had entered Italian airspace and was headed south. Derek guessed that it was making a run to Saudi Arabia, and the 767's pilots had filed a flight plan for Riyadh, at least as far as Swiss and Italian aviation authorities were concerned.

Reporting to the Saudis would be another matter. The State Department would be very busy trying to explain why a civilian 767 needed emergency airspace clearance, especially to a gun-shy post-rebellion bureaucracy that was still purging its bad apples.

"Boy, this sure beats your average movie chase, doesn't it?" said Derek, putting his seat back a bit and stretching his legs.

Catherine nodded in agreement as she shifted a pillow around, scrunching it against between the nape of her neck and the headrest.

The first officer, in shirt sleeves after shedding his uniform jacket, popped out of the cockpit door and motioned for Catherine to come forward. "Miss Hunt, there's a John Kopriva on the radio asking for you. If you'd like to come up, we can give you a headset and the jump seat."

With a look at Derek, Catherine jumped up and went forward, passing through the 767's armoured cockpit door and into the aircraft's office. The first officer unfolded a jump seat from the wall and locked it into position. Then after plugging in it to a jack, he passed her a David Clark headset. He manoeuvred himself over the centre controls and plunked back into his co-pilot seat. Catherine sat on the jump seat and pulled on the headset. The first officer nodded at her and flipped an intercom switch, one of what appeared to be hundreds of switches and toggles on the ceiling panel.

Catherine could hear Kopriva talking to someone and said hello. He did not respond. She noticed the first officer motioning at his headset mike and realized that her microphone stalk was suspended under her chin. She adjusted it to her lips and spoke again. "John, are you there?"

"Hello, Cat. Yes, I'm here. How do you like the transport?"

"Very clever."

"I can't take credit for the idea. It was on an old contingency list, but at least I remembered it."

"Well, it certainly got us back in the game. When we saw that bastard taxiing off, we thought we might never have another chance at him."

"Well, we might get another kick at the can. We have his flight plan. We got it directly from the charter company, which is European based but, fortunately, American owned. He's headed to Egypt. Abu Simbel is the flight plan's final destination."

"Abu Simbel?" replied Catherine, puzzled. "There's nothing there aside from a dam, some old statues and a lot of sand."

"Yes, but it's close to Ta'if in Saudi, and didn't you tell me he lives there?"

"He does. So what do you think he's going to do? Hijack the plane and head directly there?"

"He can't. Originally the charter service was going to provide a smaller plane than the Gulfstream, but it was out of service waiting for a part, and he made such a fuss that they decided to substitute a larger, more expensive aircraft. The smaller plane would have had to refuel at Cairo. With full tanks they could have diverted anywhere south of Cairo. The Gulfstream, on the other hand, has the range to get all the way to Aswan or Abu Simbel, so there's no need to land in Cairo, but they will be fuel critical by the time they get to the south of Egypt, probably with less that half an hour of cruise left.

"Crossing the Red Sea to Medina or Mecca is a touch too far. They'll be forced to refuel, and it's while they're gassing up that we may be able to pin back his ears. If we miss him, and he tries to make a break for Saudi, the navy will have a couple of Hornets and a supporting tanker over the Red Sea. They'll splash him. Not my first choice. I would like to have a word with him myself, but it's better than nothing. If he gets away like bin Laden did, the American people will have the president's head."

"So we're going to Abu Simbel, then," said Catherine.

"Yes. Your pilots have already been briefed and have the course laid in on their GPS. The State Department has informed the Egyptians, who have responded that they want no part of this, but — and this is very important — they will turn a blind eye both in the air and on the ground at Abu Simbel to any unauthorized aircraft that lands or anything else that happens while it's on the ground, as long as no Egyptian citizen is hurt or involved or any property damaged."

"Well, that's a relief. At least we only have to worry about al-Munajjid and his henchmen."

"Yes. Well, Cat, keep it within reason. No heroics from you or your FBI friend. Leave that to the Seals."

"I can't promise you about Derek. He has a pretty big grievance."

"Well, if he's dumb enough to get his ass shot, that's his lookout, but we have too much invested in you to have you coming back in a box. Do you understand?"

"Gotcha, Mr. Kopriva."

"Good. Now I've gotten my official duties out of the way, good luck, and watch out for that pretty ass of yours, okay?"

"Well, I do declare, Mr. Kopriva. Isn't that workplace harassment?"

"So, report me. Just make sure you come back in one piece."

"Will do, John."

Catherine pulled the headset jack out of the panel and passed the set to the co-pilot. She walked back into the first-class compartment, sat down and shared the news with Derek and the Seals.

The 767, with a clear destination now in sight, adjusted its course about fifteen degrees, aiming for Egypt instead of Riyadh. About halfway over the Mediterranean, as they were passing just south of the Greek mainland, the first officer came on the intercom.

"Lady and gentlemen, we present a special treat courtesy of Pan Global Airlines. If you look out your port windows, you'll see a set of flashing lights about five miles out and five thousand feet below us. That's the Gulfstream."

Everyone in the compartment pressed their faces to the glass of the small windows, watching their quarry flying through the night sky.

The engines of the 767 changed note for the first time since they'd reached cruise altitude, the pilot throttling back a bit to let the Gulfstream slowly pull ahead. Once its lights were almost out of sight, the pilots adjusted the engines to match speed and sat ten miles back, stuck firmly on the smaller jet's tail.

In an effort to make the big plane a little stealthier, the crew had turned off the Mode C Transponder and other alerting systems that might give them away. Behind and well out of sight of the smaller aircraft's forward-looking weather radar, they settled in to wait out the rest of chase.

One of the Seals had discovered the on-board video game terminals, and with the pilot's permission, several Seals were engaged in playing video games while several others watched an Eddie Murphy movie.

Catherine was having a nap, and Derek sat imagining the coming hours and the satisfaction he intended to have when he grabbed the Saudi by the scruff of the neck and dragged him up the stairs into the aircraft, bound him hand and foot with plastic tie wraps and left him lying in the centre aisle all the way back to the States.

He might, he conjectured, just give the old prick a good kick in the balls every time he passed by on his way to the washroom. That would be satisfying.

Chapter 30

October 8.
Rome.

The hotel phone beside his bed warbled annoyingly and persistently, waking Huang Dong from a deep sleep. It was his superior, Kuo Lin, who spoke in rapid-fire Cantonese. "Be ready, the Americans have discovered our Saudi friend and are presently tracking him. Beijing wants the problem resolved. Be in my room in fifteen minutes."

"Yes, sir." Huang hung up the phone and shook off his drowsiness.

Fifteen minutes later, he stood outside his manager's door and gave it a light knock. The door opened instantly. Liang Peng, the third member of their team, must have been waiting for him just inside the hotel door. Liang was a political officer whose job it was to monitor and report to the party. Kuo was the senior field operative, and Huang, a man of few words, was the one who dealt in persuasion and wet affairs, a well-trained assassin who was kept on a very short leash.

"Our good friend," said Kuo, who stood in front of the window looking down on the frantic Rome traffic, "who, as you remember, we last met with in Aleppo, Syria, has gotten himself into a bit of trouble. We are to intervene to ensure that his troubles do not become our troubles. He has fled Switzerland and is currently airborne. Our sources believe he is on his way to Saudi Arabia and likely does not know that an American aircraft, an airliner that disgorged its regular passengers and is now carrying a Special Forces team, took off soon after and, reason dictates, is after our dear friend.

"While we can do little right now, we are to monitor the situation and, if possible, get to him before the Americans do, which under the circumstances seems unlikely, but if they capture him and do not kill him, we are to get him away from them. All of our resources in Europe, North Africa and the Middle East have been alerted, and once we have their location, we are to secure Muhammad al-Munajjid. I have been told that we must not fail."

October 8.
Egyptian airspace, approaching Abu Simbel.

Derek had dozed off for the final a couple of hours of the five-hour flight. His sleep was disturbed by a voice that wove its way into his dream but still seemed discordant. Slowly he rose to consciousness and became aware of the stirrings around him as the other members of his party awoke. The Seal team leader shook his arm gently and said, "Time to wake up, sir. We'd better spend the next hour or so going over our next move."

While everyone else had been resting, the Seal leader and his NCO had come up with a plan formulated on a diagram of the airport at Abu Simbel, which they had found in the pilot's airport directory. That directory gave them the layout of the airfield and the terminals as well as taxi and other arrival information. The Gulfstream would likely comply with those disciplines, while the 767 would not if it did not serve their purposes. If al-Munajjid wanted to continue his journey, the Gulfstream would need to fuel.

The Egyptians had agreed not to send a fuel tender, leaving al-Munajjid and his two bodyguards exposed and helpless in the middle of a very large paved expanse. They were restricted to the interior of the aircraft until customs cleared them — which would not happen — and Egyptian ground control had made one more concession. They would direct the Gulfstream to an unoccupied area on the apron where the 767 could get very close, limiting the Seals' exposure when they made their move from one aircraft to the other.

The plan was simple. They would taxi close to the rear of the Gulfstream and halt in its largest blind spot. The Seals would then to drop to the ground from the opposite side of the airliner and rush under it to the private jet. Two of the team was tasked with pumping several 7.62-mm rounds into the jet's engines if the engines had already stopped or shooting out the tires if they had not. No one wanted the plane to blow up, but shooting out the tires risked alerting the occupants, whereas silenced rounds pumped into the rear of the engines was less detectable. Then the aircraft's occupants would be dealt with. The Seals would do everything they could to limit injury to the Gulfstream's crew, but not, they had made it quite clear, at the risk of losing al-Munajjid.

"We are currently over Aswan with about a hundred and seventy miles to go," said the co-pilot over the intercom. "We'll be beginning our descent soon and should be landing in the next half hour. The Gulfstream is ahead and on track for Abu Simbel. You might want to start your final preparations, gentlemen."

The Seal team leader rose from the centre aisle, where he had been crouched briefing the others. He headed into the cockpit to review the final plan with the pilots, making sure they would deliver his men to where they needed to be.

October 8.
Final approach to Abu Simbel.

The Gulfstream's pilot flared and touched down gently on runway 33, eating up two thirds of the 8,200-foot strip without hard braking so as to minimize discomfort to his passengers. He turned the aircraft onto a taxiway and headed for the aprons and the terminal. He switched over to the ground-control frequency and requested a slot near the terminal and fuel. After a few moments, the ground controller came back, issuing instructions to taxi to a marked spot. The pilot, seeing where they wanted him to go, asked again for a spot near the terminal. The controller told him that currently none were unavailable, because of a customs concern. The pilot, who had lengthy experience in third world countries, gave up and went with the flow.

Gregovich saw the terminal buildings as they slipped past the aircraft's port wing and receded behind them. Wondering why they were pulling up to a terminal where there were no other aircraft parked, he stuck his head into the cockpit. The pilot told him what ground control had said, and he went back and sat down. "Arabs," he said to Flannigan quietly so his employer did not hear. "The assholes can't even run an airport where there are only three arrivals a day."

The jet stopped, and the pilots cut the engines. There was a descending whine and then the uneasy silence of a closed aircraft before its door is cracked. In this case, the pilots were going to leave the doors closed. Despite the fact that it was still dark, an hour before sunrise, the outside temperature was over ninety degrees. Better to wait and enjoy the last vestiges of air conditioning.

Al-Munajjid asked Gregovich why they were not disembarking. Gregovich shrugged and offered the information he'd been given. Al-Munajjid pursed his lips and turned away, once again thwarted by circumstances.

A few minutes later, his bile rose when he saw a huge airliner landing. "That's why we are kept here," he said angrily to Gregovich and Flannigan, "so a stinking load of Western tourists can come and pat themselves on the back for the clever way they spent millions saving a bunch of old stone statues. Egypt," he spat, "stinks of old stone statues!"

October 8.
Abu Simbel.

"This is it boys. Time to rock and roll," announced McLean. The Seals, their faces blackened and their weapons held firmly across their chests with short straps, lined up at the central emergency door, which opened over the wing.

The first officer had turned off the interior lights at their request and now came back and opened the door for them. As it popped out, a blast of heat attacked the air-conditioned interior. Connor Ash secured a rope to the leg of the seat nearest the open door and then exited, running to the leading edge of the wing, playing out the rope as he went. In a twinkle, he was gone, soon followed by the rest of the team.

As instructed, Derek was last out. He eyed the rope with trepidation. What the Seals made easy work of was to him a precipitous drop to the hard concrete below. He got down on his knees and let himself over the wing's leading edge. He'd been given a Browning 9-mm, which was tucked into his waistband and stabbed him painfully in the groin until he pushed off the wing and dangled before letting himself to the ground. By the time he had himself sorted out, the Seals were grouped under the far wing tip, twenty feet back from the Gulfstream. Derek took a position behind one of the 767's massive tires, where he was to wait until the action was over. He ached to get in the middle of it, but his teammates pointed out he had neither the training nor the experience and would only be a liability.

Catherine waited on the plane, no doubt glued to a window.

The Gulfstream's occupants gave no sign of suspicion. The plane's interior lighting still burned bright through the small oval windows.

The quiet of the Gulfstream's interior had steadily eroded as the huger airliner approached them. It had come to a stop almost directly behind the Gulfstream, and its whining engines had dipped in sound as they were pulled to idle but remained running.

"It looks like they're being held away from the terminal as well," said Flannigan, looking out the window. All he could see was the back third of the airliner and didn't give it much thought. Both he and Gregovich were becoming weary. They'd been through a few very tense days, but al-Munajjid did not allow the help to sleep in his presence, because he found snoring offensive. They'd had to remain awake the whole flight when they'd have been far better off catching some sleep.

Al-Munajjid, on the other hand, had spent over three hours snoring like a pig, and whenever his own snoring awakened him, he glared at the two bodyguards, making sure they were not the cause of his disturbance. The pilots were occupied in the cockpit, going over yet another of their endless lists and flicking switches, when they heard an unusual metallic plinking from the rear of the aircraft. The pilots looked at each other in surprise.

The only one who did not react was al-Munajjid, who was too mired in his pique of bad temper to pay attention. Suddenly, the cabin door was yanked open from the outside, and two small black globes bounced into the cabin. Both Gregovich and Flannigan instantly recognized the danger and dove for cover behind the seats. Al-Munajjid leaned forward to see what was going on, when the two flash-bang grenades went off just a few feet from him. He fell back dazed — temporarily blinded and deaf — as the Seals pounced into the aircraft, guns ready to blast anyone who offered resistance.

Al-Munajjid's bodyguards, professionals who knew the futility of their situation, rolled to lay face down with their hands clasped firmly behind their heads. Gregovich looked at Flannigan and muttered, "I'm not dying for that prick." Sean smiled.

Derek scrambled into the Gulfstream and gingerly made his way through the Seals, careful not to come between the muzzles of their weapons and their prey. The endgame — the elusive Muhammad al-Munajjid sat in his opulent leather chair, a gun barrel pressed against his chest and tears streaming from his eyes as he tried to blink and relieve the impact of the bright flash and fumes of the grenade. The two bodyguards were bound hand and foot with white plastic ties, and a black hood was pulled over each of their heads. They were manhandled to their feet and pushed roughly up the aisle and out of the aircraft.

Derek stood towering over al-Munajjid. For a scant second, he felt a pang of pity for the helpless old man, but then he remembered who it was that cowered before him.

He reached down and took the Arab by the throat, digging his fingers in as he pulled him up from his seat. Once al-Munajjid was erect, Derek spun him around and grabbed his arms, pinning them to his back. One of the Seals stepped forward and threaded a plastic tie around al-Munajjid's wrists and pulled it tight. Al-Munajjid gave a little gasp of pain and then started to curse them. Despite the heavy accent, his English was clear, and his curses flowed naturally. Derek grabbed the plastic tie and gave it a violent tug that strangled the man's protests mid-utterance. "Keep your mouth shut, you evil piece of shit. Just shut it before I squeeze your black soul out of your miserable fucking hide!"

The Seals grabbed al-Munajjid and shoved him out of the aircraft. The crew members, both of them clearly confused and very scared, had not moved. One of the Seals told them with a laugh that they were free to take off. But they wouldn't be getting home in the near future, at least not in the Gulfstream. The jet's engines were full of holes and leaking hydraulic fluid, which pooled beneath the useless craft in ever-widening puddles.

With their three captives bound and hooded on the apron, one of the Seals went to find a mobile staircase. When they got back on board the 767, they were informed that a request to refuel had been denied. It seemed the Egyptians had reached the limits of their cooperation, and aside from a clearance to take off and get out of their airspace as quickly as possible, no more help would be forthcoming.

The pilots determined that they had plenty of fuel to reach Spain, where they could refuel and make the hop over the Atlantic to Washington. They were going to have to fly north over Egypt and out over the Med before turning for Spain in order to avoid Libya's airspace, but that was a small inconvenience and did little to blunt the elation they felt.

Derek did indeed lay al-Munajjid in the centre aisle at the back of the plane but refrained from kicking him in the groin. The two bodyguards were allowed seats, and all three men were guarded throughout the trip by at least two armed Seals. The 767 rose into the clear desert skies as the sun rose over the Nile River lighting the towering statues of Ramses II and the temples of Abu Simbel.

CHAPTER 31

October 8.
The White House, Washington DC.

The phone ringing on his bedroom night table woke the president from a restless sleep. Despite taking mild sleeping pills for his insomnia and antacids for his troubled stomach, he rarely got more than two hours of sleep at a time. He knew that at his age and under this stress load, even starting, as he had, from good physical condition and with the medical care available to a president, he might not have much longer before serious health issues raised their ugly heads.

He flicked on the light on and grabbed the handset. "Yes," he snapped irritably.

"I'm sorry to wake you, Mr. President, but I thought you should know immediately," said a White House aide.

"What?" he said, his mind racing to the conclusion that the operation they were running in Egypt had soured.

"They have him, sir, and they're in the air and on their way back home."

"My God. Finally," he said, a warm glow spreading through him. "Thank you. I'll be right up."

"No need, sir. They're hours away."

"No need? This is the first sleep I'll have missed in months that will be good for me. Ask them to put a fresh pot of coffee on."

"Yes, sir."

He heaved himself out of the small bed that was nearly the only furniture in the underground bunker's presidential bedroom and prepared to make his way to the White House far above to have his coffee in the kitchen and read an early edition paper no doubt full of glum news and articles critical of his administration. Tomorrow's morning editions, he was sure, would be just a shade more upbeat, at least if they were to take a leaf from his book.

October 8.
Over Barcelona, Spain.

They'd been in the air another five hours and were now entering the traffic pattern for Barcelona. The crew had determined that Barcelona was a far as they wanted to stretch their fuel reserves. The full-throttle flight from Zurich to catch up to the Gulfstream had eaten a lot more fuel than the 767 usually consumed, and they wanted to top up before continuing any farther. The authorities in Barcelona were notified, and refuelling was not going to be a problem. Of course, the pilots had told Barcelona that the airliner was on an empty maintenance rotation back to the States.

The two bodyguards had been mute throughout the trip. The same could not be said for al-Munajjid. He screamed and yelled threats and insults in Arabic and French and English, swinging from protesting his innocence to threatening the destruction of the Western world, until everyone in the plane felt like breaking his neck, an emotion never too distant even before his behaviour put a finer point on it.

Finally, having had enough, the Seal team leader rose and walked to the back of the plane. Everyone watched expectantly. Catherine started to protest, but then she realized she didn't care what happened to him, even if the Seal opened the door and threw him out. Kneeling down beside the Saudi, he yanked the hood from his head and grabbed him by the hair, pulling al-Munajjid's face to within inches of his own. He said nothing. He just looked into al-Munajjid's eyes. Al-Munajjid didn't make another sound all the way to Barcelona.

October 8.
Barcelona, Spain.

Once Kuo had received the information that the American plane was headed for Barcelona to take on fuel, he'd thrown his cigarette on the ground and scrambled into the Citation X that was sitting waiting to go at the end of a private airstrip in northern Italy. The jet leapt into the sky, throttles wide open.

The Chinese government had bought the Citation for use in Europe because it was the fastest private business jet available, flying at Mach .92, almost the speed of sound. The pilots, officers in the People's Army Air Force, had pushed it at least that hard reaching Barcelona an hour before the scheduled arrival of the 767. It was just enough time for Huang to ready himself.

Huang would make the interception solo, with Liang and Kuo acting as logistical backup. They'd had little planning time and even less information on the airport's layout and where the 767 would end up refuelling. Unlike Abu Simbel, which was tiny, Barcelona was a huge airport where the Chinese could end up over a mile from the 767's berth. Huang would have to play it by ear, but in that, he was a master. His off-the-cuff style had proven deadly and almost impossible to counter many times before. Today, they hoped, would be no exception.

They left the Citation without clearing customs, as their flight had originated in the European Union. Huang entered the main terminal and wandered around until he found a service passageway entrance. He waited a few minutes, until a cleaner with a cart loaded down with bags of garbage opened the door and started to push in. Huang held the door for janitor, who nodded in appreciation. Huang then slipped into the hall behind the man and let the door swing to and lock. The corridor was the entrance to the non-public areas that housed the various bureaucracies that accumulate at an airport like dust under a couch.

He walked briskly, not knowing exactly what he wanted but foraging for any opportunity. It came in the shape of an open door to a locker room. He entered, walked along the front of the room, looking down the rows to make sure he was alone and then started up and down the aisles, looking for lockers that were unpadlocked. He found several, but all of them empty, until at the end of an aisle he opened a locker that was in use. Hanging in it was the uniform and orange safety vest of an apron worker. The name González was emblazoned on the left chest pocket flap, and to his amazement and joy, the back was marked with the phrase, in Spanish and in English, "Fuelling Services." While he might have to take pains to hide the name on the pocket flap, the rest was perfect.

October 8.
El Prat Airport, Barcelona

The 767 pulled to a stop on the opposite side of the terminal apron, beside one of the airport's largest taxiways. Ground control had instructed them to park out of the way of the passenger-bearing aircraft while they waited for fuel services to arrive with a bowser. Airport services then informed them that the wait would be half an hour to an hour. With the plane shut down, the small auxiliary jet engine that drove the electrical systems, circulation and air conditioning was off-line. To compensate, the first officer opened the forward and the rear main doors, allowing a cool breeze blowing off the Mediterranean to enter and flush away the canned air they'd been breathing for hours. The pleasant tang of sea salt combined with the texture of shoreline detritus created a recognizable and welcoming scent.

To keep their captives out of sight and unable to escape, the Seals had provided each with additional plastic ties and closed the blinds in their section of the aircraft.

The bodyguards were bound to their armrests, and al-Munajjid to two seat legs — his wrists to one and his ankles to another. Gary Cypher taped al-Munajjid's mouth with clear cellophane tape and drew his hood over his head. He warned the old man that if he made a single noise, he'd be dead long before anyone would come to investigate. He put an exclamation mark on it by placing his boot across al-Munajjid's neck and putting a little weight on it.

The supply of sandwiches and drinks had long since disappeared, so the pilots requested a delivery of cold food plates and additional beverages. Several of the Seals were taking a nap in first class, but two were posted at the drawn curtain that divided first class and economy class, and two more, in the back of the plane: Cypher next to al-Munajjid and Wilkes in the flight attendants' service area, keeping an eye on the prisoners and the open door. As the bodyguards were tucked out of sight of any casual observation, their hoods had been removed. They proved to be model prisoners and struck up a conversation with their Seal guards. They were brothers in arms even if the bodyguards were working for the other side, and they had much in common.

In the bustle of activity that marks busy airport terminal ramps everywhere, no one in the 767 noticed the jeep-like service vehicle that wound through the baggage carts and other aircraft and airline paraphernalia.

"Here we go," the first officer said to Catherine as a loud bump reverberated though the aircraft. There were further sounds indicating that the fuelling team had arrived and tons of fuel was flowing into the wing tanks. He'd had grabbed a seat in first class, by his own admission, to stretch his legs. It was closer to the truth that, even after their adventure so far, a young man like him had enough energy reserves to try chatting up Catherine.

The captain was busy in his cockpit with paperwork and with all the other mysterious things airline pilots are tasked with when they aren't actually in the air. Catherine remained charming as she listened to the first officer's patter, but Derek knew her well enough now to know that she was only giving him a fraction of her attention.

There was a bang and a rattle announcing that a set of mobile stairs had arrived at the forward entrance.

"Oh, that's for me," the co-pilot said, flashing his most charming smile. "I guess I'm the skivvy on this flight." He rose and met a young Spanish airport worker who'd entered the aircraft carrying a clipboard with various papers on it. The first officer took the clipboard and scanned the paperwork and fuel receipts, signing them with a flourish.

Meanwhile, another pair of workers — one a short, stocky man and the other a tall, gaunt woman — arrived, both wearing Pan Global Airline service uniforms. They excused themselves as they pushed past with two aluminum airline carts, one brimming with food, the other with drink. They removed the two empty carts from the racks and locked the fully stocked carts into their respective cubbyholes. It was all standard procedure, especially to anyone who had spent time on commercial airliners.

Huang edged his stolen service vehicle very gently to the back of the 767. He managed to nose up to side of the aircraft's gleaming fuselage, a couple of feet forward of the door, so that unless someone was close to the rear bulkhead ladder or drew the blinds, he wouldn't be seen. He was further aided by the racket generated on the ramp by jets, service vehicles and various generators and electrical units, masking any noise that he made.

The aircraft's refuelling was complete, and the tanker was pulling away. The only other service personnel left were the caterers, whose delivery vehicle and ladder truck were still pressed up against the door forward of the left wing. Huang's presence would be unremarkable to any of the airport personnel engaged in their frantic, antlike activities. He noted with some satisfaction that all the window shades in the back of the plane were drawn. He reasoned, correctly, that the prisoners were being held in or near the rear of the plane and was very pleasantly surprised to find the rear door open. He'd anticipated having to open it himself, a distastefully unstealthy procedure.

He got out of his seat and stepped onto the vehicle's reinforced hood, which sported a diamond-patterned scuff plate to protect the paintwork when workers stood on it to reach a plane's ladder. Taking a casual look around to see if anyone had noticed him, he opened his vest to allow access to a nasty-looking combat knife and a lightweight Makarov 9-mm handgun, both worn by long service. He clambered up the ladder and reached the side of the open door. Pulling a dental mirror from his pocket, he gingerly slipped it around the corner at the bottom of the door frame.

He could see a man dressed in a sport shirt sitting on a jump seat about midway back in the rear flight attendants' area. He belonged no doubt to the American Special Forces unit. Drawing back the mirror very carefully so its movement would not attract the man's eye, Huang debated for a moment what he should do. Affixed to the side of the ladder was a small metal storage bin that housed various odds and sundries, including a couple of soiled rags. He wrapped his knife in a rag and balled the other rag around it. Then, leaning sideways a bit, he made circular rubbing motions against the fuselage so that his hand and the tails of the rag and would be visible from inside the plane. As he rubbed the door frame up and down, the Seal appeared.

"What are you doing?" Wilkes demanded.

Huang looked at him, shrugging his shoulders, and positioned himself.

Wilkes asked again, but this time in perfect Spanish.

Huang pretended to lose his balance, bending toward the Seal in the doorway and windmilling his arms. The Seal leaned to grab and steady him, and as he did, Huang grasped him with his left hand, as if for balance , and drove the knife concealed in his right hand deep in to the American's chest. Using the angled blade and the Seal's body as a pivot, he swung through the open door.

Wilkes grunted as Huang pulled the knife out, giving it a half twist, and driving the butt end into the Seal's chin, snapping his head back violently. The big man crumpled, tried to rise and then fell back again, unconscious. Huang crouched to one side of the entrance, pulling the Makarov from his vest in case the brief engagement had been heard and help was coming.

It apparently had not, masked by the ever-present white noise outside. Creeping forward, he used the dental mirror again and saw that the first aisle was empty. He skittered across the opening and, keeping very low, edged up to the next aisleway. Again he used the mirror. This time, he saw two men sitting in aisle seats four rows up. Casting the tiny mirror about, he found another Seal sitting in the centre section last row, in the aisle seat. He could just make out the man's arm and elbow and a bit of his shoulder. Not ideal but, provided no one opened the curtains farther up the aisle, he knew he could take the man before he rose. Huang took a deep breath and lunged around the corner and past the toilet door and swung into the Seal.

He was fast, but in this case, Cypher's reflexes were faster, and he managed to divert the blade, which punched into the seat back in front of him and lodged. Huang immediately let it go, leaving the Seal holding on, and in one fluid motion brought his hand back into Cypher's face. The heel of his hand caught the Seal, who was still struggling for purchase, right in the nose, and Huang drove it upward in a move that was rarely lethal but very debilitating. A spray of blood fountained up, and Huang lost the element of surprise. The Seal yelled in agony as he fell away from the Chinese agent.

Derek chose that moment to part the curtain and take a walk back to check on their prisoners. As he pulled the curtain aside, he heard Cypher's agonized bellow and saw Huang, who was hunched over the seat, rise and pull a gun. Derek shouted and grabbed his own firearm from his waistband.

Faced with a rapidly evaporating opportunity, Huang pulled the Makarov and fired a double tap into the surprised faces of the two bodyguards. Both Gregovich and Flannigan died instantly. As he fired at the bodyguards, he saw al-Munajjid lying on the floor bound and gagged. Al-Munajjid's eyes bulged and he made motions to the Chinese agent, whom he'd recognized as the quiet man from their meeting in the Citadel at Allepo. For a moment, he thought his salvation was at hand.

Realizing that it was al-Munajjid bound and gagged on the floor, and ignoring Derek's commands to freeze, he levelled the Makarov. Al-Munajjid suddenly grasped that Huang's intentions were not to deliver him from captivity and squealed and thrashed in his bonds in mortal fear. The Makarov spit twice in rapid succession, and then twice again. Al-Munajjid's body jumped with the impacts, and he howled, blowing the tape from one side of his mouth.

His job apparently finished and with Derek a clear and oncoming threat, Huang spun, fired a couple of unaimed rounds in Derek's direction and retreated, throwing himself into the rear compartment and sprinting for the door. Derek had second-guessed his move and was scrambling to get across a row of seats to the starboard aisle. He aimed his weapon at the passageway nearest the open door and fired, anticipating Huang's appearance. He was successful. One bullet in the spray caught Huang in the forearm as he appeared momentarily framed at the end of the aisleway. Its impact loosed the Makarov, which spun from Huang's grip, but was not enough to stop him.

He leapt through the door and soared through the air, legs and arms flailing to maintain his balance, to the hard pavement below. He hit and rolled, bleeding off the impact, but injured himself nonetheless, as his stilted run to safety testified. By the time Derek reached the door, Huang was halfway to the terminal building, and while he made an easy target, Derek held his fire and kept his pistol behind him out of sight. He turned to more important things, attending first to Wilkes, wounded at his feet.

McLean and Catherine, guns drawn, grabbed Derek and pulled him from the doorway, fearing return fire. Another Seal slammed the door into its nest. Derek was stunned. The whole thing had occurred in less than a minute, and as near as he could tell, three men lay dead and two seriously wounded.

"Jesus. What a friggin' mess," said the Seal team leader.

Swiggart leaned over al-Munajjid. "Hey, skip," he said to the team leader, "the prize is still alive."

"Son of a bitch," exclaimed Derek. Having seen the profusion of blood on al-Munajjid and the floor, he'd assumed the Saudi was dead.

"I guess we're going to have to get them all to a hospital," said Catherine. "I'll ask the pilots to radio for an ambulance."

"Excuse me, ma'am," said McLean, "our orders are not to relinquish custody of the prisoner under any circumstances. We might not be as good as a hospital, but we have a lot of experience and training stabilizing gunshot victims, and we have a pretty extensive medical kit. We can get him to a hospital, but it had better be in Washington, not Barcelona."

"Then we'd better get this plane in the air," said Derek.

Half an hour later, after the co-pilot had ascertained that none of the rounds fired on board had caused critical damage to the flight systems, the pilots nosed on to the runway, took position waiting for traffic to clear and then firewalled the throttles. The 767 climbed into a clear afternoon sky and banked to set course for the New World. The airliner and its occupants were on the last leg of their journey home.

October 9.
Andrews Air Force Base, Washington DC.

It was just a few minutes past midnight when the Boeing 767 taxied to the hangar complex at Andrews Air Force Base in Washington. The aircraft followed a brightly lit, yellow follow-me vehicle up to the front of an enormous hangar. Inside the hangar waited several ambulances, a dozen military cars and trucks and three limousines, as well as a small crowd of people.

The 767 nosed up and slowed to a stop just short of the hangar at the guidance of the ramp attendant who gave the pilots the signal to cut engines. The engines died as a set of stairs was rolled up to the forward cabin door. Moments later, the door opened inwards and a group of paramedics hustled to the top, entering with stretchers and other medical equipment.

They emerged a short time later bearing two stretchers, one carrying Wilkes and one, al-Munajjid. The Seal was going to make it. He was critical but stable, with a deep knife wound and a fractured neck vertebra. Cypher emerged with a large bandage across his nose and cheeks and pronounced bruising around his eyes, but he was walking wounded, and a huge grin was visible below the white gauze.

Al-Munajjid had been hit three times and missed once. In his hurry, Huang had not managed a fatal shot. The terrorist mastermind was gravely injured but conscious and aware of what was going on around him.

Once the stairs were clear, the first Seals, followed by Derek and Catherine, exited the plane, pausing briefly at the top of the stairs to get their bearings. Below them at the base of the stairs, a small crowd of military personnel, medical staff, the Joint Chiefs, the White House chief of staff and the commander-in-chief — the president himself — broke into applause and cheers.

Derek looked at Catherine and smiled. "We did good," he said, putting his arm around her and giving her a squeeze.

"It appears so," she said laughing.

EPILOGUE

October 14.
The White House, Washington DC.

"I am glad you came to dinner," said the president to Derek and Catherine as he pushed his half-eaten angel food cake forward for the white-gloved attendant to remove.

"It's hardly a state dinner, but it's been a wonderful opportunity to hear your whole story and for the First Lady and I to express our very real appreciation for a job well done. I hope calling you back from your brief break didn't throw a wrench into your time off, but my schedule's so tight it had to be tonight or six months from now, which wouldn't do."

"Thank you, Mr. President," replied Derek smiling. "I was pleased to come, but I know it put a strain on Cathy. Just look at her." He was now quite comfortable with the First Couple but had started off the evening as nervous as a cat. Over the last two hours, the president's easy ways and the First Lady's incorrigible laugh had rapidly put him at ease.

Catherine looked stunning in a close-fitting emerald green designer gown that glittered with hand-sewn sequins. She'd let her long red mane to fall naturally over her shoulders so that it framed her perfect features. Derek found his eyes wandering to her all evening and even the president had been taken back as he had greeted them in the main hall, a moment the First Lady found amusing and teased her husband about over dinner.

"So, our friend Mr. al-Munajjid is doing very well, although he'll never use his left arm again," said the president. "And he's been singing like a canary to save his skin. After we've finished with him, I'd be very tempted to give him to the Saudis. It's the fate he richly deserves, but we'll hold him, try him and, I sincerely hope, execute him."

"So he was the mastermind, their top man," said Catherine.

"Yes," replied the president, "but the Chinese are his main backers. Syria, Iran, Libya and North Korea also supported him, financially and with training facilities for his terrorists, and he was tapped into every major terrorist organization in the world, which is where he recruited many of his top men. He's given us some very good intelligence about training facilities and terrorist headquarters, some of which we've already acted on, as I am sure you've seen on the news." The president was referring to multiple cruise missiles and unmanned Predator attacks that had taken place all over the world in the last three days.

"Believe it or not," the president continued, playing with his spoon in the remains of a pallet-cleansing mint sorbet that sat half-melted in front of him. "He even got financing and support from Asian and European corporations who stood to make a lot of money if the United States faltered. And he planned the Saudi coup but gave up the plans and the organizers just before it kicked off. His used Abdul Aziz, a distant cousin of his, as the sop and then turned him in with the idea of taking over the older man's considerable fortune. That little plan, by the way, was thwarted by the death of Aziz's son in London."

"Yes, it's too bad about that," said Catherine. "I really liked him.'

Conversation at the table stopped dead, everyone shocked at the admission — especially since earlier, Catherine and Derek had described al-Muffaddal and his behaviour at great length. The First Lady caught the twinkle in Catherine's eye and burst out laughing. The two men fell in and laughed as well.

"What about the terrorist attacks here?" asked Derek, returning the gravity to the conversation.

"Well, we know how many of them there are now. There were around four hundred initially, and so far we can account for around three hundred and fifty. We'll get the rest, I'm sure, especially with the new information, but we were doing pretty well even before you captured al-Munajjid. Al-Munajjid doesn't have specific names for most of them — they were just foot soldiers in his own secret army — but he did give us some very significant information on how they operate and the kind of training they've had. Combined with what we know already, we should be able to track the rest down in the next week or so."

"And the Chinese?" asked Catherine.

"Well, a lot of our response is going to be classified, but I can safely tell you that we have international cooperation from much of the world in returning assets that were stolen or given away. The bastards have kept half of Taiwan, but if no one's buying anything from them, half of Taiwan isn't going to do them much good. Despite the rapid advance, the Taiwanese fought like wildcats, both in front and behind the lines, and they destroyed a lot of their own infrastructure and, more importantly, factories and research facilities before the mainland forces could secure them.

"I'm sure in a couple of years it'll be business as usual, but for now the world has turned its back on China and has promised to help us get back on our feet. The Indians, by the way, are delirious because they are one of the few countries that has a hope of picking up the industrial slack, but almost all of Southeast Asia, even Muslim Indonesia, is on board with pledges to give us a hand out and cooperate with us to increase trade with no barriers or restrictions."

An hour later, after the First Lady and her husband had given them a tour of the White House, the evening wound up. The president walked them to their waiting car and, waving aside the White House doormen, opened the door for Catherine, smiling broadly at the First Lady and sticking his tongue out at her.

"Keep that up, Mr. President, and you will lose exactly one vote and a comfortable bed," the First Lady laughed. The final jest of the night spent, Derek and Catherine climbed into the car, and it drove off.

Their driver was Special Agent Brian Good, their destination a few nightspots and a celebration with some of their FBI and CIA peers. Brian Good looked into the rear view mirror and said, "I wouldn't get too comfortable in these new social circles you two seem to be moving in these days."

"No?" said Derek.

"No. There are still bad guys out there, and you two are back out collecting them starting next week."

"Great," said Derek buoyantly while looking out the car's window at the passing monuments.

"Great," said Catherine quietly, looking at Derek.

October 15.
Atlanta.

Mohammed al-Tayeb had kept a very low profile since he destroyed the CNN building, successfully evading the hornets' nest it had aroused in Atlanta. One by one, the other members of his cell had been killed or had committed suicide to fend off capture while they were engaged in placing car bombs or planting roadside devices. Judging by the most recent news reports, many of the other cells and strike units spread across America had also been killed in action, but not without first striking hundreds of blows to the American heartland.

He had been appalled and shocked this morning when he saw newspaper headlines screaming about the capture of Muhammad al-Munajjid. He'd met al-Munajjid many times and listened to his powerful orations and considered him a great mentor. He'd been impressed and inspired by the man's piety, his great ambitions for Islam and his plans for its final blossoming when its enemies were destroyed. With the venerable elder gone, a vacuum would now exist, one perhaps he could fill.

He resided in the black heart of Islam's greatest foe. With his experience, patience and perseverance, he could perhaps assemble yet another army to strike terror into the rotting gut of the Crusaders' empire.

He swung his mop into the bucket and squeezed out the dirt swept into the entryway of the Candler Theology School on the feet of its Christian students and dreamed of the burning of America.

The End.